THE TEA ROSE

'This is a most seductive novel. You'll be charmed by the novel's heroine – her intelligence, her courage, her great heart. Despite her suffering – a lost love, a tragic family – there are moments you will want to cheer. It's the kind of novel where the writing is so fluid you feel the author simply loves telling her story. This is a splendid, heartwarming novel of pain, struggle, decency, triumph – and just what we need in these times.'　FRANK MCCOURT

'Bold, brisk and beguiling, *The Tea Rose* is a splendid brew of a book.'　SAM TWINING

'It's so much fun . . . This is London in the 1880s, the London of Charles Dickens and Edward Rutherford, a teeming, messy place full of business, dirt and poverty. Once in New York, we trip from the tenements of the Lower East Side to elegant dining at Delmonico's, with hardly a paragraph to catch our breath . . . The atmosphere of both starring cities is created in satisfying detail. One can walk the streets and listen to the people chat in the company of Jennifer Donnelly, who has done her historical homework . . . She delivers.'　*Washington Post*

'*The Tea Rose* is the kind of book that calls for a rainy day, a cozy chair and a good, steaming cup of tea. It's strong and satisfying, with a taste that lingers in the memory.'　PAULA COHEN

JENNIFER DONNELLY

The Tea Rose

HarperCollins*Publishers*

HarperCollins*Publishers*
77–85 Fulham Palace Road,
Hammersmith, London W6 8JB

www.harpercollins.co.uk

First published in the USA by St Martins Press 2002

This paperback edition 2003

1 3 5 7 9 8 6 4 2

A catalogue record for this book
is available from the British Library

ISBN 0 00 71556 5

Typeset in Sabon
by Palimpsest Book Production Limited,
Polmont, Stirlingshire

Printed and bound in Great Britain by
Clays Ltd, St Ives plc

For Douglas,
my own blue-eyed boy

Acknowledgments

I am indebted to Martin Fido, author of *The Crimes, Detection, and Death of Jack the Ripper* and *Murder Guide to London*, for a midnight tour of the lanes and alleys Jack knew and for sharing his encyclopedic knowledge of 1880s East London and its people with me. Samuel H. G. Twining, LVO, OBE, Director of Twinings Tea, and Syd Mumford, a former Senior Buyer and Blender for the firm, graciously explained the mysteries and arcana of the tea trade to me and provided a hands-on lesson in tea tasting. Thanks, also, to the staff of the Museum of London's Museum in Docklands Project for allowing me access to their library and collections. Londoners Fred Sage, a former Thames Stevedore, and Con McCarthy, an Ocean Ships Tally Clerk, walked down many a dockland street with me, sharing memories of working life on the river. Hoisting a pint with them in the Town of Ramsgate was both a privilege and an honor.

Sally Kim, my editor, is every writer's dream come true – a mentor, an advocate, a partner in crime. She has my sincere gratitude, as does the rest of the team at St. Martin's Press/Thomas Dunne Books.

Without Simon Lipskar, agent and lionheart, *The Tea Rose* would never have been. He took a chance on me and my doorstop of a manuscript. He made us better and got us heard and I appreciate his efforts more than I will ever be able to say.

Laurie Feldman, Diana Nottingham, Brian O'Meara, and Omar Wohabe were there for me from day one with advice, support, and champagne. No one could ask for truer friends. Thanks, guys. Heather, John, and Joasha Dundas read early drafts of the novel and gave me valuable criticism and confirmation, for which I am grateful.

A very loving thank-you to Wilfriede, Matt, Megan, and Mary Donnelly, and Marta Eggerth Kiepura, my wonderful family, for believing in me, encouraging me, and always telling me stories.

And to Douglas Dundas, for teaching me what faith means, the biggest thank-you of all.

Deep in the roots all flowers keep the light
–Theodore Roethke

The Tea Rose

Prologue

London, August 1888

Polly Nichols, a Whitechapel whore, was profoundly grateful to gin. Gin helped her. It cured her. It took away her hunger and chased the chill from her joints. It stilled the aching in her rotten teeth and numbed the slicing pains she got every time she took a piss. It made her feel better than any man ever had. It calmed her. It soothed her.

Swaying drunkenly in the darkness of an alley, she raised a bottle to her lips and drained it. The alcohol burned like fire. She coughed, lost her grip on the bottle, and swore as it smashed.

In the distance, the clock at Christ Church struck two, its resonant chime muffled in the thickening fog. Polly dipped her hand into her coat pocket and felt for the coins there. Two hours ago, she'd been sitting in the kitchen of a doss-house on Thrawl Street, penniless. The landlord's man had spotted her there, asked for his fourpence, and turned her out when she couldn't supply it. She'd cursed and screamed at him, telling him to save her bed, he'd get his doss money, telling him she'd earned it and drunk it three times over that day.

"And I got it, too, you bastard," she muttered. "Didn't I say I would? Got yer poxy fourpence and a skinful to boot."

She'd found her money and her gin in the trousers of a lone drunk wending his way down the Whitechapel Road. He'd needed a bit of coaxing. At forty-two, her face was no longer her fortune. She was missing two front teeth and her pug nose was thick and flattened across the bridge like a fighter's, but her large bosom was still firm and a glimpse of it had decided him. She'd insisted on a swig of his gin first, knowing a mouthful would numb her throat, get up her nose, and block the beer and onions stink of him. As she drank, she'd unbuttoned her camisole, and while he was busy groping her, she'd slipped the bottle into her own pocket. He was clumsy and slow and she was glad when he finally pulled away and staggered off.

Christ, but there's nothing like gin, she thought now, smiling at the memory of her good fortune. To feel the weight of a bottle in your hands, press your lips against the glass, and feel the blue ruin flowing down your throat, hot and harsh. Nothing like it at all. And close to full that bottle had been. No mean thru'penny swig. Her smile faded as she found herself craving more. She'd been drinking all day and knew the misery that awaited her when the booze wore off. The retching, the shaking, and, worst of all, the things she saw – black, scuttling things that gibbered and leered from the cracks in the walls of the doss-house.

Polly licked her right palm and smoothed her hair. Her hands went to her camisole; her fingers fumbled a knot into the dirty strings threaded through the top of it. She tugged her blouse together and buttoned it, then lurched out of the alley and down Buck's Row, singing to herself in a gravelly, gin-cracked voice:

> "Oh, bad luck can't be prevented,
> Fortune, she smiles or she frowns,
> 'E's best off that's contented,
> To mix, sir, the ups and the downs . . ."

At the corner of Buck's Row and Brady Street, she suddenly stopped. Her vision blurred. A buzzing noise, low and close like the wings of an insect, began in her head.

"I've the 'orrors of drink upon me," she moaned. She held her hands up. They were trembling. She buttoned her coat up around her neck and began to walk faster, desperate for more gin. Her head lowered, she did not see the man standing a few feet ahead of her until she was nearly upon him. "Blimey!" she cried. "Where the 'ell did you come from?"

The man looked at her. "Will you?" he asked.

"No, guv'nor, I will not. I'm poorly just now. Good night."

She started to move off, but he grabbed her arm. She turned on him, her free arm raised to strike him, when her eyes fell upon the shilling pinched between his thumb and forefinger.

"Well, that changes things, don't it?" she said. His shilling plus the fourpence she already had would buy booze and a bed tonight, tomorrow, and the day after, too. As sick as she felt, she couldn't turn it down.

Polly and her client walked back the way she'd come in silence, past tumble-down dwellings and tall brick warehouses. The man had a powerful stride and she found herself trotting to keep pace. Glancing at him, she saw he was expensively dressed. Probably had a nice watch on him. She'd certainly have a go at his pockets when the time was right. He stopped abruptly at the end of Buck's Row, by the entrance to a stable yard.

"Not 'ere," she protested, wrinkling her nose. "By the metal works . . . a little ways down . . ."

"This'll do," he said, pushing her against two sheets of corrugated metal, secured by a chain and padlock, that served as the stable's gate.

His face shone weirdly bright in the thickening darkness, its pallor broken by eyes that were cold and black. A wave of nausea gripped her as she looked into them. Oh, Jesus, she pleaded silently, don't let me be sick. Not here. Not now. Not this close to a whole shilling. She forced herself to breathe deeply, willing the nausea to subside. As she did, she inhaled his scent – Macassar oil, sweat, and something else . . . what was it? Tea. Bloody tea, of all things.

"Let's get on with it then," she said. She lifted her skirts, fixing him with a look of weary expectation.

The man's eyes were glittering darkly now, like shiny pools of black oil. "You filthy bitch," he said.

"No dirty talk tonight, pet. I'm in a bit of an 'urry. Need some 'elp, do you?" She reached for him. He slapped her hand away.

"Did you really think you could hide from me?"

"Look 'ere, are you going to –" Polly began. She never finished. Without warning, the man grabbed her by the throat and slammed her into the gate.

"Leave off!" she cried, flailing at him. "Let me go!"

He tightened his grip. "You left us," he said, his eyes bright with hatred. "Left us for the rats."

"Please!" she rasped. "Please don't 'urt me. I don't know about any rats, I swear it . . . I . . ."

"Liar."

Polly never saw the knife coming. She had no time to scream as it plunged into her belly, biting and twisting. A soft gasp escaped her as he pulled it out. She stared at the blade, uncomprehending, her eyes wide, her mouth a great, round O. Slowly, delicately, she touched her fingers to the wound. They came away crimson.

She lifted her eyes to his, her voice rising in a wild, terrified keen, and looked into the face of madness. He raised his knife; it bit into her throat. Her knees buckled and all around her darkness descended, enveloping her, dragging her into a thick and strangling fog, a fog deeper than the river Thames and blacker than the London night that swirled down on her soul.

PART ONE

1

The scent of Indian tea leaves – black, crisp, and malty – was intoxicating. It floated out of Oliver's, a six-story wharf on the Thames's north bank, and wafted down the Old Stairs, a flight of stone steps that led from Wapping's winding, cobbled High Street to the river's edge. The tea's perfume overpowered the other smells of the docks – the sour stench of the mud bank, the salty tang of the river, and the warm, mingled scents of cinnamon, pepper, and nutmeg drifting out of the spice wharves.

Fiona Finnegan closed her eyes and inhaled deeply. "Assam," she said to herself. "The smell's too strong for a Darjeeling, too rich for a Dooars."

Mr. Minton, the foreman at Burton's, said she had a nose for tea. He liked to test her by holding a handful of leaves under her nose and making her name it. She always got it right.

A nose for tea, maybe. The hands for it, surely, she thought, opening her eyes to inspect her work-roughened hands, their knuckles and nails black with tea dust. The dust got everywhere. In her hair. Her ears. Inside her collar. She rubbed at the grime with the hem of her skirt, sighing. This was the first chance she'd had to sit down since six-thirty that morning, when she'd left her mother's lamplit kitchen for the dark streets of Whitechapel.

She'd arrived at the tea factory at a quarter to seven. Mr. Minton had met her at the door and put her to work readying half-pound tins for the rest of the packers due in on the hour. The blenders, who worked on the upper floors

3

of the factory, had mixed two tons of Earl Grey the day before and it had to be packed by noon. Fifty-five girls had had five hours to pack eight thousand tins. That worked out to an allotment of about two minutes' labor per tin. Only Mr. Minton thought two minutes was too much, so he'd stood behind each girl in turn – timing her, shaming her, bullying her. All to gain a few seconds on the output of a tea tin.

Saturdays were only half-days, but they seemed endless. Mr. Minton drove her and the other girls terribly hard. It wasn't his fault, Fiona knew, he was only following orders from Burton himself. She suspected her employer hated having to give his workers half a day off, so he made them suffer for it. They got no breaks on Saturdays; she had to endure five long hours on her feet. If she was lucky, her legs went numb; if not, they ached with a slow, heavy pain that started in her ankles and climbed to her back. And worse than the standing was the grindingly dull nature of the work: glue a label on a tin, weigh out the tea, fill the tin, seal the tin, box the tin, then start all over again. The monotony was agony to a mind as bright as hers and there were days, like today, when she thought she'd go mad with it, when she doubted she'd ever escape it, and wondered if all her big plans, her sacrifices, would ever amount to anything.

She pulled the hairpins from the heavy knot at the back of her head and shook her hair free. Then she loosened the laces on her boots, kicked them off, peeled her stockings off, and stretched her long legs out before her. They still ached from standing and the walk to the river hadn't helped any. In the back of her mind, she heard her mother scolding. "If you 'ad any sense, child, any sense at all, you'd come straight 'ome and rest yourself instead of traipsing off down the river."

Not come to the river? she thought, admiring the silvery Thames as it shimmered in the August sunshine. Who could resist it? Lively waves slapped impatiently at the bottom of the Old Stairs, spraying her. She watched them inching toward her and fancied that the river wanted to touch her toes, swirl up over her ankles, draw her into its beckoning waters, and carry her along with it. Oh, if only she could go.

As she gazed out over the water, Fiona felt the weariness in her ebb – a weariness that left dark smudges under her brilliant blue eyes and a painful stiffness in her young body – and a sharp exhilaration take its place. The river restored her. People said that the City, the center of commerce and government to the west of Wapping, was London's heart. If that was true, then this river was her lifeblood. And Fiona's own heart quickened and leaped at its beauty.

Everything exciting in the world was right here before her. Watching ships traverse the river, their holds laden with cargo from all the far-flung reaches of the Empire, filled her with wonder. This afternoon the Thames was choked with traffic. Punts and lighters – small, quick boats – were plying the waters, ferrying men to and from ships moored midstream. A hulking steamer, intent upon her berth, shouldered smaller craft out of the way. A battered trawler, back from chasing cod in the icy waters of the North Sea, steamed upriver to Billingsgate. Barges jostled for right-of-way, moving upriver and down, discharging cargo – a ton of nutmeg here, sacks of coffee there. Barrels of treacle. Wool, wine, and whiskey. Sheaves of tobacco. And chest upon chest of tea.

And everywhere, standing on the jutting docks conferring with their captains, or moving between the casks and crates and towering pallets, were merchants – brisk, imperious men who swooped down from the City to examine their goods the second their ships arrived. They came in carriages, carried walking sticks, and flipped open gold watches with hands so fine and white, Fiona could hardly believe they belonged to men. They wore top hats and frock coats and were attended by clerks who dogged their heels, carried their ledgers, and poked into everything, frowning and scribbling. They were alchemists, these men. They took raw goods and changed them into gold. And Fiona longed to be one of them.

She didn't care that girls weren't supposed to involve themselves in business matters – especially girls from the docks, as her mother was always reminding her. Dock girls learned to cook, sew, and keep house so they could find husbands who'd look after them at least as well as their fathers had. "Foolishness," her mother called her ideas, advising her to spend more time improving her short crust and less time at the river. But her da didn't think her dreams were foolish. "Got to have a dream, Fee," he said. "The day you stop dreaming you might as well take yourself down to the undertaker's, for you're as good as dead."

Lost in the river's spell, Fiona didn't hear a pair of feet approach the top of the Old Stairs. She wasn't aware that the young man standing there smiled as he watched her, not wanting to disturb her, just wanting to gaze at her for a moment before he made his presence known, wanting to savor the image of her – slender and straight-backed against the backdrop of mossy stones and black mud banks.

"Coo-eee," he called softly.

Fiona turned around. Her face lit up at the sight of him, softening for a few seconds the resoluteness, the determination that was always present in her expression – a determination so apparent that neighbor women remarked upon it, clucking and sighing and gravely saying that a strong face meant a strong will. And a strong will meant trouble. She'd never get a husband, they said. Lads didn't like that in a lass.

But this lad didn't seem to mind it. No more than he minded the glossy black hair that curled around her face and tumbled down her back. Or the sapphire eyes that seemed to sparkle with blue fire.

"You're early, Joe," she said, smiling.

"Aye," he said, sitting down beside her. "Me and Dad finished up early at Spitalfields. The veg man's miserable with a cold, so 'e didn't 'aggle. I've got the next two hours to call me own. 'Ere," he added, handing her a flower. "Found that on me way over."

"A rose!" she exclaimed. "Thank you!" Roses were dear. It wasn't often he could afford to give her one. She touched the crimson petals to her cheek, then tucked it behind her ear. "What's the weekly report, then? 'Ow much 'ave we got?" she asked.

"Twelve pound, one shilling, sixpence."

"Add this to it," she said, pulling a coin from her pocket, "then we'll 'ave twelve and two."

"Can you spare it? Not skipping dinners again to save money, are you?"

"No."

"I mean it, Fee, I'll be angry if you are –"

"I said I'm not!" she bristled, changing the subject. "Before long we'll be at fifteen pounds, then twenty, and then twenty-five. It's really going to 'appen, isn't it?"

"Of course it is. At the rate we're going, another year and we'll 'ave our twenty-five quid. Enough for three months' rent, plus start-up stock."

"A whole year," Fiona echoed. "It sounds like forever."

"It'll go quick, luv," Joe said, squeezing her hand. "It's only this part that's 'ard. Six months after we open our first shop, we'll 'ave so much money, we'll open another. And then another, until we 'ave a whole chain. Be making money 'and over fist, we will."

"We'll be rich!" she said, brightening again.

Joe laughed. "Not right away. But one day we will. I promise you that, Fee."

Fiona hugged her knees to her chest, grinning. A year wasn't so long, not really, she told herself. Especially when she thought of how long they'd been talking about their shop. For ages, ever since they were children. And two years ago, they'd begun saving, putting money away in an old cocoa tin that Joe kept under his bed. Everything had gone into that tin – wages, Christmas and birthday coins, errand money, even a few farthings found in the street. Bit by bit, the coins had mounted up, and now they had twelve and two – a fortune.

Over the years, she and Joe had painted a picture of their shop in their imaginations, embellishing and refining it until the picture was so real she could close her eyes and smell the tea in its chest. She could feel the smooth oak counter under hand and hear the little brass doorbell tinkle as people came in. It would be a bright and gleaming place, not some tatty hole-in-the-wall. A real beauty, with the windows done up so nicely that people simply couldn't walk by. "It's all in the presentation, Fee," Joe always said. "That's what brings the punters in."

The shop would be a success, she knew it would. As a costermonger's son, Joe knew everything there was to know about selling. He'd grown up on a barrow, spending the first year of his life propped up in a basket between the turnips and the potatoes. He could bellow "Buy my fine parsley-o!" before he could say his name. With his know-how and their combined hard work, they couldn't possibly fail.

Our shop, ours alone, Fiona thought, gazing at Joe as he gazed at the river. Her eyes caressed his face, delighting in every detail – the strong line of his jaw, the sandy stubble covering his cheeks, the tiny scar above his eye. She knew its every plane and angle. There wasn't a time when Joe Bristow hadn't been part of her life and there never would be. She and Joe had grown up on the same shabby street, one house apart. From childhood they'd played together, roamed Whitechapel together, eased each other's hurts and heartaches.

They'd shared pennies and treats as children, now they shared their dreams. Soon they would share a life. They would be married, she and Joe. Not right away. She was only seventeen and her father would say that was too young. But in another year she'd be eighteen, and Joe twenty, and they would have money saved and excellent prospects.

Fiona stood up and jumped from the steps onto the stony flat below. Her body was humming with excitement. She trotted to the river's edge, scooped up a handful of stones, and skipped them across the water as hard and fast as she could. When she'd skipped them all, she turned to Joe, who was still sitting on the steps, watching her.

"One day, we'll be as big as all this," she shouted, thrusting her arms out wide. "Bigger than Whites or Sainsburys. Bigger than 'Arrods, too." She stood still for a few seconds, taking in the warehouses on either side of her, the wharves across the river. At a glance, she seemed so slight and fragile, nothing but a slip of a girl standing at the river's edge, dragging her hem in the mud. But eyes that lingered upon her as Joe's did could see the force of her ambition in her every expression, her every gesture, from the thrust of her chin to her rough worker's hands, now clenched into fists as if someone had challenged her.

"We'll be so big," she continued, "that every merchant on the river will be falling over 'imself to sell us 'is goods. We'll 'ave ten shops in London . . . no, twenty . . . and more all over the country. In Leeds and Liverpool. In Brighton and Bristol and Birmingham and . . ." She stopped, suddenly aware of Joe's gaze, suddenly shy. "Why are you looking at me like that?"

"Because you're such a queer lass."

"I'm not!"

"You are. You're the fiercest little lass I've ever seen. You've more bottle than most lads." Joe leaned back on his elbows and gave her an appraising look. "Maybe you're not a lass at all, maybe you're really a lad in disguise."

Fiona grinned. "Maybe I am. Maybe you better come down 'ere and find out."

Joe stood up and Fiona, full of mischief, turned and ran down the shore. A gravelly crunch behind her told her he'd jumped down and was pursuing her. She squealed with laughter as he grabbed her arm.

"You certainly run like a lass." He pulled her close and

9

made a big show of inspecting her face. "And I guess you're pretty enough to be a lass –"

"You *guess*?"

"Mmm-hmm, but I could still be wrong. I'd better make sure . . ."

Fiona felt his fingers brush her cheek. Ever so gently, he tilted her chin up and kissed her lips, parting them with his tongue. She closed her eyes and gave herself over to the pleasure of his kiss. She knew she shouldn't be doing this, not until they were married. Father Deegan would give her a string of Hail Marys to say at confession, and if her da found out he'd skin her alive. But oh, how lovely his lips felt, and his tongue was like velvet, and how sweet his skin smelled, warm from the afternoon sun. Before she knew what she was doing, she was up on her tiptoes, arms around his neck, kissing him back. Nothing felt as good as this, her body pressed against his, his strong arms around her.

Hoots and catcalls interrupted their embrace. A barge had come out of Wapping Entrance, gateway to the nearby London docks, and was sailing past. Its crew had caught an eyeful.

Beet-faced, Fiona pulled Joe into a maze of pilings, where they stayed until the barge was past. A church bell sounded the hour. It was growing late; she knew she should be home helping her mother get the dinner. And Joe had to get to the market. After one last kiss, they walked back to the Old Stairs. She scrambled up the steps to put her stockings and boots back on, tripping over her skirts as she did.

As she stood to go, she stole one final glimpse of the river. It would be a week before she could return – a week of rising in the darkness, trudging to Burton's and trudging back home, where chores of every description were always waiting. But it didn't matter, none of it mattered; one day she would leave it all behind. Out from the shore, white froths rose and curled on the water's surface. Waves danced. Was it her imagination, or did the river seem to leap with excitement for her, for them?

And why wouldn't it? she wondered, smiling. She and Joe had each other. They had twelve pounds, two shillings, and a dream. Never mind Burton's or the dreary streets of Whitechapel. In a year, the world would be theirs. Anything was possible.

"Paddy? Paddy, what time 'ave you got?" Kate Finnegan asked her husband.

"Hmmph?" he replied, his head buried in the day's newspaper.

"The time, Paddy," she said impatiently, one hand gripping the edge of a yellow mixing bowl, the other whisking together its contents.

"Kate, luv, you've just asked me," he sighed, reaching into his pocket. He pulled out a dented silver watch. "It's two o'clock exactly."

Frowning, Kate banged the whisk on the side of the bowl, knocking globs of cream-colored batter from its wires, then tossed it in the sink. She picked up a fork and poked it into one of the three mutton chops sizzling on top of the stove. A rivulet of juice ran down the side of the chop, sputtering into steam as it hit the hot metal of the frying pan. She speared the chops, dropped them onto a plate, and put them into a warming hatch next to the oven, alongside a jug of onion gravy. Next she picked up a rope of sausages and cut the links into the pan. As they began to fry, she sat down at the table across from her husband.

"Paddy," she said, lightly banging the palm of her hand on the table. "Paddy."

He looked over the top of his paper into his wife's large green eyes. "Yes, Kate. What, Kate?"

"You really should get after them. They can't just trundle in when they please, keeping you waiting for your dinner. And me standing 'ere, not knowing when to start the toad."

"They'll be along any minute now. Start the dinner. If it's cold when they get here, they've only themselves to blame."

"It's not just the dinner," she confessed. "I don't like them larking about with all this murder business going on."

"Sure, you don't t'ink the Whitechapel Murderer is running about in broad daylight? And stalking a tough little bugger like Charlie? God help him if he is, it'll be the murderer screaming murder after two minutes with that lad. To say not'ing of Fiona. Remember what happened to that bully Sid Malone when he tried to take her into an alley? Busted him in the nose, she did. Broke it. And him twice the size of her."

"Yes, but –"

"Here, Kate, there's an article on Ben Tillet, the union lad, organizing the men down the tea warehouses. Listen to this . . ."

Kate looked at her husband reproachfully. She could've told him the roof was on fire and received the same response. Whatever the paper said, she didn't want to hear it. Talk of unions worried her; talk of strikes terrified her. With a husband, four children, and a lodger to feed, she barely made it through the week as it was. If a strike was called, they'd starve. And if that wasn't enough to worry about, there was a murderer on the loose. Whitechapel had always been a tough neighborhood, a two-fisted mixture of Cockneys, Irish, Polish, Russians, Chinese, and a smattering of others. No one was rich, most were hardworking. Many were hard-drinking, too. There was plenty of crime, but it was mainly thieving. Thugs sometimes killed each other or a man died in a brawl, but nobody did this sort of thing, cutting up women.

With Paddy still reading, she stood up, moved to the stove, and prodded the sausages, grizzling in a slick layer of juices and fat. She picked up the mixing bowl and poured the batter into the frying pan, blanketing them. The batter hissed as it hit the hot drippings, then spread to the edges of the pan, where it bubbled and puffed. She smiled. The batter was airy and would brown nicely. A cup of ale always did the trick. She shoved the skillet into the oven, then

12

turned her attention to a pot of potatoes. As she mashed them, she heard the front door bang open and her daughter's steps, light and quick, in the hallway.

" 'Ello, Mam. 'Ello, Da," Fiona said brightly, depositing her week's wages minus sixpence in an old tea tin on the mantel.

" 'Ello, luv," Kate said, looking up from the potatoes to greet her.

Paddy grunted a greeting from behind his paper.

Fiona grabbed a pinafore from a hook near the back door. As she tied the strings behind her, she checked on her baby sister Eileen, asleep in a basket by the hearth, then bent down next to her four-year-old brother Seamus, who was sitting on a rug playing soldiers with some clothespegs, and gave him a kiss.

"Now give me one back, Seamie."

The little boy, all red hair and mischief, pressed his lips against her cheek and blew a loud, wet raspberry.

"Oh, Seamie!" she cried, wiping her cheek. "That wasn't very nice! Who taught you that?"

"Charlie!"

"That figures. What needs doing, Mam?"

"You can slice the bread. Then set the table, start the tea, and get your da 'is porter."

Fiona set about her work. "What's the news, Da?"

Paddy lowered his paper. "The union. Numbers are growing every day. Won't be long before the Wapping lads are in. Mark my words, we'll see a strike before the year's out. The unions will save the working class."

"And 'ow will they do that? By giving us an extra penny an hour so we can starve slowly instead of getting it over with all at once?"

"Don't start, Fiona . . ." Kate cautioned.

"Fine attitude, that. It's that Joe Bristow puts them anti-union ideas in your head. Costers, they're all the same. Too independent. Don't care about the rest of their class."

"I don't need Joe to put ideas in me 'ead, I've plenty of

13

me own, thank you. And I'm not anti-union. It's just that I prefer to make me own way. Whoever waits for dock owners and factory owners to answer to a bunch of ragtag unionists is going to wait a good long time."

Paddy shook his head. "You should be joining up, paying dues, putting some of your wages to work for the common good. Otherwise, you're behaving just like one of them."

"Well, I'm not one of them, Da!" Fiona said hotly. "I get up and work every day but Sunday, just like you. I believe working people should 'ave better lives. Of course I do. I'm just not prepared to sit on my arse and wait for Ben Tillet to bring it all about."

"Fiona, watch your tongue," Kate scolded, checking on the batter.

"Do you really think, Da, that William Burton will allow 'is premises to go union?" she continued, unheeding. "You work for 'im; you know what 'e's like as well as I do. Tighter than bark to a tree. 'E wants to keep 'is profits, not share them."

"What you don't see, lass, is you have to start somewhere," Paddy said heatedly, straightening in his chair. "You go to meetings, spread the word, get all of Burton's workers behind the union – the lads at the docks, the lasses at his factories – then he'll have no choice but to accept it. You have to make the small gains before you make the big ones. Like the match girls at Bryant and May's. Protesting against the terrible conditions and the fines for talking or going to the loo. They won after only a t'ree week stoppage. A bunch of wee lasses! There's power in numbers, Fiona, mark my words. Unions will save the dockers, the whole working class."

"Never mind saving it," she said. "Just save me from it."

Paddy brought his fist crashing down on the table, making his wife and daughter jump. "That's enough!" he thundered. "I won't have talk against me own class in me own house." Glowering, he took up his newspaper and snapped the creases out of it.

Fiona was steaming, but knew better than to open her mouth.

"When will you learn?" Kate asked her.

She shrugged as if none of it mattered and started to lay the knives and forks, but Kate wasn't fooled. Fiona was angry, but she ought to know by now to keep her opinions to herself. Paddy always said he encouraged his children to think for themselves, but like all fathers, he actually preferred they think like him.

Kate glanced between her husband and daughter. Lord God, are they alike, she thought. Same jet-black hair, same blue eyes, same stubborn chin. Both of them with their big ideas – that's the Irish in them. Dreamers, they are. Himself always dreaming after tomorrow, when the capitalists repent their evil ways and pigs fly. And that lass, scheming for that shop of hers. She has no idea how hard it will be to make a go of it. You can't tell her anything. But it's always been that way with her. Too big for her britches.

Her eldest daughter worried Kate greatly. Fiona's single mindedness, her sense of purpose, was so strong, so directed, it was frightening. A sudden stab of emotion, fierce and protective, pierced her heart. How many dock girls make a go of a shop? she wondered. What if she gets as far as opening it only to see it fail? It'll break her heart. And then she'll spend the rest of her life bitter over something she never should have wished for in the first place.

Kate confided these worries to her husband on many occasions, but Paddy, proud of the fire in his eldest girl, always argued that spirit was a fine thing in a lass. Spirit a fine thing? She knew better. Spirit was what got lasses sacked from their jobs or got them black eyes from their husbands. What good was spirit when the whole world was just ready and waiting to knock it out of you? She sighed deeply – a long, noisy mother's sigh. The answer to those questions would have to wait. Dinner was ready.

"Fiona, where's your brother?" she asked.

"Down the gasworks after lumps of coke. Said 'e was going to sell them to Mrs. MacCallum for 'er fire. She won't pay for coal."

"That lad's got more ways to make two bob than the Bank of England. He'd skin a turd for a farthing," Paddy commented.

"Enough! This is my kitchen, not a gutter!" Kate scolded. "Fiona, put the gravy on the table."

There was the sound of trundling from the front of the house. The door opened and the trundling came inside. Charlie was home, with his wooden cart in tow.

Little Seamie's head snapped up. "The Whitechapel Murderer!" he shouted gleefully.

Kate frowned. She did not approve of this, her sons' ghoulish new game.

"Yes, little boy," came a ghostly voice from the hallway. "It's the Whitechapel Murderer, guv'nor of the night, come to look for naughty children."

The voice broke into evil laughter and Seamie, squealing with terror and delight, charged about on his stubby legs, looking for a place to hide.

"Come 'ere, pet!" Fiona whispered, running to the rocker in front of the hearth. She sat down and spread her skirts out. Seamie crawled under, but forgot to pull in his feet. Charlie tramped into the kitchen, still cackling like a fiend. When he saw the little boots sticking out from under his sister's skirts, it was all he could do to keep from laughing and wreck the game.

" 'Ave *you* seen any naughty little boys, missus?" Charlie asked his mother.

"Go on with you," Kate said, swatting him. "Don't scare your brother so."

"Oh, 'e loves it," Charlie whispered, shushing her. "Oh, Shaaymeeeee," he called, wheedling and coaxing, "come out, come out!" He opened the cupboard door. " 'E's not in 'ere." He looked under the sink. "Not in 'ere." He walked over to his sister. " 'Ave *you* seen any bad little boys?"

"Only the one I'm looking at," Fiona replied, smoothing her skirts.

"Is that so? Are these your feet sticking out 'ere, then? Seems like awfully small feet for a big fat cow of a lass like yourself. Let me 'ave a closer look . . . aha!"

Charlie grabbed Seamie's ankles and pulled him out. Seamie screeched and Charlie commenced tickling him to within an inch of his life.

"Take it easy, Charlie," Kate cautioned. "Let 'im catch 'is breath."

Charlie paused and Seamie kicked him in the leg to get him to start again. When he was truly breathless, Charlie stopped, giving him a fond pat on the head. Seamie, sprawled out on the floor panting, regarded his brother with utter adoration. Charlie was the center of his universe, his hero. He worshiped him, followed him around, even insisted on dressing like him, right down to the bit of fabric he made his mother tie around his neck in imitation of Charlie's kingsman – a bright red neckerchief that all the flash lads wore. The two boys were almost identical, both taking after their mother with their red hair, green eyes, and freckles.

Charlie hung up his jacket, then took a handful of coins from his pocket and dropped them into the tea tin. "A little bit more than usual, Mam. Got a few extra hours this week."

"Thank you, luv, I'm glad of it. I've been trying to put something aside for a jacket for your da. Malphlin's 'ave got some nice second'and ones. I've mended 'is old one so many times it's nothing but thread and patches."

He sat down at the table, picked up a thick slice of bread and began to wolf it. Paddy looked over his paper, saw him eating, and cuffed the top of his head. "Wait for your mother and sister. And take off your hat when you eat."

"Fiona, get Seamie settled, will you?" Kate said. "Where's Roddy? Still asleep? Usually the smell of dinner gets 'im moving. Charlie, go shout 'im down."

17

Charlie got up from the table and went to the staircase. "Uncle Rodd-eee! Dinner's ready!" There was no response. He tramped upstairs.

Fiona washed Seamie's hands and sat him at the table. She tied a napkin around his neck and gave him a piece of bread to keep him quiet. Then she went to the cupboard, took down six plates and carried them to the stove. Three plates got a chop each, mashed potatoes, and gravy. Kate pulled the skillet from the oven and divided its contents and the rest of the potatoes and gravy between the remaining three.

"Toad in the 'ole!" Seamie crowed, regarding the crispy puff of batter, hungrily counting the nuggets of sausage peeping out from their doughy covering like so many timid toads.

Neither Kate nor Fiona ever thought to question the chops on the men's plates and the batter on their own. Men were the breadwinners and needed meat to keep up their strength. Women and children got a taste of bacon or sausage on the weekends if the week's wages stretched that far. The fact that Kate worked over a copper and mangle hefting and wringing loads of wet laundry all day long or that Fiona stood on her feet packing tea for hours at a stretch was not considered and would have made no difference if it had been. Paddy's and Charlie's wages made up the lion's share of the household income; they paid the rent, bought clothes, and provided most of the food. Kate's and Fiona's earnings went for coal and household necessities like boot black, kerosene, and matches. If Paddy or Charlie took ill and missed work, everyone would suffer. It was the same in every home on every street in East London – men got the meat and women got what they could.

Kate heard Charlie's heavy steps on the stairs again.

" 'E's not 'ere, Mam," he said, returning to the table. "Doesn't look like 'is bed's been slept in, either."

"That's odd," Paddy said.

"And 'ere's 'is dinner getting cold," Kate fretted. "Fiona, pass it back to me, I'll put it in the oven. Where is 'e? Wasn't 'e 'ere this morning, Paddy?"

"No, but he usually doesn't come in till after I leave, so I wouldn't have seen him."

"I 'ope 'e's all right. 'Ope nothing 'appened to 'im."

"I t'ink we'd have heard by now if somet'ing had," Paddy said. "Maybe somebody on the next shift was sick and he had to take his place. You know Roddy, he'll turn up."

Roddy O'Meara, the Finnegans' lodger, was not related to the family, but the children still called him Uncle. He'd grown up with Paddy and Paddy's younger brother, Michael, in Dublin, and had emigrated first to Liverpool and then to London with them, staying in Whitechapel with Paddy while Michael continued on to New York. He had known the Finnegan children all their lives – had dandled each one on his knee, rescued them from bullies and mean dogs, and told them ghost stories by the fire at night. He was more of an uncle to them than their real uncle, whom they'd never seen, and they adored him.

Kate mashed the tea and sat down. Paddy said the blessing and the family began to eat. She regarded her brood and smiled. When they were eating, they were quiet. There might actually be two minutes of peace now. Charlie was tearing through his dinner. There was no filling him up. He wasn't a tall lad, but he was big for his sixteen years. Broad-shouldered and just as tough and scrappy as the bull terriers some of the neighborhood men kept.

"Any more spuds, Mam?" he asked.

"On the stove."

He got up and shoveled more potatoes onto his plate. Just then the front door opened.

"Roddy, that you?" Kate shouted. "Charlie, get your uncle 'is plate . . ." Her words trailed off as Roddy appeared in the doorway. Fiona, Paddy, even Seamie stopped eating and looked at him.

"Jaysus!" Paddy exclaimed. "What the divil happened to you?"

Roddy O'Meara didn't answer. His face was ashen. He

held his policeman's helmet in one hand. His jacket hung open and there was a crimson smear across the front of it.

"Roddy, lad . . . speak, would you?" Paddy said.

"Another murder," Roddy finally said. "Buck's Row. A woman named Polly Nichols."

"Jaysus," Paddy said. Kate gasped. Fiona and Charlie were wide-eyed.

"She was still warm. You can't imagine what he'd done. The blood – it was everywhere. Everywhere. A man found the body on his way to work just before dawn. I spotted him running down the street, yelling. Woke the whole place up. I went back with him and there she was. T'roat cut. Rest of her opened up like somet'ing in a slaughterhouse. Lost me dinner right there. Meantime, it's getting lighter and people are gathering. I sent the man down the station to get more help and by the time it arrived, I nearly had a riot on me hands." Roddy paused, passing a hand over his weary face. "Couldn't move the body till the detectives in charge of the case came. And the coroner. By the time they were done, we had a whole squad out front just to keep the people back. Furious, they were. Another woman dead. This boyo's dancing circles round us."

"Papers t'ink so," Paddy said. "All righteous, they are. Going on about the squalor and depravity of the poor giving rise to a fiend. Them damn rags never paid any attention to East London before. Takes a lunatic on the loose to get the upper classes to take any notice of Whitechapel. And they're only talking about it now because they'd like to put a fence around it, keep your man inside so he can't take a walk west and trouble the quality."

"No chance of that," Roddy said. "This lad sticks to his pattern. Always goes after the same kind of woman – drunk and broken-down. He sticks to Whitechapel, knows it like the back of his hand. Moves like a ghost, he does. A brutal murder happens and nobody's seen not'ing, heard not'ing." He was silent for a few seconds, then he said: "I'll never forget the sight of her."

20

"Roddy, luv," Kate said gently, "eat something. You need some food inside you."

"I don't t'ink I could. I've no appetite at all."

"Cor, it's 'orrible," Fiona said, shuddering. "Buck's Row isn't so far away. Makes a body jumpy to think about it."

Charlie snorted. "What are you worried about? 'E only goes after whores."

"Give over, Charlie," Kate said testily. Blood and guts at the table. Now whores.

"Christ, but I'm tired," Roddy said. "Feel like I could sleep for a week, but I have to appear at the inquest this evening."

"Go up and rest," Paddy said.

"Aye, I t'ink I will. Save me dinner, will you, Kate?"

Kate said she would. Roddy stripped off his suspenders and undershirt, gave himself a quick wash, then went upstairs.

"Poor Uncle Roddy," Fiona said. "What a shock that must've given 'im. Probably take 'im ages to get over it."

"It would me. Can't stand blood. I'd have passed right out beside her," Paddy said.

I hope they catch him, whoever he is, before he does someone else, Kate thought. She glanced down the hallway toward the door. He's out there right now. Maybe sleeping or eating or out at a pub like everyone else. Maybe he works at the docks. Maybe he lives two streets over. Maybe he walks past our house at night. Though she was warm from cooking, she suddenly shivered. "Someone just walked across your grave," her mother used to say when that happened.

"I wonder if the murderer –" Charlie started to say.

"For God's sake, no more!" she snapped. "Now finish the dinner I cooked for you."

"Kate, what's the matter?" Paddy asked. "You look as white as a ghost."

"Nothing. I just wish this . . . this monster would go away. I wish they'd catch 'im."

"Don't worry, luv. No murderer's going to come after you or anyone else in this family," Paddy soothed, taking his wife's hand. "Not as long as I'm around, he isn't."

Kate forced a smile. We're safe, she told herself, all of us. In a sturdy house with strong locks. She knew they were strong, for she'd had Paddy test them. Her children slept soundly at night with their father upstairs, and Roddy, too. No fiend would be reaching in to harm any of them. But still, Fiona was right. It made a body jumpy to dwell on him. It chilled one to the bone.

"Pippins! Lovely pips 'ere! Four a penny, none finer in London!"

"Cockles, fresh cockles, all alive-o!"

"Who'll buy me fine 'errings? Still jumping! Still breathing!"

It was the same every Saturday evening; Fiona could always hear the market before she saw it. From two streets away, the cries of the costermongers had already begun to reach her ears. Spilling from stalls and barrows, they echoed and bounced over rooftops, down alleyways, around corners, beckoning.

"The best parsley right 'ere, ladies! Buy my fine parsley-o!"

"Orrrrrranges, two a penny! Who'll buy me fat oranges?"

And over the music of the market a new, discordant note rose, one that quickened the steps of the evening shoppers and made them eager to be home by their fires, their doors bolted behind them. "Another 'orrible murder!" cried a ragamuffin newsboy. "Only in the *Clarion!* Get'cher news 'ere! Drawings of the murder scene, blood everywhere! Buy the *Clarion!*"

As they turned onto Brick Lane, Fiona's excitement grew. Here was the market, all lit up and stretched out before her. A laughing, bawling, wheedling creature. A big, roistering, ever-changing being that she could step into and

22

become a part of. She tugged at her mother's arm.

"Give over, Fiona. I'm walking as fast as I can," Kate said, eyeing her shopping list.

Cockney voices, brash and bluff, continued their lusty bellowing. Strutting and crowing like prizefighting cocks, the costers dared market-goers to find fault and challenged other costers to better their prices – practicing the East London trick of fending off trouble by inviting it. "Old trout?" Fiona heard one coster shout at a customer who'd questioned his wares. "Them trouts is fresh as a daisy. You want to see an old trout? Look in a mirror!"

Fiona saw the fishmonger with his trays of crinkled whelks, tiny blue-tipped cockles, fat herrings, and buckets of oysters – a sample few shucked and glistening on the half shell. Next to it was a butcher's stall – its edges festooned with crimson and white crepe paper, its boards stacked with neat rows of plump chops, stubby sausages, and grisly dripping pigs' heads.

A multitude of greengrocers – the more ambitious with barrows boasting carefully constructed pyramids of fruit: shiny pippin apples, fragrant pears, bright oranges and lemons, damsons and grapes. And, in front, baskets of nubby cauliflowers, broccoli heads, purple pickling cabbages, turnips, onions, and potatoes to boil or bake.

Flickering light from gas lamps, naphtha flares, and even bits of candle stuck into turnips illuminated the scene. And the smells! Fiona stood still, closed her eyes and inhaled. A salty ocean smell – cockles soused with vinegar. A whiff of spice – apple fritters sprinkled with cinnamon sugar. Fried sausages, jacket potatoes, warm ginger nuts. Her stomach growled.

She opened her eyes. Her mother was making her way toward a butcher's stall. As she watched her move through the mass of people, it seemed to her that the entire East End was there – familiar faces and foreign ones. Solemn, pious Jews hurried from their worship; sailors bought jellied eels or hot pea soup; workingmen of all sorts, clean-shirted and clean-shaven, idled in pub doorways, some with squirming terriers tucked under their arms.

And everywhere countless numbers of women of every age and description squeezed, prodded, bartered, and bought. Some were attended by their husbands, who held baskets and puffed on pipes. Others were beleaguered by children, yowling in their arms, pulling at their skirts, pestering for cakes, candies, or hot muffins. Cockney kids crying Mum and Irish kids crying Mam. For Italian and Polish and Russian kids it was Mama, but their pleas were all the same – a pretty sweet, a colored lolly, a shiny brandy snap. And the harried mothers without enough money for the week's meals buying an iced bun to be split among three, just so their children could have a taste of something nice.

Fiona looked around for her mother and spotted her at the butcher's. "Roast beef tomorrow, is it, Mrs. Finnegan?" she heard the man ask as she joined her.

"Not this week, Mr. Morrison. Me rich uncle 'asn't died yet. But I do need a cut of brisket. About three pounds or so. Five pence a pound's my limit."

"Mmmmm . . ." The man pressed his lips together and frowned. "All me cuts is on the large side tonight . . . but I'll tell you what I could do, luv . . ." He paused dramatically, leaning forward on spread-fingered hands. ". . . I could do you a five-pounder for a very nice price."

"I'm sure that's too dear for me."

"Nonsense, duck," he said, his voice dropping conspiratorially. "Y'see, the bigger the piece, the less I 'as to charge per pound. It's 'olesale economicals. You pay more for the 'ole thing because it's bigger, but you pay less, really . . ."

With her mother and the butcher busy dickering, Fiona searched the street for Joe. She spotted him five barrows down, hawking his goods. Although the night was no longer warm, his collar was open, his sleeves rolled up, the color high in his cheeks. For the last year or so, at Joe's insistence, Mr. Bristow had let him do more of the patter instead of keeping him behind the stall. And wisely so, for he was a natural. Every week he single-handedly moved hundreds of pounds of produce – more than any clerk at a fancy West End shop moved in a month. And he did it without the benefit of a high-end shop name behind him, or pretty window displays, or billboards, ads, anything. He did it with nothing but his own raw talent.

Fiona felt a thrill of excitement as she watched him work, coaxing customer after customer out of the crowd. Catching a lady's eye. Reeling her in. All the time joking and laughing – keeping the patter going, the interest high. Nobody played the game like Joe. He knew how to entertain and flirt with the brassy ones, and how to make his voice serious and sincere for the suspicious ones, feigning hurt and disbelief if a woman wrinkled her nose at his offerings, daring her to find a better bunch of carrots, a finer onion, anywhere in London. He had a showman's way of slicing open an orange and squeezing its juice in an arc across the cobblestones. Fiona saw that it caught the eyes of passing shoppers ten feet away. Then he'd snap open a sheet of newspaper, shovel "not two, not three, but four large and lovely oranges, all yours for tuppence!" into it, twist it closed, and hand it over with a flourish.

Of course, his beautiful sky-blue eyes and his smile don't hurt business, either, Fiona thought. Nor did the mass of dark blond curls caught up in a ponytail and spilling out from under his cap. A warm flush came over her, coloring her cheeks. She knew she should keep her thoughts pure, as the nuns had warned, but that was getting harder to do. There was a triangle of skin showing in his open collar, underneath the red neckerchief he wore. She imagined touching him there, pressing her lips against him. His skin would be so warm and smell so good. She loved the way he smelled – of the fresh green things he handled all day. Of his horse. Of the East London air, tinged with coal smoke and the river.

He had touched her inside her blouse once. In the dark,

behind the Black Eagle Brewery. He'd kissed her lips, her throat, the hollow of her neck, before undoing her blouse, then her camisole and slipping his hand inside. She'd felt as if she would melt from the heat of his touch, from the heat of her own desire. She'd pulled away, not from any sense of shame or modesty, but from a fear of wanting more and not knowing where that desire would lead. She knew that there were things men and women did together, things that were not allowed before marriage.

No one had ever told her about these things – what little knowledge she had, she'd picked up from the street. She'd heard neighborhood men talking about mating their dogs, heard the lads' rude jokes and, together with her friends, had eavesdropped on the conversations of their sisters and mothers. Some of them spoke of being in bed with a man with the long-suffering air of a martyr, others giggled and laughed and said they couldn't get enough.

Joe suddenly caught sight of her and flashed a smile. She blushed, certain he knew what she'd been thinking.

"Come on, Fee," her mother called. "I've still got the veg to get . . ." Kate headed across the street to Bristows and Fiona followed.

" 'Ello, luv!" Fiona heard Joe's mother call to her mother. Rose Bristow and Kate Finnegan had grown up together on the same dreary close off Tilley Street in Whitechapel, and now lived only doors down from each other on Montague Street. From stories her mam had told her, Fiona knew they'd been inseparable as girls, always giggling and whispering together, and even now, as married women, easily fell back into their old ways.

"Thought the murderer might've got you," Rose said to Kate. She was a small, plump hen of a woman, with the same easy smile and merry blue eyes as her son. "Seems like 'e's decided to work overtime this week. 'Ello, Fiona!"

" 'Ello, Mrs. Bristow," Fiona replied, her eyes on Joe.

"Oh, Rose!" Kate said. "Don't even joke! It's 'orrible! I wish to God they'd catch 'im. I'm jumpy just coming to

26

the market. Ah, well, we still 'ave to eat, don't we? I'll 'ave three pounds of spuds and two of peas. 'Ow dear are your apples, luv?"

Joe handed the broccoli he'd been holding to his father. He came over to Fiona, took off his cap and wiped his brow on his sleeve. "Cor, but we're busy tonight, Fee. Can't move the stuff fast enough! We'll run out of apples before closing time. I told Dad we should buy more . . ."

". . . but 'e didn't listen," Fiona finished, giving his hand a sympathetic squeeze. This was a familiar complaint. Joe was always pushing his father to expand the business and Mr. Bristow was always resisting. She knew how much it upset Joe that his father never listened to him. "Twelve and two . . ." she said, using their secret code – the current amount of money in their cocoa tin – to cheer him up, ". . . just think of that."

"I will," he said, smiling at her. "It'll be more after tonight, too. Bound to 'ave a little extra brass with this crowd. They 'ardly let you catch your breath." He glanced over at his father and younger brother Jimmy, swarmed by customers. "I'd better get back. I'll see you tomorrow after dinner. Will you be around?"

"Oh, I don't know," Fiona said airily. "Depends on if my other suitors come calling."

Joe rolled his eyes. "Oh, aye. Like the cat's meat man," he said, referring to the gnarled old man two stalls down who sold offal for pet food. "Or was it the rag-and-bone man?"

"I'll take the rag-and-bone man any day over a good-for-nothing coster," Fiona said, nudging the toe of Joe's boot with her own.

"Oh, I'd take the coster!" a girlish voice chirped.

Fiona turned her head and stifled a groan. It was Millie Peterson. Spoiled, arrogant, full-of-herself Millie. So blond, so buxom, so bright and pretty. Such a bloody little bitch. Millie's father Tommy was one of the biggest produce men in London, with wholesale concerns in both the East End

27

and Covent Garden. A self-made man, he'd started out with only a barrow and his own ability, and with hard work and a bit of luck he'd made it to the top. As businessmen went, there was none shrewder. As busy as he was, he spent as much time as possible on the streets, getting his knowledge firsthand by watching his customers and their customers.

Tommy had grown up in Whitechapel. As a newly married man, he lived on Chicksand Street, only a street away from Montague. As a child, Millie had played with Fiona and Joe and all the other children in the neighborhood. But as soon as he started to make some money, Peterson moved his family to a better locale – up-and-coming Pimlico. Shortly after moving, Tommy's wife became pregnant with her second child. She died in child-birth and the infant with her. Tommy was shattered. Millie was all he had left and she became the focus of his existence. He showered her with affection and gifts, trying to make up for the mother she'd lost. Whatever Millie wanted, Millie got. And ever since she'd been a little girl, Millie had wanted Joe. And although Joe did not return her feelings, Millie persisted, determined she would get what she wanted. She usually did.

There was no love lost between Fiona Finnegan and Millie Peterson, and if she could've, Fiona would've told her where to go right then and there. But she was at the Bristows' pitch, and the Bristows bought much of their stock from Millie's father and getting good prices depended to a large degree on good relations. She knew she would have to behave herself and hold her tongue. At least she'd have to try.

"Hello, Joe," Millie said, smiling sweetly at him. "Hello, Fiona," she said, nodding curtly. "Still on Montague Street, are you?"

"No, Millie," Fiona answered, poker-faced. "We've taken up residence in the West End. A lovely little place. Buckingham Palace it's called. It's a long walk for me da to the docks every morning, but the neighbor'ood's ever so much nicer."

Millie's smile soured. "Are you making fun of me?"

"Whatever gave you —"

"So then, Millie," Joe cut in, shooting a look at Fiona, "what brings you 'ere?"

"Just out for a stroll with my father. He wants to have a look around, see who's doing well, who isn't. You know him, always an eye on the main chance."

Out for a stroll, my arse, Fiona thought acidly. Turned out like that?

All eyes were upon Millie, Joe's included. She was dazzling in a moss-green skirt and matching jacket, cut tight to show off her small waist and full bosom. No woman in Whitechapel owned an outfit like that, much less wore it to the market. Her golden curls were swept up under a matching cap. Pearl earrings complemented the ruff of lace at her throat and the ivory kid gloves encasing her dainty hands.

Looking at her, Fiona felt a sharp stab of self-consciousness at the drabness of her own woolen skirt, her white cotton blouse, the gray knitted shawl around her shoulders. She squashed the feeling immediately; she would not allow the likes of Millie Peterson to make her feel inferior.

"Is 'e finding any new customers, then?" Joe asked, his eyes, and a dozen others, straying from Millie's face to her chest.

"A few. But it's not only customers he's after. He likes to come to the market to spy out new talent. He's always looking for lads with promise. I'm sure he'd be taken with you," she said, laying her hand on his forearm.

A jealous anger surged through Fiona. Sod good relations; Millie Peterson had just crossed the line. "You feeling ill, Millie?"

"Ill?" Millie asked, eyeing her like so much rubbish. "No, I'm fine."

"Really? You look like you might fall over, leaning on Joe

like that. Joe, why don't you get Millie a crate to sit on?"

"There's no need, thank you," Millie snapped. She removed her hand from Joe's arm.

"If you say so. Wouldn't want you to faint away. Maybe your jacket's too tight."

"Why, you little cow!" Millie cried, her cheeks turning red.

"Better a cow than a bitch."

"Ladies, that's no way to be'ave. Can't 'ave a row in the market, now, can we?" Joe joked, trying to defuse the two girls, who were regarding each other like bristle-backed cats ready to strike.

"No, we can't," Millie sniffed. "That's gutter behavior. For guttersnipes."

"Watch who you call a guttersnipe. You came out of the same gutter, Millie," Fiona said, her voice low and hard. "Maybe you've forgotten that, but nobody else 'as."

Sensing defeat, Millie changed her tack. "I should go. It's plain I'm not wanted here."

"Aw, Millie," Joe said awkwardly. "Fiona didn't mean it."

"Yes, I did."

"It's all right," Millie said mournfully, turning her huge hazel eyes on Joe. "I've got to find my father anyway. I'll see you about. Hopefully in better company. Ta-ra."

"Ta-ra, Millie," Joe said. "Give me regards to your dad."

As soon as Millie was out of earshot, Joe turned to Fiona. "Did you 'ave to do that? Did you 'ave to insult Tommy Peterson's daughter?"

"She 'ad it coming. Thinks she can buy you with 'er father's money. Like a sack of oranges."

"That's ridiculous and you know it."

Fiona kicked at the ground.

"You ought to watch that temper of yours. Are you going to be'ave like that when we 'ave our shop? Putting your nonsense before good business?"

Joe's words cut Fiona. He was right. She had behaved stupidly.

30

"Joe! 'Elp us out, will you?" Mr. Bristow shouted.

"Right away, Dad!" Joe shouted. "I've got to go, Fee. See if you can finish your marketing without causing any more trouble, all right? And don't be so jealous."

"Who's jealous? I'm not jealous, it's . . . it's just that she's unbearable, that's all."

"You're jealous and you've no reason to be," he said, returning to his pitch.

"I'm not!" Fiona shouted, stamping her foot. She watched Joe take his place out in front of the barrow again. "Jealous," she huffed. "Why should I be jealous? She's only got pretty clothes and jewelry and big bubs and a pretty face and all the money in the world."

Why in the world should Joe fancy her, when she had so much less to offer him than Millie did? Millie, with her big important father and his big important money, could get Joe a shop just like that. Ten shops. He'd probably call the whole thing off any day now – their plans, their shop, everything – to take up with Millie. Especially now that she had behaved so badly and made him angry. Well, let him. She wouldn't be dumped like a sack of rotten spuds. She'd beat him to it. She'd tell him she liked Jimmy Shea, the publican's son, better. Tears pricked behind her eyes. They were just about to spill over when her mother came up behind her.

"Was that Millie Peterson I just saw?" Kate asked, glancing at her daughter's face.

"Aye," Fiona said glumly.

"Lord, but she puts 'er goods on show, doesn't she? Overbearing sort of lass."

Fiona brightened a little. "You think so, Mam?"

"Aye, I do. Come on, let's 'urry, I want to get 'ome . . ." Her mother's voice trailed off as she moved toward another stall, and Fiona heard Joe's voice rising above the general din as he resumed his patter. He sounded livelier than ever. She turned to look at him.

He smiled at her and even though she was standing in

the dark, Fiona felt as if the sun had just come out. "This smashing cabbage . . ." he was saying, ". . . usually I'd charge thruppence for a specimen of this quality, but tonight it's free! Free, that is, to the prettiest girl in the market. And there she is!" He lobbed the cabbage at her. She caught it. "Ah, ladies," he sighed, shaking his head. "What can I say? She stole me cabbage and me 'eart, but if she won't 'ave me, I'll take you instead, me darling," he said, winking at a customer who was at least seventy and nearly toothless.

"I'll take you, too, laddie!" the old lady shouted back. "But keep your cabbage, I'd rather 'ave yer cucumber!" The women at Bristows' screeched bawdy laughter and Joe's mother and father were once more wrapping produce as fast as they could.

The prettiest girl in the market! Fiona was beaming. How silly she'd been, getting so jealous over Millie. Joe was hers and hers alone. She waved good-bye to him and ran off to catch up with her mother. She felt happy and sure of herself again. Her emotions had boiled up, then spent themselves like a sea fret and were now forgotten.

Fiona's happiness would certainly have been dampened if she'd remained at the Bristows' pitch a few seconds longer. For just as she left to follow her mother, Millie reappeared, her father in tow. She tugged on his sleeve and pointed at Joe, as if she were pointing at something in a shop window, something she meant to have. But Tommy Peterson didn't need to have his attention directed to Joe. His sharp eyes had already fastened upon him, noting with approval how quickly he moved his stock. For the first time that evening, Tommy smiled. How right his daughter was; here was a lad with promise.

2

"Five bloody pence an hour for slaving our guts out, lads," Paddy Finnegan said, slamming his glass on the bar. "No overtime pay. And now the bastard holds back our plus money."

"Bloody Burton's got no right," said Shane Patterson, a man who worked with Paddy. "Curran said if we got the boat unloaded by five o'clock tonight we'd get our plus. We was done by four. Then 'e says 'e ain't paying!"

" 'E can't do that," Matt Williams, another workmate, said.

"But he did," Paddy said, remembering the anger, the shouts and curses, when their foreman told them that their plus – a bonus paid for the quick unloading of cargo – was being withheld.

The pub door opened. All eyes fastened on it. The Lion was a dangerous place to be tonight. Ben Tillet, the union organizer, was speaking, and every man in the place was jeopardizing his job by being here. The newcomer was Davey O'Neill, another docker from Oliver's. Paddy was surprised to see him. Davey had made it clear he wanted nothing to do with the union. A young man, he already had three small children. It was all he could do to feed them and he was terrified of losing his job.

"Hey, Davey lad!" Paddy shouted, motioning him over.

Davey, a slim man with sandy hair and anxious eyes, greeted them all.

"A pint for me, Maggie, and one for me mate," Paddy called to the barmaid, jostling the man on his right and knocking his glass. He apologized for the spilled beer and offered to buy him a new pint, but the man shook his head. "No harm done," he said.

The pints arrived, thick and foamy, and the barmaid took their price from a pile of coins on the bar. Davey protested, but Paddy waved him off. "What brings you here?" he asked. "T'ought you were steering clear."

"I was till today. Till Curran robbed us." Davey said. "Thought I'd come and 'ear what Tillet 'as to say. I'm not saying I'm joining, but I'll 'ear 'im out. Don't know who to believe. Union says it'll get us sixpence an hour, but Burton says 'e'll give us the sack for joining. If I lose me job I'm done for. Lizzie, me youngest, she's taken ill again. Weak lungs. I can't afford the medicine. Me wife does what she can, putting poultices on 'er, but it's not enough, the poor wee thing cries . . ." Davey stopped talking; his jaw was working.

"You don't 'ave to explain, lad. We're all in the same boat," Paddy said.

"Aye," Matt said. "The one with the 'ole in it. You 'eard Curran at dinnertime."

Paddy remembered the lecture their foreman had given them earlier. "Think of your families, lads. Look at the risks you're taking," he'd said.

"It's them we are t'inking of," he'd shot back. "We'll never get anywhere if we don't take a stand. We know Burton's talking to banks, Curran. Looking for money to build up Burton Tea. You tell him we are Burton Tea, and if he wants to make improvements, he can start with our wages."

"Lads, lads," Curran had said. "Burton'll never have his arm twisted by the likes of you. Give up this union stuff. You'll never win."

"I heard him, Davey," Paddy said now. "It's all talk. He's on a big push to expand the company. A mate down the tea auctions tells me he's t'inking of buying a whole bloody estate in India. Says he's talking about putting Burton Tea on the stock exchange to pay for it all. Believe you me, if anyone's scared, it's him. Scared we'll go union and squeeze an extra penny out of him, so he t'reatens to sack us. But just t'ink for a minute . . . what if we all joined? All the lads at the wharf, all the lads in Wapping? He couldn't fire us then. How would he replace us? All the men would be union, y'see, and no union man would take the job. That's why we've got to join."

"I don't know," Davey said. "Listening's one thing, joining's another."

"All right, then," Paddy said, looking at each of his mates in turn. "This is what we'll do. We'll hear the man out. He's a docker. He knows what we're up against. If we don't like what he says, no harm done. If we do, then he's got himself four new members."

They all agreed. Shane said he'd look for a table; Matt and Davey followed him. Paddy ordered another pint. As the barmaid refilled his glass, he looked at his pocket watch. Seven-thirty. The meeting was supposed to have started half an hour ago. Where was Tillet? He glanced around the pub, but didn't see anyone he thought might be the union leader. Then again, all he'd ever seen of him were drawings in newspapers, and you wouldn't recognize yourself from those.

"I think you've convinced your mates to join," said the man on his right, the one he'd jostled earlier. Paddy turned to him. He was a younger man, slight and clean-shaven, with an earnest expression. He wore the rough clothes of a docker. "Are you in charge here?"

Paddy laughed. "In charge? Sure, no one's in charge here. That's part of the problem. Supposed to be organized labor. Here in Wapping, it's disorganized labor."

"You should be. I couldn't help but overhear. You're a good speaker. Persuasive. You must really believe in the union."

"Aye, that I do. You from round here?"

"From the south originally. Bristol."

"Well, if you worked in Wapping, you'd know what the

union means to us. It's our only chance for decent wages, for fair treatment. Look at that old man there," he said, pointing to a far corner. "Spent his whole life unloading boats and then a crate fell on him. Cracked his head. Made him barmy. Foreman tossed him out like so much rubbish. See that one by the fire-place? Wrecked his back at the Morocco Wharf. Couldn't work. Five kids. Didn't get one bloody penny in compensation. Kids were so hungry the wife finally went into the workhouse with them . . ." Paddy fell silent for a second, overcome by emotion, his eyes bright with anger. "They work us hard. Ten- and twelve-hour days in all kinds of weather. They wouldn't work an animal like that, but they do it to men. And what've we got to show for it? Fuck all."

"And the others? Do they feel like you do? Do they have the heart for the struggle?"

Paddy bristled. "They have heart, mate, plenty of it. It's just they've been beaten down so long, it might take them a little while to find it again. If you could see these men, what they endure . . ." His voice trailed off. "They have heart, all right," he finished softly.

"And do you –"

"Sure, but you ask an awful lot of questions," he cut in, suddenly suspicious. Dock owners paid good money for information on the union. "What's your name, then?"

"Tillet. Benjamin Tillet," the man answered, extending his hand. "Yours?"

Paddy's eyes widened. "Oh, Christ!" he spluttered. "Not *the* Ben Tillet?"

"I suppose so."

"You mean all this time I've been standing here preaching to the choir? Sorry, mate."

Tillet laughed heartily. "Sorry? What for? The union's my favorite topic. I like listening to you. You've got a lot to say and you say it well. I still didn't get your name."

"Finnegan. Paddy Finnegan."

"Listen, Paddy," Tillet said. "I've got to get this meeting underway, but what you said earlier was right; we are disorganized down here. We need leaders on the local level. Men who can inspire their mates, keep their spirits up when the going gets tough. What do you say?"

"Who? Me?"

"Aye."

"I . . . I don't know. I've never led anybody anywhere. Wouldn't know how."

"Yes, you would. You do," Tillet said. He drained his glass and put it on the bar. "Earlier, when your mates were unsure, you asked them to think about it. Now I'm asking you. You'll do that much, won't you?"

"Aye," Paddy said, dumbfounded.

"Good. I'll see you afterward." He moved off through the crowd.

Well, I'll be blowed, Paddy thought. He had to admit he was flattered and honored that Tillet would ask him to lead the men. But being flattered was one thing, and actually taking over was another. Could he do it? Did he even want to?

"Brother dockers . . ." It was Tillet. He warmed up by telling everyone about the withheld plus money at Oliver's, then moved on to the threatened wage cuts at the Cutler Street Tea Warehouse. With a full head of steam up, he chronicled the poverty and deprivation of the dock worker's life, then lambasted the ones responsible. All talking had stopped. Men held their pints or put them down. The quiet-spoken, earnest man had turned into a firebrand.

As Tillet railed against the enemy, Paddy's mind worked its way back to his request. What would he do? He looked around at the faces of the men who worked the docks, faces like anvils, hardened by the constant hammering life had given them. Usually it was porter or stout that erased the cares from those faces. Pint after pint. Washing away the bellowing foreman, the sad-eyed wife, the underfed children, the constant, aching knowledge that no matter how hard you worked, you'd only ever be a docker and there'd never be enough – enough coal in the bin, enough meat on the table. But tonight something else had lit up these faces – hope. Tillet had made them see the possibility of winning.

Paddy thought about his family. He had a chance to fight for them now on the front lines. For more money, but for something bigger, too. For change, for a voice. Dockers had never had that before. If he turned down Tillet's request, how could he live with himself knowing he'd done less than his best for his children?

A cheer burst from the men; they were applauding. Paddy looked at Tillet, thundering at his audience, on fire, and saw that fire reflected in the scores of faces watching him. There was no longer any doubt in his mind. When Tillet came for his answer, he knew what he would say.

"Surrender now, Jack Duggan, for you see we're
  t'ree to one,
Surrender in the Queen's high name for you're a
  plundering son . . ."

Fiona woke with a start to the sound of singing. It was coming from the back of the house. She opened her eyes. The room was dark. Charlie and Seamie were asleep; she could hear them breathing. It's the middle of the night, she thought, her mind thick with sleep. Why's Da singing in the bog?

She sat up, groping blindly for the lamp and the box of Vestas next to it. Her fingers were clumsy and it took a few scrapes along the edge of the box before the match flared. The lamp's flame cast only a feeble light over the small room that served as a parlor during the day and as sleeping quarters for herself, Charlie, and Seamie at night. She drew back the makeshift curtain – an old sheet draped over a piece of twine – that separated her from her brothers, and headed for the kitchen.

"Jack drew two pistols from his belt and proudly waved them high . . ."

She heard the jakes door bang back on its hinges, and then the grand finale.

"I'll fight but not surrender said the Wild Colonial Boy!"

"Da!" she hissed, stepping out into the dark yard. "You'll wake the whole house with your noise. Come inside!"

"Right away, mavourneen!" Paddy bellowed.

"Da! Shush!" Fiona stepped back into the kitchen, put the lamp on the table, and filled the kettle with water. Then she stoked the small pile of coals glowing under the hearth grate.

Paddy came into the kitchen, smiling sheepishly. "Seems the booze got the better of me, Fee."

"I can see that. Come and sit down. I've put the kettle on. Would you like some toast as well? You should put something in your stomach."

"Aye, that would be grand." Paddy sat down by the fireplace, stretched his legs out, and closed his eyes.

Fiona took a loaf of bread from the cupboard, cut a thick slice and stuck it on a toasting fork. " 'Ere, Da," she said, nudging her dozing father. "Don't let it catch fire."

The water boiled. She mashed the tea. Then she pulled a chair from the table to the hearth and father and daughter sat together in companionable silence, Fiona warming her feet on the iron fire surround, Paddy turning his toast over the coals.

Fiona cast a sideways glance at her father and smiled. If her mam and Roddy hadn't been asleep, she wouldn't have shushed him. She loved to hear him sing. His voice was the sound of her earliest memories. It was he, not her mam, who'd sung her lullabies. He sang on his way home from work – you could hear him a street away – and from the pub. On evenings when he didn't go out, when he stayed in to mend their boots, or carve a toy for Seamie, he sang in the kitchen. How many nights had she fallen asleep, snuggled down in her covers, listening to his voice rising and falling? Too many to count.

"Well, lass," Paddy said through a mouthful of toast. "Shall I tell you me news?"

"What news?"

"It's not any regular old dock rat you're taking tea with tonight."

"Oh, no? Who am I taking tea with, then?"

"The new leader of the Wapping Tea Operatives and General Laborers' Association."

Fiona's eyes widened. "Da, you're joking!"

"Sure, I am not."

"When?"

Paddy wiped his mouth with the back of his hand. "This evening. Down the pub. I spent some time talking to Ben Tillet before the meeting. Bent his ear off, I did, but he must've liked what I had to say, because he asked me would I lead the local chapter."

Fiona's eyes were shining. "That's grand," she said. "Me own da's a guv'nor! I'm ever so proud!" She started to giggle. "Wait till you tell Mam, she'll faint! Father Deegan says the unionists are a bunch of godless socialists. You've as good as got 'orns and a pointy tail now. She'll 'ave to do double time with 'er rosary."

Paddy laughed. "Deegan would say that. William Burton just gave him a hundred quid to fix the church roof."

"What do you 'ave to do?"

"Try to get as many men to join up as I can. Hold regular meetings and collect dues. And go to meetings with Tillet and the other leaders, too." He paused to take a sip of tea, then said, "Maybe, I can even get me own lass to join a union."

"Oh, Da," Fiona sighed. "Don't start that again. You know it's all I can do to save a bob or two for me shop. I've got nothing left for dues."

"You could just go to meetings to start. Wouldn't have to give them anyt'ing –"

"Da," she cut in, determined to nip his unionizing in the bud before it turned into another argument. "I'm not going to be a factory girl forever. Remember when we were little – me and Charlie? ' 'Ave to 'ave a dream,' you would tell us. 'Day you stop dreaming you might as well take your-self down to the undertaker's, for you're as good as dead.' Well, the union is your dream and it means a lot to you. But 'aving a shop is my dream and it means the world to me. So, your way for you and my way for me . . . all right?"

Paddy gave his daughter a long look, then covered her hand with his own. "All right, stubborn lass. Is there any more tea in the pot?"

"Aye," Fiona said, pouring her father another mugful, relieved the discussion would go no further. "Oh! We got a letter from Uncle Michael!" she said excitedly. "Auntie Molly's expecting a baby! 'E says the shop's doing well. Do you want to see it?"

"I'll read it in the morning, Fee. Can't see straight enough to do it now."

"New York sounds grand," Fiona said, thinking about her uncle in America and his wife and their tidy little shop. He'd sent a picture of them standing in front of it last year. M. FINNEGAN – GROCERIES, it said. The idea that her own uncle owned a shop inspired her. Maybe it ran in the blood. "Do you suppose I could write to 'im and ask 'im about shopkeeping?" she asked.

"Sure you could. He'd be tickled. Probably write you a twenty-page letter back. Loves to go on, does Michael."

"I'll save a few pennies for paper and a stamp . . ." Fiona said, yawning, her voice trailing off. A few minutes ago, the urgency of getting her father inside before he woke the whole street had made her feel wide awake. But now, sitting by the hearth, warmed inside and out, she felt tired again. If she didn't go back to bed soon, she'd be exhausted when her mother rose to go to Mass and woke the rest of the household for work.

Her mam went to Mass nearly every morning of the week and Seamie and Eileen went with her. Her da never did. Not even on Sundays when she and Charlie went. He made no secret of his dislike for the Church. He hadn't even gone for their baptisms. Uncle Roddy had had to go.

She wondered how her mother had got him to go for their wedding.

"Da?" Fiona asked drowsily, twirling a strand of hair around her finger.

"Mmm?" Paddy mumbled through a mouthful of toast.

"Why is it you never go to church with us?"

Paddy swallowed. He stared at the coals. " 'Tis a hard question, that. I was going to say that I've never liked the idea of being told what to do, or how to do it, by a bunch of old men in long dresses, but there's more to it than that. T'ings I've never told you, nor your brother."

Fiona regarded her father, feeling surprised and a little apprehensive.

"You know that me and your Uncle Michael lived in Dublin when we were lads. And that we were brought up by me mother's sister, me Auntie Evie, right?"

She nodded. She knew that her father had lost his parents when he was small. His mother had died in childbirth and his father soon after. "Of what?" she'd once asked. "Grief," he'd replied. He never said much about his parents. She always assumed he'd been too young to remember them.

"Well," he continued, "before me and Michael went to Dublin, we lived with our mam and da on a small farm in Skibbereen. On the coast of County Cork."

Fiona listened, her eyes wide and curious. She'd known her mother's parents before they died, but knew nothing of her father's side.

"Me parents married in '50," he said, taking a sip of tea, "one year after the last bad potato blight. Me da wanted to marry sooner but couldn't on account of the famine. It was so bad then . . . well, you've heard plenty of stories, Fiona, but a man could hardly find enough food to fill his own belly, never mind providing for a family. They both had a hard time of it, both lost family. Me da often said the t'ing that pulled him t'rough was the hope of marrying me mam."

Paddy set his mug down and leaned forward in his chair,

his elbows on his knees. A faint, sad smile tugged at his mouth and crinkled the corners of his eyes. "He was wild about her, y'see. Adored her. They'd known each other since they were wee children. He was forever bringing her t'ings. Daft t'ings. Wild violets in the spring and the empty shells of blue robins' eggs. Smooth rocks from the seashore and tiny birds' nests. He had no money, me da. These t'ings cost not'ing to give, and yet to me mam, they was priceless. She saved everyt'ing he gave her.

"They worked hard together, me mother and father. They both knew what hunger was and wanted to make damn sure it never troubled them again. I was their first. Then Michael came. I was four when he was born. When I was six, me mam was expecting again. She was poorly during much of it. I remember that even though I was only a lad."

As Paddy spoke about his childhood, his face began to change. Memories of the past faded his bittersweet smile; his eyes became dark and troubled and the shallow lines that barely creased his cheeks and forehead suddenly appeared deeper.

"When her time came, me da went after the midwife. He left me to look after me mother and brother. Me mam was taken badly while he was gone. Twisting and gripping the sides of the bed. And trying so hard not to cry out. I was trying to help her, running outside and wetting Da's handkerchiefs under the pump and pressing them to her forehead."

"When the midwife finally arrived, she took one look at me mother and told Da to fetch the priest. He didn't want to leave her. Wouldn't budge an inch till the woman screamed at him, 'Go on, man! Go, for God's sake! She needs a priest!' "

"He didn't have to go far and it wasn't long before he was back with Father McMahon. A tall, stiff stick of a man he was. Me and Michael were sitting at the kitchen table; the midwife had chased us out of the bedroom. Me father and the priest went in, but she chased me father out, too.

He came into the kitchen and sat in front of the fire, never moved, just sat there staring into the flames."

Just like you, Da, Fiona thought, her heart aching for her father, at the way he sat, his broad shoulders slumped, his huge, strong hands clasped in front of him.

"I was sitting closest to the bedroom and I could hear them. The midwife, Mrs. Reilly was her name, and the priest. She was telling him that me mam was bleeding too much, that she was weak, that it would have to be one or the other."

" 'Save the child,' the priest said."

" 'But Father,' I heard her say, 'she's got two others need looking after and a husband, surely you don't – ' "

" 'You heard me, Mrs. Reilly,' " he said. " 'The baby is not baptized. You imperil its immortal soul, and your own, by waiting.' "

"Well, Mrs. Reilly got the baby out of her. God knows how. He hardly made a sound, poor t'ing. A few minutes later, I smelled candles burning and heard the priest reciting in Latin. Me da heard it, too. He ran into the bedroom. I followed and saw him push the priest aside and take me mother in his arms and cradle her like a child, crooning and whispering to her as she slipped away . . ." Paddy's voice caught; he swallowed hard. "The baby was baptized Sean Joseph, after me da. The priest named him. An hour later, he was gone, too.

"Me da stayed with me mother for a long time. It was twilight when he finally let her go. The priest had already gone to the neighbors', the McGuires, to get some supper and to ask Mrs. McGuire to look after us. Mrs. Reilly was laying out the baby. Me da put on his work coat and told me to look after me brother. There was this terrible quiet about him. Maybe if he'd raged and wept and broke the furniture, he could've got out some of the grief that was twisting in him. But he couldn't. I saw his eyes. They were dead. There was no light in them anymore, no hope."

Paddy paused, then said, "He told Mrs. Reilly he was going to see to the animals. He never came back. When it

44

got dark, she went into the barn after him. The animals had been fed and watered, but he wasn't there. She ran across the field and got Father McMahon and Mr. McGuire to go looking for him. They found him early the next morning. At the foot of a cliff where he and me mam used to walk before they were married. His back was broken and the sea was lapping at his head, all smashed open."

Paddy, his eyes dull, picked up his mug and took another sip.

That tea must be cold by now, Fiona thought. I should top it up for him. Get him some more toast. She did neither.

"The priest sent to Dublin for me aunt and we went to stay with the McGuires until she came, two days later. The funeral for me mother and the baby was the same day she arrived. I remember it so clearly. I got t'rough the whole thing, the open coffin, the Mass, watching them lower me mother into the ground and me baby brother in a tiny wooden box next to her. I didn't shed a tear in the churchyard. I t'ought," he said, suddenly laughing, "I t'ought maybe they could see me, and I wanted to be brave and not cry so they'd be proud.

"The next day, the priest held me father's funeral, if you could call it that. I watched them bury him in a patch of nettles by the cliff where he'd jumped. And then, oh, Christ, lass, the tears started to come and I was standing there weeping, wondering why he wasn't being put in the earth next to me mother where he belonged. With Sean Joseph. I didn't understand. Nobody told me that the priest wouldn't allow a suicide to be buried in the churchyard. All I could think of was me da out there all alone, with not'ing but the sound of the waves for company. So cold . . . so lonely . . . without me mam beside him . . ." Tears welled up in Paddy's anguished eyes and coursed down his cheeks. He lowered his head and wept.

"Oh, Da . . ." Fiona cried, choking back her own tears. She knelt beside him and rested her head on his shoulder. "Don't cry, Da," she whispered, "Don't cry . . ."

"That bloody priest had no right to do that, no right," he said hoarsely. "Their life together was holy, holier than anyt'ing in that miserable bastard's whole miserable church."

Fiona's heart ached with sadness for that little boy, her father. She had never seen her da cry, not like this. His eyes had been watery during her mother's long, difficult labors with Eileen and Seamie. And during the two miscarriages she'd had before Seamie. Now she knew why. And why he never went out to the pub while her mam was lying in as other fathers did.

Paddy raised his head. Wiping his eyes with the back of his hand, he said, "I'm sorry, Fee. Must be the beer making me daft."

"That's all right, Da," Fiona said, relieved he was no longer weeping. She sat down again.

"You see, Fiona, the reason I told you all this is that when I got older and t'ought about everything that had happened, I t'ought that me mother and father might still be alive if it wasn't for that priest. If he hadn't told the midwife to save the child instead of me mam, she might've lived and me Da wouldn't have done what he did. I still t'ink that. And that's the reason I don't go to church."

Fiona nodded, taking in all that her father had said.

"Of course, none of this sits well with your mam," Paddy said, regarding his eldest levelly. "And it might be a good idea for you to keep this conversation to yourself. The Church means a lot to her."

"Oh, aye, Da." She certainly would keep it to herself. Her mother was very devout, never missed Mass, and said her rosary morning and evening. She believed that priests were above reproach, that they carried the word of God and were special to Him. Fiona had never questioned this, no more than she would have questioned the sky or the sun or the existence of God Himself.

"Da . . ." she began hesitantly. A frightening thought had gripped her.

"Yes, Fee?"

"Even though you don't like the priests or the Church, you believe in God, don't you?"

Paddy considered his answer, then said, "Do you know what I believe, lass? I believe that t'ree pounds of meat makes a very good stew." He chuckled at her puzzled expression. "I also believe it's time for you to be in bed, mavourneen. You'll be falling asleep at work tomorrow. So go on now and I'll clear away these tea t'ings."

Fiona didn't want to go to bed, she wanted to stay and make her father explain what he meant about three pounds of meat, but he was already picking up the teapot and looked too tired to do any more talking. She kissed him good night and returned to her bed.

She soon fell asleep, but did not sleep well. She tossed and turned, disturbed over and over again by a dream in which she was running toward St. Patrick's, late for Mass. When she got to the church, she found the doors locked. She ran around the building, shouting up at windows, trying to get in. She came back to the doors and pounded her fists against them until her hands were ripped and bleeding. Suddenly the doors creaked open and there stood Father Deegan with a large iron pot. She reached into her skirt pocket, pulled out her rosary and gave it to him. He handed her the pot and withdrew, locking the doors behind him. The pot was heavy; it took all her strength to carry it down the church steps. At the bottom, she set it down and took off the lid. Billows of steam rushed up at her face, fragrant with the smell of cooked lamb, carrots, and potatoes. The pot was full of stew.

3

A thick, roiling fog swirled around the High Street gas lamps, muting their glow, as Davey O'Neill followed Thomas Curran into Oliver's Wharf. It was dangerous to be walking about the docks on a night like this; one wrong step and a man could fall into the river with no one to hear him, but he would take that risk. The foreman had a job for him, a little something on the side. Moving stolen goods, no doubt. It wasn't the sort of thing he wanted to be involved with, but he had no choice. Lizzie was ill and he needed the money.

Curran closed the street-side door behind them and fumbled for a lantern. Its glow illuminated a path through the stacks of wooden tea chests to the waterside doors. Outside again, Davey saw that the fog completely blanketed the Thames, engulfing most of the dock. He wondered how anyone would even *find* Oliver's in this murk, never mind bring a boat alongside it and unload. He stood quietly for a few seconds, waiting for Curran to tell him what to do, but the foreman didn't say anything. He merely lit up a cigarette and leaned against the door. Looking at him, Davey realized that if for some reason he wanted to get back through that door, he wouldn't be able to – not with the man blocking it like that. The thought made him uneasy.

"Isn't anyone else coming, Mr. Curran?" he asked.

Curran shook his head.

"Do you want me to get some 'ooks? A sling?"

"No."

Davey smiled uncertainly. "What do you want me to do, then?"

"Answer some questions, Mr. O'Neill," said a voice from behind him.

Davey whipped around, but there was nobody there. The voice seemed to have come from the fog itself. He waited, listening for the sound of footsteps, but heard nothing, only the sound of the river swirling and lapping about the pilings.

He turned back to Curran, fearful now. "Mr. Curran, sir . . . what's 'appening . . . I . . ."

"Davey, I'd like you to meet your employer," Curran said, inclining his head to Davey's right.

Davey looked and saw a dark figure emerge from the fog – a man of average height, powerfully built. He had black hair combed back from his face, a hard brow, and black, predatory eyes. Davey guessed him to be in his forties. His clothes gave him the appearance of a gentleman – he wore a black cashmere greatcoat over a gray wool suit, and a heavy gold watch dangled from his vest – but there was nothing gentle-looking about the man himself. His bearing and expression spoke of a contained brutality; a coiled, latent violence.

Davey took his cap off and held it in both hands, squeezing it to keep them from shaking. " 'Ow . . . 'ow do you do, Mr. Burton, sir?"

"Do you listen to what Mr. Curran tells you, Mr. O'Neill?"

Davey looked anxiously from Burton to Curran, then back again. "I don't understand, sir . . ."

Burton walked away from the two men toward the edge of the dock, his hands clasped behind his back. "Or do you do what Ben Tillet tells you?"

Davey's stomach lurched. "Mr. B-Burton, sir," he stammered, his voice barely a whisper. "Please don't give me the sack. I only went to one meeting. I – I won't go to another. Not ever. Please, sir, I need me job."

Burton turned back to him. Davey could read nothing from his face. It was absolutely expressionless. "What does

Tillet tell you, Mr. O'Neill? To strike? And what does this *union*" – he spat the word – "of his want? To shut me down? To let my tea rot on the barges?"

"No, sir . . ."

Burton began to circle him slowly. "I think it does. I think Tillet wants to destroy me. To ruin my business. Am I right?"

"No, sir," Davey said.

"Then what *does* the union want?"

Davey, sweating now, looked at Burton, then at the dock, then mumbled an answer.

"I didn't hear you," Burton said, leaning in so close that Davey could smell his anger.

"M-more money, sir, and shorter hours."

In the years to come – the bitter, shriveled, soul-destroying years ahead of him – Davey would try to remember how the man had done what he had. How he'd gotten his knife out of his pocket so quickly and used it so expertly. But now all he felt was a searing heat on the side of his head, a wetness on his neck.

And then he saw it . . . his ear . . . lying on the dock.

Pain and shock dropped him to his knees. He clutched at the wound, blood coursing through his fingers and over his knuckles, and his hands told him what his mind refused to believe – that there was nothing, nothing at all, where his left ear used to be.

Burton picked up the pale piece of flesh and tossed it off the dock. It made a small, soft splash. Certain he would never see his wife and children again, Davey began to sob. He stopped when he felt the thin, cold point of the knife under his remaining ear. He looked up at Burton in bald terror. "No . . ." he croaked. "Please . . ."

"Am I to be told how to run my business by union scum?"

He tried to shake his head no, but the knife stopped him.

"Am I to take orders from extortionists and thugs?"

"N-no . . . please don't cut me again . . ."

"Let me tell you something, my young friend. I fought hard to make Burton Tea what it is and I will smash anything, and anyone, who tries to interfere with me. Do you understand?"

"Yes."

"Who else was at the meeting? I want every name."

Davey swallowed hard. He said nothing.

Curran stepped in. "Tell 'im, lad!" he urged. "Don't be a fool. What do you care for them, Davey? They ain't 'ere to 'elp you."

Davey closed his eyes. Not this. Please, not this. He wanted to talk, he wanted to save his life, but he couldn't shop his mates. If he did, Burton would do to them what he'd done to him. He clenched his teeth, waiting for the upward jerk of the knife, for the pain, but it didn't come. He opened his eyes. Burton had moved away. He no longer held the knife. When he saw Davey looking at him, he nodded to Curran. Davey shrank away from him, thinking he was signaling the man to finish him off, but Curran merely handed him an envelope.

"Open it," Burton said.

He did. There was a ten-pound note inside.

"Should help with Elizabeth's doctor bills, no?"

" 'Ow . . . 'ow do you know . . . ?"

"I make it my business to know. I know you're married to a pretty girl named Sarah. You have a son, Tom, aged four. A daughter Mary, who's three. Elizabeth is just over a year. A fine family. A man should take care of a family like that. Make sure nothing happens to them."

Davey stiffened. More than pain now, more than anger or fear, he felt hatred. It was in his heart and on his face. He knew Burton could see it and he didn't care. Burton had him. If he didn't give the man what he wanted, his family would pay the price. He would've sacrificed himself, but he wouldn't sacrifice them. And the man knew it. "Shane Patterson . . . ," he began, ". . . Matt Williams . . . Robbie Lawrence . . . John Poole . . ."

When he had finished reciting the names, Burton said, "Who's in charge?"

Davey hesitated. "No one. No one's been appointed yet . . . they 'aven't . . ."

"Who's in charge, Mr. O'Neill?"

"Patrick Finnegan."

"Very good. Continue to attend meetings and keep Mr. Curran informed. If you do, you'll see my appreciation in your wage packet. If you don't, or if you're foolish enough to tell anyone what went on here tonight, your wife will wish you hadn't. Good night, Mr. O'Neill. It's time you went home and saw to yourself. You've lost quite a bit of blood. If anyone asks about your ear, you were set upon by a thief. When he found you had nothing to give him, he cut you. You didn't see which way he went in the fog."

Davey got to his feet, dazed. He pulled his handkerchief from his pocket and pressed it to his head. As he staggered across the dock, he could still hear Burton talking.

"The leader . . . Finnegan. Who is he?"

"An uppity bastard. Always 'as something to say. Good worker, though. I'll give 'im that. One of me best."

"I want an example made of him."

" 'Ow's that, sir?"

"I want him dealt with. I'll have Sheehan handle it. You'll be hearing from him."

Paddy . . . my God . . . what have I done? Davey cried silently, sick with shame. He stumbled through the wharf and out into the fog-shrouded street. He felt dizzy and weak. He caught his toe on a cobble and tripped, but managed to right himself against a lamppost. His heart heaved in his chest. He put a bloodied hand over it and uttered a cry of anguish. He was a traitor now, a Judas. And under the shell of his skin, the bones of his rib cage, there was no longer a heart – just a rotten, twitching thing, black and broken and rank.

4

Fiona's hands shook as she poured the tea leaves she'd just weighed into a tin. She knew she mustn't look up. If he saw her do it, she'd get the sack. Surely that was why he was here – to sack someone. Why else would William Burton pay a surprise visit? To give them all a raise? She heard his slow, measured footsteps as he passed by. She felt his eyes on her hands as she sealed the tin and stamped it. He reached the bottom of the table, turned, and started up the other side. Halfway up the row, he stopped. Her heart lurched. She didn't have to see him to know where he was – behind Amy Caldwell. Walk on, she silently urged him. Leave her alone.

Amy was fifteen years old and simple. Her fingers weren't nimble and sometimes she bumped her scale pan, spilling its contents, or glued a label on crookedly. All the girls compensated for her, each doing a bit more than her share to make up for Amy's slowness. It was their way to look out for one another.

Fiona weighed more tea, praying for Amy to not make a mistake. Then she heard it – the unmistakable clang of a scale pan. Her eyes darted up; Amy had dumped tea all over the table. And instead of cleaning it up, she was standing there helplessly, her chin quivering.

"Wipe it up, luv," Fiona whispered to her. "That's a good girl. Go on . . ."

Amy nodded, then cleaned up the tea and Burton moved off to terrorize someone else. Fiona looked after him, fuming. Amy's accident was entirely his fault. She would've been fine if only he hadn't stood there so long, making her nervous, the poor thing.

William Burton was one of the wealthiest, most successful tea merchants in England. He had come up from nothing and made himself a rival to the most esteemed names in the business – Twining, Brooke, Fortnum & Mason, Tetley. Fiona knew his story, everyone did. He'd been born and raised in Camden Town, the only child of an impoverished seamstress, now dead, whose husband, a sailor, had perished at sea. He'd left school to work in a tea shop at the age of eight, and by eighteen, through hard work and thrift, had been able to buy the shop and turn it into the foundation of what would become Burton Tea. He had never married and had no family.

Fiona admired the determination and perseverance that had propelled him to his success, but she despised the man himself. She could not understand how someone who'd endured and escaped the sinkhole of poverty could have no compassion for those he'd left behind.

Burton finished his tour, then called for Mr. Minton. Fiona heard them conferring. There was another man with them, too. She could hear his voice. She risked a glance and saw Burton pointing at various girls and Minton nodding as he did and the third man, brisk and portly, expensively dressed, looking at his watch. Then Minton, awkward and self-important, said: "Your attention, girls. Mr. Burton 'as informed me that various projects and expansions recently undertaken 'ave forced the need for drastic economic measures . . ."

Fifty-five worried faces, Fiona's included, regarded the foreman. They didn't understand what his mumbo-jumbo meant, but they knew it couldn't be good.

". . . which means I 'ave to let some of you go," he said, causing a collective gasp to go up. "If your name is called, please go to my office to collect your wages. Violet Simms, Gemma Smith, Patsy Gordon, Amy Caldwell . . ." The list went on until fifteen names had been called. Minton, who,

Fiona saw, at least had the decency to look shamefaced, paused, then said, "Fiona, Finnegan . . ."

God, no. What was she going to tell her mam? Her family needed her wages.

". . . will be fined sixpence for talking. If there's any more talking, any noise whatsoever, the offenders will all be fined. Back to work now."

Fiona blinked at him, giddy with relief at not being sacked, furious at being fined just because she'd tried to help Amy. Around her she heard choked sobs and soft shufflings as the fifteen girls gathered their things. She closed her eyes. Little dots of light, small and bright, surged behind her eyelids. Rage, pure and strong, welled up inside of her. She tried to push it down.

Taking a deep breath, she opened her eyes and picked up her tea scoop. But she couldn't keep herself from looking at her workmates, white-faced and trembling, as they filed into Minton's office. She knew that Vi Simms was the sole support of herself and her sick mother. Gem had eight younger siblings and a father who drank his wages. And Amy . . . she was an orphan who lived in one tiny room with her sister. Where on earth would she find another job? How would she eat next week? It was the sight of her, standing bewildered in her shabby bonnet and threadbare shawl, that made Fiona snap. She slammed her tea scoop down. If Burton wanted to fine her for talking, she'd give him something to listen to.

She marched to Minton's office, right past all the girls waiting for their wages. For a supposedly smart man, William Burton is damn shortsighted, she thought. He'd watched them all pack – didn't he see how inefficient the whole process was? Obviously, he had no understanding of this part of his business. He thought he had to sack those girls to save money, but if he just put their labor to better use, he could *make* money. She'd tried to tell Mr. Minton this before, time and again, but he never listened. Maybe he would now.

"Excuse me," she said, squeezing by the girl in the doorway.

Mr. Minton was at his desk, doling out shillings and pence. "What is it?" he asked brusquely, not bothering to look up. Burton and his companion, absorbed in a ledger, raised their eyes.

Fiona swallowed, shrinking under their scrutiny. Her anger had carried her in here, now fear nudged it aside. She realized she was probably going to get herself fired. "Begging your pardon, Mr. Minton," she began, struggling to keep her voice steady. "But sacking those girls is a false savings."

She had Minton's attention now. He gaped at her for what seemed like an eternity before he found his voice. "I'm terribly sorry about this, Mr. Burton, sir . . ." he sputtered, standing up to see her out.

"Just a moment," Burton said, closing the ledger. "I'd like to hear why one of my tea packers thinks she knows my business better than I do."

"I know my part of it, sir. I do it every day," Fiona said, forcing herself to look first into Burton's cold, black eyes, then into the other man's, which were a startlingly beautiful shade of turquoise and completely at odds with his hard, rapacious face. "If you kept the girls and made a few changes in the work routine, you could get more tea packed faster. I know you could."

"Go on."

She took a deep breath. "Well . . . every girl assembles 'er own packaging, right? If it's a box, she 'as to glue it together; if it's a tin, she 'as to put a label on it. Then she fills the package with tea, seals it, and stamps the price. The trouble is, we're always leaving our stations to get more supplies. It takes too much time. And sometimes tea gets into the glue brush. It's a waste of material. What you should do is take some of the girls – say twenty out of the fifty-five – and 'ave them assemble the packaging. Then 'ave another fifteen weigh the tea and fill the packages.

Another ten could seal and stamp them, and the last ten could run the supplies to the tables as they're needed. Every girl would get more done, you see. It would speed up output and lower the cost of packing, I'm sure of it. Couldn't we at least try, sir?"

Burton sat silently. He looked at her, then he looked off into the air, mulling her words.

Fiona took this as a hopeful sign. He hadn't said no, and he hadn't sacked her, either. At least, not yet. She knew the girls had heard her. She felt their eyes on her back, felt the weight of their desperate hopes on her shoulders. It made sense, her idea, she knew it did. Oh, please, please let him think so, too, she prayed.

"It's a good idea," he finally said, and Fiona felt her heart soar. "Mr. Minton," he continued, "when you're finished here, I want you to implement it with the remaining girls."

"But Mr. Burton," she said, her voice faltering, "I – I thought you might let them stay . . ."

"Why? You've just shown me how to get forty girls to do the work of a hundred. Why should I pay fifty-five?" He smiled at his companion. "Higher productivity at a lower cost. That should make the bank very happy, Randolph."

The fat man chuckled. "Quite," he said, reaching for another ledger.

Fiona felt as if she'd been slapped. She turned and walked out of Minton's office, humiliated. She was a fool. A bloody great fool. Instead of restoring her friends' jobs, she'd confirmed they weren't needed. She'd walked right up to William Burton and handed him a way to get more work done with fewer people. And when he was done here, he would probably go to his other factories in Bethnal Green and Limehouse, implement her ideas, and sack girls there, too. Would she ever, *ever* learn to keep her temper under control, to keep her mouth shut?

As she walked by the girls, her cheeks burning, ashamed

of herself, she felt someone take her hand. Thin, fragile little fingers wrapped around her own. It was Amy. "Thank you, Fee," she whispered. "For trying, I mean. You're so brave. I wish I was brave like you."

"Oh, Amy, I'm daft, not brave," Fiona said tearfully.

Amy kissed her cheek, and Violet did, too. Then Gem told her to get back to work, quick, before she found herself in line with the rest of them.

The evening sunshine that warmed Joe's back seemed ill-suited to the squalid lanes and narrow streets of Whitechapel where he and Fiona walked. Unkind rays slanted onto tumbledown houses and shops, exposing the crumbling rooftops, scarred brick walls, and stinking gutters better left concealed by mist and rain. He could hear his father's voice saying, "Nothing like the sun to make this place look dreary. It's like rouge on an old whore, only makes things worse."

He wished he could do better for her. He wished he could take her to someplace stylish like one of those pubs with red velvet wallpaper and etched glass. But he had very little money and all he could muster by way of entertainment was a walk down Commercial Street to window-shop and maybe a penny's worth of chips or ginger nuts.

He watched her as she looked in the window of a jeweler's, saw the hard set of her jaw, and knew she was still torturing herself over Burton, over those girls who'd been sacked. He'd called for her just after supper, and she'd told him about it as they walked.

"You didn't really expect to win, did you?" he asked her now.

She'd turned to him, disconsolate. "That's the thing, Joe, I did."

Joe smiled and shook his head. "I 'ave myself a lass with brass balls, I do."

Fiona laughed and he was glad of her laughter. She'd been crying over her workmates earlier, bitter tears of sorrow and rage. He couldn't stand to see her cry. It made him feel useless and desperate. He put his arm around her, pulled her close, and kissed the top of her head. "Twelve and six," he whispered to her, as they resumed their walk. "Sod William Burton."

"Twelve and *six?*" she said, excited.

"Aye. I added a bit. Business was good this week."

" 'Ow are things with your father?"

Joe shrugged. He didn't feel like getting into that, but she pressed him and he finally told her that they'd had a big row today.

"Again? What was it over this time?"

"Getting a second barrow. I want to and 'e doesn't."

"Why not?"

"Well, it's like this, Fee," he began, agitated. "We're doing all right with the one barrow, but we could be doing a lot better. The business is there. Last Saturday – you saw it – we couldn't even keep up with the punters. We actually ran out of stuff – ran out, Fee – with people wanting to buy! We could've turned over another crate of pippins, plus figs, potatoes, broccoli – but you can't sell off an empty cart. For two months I've been telling Dad to get another barrow and divide the goods between them – fruit on one, veg on the other. But 'e won't 'ear of it."

"Why not? It makes sense."

" 'E says we're doing fine as is. We make a living and there's no need to do anything risky. 'Don't tamper with success,' 'e says. Christ, 'e's always dragging 'is feet! 'E just doesn't see the bigger picture. I don't want to just make a living, I want to see a profit and make the business grow."

"Never mind your father, Joe," Fiona said. "Another year or so, and 'e won't be sitting on you anymore. We'll be out on our own, making the biggest success ever out of our shop. For now, you've just got to put up with it. There's nothing else you can do."

"You're right about that," he said gloomily. But he wondered if he *could* put up with it. The tension was getting worse. He didn't want to tell Fiona – she'd had enough upsets for one day – but he and his father had almost come to blows.

He didn't tell her, either, that right after their row, after his dad had stalked off for a pint leaving Joe all on his tod, Tommy Peterson had appeared. He'd complimented the barrow, noted the brisk business Joe was doing, and invited him to come round to his Spitalfields office tomorrow. Joe was certain Tommy was going to suggest they get another barrow, and maybe even offer them better terms on larger orders to fill it. What would he tell the man? That his father wouldn't let him? He'd look a right git.

Joe and Fiona walked on in silence as the evening turned cool. Summer was on the wane. It would be autumn soon, and the cold weather and rainy skies would curtail their evening walks. Joe was wondering how on earth he could get more money so they could open their shop and get married sooner, when Fiona suddenly said, "Let's take a shortcut."

"What?"

She was grinning at him mischievously. "A shortcut. There." She pointed at a narrow alley that cut between a pub and a coal seller's office. "I'm sure it leads back to Montague Street."

He raised an eyebrow.

"What? I'm just trying to get 'ome faster," she said innocently, pulling him after her.

As they entered the alley, something with tiny scrabbling feet shot out from between the beer barrels stacked inside. Fiona squealed and stamped her own feet.

"It's just a cat," Joe said. "Of the . . . um . . . pygmy variety."

Giggling, she pushed him against the wall and kissed him. It wasn't like her to be so bold. Usually he kissed her first, but he found he didn't mind it a bit. In fact, he quite liked it. "Is that what this is about?" he asked. "Are you trying to 'ave your way with me?"

"If you don't like it, you're free to go," she said, kissing him again. "You can leave anytime you want." Another kiss. "Just say the word."

Joe considered her offer. "Maybe it's not so bad," he said, putting his arms around her. He kissed her back, long and deep. Her hands were on his chest, he could feel the warmth of them through his shirt. Gently, he moved his hand to her breast, expecting her to stop him, but she didn't. He could feel her heart beating. The feel of it under his palm, so strong and yet so vulnerable, completely in his keeping, overwhelmed him. She was his soulmate, as much a part of him as the very flesh and bone that made him. She was with him, in him, in everything he did. She was everything he wanted from his life, the very measure of his dreams.

Hungry for her body, he pulled her blouse and camisole free of her skirt and slipped his hand underneath. Her breast was soft and heavy in his hand, like wine in a skin. He kneaded her flesh gently. A small breathless moan escaped her. The sound of it, low and urgent, made him painfully hard. He wanted her. Needed her. Here. Now. He wanted to lift her skirt and thrust into her, right against the wall. It was so hard to control his desire for her. The softness of her, the smell and taste of her drove him mad. But he wouldn't. He didn't want their first time to be like that – quick and hard in some filthy alley. But something had to happen, and fast, before the ache in his balls turned into a crippling, blue agony.

He took her hand and guided it. She touched him over his trousers, then inside. He showed her how to move her hand, and she did, rubbing him there, stroking him until his breath came hot and hard, and he groaned into her neck and his whole body shuddered in a sweet release. Then he leaned back against the wall, eyes closed, his chest heaving.

"Joe," he heard her whisper anxiously. "Are you all right?"

He chuckled. "Oh, aye, Fee. Never better."

"You sure? I . . . I think you're bleeding."

"Crikey! You pulled it off!"

"Bloody 'ell!" she screeched.

He couldn't help laughing. "Sshh, I'm just teasing you." He wiped at himself with his handkerchief, then tossed the crumpled cloth. "Can't take that 'ome to me mum to wash."

"You can't?"

"Oh, Fiona, you don't know anything about it, do you?"

"You don't know so much, either," she said crossly.

"I know more than you do," he said, bending to kiss her neck. "I know 'ow to make you feel as good as you just made me feel."

"It felt good, then?"

"Mmm-hmm."

"What was it like?"

He lifted her skirts, and fumbled with her drawers for a few seconds, before getting his hand inside. He caressed the insides of her thighs, amazed that skin could feel so silky, then his fingers found the soft, downy cleft between them. He felt her stiffen. She looked at him, her eyes wide and questioning. He heard her breath quicken, heard himself whispering to her in the darkness . . . heard the church bell, two streets over, strike the hour.

"Oh, no . . . oh, blimey!" she cried, pulling away from him. "I forgot the time! It's nine o'clock! Me mam'll skin me. She'll think I've been murdered. Come on, Joe!"

They fumbled themselves back together in the dark, buttoning blouses, tucking in shirts. Why was it always like this? he wondered. Why were they always snatching a kiss in an alley or down by the river in the mud?

Fiona fretted, wondering aloud how she was going to explain being late. They ran all the way back to Montague Street. "There, Fee, got you back before you were even missed," he said, giving her a quick kiss on her step.

"I 'ope so. At least me da's not 'ome. See you tomorrow." She turned to go, but before she did, she looked back at him one last time. He was still watching her, waiting to see that she was inside with the door closed before he went.

"Twelve and six," she said.

He smiled back. "Aye, luv. Twelve and six."

5

Kate Finnegan looked at the huge pile of laundry in front of her and groaned. Bedsheets, tablecloths, serviettes, blouses, frothy nightgowns, camisoles, petticoats – she'd have to pack them with the skill of a stevedore to fit them all into her basket. And what a treat the long walk home would be with it all balanced on her shoulder.

"Lillie, you tell your missus it's going to cost 'er double for a load this size," she shouted from Mrs. Branston's pantry.

Lillie, Mrs. Branston's maid, a gangly, red-haired Irish girl, poked her head in. "Sure, I'll tell her, Mrs. Finnegan, but good luck getting it. You know what she's like. Tighter than a duck's arse. Will you have a cup of tea before you go?"

"That sounds lovely, but I don't want to get you in any trouble."

"Oh, no fear of that," Lillie said cheerfully. "The missus has gone up to Oxford Street shopping. She won't be home for ages."

"Then put the kettle on, lass."

When she finished packing, Kate took a seat at the kitchen table. Lillie mashed the tea and brought the pot to the table along with a plate of biscuits. They talked the pot dry – Kate about her children, and Lillie about her young man, Matt, who worked at the Commercial Docks.

"Do you see 'im much?" Kate asked. "With you 'ere all day and 'im across the river?"

"Oh, aye, Mrs. Finnegan. He's like me shadow these

64

days, with them murders going on. Walks me here in the morning on his way to the docks and he's back again at night. And to tell you the truth, I'm awfully glad of it. I don't like being out after dark anymore."

"I don't blame you. You'd think those women would be too scared to walk the streets, wouldn't you? But Paddy says 'e still sees them out at night."

"They don't have much choice. If they get off the game, they go hungry."

"Father Deegan was going on about the murders on Sunday," Kate said. "The wages of sin is death, and all that. I wouldn't go against 'im, 'im being the priest, but I feel sorry for those women. I do. I see them sometimes, yelling and cursing, all drunk and broken-down. I don't think any of them chooses the life. I think they end up there because of drink or 'ard times."

"You should hear Mrs. Branston going on about it," Lillie said angrily. "Handmaids of Satan she calls those poor murdered women. T'inks they deserved what they got because they were hoors. It's fine for her, all tucked up in a nice warm house, money coming out of her arse." Lillie paused to take a sip of tea and calm herself. "Ah, well, no use in getting worked up over the missus. As me gran used to say, 'Morality is for them who can afford it.' And anyway, Mrs. Finnegan, it's not the murders, it's what's going on down the docks that's really got me worried."

"Don't I know it."

"They're doing the right t'ing, I know they are, but if they strike, God knows when me and Matt will be able to get married," Lillie said anxiously. "Likely be another year."

Kate patted her hand. "Won't be that long, luv, don't you fret. And even if it takes a little longer than you thought, your Matt's a good lad. 'E's worth the wait."

Her reassurances to Lillie made Kate sound easier about the threat of a strike than she felt. Paddy believed a strike was a certainty, the only question was when. Just last week she'd sat down with pencil and paper and tried to figure how long they could last if he walked off the docks. A few days. A week at the most.

He usually earned about twenty-six shillings a week for sixty-odd hours of cargo work. A bit more when the wharf was busy, less when it was not. In addition, he often picked up another three shillings by taking a shift as a night watchman or by taring tea – dumping the crates and raking the leaves into piles – for the graders, which brought the total to twenty-nine shillings or so. He kept two back for beer, tobacco, and newspapers, and one for the union, and handed the rest over to Kate, whose job it was to stretch them out farther than the Mile End Road.

She supplemented her husband's wages by taking in washing, which netted her four shillings a week after paying for soap and starch, and by renting a room to Roddy and cooking his meals – for which he paid her five shillings a week. She also had Charlie's wages at about eleven shillings and Fiona's at seven, minus what they kept back – Charlie for beer and his kingsmen, Fiona for her shop – that came to another fifteen, which gave her about two and ten, give or take a shilling.

Weekly expenses included the eighteen-shilling rent. The house was very dear – many families only rented one floor for eight or ten shillings – but it was a warm, dry house, free of bugs, and Kate was convinced that crowding was only a false economy, for whatever you saved in rent, you'd lose again on doctors and missed work. Then there was coal – a shilling a week now, but that would go up to two in the winter, and lamp oil – another sixpence.

That left about one and nine, all of which she could've spent on food and still not provided the kinds of meals she wanted to. She limited herself to twenty shillings for the weekly purchase of meat, fish, potatoes, fruit and veg, flour, bread, porridge, suet, milk, eggs, tea, sugar, butter, jam, and treacle to make three meals a day for six people – not counting the baby. There was the shilling for burial insurance, and another for the clothing fund – a little tin in which she faithfully deposited a shilling a week against the day somebody's coat or boots wore out, and two more for the strike fund. She'd started that one two months ago and it got its coins every week now, even if she had to scrimp on meals to find them. That left about four shillings to cover everything else: doctor's bills, boot black, rusks, throat lozenges, matches, needles and cotton, collars, soap, tonic, stamps, and hand salve. Often there were only a few pennies left by the time Saturday rolled around.

She and Paddy had struggled so hard together to reach their current standard of living. He was a preferred man at the docks now, a man with steady employment. He was no longer the casual he'd been when they were first married – tramping down to the waterfront at dawn every day for the call-on, where the foreman picked out the strongest for a day's work and paid them threepence an hour. Fiona and Charlie both worked now and their wages helped immensely. They were poor, but they were among the respectable working poor, and that made all the difference in the world. Kate didn't have to pawn things to eat. Her children were clean, their clothes were neat, their boots were always mended.

The constant struggle to stay ahead of the bills wore her down at times, but the alternative was unthinkable. Real poverty. The crushing, inescapable kind where your furniture was thrown out in the street when you couldn't pay the rent and you caught lice from sleeping in dirty lodging houses. The kind where your kids were raggedy and your husband stayed away because he couldn't bear the sight of his thin, hungry children. Kate had seen these things happen to families on her street when a man lost his job or took ill. Families like hers, with no savings to speak of, just a few coins in a tin. Poverty was an abyss that was much easier to slide into than crawl out of and she wanted to keep as much distance between it and her family as possible. She was terrified the strike would take them right to the edge of it.

"I know what we'll do, Mrs. Finnegan," Lillie said, giggling. "I read in the papers that there's a reward offered for the one who catches the Whitechapel Murderer. It's a lot of money – a hundred quid. We could catch him, you and me."

Kate laughed, too. "Oh, aye, Lillie, what a pair we'd make! The two of us going down an alley at night, me with a broom and you with a milk bottle, one more terrified than the other."

The two women talked for few more minutes, then Kate drained her cup, thanked her friend, and said she had to be off. Lillie opened the kitchen door for her. She would have to go around to a gate, then down a narrow alley that ran alongside the house into the street. She never failed to scrape her knuckles on the brick wall. She wished she could just walk through the house and use the front entry, but a neighbor might see and tell Mrs. Branston. This was a middle-class house on a good street and the help did not come and go through the front door.

"Ta-ra, Mrs. Finnegan."

"Ta-ra, Lillie. See that you lock the door," Kate called, her head hidden, her voice muffled by the large basket of linens on her shoulder.

6

Autumn is on its way, Fiona thought, pulling her shawl around her shoulders. The signs were unmistakable – falling leaves, shorter days, the coal man bellowing from his wagon. It was a gray September Sunday and the damp, creeping air had turned chilly. "THE SEASON OF DEATH," the headline screamed from the newspaper, "WHITECHAPEL MURDERER STILL AT LARGE."

Sitting on her step reading her father's paper while Seamie played next to her, Fiona wondered how anyone could go off down an alley with a stranger while a murderer was on the loose. "The devil is a charming man," her mam said. He'd have to be, Fiona thought, to get any woman round here to take a walk with him in the dark, in the fog, all alone.

On her street, and all throughout Whitechapel, people found it impossible to believe that anyone could commit such acts, then simply disappear. The police looked like buffoons. They were criticized by Parliament and by the press. It was taking a toll on Uncle Roddy, she knew. He hadn't gotten over finding the Nichols woman's body. He still had nightmares.

The murderer was a monster. The press had also turned him into a symbol of all that was wrong with society – violence and lawlessness in the working classes, profligacy in the upper ones. To the rich, the killer was a member of the vicious lower orders, a raging brute. The poor saw him as a member of the quality, a gentleman who derived obscene pleasure hunting streetwalkers like prey. To

Catholics, he was a Protestant; to Protestants, a Catholic. To the immigrants who lived in East London he was a crazy Englishman, liquored up and dangerous. To John Bull, he was a dirty, godless foreigner.

Fiona had no image of the murderer. She didn't want to know what he looked like. She didn't care. All she wanted was for him to be caught so she could walk out at night with Joe without her mam thinking she was lying dead in an alley if she got in five minutes late.

The noisy crash of building blocks next to her startled her.

"Bugger!" Seamie yelled.

"Charlie teach you that?" she asked.

He nodded proudly.

"Don't let our da 'ear you say it, lad."

"Where is Charlie?" Seamie asked, turning his face up to hers.

"Down the brewery."

"I wish 'e was 'ome. 'E said 'e was going to bring me some licorice."

" 'E'll be 'ome soon, luv." Fiona felt a twinge of guilt for fibbing. Charlie wasn't at the brewery. He was at the Swan, a riverside pub, giving some lad a thrashing; but she could hardly tell Seamie. He was too little to keep secrets and might blurt it to their mam. Charlie was fighting for money. Fiona had heard it from Joe, who'd heard it from a friend who'd placed bets on him and won. It explained his sudden propensity for coming home with black eyes, which he always put down to "just lads scrapping."

She wasn't supposed to know her brother was fighting, so she couldn't ask him what he planned to do with his winnings, but she had an idea: Uncle Michael and America. She'd seen his eyes light up the other day when their mam opened the letter and read aloud their uncle's description of his shop and New York. She'd seen him later, too, rereading the letter at the kitchen table. He didn't even look up when she passed by, just said, "I'm going, Fee."

"You can't. Mam'll cry," she replied. "And you don't 'ave the money for a ticket anyway."

He'd ignored her. "I bet Uncle Michael could use a lad the way 'is business is going. And with Auntie Molly 'aving a baby and all. Why not 'is own nephew? I'm not staying 'ere working for shite wages in the brewery me whole life."

"You can work for me and Joe in our shop," she said.

He'd rolled his eyes.

"Don't make faces! We'll 'ave our shop, you wait and see."

"I want to make me own way. I'm going to New York."

Fiona had forgotten all about that conversation until she learned he was fighting. The little bleeder was serious. America, she thought, where the streets were paved with gold. If he went there, he'd become a toff in no time. She would try to be happy for him when the day came, but she hated to think of her brother going so far away. She loved him dearly, even if he was a troublemaker, and people who went to America almost never came back. Memories and the odd letter would be all they'd have of him when he was gone.

She would miss him if he went, but she understood his wanting to go. Like herself, he couldn't accept a future of nothing but back-breaking labor. Why should that be her lot? And Charlie's? Because they were poor? It was no crime to be poor – the Lord himself had been poor and working-class, as her da always reminded her. Father Deegan also said poverty was no sin; but he expected you to be humble about it. If you were poor, it's what the Lord intended for you, and you should be accepting of His will. Keep your place and all that.

She looked up and down Montague Street at the shabby, soot-blackened houses with their cramped rooms, thin walls, and drafty windows. She knew the lives of almost all their inhabitants. Number 5 – the McDonoughs – nine children, always hungry. Number 7 – the Smiths – he was a gambler, she was always at the pawnshop and the kids ran wild. Number 9 – the Phillipses – struggling, but respectable. Mrs. Phillips, who never smiled, was forever washing the stoop.

Was this her place? She sure as hell hadn't asked for it. Let somebody else keep it. She would find a better one, she and Joe together.

Joe. A smile came to her lips at the memory of what they'd done in the alley the other night. She felt warm and achy inside whenever she thought of it and she thought of it constantly. She'd gone to church intending to confess what she'd done to Father Deegan, but on the way decided it wasn't any of his damn business, for it wasn't a sin. He would say what they'd done was wrong, but she knew it wasn't. Not with Joe.

What's gotten into me? she wondered. One minute she was convinced she shouldn't be doing anything like that, not even thinking about it. The next minute, she was imagining herself alone with Joe again – his kisses, his hands on her, touching her where he wasn't supposed to. Had they done everything you could do before the final thing? And what was that like? She had a vague notion of what went on. The man pushed a lot, she'd heard, but why? Because it didn't fit? And if it didn't fit, did that mean it hurt? She wished there was somebody who could tell her. Her friends didn't know any more than she did, and she'd rather die than ask Charlie.

She felt Seamie lean into her. He was blinky-eyed and yawning. It was time for his nap. She gathered his blocks, then took him inside and put him to bed in the parlor. He was asleep before she even got his boots off. She crept quietly out of the room and pulled the door closed. Charlie was out. Uncle Roddy was at the pub. Eileen, upstairs in her parents' bedroom, was asleep. Even her mother and father had gone up for a nap, just as they did every Sunday – the sort of nap that she and Charlie knew better than to disturb.

For the next hour at least, she was free. She could make herself a cup of tea and read. She could take a walk to Commercial Street and look in the shop windows, or she could visit with friends. She was standing in the hallway trying to make up her mind when she heard a knock on the door. She opened it.

" 'Ello, missus," said the lad on the step. "Fancy any fruit and veg today? Turnips? Onions? Some Brussels sprouts?"

"Be quiet, you fool, you'll wake me brother and the rest of the 'ouse, too," Fiona said, delighted to see Joe. "You're off early today. Business bad this morning?"

"Business? Um, no, not exactly, just, uh . . . finished up early, that's all. Finished up early and thought I might take a walk. To the river," he said, smiling brightly.

Too brightly, she thought. And he never finishes early. Or takes a walk to the river on a Sunday when he's dead on his feet after a whole weekend of selling. Something's up.

"Come on, then," he said, tugging at her arm.

His pace was brisk. He was silent, too. Fiona had no doubt that something was on his mind. Had he fallen out with his father again? She was anxious to know, but he wasn't one to speak until he was good and ready.

The docks were quiet when they arrived at the Old Stairs. The river, too. The tide was out. Only a few barges and wherries plied the waters. Along the wharves, loophole doors were pulled shut; cranes were silent. The river, like the rest of London, was doing its best to observe the Lord's day.

They settled themselves halfway down the stairs. Joe leaned forward, elbows on his knees, silent. Fiona looked at the side of his face, then turned her gaze to the river, waiting for him to speak. She took a deep breath and smelled tea. Always tea. Crated in Oliver's or loose in small mountains on the floor. She imagined the brown dust sifting down through floorboards, floating out of cracks in the loophole doors. She closed her eyes and inhaled again. Sweet and bright. A Darjeeling.

After a minute or so, Joe said, "I 'ear Charlie's getting 'imself quite a reputation down the Swan."

She knew he hadn't come to the river to talk about Charlie. This was just his way of getting around to what was eating him. " 'E better 'ope our mam doesn't find out," she said. "She'll drag 'im out by 'is ear."

"What's 'e do with 'is winnings?"

"I think 'e's saving up for a boat passage to America. 'E wants to work for me da's brother in New York –"

"Fiona . . ." Joe interrupted, taking her hand.

"Aye?"

"I asked you to come walking with me because I wanted to tell you that I might . . ." He hesitated. "There's a chance that I . . . there's this job come up, y'see . . ." He stopped again, scraping the heel of his boot on the step below him. He looked at the lapping water, took a deep breath, then blew it out. "This is no good. You're not going to like what I 'ave to say no matter 'ow I put it, so 'ere it is: Tommy Peterson offered me a job and I took it."

"You what?" she asked, stunned.

"I took the job." He started speaking quickly. "The pay's good, Fee, much more than I make at the market with me father –"

"You took a job with Tommy Peterson? Millie's da?"

"Aye, but –"

"So our shop's off?" she said angrily, pulling her hand away. "Is that what you're telling me?"

"No, no, that's not what I'm telling you! Sod it, Fiona! I knew you'd make this ten times 'arder than it 'as to be. Shut up and listen, will you?"

She stared ahead at the river, refusing to look at him. Millie Peterson had a hand in this; she just knew it. Joe grabbed her chin and turned her face back to his. She slapped his hand away.

"I'll be doing pretty much what I do right now – 'awking

goods," he explained. "Tommy saw me working at me dad's pitch and liked my style. Only I'll be selling to other costers, not the public . . ."

Fiona stared at him stonily, saying nothing.

". . . so I'll be learning a lot about the 'olesaling business – 'ow to do business at the source. With the farmers in Jersey and Kent. With the French. I'll be able to see 'ow the buying and selling works in the biggest market in London, and –"

"Where? At Spitalfields?" Fiona cut in, referring to the nearby market.

"Well, that's something else I 'ave to tell you. I won't be working at Peterson's Spitalfields pitch. 'E wants me at Covent Garden."

"So you'll be leaving Montague Street," she said dully.

"I don't 'ave any choice, Fee. We start at four in the morning. I'd 'ave to leave Whitechapel at two to get there on time. And with 'arvest wagons coming in at all hours now, we'll be working way into the night. I'll 'ave to grab me sleep when I can."

"Where?"

"In a room Peterson's got in 'is market building. Over the offices."

"Complete with bed, washstand, and daughter."

"I'll be sharing it with 'is *nephew,* a lad my age. It won't cost me a penny."

Fiona said nothing. She returned her gaze to the river.

"It could be a good thing, this job, Fee. Why are you carrying on so about it?"

Why? Fiona asked herself, staring hard at a barge. Because my whole life you've never not been on Montague Street, because my heart thumps every time I see you, because your face, your smile, your voice all take away the dreariness of this place, because our dreams give me hope and make everything bearable. That's why.

She swallowed hard, trying to hold back the tears that were just underneath her anger. "It's just a lot to take in, isn't it? It's so sudden. You just take a whole new job and move away. You won't be right down the street anymore or at the market. Who's going to sit 'ere with me after work on Saturdays and . . . and . . ." Her voice caught.

"Fiona, look at me," Joe said, brushing a tear from her cheek. She turned her face to his, but would not meet his eyes. "I didn't take this job without thinking about it. Peterson offered it to me two days ago. I've been turning it over in me mind ever since, trying to figure out the best thing to do. Not for me, for *us*. And this job's it. I can't stay 'ere, Fee. I'm fighting with me dad all the time. And I can't set up on me own. I'd be the competition, taking food out of me own family's mouth. At Peterson's I'll make twice what I did with me father. I'll be able to put away money for our shop faster than ever. And I'll be learning things we can use when we go into business." He squeezed her hand tightly. "Don't you see 'ow this can 'elp us?"

Fiona nodded; she did see. Despite her initial anger, she saw that he was right – it was a good step even if it was a hard one. Anything that helped them get their shop sooner rather than later was good. But she still felt sad. The idea might make sense to her head, but her heart felt like it was breaking.

"When do you go?"

"Tomorrow."

"Blimey, Joe."

"Don't look so sad, misery," he said, desperate to cheer her up. "It won't be forever and I'll come 'ome soon as I can. And I'll bring you something, all right?"

"Just yourself. That's all I want. And promise not to fall for Millie. I'm sure she'll find some reason to show up at Covent Garden now and again, fawning and flirting," she said.

"Don't be daft."

She jumped off the stone steps and walked downriver toward the Orient Wharf. She bent down to scoop up a

76

handful of stones to skip and resolved to stop carrying on. She'd been selfish, only thinking of her own feelings. She ought to get behind him; it wouldn't be easy for him. The Covent Garden job would be new and exciting, but also tough. From what she'd heard of Tommy Peterson, he'd be working every hour God sent.

Joe joined her and began to skip stones, too. After he'd pitched his entire pile, he bent down for more. One stone, deeply embedded in the river mud, gave a loud wet sucking noise as it came up. In the split second before the muddy hollow it left was filled by a lap of water, he saw a glint of blue. He dropped the stone and probed the silty mud. His fingers found a small hard lump. After a few seconds, he freed it.

"Look, Fee," he said, washing the object clean. Fiona bent over next to him. He held in his hand a smooth, oval stone, flat on the bottom and humped on the top. A long groove ran from its top to its middle, where it split into two grooves that curved out toward its sides. It was indigo blue and just over an inch long. As it dried, its surface took on a frosted look, evidence of long and constant abrasion from sand and water.

"What a pretty blue," Fiona said.

"Don't know what it's from. Maybe the bottom of on old medicine bottle," he said, frowning as he turned the stone between his thumb and forefinger. He took Fiona's hand, placed the stone on her palm and curled her fingers around it. "There. A jewel from the river for you. It's the best I can do right now, but someday I'll do better. I promise."

Fiona opened her hand and regarded her treasure intently, enjoying its weight in her palm. She would carry it with her everywhere when Joe left. When she was feeling lonely, she could slip her hand into her pocket and it would be there, reminding her of him.

"Fiona . . ."

"Mmmm?" she said, engrossed by the stone.

"I love you."

She looked up at him in amazement. He had never said that before. Their feelings for each other had been something understood between them, but never spoken aloud. It wasn't the Cockney way to wear your heart on your sleeve, to speak of your deepest feelings. He loved her. She had always known it and never doubted it, and yet to hear those words from his own lips . . .

"I love you," he said again, fiercely this time. "So, take care of yourself, right? Because I won't be around to. No shortcuts 'ome from Burton's. No alleyways. You stay on Cannon Street and get across the 'ighway quick. No coming to the river unless it's to meet your da. And you make sure you're inside by dark with that bastard on the loose."

Suddenly, her sadness was unbearable. Tears stung behind her eyes again. He was only going across London, to the West End, and yet it might as well be China. She couldn't go there; she had no money for bus fare. She couldn't bear the thought of the days to come. Days without him in them, dragging by one after another, so dreary and lifeless without a glimpse of him in the morning trundling the barrow off to the market, or in the evening out on the step.

"Joe," she said quietly.

"What?"

She took his face in her hands and kissed him. "I love you, too."

"Of course you do," he growled, flustered. "Goodlooking lad like meself, 'ow could you 'elp it?"

Looking at him, Fiona was suddenly overcome by a wild and desperate fear of losing him. She felt as if he were being taken from her. She kissed him again, more passionately than she ever had, her hands clutching bunches of his shirt. She was overwhelmed by a blind and powerful need for him. She wanted to pull him to her and keep him there forever. To mark him as hers, to claim him. These were dangerous feelings, she knew where they would lead, but she didn't care. He would go, he would have to. But she

78

would make sure he took a part of her with him and that she kept a part of him here.

It was only a short distance from where they were standing to the shadows and shelter of the Orient Wharf. She took his hand and pulled him into the pilings that supported the jutting dock. It was dark and silent underneath, the only sound was of the river gently lapping. There was no one to see them there, no sailors or bargemen to whistle and hoot.

She pulled him to her again, kissed his lips, his neck, his throat. When he moved his hand from her waist to her breast, she covered it with her own and pressed it tightly against herself. Her girlish fears had disappeared. She had always been eager for his lips, his touch, but also afraid. Now it seemed as if her body had a purpose of her own, fierce and urgent; the pounding of her heart, and the aching heat that had started in the pit of her belly and now surged in every vein drowned out the warning voices in her head. She could not get him close enough; kissing him, touching him, feeling his hands upon her did not satisfy this new and powerful craving, it only made it stronger. She felt unbearably hot and breathless and thought she would die if she did not fill up this empty, aching void within herself.

Her hands pushed his jacket off his shoulders. He shrugged out of it and tossed it onto the ground. Her fingers sought the buttons of his shirt, and one by one, quickly undid them. She slipped her hands inside, running her palms over his chest and back. She touched her lips to his bare skin and inhaled the smell of him. It was as if her senses wished to know every inch of him and imprint the smell and taste and feel of him on her memory. And still it wasn't enough.

She unbuttoned her blouse, then undid her camisole, her fingers fumbling with the ribbons. The white cotton parted and slipped from her body to the ground, leaving her naked to the waist. She raised her eyes to his and saw the desire in them, but she couldn't possibly know how deep, how strong that desire was. Joe had seen her nearly every day of his life, knew all her moods, her expressions and gestures, but he had never seen her like this – her hair tumbling down her shoulders, jet-black against her ivory skin. Her bare breasts, round and ripe and pretty. And her eyes, as deep and darkly blue as the ocean.

"God, lass, but you're beautiful," he whispered.

Gently, with infinite tenderness, he cupped her breasts with his hands and kissed them, and the place between, and finally, he kissed the place over her heart. Then he bent down, gathered her clothes, and handed them back to her.

"Why?" she asked, wounded. "Don't you want me?"

He snorted laughter. "Don't I?" He took her hand roughly and pressed it between his legs. "Does this feel like I don't want you?"

Fiona drew her hand back, blushing furiously.

"I want you more than I've ever wanted anything in me whole life, Fiona. A second ago, I almost took you right there on the ground. And God only knows where I found the strength to stop."

"Why did you? I didn't want you to stop."

"Because what if we did, and something 'appened? And then I'm in Covent Garden and you're 'ere with a big belly and a father fit to kill us both."

Fiona bit her lip. It was no use telling him she'd wanted him so badly, she'd been ready to take that chance.

"I'd marry you in a second if that 'appened, Fee. You know I would, but 'ow could we take on a baby right now? We can't afford to. We've got to stick to our plan – the savings, and then the shop, and then we'll get married. And that way, when the babies come, we'll 'ave the money to give 'em what they need. Right?"

"Right," she said quietly. She slipped her camisole back on, then her blouse. Then she gathered her hair back into a neat plait and tried to affect a calm, collected manner. Her mind agreed with what Joe said, but her body did not.

It was hot, uncomfortable, and deeply unsatisfied. It still ached for what it wanted, regardless of reason.

"Come on, then," he said, offering her his hand. He pulled her to him, and they stood that way for a long time before he led her out of the pilings. They walked back to the Old Stairs, climbed them, then paused briefly at the top, while he cast one last glance over the barges, the tea wharves, and the river. He wouldn't be seeing them again for a while.

As they walked home, Joe, as always, could not resist teasing her. He kept looking at her and grinning. And when she finally turned to him and demanded to know what he was looking at, he laughed and shook his head. "I never knew," he said.

"Never knew what?"

"Never knew that my shy little violet, the lass who once was worried lest I go too far be'ind the brewery wall, is really as randy as a goat."

"Oh, Joe!" she cried, reddening. "Don't you dare tease me!"

"I think it's grand. I do. And you better be at least that randy the day I marry you or I won't 'ave you. I'll take you back to your father's. Return you like a crate of bad apples."

"Be quiet, will you? Somebody will 'ear!"

A couple, an older man and woman, passed them on the sidewalk. Joe affected a serious, businesslike voice for their benefit. "Oh, well, even if I couldn't close the deal today, at least I got a good look at the merchandise. And fine goods they are, lass."

He made her laugh so much all the way from Wapping to her home that she almost forgot he was leaving. But when they rounded the corner of Montague Street, it came back to her. He was going tomorrow. When she got back from Burton's, he wouldn't be here.

As if sensing her feelings, he took her hand and said, "Remember what I told you. It's not forever. I'll be back to see you before you know it."

She nodded.

"Take care of yourself," he said, kissing her good-bye.

"And you," she murmured, watching him as he walked down the street, watching as he walked away from her.

Roddy O'Meara doubled over and groaned. With one great, wrenching heave, his stomach emptied itself of the beef-and-onion pie he'd eaten for supper. He leaned against the pitted brick wall in the yard behind 29 Hanbury Street and forced himself to breathe deeply, willing the nausea still gripping his gut to subside. As he passed a hand over his damp brow, he became aware that his helmet had fallen off.

"Jaysus, I hope I haven't puked on that."

He hawked a gob of spit, located his helmet, and after a quick inspection placed it back on his head, tightening the strap under his chin. Then he forced himself to walk back to the body. He wasn't about to allow his weak stomach to keep him from doing his job.

"Better?" George Phillips, the police surgeon, asked him.

Roddy nodded, picking up the bull's-eye lantern he'd left next to the body.

"Good man," Dr. Phillips said, crouching by the corpse. "Shine that over here."

He directed the beam to the woman's head. As the doctor began to scribble in his notebook, trading questions and comments with the officer in charge, Inspector Joseph Chandler, and various detectives, Roddy's eyes swept over the body. What had only hours ago been a living, breathing woman was now a gutted carcass. She lay before them on her back, her legs obscenely splayed, her abdomen yawning. Her killer had disemboweled her and deposited her glistening intestines beside her. He'd sliced into her thighs and hacked at the flesh between them. A gash lay across her throat like a garnet choker, the congealing blood glinting darkly in the lantern's light.

"Good Christ," one of the detectives said. "Just wait

until the papers get hold of this one, with her guts all over the place."

"There's to be no press in here. None," Chandler barked, looking up from the body. "Davidson," he said to the detective. "Take a dozen men and position them in front of the building. No one's to come in here unless they're on police business."

It was the worst murder yet. In spite of all the extra officers on patrol after Polly Nichols was found cut up in Buck's Row nine days ago, the murderer had hacked another streetwalker to death.

Roddy had seen death before. Women beaten lifeless by their husbands. Children starved and neglected. Victims of fires and accidents. Nothing approached this. This was hatred – black and insane and staggering. Whoever had killed this woman, and the others, hated them with an incomprehensible fury.

He now had another image of the killer's work to store in his brain. But this time, he wouldn't let it keep him up at night; this time he would channel the horror and anger into his casework. They'd catch the man; it was only a matter of time. And when they had him, he'd hang for what he'd done. Even now, as Dr. Phillips examined the body, scores of constables and detectives were fanning out through the area, searching for clues, knocking on doors, rousing residents to find out if they'd heard anything, seen anything.

"Over here," Dr. Phillips said, moving from the woman's neck to her abdomen.

Roddy followed, stepping over a puddle of blood. He shone the lantern into the cavity. His stomach twisted again, tightening itself to the size of a walnut. The sweet, coppery smell of her blood, the stench of human organs and their contents were overpowering.

"Her throat was cut left to right. She's only been dead a half hour, no rigor yet," Phillips told the inspector, still scribbling as he talked. "Abdominal mutilation is worse than the last time. It appears as if –"

Above their heads, a sticky window was forced open. Dr. Phillips looked up; Roddy and the others followed his gaze. Out of almost all the windows in the upper stories of the houses that bordered the tiny yard, heads protruded and fingers pointed.

"Please go back inside!" the doctor shouted. "This is no sight for decent folk!"

Some of the heads were withdrawn, most remained.

"Did you hear the man? Go inside or I'll have you brought up on charges of obstructing police inquiries!" Chandler bellowed.

"You can't do that, guv'nor!" came one indignant reply. "I paid the geezer what lives 'ere tuppence for a gander."

"Good God," Phillips groaned. He turned back to the body, a scowl darkening his face. "Come on, let's finish and then we'll cover her. Give them less to gawk at, the bloody ghouls."

He finished his examination and dismissed Roddy, who joined the other constables in front of the building. While the inspector and his detectives searched the area around the body for evidence, Roddy and his fellow officers faced down an ugly crowd.

A woman wearing a man's greatcoat over her nightdress glared at him, a mixture of fear and anger in her eyes. "Constable!" she shouted, taking a few steps toward him. "It's 'im, ain't it? The Whitechapel Murderer. 'E's struck again, 'asn't 'e? Why don't you coppers get 'im?"

In keeping with official policy, Roddy made no reply. He trained his gaze on the house across the street.

"You're doing nothing!" the woman cried, her voice as shrill as a rook's. "And it's because it's all poor women, ain't it? Nobody cares about us. Just wait till 'e goes west and threatens the fine ladies there. Then you'll catch 'im!"

"Aw, missus," a man shouted, "them peelers couldn't catch clap in a whorehouse."

The crowd threw more taunts and jeers, growing larger – and surlier – by the minute. Inspector Chandler pushed his way through the officers to check on the source of all the noise. He looked at the crowd, then turned to his men and told them that the ambulance should arrive momentarily. "As soon as the body's gone, the rabble will disperse," he said.

" 'Ow many more will 'e get?" a woman screeched. " 'Ow many?"

Giving the crowd a filthy look, Chandler turned to rejoin his detectives. Before he could leave, however, a new voice piped up.

"Yes, Inspector, how many more?"

Roddy saw Chandler grimace.

"How many more, sir? The public have a right to know!"

Roddy's eyes darted to the speaker. He knew that voice. Brisk, excited, almost cheerful in tone, it belonged to a wiry, rumpled figure hastily making its way toward Chandler.

"I've nothing for you, Devlin," the inspector growled.

"Was her throat cut?"

"No comment."

"Body slashed?"

"I said no comment!" Chandler snapped. He shouted orders at his men to stand firm and rejoined Phillips.

Undaunted, the reporter sized up the row of constables before him. "How about you men? Seems like our boy got another one, eh? And the police were nowhere in sight as usual. Heard she only just died. Might've lived if you lot had been faster. Too slow off the mark . . ."

Devlin's fishing expedition paid off. One young constable, offended by his words, took the bait. "We wasn't too slow! She died right away from the wound to 'er throat. She –"

Devlin pounced. "What time? Who found her?"

A quick elbow in the ribs reminded the lad to close his mouth and left Devlin, pad in hand, to try his luck elsewhere.

Roddy sighed. He felt edgy and restless. He didn't want to stand here. He wanted to be out, pounding on doors.

He needed to move, to be active; that was the only thing that would erase the sights that plagued his memory – her torn body, her splayed legs, the little red flower pinned to her jacket. Would he be able to sleep when this night was over? He closed his eyes and found that the images persisted behind his shuttered eyelids, and that Devlin's voice, badgering, relentless, echoed in his head: "How many more will he get? How many more?"

7

Hot water straight from the tap. Drains that never backed up. It was bloody amazing. Bloody wonderful! Joe dipped his razor into a basin of warm soapy water and marveled again at the miracle of modern conveniences. A sink. A bathtub. A flush toilet. All indoors! Eyeing himself in the bathroom mirror, he puffed out his cheek and scraped away the blond stubble covering it.

When Peterson told him he'd be living in a room over the company offices, he expected a dark, drafty rathole with a dank privy in the backyard. He couldn't have been more wrong. The room – the top floor of a three story brick building – had been used for storage, then as sleeping quarters for farmers in from the country. When his nephew Harry came up from Brighton to work for him, Peterson had had it renovated into serviceable bachelor's quarters. It was sparsely furnished, but bright and clean. The walls were painted a warm cream. There was a cast-iron stove to warm the room and heat a dinner or water for tea. An old braided rug covered the floor in front of it and a pair of worn leather wing chairs – pulled from the attic of Peterson's house – flanked it. Each lad had a bed and a narrow wardrobe to call his own, plus a fruit crate for a night table and an oil lamp.

Tommy's done right by me so far, Joe thought. The pay's good and the quarters are first-rate. But Peterson had given him something more than a room and wages, something he valued greatly. He listened to him. The man was mind-bogglingly busy – he oversaw an entire army of workers:

buyers, sellers, porters, drivers – yet he took the time to hear his employees' ideas, from the lowliest porter to the head buyer. When Joe suggested that the pea-shellers might get more done if they had a boy to keep them stocked rather than getting up from their stools to get the pods themselves, a boy was hired. Output increased and the whole experiment earned him a "Good lad!" and a slap on the back. When he noticed that the chefs from the grand hotels and restaurants – a picky, impatient bunch – tended to move around from seller to seller, buying apples here and broccoli there, he asked if he could have tea available for them. Tommy agreed, and the chefs, grateful for a hot drink at four in the morning, lingered and bought.

The money, the room – they both pleased him greatly, but the encouragement he got from Tommy – that made him happiest of all. His father had never been interested in his ideas; he'd resisted every one. Now Joe was seeing his good ideas confirmed, commended even.

The first free moment he had, he wrote to Fiona and told her about his new life: "Hot baths whenever I want, a bed all to myself, and a warm room with buckets of coal," he wrote. "We'll have all this someday and more besides." He told her about the job, his roommate, the farmers from Devon and Cornwall, and the incredible commotion of Covent Garden. It took four pages to tell her these things and a fifth to tell her that in a fortnight, when he had a full weekend off – Tommy only gave one full weekend off a month – he was going to take her to see the shops on Regent and Bond Streets. And this was just the beginning. He was able to put more money aside, just as he'd said. They would have their shop sooner than they thought, and when they were rich they would have a nice house with a modern bathroom. He closed the letter by saying that he hoped she missed him, for he missed her.

And he did. Terribly. He was lonely for his home and his family, but mainly for her. Every day he was bursting with new things to tell her. So many new people, so many new experiences. He wished he could talk to her at night, share it all with her and see what she made of it. He missed the sound of her voice and her excited eyes. He thought of her every night before he fell asleep, picturing her pretty face, her smile. Most of all, he thought about the way she had looked by the river, under the pilings, when she'd wanted to give herself to him. Part of him knew he'd done the right thing, but another part said he'd been a fool. What lad in his right mind would turn down a beautiful, half-naked girl? One thing was certain: the next time they were alone and she took off her blouse, he wouldn't be handing it back to her. He'd learned one or two things since he'd come to Covent Garden that had nothing to do with produce, thanks to his new roommate.

Joe's thoughts of Fiona were interrupted by a gust of rain against the bathroom window. It was a foul day. He'd planned to go walking with Harry, who was snoozing in front of the stove, but they weren't going anywhere in this. It was a shame. Today – Sunday – was their only day off for the week and it would've been nice to stretch their legs, maybe get a pint. But staying in and reading the paper would be all right, too. After all, they were both exhausted. Peterson was a demanding employer and he worked them hard – especially on Saturdays, when he wanted to clear out leftover stock. Joe's voice was always raw by the end of the day, his body weary and sore. Neither he nor Harry had gotten up until noon; they'd snored through the church bells, the newsboys, and the muffin man singing his wares beneath their window.

Joe toweled his face dry. His stomach growled. He wondered if Harry wanted to brave the weather to go after some dinner. He was just about to ask him when he heard a loud banging on the downstairs door. He put on his shirt, hitched up his suspenders, and came out of the bathroom. Harry was sitting in his chair, blinking.

"Who is it?" Joe asked him.

"Haven't a clue," he said, yawning. "Go see, you're closest."

Joe opened the door to the stairway and skipped down the steps. "Harry! Let me in, I'm half drowned!" a woman shouted. He yanked the door open and found himself face-to-face with a drenched Millie Peterson. "Joe, luv!" she exclaimed, handing him a wicker hamper. "Take this, will you? There's one more. Harris will help you get it." She bustled by him, all smiles, and ran upstairs. Joe and the driver got the second hamper out of the carriage. He thanked the man, then staggered upstairs with both baskets.

"Silly Millie!" he heard Harry shout. "You've come to visit us!"

"Indeed, I have. I wanted to surprise you, Harry. I brought a picnic. I was hoping we could go to the park, but we'll have to have it indoors."

Joe, panting, closed the door to the landing, put Millie's baskets down, then laughed as Harry swept her up in a big bear hug, lifting her clear off the floor.

"Harry, put me down! You'll crush me!"

Instead, he spun her around until she was screeching and begging him to stop. When he finally did put her down, they both staggered, completely dizzy, then burst into laughter at the sight of each other.

"Ohhh, Harry Eaton, you're going to get it. Just as soon as my head stops spinning."

"Why? You used to love it when I spun you around."

"When I was five years old, you fool!"

"It's good to see you, Mills," Harry said, looking at her with genuine affection. "It's ever so dull here, with just the two of us. You're a ray of sunshine in this dreary place."

"Dull? Dreary? Thanks a lot, mate," Joe said.

"Sorry, lad, you're a cracker of a roommate, but my cousin's much prettier."

Millie did indeed brighten the room. She had taken off her wet cloak and was wearing a butterscotch plaid skirt and jacket, with ivory lace at the collar and cuffs. The color was rich and played up her hazel eyes and honey-blond hair beautifully. Little topaz drops dangled from her earlobes and a matching bracelet, small and tasteful, circled her wrist. Her hair was pulled back into an ornate knot, secured by tortoiseshell combs. She was a picture, there was no denying. Thinking Millie and Harry might like to have their dinner, Joe decided to make himself scarce. He walked to his wardrobe to get his jacket.

"Where are you going?" Millie asked, looking up from her basket.

"I thought I'd take a walk."

"On a day like this? In the rain? You'll do no such thing. You'll catch your death. Stay and have dinner with us. I hoped . . . I thought you might be here and I brought tons of food just in case you were. You won't disappoint me after I came all this way, will you?" She turned to her cousin. "Harry, make him stay."

"I'm afraid you'll have to, squire. Millie has made her wishes clear and there'll be no peace for either of us if you don't."

Joe saw that to insist on leaving would be rude. Millie had begun to unpack all sorts of things and he *was* awfully hungry. "Well, if you're sure it's no bother . . ."

"None at all," she said. "Here, take this cloth and spread it out in front of the stove. Harry, can you build the fire up a little?"

With Millie directing them, Joe and Harry soon had the picnic set up. Harry shoveled coal into the stove and stoked the fire until it was blazing. He left the door open, the better to warm the room. Joe spread the white tablecloth on the rug and opened bottles of ginger beer. Millie placed all the goodies she unpacked on the cloth, bade her companions sit down, gave them napkins and cutlery, then served them their dinner.

"Cor, Millie, you've enough 'ere to feed an army," Joe exclaimed.

"An army named Harry," she said, cutting into a pork

91

pie. "It's my Auntie Martha's – Harry's mum's – fault. She wrote and asked me to make sure that her darling lad was getting enough to eat. She gave me a list of his favorite things."

"Well, she didn't mean for me to eat them all at once! Even I couldn't get through this spread," Harry said.

In addition to a large pork pie, there were Scotch eggs, sausage rolls, plump meat pasties, roast chicken, cold lamb, kippers, brown bread, Stilton and cheddar, gingerbread, and lemon biscuits. Joe and Harry were hungry, and as soon as Millie had handed them their plates, they tucked into their dinners with relish.

"This is grand, Millie, thank you," Joe said.

"Aye," Harry mumbled through a mouthful of food. "A damn sight better than the slop from the cookshop."

While Joe and Harry ate, Millie talked. She asked how their work was going and told funny stories about her and Harry's childhood that made them all laugh. Joe learned that Harry's mother was Millie's late mother's only sister, that Harry was only six months older than she was, and that the two cousins had been playmates since childhood, but had seen less and less of each other in recent years, as Harry's family had moved to Brighton.

Joe looked from Millie to Harry – two blond heads, two laughing faces. There was a strong resemblance between them. Like Millie, Harry was fair, but he was big and brawny. He liked sport, horses, and pretty girls. He didn't like the produce business and had told Joe as much, making him swear not to say anything to his uncle. Harry wanted to be an explorer. He wanted to go to India and Africa. He'd told Joe he would, too; in December, when he turned twenty.

As soon as Joe cleaned his plate, Millie filled it again. He took a swig of his ginger beer, then leaned back against one of the wing chairs, determined to eat his second helping a bit more slowly than his first. A pleasant lassitude settled on him as the afternoon lengthened. The food, the blazing fire, and Millie's lively presence had taken the gloom off the day and dispelled his loneliness. He felt warm, well-fed, and contented. He'd never had a day like this, with no work and no worries and nothing to do but sit in front of a fire with two friends. He felt as if he didn't have a care in the world, here with Harry and Millie.

He looked at Millie, chattering on, and wondered if she had a care in the world, if she'd ever had one. Although she was looking at Harry, she was sitting so close to Joe, he could smell her perfume. Lilac. Her color was high; her blond hair shone in the firelight. He closed his eyes and thought of Fiona and how she would enjoy all the little luxuries – the ginger beer, the Stilton, the lemon biscuits. He wished she were here. He would write and tell her all about it. But, no, he thought, maybe not. The fact that he'd been with Millie all afternoon wouldn't go over well. Even if he said Millie had only come to visit her cousin, which, of course, was true, Fiona would be jealous. She couldn't see that Millie was just a nice, sweet girl. He would keep this to himself.

Joe felt a soft pinch on his leg and heard Millie and Harry laughing. He realized that they were laughing at him.

"I say, Bristow, are we keeping you up?" Harry asked.

Joe opened his eyes, smiling. "Not at all," he said, stretching. "Just resting me eyes."

"What time is it, Harry?" Millie asked.

"Just gone five."

"I'd better get going," she said, beginning to wrap up the leftovers. "I told Harris to fetch me at five. He's probably outside right now."

Harry reached over and grabbed her hand. "No, I'm sorry but you can't go. You'll have to stay here with us forever."

"That would hardly be proper, now would it? Will you stop it, Harry? Let me pack . . ." she giggled, trying to twist free of his grasp.

"Only if you promise to come visit again. Soon. Promise, Mills."

"All right, but only if Joe wants me to."

"Of course I do, Millie," Joe said, coloring. "It's been nice 'avin' you 'ere." And it had. Millie's company had made the afternoon fly by.

She smiled at him, then resumed her tidying. Harry and Joe helped. "I'm not taking this back with me," she said. "Just put it on the landing where it's cool and it'll keep."

"Smashing! We'll be set for days," Harry said.

"I'm leaving the other basket, too. It's got wool blankets in it. It's getting chilly and Dad never thinks about who's cold unless it's his apples and oranges."

After they had packed up their picnic and folded up the cloth, Harry helped Millie put her cloak on, pulling the hood up and tying it under her chin.

"Take care getting home," he cautioned. "We'll walk you down."

Harry led the way down the stairs; Millie and Joe followed. Outside, the rain had stopped, but the evening was dark and drizzly. Gas lamps flickered, their flames reflected in the slick surface of the cobbles, and lanterns glowed on either side of Millie's carriage.

"Evening, Harris," Harry said to the driver.

"Evening, sir," Harris replied, tipping his hat.

Harry opened the carriage door. "Bye, Silly Millie. I wish you didn't have to go."

"I'll come again. On a better day. And we'll all go out for tea, or a walk in the park." She went up on tiptoes to give Harry a peck on the cheek, then turned to Joe and gave him a quick kiss, too. He smelled her perfume again as she pressed against him; felt her lips brush his cheek and her hand squeeze his arm. Then Harry bundled her into the carriage, rapped on the side, and she was gone.

Harry and Joe looked after the carriage for a few minutes, until it was out of sight, then headed back upstairs. Their room seemed gray and hollow now.

"She's quite a character, isn't she?"

"Oh, aye," Joe said. "That she is. Place feels empty without 'er."

"She's a bonny lass," Harry said, settling himself in front of the fire. "I'll tell you, whoever gets her has it made. A pretty face, a wealthy father, and a fine pair of tits to boot."

"I 'adn't noticed," Joe said. He picked up the coal bucket and fed a few lumps to the stove.

Harry smirked. "Of course you hadn't." He stretched his legs out before him, patted his stomach, and sighed contentedly. "A man could do a lot worse than Millie in the wife department. If she wasn't my cousin, I'd marry her myself."

Suddenly Joe felt uncomfortable; Harry's tone had turned too serious. "Maybe you ought to, old son. No other woman will 'ave you."

Harry made a face. "Unfortunately, you're wrong. There's the dreaded Caroline Thornton."

"Who?" Joe closed the oven door and sat down on the other side of it.

"The girl my dear mother has picked out for me. In Brighton. Pop-eyed, flat-chested, teeth like an old picket fence, but pots and pots of money. And head over heels in love with me."

Joe laughed. "Sounds like an angel."

Harry snorted. "A devil, rather. But she won't get her claws in me. No, sir. I'm telling you, Joe, I'm joining the foreign service. Swear you won't tell my uncle –"

"I already swore."

"Swear again."

"I swear," Joe said, rolling his eyes.

"I'll be off before the end of the year. Far away from London and Brighton and Miss Caroline Thornton. And apples and oranges, too. I can't take this business. I don't give a damn for it and I never will."

"Maybe you should tell your uncle," Joe suggested. "Maybe 'e'd understand."

"Never. Uncle Tommy'll kill me when he finds out, but it'll be too late by then. I'll be on a steamer bound east." Harry was silent for a moment, gazing into the fire. "He wants me to be the son he never had . . . the son he lost . . . but I'm not."

" 'E can't expect that of you, 'arry, you've got to live your life. 'E'll get over it. 'E'll just 'ave to find somebody else, won't 'e?"

Harry nodded slowly, then turned to Joe and smiled. "Maybe he already has."

8

Nothing in London could compete with the sheer spectacle, the dizzying variety, the tumult and commotion of Harrods's food hall on a Saturday morning. It was a veritable cathedral of food, where fine ladies selected pretty cakes and biscuits, and imperious housekeepers piled package after package in the arms of the hapless grooms who trailed them, brisk shopgirls wrapped purchases at lightning speed, and aproned lads raced up and down, replenishing shelves.

To Fiona, the sight was nothing short of magical. As she walked up one aisle and down the next, she had to hold on to Joe's arm to keep from stumbling. She simply couldn't keep her eyes ahead of her. "Look!" she said, pointing to an artful mosaic of fish on a mountain of crushed ice. Beyond it, rabbits, pheasants, geese, ducks, and partridges hung from steel hooks. To the left was the meat counter – no necks and backs here. This was rich man's meat – tender fillets, tawny hams, chops as thick as a fist. They strolled past the spice counter, past bottles of the finest ports and Madeiras, into the produce section where Joe proudly pointed out the blushing Bramleys and golden Boscs from Peterson's of Covent Garden.

Their last stop was the pastry hall, where Fiona was taken by a beautiful wedding cake. Cascades of red sugar roses, so well done they looked real, decorated its ivory fondant sides. A card at its base informed the curious that it was a replica of one done for the wedding of Lilian Price Hammersley of New York to George Charles Spencer-Churchill, the Eighth

Duke of Marlborough. The sugar roses, it said, were modeled after a new specimen of rose from the United States – the American Beauty.

"We'll 'ave one just like it," Joe said. "Only with White-chapel Beauties on it."

"Whitechapel Beauties? Never 'eard of them."

"Also known as daisies."

"Do 'Arrods deliver to Whitechapel?" Fiona asked, giggling.

"Wouldn't that be a sight?" Joe said, laughing himself. "The 'Arrods van trying to get to Whitechapel? They probably don't even know it's in London."

They were convulsed with laughter as they walked out of the store at the idea of the green Harrods van, with its straight-backed, white-gloved driver, bumping and bouncing over the pitted dockland streets, mobbed by urchins and stray dogs.

"Where will we go next?" Fiona asked, her blue eyes sparkling.

"Past Hyde Park to Bond Street and Regent Street, and then a surprise. Come on."

Everything had been a surprise since early that morning when Joe arrived at Montague Street and knocked on her door. She'd flown to answer it, knowing it would be him, for he'd written a fortnight ago to tell her he wanted to take her on an outing.

She'd asked her mam, who'd said, "Ask your da," who'd huffed a bit, but finally said she could go. Then she'd pleaded with Mr. Minton for a half-day off from work. He made her grovel, but finally agreed – with a dock in wages, of course.

At first, she'd been so excited she could barely wait for the day to arrive. But she soon realized she didn't have anything nice to wear and that she'd have to go in the better of her two skirts and a plain cotton blouse. Her mother noticed her sudden glumness and guessed what was wrong. An expert at making something out of nothing, she soon remedied the problem. She took Fiona into her bedroom and rummaged in a trunk until she found what she was after – a navy-and-cream-striped peplum jacket that she'd worn the day she was married. It was too small for her now – four children had broadened her bosom and waist – but it fit Fiona perfectly, showing off her slender figure. Fiona had also borrowed a little brass-and-enamel pansy brooch from her friend Bridget, and Uncle Roddy's lady friend, Grace, had lent her a pretty embroidered purse.

Her father and her Uncle Roddy had provided the finishing touch – a navy velvet wide-brimmed hat and two red milliner's roses. She'd come in late from work on Friday evening and found them sitting on the table, in her place. Her da had his face behind a newspaper, as always, and her Uncle Roddy was pouring himself some porter. Charlie and Seamie were at the table. Kate was at the stove. Fiona looked, wide-eyed, from the hat to her mother.

"From your da," her mam had said. "And your Uncle Roddy."

She'd picked up the hat. It was secondhand and there was a little fray in the velvet on one side where some trimming had come off, but it was nothing the roses wouldn't hide. She knew her mam had picked them out and that her father and Roddy had paid for them. She tried to say thank you, but her throat was tight and her eyes were glistening.

"Don't you like them, lass?" Roddy asked, concerned.

"Oh, yes, Uncle Roddy!" she said, finding her voice. "I love them! Thank you ever so much. Thank you, Da!"

Roddy smiled. "Picked them flowers out meself," he said. Paddy snorted.

Fiona gave Roddy a hug, then got between her father and his newspaper and gave him one, too. "You shouldn't 'ave, Da. Thank you."

"It's only a little somet'ing," he said gruffly. "You enjoy yourself tomorrow. And tell Bristow he'd better take care of you or he'll be answering to me."

Still holding the hat, Fiona ran her hand over its soft

velvet brim. Just when she thought her tears would certainly spill over, Charlie produced a pair of navy kid gloves and they did.

"Aw, don't be so daft," he said, embarrassed. "They ain't nothing grand. Bought 'em second'and. Just don't want you looking like a dosser."

Later that night, Fiona bathed and Kate washed her hair for her. Then she ironed her skirt, blouse, and jacket while her mother stitched the roses to her hat. She thought she'd never sleep, but she did and was up early. She washed her face, combed her hair out and pinned it up with her mother's help. Then she dressed, tried her hat on, took it off, then tried it on again, her mother protesting all the while that she would ruin her hair if she didn't stop. Finally, she was ready.

"Oh, just look at 'er, Paddy," Kate had said wistfully, pinning the borrowed brooch onto her lapel. "Our first is all grown up. And just as bonny as a June rose."

Charlie, sitting at the table wolfing his breakfast, made a gagging noise. Paddy, buttoning his shirt for work, looked at his girl and smiled. "Aye, she's a fine lass. Takes after her mam."

Fiona stole a shy glance in the small mirror on top of the kitchen mantel and was pleased. Her mam had done a nice job with her hair and the jacket looked crisp and smart.

She didn't have long to admire herself, for there was a knock on the door and then she was running down the hall to meet Joe. His eyes widened when he saw her and he couldn't stop himself from kissing her. "You look smashing," he whispered. "Bonnier than I even remembered." Fiona was so happy to see him; it had only been two weeks since he'd left, but it felt like months. He looked different – his hair was longer, he'd lost weight. She couldn't wait to have him all to herself, but first, he'd have to chat with her parents. He came into the kitchen, had a cup of tea, and told them all about his new job.

When her father started holding forth on the union,

Fiona decided it was time to go. They headed off to Commercial Street, where they would pick up a city bus. But first, Joe made a detour. At the end of Montague Street, he pulled her into an alley and kissed her long and hard. "Blimey, but I missed you," he said, standing back for a few seconds to look at her face. Then, before she could tell him she'd missed him too, he pulled her close and kissed her again. Finally he took her hand and said, "Come on, stop mauling me. We've got a bus to catch."

He told her more about Covent Garden as they walked to the bus stop, about the chefs from Claridge's and the Café Royal and the St. James's gentlemen's clubs who wrinkled their noses at everything, about the market porters who carried their baskets stacked on their heads, and the loud and bawdy ladies who made their living shelling peas and walnuts. The bus came, drawn by a team of horses. Joe helped Fiona on and paid their fares, then they climbed to the top deck. It was a fair September day, not too chilly, and they'd be able to see all of London from there.

Fiona, who'd never ridden on a bus, was beside herself. "Are you sure it's not too dear?" she whispered, worried. "Are you sure you can afford it?" Joe shushed her. The bus took them toward the City, London's center of commerce, and he pointed out the offices of various merchants. She clutched his hand tightly, excited by all the new things she was seeing. One building, taller and grander than the rest, caught her attention. "That's Burton's," he said. "Renovations cost the earth, I'm told. I don't think your father should count on 'is union squeezing an increase out of that bloke anytime soon."

Now, as they walked down the Brompton Road away from Harrods, Fiona could not keep her eyes off Joe. He was talking about Peterson's again, but stopped suddenly when he realized she was looking at him, and smiling, and not hearing a word he was saying.

"What?"

"Nothing."

"Tell me."

"I just like looking at you, that's all. You've been away. And now 'ere you are – the same but different. All excited about new things and new people."

"Well, stop it. You're embarrassing me. If I'm excited, I'm excited for us. For our shop. I'm learning so much, Fee, so much more than I would've if I'd stayed on with me dad, and I'm getting paid well, too. Remember our cocoa tin?"

"Aye. I've money to give you for it."

"Wait till you see 'ow much is in there."

" 'Ow much?"

"You'll see."

"Tell me!"

"No."

"Why not?"

"Because I 'ave to 'ave something to tempt you to me room with, don't I?" he said, smiling slyly. "Some way of getting you to me lair."

"So I can meet your mate? 'Arry?" Fiona asked, purposely misunderstanding him.

" 'E's gone out for the day."

"Really? What a coincidence."

"Isn't it?"

"Why would you want me in your room, then?" she asked, trying not to giggle.

"Because it needs cleaning and I can't afford a charlady."

"You bleeder!"

Fiona and Joe paused at Hyde Park to watch the fine ladies and gentlemen on horseback. When they got to the end of Knightsbridge, they stole a quick look at Buckingham Palace – Fiona wanted to see where the Queen lived – then continued up Piccadilly toward Bond.

There they looked in the windows of Garrard's, jewelers to the royal family; Mappin & Webb, silver- and gold-smiths; and Liberty's, where all the fashionable people shopped. They passed fabric stores with bolts of silk, damask, and velvet; shoe stores with boots of the softest kid. Fiona was amazed by the colors – red, pink, pale blue. She had only ever seen boots in black or brown. There were windows full of laces and trim, silk flowers for hats, pretty handkerchiefs, lace gloves, beaded purses. There were soap and scent shops, bookshops, flower shops filled with hothouse blooms, and shops that sold gorgeous cakes, biscuits, and candies in pretty boxes.

Fiona wanted to buy something to take home for her family and agonized over what it would be. She only had a shilling. She wanted a lace handkerchief for her mam, but that wouldn't leave much to get something for her father and brothers and Uncle Roddy. And if she bought the fancy cigarettes she'd seen for her da, what would she do about her mother? With Joe's help, she decided on a pretty tin of cream toffees. Everyone could enjoy those except the baby, but she was too little to care so that was all right.

Their eyes roved over everything, storing every scrap of knowledge for future use. At the high-class grocer's they noted how the apples were stacked, how each was wrapped in a square of blue tissue. They read ads on buildings and buses. They argued over what was a nicer way to wrap candy – in a white box with a pink satin ribbon or a navy box with a cream one.

And just when Fiona thought she had seen everything beautiful in the entire city, that the day could hold no more surprises, they found themselves outside of Fortnum & Mason's. A uniformed doorman held the door open. Joe motioned for her to go in.

"What? In 'ere?" she whispered, uncertain.

"Aye, go on, will you?"

"But Joe, it's awfully grand . . ."

The doorman cleared his throat.

"Go on, Fee, will you? You're blocking the door." With a nudge, he got her inside.

"Blimey, but it's first-rate, isn't it?" she whispered, looking at the high arched ceilings, the glass cases, the intricately tiled floors. "What are we going to do 'ere?"

"We're 'aving tea. It's a treat. My surprise. Come on."

Joe led her from the front of Fortnum's, past all manner of expensive delicacies, toward the tearoom. The hostess seated them in two tufted chairs that faced each other across a low table, and Fiona was so taken by the beauty of the room, and the people in it, that she forgot to be nervous about the expense. The tearoom was a revelation to her. She had no idea things like this existed – this pretty, perfect world where people had nothing better to do than sip tea and nibble cakes. She looked around, her eyes shining, taking it all in, carefully stowing each image away to memory as if she were putting jewels in a safe: the room, done in pale pinks and greens with snowy linens and real roses on the tables; the handsome men and stylish women. The soft music from a piano, snatches of conversation, silky laughter. And best of all, Joe, right across the table from her. It was a beautiful dream, this day, and she wished she could stay in this lovely world and not go back to Whitechapel to be without him again. But she wouldn't think about that now, it would only ruin things. It wasn't Monday yet. She still had him for the rest of today and tomorrow as well, as he was coming back to Whitechapel to spend the night with his family.

It was nearly half past four when they left Fortnum's, stuffed with finger sandwiches, scones, and cake. The dusk was coming down and the air had turned nippy. They walked for a little ways, then caught a bus. Fiona leaned her head on Joe's shoulder and closed her eyes. Before long, they arrived at Covent Garden; his flat was only two streets from the stop. It took him a few seconds of fumbling with the key to get the door open. Once inside, he lit the gas lamps and made a fire in the stove. While the room was warming, she inspected the flat.

"This is all yours?" she asked, walking around.

"Aye, mine and 'Arry's. We've each got our own bed. Couldn't get used to it at first. Too comfortable, too much room. No little brother to kick you all night."

"And you've a loo? Right inside?"

Joe laughed. "Aye. Go take a look. It's a wonder."

When she returned, he had her sit down in front of the stove – its door was wide open and a fire was blazing brightly inside it. Her eyes roved over the mantel. There were masculine odds and ends on it: razors, a clasp knife, a whiskey flask engraved with "H. E.," and a pretty silk purse.

"Is that your purse or 'Arry's?" she jokingly asked.

"What?" Joe asked, following her gaze. "Oh. That's . . . um . . . that's probably Millie's."

"Millie! Millie Peterson?"

"Aye," he said, giving the coals a shove with a poker.

"What's Millie's purse doing 'ere?" she asked indignantly.

"Well . . . she comes to visit 'Arry . . ."

" 'Ow often?"

"I don't know! Last Sunday. A few times during the week. And it looks like she came today, too."

"I see."

"What do you see?" he asked, still prodding the coals.

"She doesn't come to visit 'Arry, she comes to visit *you*."

"Oh, Fiona," he groaned. "Don't start this again."

Fiona was livid. Millie Peterson came here every weekend. She got to see Joe during the week, too – the cunning little bitch! – while she herself hadn't seen him in a fortnight

"What do you do when she comes to visit?"

"I don't know. Nothing, really."

She raised an eyebrow.

"Well, we talk, all of us, or take a stroll. Fiona, don't look at me like that. Millie's a nice, chattery girl. It gets boring being all on me own. And spending a few hours with Millie and 'Arry takes me mind off it. All right? 'Arry's a good bloke and Millie's 'is cousin. She comes to visit *'im*. So will you please give over now and not wreck our nice day?"

"Why didn't you tell me she's been 'anging about?" Fiona asked reproachfully.

"Because I knew you'd raise 'ell over nothing, like you are now. I didn't take Millie out on the town, did I? And it's not Millie I'm sitting with now, is it?"

"No," she admitted. She realized she was behaving foolishly again, that her jealousy was getting the better of her. Joe wasn't to blame because Millie came to the flat, but he just didn't understand: Millie would sell her soul to get him. Well, she wouldn't argue the point. Not today; today was too special. But because she decided to behave didn't mean she would close her eyes to Millie's scheming ways. That purse was a calling card. She was pursuing Joe as eagerly as ever.

They sat quietly for a few minutes, staring into the fire – Fiona in the chair, Joe on the floor beside her. She ran a conciliatory hand through his hair, playing with his curls. He leaned against her legs and closed his eyes. "Did you like your day out?" he asked her.

"Like it? It was the best day I ever 'ad – just like a dream! I don't even think it's all sunk in. I can't wait to tell me mam about everything. It's London, the same city I live in, but it's a whole different world. 'Arrods, and all the shops, and tea at Fortnum's. I barely catch my breath from one thing and something else is 'appening. So many surprises!"

"Well, there's another one," Joe said, getting to his feet.

Fiona watched him as he crossed the room to his bed, flipped up the mattress, and produced an old cocoa tin. "Our tin!" she exclaimed, sitting up in her chair. "Let's see it! 'Ow much 'ave we got now? 'Ere, I've a shilling for it."

Joe sat down by her feet again, smoothed her skirt over her knees, and dumped the contents of the can into her lap. He smiled as she excitedly counted their money. "Like a greedy squirrel with a pile of peanuts, you are . . ."

"Shush, Joe! Twelve pounds, twelve shillings, fourpence . . . twelve and fifteen . . . twelve and eighteen . . . nineteen . . ." she counted. She looked up at him in amazement. "Thirteen pounds?"

"Go on, there's more . . ."

"Thirteen and six . . . fourteen and ten . . . fifteen . . . blimey! We've got nearly fifteen quid 'ere!" she cried. "Where'd it all come from? We only 'ad twelve and six when you left!"

"Peterson pays me sixteen shillings a week, Fiona. Same as 'e pays 'is own nephew," Joe said. "And if I 'ave to make a delivery to an 'otel or a restaurant, I get a tip. My room is free. I spend a little on meals and the odd paper or a pint, and that's it. The rest goes in the tin."

"Joe, this is so much more than we thought we'd 'ave by now . . . you saved up so much . . . maybe we can 'ave our shop sooner," she said breathlessly. "You said a year, but at this rate . . ." She was chattering so fast, so carried away by her visions of their shop, that she didn't see him pull a small piece of tissue out of his waistcoat pocket, and hardly felt it as he took her left hand and pushed a thin gold band over her ring finger.

"Just one last little surprise," he said softly.

She looked at the ring and gasped. "It's for me?" she whispered.

"It ain't for your mam."

"Oh, Joe!" She threw her arms around his neck and kissed him. "It's lovely! The loveliest thing I've ever 'ad. What's the stone?"

"Sapphire. Like your eyes. Remember the blue stone we found by the river? I told you I'd do better and I 'ave. It's only second'and, mind, but just you wait, one day you'll 'ave a brand-new one from a fancy jeweler's with a stone as big as a shilling."

"I couldn't like it any more than I like this one." It was an impossibly thin gold band, with a tiny sapphire, just a chip. But to Fiona, it was breathtaking.

Joe said nothing as he took her hand and examined the ring, twisting it back and forth on her finger. After a minute or so, he cleared his throat. "You're right about our savings. They'll mount up faster now that I'm earning more money, and it looks like we'll be ready to open our shop sooner than we thought. So . . ." he said, looking up at her, ". . . I want us to be courting now – all official-like."

Fiona grinned ear-to-ear. "Courting? You mean, I'll 'ave to tell me da? For real?"

"Yes, for real," Joe said, smiling at her reaction. "If you'll 'ave me, silly lass."

"And I'll 'ave to tell all me other suitors that they 'aven't a chance anymore?"

"Oh, aye," he said, rolling his eyes. "I'm sure they'll all be 'eartbroken."

"You had this planned all along, didn't you?" she asked, still unable to take her eyes off her ring. "You knew you were going to do this all day and I 'adn't a clue."

Joe nodded, pleased with himself.

"Well, I 'aven't made up my mind yet," she teased, determined not to let him think he had the upper hand completely. "Why do you want to go courting with me?"

"What do you mean, *why*?"

"Just . . . why?"

"Feel sorry for you. Plain girl like yourself, you'll never find anybody else."

"That's not it, Joe."

"No?"

"No. It's because . . ."

". . . your da paid me to."

Fiona started to giggle. "It's because you love me, so say it."

Joe snorted. "Who told you that?"

"You did, remember? By the river? You said it, I 'eard you – you love me."

"I never said that."

"You did. You love me, I know it. So tell me one more time and I might say yes . . ."

Joe, who'd been sitting, got up on his knees, pulled her close, and kissed her.

Fiona broke away. "Say it, Joe," she insisted.

He kissed her again.

"Say it . . ."

He silenced her with another kiss, and another, until she gave up altogether and surrendered to his kisses. It felt wonderful to be with him like this, in a warm room all by themselves. She'd wanted to touch him, to hold him, all day. And now there was no one to see them – no parents, no one to interfere. Free of any constraints, she kissed him passionately, with her lips, her tongue. She ran her hands over him – his shoulders, his chest, claiming him again. She felt his hands on her breasts. They moved to her neck, where he undid the buttons of her jacket, one by one. As he pulled the jacket off her arms, she gave him a long look, then said, "If I take me camisole off, are you going to 'and it back to me? Like you did at the river?"

"Not a chance."

She untied the strings that kept the garment together and slipped it off, letting it hang about her waist. "Now you," she said, crossing her arms over her breasts.

In a flash, Joe had his vest and shirt off. Looking at him, Fiona felt a familiar desire stir deep inside. Could you call a man beautiful? she wondered. Because that's what he was – more than handsome – beautiful. From the line of his jaw to the curve of his strong shoulders, to the rippling muscles of his belly.

"What are you looking at?" he asked self-consciously.

"You." She pressed her palm to his chest, fascinated to find that the bit of hair he had there was darker than that on his head. And under his arms, too. And lower, under his belly button. The sight of his naked skin thrilled her and she could feel the heat in the pit of her belly grow. She kissed the hollow beneath his throat, and then the shallow indentation in the middle of his chest. Then she pressed her ear against him and listened for the sound of his heart. When she kissed him there, she heard him groan softly, felt his fingers tighten on her waist.

And then his lips were on hers again, hard and insistent.

He kissed her mouth, her throat. He brushed tendrils of her long black hair aside and nuzzled her breasts. Eyes half-closed, she said a quick prayer that this time he wouldn't stop. Then she stifled a giggle. God was hardly the person to ask for assistance at a time like this. She knew what she wanted – Joe's touch, his kisses. She wanted him to make love to her. He raised his head, and she sighed at the loss of his lips.

"Fee, I want you . . . I want to make love to you . . ."

She nodded, drunk with pleasure, eager for his kisses again.

"I know a way . . . nothing will 'appen . . ."

He scooped her out of the chair and carried her to his bed. She watched as he unbuckled his belt, his back to her, dropped his pants and then his drawers. And then he turned around and she felt a sudden knot of fear in her stomach. Good God, she thought. Look at the size of it!

He began to undress her. He was quick and intent on his purpose and had her skirt, boots, and stockings off in no time. And all the while, she couldn't take her eyes off the object of her uneasy interest. She'd never seen one, never imagined it would be so large and . . . well, protruding. As he tugged at her knickers, she started to feel very much like a drunk when the gin wears off. The burning desire she'd felt just minutes ago had disappeared. Now she only felt nervous. They were going to make love, not just touch and kiss, and she had only the vaguest idea of what was done and not the first clue how to do it.

When she was naked, Joe nudged her over on the bed, laid down beside her, and pulled her to him. She could feel it against her thigh. He was so quiet; there was an urgency about him and she wished he'd say something. Was he nervous at all? He didn't seem it. It had all felt so good a minute ago, maybe it would again if she could just relax.

She felt his kisses on her neck, felt him stroke her back, her bottom, and then her thighs. His hand was between her legs, his fingers gently opening her . . . and then some-

110

thing else was there, pushing itself against her and her whole body tensed.

"Fee, what's wrong?"

She looked away, not answering.

"What's the matter? Do you not want to? It's all right, we don't 'ave to . . ."

"No, I . . . I want to think . . . it's just . . ."

"What, luv?"

"Well . . . that, Joe!" she blurted out, pointing between his legs. "It's huge! Where the 'ell's it going to go?"

Joe looked down at himself, then burst out laughing. He rolled over onto his back and laughed harder, until there were tears in his eyes.

"What's so bloody funny?" she asked, sitting up.

When he could catch his breath, he answered her. "I don't know where it's going, Fee. I was 'oping you did."

" 'Aven't a clue," she said, giggling herself now, relieved. When their laughter subsided, he took her in his arms and said again that she didn't have to do anything she didn't want to; they could stop right now and get dressed and it would be fine, but she said she did want to, and then he kissed her mouth and said, "Thank God," because he wanted her so badly, he didn't think it would ever go down on its own.

After a few false starts, they got it right. Fiona felt a sharp pain, just for a second, but he kissed her, and told her it was all right and she relaxed, and then there was no more pain, and he was inside of her. It felt nice, having him so close, possessing him. She felt him move inside of her, heard him whisper her name, and was warmed again by her desire for him. But then, after what seemed to her like only seconds, it all ended. He groaned and pulled out of her. Then he rolled onto his back; his eyes were closed, his chest heaving. Something had happened for him – she felt it on her belly, all warm and wet. Was something supposed to happen for her? Was that it?

"Was it all right?" she asked in a whisper.

Joe opened his eyes and turned his head toward her. He was smiling. "More than all right. I almost didn't make it out in time. I can 'ardly see straight."

Fiona smiled, pleased that he was pleased. She hoped that when he caught his breath, he might kiss her again. She felt so warm and restless, so uncomfortable. After a minute or so, he got out of bed, fumbled in his pants, and produced a handkerchief. He mopped up the puddle on her belly, folded the cloth over, then pressed it between her legs.

"Only a bit," he said, examining the cloth.

"Bit of what?"

"Blood."

"*Blood?* Jesus, Joe!"

"It's nothing, Fee. It 'appens to lasses the first time," he said knowledgeably.

"Oh, really? Since when are you such an expert?"

"Lads' talk. The blokes 'ere are a bawdy lot." He winked at her and got back into bed. "I've learned a few things since I started working 'ere and not just about cabbages."

He took her in his arms again, kissed her mouth, her ears, her neck, her rosebud nipples, and when he felt her breath coming hot and hard, he moved down lower.

She sat up; her hands flew down to cover herself. "Joe! Don't," she whispered.

Gently, he moved her hands away, kissing her palms. "Let me, Fee. It'll be nice."

She protested, and tried to pull her hands free of his grip, but he held them firmly. He kissed her where she did not want him to, and then tasted her there. And slowly, her protests turned into soft moans as his tongue explored her, teased her, taught her what this part of herself was for. She sank back on the bed, helpless against the hot, liquid sensations rippling through her, the sweet shuddering tremors that seemed to come from her very core. And then it was she who was gripping his hands tightly, and calling his name, and twisting and thrusting herself against him, until the fire inside of her crested and broke, engulfing her in wave after molten wave of the sweetest pleasure she had ever known.

Panting, her eyes still closed, Fiona felt Joe's mouth on her belly, her chest, her throat, as he made his way to her mouth. He propped himself up on one elbow, kissed her, and kissed her again, until she opened her eyes and smiled at him.

"I love you, Fee," he said, his eyes filled with tenderness. "I always 'ave and I always will."

"I love you, too, Joe," Fiona murmured. "Always . . ."

She closed her eyes. So that's what it was all about; now she knew. No wonder everyone made such a fuss. She felt so good, so warm and sleepy and happy.

She felt Joe smoothing back wisps of hair from her face. "Sleep for five minutes, luv. And then we 'ave to go. Told your father I'd 'ave you back by eight and it's getting on."

"Mmm-hmm," she mumbled, nestling into his pillow. She heard him rummaging around, sorting out his clothes from hers, and felt him sit down on the bed to put his socks on. She heard him padding back and forth, clearing up. And then she heard him stop abruptly. He was still for a few seconds, then he bolted over to one of the street-side windows.

"Christ!" he yelled, peering out the window down the street. "Fee, get up! Quick! It's 'Arry, me mate!"

Fiona sat up groggily and blinked her eyes. She heard laughter from the street, a male voice and a female one. "I thought 'e was out for the day," she said.

"Well, now 'e's in," Joe said, hustling her out of the bed. " 'Ere, take your things and go in the loo," he ordered, piling her clothes into her arms. "You can dress in there. 'E'll never know. It'll look like you're 'aving a piss."

Fiona, stark-naked, stumbled off toward the bathroom. Just as she got to the door, she stopped. "Joe! Me camisole . . . it's not 'ere . . ."

Joe tore up the bed he was frantically making, but there was no camisole. He flipped up the mattress; still no

113

camisole. Then he ran over to the chair; it was on the floor. He balled it up and tossed it to Fiona just as they heard the downstairs door open. She caught it and he dashed across the room once more to straighten out the bed. When Harry and Millie came in, the door to the loo was closed and Joe was seated in front of the fire reading the paper.

"Old chap!" Harry exclaimed.

"Hello, Joe," Millie trilled, smiling warmly.

"Didn't expect to find you here," Harry continued. "Thought you were gadding about town with a lady friend . . ."

"A what?" Millie cut in brusquely.

"A lady friend," Harry said. Millie, staring at her cousin, said nothing. Harry, obviously thinking she hadn't heard, or didn't understand, added: "A señorita. A demoiselle. A girl."

"I heard you," Millie said, looking daggers at her cousin. Her sweet smile and merry chatter were gone. "You told me a friend, Harry. You said Joe was out with a friend."

There was an embarrassing silence. Harry shifted from foot to foot. Joe pretended to be absorbed in his newspaper.

"Well." Harry shrugged. "He was."

"But you told me –"

"What does it matter, Mills?" Harry was smiling, but his tone and expression told her she was being difficult.

At that, Millie collected herself. As quickly as they'd come, the angry tone and black looks were gone and the smile was back. "Well," she said brightly, rubbing her hands together. "The night's turned chilly. And I, for one, need a cup of tea. Anyone else?"

"I will," Harry said. Joe declined, saying he'd drunk enough to sink a ship.

"Have you?" Millie asked, bustling about proprietarily with the teapot. "Why? What were you doing that required so much tea-drinking?"

Joe told Millie and Harry about his day, what he'd seen, where he'd been. Neither Millie, Joe, nor Harry heard the bathroom door open; none of them was aware of Fiona standing in the doorway. She'd finished dressing and was watching Millie flutter about Joe. As she did, her jaw tightened. Millie Peterson, she decided, was a poaching bitch who never knew when to quit. Well, she'd learn. No scenes, no brawls, nothing that would reflect badly on Joe. There were other ways. She undid the brooch from her lapel and dropped it into her skirt pocket.

As Joe finished telling them about his adventures, Millie asked, "And what lucky girl had the honor of accompanying you?"

"I did," said Fiona.

Harry jumped to his feet. "I say!" he exclaimed. "Forgive my dreadful manners, I didn't know you were here. Joe didn't tell us, but then, we never gave him the chance, did we? Harry Eaton, pleased to meet you. Please take my chair. This is my cousin, Millie Peterson."

"Pleased to meet you, 'Arry Eaton. I'm Fiona Finnegan and I already know Millie."

"Do you? Isn't that wonderful?" Harry exclaimed. He turned to Millie and blanched. Her mouth was smiling, but her eyes . . . the fury in them was sharp enough to impale somebody.

"Delightful," Millie said.

"Do sit down. You must have a cup of tea with us."

"Thank you, but I can't," Fiona demurred. "It's getting on and we – Joe and I – 'ave to get back to Whitechapel. We're expected shortly."

Fiona and Harry continued to make small talk as Joe gathered his jacket and cap. Millie stared at Fiona, saying nothing. When Joe was ready, they said their good-byes and headed for the door. As Joe opened it, Fiona turned and cried, "Oh, no! Me brooch! It's gone, I've lost it!"

"Did you 'ave it on when we got 'ere?" he asked her.

"I'm sure I did. It must've come off somewhere inside."

"Where were you sitting?" Harry asked. "Maybe it's there."

Millie didn't budge. "What kind was it?" she asked archly. "Ruby? Emerald?"

"Brass," Fiona answered.

"How appropriate."

With Harry down on his hands and knees and Joe searching the loo, Fiona, aware that Millie was watching her, walked over to Joe's bed, flipped back the pillow and said, "Found it!"

Walking back across the room, she pinned the brooch to her lapel, smiling. As she passed the stove, Millie, acid-eyed, said, "I wonder how it got there?"

Fiona winked at her. "I don't," she said.

Harry, dusting himself off, and Joe, emerging from the loo, both missed the exchange.

"Where was it?" Joe asked.

"Oh, just over by . . . blimey! Is that the time?" she exclaimed, looking at the carriage clock. "We'd better 'urry, Joe. My da will kill us."

When they were outside, Joe clapped Fiona on the back and said, "I'm real proud of you, Fee. You were polite to Millie and didn't row with 'er. Be'aved just like a lady."

More like a dockside tart, Fiona thought. She smiled sweetly.

"I hope you see how daft you've been. Millie knows what's what."

She does now, Fiona thought.

As they approached the main thoroughfare, they heard the noisy clopping of horses. Joe grabbed her hand. "C'mon, there's the bus. We can still make Whitechapel by eight if we catch it and your father won't skin me alive."

"No, but 'e'll skin me when 'e finds out I'm courting with a no-account coster."

"No, 'e won't, 'e'll be proud of you, Fee. You made a good deal," he said, running faster, for the bus was slowing just yards from the stop.

116

"I what?" she asked breathlessly.

He grinned at her. "You made a good deal . . . traded one cherry for a lifetime of apples and oranges."

Fiona turned bright red. They reached the back of the bus just as the driver snapped the reins. Joe hoisted her on, then jumped on himself. Laughing and panting, they tramped down the aisle, garnering a disapproving stare from a prim matron, then settled themselves into a seat as the horses nosed their way east, toward the river and Whitechapel.

Millie Peterson ran up the curving staircase from her front hall, trailed by her maid, Olive. She burst through the door of her bedroom, grabbed a crystal scent bottle from her dresser and hurled it against the wall. It shattered loudly, spraying lilac water everywhere.

"Oh, miss," Olive cried, her plain face a picture of dismay.

"Never mind that!" Millie snapped. "Help me get my boots off." She sat down on her bed. Olive knelt beside her with a buttonhook. "I *knew* it, Olive. The second I got to the flat, and saw how clean it was, I knew she was coming to see him. And I was right! Harry invited me to lunch – all the way in Richmond. 'We'll take a train,' he said 'I fancy a jaunt to the country.' The dirty little collaborator."

"But that sounds like a nice invitation, miss," Olive said, pulling a boot off.

"Well, it wasn't. He only wanted to get me out of the flat for the day so that Joe could be alone with his little trollop."

"But if you were in Richmond, miss, 'ow do you know she was at the flat?"

"Before we left, when Harry's back was turned, I put my purse on the mantel. After lunch I told him I'd lost it and acted upset. We went back to the restaurant and when it wasn't there, he said I must've left it on the train or in

117

the flat. We checked at the station, and no one had turned it in, of course, so he had to bring me back to the flat. And when we got there . . ." – Millie's eyes narrowed – ". . . *she* was there. They'd *made love*, Olive."

"They didn't!" Olive whispered, her eyes widening.

"They did. I'm certain of it," Millie said. She sniffed, then made a face. "God, that smells strong. Clean it up, will you? And open the window. I'm going to choke soon."

Olive gave her a look that said soon couldn't possibly be soon enough.

Millie collapsed on her bed and groaned in frustration. After Joe and Fiona left, she'd sat in silence, staring at Joe's bed, imagining them in each other's arms. Now, in her own room, fury boiled up inside her. "I don't know why he prefers her, Olive," she said. "Honestly, I don't."

"Maybe you 'aven't given 'im the right signs, miss."

"I've given him every sign I can think of. He must be blind."

"If you ask me," Olive said, picking up pieces of glass, "it's not the lad who's blind."

Millie sat up. "What do you mean by that?"

"Well . . . 'e works for your father, doesn't 'e?"

"So?"

"It's not *right*, miss, is it? It's not proper to chase after your employer's daughter. Try and see it from 'is angle. 'E probably thinks your father would be angry. Probably thinks 'e 'as someone better than 'imself picked out for you."

Millie looked at Olive in amazement. She was right. It wasn't that Joe wasn't interested in her, of course it wasn't. It was that he thought he wasn't good enough for her! She was an heiress; she could have anyone, so why would she pick a penniless coster? It was all so clear now. Joe admired her father and looked up to him and it was out of respect for him that he'd never forced his attentions on her. How could she have been so stupid?

"Olive, you clever girl! That's it exactly!" She plumped

118

herself down at her vanity. She needed time with Joe and the right opportunity. Had he found her untouchable? Well, she would show him just how touchable she was. Oh, how she would! Men had powerful, uncontrollable urges. They simply couldn't help themselves. That's what her aunt told her when she'd started to bleed and they'd had their talk. "I've got to be bolder, Olive," she said, regarding herself in the mirror. "Show him I'm his for the asking." She bit her lip. "If only I could get him alone without Harry or Dad hovering."

"What about Guy Fawkes night, miss?"

Every autumn Millie's father held a huge Guy Fawkes party for his employees and customers. It was only about a month and a half away. As always, there would be an enormous bonfire, piles of food, and rivers of drink. Joe would come to the party; he'd have to. And in the dark, amid all the frolicking and fireworks, she would get him alone. She'd ask him if he wanted to see the house or some such thing. He'd have plenty of liquor in him by then and fewer inhibitions. Some men needed a push; she'd give him one.

Guy Fawkes night was eagerly anticipated by all who worked for Tommy Peterson. It was the night he handed out bonuses. Most companies did it at Christmas, but he was too busy with holiday business to spare the time then. It was also the night he gave out promotions. Joe was in line for one even though he was only newly hired. Millie knew this from suppertime conversations with her father. He spoke constantly of Joe's talent and ambition. He noted how the Covent Garden business was already making gains as a result of his ability. Millie guessed he saw a lot of himself in Joe. She couldn't say the same for Harry; he'd been there for three months and still wasn't making much progress, poor dear. She knew his heart wasn't in it, and little by little, her father was discovering that, too. He'd had great hopes for Harry, but those hopes were now being transferred to Joe. Although she hadn't discussed it with her father, she knew that were Joe to come to him with a proposal of marriage one day, he would be delighted. Joe was fast becoming the son her father had always wanted.

"Olive, has my dress for the party come yet?"

"Yes, miss, it's in your closet. It's ever so pretty."

Millie asked her to get it. She inspected it, frowning. It was a royal-blue taffeta with cap sleeves and a full skirt. It was pretty, but pretty wasn't good enough. She needed something stunning. She wouldn't go to her dressmaker, she'd go to Knightsbridge for something truly spectacular. It would cost, but with any luck, by the time the bill came her father would be too delighted with the news of her engagement to scold her.

"Are you still cleaning up that perfume? Go downstairs and tell Harris I'll need the carriage first thing tomorrow. I'm going shopping."

"Shopping? For what, miss?"

"Well, for a new perfume bottle, for one thing," she said. "And a dress. A very special dress."

"Another dress? What's the occasion, miss?"

"With any luck, Olive, my engagement."

9

From where she stood, near the window in the parlor, Fiona
could hear the rustle of dead leaves being swept along the
street by a forceful wind. She drew the curtains against the
encroaching night, shivering at the thought of the solitary
figure who had made the darkness his own.

The Whitechapel Murderer had a new name now. He'd
written a letter to the police exulting in the carnage he'd
wreaked. It had been published in all the papers. He'd saved
blood from one of his victims to write with, he'd explained,
but it had gone hard in the bottle, so he'd had to use red
ink. He'd signed it, "Yours truly, Jack the Ripper."

Bloody ghoul, Fiona thought. She wasn't allowed to sit
on the step with her friends past dark anymore or go to
the river by herself. Her evenings were spent inside now
and she didn't like it one bit. Kneeling down by the settee,
she reached underneath it and pulled out a cigar box. In it
were a few sheets of paper and two envelopes she'd bought
to write to Joe and her Uncle Michael. She returned to the
kitchen. A fire was blazing in the hearth; her whole family
was there except her father, who was working.

Curran, the foreman at Oliver's, had asked him to fill
in for the night watchman, who was sick with influenza.
Fiona missed him being home in his usual spot by the fire,
but she'd see him in the morning. She'd hear him come in.
She liked the sound of him coming home, his approaching
steps on the cobblestones, his whistling. It made her feel
safe and secure.

She got a pen and a bottle of ink from the cupboard

and sat down at the table. Her mother was in her rocker darning. Charlie sat in his father's chair, reading a book he'd borrowed from Mr. Dolan, next door, on America. Normally he would've been out with the lads, but with both his father and Roddy gone, he'd stayed home to keep his mother company and make sure Jack didn't slide down the chimney and murder them all. Seamie was playing with his soldiers. Eileen was in her basket.

Fiona thought for a minute about what she would write to Joe. There wasn't much to report. Not much had happened on Montague Street in the few days since she'd last seen him. The biggest news was their courtship. She remembered that night with a smile. Her mother had been all misty-eyed, delighted that Fiona would have such a good, hardworking lad for a husband, happy that she would have her heart's desire, her childhood sweetheart. No mother could wish for more, she'd said. If all her children made such good matches, she would count herself lucky.

Her da, however, had been a different matter. When she'd come in bursting to show off her ring and tell her news, he'd sat in his chair looking gruff and saying nothing. After Joe left, he let it be known that seventeen was far too young for any lass of his to be getting married. And he hoped she had a long courtship in mind, because to his thinking, nineteen was the youngest a girl should marry. Her mother had put a finger to her lips, warning her not to start. Later, when he went out to the pub, she reassured Fiona that he'd come around, that he was not quite ready to lose his girl yet. "Give him a little time to get used to the idea," she'd said. And for once, Fiona followed her mother's advice. She hadn't argued, knowing if she did, he'd suddenly decide thirty was the right age to marry. The next day he invited Joe for a pint. She didn't know what transpired, but he was in a cheerful mood when he got back. The following day, he'd revised nineteen to eighteen.

Was this the way you handled men? she wondered. Nod, agree, tell them what they wanted to hear, then go about your business just as you'd planned? It was how her mother handled her da. She put her pen to paper and started telling Joe all about her father's change of heart.

"Who you writing to, Fee?" Charlie asked.

"Joe and then Uncle Michael."

"Let me write a page to Uncle Michael when you're done, would you?"

"Mmm-hmm," she said, bent over her paper, writing carefully so the pen didn't blot.

"Wish they lived 'ere, your aunt and uncle," Kate sighed. "Especially now that they're expecting. 'E'll be your cousin. Or she. 'E's a lovely man, your father's brother. A bit of a devil, as I recall. Though maybe 'e's settled 'imself down by now –"

Her words were cut off by a frantic battering on the door.

"Blimey!" Charlie exclaimed, jumping to his feet.

"Missus! Missus!" a man's voice shouted. "Open up!"

"Stay put, Mam," Charlie said, moving off down the hallway. Within seconds, he was back in the kitchen with a policeman in tow.

"Mrs. Finnegan?" the officer asked breathlessly. "I'm P. C. Collins . . ."

"Aye?" Kate said, standing.

"Can you come quickly, ma'am . . . it's your 'usband . . ."

"My God! What is it?"

" 'E's 'ad an accident down the docks. They've taken 'im to 'ospital. Can you come along right quick?"

"What 'appened?" Fiona cried. Her pen clattered to the table, splashing ink on her letter. An ugly blot spread across the page.

" 'E fell, miss. From a loop'ole . . ." the bobby said.

She held his gaze, waiting for him to finish. Oliver's was a tall building, six stories high. It could've been the first story. Oh, please God, she prayed, let it be the first story.

The bobby looked away. "From the fifth story."

"Noooo . . ." Kate shrieked, covering her face with her hands. Fiona ran to her mother, catching her as she sank to the floor.

The officer looked at Charlie. "Please, son . . . there isn't much time . . ."

Charlie snapped into action. "Mam . . . Mam!" he barked. "Get your shawl on. Fee, get Eileen wrapped up. Come 'ere, Seamie . . ." As he put Seamie's boots on, Fiona knotted their mother's shawl around her shoulders. She picked up Eileen, tucked a blanket around her, snuffed the lamps, and banked the fire. Officer Collins led Kate outside. Charlie ran to the Bristows. Within minutes, Mr. Bristow was in his shed at the bottom of the street harnessing his horse.

The noise and commotion brought several of the neighbors out. Anne Dolan came running over. "Fiona, what is it? What's 'appened?" she asked.

"Me da's 'ad an accident. We've . . . we've got to get to 'ospital . . ."

" 'Ere," Mrs. Dolan said, reaching into her skirt pocket, " 'ere's money for an 'ackney cab."

"Thank you, Mrs. Dolan, but Mr. Bristow's bringing 'is cart round."

They heard the sound of clopping hooves from the end of the street and then Peter Bristow was at their door. Rose Bristow had come outside and was trying to comfort Kate. "Climb up next to Peter, luv, 'urry," she said. "I'll come right after. Soon as I can get the kids seen to. It'll be all right. Your Paddy's a tough old bugger."

P. C. Collins helped Kate up, then he piled onto the back of the cart with Fiona, Charlie, and the little ones.

"Giddyap!" Mr. Bristow barked, snapping the reins sharply. The cart lurched forward. As they trotted along through the dark streets, Fiona, cradling a whimpering Eileen, looked at Charlie, who held a frightened Seamie in his lap. She didn't dare speak her thoughts aloud, for fear of further upsetting their mother, but her eyes told her brother that she was terrified. She heard Mr. Bristow urging his horse on, heard him talking to Kate, and then she heard traffic and saw more streetlights, and knew they were near the Whitechapel Road. Her thoughts raced. How could her father have fallen? He knew Oliver's like the back of his hand. Only fools or drunks fell. Maybe he landed on a pile of sacking or coils of rope, something to break his fall. Maybe it wasn't as bad as the constable said. She started to pray again, feverishly, to Jesus, the Virgin Mary, Saint Joseph, Saint Francis, any saint she could think of, to please, please help her da.

The cart finally pulled up in front of the hospital. Charlie was out of it before it stopped. P. C. Collins swung Seamie down. Fiona jumped down with Eileen in her arms. Kate was up the steps immediately. Mr. Bristow shouted that he'd be in as soon as he secured the cart. Inside, one of the two sisters who staffed the front desk stopped them and asked Kate which patient she was here to see.

"Paddy Finnegan. 'E's me 'usband. 'E 'ad an accident . . ." Her voice caught.

"Finnegan . . ." the sister repeated, running a finger down her roster. She looked up at Kate. "The one from the docks?"

"Aye," Charlie answered.

"First floor. Top of those stairs and turn left. There's a man up there already. A constable. He said he was your lodger."

Kate nodded and turned toward the stairs.

"Just a minute," the second sister said officiously. "She can't go up there with all those children. It's a hospital ward . . ."

"Sister Agatha!" came the sharp reprimand. "Never mind, Mrs. Finnegan. Go, dear. Hurry!"

Kate ran to the stairs. Fiona followed, slowed down by the baby. She was closer to the sisters' station than they thought and she could hear them even as she neared the staircase. ". . . at times we must bend the rules for reasons of compassion, Sister Agatha . . . this is the last chance those children have to see their father . . ."

"Oh, no . . . no!" Fiona sobbed, her voice echoing off the walls of the cavernous lobby. She handed Eileen to P. C. Collins, and then she was running, right behind her mother. They pushed the doors to the ward open together. A shattering sight greeted them.

Paddy lay in a bed near the front of the long, open room that was the men's ward. His eyes were closed. He was mumbling, rolling his head from side to side. His breathing was shallow and labored and his face, drained of all color, was slick with sweat. As they drew near, a wave of pain gripped him. He writhed against it, pleading for it to stop. Fiona saw that his arms were scraped raw, and that there was nothing, absolutely nothing, where his right leg used to be.

Sitting next to his bed, in his blue uniform, was Roddy. He turned when he heard them approach. His face was wet with tears. "Oh, Kate . . ." he said.

Kate stumbled to the bed. "Paddy?" she whispered. "Paddy, can you 'ear me?"

He opened his eyes and looked at her, but didn't know her. Another wave of pain slammed into him and this time he screamed, arching his back against it.

Unable to bear it, Fiona covered her ears. " 'Elp me da," she moaned. "Somebody please 'elp 'im." Eileen, terrified, was shrieking in the constable's arms. Seamie buried his head in Charlie's legs. Seconds later, two sisters and a doctor were at her father's bedside. While the sisters held him, the doctor injected a syringe of morphine into his arm. After what seemed like an eternity but was only seconds, his agony eased.

"Mrs. Finnegan?" the doctor, a tall, gray-haired man, asked.

"Aye . . ."

"I'm afraid I must tell you . . . your husband doesn't have much longer. His legs were crushed in the fall. We were

126

forced to amputate the right one immediately or he would have bled to death." He paused. "He has other injuries as well and he's hemorrhaging . . . bleeding inside. We're trying to keep him out of pain, but he can't take much more . . . I'm sorry."

Kate covered her face with both hands and sobbed. Fiona went to her father's bedside and took his hand. She was dizzy with shock. Her mind could not understand this. Hadn't she just said good bye to him on his way to work? Now he was in a hospital bed, his body broken. It can't be, she thought, staring at his hand, so big against hers. It's not possible . . .

"Fee . . ."

"Da! What is it?"

He swallowed. "Water."

She snatched a jug of water from another patient's night table. "Mam! Mam!" she shouted, pouring some into a glass. She supported her father's head with one hand and held the glass to his lips with the other.

Kate was at his side in an instant. "Paddy?" she said, trying to smile through her tears. "Oh, God . . . Paddy . . ."

"Kate . . ." he rasped, his chest heaving with the effort of talking. "Sit me up." The wild, glassy look in his eyes had receded; he knew his family.

Slowly, gently, Kate and Fiona eased him forward, stopping when he cried out, and propped his pillow behind him. His breathing became frighteningly ragged; he closed his eyes for a few seconds until the hitching in his chest lessened. Marshaling his remaining resources, he drew his family around him.

He motioned for Eileen. P. C. Collins gave her to Kate, who set her gently down on the bed. He held her close in his damaged arms, kissed her hand and her forehead, then gave her back to Kate. Seamie, relieved to hear his father's voice, went bounding toward him. Fiona grabbed his arm to slow him and told him in a faltering voice to be careful.

"Why?" he asked reproachfully, backing away.

"Because Da 'as a bad 'urt."

"Where?"

"On 'is leg, Seamie."

Seamie looked at the lower half of his father's body. Sucking on his lower lip, he looked at Fiona, then said, "But Da's leg is gone."

Fiona, in shock, awkward, but tender with her baby brother, said, "One leg's gone, Seamie, but the 'urt is on the other one."

Seamie nodded. Then, soft as a mouse, he went to his father. He kissed his knee and patted it, his tiny fingers light and gentle. "All better, Da?" he asked.

"Aye, Seamie," Paddy whispered, reaching for his son. He clutched the boy, kissed his cheek, and let him go.

He called for Charlie next and told him that he was the man of the house now and that he must take care of his mother and brother and sisters.

"No, Da, you'll get better . . ."

Paddy shushed him, then asked him to go to his waistcoat, hanging on a chair at the foot of his bed, and get his watch. Charlie did so. Paddy told him it had once been his grandfather's, now it was his. "You're a good lad, Charlie. Take care of them. Look after them."

Charlie nodded and turned away from the bed. His shoulders were shaking.

Paddy turned to Fiona, still at his bedside, and took her hand. She looked down at their two hands, her tears flowing.

"Fee . . ."

She looked up at her father's face. His blue eyes held hers. "Promise me, lass," he said, with violent emotion, "that you'll keep hold of your dream no matter what it takes. You can do it. Get your shop, you and Joe, and never mind about people who tell you you can't . . . promise me . . ."

"I promise, Da," Fiona said, choking back her tears.

"Good lass. I'll be watching you. I love you, Fiona."

"I love you, too, Da."

Paddy turned to Roddy; he took his hand. The two men looked at each other. No words passed between them; none were needed. Paddy released him and Roddy walked silently away. Paddy's breathing was labored again. He lay quiet, not speaking for a moment, just gazing at Kate. She was crying and could not lift her head to look at him.

When he could speak again, he touched his fingers to her face. "Don't cry, luv, don't cry," he said softly. "Do you remember that day at the church, all those years ago? The day I first laid eyes on you? You were no more than a girl. So bonny. Running in the snow, late for Mass. And me, back from the tuckshop with a bacon sandwich. I stuffed it in me pocket, followed you in and stunk up the whole church with the smell of it. You were the most beautiful t'ing I'd ever seen."

Kate smiled through her tears. "And ever since, you wished you'd never laid eyes on me. I kept you from roaming. From America. Kept you 'ere in London."

"You stole my heart. And I've never once wanted it back. Only happiness I've known, I've known because of you. Loved you from that day at St. Pat's and I always will."

Kate bowed her head and wept.

The hitching started in Paddy's chest again. A drop of blood appeared in the corner of his mouth and trickled down his jaw. Fiona wiped it away with the edge of his bedsheet.

"Kate," he said, his voice a whisper now. "Listen to me . . . there's two quid in the lining of me old suitcase. The lads at Oliver's will take a collection; you're not to be too proud to take it. You'll need it." Kate nodded, struggling with her tears. "Write to Michael and tell him . . ." he started to say, but his pain cut him off. He gasped and gripped her hand. ". . . tell him what's happened. He'll send money. And make sure I'm not buried with me wedding ring on. It's in the little dish on top of the mantel. Take it and pawn it."

"No."

"Do it, it's just a ring . . ." he said fiercely.

Kate said she would and he slumped back against his pillow. She dug in her pocket for her handkerchief and wiped her eyes, then she turned back to her husband. His chest was still, his face was peaceful. He was gone.

"Oh, Paddy, no!" she wailed, throwing herself upon his body. "Don't leave us! Please, please, don't leave us!"

Fiona saw her father's face, heard her mother's cries, and felt the bottom drop out of her world.

10

"Fiona, luv . . . eat a little something," Rose Bristow pleaded. "A bit of stew, a sandwich?"

Fiona, sitting at her kitchen table, smiled wanly. "I couldn't, Mrs. Bristow."

"Child, you 'ave to eat. Your clothes are 'anging off you. Just a bite? Come on, lass. Joe'll be furious with me when 'e sees you, nothing but skin and bones."

Fiona gave in and allowed Rose to fix her a bowl of beef stew, just to please her. She wasn't hungry and couldn't imagine ever being hungry again. Their kitchen was full of food. Neighbors had brought meat pies, sausage rolls, stews, cold meats, potatoes, boiled cabbage, and soda bread for her family, so that they would have enough for themselves and the mourners through the three days of the wake, the funeral, and the burial. Under Rose's watchful eye, she lifted a forkful of stew to her mouth, chewed it, and swallowed it.

"That's a good lass. You polish that off and I'll go see to your mother. 'E'll be 'ere soon, Joe will. I sent the letter two days ago. Don't you worry, luv, 'e'll be 'ere."

Mrs. Bristow quit the kitchen for the parlor to tend to the mourners who had walked back with Fiona and her family from the churchyard. Fiona put her fork down and covered her face with her hands. Images of her father's burial replayed themselves in her mind. The long procession to the graveyard, his coffin going into the ground, her mother's legs buckling as the priest dropped a handful of dirt upon it. Her da had spent his last night under

131

their roof and was gone now, buried in the cold earth.

She didn't cry as these pictures swam before her eyes; she was too tired. She had cried in the hospital, cried until her eyes had swelled shut, and again at the wake. The wild tearing pain she had felt the night of his accident had become a dull and heavy ache that suffused her entire being – body and soul – and made her leaden and unaware of everything except that her da was gone and would never be coming back. There was no relief from this pain. She would be all right for a moment or two, occupied with Seamie or Eileen, and then she'd remember, and her breath would catch. It felt like a deep wound splitting open and bleeding afresh. Everywhere she looked there were reminders of him – his chair at the hearth, his tobacco pouch, his grappling hook. How could his things be here when he was not? She went to the mantel and took the hook down, curling her fingers around the wooden handle, worn smooth by use.

What would become of them? Her mam . . . for two days she'd barely known them. She'd refused to feed Eileen. Mrs. Farrell across the street, herself with a newborn, had nursed the baby. Kate had lain in her bed, weeping and calling for her husband, out of her mind with grief. On the eve of the second day, she'd come downstairs, her face white, her eyes dark hollows, her long auburn hair tangled and matted, and had taken her place by her husband's coffin. There she had joined in the unearthly shrieking and wailing that the Irish make for their dead, so that the dead will hear them and know their grief. It was a terrifying thing to witness, the sound of a human soul, bereft, howling its agony to the heavens.

Afterward, she had allowed Rose to bathe her, apply warm compresses to her milk-swollen breasts, and comb her hair. Still dazed, she'd asked after her children and insisted that Eileen be brought to her. She talked to Roddy about the burial arrangements, then she returned to her bed and slept for the first time in days.

Charlie was trying hard to be strong and carry his family through. He'd helped with the funeral and burial. He'd been a pallbearer. Fiona hadn't seen him weep, but she'd seen him sitting in the kitchen by himself, staring into the fire, holding their father's watch.

Seamie had reacted like any four-year-old. There were times when he was frightened and confused, crying for his father, and times when he sat in front of the hearth and played with his toys, oblivious to everything. Fiona's heart ached for him and Eileen, for all the things they'd never know of their father – the tales he told of Ireland, the ghost stories on All Hallows' Eve, the walks to the river. So many things. Things she would try to tell them, things she couldn't begin to tell them.

A soft hand on her shoulder interrupted her thoughts. "Fiona, could you put the kettle on?" Mrs. Bristow asked. "Ben Tillet's 'ere with 'is lads. They could use a cup of tea."

"Aye," she said, returning the hook to the mantel.

Rose disappeared again and Fiona prepared the tea, relieved to have a job to occupy her. As she carried the pot into the parlor, she saw that there were still many mourners in the house; their presence now and throughout the last three days was a tribute to her father, evidence of their esteem. She forced herself to talk to her neighbors and friends. Old ladies squeezed her arm, others whispered condolences and told her how much she looked like him. She looked up every now and then, searching for Joe. How she wished he were here. Mrs. Bristow had sent a letter to Covent Garden, telling him what had happened. She would've gone to get him, if she could've, but she had no money for bus fare and was too worried about Kate to leave her. Mr. Bristow couldn't go after him, either. He'd missed a day of work to help with the funeral arrangements. Any more days away from the market and another coster would claim his space. Fiona listened politely, trying to conceal her weariness, as Mrs. MacCallum told her about the kindnesses Paddy had shown her.

As the old woman talked on, another conversation caught her ear. Two men, Mr. Dolan and Mr. Farrell, neighbors and dockers, were standing in a corner, also talking about her father.

"Fifteen years on the docks and 'e never 'as so much as a slipup," Mr. Dolan said. "No fingers gone, no broken bones. And then 'e falls from a loop'ole. It just don't make sense, Alf."

"I 'eard the coppers found grease on the platform," Alfred Farrell said. "They think it dripped from a winch and that's what caused 'im to slip."

"Bollocks! You ever know anyone at the docks to fling grease about? It just ain't done. It's like a wedding ring – no one wears one 'cause it's dangerous. Get it caught and there goes your finger. Same goes for grease. Spill any and it's wiped right up, spot's covered with sand. Any man at Oliver's would know better than that."

Fiona was struck by what they were saying. They're right, she thought; it doesn't make sense. She knew enough about her father's work to know a docker would never be sloppy with grease, no more than he would stack a crate of nutmeg on top of a chest of tea, lest the leaves pick up the flavor. She'd heard Roddy talking about the inquest, how the police had found the loophole door unbolted and a splodge of black grease on the floor near it. The foreman, Thomas Curran, said he figured one of his men hadn't secured the door properly. It was a windy night and her father must've heard it banging against the side of the building. He would've gone up to latch it, and with it being dark and him having only a lantern, he wouldn't have seen the grease. Curran said he had told one of his men – Davey O'Neill – to grease the winches earlier in the day. Davey may have dripped some. It was a tragedy, Mr. Curran said. The lads would take up a collection and he was certain Mr. Burton himself would find something for the family in the way of compensation. Satisfied with this explanation, the coroner had returned a verdict of accidental death.

Fiona had heard all this, but overwhelmed by the shock of her father's death, it had barely registered. Her da had fallen from a loophole. The particulars hadn't mattered; all that mattered was that he was dead. But now that her mind was a little clearer . . .

"Excuse me, Mrs. MacCallum," she said brusquely. She left the woman rattling and returned to the kitchen. She had to be by herself for a minute to think.

She sat down in her father's chair. It was clear as day: somebody had put grease on the floor so he would slip. Why hadn't anybody seen this? It almost hurt to think, her mind was so thick and fuzzy, but she would write down her thoughts, get them all straight. And then she would tell Uncle Roddy and he'd have the ones in charge do another inquest. It was obvious what had happened, it was plain as the nose on her face . . . it was . . . ridiculous.

Why would anybody injure me da? she asked herself. Least of all one of his workmates. Was she mad? Yes, that was it. She was losing her mind. She was looking for a reason for her father's death, grasping at straws.

She leaned forward, elbows on her knees, and rested her head in her hands. She still couldn't accept what had happened; part of her still expected her father to come through the front door, home from the docks. He'd sit down, read his paper, and this whole nightmare would be forgotten. When she was a child, he had been the center of her universe and she had assumed he would always be there – to take care of them, put food on the table, shield them from the world and its dangers. Now they had no father. Their mother had no husband. He was gone. Who would look after them? Where would they go from here?

Now, as it had over and over again during the last three days, the pain of his death came crashing in upon her like an avalanche. She tried to hold it back, but the emotion was too great. Crying bitterly, she wasn't aware that Joe had come into the kitchen.

"Fee?" he said softly, kneeling down beside her.

She lifted her head. "Oh, Joe," she whispered. Her eyes were so full of pain that tears came to his eyes for her. He wrapped his arms around her and held her as she wept. He rocked her gently, stroking her hair, as her grief wrenched sobs out of her.

When she could weep no more, he held her face between his hands, wiping the tears from her eyes with his thumbs. "My poor lass," he said.

"Why, Joe? Why me da?" she asked, her eyes bright blue through her tears.

"I don't know, Fiona. I wish I 'ad an answer for you."

"God, I miss 'im," she whispered.

"I know you do, luv. I miss 'im, too. 'E was quite a man, your da."

They sat quietly together for a few minutes, Joe holding Fiona's hand, Fiona sniffling. No flowery words, no platitudes passed between them. Joe would have done anything to ease her suffering, but he knew nothing he might do, or say, could. Her grief would run its course, like a fever, and release her when it was spent. He would not shush her or tell her it was God's will and that her da was better off. That was rubbish and they both knew it. When something hurt as bad as this, you had to let it hurt. There were no shortcuts. He sat down heavily in Kate's rocker.

Fiona looked at him and saw he was tired and unwashed. "Peterson working you 'ard?"

"Aye. Got 'arvest wagons coming in. Unloading them round the clock. I would've been 'ere sooner otherwise. Got me mum's letter yesterday morning, but I couldn't get away. If I'd 'ave left, I'd 'ave got the sack. Tommy P. don't give a damn for anyone's funeral, less it's 'is own. 'Aven't slept since I read what 'appened. I'm sorry, Fee. I wish I could've come sooner."

Fiona nodded; she understood. He was here now.

"When do you 'ave to get back?"

"Tonight. Not right now, later. I left 'Arry to finish up,

136

but there's another load due in early tomorrow morning."

She was disappointed. She'd hoped he'd be able to stay. God, how she wished he were still in his parents' house instead of all the way across London. She needed him so much now – to talk to her, to comfort her. She'd need him in the days ahead, too. But he wouldn't be here.

As if reading her mind, he took out a shilling and pressed it into her hand. " 'Ere. For paper and stamps. You can write me. Every night. When you can't stand it anymore, just write me a letter and it'll be like we're talking to each other, all right?"

"All right."

"I've got time for a walk," he said, standing up. "Let's get out of 'ere. All this whispering and moaning won't do you any good. Let's go to the river and watch the boats. We've still got an hour or so before it's dark."

Fiona stood up and took her shawl off its hook by the back door. He was right; it would be good to get out of the house. As she readied herself, she was possessed by the strangest feeling that her da would be at the waterside, present in all the things he loved – the rolling gray waves and the scudding clouds, the gulls wheeling and soaring, the eager prow of a ship nosing its way out to sea. He wasn't here in this house of pain, he was there, by the river – she was certain of it. And as Joe took her hand and led her out of the house, that certainty soothed her and gave her some small measure of peace.

11

Kate checked the number on the scrap of paper she held: 65 Steward Street. That was the number on the door. Why was no one answering? She knocked again.

" 'Old on, will you?" a voice shouted from within. "I 'eard you the first time."

The door was wrenched open and she was face-to-face with a fat, disheveled woman who, judging from her appearance, had been asleep and was not pleased to have been roused.

"Are you Mrs. Colman?"

"I am."

"I'm Mrs. Finnegan. I'm 'ere about the room."

"Come in, then," the woman said, ushering her into a hallway that was dark and stank of cabbage. "Room's upstairs. Top floor. Door's open. It's a nice room, Mrs. Flanagan," the woman said. Her teeth were black. She reeked of whiskey.

"Finnegan."

"Flanagan, Finnegan, it's all the same to me. Go on up."

"Thank you, Mrs. Colman," Kate said, mounting the stairs. The banister wobbled under her hand as she climbed to the first landing. The stairs shuddered and creaked. She glimpsed a young woman through an open door, gnawing on a crust as she nursed her baby. In another, a man was stretched out on a cot, snoring.

She continued up to the second landing. One of the three doors there was open wide. She walked in. Something crunched under her feet. Probably a bit of plaster, she thought. The room was dark; shutters covered its only window. She pulled them open and screamed.

The entire room was crawling with black beetles. They ran madly over the floor and ceiling, shying away from the light. They scuttled over the filthy wallpaper that was hanging down in strips. They darted into the fireplace and swarmed over a stained mattress. She was back downstairs in seconds, tugging at the front door.

"Did you like the room, then?" Mrs. Colman shouted, waddling after her.

"It's crawling!"

"Oh, the bugs won't 'urt you. Tell you what, I'll let you 'ave it cheap. Includes use of the kitchen, too." She leaned in close to Kate. "And there's another advantage to taking that room. If you're ever 'ard up, you can make a few bob without leaving it." She gave her an oily smile. "Mr. Daniels, second landing. Pays well, I'm told."

Kate wrenched the door open and ran out. The beetles, the dirt, the stink of the place all made her nauseous. That filthy bitch, she fumed, making her filthy propositions. If Paddy'd heard her, he'd have knocked her rotten teeth out.

Paddy. At the thought of him, tears welled. She drew her handkerchief out of her pocket and dabbed at her eyes. She could not afford to start weeping now. She had to find a room, for she was nearly out of money and could no longer afford the rent on the Montague Street house.

The loss of Paddy's wages alone would've been enough to cause her hardship, but she had been hit immediately after his death with a hospital bill, the cost of a coffin and a hearse, a plot in the churchyard, and a marker for the grave. She had found the two pounds he'd told her about, and as he said, the men at Oliver's had passed the hat and presented her with three more, plus there was a pound from the union, and the burial insurance. Fiona and Charlie were giving her everything they earned and she had started laundering again, but it wasn't enough.

She had hoped that Burton Tea might pay her ten or

twenty pounds' compensation for her husband's death. After nearly two weeks had passed and she'd heard nothing, she'd summoned her courage and walked to the company's offices. She'd waited for three hours before being seen by a junior clerk, who told her she'd have to come back the next day and speak with a senior clerk. When she returned, she was made to wait again. Another clerk then gave her documents to fill out. She wanted to take them home to have Roddy read them, but the clerk said she couldn't, so she handed them in and was told to come back in a month to check on her claim.

"A month! Sir, I need the money now," she'd protested.

The clerk, a severe-looking man with muttonchop whiskers, told her that by signing the papers she'd consented to follow Burton's procedures for awarding compensatory monies. If she did not follow these procedures, her claim would be forfeited. She'd had no choice but to wait.

The time she'd spent at Burton's had exhausted her. It was all she could do these days not to come apart at the seams. Every morning when she opened her eyes, the pain hit her again and she would weep. Then, dazed by grief, but driven by necessity, she would get up, feed her children, and start the laundering, keeping herself going as best she could. She wore no mourning clothes, no jet beads or brooches. There was no languishing in darkened parlors with mementos of the dearly departed. That was for her upper-class sisters. Women like herself, they might be mad with sorrow, but they got up and got going or their children went hungry.

Whenever she thought about her children, she was plagued by fears for their future. How would she support them? She could sell some of their furniture when they moved – that might bring a few shillings. If she had to, she could pawn Paddy's wedding ring, but only if she had to. She could sell her mangle and copper. There wouldn't be room for those when they were all living in one room. Without them, she wouldn't be able to take in laundry, which would mean another loss of income, but maybe she could do piecework or launder for her customers at their houses. But then who would watch Seamie and Eileen?

I can't cope with this, she thought, I can't. I've spent two days at Burton Tea and I've got nothing to show for it. I spent yesterday and today looking for a room and I haven't found a thing. They're either too dear, too small, or too horrible. Her tears came again. And this time they were tears of desperation and there was nothing she could do to stanch them.

"Come on, Bristow, come out with me and the lads. It'll be fun," Harry Eaton said, straightening his tie in the mirror.

"No thanks, mate. I'm knackered," Joe said, eyes closed, stifling a yawn.

"Oh, bollocks! You're not tired. I know what the real reason is."

Joe opened one eye. "What?"

"It's that pretty little lass of yours. Fiona. She wouldn't like it. You tell her your cock's not a bar of soap. You won't use it up just because it gets wet now and again."

Joe laughed. This was Harry's Saturday-night ritual. No matter how tired he was, he still found the time and energy to go wenching . . . and to rib him for not going.

"Just think of it, squire," he cackled. "A pretty tart with big tits and a nice tight cunny, all yours for three bob. Blond or brunette, whatever you fancy. I know a ginger-haired girl who does all sorts of tricks. She can suck the paint off a lamppost . . ."

"Control yourself, would you?"

But Harry Eaton never worried about controlling himself. He was more than willing to pay for sex and there was no shortage of women in London to accommodate him. There were two types of women in Harry's book – the ones who made you merry and the ones who made you marry – and he preferred the former.

Joe had his reasons for not joining Harry – namely Fiona,

but he also had no desire to come back from a Haymarket whorehouse with a nice dose of clap. He'd heard Harry groaning in the loo some mornings when his cock hurt him so much he could barely piss out of it. He said the treatment hurt even more – his wallet as well as his member. It didn't stop him, though. He still went out with blokes from the market in pursuit of "a sheath for my sword," as he put it, and there was always a ribald joke to be endured as he departed. Little witticisms about how he would leave Joe to take matters into his own hands, or that he hoped he'd have a wonderful evening with the lovely Rosie Palm.

"All right, I'm off."

"I thought something smelled."

"Very funny. Don't wait up. And, Joe . . ."

"What, 'Arry?"

"Have you had your eyes checked lately?"

"No."

"You ought to, lad. Too much of this . . ." – Harry, smirking, made an obscene gesture – ". . . leads to blindness."

"Thanks. Now get out and give me some peace."

Harry left, whistling as he trotted down the stairs.

I pity the poor girl who gets him tonight, Joe thought, he'll be at her like a bull. He yawned again. He should go to bed, but he was too tired to get up. The stove door was open, the fire was toasting his feet nicely. He was feeling full and warm . . . and guilty.

He and Harry had started work at four that morning. Harvest season was ending, but wagons were still coming in nonstop. Farmers were eager to sell off the last of their crops. He hadn't seen a proper day off in ages. He could've insisted on one, but it wouldn't be smart. Not now. Peterson was dropping hints about a promotion. Martin Wilson, the man who negotiated the final price they paid for produce, was leaving. Joe hadn't even thought about taking over from Martin; he assumed he was too new to expect advancement, but the signs were unmistakable. Peterson was taking every opportunity to compliment his work. And today, he'd had him do Martin's job because Martin had been needed inside. He'd seen both Tommy and Martin observing him. At quitting time, Tommy had gone over the tally sheet, pointed out two transactions where he'd overpaid, gleefully noted four where he'd underpaid, and pronounced his work "all in all, first-rate." He'd nearly burst with pride. Peterson's approval had become very important to him.

He and Harry had closed down late, just after seven. Tommy had still been around when they finished, and Millie was with him. He'd invited both lads to join them for supper. Joe's heart had sunk. He'd planned to race to Whitechapel to see Fiona. He hadn't been back to see her for a fortnight and he was worried about her, but he couldn't refuse Peterson's invitation. Tommy told them to get cleaned up and meet them at Sardini's, an Italian place two streets over. Joe was panic-stricken; he'd never been to a restaurant in his life. He told Harry that maybe he shouldn't go, for he only had his work clothes to wear. Harry gave him a jacket he'd outgrown and lent him a shirt and tie. He wore the nicer of his two pairs of trousers.

Sardini's was dark, lit only by candles stuck in wine bottles, so nobody noticed that his trousers didn't go with his jacket. Tommy ordered for everyone. Joe got through the soup and starter beautifully, but was stumped when the pasta arrived. Millie, Tommy, and Harry all laughed as they watched him fight with the noodles, then Millie showed him how to twirl them on a fork. She sprinkled Parmesan on his spaghetti and wiped tomato sauce off his chin. She was her chatty self, telling them how plans for her father's Guy Fawkes party were progressing. When they finished eating, they walked back to Covent Garden together, then Tommy and Millie departed.

Joe had enjoyed himself immensely, but now he felt terrible. He should've been with Fiona in Whitechapel tonight. Fiona, who was pale and thin and grieving for her father. He was a first-class turd. She needed him and where was he? Living it up at Sardini's. He remembered walking her home from the river the night of her father's burial, remembered how she had clutched at him when he left. It broke his heart. He couldn't stand leaving her when she needed him so. But what could he do? For a day or two, he'd been tempted to quit his job so he could go back to Montague Street and be with her. But where would that get them? He'd be back with his father, scrimping to put pennies in their tin, when he was now putting in pounds. And Martin Wilson's job – if he got it – paid even more. Wasn't it more important that he stay the course? Fiona would do her grieving with or without him; his presence would be a comfort, but it wouldn't take away her pain.

He rose from his chair, stoked the coals, and walked to the loo to wash up. He had to get some sleep. As he dried his face, he looked out of the bathroom window. The London sky was remarkably clear. Stars shone against the black night. He stared at one twinkling brightly. Did the same star shine down on her? he wondered. Was she maybe looking at it out of her window and thinking of him? He told the star he loved her, he told it to watch over her and keep her safe.

He undressed and got into bed. Images of Fiona flooded his mind as he drifted off. One day soon he'd have the money they needed for their shop and he'd be done at Peterson's and then they'd be together always. They'd be married and this difficult time of separation and struggle would be behind them. One day. One day soon.

12

Fiona eyed the smoked herrings arranged in a row on the fishmonger's barrow. She was at the Friday night market alone. Her mother had a terrible cough, one she couldn't seem to shake, and Fiona didn't want her out in the damp October air. She took no pleasure in the costers' songs, showed no interest in their pretty displays. She was too busy trying to figure out how to buy tea for four with only sixpence.

" 'Ow much are your bloaters?" she asked the fishmonger.

"The large ones are tuppence," he said. He pointed to some smaller ones. "These 'ere are two for thruppence."

"I'll 'ave two of those." She put the fish in her shopping bag, on top of the potatoes she'd bought at Bristows and the pears Mrs. Bristow had tucked in beside them.

Fiona appreciated the pears, but Mrs. Bristow's kind gesture made her feel like a charity case. Still, she wasn't too proud to accept them. Seamie liked pears and she wanted him to have them. She'd chatted awhile with Mrs. Bristow about Joe and his much-hoped-for promotion. They both received letters every week, but neither one had seen him in nearly a month. Fiona missed him terribly. She wanted to write to him; it helped relieve her loneliness. But every time she saved a few pennies for paper and stamps, they were needed to buy socks for Seamie or throat lozenges for her mam or bread.

Fiona was certain her mother's cough was due to the damp walls of their new room in Adams Court. It was next to the court's single water pump, which leaked night and day, making the cobbles slick and the walls of the houses near it wet and cold.

Adams Court was a short, gloomy cul-de-sac accessed from Varden Street by a narrow brick passage. Its houses were squat two-up-two-downs that faced each other across seven feet of cobblestones. Theirs was the downstairs front room in number twelve. Her mother had taken her to see it before they moved in. She had heard about it from her friend Lillie. Lillie's fiancé had lived in it, but had given it up after their wedding to move into a bigger one across the river. There was no sink. No closet, either. They had to hang their clothing on nails. It measured about fourteen by sixteen feet. They'd had to sell most of their furniture. Fiona hated the room, but when her mother had asked her what she thought, her face hopeful and anxious all at once, she'd told her that once they got used to its size, it would do very nicely. Of course it would.

Their old friends and neighbors had done their best to keep them on Montague Street, offering them spaces in houses that were already full. But their offers came from good-heartedness, not practicality, and her mother would not take advantage of them. Roddy had tried to help, too. Fiona wasn't supposed to know about it, but she did. He'd come in late from a shift one night, while they were still in the old place, and Kate had fixed him his tea. The door to the parlor was open and she'd heard them discussing her mother's trials with Burton Tea. And then, out of the blue, Roddy had asked her mam to marry him.

"I know you don't love me, Kate," he'd said. "And I don't expect you to. Not after Paddy. I know how it was between the two of you. It's not about that. It's just that, well . . . I could take care of you and the children. I'd stay in me own room and you could stay in yours and we could all go on just as we always have. You don't have to go."

And then Fiona had heard the sound of her mother crying and Roddy's anxious voice: "Oh, Jaysus, I'm sorry. I didn't mean to make you cry, I only wanted to help. Christ, I'm an eejit . . ."

"No, Roddy, you're not an eejit," her mother said. "You're a good man, and any woman would be glad to 'ave you. I'm only crying because it touches me. There aren't many in this world who would put their own happiness second to another's. But you can't saddle yourself with another man's family. You should 'ave your own with Grace. You're sweet on 'er as can be and everyone knows it, so go on and marry that lass. We'll make out fine."

But would they? Fiona wasn't so sure. These days, a voice gibbered at her constantly from deep inside, reminding her over and over again that they had so little money. Hers and Charlie's wages barely covered the rent, with a bit left over for food. Where was the rest to come from? What would they do when the baby needed new clothes or somebody's boots wore out? It was paralyzing, this voice. It screamed and shrieked and she never had the answers it demanded. She had prayed to God, asking Him for help. For strength to endure everything she'd lost and courage to face everything that lay ahead. But she'd received no reply. God, it seemed, wasn't listening.

Whenever her spirits sank, she would reach into her pocket and feel for the blue stone Joe had given her. She would squeeze it tightly, picture his face and remind herself of their shop, their dreams, the life they would have together. One day. One day soon. The money in their tin continued to grow. Every time he wrote, the amount was higher. In his last letter he'd said if things kept going well, they'd be able to marry before much longer. She'd been so happy when she'd read that, but her happiness faded as she realized she couldn't get married anytime soon. Her family needed her wages. Her mam was still waiting for compensation from Burton Tea for her father's death. It could be as much as twenty pounds and would enable her to find a better place to live and establish surer footing for herself and the little ones. Fiona knew she couldn't think of leaving until that money came through.

Walking past the butcher's stall, she wished she could buy a nice cut of beef for her mother to fix with potatoes and gravy, but their budget no longer stretched to pricey cuts, and even if it had, there was no way to cook them. The room had no stove, only a fireplace with a narrow grate that held one pot at a time. She missed the nourishing meals her mam used to make. Sometimes the only thing hot about what should've been a hot meal was a cup of tea.

Tonight's supper would be meager. She and Seamie would have boiled potatoes with bread and margarine. No butter – too dear. Charlie and her mam would get the same plus the bloaters – Charlie to keep up his strength for the brewery and Kate because she needed some building up. The cough she'd caught was draining her. She coughed so hard sometimes that her face turned red and she could barely catch her breath. Maybe Charlie would have a few extra pennies tomorrow. If he did, she'd get some cheap mutton pieces for a stew. They could be boiled in a pot with carrots and potatoes. That might be the thing to set her mam to rights.

She finished her marketing with a loaf of bread and a quarter pound of margarine, then started for home. Creeping fingers of fog curled around the hot orange flames of the gas lamps, casting an eerie flickering light over the street. Like a living thing, the fog moved, dipping and swirling around the market stalls, squelching sound, obscuring vision.

The fog made her shiver. Walking through it was like being wrapped in a cold, wet blanket. Her marketing was heavy, she was hungry, and her legs ached from standing all day. Ever since she had inadvertently told Mr. Burton how to get more labor from fewer girls, Mr. Minton – feeling shown up – had worked her extra hard, requiring her to wash the tea scoops at night, wipe the tables, and sweep the floor. She was weary and wanted to be home. On impulse, she decided to take a shortcut.

Veering off the High Street, she walked through the roiling mist down Barrow Street, a derelict lane of ruined lodging houses, each with its door torn off, its windows vacant. There were no gas lamps, they'd all been broken. The street was dark and quiet, and twenty yards down it Fiona began to think that maybe taking a shortcut hadn't been such a great idea. She remembered how frightened she'd been the time that horrible Sid Malone had grabbed her. What if he'd seen her at the market and followed her? And then there was Jack. Three weeks ago, at the end of September, he'd murdered two more women, both on the same night – Elizabeth Stride in Berner Street and Catherine Eddowes in Mitre Square. It was all anyone talked about. Fiona hadn't paid much attention to the news – she'd been grieving for her father – but she thought about it now. Neither Berner Street nor Mitre Square was very far from Barrow Street. Jack hadn't been caught yet. He could be anywhere. There was no one to hear her if she screamed and . . . oh, stop it, she scolded herself. You're being silly. You'll be home in ten minutes instead of twenty this way.

She made herself concentrate on other things. She thought about their new neighbors. There was Frances Sawyer on one side, who, Charlie said, was on the game. Then there was Mr. Hanson on the other. Mr. Hands-on, Fiona called him. He was awful, always leering and feeling his crotch, trying to look at her and every other woman through the cracks in the privy. At least the people who shared their house were decent. Mr. Jensen, a bricklayer who had the upstairs back room, kept to himself. Mrs. Cox, a widow – upstairs front – shouted at her two boys a lot. Jim and Lucy Brady, who occupied the back downstairs room, were the nicest of all. Jim always found time to play with Seamie, and Lucy, who was expecting her first child, had a daily cup of tea with Kate and asked her questions about birthing and babies.

It was hard to live cheek-by-jowl with so many strangers They had to find a better place, but to do that, they needed more money. Not willing to simply sit and wait for the check from Burton Tea to arrive, Fiona had gone to see about weekend work in some of the local shops. She'd had no luck yet, but a few shopkeepers had taken her name. Her mother had started doing piecework, assembling silk poinsettias for Christmas trimming. Charlie helped out, too. Sometimes when she thought she only had enough money for bread and marge, he would come up with a few shillings – his fighting winnings – and then they had meat pies or fish and chips.

Fiona was lost in her thoughts, and only halfway down Barrow Street, when she heard the footsteps behind her. It's nothing, she told herself hastily, just another lass on her way home from the market. But a little voice inside pointed out that the footsteps were too heavy to be a girl's. Well, she countered, they can't be too close, not by the sounds of them. But then again, the voice whispered, that could be the fog. It muffles noise, makes things sound farther away than they really are. Fiona clutched her marketing tightly and picked up her pace. The footsteps picked up theirs. Whoever was behind her was following her. She broke into a run.

She couldn't see the end of the street through the fog, but she knew it wasn't far. Somebody will be there, she told herself, somebody will help me. She was pounding down the street now, but the person behind her was gaining. The footsteps grew louder and suddenly she knew she wouldn't make it. Terrified, she spun around. "Who's there?" she cried.

"Sshhh, don't be afraid," a man's voice answered. "I won't 'urt you. My name's O'Neill. Davey O'Neill. I 'ave to talk to you."

"I – I don't know you. S-stay away from me," she stammered. She tried to run again, but he grabbed her. She dropped her marketing and tried to scream, but he clapped a hand over her mouth.

"Don't!" he hissed. "I said I 'ave to talk to you."

She looked into his eyes. They were desperate. He was crazy. He was Jack; he had to be. And he was going to kill her right here. A terrified whimper escaped her. She squeezed her eyes shut, not wanting to see his awful knife.

"I'll let go of you, but don't run away," he said. She nodded. He let go and she opened her eyes. "I'm sorry I frightened you," he said. "I wanted to talk to you at the market, but I was afraid. You never know who's watching."

She nodded again, trying to stay calm. Trying to keep him calm. She hardly heard what he was saying; it made no sense. He was obviously a loony, but loonies could be dangerous. She must not upset him.

The man looked at her frightened, uncomprehending face. "You don't know me, do you? I'm Davey O'Neill. O'Neill . . . don't you remember?"

Suddenly, she realized she did know him, or rather his name. O'Neill, from the inquest. He was the one who had spilled the grease her father had slipped in.

"Y-yes, I do. But –"

"They blamed me for Paddy's accident, but I didn't do it. I greased the winches, like Curran told me to, but I didn't drop nothing. I wiped all the gears down to be safe, just like I always do. When I was done, there wasn't any grease anywhere. I swear it!"

"But if you didn't . . . then 'ow –"

"I 'ad to tell somebody it wasn't my fault. There's some won't even talk to me. You're Paddy's lass, you're the right one to tell." He looked around himself. "I've got to go now."

"Wait!" She clutched at his sleeve. "What are you saying? If you didn't drip the grease, then 'ow did it get there? I don't understand . . ."

O'Neill pulled free. "I can't say no more. I 'ave to go."

"No, wait! Please!"

"I can't!" He looked like a hunted creature. He made

151

as if to leave, then turned back and said, "You work down the tea factory, don't you?"

"Aye . . ."

"You stay away from the unions, you 'ear me?" His voice was low and harsh. "The Wapping branch is all in pieces now without your father, but Tillet's trying to mend it. There's talk of organizing the tea girls, too. You stay away! Promise me . . ."

"What 'ave unions got to do with anything?"

"Promise me!"

"All right, I promise! But at least tell me why!"

Without another word, he disappeared into the fog. Fiona wanted to run after him, but she couldn't make her trembling legs move. What a flipping fright he'd given her! She must get hold of herself or her mam would see she was upset and ask her what happened and she didn't dare tell her. She was terribly confused. She didn't know what to make of O'Neill and the crazy things he'd said. He was out of his mind; he had to be. Following her down the street like that, coming out of the fog like a bloody ghost. He must be suffering from a guilty conscience.

Or maybe he *was* telling the truth. And if he was, then how did her father slip? The question made her uneasy. She'd wondered about this before, after his burial, when Mr. Farrell and Mr. Dolan said how strange it was that her father, who'd never had an accident at the docks, had fallen to his death. She'd dismissed their conversation – and her wild suspicions – as ridiculous, the product of a grief-stricken mind. Were they?

Was Davey O'Neill saying that he himself hadn't dripped the grease – or that there was never any grease at all? It couldn't be the latter; the constables who investigated the accident found some. Uncle Roddy himself had gone over the report and said it was sound. What else had O'Neill said? "There's some won't even talk to me . . ." Fiona felt anger displacing her fear. It was clear now what was going on – there were dockers who were angry with O'Neill; they blamed him for her father's death. They were giving him the cold shoulder; he might even be having trouble finding work. And he wanted her to make it all better. He wanted her to tell people that it wasn't his fault. The selfish bastard. Her father was dead, her family was struggling, and all he cared about was getting back into his workmates' good graces. Well, sod him. As if she had no other worries than Davey O'Neill's hard luck. The barmy git! Sneaking up on her and rattling on about unions. Telling her not to join one. As if she had the money to spend on dues!

She passed a shaking hand over her forehead, brushing back wisps of hair. She knew she should get off Barrow Street. One run-in with a loony was plenty – was she going to stand around and wait for the next one? She was still angry and she wished she could tell somebody what had happened. Charlie would know what to make of O'Neill, but he'd be livid with her for taking a shortcut and she was in no mood for a tongue-lashing. She wouldn't tell anyone, she'd just forget the whole thing. She picked up her marketing. Nothing had rolled out of the bag, but the pears were probably bruised. She resumed her walk, feeling for the bloaters. Luckily, they weren't smashed. As she neared the end of the street, she was still cursing O'Neill, vowing to give him a good piece of her mind if she ever had the misfortune of seeing him again.

13

A troop of raggedy boys, mudlarks, poked about birdlike in the soft silty mud below the Old Stairs, turning up bits of copper, old bottles, and chunks of coal. Fiona watched them as they chased the ebbing tide, filling their pockets and scurrying off, eager to sell their treasures to the rag-and-bone man.

She was sitting with Joe in their special place. She knew this part of the river like the back of her hand. Everything here was familiar to her – the frothing waves, Butler's Wharf across the water, the rich scent of tea. Everything was familiar, yet nothing was the same.

She couldn't shake the feeling she had, ever since Joe had arrived on her doorstep that morning, right out of the blue, that he'd changed somehow. She couldn't put her finger on it; he just seemed different. He had a new jacket – a beautiful moss-green tweed that Harry had given him. He was also wearing a crisp white shirt and new wool trousers that he'd bought for a trip to Cornwall with Tommy Peterson. In them, he didn't look like a rough-and-tumble barrow boy anymore, but a confident young man on the rise.

Fiona was wearing her navy skirt, a white blouse, and her gray shawl. It was a blustery autumn Sunday and she was glad of an excuse to wear the shawl; it covered up a clumsily mended tear in her sleeve. She was uncomfortably aware of her shabby clothes and of Joe's nice new ones. It made her feel self-conscious, something she'd never felt with him before.

Joe seemed excited, pleased with his job, with Peterson, and with himself. As he should be, she thought, he hasn't even been there two months and already he's up for an advancement. He'd gone on and on about Peterson's – Tommy-this and Tommy-that – talking a mile a minute. His face glowed as he spoke about the possibility of getting the buyer's job. He talked about the Cornwall trip, and how he'd stayed in a fancy hotel. He used all sorts of buying and selling terms that she didn't understand. She tried to feel happy for him, tried to share in his excitement, but it seemed all his and none of hers.

". . . and our tin now contains eighteen pounds and sixpence, I'm 'appy to report," he said, snapping her out of her thoughts.

Fiona looked apologetic. "I 'aven't any money for it. Maybe next week . . ."

"Don't worry. I'm putting in enough for the two of us."

She frowned. That wasn't it at all; that he was putting in enough for them both. It was *their* dream, wasn't it? *Their* shop. She wanted to contribute, too. When they got it, she wanted it to be because of her efforts and sacrifices, as well as his. Didn't he understand that?

He took her hand and rubbed it between his. "Cor, luv, your 'and is rough," he said, inspecting it. "We'll 'ave to get you some salve."

"I 'ave some, thanks," she said curtly, pulling it away.

She shoved both hands into her skirt pockets. It wasn't true, she didn't have any salve. But she didn't want any from him. She felt hurt, as if he had criticized her. Her hands had always been rough. Weren't everyone's? Everyone who worked, at least. Fine ladies had soft hands, not tea packers like herself. Millie's hands would be soft, she thought darkly.

"Fee, what's wrong?" Joe asked, noticing her sullen expression.

God, she was being miserable. He was only trying to be nice, only trying to take care of her. He'd surprised her family with a huge basket of fruit and vegetables. He made it seem like a gift, though he'd known it was a necessity. He brought candies for her mother and a painted wooden soldier for Seamie, whose face had lit up like a lamp at the sight of it. For her, he'd brought six red roses. He'd been so good to her, so why did she feel so upset, so defensive?

"Nothing," she lied, forcing a smile, determined not to give in to her rotten thoughts and spoil the first afternoon they'd had together in ages.

"I'm going on about me job too much. Probably boring you. I'm sorry, Fee." He put his arm around her, pulled her close, and kissed her.

In his arms, her fears dissipated. She felt as if she and Joe were themselves again. Just the two of them . . . loving each other, possessing each other, with no thoughts of Peterson's. No worries about her mam and their cramped room and money.

"I wish we 'ad more time together, Fee. I 'ate never seeing you."

"Well, at least you're 'ere now," she said brightly. "And you'll be back for Guy Fawkes. That's not far away at all – only about a fortnight." She was so looking forward to the holiday, she became animated just talking about it. "We're all going back to Montague Street for the bonfire. I can't imagine not being there for Guy Fawkes." She squeezed his hand. "Will you be getting the whole day or just the night?"

He looked away.

"Joe?"

"I won't be able to come, Fiona."

"Not come?" she cried, crushed. "But why? Don't tell me Peterson 'as you working on Guy Fawkes night!"

"No, not exactly. Tommy's 'aving a big do and I 'ave to go."

"Why? Can't you just say 'No, thank you' and come 'ome?"

"No, I can't. It's a big party for all the employees. It's the night Tommy 'ands out the bonuses and promotions. It's a slap in the face if I don't go, Fiona. Please don't be mad, there's nothing I can do about it."

But she was mad, she couldn't help it. And sad and disappointed. Guy Fawkes was a big event on Montague Street; it always had been. All the children made their Guys; all the neighbors came out to watch the bonfire and set off firecrackers. Courting couples held hands in the light of the fire and she had hoped to do the same with Joe. It had been something to look forward to, a little promise of fun to hold on to, and now she had nothing again.

"Will Millie be there?"

"I would think so. It's at their 'ouse."

She was silent for a few seconds, then said, "Are you sweet on 'er?"

"What?"

"Are you?"

"No! Bloody 'ell, Fiona! Are you starting that again?"

"Sorry, I got it wrong," she said acidly. "Tommy's the one you really love, not Millie, right? Must be. You spend all your time with 'im."

Joe exploded. "Fiona, what do you want me to do?" he yelled. "Do you want me to quit?" He didn't give her a chance to answer. "I've thought about it, because I want to be back 'ere with you. But I 'aven't because I'm trying to do the right thing for us. I'm trying to get the promotion Tommy's dangling so I can earn more money. So we can get our shop. So I can take care of you."

"I'm not asking you to take care of me," she shouted back. "I'm just asking you to be around once in a while . . ." She could feel her lip trembling. She wouldn't cry, sod it, she was too angry. "It 'asn't been easy after me da and all. If you were only 'ere sometimes . . . just to talk to."

"Fee, you know I would be with you if I could. You *know* that. It won't always be like this. Just be patient a little longer. I feel terrible, but I can't do anything about it, I can't be in two places at once. Please don't make me feel guiltier than I already do."

Fiona had been about to reply, but his words stopped her. Guilty. She made him feel guilty. Her stomach lurched. She felt sick and ashamed. She closed her eyes and in her imagination she saw him with Harry and Millie. They were strolling and laughing, free and easy, talking about Tommy, making jokes, looking in the brightly lit shop windows they passed, stopping for tea. Why in the world would he want to come back here, to the dingy streets of Whitechapel, when he could be with them? Why would he want to be with her and listen to her worries and fears when he could listen to Millie's laughter? She couldn't compete with the likes of Millie; she looked like a ragpicker in her worn clothes. Her old shawl, her rough hands – he was probably making a hundred unfavorable comparisons, she thought, cringing inside. She couldn't even give him sixpence for their cocoa tin. She understood now; he was leading an exciting new life, full of interesting people and new experiences. He was moving ahead, away from her, and didn't want to be burdened. She was an obligation. He hadn't said that, but he didn't need to. Well, she was too proud to be anybody's bloody burden. She blinked hard, several times, then stood up.

"Where are you going?"

" 'Ome."

"You're still angry at me."

"No, it's all right," she said quietly, not wanting to lose her temper and raise her voice again. Millie probably never yelled. "You're right, you should go to Peterson's. It's just . . . I've 'ad enough of the river and I want to go back."

He got up to go with her.

"I'll go meself, thanks."

"Don't be daft. It's a long way. If you insist on going 'ome, I'll walk you."

Fiona turned on him. "I said no! Leave me alone! Go back to bloody Covent Garden! I don't want to 'ear that my 'ands are rough or that I should be patient or that you'll be spending Guy Fawkes with Millie Peterson!"

"I'm not spending it with Millie! I'm just going to a party! What is wrong with you? I can't please you no matter what I do!" Joe said, exasperated. "You say you want me around more, but now I'm 'ere and you want to go 'ome. Why are you so bloody touchy?"

"No reason, Joe. None at all! I've lost me da, lost me 'ome, and now I'm losing me lad. Everything's just bloody grand!"

"Fiona, I'm sorry about things, I am. But you're not losing me; I'm trying to make things better. What the 'ell do you want from me?"

"I want my Joe back," she said. Then she ran to the top of the stairs and disappeared from his sight. She ran across the High Street, past wharves and warehouses, toward Gravel Lane and Whitechapel. She didn't understand anything anymore. Nothing made sense. Joe said he was working hard for them, for their shop. That should comfort her, but it didn't.

If he was truly working toward their shop, why was he so bent on getting that promotion? Hadn't he told her that they had eighteen pounds and sixpence? That was only about seven pounds shy of the twenty-five they needed. He didn't need the buyer's job, all he needed was a few more months' wages. Then he could quit and they could open their shop. What was he doing? Why was he after that job?

A half mile up Gravel Lane, she started to run faster. She was out of breath, and her legs were weak, but still she ran, trying to escape the voice in her head, the one with the answer to her questions: "Because he doesn't want the shop anymore. And he doesn't want you."

In front of scores of hard, appraising eyes, Charlie Finnegan removed his shirt and tossed it over a chair. He pulled his elbows behind his back, loosening his shoulders, opening up his chest. The eyes roved over his rippling muscles. They noted the thick arms, the powerful hands. A murmur of approval moved through the crowd. Odds increased, bets changed, coins leaped from hand to hand.

Impassive, Charlie's own eyes roved around the room. He liked what he saw. This was his first fight at the Taj Mahal – an old music hall newly converted to a sporting hall. The owner, Denny Quinn, had gutted the building, ripping out the stage and the seats, but leaving the fancy gas chandeliers and sconces and the florid wallpaper. The end result was a large, well-lit space, perfect for dogfights, ratting matches, cockfights, and bare-knuckle brawls.

He liked the crowd, too – mostly workingmen, but also some toffs. He spotted Thomas "Bowler" Sheehan in the crowd. Bowler, named for the black hat he always wore, was the most notorious criminal in East London. There wasn't a whorehouse, dicing parlor, gaming hall, or fencing ring that he didn't have a piece of. Wharfingers paid him to "protect" their property. Publicans paid him to keep their windows from going in. And those foolish enough deny him a piece of their pie usually turned up facedown in the Thames.

Sheehan's presence was a testimony to the amount of money in the hall. He didn't squander his evenings on small-time fights. Charlie was pleased to know that interest in him was high. He knew that lads Quinn liked, boxers who became his regulars, got a piece of the nightly draw, in addition to prize money. He was fighting for nothing tonight. Quinn made the new lads do a tryout before he took them on. Charlie was determined to make an impression.

A bell sounded. Amid cheers and catcalls, he and his opponent came together in the center of the room. They held out their hands for the referee, who turned them palm-up to make sure they weren't concealing anything, then sent them back to their corners – opposite sides of the circle formed by the spectators.

Charlie sized up the lad. He knew him. His name was

Sid Malone. He worked with him at the brewery. Sid lived across the river in Lambeth. He wasn't a native Londoner. According to Billy Hewson, their foreman, he'd come up from the countryside after his mother died. He had no family. No friends, either. He was a bully, always picking fights, though Charlie never had any trouble from him. At least not until the day, several months ago, that Sid had taken a fancy to Fiona. He'd asked her to a pub, and when she declined, he'd tried to drag her into an alley. She'd broken his nose with a single, well-placed punch that had everything to do with luck, not strength, but Malone had never lived it down. He wanted to recover his pride and knew no better way of doing it than by beating Fiona's brother to mush. Sid was about Charlie's age and height. He had red hair, too, but he wasn't built as solidly. Charlie knew his style and thought he could take him, but any fighter, Sid included, was better when he was angry.

Some boxers had to work up their anger. They needed a reason – a score to settle, a few jeers from the crowd. All Charlie had to do was open the box where his rage lived. Always a good fighter, he'd gotten even better in the weeks since his father's death.

Fighting cleansed him. Of his fury, his guilt, his hopelessness. When he fought, he forgot his anxious sister and his pale, tired mother. He forgot his sad-eyed little brother, mutely reproaching him for never being around. He forgot New York and the life he'd hoped to build there. He lost himself completely in the circling, the faking, the crack of his knuckles against somebody's jaw, in the smoke and the sweat and the bright, brilliant pain.

The referee took the center of the ring and raised his arm. The air crackled with tension. Charlie could feel it raising the hairs on his arms. The crowd surged in closer, voices urged him on. A bell sounded and the fight was on. Sid was like a marionette. Hurt pride and anger pulled his strings, jerking him toward Charlie, making him throw stiff, shaky punches. Charlie withdrew into the defensive, easily parrying Sid's thrusts. From this position, he could watch him, conserve his energy, and decide exactly when to nail the bastard.

"C'mon, ya' coward," Sid hissed. "Fight me."

The crowd didn't like it; they wanted more aggression. Men booed and shook their heads. Charlie didn't give a damn. He could've thrown a dozen giveaway punches, cutting a lip, swelling an eye, but he wanted to give them something memorable, so he held back, teasing the crowd, drawing the whole process out like a skilled lover who increases pleasure by delaying it.

But then, out of nowhere, Sid landed a punch under Charlie's left eye. His knuckles drove in against the socket and split the skin. Charlie's head snapped back. Blood streamed from the cut; the crowd roared. Charlie shook his head, throwing off a red spray. He was glad the cut was under his eye so the blood wouldn't blind him. Sid was confident now, strutting. Charlie watched the position of his fists. There was more room between them. His cover was loosening.

Sid got a few more jabs in, harmless hits that Charlie let him have, all the while watching him like a hawk. His left fist dropped lower every time he threw a right. He was winded, jabbing in a pattern to preserve his breath. Charlie kept his own fists close to his face. Now was not the time to give Sid another crack at his eye. He took a deep breath, steadying himself, still watching Sid's pattern. Right, right, right. The left fist lowered as he punched, then went up, then he took a rest. Another pattern. Right, left, right. Once more. Then all rights again. Lower and rest. He waited. Sid punched with his right again, his left fist dropped, and Charlie delivered a hurtling freight train of a punch directly to his temple.

Sid dropped to the floor like a sack of rocks. He groaned once, his eyes fluttered closed, he was out. There were a few seconds of stunned silence as the referee counted to ten, then he ran to Charlie, hoisted his arm, and declared him the winner. The crowd erupted into cheers, with many exclaiming they'd never seen the like. Men who only minutes ago had been jeering Charlie now praised his restraint and timing.

Sid was carried off to a table, where his mates worked to revive him. Charlie spat out the blood that had leaked into his mouth. In no time, admiring punters brought him a chair, a pint of porter, clean towels, and water. He wiped his face. A stout man in a waistcoat and shirtsleeves, carrying a battered black bag, introduced himself as Dr. Wallace, Denny Quinn's barber-surgeon, and attended to his eye. He cleaned it with soap and water, then patted it with whiskey, which made Charlie wince. When he got out a needle and thread, Charlie asked what the hell he was doing.

"It's a deep one," Wallace said. "If we don't stitch it up now, it'll take forever to 'eal. Open right up on you the next time you fight."

Charlie nodded, steeling himself as Wallace poked the needle through his skin.

"Sit still, lad. We want to keep your face pretty for the ladies." He put in a few more stitches, five in all, then knotted the thread. "Nice wallop you gave that lad. Don't see many like that and I see a lot. Needlework's on the 'ouse. And there's a plate of chops coming your way, courtesy of Mr. Quinn." Wallace nodded toward Sid, splayed out on a table. "I'd better go see if I can wake up Sleeping Beauty. Keep that cut clean."

Charlie thanked him, then downed his pint. As soon as the glass was empty, another appeared. And then a heaping plate of pork chops. He tore into them; he'd had nothing to eat but bread and marge for days. A man brought him his shirt, which he put on but didn't button; he was too hot. Men who'd won money came over to express their appreciation.

"The odds changed twice during the match," one told him, gleefully tousling his hair. "But I stuck by you and won meself a pot! You've got the makings of a great, lad."

The man was so happy, he gave Charlie two shillings of his winnings. He pocketed the money and smiled. The fight had gone just as he'd hoped – he'd made his impression. He leaned back in his chair and closed his eyes. The mad excitement of the match had worn off and he was tired. He took a deep breath, inhaling the stifling air. Like every other establishment of its kind, the Taj Mahal reeked of men and their activities – beer souring in the floorboards, sweat, smoke, greasy chops, and . . . perfume. Perfume? Charlie opened his eyes to see where it was coming from.

A pretty strawberry-blonde stood before him. She was wearing a tightly laced pink corset, a flouncy white petti-coat, and not much else. Her long curls were pulled up in a loose knot; a few corkscrewed free. She had warm brown eyes, freckled skin, and a sweet smile. Charlie could not take his eyes off her bare arms, the tops of her freckled breasts. He'd never seen so much woman.

"Mr. Quinn said you might like some company," the girl said, smiling. "I'm Lucy."

Charlie couldn't speak. God, was she pretty. He could see through her corset.

"Do you want me to go away?" she asked, frowning. "Do you want someone else?"

He found his voice. "No! No, not at all. Sit down, won't you? Excuse me manners, I'm a bit tired. Fight takes it out of you." But suddenly, Charlie found he was not tired in the least.

"I didn't see the fight. Den doesn't want us downstairs till it's over. Says we distract everyone and mess up the betting. But I 'eard you was smashing!"

So, Lucy was one of Denny's girls. He was tongue-tied; he didn't know what to say, but he had to say something. He desperately wanted to keep her here, where he could look at her and talk to her. Where all the other blokes could see him with her. So he started talking about the fight, and Sid Malone, and how his sister had broken Sid's nose. He made Lucy laugh and she didn't go away. Instead she leaned closer and he saw even more of her cleavage.

Charlie felt a hand on his back and looked up. The hand belonged to a rangy man wearing a flash jacket. It was Quinn. He pushed his chair back to stand up, but Quinn told him to sit still.

"That was good work, lad," he said. "Unexpected. Kept the betting 'igh. I like that. I want to take you on. Give that eye time to 'eal and then I'll set you up, all right?"

"Yes, sir. Thank you, Mr. Quinn."

"My terms are generous," Quinn continued, his sharp eyes moving around the room as he spoke. "A set purse, plus a piece of the night's draw. Now listen, Charlie. You're good and others will want you, but I want you exclusively and I'll make it worth your while." He pulled a wad of notes out of his pocket, peeled off a fiver, and gave it to Charlie. Charlie started to thank him, but he held up his hands. "If you're not too knackered, the services of our lovely Lucy are on the 'ouse. She'll get you a good 'ot bath, won't you, luv? And if you're nice to 'er, she'll do one or two other things, I imagine."

Before a red-faced Charlie could say a word, Quinn was off, moving through the crowd. He'd spotted one of his girls alone. "Get a man and get upstairs," Charlie heard him yell. "What do you think this is? A church social?"

Lucy put an arm around Charlie, drawing him close. His heart was hammering. " 'E must really want you, Charlie. It's not often I see Denny Quinn willingly part with five quid."

Charlie couldn't believe his luck. All he'd wanted was to get Quinn to take him on. And now he had five pounds, two shillings, and the promise of more to come. And Lucy. He had Lucy. They would go upstairs and he could take off her corset and look at her. He could kiss her. He could take off her petticoat and lie down next to her and . . . and more.

He was nervous. For all his bragging with the lads on Montague Street about the fourpenny whores they'd had, he'd never done more than kiss his sister's friend Bridget and grope her small breasts. He drained his pint. That made three. Four more and he might actually be ready for this.

"Come on," Lucy whispered, taking him by the hand. She led him upstairs, to a narrow hallway with doors on either side of it. She paused by one door, drew him to her, and kissed him, trailing her hands through his hair and down his back to his bum, which she squeezed and kneaded like a batch of dough, pressing him into her.

"Want your bath now or later?" she whispered, moving her hands to his front.

"What bath?" he croaked, thinking of Denny Quinn and the five-pound note in his pocket, thinking of anything at all to take his mind off what she was doing to him with her hands. Because if he didn't, he wouldn't make it to her bed. To his relief, she stopped to fish in her corset for her room key. Giggling, she unlocked the door and pulled him inside. And in Lucy's plump feather bed, in her soft, freckled arms, Charlie Finnegan found an entirely new way to lose himself.

14

Over a breakfast of toast and tea, Fiona, her face beaming with happiness, reread her letter from Joe for the fifth time.

Dear Fiona,

Here's two bob. Come to Covent Garden on Sunday morning. Take the number-four bus from Commercial Street where we took it the day I brought you here. Get off at Russell Street and I'll be there waiting. I'll only have half a day – I've got to leave for Jersey with Tommy at one, but if you got here by nine, we could have the morning. I'm sorry about the other day and Guy Fawkes. I know this is a hard time for you. I miss you and hope everything's all right.

Love, Joe

The letter arrived yesterday afternoon. It was really more of a package – a small box wrapped with brown paper and twine containing the letter and two shillings, each wrapped in tissue paper so they didn't rattle and tempt the postman.

Fiona was over the moon. For six days, ever since their awful fight, she'd neither seen nor heard from him and she'd been imagining the worst. He didn't love her anymore. He didn't want their shop. He'd taken up with Millie. These thoughts had tortured her during the day and kept her awake at night, staring at the ceiling, lonely and miserable and heartsick. Maybe she'd driven him away for good. Why had she fought with him when they had so little time together? It was all her fault; all he'd done was talk about his job. She'd let her jealousy overwhelm her again. She was so anxious to make things right, but she couldn't travel to him. She couldn't even write, there was never enough money for paper. But now he'd written to her and she was hopeful and excited. She would see him. They would talk and everything would be all right. She needed him, needed the security of his love, so much.

He was right; it *was* a hard time, the hardest of times. Terrible, in fact. Every day there seemed to be a new crisis to deal with: Seamie needed mittens, a sweater. Charlie needed a jacket. The cold weather had come and with it the need for more coal. The little factory that supplied her mother with piecework had gone out of business. She'd looked everywhere – pubs, shops, cookshops – for a second job, but no one was hiring.

And, worst of all, Eileen had caught their mother's cough. The other night she'd taken a very bad turn, hacking until she could hardly catch her breath, bringing up bloody phlegm. They'd rushed her to a doctor. He wasn't sure what it was, he said, they'd have to watch her closely to see if the medicine he'd prescribe would help or not. Fiona had taken hope at this, but her mam had been strangely quiet. When they got home, she'd sat down by the fire and wept. Fiona, frightened more by her mother's tears than the baby's coughing, asked what was wrong.

"It's my fault. Eileen caught my cough and it's turned into consumption," she said. "The doctor won't say it, but I know it."

"No, it's not, Mam," Fiona said forcefully, as if her words themselves could squash the possibility of that dread disease. "The doctor said it could be just that 'er throat's raw or that she's got an infection. 'E said to watch what the medicine did and come back in a week. That's what 'e said and 'e knows more about it than you do."

Her mam had wiped her eyes and nodded, but she hadn't

looked convinced. She'd watched Eileen anxiously ever since, getting little sleep, growing increasingly distracted and depressed. She'd lost weight, too. They all had. There was so little money for food. They'd eaten a steady diet of bread and tea for days until Charlie came home the other night with a five-pound note and a cut under his eye. A moving job, he'd said. The doctor's bills and the cost of Eileen's medicine plus three weeks' back rent and a trip to the market had eaten up most of their windfall, but now, at last, something good had happened. Joe had written and she would see him in only a few hours. She could bear whatever hardships came her way, as long as she had his love and their dreams to hold on to.

As she was wrapping her shawl around her shoulders, trying to remember how long the number-four bus took to get to Covent Garden, a boy's face appeared in the window.

He knocked on the glass. "Is this the Finnegans'?" he shouted.

"Aye. Who are you?"

"Mr. Jackson from the Bull sent me. Said I was to tell Fiona Finnegan that 'e wanted to see 'er about the job. Said she was to come right away if she still wanted it."

"What . . . this minute?"

"That's what 'e said." The boy's eyes strayed to the loaf of bread on the table.

Fiona cut a slice, spread some margarine on it, and handed it to him. He ate it greedily and left to find himself another penny errand.

"Ta-ra, Mam," she said, bending over the bed to kiss her mother good-bye. She wasn't asleep, she was just lying on her side, eyes closed.

"Ta-ra, luv."

Fiona sighed. Once her mother would have peppered her with questions about a new job – especially one in a pub – before ever letting her out the door. Now she was too tired to care. She hadn't even asked about Charlie's eye, or noticed that Seamie's vocabulary now included "bloody" and "bastard." We have to get out of here, Fiona thought. Life in Adams Court was harsh and defeating. It was changing them, doing them in.

She closed the door behind her and set off for the Bull, her fingers crossed. If she hurried, maybe she could get to the pub, talk to Mr. Jackson, and still get to Covent Garden before nine. When she'd spoken to him a few days ago, he hadn't anything available. Someone must've left. His timing could've been better, she thought. Today of all days! But it couldn't be helped and Joe would understand if she was a bit late. If she got the job, she'd have a few extra shillings in her pocket and maybe she could get some meat for their tea during the week or get her mam a bottle of tonic. Maybe, just maybe, she'd get this job. Maybe two good things in a row would happen. She was overdue for a bit of luck.

When she got to the pub, she rapped on the door, and within seconds a burly, ruddy-faced man with a big walrus mustache was ushering her in.

"You're 'ere quick," Ralph Jackson said. "Only just sent that boy off after you."

"Yes, sir," Fiona said, smiling, hoping to make a good impression. "I didn't want to keep you waiting." The truth was she didn't want to keep Joe waiting, but what Mr. Jackson didn't know wouldn't hurt him.

"Good, I like that in me workers. So, you think you're up to the job, then?" he asked. "It's not easy work. And it's not pleasant. Takes lots of elbow grease to get a boozer clean."

"Oh, aye, Mr. Jackson. I can manage it. I'll do a first-rate job for you." I'll wash the windows until they sparkle, I'll scrub the floor until it gleams, she thought. I'll wash the glasses and polish the bar, and kiss your big hairy arse, too. Just give me the bloody job!

"It's three evenings a week, plus Saturday afternoon and Sunday morning. The rate's two and an 'alfpence an hour, plus a meal and a pint of whatever you like when you're finished."

"Yes, sir."

Mr. Jackson chewed his lip, ran his eyes over her as if he were sizing up a plowhorse, then gave her the nod. "All right, then. Scrub brush and bucket are be'ind the door. Bar needs polishing, too, but you'll need to get the dirty glasses off it first."

Fiona blinked. "You mean right now?"

"Yes, of course right now. Something wrong with that? I said the hours included Sunday mornings and today's Sunday."

She wouldn't get to see Joe. He was waiting for her. He'd sent her the fare. They were going to talk and he'd hold her and make things better. She pictured him standing at the bus stop, searching for her face as bus after bus stopped to discharge its passengers. Not finding her. Giving up and going home.

"It's just . . . I was going . . . I didn't think the job would start right away . . ." Fiona said.

"Look, lass, I just lost me charlady," Mr. Jackson said impatiently. "She was expecting and dropped the sprog early. I need me pub cleaned. Makes no difference to me who cleans it. If you don't want the job, I'll give it to the next one who does."

"Oh, no, I do want the job," she said hastily, forcing herself to smile. "I'm grateful to you for remembering me and I'll get right to work."

As soon as she was out of his sight, Fiona allowed her fake smile to drop. Bitter tears stung behind her eyes and slipped down her cheeks; she couldn't hold them in. She was so desperate to see Joe, to make it up with him. Now it all seemed hopeless again. Why did the job have to come through now? This very day? She had no way of telling him what had happened. He'd be standing there waiting for her and she wouldn't come.

But there was no other choice. It had taken weeks to get the job. If she turned it down, it would be ages until something else came up and she didn't have ages. She needed

Joe, but her family needed money. She would just have to write him and explain what happened. She could use the money he sent to do it. She'd tell him she was sorry about the other day, too. And that she loved him and wanted to see him just as soon as he could manage it. And hopefully, he'd understand.

She filled up the wooden bucket with soap and water, grateful that she was alone in the pub, that Mr. Jackson had things to attend to in his office. She rolled up her sleeves, knotted her skirt and got down on her hands and knees. She dunked the brush into the water and began to scrub, her tears mingling with the soapy water on the dirty, beer-soaked floor.

15

"Glass of punch, sir?"

"No. No, thank you," Joe said quickly. His head already felt as if it were floating on a string. "I'll 'ave a lemonade, please."

"Very good, sir," the waiter said, turning crisply on his heel to fetch it.

Joe was finished with the punch. He wasn't used to hard liquor and the two cups he'd had already had made him tipsy. He wanted to stay clearheaded. Tommy had been squiring him about all evening, introducing him to one nob after another. He'd met the head buyers for Fortnum's and Harrods, various chefs and maître d's from the bigger hotels, restaurateurs, and countless wives and sons and daughters and it had taken all his concentration to keep their names straight.

The party was fun and boisterous, not at all the stuffy affair he'd expected. Spirits were high. All the guests truly seemed to be enjoying themselves. But how could they not? Everything was exceptional – the staggering amount of food, the drink, the music, the house all decorated with flowers, the yard aglow with torches and candles. It was a dazzling sight and he wished Fiona were there to share it with him. Fiona. His heart ached at the thought of her.

Why had everything become so bloody difficult between them? He'd hooked himself a good job in hopes of getting them their shop sooner than they'd planned. So they could be together. And now they were coming apart.

He'd sent her money to come to him at Covent Garden

over a week ago and she hadn't – without any explanation at all. She could've at least written to him to say why. She must still be angry. Maybe she hated him and never wanted to see him again. Maybe she'd found someone else.

The last time he'd seen her, the day they'd fought, she was so distracted he couldn't even talk to her. And then, like a clod, he'd told her that she made him feel guilty. He shouldn't have said that – she was very proud and his words had cut her – but the truth was, he *did* feel guilty.

Some of his guilt, he knew he deserved for hurting her feelings at the Old Stairs. But there was a deeper, larger guilt – one that he struggled against. It came from not being there for her after her father's death. From not being able to take care of her. He wanted to rescue her, but how? She couldn't leave her family, she'd told him as much. And he couldn't take them all on. If he did, they'd never get their shop.

Was it selfish to not want these burdens? He wasn't prepared to shoulder a family man's worries yet, but he was doing just that. He worried every minute about Fiona: Was she walking home too late at night? Did she have enough to eat? Did her family have enough money? He'd brought them food when he visited. And he'd slipped four shillings into their money tin when no one was looking. He knew it wasn't enough, but he didn't know what else to do.

He was young; he was going somewhere. His boss liked him, respected him, even. He didn't want all these worries. He wanted, just for a bit, the young man's freedom to work at his job, to learn it and excel at it. To hear that he was smart and talented from someone like Tommy and to bask in the glow of that praise. Just for a bit. But he even felt guilty for wanting that. Christ, it was all too much. A big, overwhelming burden. One he couldn't resolve no matter how many times he went over it in his mind.

The waiter reappeared. Joe took his drink and walked from the living room out onto the balcony to get some air. The November night was crisp and clear. From his vantage point he could see the bonfire blazing in Tommy's enormous backyard. Girlish laughter attracted his attention. He knew that laughter; it was Millie's. Now there was a girl who had no burdens and never would. She was always laughing, always merry. His eyes searched the groups of people clustered around the bonfire and found her. She was hard to miss for she was wearing a spectacular dress. He didn't know the first thing about dresses, but he knew expensive when he saw it. It was a shimmering midnight-blue silk cut low and fitted to her every curve. But the most dazzling thing about it was the fireworks motif embroidered onto it. Thousands upon thousands of tiny iridescent glass beads had been stitched onto the skirt to form one large colorful burst with several smaller ones around it. It looked just like real fireworks exploding in a night sky. The dress was the talk of the party and Millie was the center of attention in it.

She was with her father and a lad who worked for him at his Spitalfields pitch. The lad had obviously said something entertaining; Millie and her father were laughing uproariously. Watching them, Joe felt a sudden stab of jealousy, of possessiveness. But over whom? Tommy? Millie? Tommy had his hand on the lad's back and Joe resented it. Is he as good as I am? he wondered. Better? Looking at Millie standing next to her father, he knew that whoever got her got the family business. Officially, the word was that Harry would take over the firm, but Joe knew better. Harry had purchased a ticket to India and would depart next month. If this lad won Millie's heart and married her, he would become Peterson's son. And what of it? Joe asked himself, watching as Peterson broke away from the group and headed for the house. Why did he suddenly care? He was only in this until he could strike out on his own. He turned away and helped himself to a smoked oyster on a toast point from a passing waiter's tray.

"There you are, Bristow! I've been looking all over for you!"

It was Tommy. He placed his hands on the balcony and smiled. "Smashing party, if I say so myself," he said, observing his guests. A waiter scurried up and asked what he could get him. "Scotch. A double. And the same for my young friend here."

Uh-oh, Joe thought. He was already half pissed. He'd have to dump some out when Tommy wasn't looking or he'd be legless. The waiter was back in an instant, handing him a glass. He took a swallow and winced. It packed a kick.

"I've got news," Peterson said, licking whiskey from his lips. "Just before I left the office tonight, I received an inquiry from Buck Palace. Can you believe it, Joe? I don't even dare hope," he said, flapping his hand as if it didn't matter, but he couldn't keep the gleam out of his eyes. "If they liked our goods, if we got the nod, it could lead to a Royal Warrant on the Peterson sign. Never in my wildest dreams did I see that. Wouldn't it be something?"

"I'll say it would," Joe replied, just as excited as his boss was about a crack at a warrant – the right to display the royal crest and proclaim to all the world that "the Queen shops here." He was already envisioning ways to convince the palace to buy. "We could send them samples of our best produce arranged in baskets on the good wagon, the one that just got painted. We could get Billy Nevins to drive it in uniform. 'E's a good-looking lad, clean and neat. Before they ask, I mean. Bring the goods to them so they don't 'ave to come to us."

"Good idea . . ." Peterson said, signaling for the waiter. He'd finished his drink and was ready for another. He looked at Joe, who'd only gotten halfway through his. "You ready?"

Joe knocked more of his whiskey back and said he was. "We should give them a ridiculous price, cut it way down . . ." he continued, as the waiter handed him a fresh drink. ". . . doesn't matter if we only break even. Or if we lose money. The new business we'd get from the warrant

176

would more than make up for lost profits on the palace . . ." He saw Peterson frown and wondered if he'd gone too far. After all, it was Peterson's profits he was offering to cut. "That is, if you agree, sir."

"Of course I agree," Tommy said. "I was just wondering why none of my senior men came up with these ideas. I guess it takes a young bloke to suggest that we lose money in order to make some. Let's go over your ideas again tomorrow morning. The reason I came over here in the first place was to give you this" – he reached into his jacket, produced an envelope and handed it to him – "and to be the first to congratulate my new head buyer."

Joe was stunned. He'd hoped for the promotion, thought he might have a shot at it, but he'd never assumed the job was his. Now it was. He was Peterson's head buyer. A grin spread across his face. "Thank you, Mr. Peterson, sir. I . . . I don't know what to say."

"You don't need to say anything, lad. You've earned it." He raised his glass. "Here's to your future with Peterson's. You're a bright young man. Always thinking on behalf of the business and I appreciate it."

Joe clinked his glass against Tommy's, then took another swallow. Tommy, a little maudlin now, put an arm around him and launched into the story of how he began his business. Joe, smiling and nodding, appeared to be entranced by the tale, when really he was barely listening.

He simply could not believe his good fortune. Once, he could not even convince his own father to rent another barrow and put fruit on one and vegetables on the other. Now he was head buyer for one of London's biggest fruit-and-veg men. He had the talent and the drive to make it in this world. He'd proved it. He was the guv'nor. Well, not *the* guv'nor, he thought, let's not get carried away . . . but *a* guv'nor, anyway. And he was still only nineteen. He'd have a raise in wages and had what was bound to be a nice bonus in his back pocket, too. He took another swallow of whiskey; it was going down a lot smoother now.

He felt like a million quid. Everything was smashing. This party, the food, the whiskey. Just fucking smashing!

"Oh, Dad, you're not boring poor Joe with those old stories, are you?"

Millie had joined them. Peterson put his other arm around his daughter. "Certainly not," he said, swaying slightly. "Joe loves to hear about the business." He pronounced it "bishnesh." "Don't you, lad?"

"I do indeed, sir," Joe said righteously. He pronounced it "shir."

Millie looked from her father to Joe and giggled. He wondered if they looked drunk. He felt drunk.

"Well, I don't," she said, tossing her head. "There's too much talk of business. Let's talk of bonfires. And Guys. Like the one your faithful employees are marching about the yard right now, Dad. The one that looks just like you."

She was laughing again. Silly Millie, Joe thought. Always laughing. Eyes sparkling. Big round bosoms about to burst out of her dress. A beautiful, giggling girl.

"Well, we'll have to see about that," Tommy said, pretending to be offended. He put his whiskey down and straightened his tie. "We'll sort that bunch out. And you, young man . . . ," he added, pointing at Joe, ". . . you are not to talk about fruit and vegetables anymore tonight. Millie's right. Young people ought to be enjoying themselves at a party, not talking shop." He waved his hands at them, shooing them off the balcony and back into the house. "Millie, show Joe around. Get him something to eat. Get him a drink."

"Yes, Dad," she said. As soon as he'd disappeared down the balcony stairs into the yard, she turned to Joe and said, "I hope he doesn't trip and break his neck. He's pissed as a newt." She threaded her arm through his and led him from the living room. "Come on, I'll show you the house."

Joe let himself be led. It was the easiest course of action. Tommy wasn't the only one who was pissed as a newt. He'd have to pull himself together. Hopefully, Millie hadn't noticed how bad he was. He didn't want her telling her father he'd gotten himself blind drunk.

People looked at them and smiled as they walked from room to room. Joe smiled back; he enjoyed the attention. They must know I'm the new head buyer, he thought giddily. Women whispered and nodded approvingly. Harry waved from a corner. Everyone was so nice. This house was nice. Millie was nice. He stubbed his toe on the carpet and almost tripped, which set her giggling again. Why couldn't he make his feet work right? Another glass of Scotch appeared and she put it into his hand. He took a sip, just to be polite.

Millie showed him the parlor, which she said she planned to do over à la Japonaise, whatever that meant. She showed him her father's study, with its immense mahogany desk, rich rugs, and heavy draperies, and she showed him the kitchen, which was vast and swarming with an army of cooks and waiters. And then she led him to the stairway. Halfway up, he knew he was in trouble. His head had started to spin.

Millie noticed his discomfort. To his relief, she wasn't angry. "Poor duck," she said. "Don't worry. We'll find you a place to rest until it wears off."

They walked past door after door, but she wasn't showing him any more rooms, she was leading him down the hall to a room at the end. He felt very bad. He was swaying back and forth like a sailor who hadn't got his land legs. Millie opened the door to the last room and ushered him in. There was a bed, soft and inviting, and he sat down on it, expecting her to leave him to his devices. Instead, she sat down next to him and started to remove his jacket. He protested, telling her he'd be fine, he just needed to sit for a minute, but she shushed him, saying he'd be much more comfortable this way. She took his jacket from him, loosened his tie, then pushed him back on the bed, telling him to lie still and close his eyes, in that sweet, soft voice of hers.

He did as he was told. Breathing deeply, he willed his

brain to stop doing somersaults. Little by little, the spinning feeling eased. He still felt very drunk, almost as if he were outside of his body, but at least he wasn't so dizzy anymore. He was dimly aware of Millie moving about the room; he heard her skirts rustling. He opened his eyes. It was dark. She must've doused the lamp. He focused on a pile of pillows at his left. They were lacy and embroidered. They smelled of lilacs. Millie always smelled of lilacs. He closed his eyes again. This must be her bedroom, he thought uneasily. He shouldn't be here. But it was so easy to lie here and so hard to get up.

"Millie?"

"What is it?"

"I better go back downstairs. Your father wouldn't like this."

"How will he find out?" she asked, her voice closer now. "I won't tell him." She sat on the bed beside him. The smell of lilacs was stronger. Joe felt something brush his lips. His eyes flew open. It was Millie, she'd kissed him. She raised her head, smiling at him, and he realized she no longer had her dress on. She was wearing only a camisole and petticoat. As he stared at her, she began unbuttoning her top, exposing more and more of herself. He could not tear his eyes away from her. Her breasts were beautiful and lush, with small pink nipples that hardened in the cool air of the room. He let out a groan at the sudden, deep ache in his groin. She shrugged the camisole off her shoulders, took his hand and pressed it against herself. She leaned over him and kissed him again, flicking her tongue over his lips.

Don't do this, he told himself. Don't. He pushed her away and struggled to stand on his wobbly legs. She smiled at him, eyes glittering like a cat who's released a mouse it means to kill just to watch it run one last time. "I'm yours, Joe," she whispered. "I want you. And I know you want me. I can see it. I've seen it in your eyes from the beginning. You can have me. You can have anything you want . . ."

He had to leave. Now. This instant. But he wanted her. He wanted to fuck her so badly he could hardly breathe. It was easier to give in, wasn't it? It was a lot easier here on Easy Street. Everything else was hard. It was easy here, in Peterson's house, where maids and waiters brought you things to eat and lots of whiskey. It was easy in Millie's big bed, with her sweet lips and her big, lovely tits. It was all right. He could have her. He could have anything. Isn't that what she'd said?

Millie stood up, unbuttoned her petticoat and let it drop to the floor. She was now completely naked. In the darkness, he could see the curve of her small waist, her thighs, the tuft of blond hair between them. She pressed herself against him and kissed him again, snaking her hand between his legs, unbuttoning his trousers. His hands sought her breasts. He had to have her. Now. He pushed her down on the bed, parted her legs, and entered her roughly. And then he was inside of her, plunging into the deep, soft velvet of her again and again. She was his. The buyer's job was his. Peterson's was his. Everything was his. He came hard and quick, biting her shoulder as he did.

When it was over, he lay still, breathing heavily. The whiskey was playing tricks again. Where was he? He wasn't quite sure. Oh, yes, he was with Fiona, of course. In their big house. In their big bed. They had their shop, scores of shops, in fact. They were rich and everything was lovely. He felt calm, contented, his face buried in Fee's soft neck.

But something was wrong. He felt so dizzy, so sick. There was that smell again – something cloying. Lilacs. He raised his head and looked through bleary eyes at the woman beneath him. This isn't Fiona, his mind screamed. My God, what have I done? He rolled off her and backed away from the bed. He knew he was going to be violently sick. Holding his pants up with one hand he unlocked the door with the other and ran from the room.

On the bed, Millie massaged the bite mark on her shoulder. There was a wetness between her legs from what they'd done, she could feel it. Good thing she'd covered her bedspread with an old sheet earlier. She raised her knees, her feet flat on the bed, then tilted her hips up, just as she'd read in the book she'd got from her married friend, Sarah. She closed her eyes, savoring the taste of him on her tongue, and smiled.

16

"Don't you want some, Fee? They're nice and salty," Charlie said, holding a paper cone of chips out to his sister. "Come on, 'ave one . . ."

"No, thanks."

Something was wrong. She hadn't told him so, but he could see it in her face. Something was making her sad. He'd hoped a Sunday afternoon walk to the river would lift her spirits, but the things that usually made her smile – a chantey carried on the wind, gulls pestering for chips – seemed to have no effect. If anything, she looked lower now than when they'd left Adams Court.

He followed her gaze out over the whitecapped water. A pair of barges were crossing midstream. Two ships passing in the shite, he thought. For the life of him, he could not understand what she saw in this poxy river. He finished his chips, then looked to see where Seamie had got to. He was chasing seagulls by Oliver's. "Oi! You! Don't go too close to the water," he shouted. Seamie paid him no attention. He followed a bird into the waves, soaked his boots, and laughed. Charlie swore. He couldn't even make a four-year-old mind.

It wasn't easy being the man of the family. He worked all day at the brewery, fought like a tiger at the Taj, and still didn't make enough money to pay all the bills. And though he needed every penny he could earn, work kept him out of the house too much. This afternoon, at dinner, was the first time he'd talked to his mother in days. He'd looked at her face, really looked at it, as she poured him a cup of tea, and he'd been shocked to see how pale she was. And then he'd looked at his sister, who seemed to be constantly fighting tears. His brother was sulky and whiny, having been cooped up for too long. Even the baby was ailing.

How had his da done it? he wondered. How had he kept them all fed and clothed? How had he made them feel cared for and safe? And all on a docker's wages? He'd promised his father he'd look after them and he was trying his best, but no matter how hard he tried, he failed. If only he could put away a few pounds. Then he could move his family out of Adams Court, into a decent room, or maybe even a whole floor in a better house. The other day, Denny Quinn had offered him the chance to make a few extra bob. There was a man who owed him a considerable amount of money, he'd said. He wanted Charlie and Sid Malone to collect it for him. Charlie had turned him down. He had no desire to knock on some stranger's door in the middle of the night and beat him senseless over an unpaid gambling debt. But that was before his mother had grown so pale. Before the baby had taken ill. Now, he wondered if he'd been daft to say no.

Fiona sighed, taking his thoughts away from Quinn. Looking at her, he decided to take another tack. Maybe if he could get her to talk about something – anything at all – he could eventually get her to tell him what was bothering her.

" 'Ow's it going at the Bull?" he asked.

"Fine."

" 'Ard work, is it?"

"Aye."

A long silence followed. He tried again. "Saw Uncle Roddy yesterday."

"Did you?"

"We talked about the murders. 'E said the latest one – the Kelly woman from Dorset Street – was the worst yet. 'E said what was left didn't even resemble a woman."

"Really?"

"Aye. And they're no closer to catching the bloke, either."

"Hmm."

So much for that idea. Well, there was no help for it. He'd have to take the direct route. Get all blabbery and emotional, just like a lass. He dreaded it.

"All right, Fiona . . . what's up?"

She didn't look at him. "Nothing," she said.

"Look, something is. You're not yourself. You'd tell da if 'e were 'ere, so you better tell me. I'm the man of the 'ouse, remember? 'E left me in charge."

Fiona laughed at that, which he did not appreciate. Then, even worse, she started to cry. Flustered, he gave her his handkerchief, then awkwardly put an arm around her, hoping that none of his mates was around to see him.

"It's over between us . . . me and Joe," she sobbed.

"Did 'e break it off?"

"No, but 'e will. I'm sure of it."

She told him all about Joe's letter. "It's been ages since 'e sent it," she said. "I want to see 'im, but every time I get two pennies together something 'appens or somebody's 'ungry and they're gone. I know 'e doesn't care for me anymore . . . 'e'd come see me if 'e did . . ." She pressed his handkerchief to her face as fresh tears overtook her.

"Aw, Fiona, is that all it is?" he said, relieved. He was worried she might be up the pole. "Joe cares for you. 'E always 'as. Just go see 'im and make it up, will you?"

"Charlie, I 'aven't got the money. Did you listen to anything I said?"

"I'll give you the money. I've got a bit of a sideline going . . . a way of making some extra brass. I can't tell you what it is, but . . ."

"Oh, I know all about it."

He looked at her, surprised. "What do you know?"

She touched the scar under his eye. "I know 'ow you got that."

"I got it from the rim of a beer barrel I was lifting. It slipped and 'it me in the face."

185

Fiona smirked. She pulled his collar open and peered at the love bite on his neck. "Beer barrel give you that, too?"

He slapped her hand away, scowling. "All right, so I'm fighting. Just don't tell Mam. I've got a match next Saturday. If I win, you'll 'ave bus fare to Covent Garden."

"Oh, Charlie . . . really?"

"Aye."

She hugged him tightly. "Thank you . . . oh, thank you!"

"That'll do, Fee," he said, extricating himself.

She blew her nose in his handkerchief then handed it back to him.

"Um . . . that's all right. You keep it," he said.

"Where's Seamie?" she asked, suddenly worried.

He nodded at the riverbank. " 'Alfway to Lime'ouse, the little bugger. Let's go get 'im. And then we'll go 'ave a pint at the Black Dog."

"With what for money?"

He gave her a superior smile. "Unlike yourself, Fiona, a person as 'andsome as I am needs no coin. The barmaid's sweet on me. She'll give us a couple of pints for free."

"Is that who put those marks on your neck? Is she a girl or a flipping vampire?"

"No, that was another lady friend."

"You better watch yourself, Charlie."

He rolled his eyes. He did not need a lecture on this topic from his sister.

"I mean it! All we need now is some lass showing up on the doorstep with an ugly red-'aired baby in 'er arms."

He shook his head. "It'll never 'appen."

"Because you're . . ." She blushed slightly at the words. ". . . you're being careful, right?"

Charlie snorted. "Aye, careful not to tell 'er where I live!"

"Turn," Ada Parker, Millie's dressmaker, commanded through a mouthful of pins.

Millie did and Ada deftly hemmed the last few inches

of the mauve satin skirt she was fitting. When she was done, she sat back on her heels to appraise her work and frowned.

"What's wrong?" Millie asked.

"I don't know. The skirt's loose around your waist. I can't understand it. Everything looked fine at the last fitting. I *know* I cut it properly. I know your measurements by heart."

She unhooked the skirt and made Millie step out of it. Then she took a tape measure from her pocket and wound it around her waist. "There's the answer," she said, batting her on the rump. "You've lost weight! What's wrong? Why aren't you eating?"

"Nothing's wrong, Ada. My . . . my appetite's a little off, that's all."

"You should see a doctor. You don't want to get too thin or you'll ruin your beautiful figure. And then how will you find a husband?"

Millie smiled. "I've already found one. I'm expecting a proposal of marriage any day."

"That's wonderful! Congratulations, my darling," Ada said, hugging her. Then she shook a finger at her. "But you won't keep him if you lose more weight!"

Millie skimmed her hands over her belly. "Oh, I think I will," she said. "In fact, Ada, let me see your taffetas before I leave. An ivory, maybe. Or possibly a cream. White doesn't suit me. Not at all."

17

Fiona mopped up the last bit of gravy on her plate with a crust of bread and washed it down with a swig of weak beer.

"Like that, did you?" Ralph Jackson asked her.

"It was delicious. Mrs. Jackson makes a smashing steak pie."

"Don't I know it!" he exclaimed, patting his impressive belly. "I'm glad you liked it, lass. You could use a little building up."

Fiona smiled. Any girl under two hundred pounds was in need of building up in Mr. Jackson's eyes. She washed her dishes, grabbed her shawl, and bade him ta-ra. It was chilly outside, but the supper had filled her up and she felt a warmth throughout her body that only came from a good hot meal. It was Saturday, just after six, and she started down the sidewalk toward her home with a spring in her step. Her spirits were improved, she was hopeful. If Charlie won tonight, and she had prayed so hard that he would, she'd be on her way to Covent Garden tomorrow afternoon, right after she finished at the pub, to see Joe. She hated that her fare would be earned from his cuts and bruises, but she was desperate. She would make it up to him somehow. As soon as she and Joe had their shop, she would start putting aside money for his passage to New York.

She had only gone a few yards down the sidewalk when she heard someone call her name. She turned. It was Joe. He was standing about ten yards behind her. He looked at her, then looked away again. She called to him. Her heart filled with love and happiness at the sight of him. Joe, her Joe! He was here, oh, thank God, he was here! He didn't hate her; he'd come to see her. He still loved her. He did! She ran to him, beaming. But as she got closer, her steps slowed. Her smile faded. Something wasn't right. He looked thin and haggard. He was unshaven.

"Joe?" He raised his eyes to hers. The look she saw in them terrified her. "What is it? What's 'appened?"

"Come on, Fee. Come to the river," he said, in a voice so hopeless, so dead-sounding, she barely recognized it. He turned in the direction of the Thames and started to walk.

She grabbed his arm. "What's going on? Why are you 'ere and not at work?"

He wouldn't look at her or answer her questions. "Just come for a walk," he said and she had no choice but to follow.

When they got to the Old Stairs, they sat in their usual place, halfway down. Joe took her hand and squeezed it so tightly, it hurt. He tried to speak, but no words came. He lowered his head and wept. Fiona was so frightened, she could hardly find her own voice. She'd only seen him cry once, when his grandmother died. Was that it? Had someone died?

"Luv, what is it?" she said, her voice trembling. She put her arms around him. "What's wrong? Is it your mam? Is your father all right?"

He looked at her through his tears. "Fiona . . . I've done a terrible thing . . ."

"What? What 'ave you done? 'Ow bad can it be? Whatever it is, I'll 'elp you. We'll fix it." She tried for a smile. "You didn't kill anyone, did you?"

"I've made Millie Peterson pregnant and now I've got to marry 'er."

Fiona would later remember that the seconds that followed his words were without sound. She heard nothing of his voice, nothing of the river traffic or the noise

189

from the nearby pub. It was as if her ears had been seared by those words, permitted to hear no more. She sat upright, arms wrapped around her legs, rocking slightly. Hearing nothing. Nothing. Part of her knew Joe had just said something, something bad, but if she didn't think about it, she'd be all right. She knew he was still speaking, but she wouldn't listen, because if she did he would tell her about . . . he would say that he'd . . . Millie . . . that they'd . . .

A low cry escaped her throat, an animal sound of deep, crushing pain. She doubled over as if she'd been punched in the stomach. She heard him now, crying her name, felt his arms around her, pulling her to him. He'd made love to Millie Peterson. What they had done because they loved each other, he had done with her. Seconds ago, her mind would not accept it, now it tortured her with images of them together – his lips on her, his hands on her. She pushed him away, staggered to the water's edge, and vomited.

When her stomach stopped heaving, she dipped her hem in the water and wiped her face. She tried to straighten, to walk back to the stairs, but then her mind seized on the rest of what he'd said. Millie was pregnant. He was going to marry her. Be her husband. Go to bed with her, wake up with her. Spend the rest of his life with her. Like a glass vase dropped on a hard stone floor, her heart shattered into a million jagged pieces. She covered her face with her hands and sank to the ground.

Joe jumped down from the steps, lifted her up, and held her. "I'm sorry, Fiona, I'm so sorry. Forgive me. Please, please forgive me . . ." he said brokenly. She struggled against him, kicking him, pummeling him. She broke away, stumbling backward. A murderous rage filled her. "You bastard!" she screamed. "All those times you told me I was jealous, told me I 'ad no reason to be! Looks like I 'ad a bloody good reason! 'Ow long 'as this been going on, Joe? 'Ow many times did you fuck 'er?"

"Once. I was drunk."

"Oh, just once? And you were drunk . . . well, that's all

right then, isn't it? That excuses it completely . . ." Her voice cracked, she had to swallow before she could continue. "And did you kiss 'er like you kissed me? On 'er lips? 'Er 'eart? Between 'er legs?"

"Fiona, don't. Please. It was nothing like that."

She walked up to him, her whole body twitching with fury. She wanted to slap his face, kick him in the balls, do something to him that would make him feel one tiny fraction of the pain, the humiliation, she felt. Instead she burst into tears. "Why did you do it? Why, Joe, why?" she wailed piteously, her beautiful blue eyes red and swollen.

"I don't know, Fiona," he cried. "I go over and over it in my 'ead and I still don't know." He told her everything in a gush of words. About being at the party and missing her and worrying that she hated him. He told her about wanting his promotion so badly and feeling like a king when he got it. About drinking too much and Millie showing him around and his head spinning and ending up in her room. And then realizing what he'd done and being so violently ill that he'd retched up blood. "I was so drunk . . . and it felt like everything I wanted was right there before me . . . all the attention, the money, the ease of everything, but it wasn't. Everything I want is right 'ere in front of me. I thought I'd lost you, Fiona. I waited and waited for you at the bus stop and you didn't come. I thought it was over, thought you 'ated me. Why didn't you come?"

"I tried," she said dully. "I was on my way when Mr. Jackson, the publican, sent for me. I'd asked about a job there and 'e told me I could 'ave it, but I 'ad to start right away. I was going to write you, but we needed the money you sent to buy Eileen medicine. I'm sorry," she said. Fresh tears coursed down her face. "If only I'd come." Sobs racked her entire body. She could not speak. When she could finally get the words out, she asked, "Do you . . . do you love 'er?"

"No! God, no!" he shouted. "I love you, Fiona. I made a mistake, a stupid fucking 'orrible mistake and I'd give anything to be able to go back and undo it. Anything! I love you, Fee. I want to be with you, I want things to be like they were before everything went wrong. I can't . . . I can't go through with this . . . I can't . . . oh, God . . ." He turned away from her and his words were lost in his weeping.

But you will, Fiona thought. You have to. There's a baby coming. Your baby. She watched him as he cried like a child and into the maelstrom of emotion engulfing her – sorrow, rage, fear – came a new feeling, one of pity. She didn't want to feel it. She wanted to hate him, because if she could just hate him, she could walk away from him. But it was impossible. Instinctively, her hand went out and stroked his back. He felt it, turned to her, and pulled her to him. He wrapped his arms around her and buried his face in her neck. She felt sick and quaking in her very soul. "Do you know what you've done?" she whispered. "Do you know what you've thrown away? Our dreams. Our lives, past and future. Everything we were, everything we 'oped for. The love we 'ad for each other . . ."

"No, Fee," Joe said, taking her face in his hands. "Don't say that. Please don't say you don't love me anymore. I've no right, I know it, but please, please still love me."

Fiona looked at the man she'd loved her entire life, the man she needed more than anything or anybody. "Aye, I love you, Joe," she said. "I love you and you're going to marry Millie Peterson."

As the sun went down over London, darkening the sky and chilling the air, Joe and Fiona remained by the river's edge, holding each other as if they would never let go. Fiona knew it was for the last time. When they left the river, it would be over. She'd never know the feel of him, the smell of him again. She'd never sit at the Old Stairs with him again, hear his voice call her name, see his quick blue eyes crinkle with laughter. They'd never have their shop, a home, children, a life. Her dreams were gone forever, stillborn. Out of the blue, her best friend was leaving; her hope, her love, her very life was leaving her.

She couldn't bear it. It hurt too much. Without Joe in it, her life was no longer worth living. It was nothing to her. With sudden clarity, she knew what she would do. She would tell him to go, and when he had, she would walk into the Thames and let it swallow her. It would be quick. It was nearly December and the water was cold. She wanted an end to this blinding, tearing pain.

"When is your . . . your wedding?" she asked, not believing that these words were coming from her mouth.

"A week from today."

So soon. My God, it's so soon, she thought. "I need something from you," she said.

"Anything."

"I need the money. My part of our savings."

"You can 'ave it all. I'll bring it round."

"Give it to me mam if I'm not . . . if I'm not there." She looked at him one last time, then trained her gaze on the river. "Go now. Please."

"Don't send me away, Fiona. Let me 'old you while I can," he pleaded.

"Go. Please, Joe. I'm begging you."

And then he was standing, looking at her and sobbing. And then he was gone and she was alone. Suicide was a sin, a small voice told her, but she didn't care. She thought of her grandfather, her father's father, who'd jumped from a cliff when his wife died. People said time healed anything. Maybe those people had never loved anyone. Time wouldn't have healed her grandfather, she was sure. And it wouldn't heal her.

She walked to the water's edge and took a last look at the river she loved, at the wharves and the barges and the stars coming out in the dark London sky. She was in the water up to her ankles before she heard the shouting from the top of the stairs.

"There you are, you sorry little cow!"

She spun around. It was Charlie. He was standing at the top of the steps and he was furious. "Where the fuck 'ave

193

you been?" he shouted, walking down them. "I've been looking for you since seven o'clock and it's just gone nine. 'Ave you lost your bleeding mind? Mam's out of 'er 'ead with worry. We thought you was murdered. Thought the Ripper 'ad got you. I missed me fight at the Taj because of you. Quinn's going to kill me . . ." He stopped and looked at her pale face, saw her eyes swollen with crying, her hair all wild. "What 'appened to you?" His expression changed from anger to frantic concern. "It wasn't a bloke interfering with you, was it, Fee?" He took her by the shoulders. "Nobody touched you, did they? Did Sid Malone . . ."

Fiona shook her head.

"Well, what's going on, then?"

"Oh, Charlie," she cried, collapsing into her brother's arms. "I've lost my Joe."

18

Joe stood at the altar, handsome in a dark gray suit. He faced the entrance to the church, awaiting his bride. Harry Eaton stood at his side.

"All right, old man?" Harry whispered, eyeing his green complexion.

He nodded, but he was far from all right. He felt numb, as if he were in a nightmare, the kind where he couldn't scream or run away. He was trapped, utterly and absolutely. His father hadn't raised him to shirk his responsibilities. He was an adult and he had to face them. He had made one fatally stupid mistake and now he would spend the rest of his life paying for it. The rest of his life for one fuck. What an obscenely high price. And Harry thought his whores were expensive. Hysterical laughter burbled up inside him, he had to bite the inside of his cheek to keep it in.

"Not going to pass out, are you?" Harry asked, concerned.

He shook his head.

"Don't worry. It's not a death sentence. You can always play around."

Joe smiled ruefully. Harry assumed he shared his own fear of monogamy. Oh, Harry, he thought, if it were only that simple. He knew that with his new position at Peterson's and the money Tommy had settled on them, he could have plenty of women. It didn't matter. He couldn't have the one woman he wanted.

His eyes took in the rows of faces before him. He saw his parents, his brother Jimmy, his sisters, Ellen and Cathy, all dressed in the new clothes he'd bought them. His father was tight-lipped; his mother was crying off and on, just as she had been doing ever since he'd broken the news to her. He saw people he knew from work, important customers of Tommy's, friends and relatives of Millie's. It was a small crowd by Tommy's standards, only about a hundred people. But it was a rushed affair and there hadn't been time to organize anything larger.

Tommy had been angry when he first found out, but he calmed down when he learned that Joe intended to marry his daughter. Millie later said it was all bluster. He was thrilled to be getting Joe for a son-in-law, but wanted to play the outraged father for the sake of appearances.

Her pregnancy became an open secret. Men elbowed each other, joking that that devil of a Bristow just couldn't wait. Women smiled among themselves, smugly talking about an early arrival. No one was overly scandalized, they were happy for the handsome couple, pleased that Tommy's daughter and his protégé were marrying. Soon there'd be a third-generation son with selling in his blood. It was a brilliant match, people said.

Joe became aware of organ music. The guests stood up and looked toward the entrance. He followed their gaze. A flower girl came out, followed by Millie's maid of honor, followed by Millie herself, escorted by her father. His eyes held no joy in them as he looked at her, only dread. He might have been watching his executioner walk toward him. She wore an ivory taffeta dress with leg-o'-mutton sleeves, a long train, and a full veil, and carried an enormous bouquet of white lilies. He thought she looked like a ghost, shrouded in white from head to toe. Like the ghost in that Christmas story by Charles Dickens, the ghost of Christmas Future, of all his days to come.

He was barely aware of himself during the ceremony. He got through his vows, exchanged rings, kissed his new wife on her cheek, then led her down the aisle to receive their guests as Mr. and Mrs. Joseph Bristow. He managed a hollow smile now and again. It was all unreal, he was still moving in a nightmare. Surely, he would wake up any minute now, sweating, twisted up in his sheets, so relieved it was over.

But it wasn't. He rode with Millie in a carriage to their reception at Claridge's. He suffered through dance after dance with her, drank toasts, ate his supper, kissed her perfunctorily, smiled at people he didn't know. He escaped once, for a few minutes, to have a drink with Harry on a balcony. Harry told him that he'd be leaving in a week's time. He tried to be happy for his friend, but he didn't want to see him go, he'd miss him. And he envied him.

Finally it was time to leave. Amid bawdy jokes and raucous laughter, Joe and Millie were bundled off to the sumptuous suite Tommy had rented for them. They were to spend the night there before setting off for Paris the following morning for a two-month honeymoon. Millie wanted to go for three, but Tommy said he needed Joe back at work, and Joe had quickly agreed. He had no idea how he was going to get through two months with Millie; two hours seemed unbearable.

Once inside their suite, she disappeared to change. Joe shrugged off his jacket, loosened his tie and poured himself a glass of whiskey. He stepped through a set of French doors onto the balcony and looked out at the London skyline. Eastward. Where she was.

Attired in a frothy negligee, Millie rejoined him. "Come to bed," she whispered, putting her arms around him.

He stiffened. "I'm fine where I am."

"Is something wrong?" she asked, her eyes seeking his.

"No. Nothing. I'm tired. It's been a long day."

"I can wake you up," she said, pressing herself against him.

Joe closed his eyes lest she see the loathing in them. "I need a bit of air, Millie. Why don't you go in and lie down? You must be tired. I'll be in shortly."

"Promise?"

"Yes."

The first night in a lifetime of lies. God, how would he keep this up? What would he say when the getting-some-air excuse wore thin? That he couldn't bear the sight of her? That her voice, her smile, everything about her sickened him? That he didn't love her and never would? He looked into his whiskey glass, but it had no answers for him. He reminded himself that it was his fault she was pregnant. She would soon be the mother of his child; he mustn't be cruel to her. If only he could take it all back; if he could just go back to that night and walk out of her bedroom before anything happened.

This should have been his wedding night with Fiona. His soul cried out for her. The wedding, the fact that Millie was now his wife, changed nothing. In his heart, Fiona still belonged to him and he belonged to her even though he would never again look at the face that he loved. Or see her eyes light up, hear her excited voice, touch her, love her. What would become of her? He knew the answer. In time she would get over him and find another man. And then he, whoever he was, would be the one to see her smile, to share her days, to reach for her in the dark. The thought made him feel physically ill.

He had to get out of here, out of this room, away from Millie. The hotel had a bar. He would drink himself silly tonight and every night of this godforsaken honeymoon. Soon she'd be too big to want him anyway. And after the baby came, he'd find some new excuse. He'd travel for Tommy, work twenty-four hours a day. He knew he could never bear to touch her again. He stepped inside the sitting room and closed the balcony doors. He rummaged around for his jacket, fixed his tie, and pocketed the room keys.

"Joe?" he heard her call sleepily from the bedroom. Her only answer was the sound of the door slamming.

Eileen's breathing sounded thick and wet. Kate listened intently, waiting for the sudden catch that signaled a fit of coughing, but it didn't come. Maybe the poor little thing will actually sleep through the night, she hoped. It was ten o'clock now; if Eileen remained peaceful for another half hour, she would turn in. Sitting in her rocker, she sipped from a cup of tea, keeping her eyes on the baby. The last few months had not been kind to her. There were dark circles under her eyes and lines where there had been none. She had been racked with worry for weeks over the health of her baby daughter, and now Eileen was not the only child she worried about. She raised her eyes to the bed. Fiona had cried herself to sleep again. A week had passed since Charlie had brought her home from the river and she was no better. Her temperature remained high despite every attempt to bring it down. Her color was poor. She refused to eat. It was all Kate could do to get her to take some broth.

The fever worried Kate, but what worried her more was Fiona's emotional state. She wasn't fighting her illness; she was making no effort at all. Her bright, cheerful girl was gone and a dead-eyed stranger had taken her place. It broke her heart to see it. She'd always fretted over her high spirits, her determination to open a shop. Now she longed to hear her daughter speak of a shop, or anything at all, with just a little of her old enthusiasm.

Kate had nursed her children through many illnesses, but she'd never seen anything like Fiona's ailment. There was no reason for the fever; she had no cough, there was nothing wrong with her chest. She had no stomach pains, no vomiting. Her boots and stockings had been soaked when Charlie brought her home, but Kate didn't think her fever came from taking a chill. No doctor would agree with her, but she was certain it came from a broken heart.

When she'd found out what had happened, she'd wanted to wring Joe Bristow's neck. Eventually, her anger had given way to sorrow. Mainly for her daughter, but also for Joe. Rose Bristow had come to see them. She'd brought nearly twenty pounds from her son. Money that would have financed

Fiona's dream. Now it would go toward doctor bills, medicine, food, a new place to live. Fiona insisted they use it. Kate had argued with her, telling her to hang on to it, but she was adamant.

Rose had dissolved into tears at the sight of Fiona. She didn't want her son to marry Millie, not when she knew how much he loved Fiona. "The stupid, stupid sod," she'd said bitterly. " 'E's ruined 'is life. You're luckier than 'e is, Fiona. You're still free to find someone to love and in time you will. 'E never will."

Kate leaned her head against the rocker's high back and closed her eyes. She would give anything to be able to take away her child's grief. She knew her daughter had adored Joe ever since they were little. Her whole life had been Joe and the dreams they shared. Maybe there was no getting over a loss like that. Maybe the wound healed, but the scar ached forever. She had not gotten over Paddy's death and did not expect to. How did you get over losing the one man you loved body and soul? You went on, moving numbly through a gray world. That was all you could do.

She heard the faint sound of singing coming through the wall. Frances must be home, she thought. The walls between the houses were so thin that she often heard her singing or clattering pots, or, worse, entertaining a paying gentleman. She was glad to know that Frances was in, however. Charlie was never around these days and Lucy Brady had gone to the lying-in hospital to have her baby. She liked knowing there was someone close by she could call on to sit with Seamie and Fiona in case she needed to fetch Eileen's doctor.

She yawned. Lord, I'm tired, she thought, I'll get myself to bed now. Instead she drifted off. She stirred once, a few hours later, thinking she'd heard somebody scream, then dropped off again, convinced she'd dreamed it. A few minutes later, she snapped awake. The baby was wheezing; her face was red. Kate picked her up, trying to comfort her, trying not to panic. She decided to go for the doctor now before the wheeze turned into a gasp. Moving quickly, she laid Eileen back in her basket and grabbed her shawl.

"What is it, Mam? What's wrong?" Fiona asked groggily.

"It's Eileen. I'm going to the doctor's."

"I'll fetch 'im 'ere," she said. She stood up, keeping one hand on the bed to steady herself.

"Get back in bed. Right now. I'm going to get Frances to sit with you."

Kate picked up the baby's basket and ran to Frances's. She banged on the door. There was no response. Frantic, she peered into the small, grimy window next to it, wiping a pane clean with her sleeve. In the glow of a small fire, she saw Frances on the bed and a man in his shirtsleeves bent over her. She had a client; he was just finishing his business from the look of things. Kate was too desperate to be embarrassed. She put the basket down and yelled for her friend, rapping on the window. Frances did not move, but the man straightened. He's heard me, thank God! she thought.

Slowly, as if in a trance, the man moved toward the door and Kate's relief turned to horror as she saw he was holding a knife. Its blade was dark and slick. The same substance that was on it covered his hands and his shirtfront and ran in a rivulet down his cheek.

"It's blood," she whispered. "Oh, my God, look at it all!"

Shrieking, she stumbled away from the window, caught her boot heel in the hem of her skirt and fell to the ground. The door was wrenched open and the man was on her. She held her hands up, trying to save herself, but it was no use. In the instant before he slid his knife between her ribs, she glimpsed his mad, inhuman eyes and knew him. He was Jack.

19

Fiona stared at the stark wooden markers sticking out of the snowdusted ground. On the left, her father's, already weathered by the elements. Next to his, her mother's and the baby's, just starting to darken. And next to theirs, a brand-new one, the wooden cross still pale and unweathered. Her brother Charlie's.

Roddy had come from work three days ago with the news. River police had pulled a body from the Thames – the corpse of a young man, about sixteen years old. He'd gone to the morgue to identify the body – a task he'd said was nearly impossible in light of the time it had spent in the river. The face was gone. What hair remained was red. A search of the corpse's clothing confirmed the identity. In one of the pockets was a battered silver watch with the inscription: "Sean Joseph Finnegan, Cork, 1850." Her grandfather's name. Her brother's watch. She'd known immediately what it meant when Roddy placed it in her hands.

She closed her eyes now, despair descending, and wished herself in the ground with them. Day after day after day, the black, suffocating grief engulfed her and her longing for her family, and Joe – always Joe – was unbearable. Mornings, she would sit and stare into space and wonder how she would make it through the day. She had wanted to end her life the night Joe told her he was going to marry Millie. And again, right after her mother's death, unable to face the loss of her mam and the horrible manner in which she died, she wished herself dead. There were moments now, even as she tried to pull herself together for Seamie's sake, that she still contemplated taking her life, for there was never any relief from her pain.

To comfort herself, she tried to picture her mam's face as she wanted to remember her – smiling and laughing. But she couldn't. Those images were gone. All that came was the memory of her mother lying in the street, struggling to live as the blood poured from her side. Fiona had heard her cries and had come stumbling out of their room after her. She'd dropped to her knees beside her, pressed her hands over the wound and screamed for someone to help them. People had come, they'd done what they could, but Jack had pierced her mother's heart. The end had come quickly at least. Her mother had touched her face with trembling fingers, smearing blood across her cheek, and then her body had gone slack, and her eyes had turned dull and empty.

Fiona didn't want to remember that night, but it kept playing in her head over and over and over again. She kept seeing her mother's body in the street, kept hearing the baby wailing and Seamie shrieking from a policeman's arms.

And Charlie . . . she kept seeing him as he ran into Adams Court, shouting and pushing people aside. She saw his face, uncomprehending, as he gazed upon their mother. She'd called to him and he turned to her, but his eyes were wild and he seemed not to know her. He had picked their mother's body up off the street and held her tightly, moaning and keening. He refused to let the officers take her away from him and fought them off until three of them finally over-powered him. When they released him, he tried to pull the body out of the coroner's wagon. "Stop it, Charlie!" Fiona had screamed at him. "Stop it, please!" But he'd didn't stop. He dashed himself against the wagon as it drove off, and then he ran. Out of Adams Court and into the night. No one knew where he'd gone. Roddy had searched for him for days, then weeks. And then the body had been found. There was no money on it and the skull had been fractured. Roddy guessed that in his shock and grief, Charlie had wandered down a dangerous street and become the victim of thieves – coshed, robbed, and pushed into the river. Fiona was thankful they'd missed his watch, thankful she had something with which to remember her brother.

Up until the day Charlie's body was found, Fiona had clung tightly to the hope that he was still alive. She grieved for him deeply. She missed his cocky swagger, his grin, all his daft jokes. She missed his strength and wished to God she had him there to lean on. It was just she and Seamie now. Poor little Eileen had survived her mother by a mere five days before the infection in her chest killed her.

Fiona doubted that she or Seamie would have survived at all if it hadn't been for their Uncle Roddy. He'd taken them in right after the murder. He'd lied to the parish authorities, telling them that he was a blood relative, their mother's cousin, and demanding they all be released into his care. Fiona had been in no condition to look after Seamie and Eileen and he feared that the authorities would put them all in the workhouse.

He had given them a home, fed them, cared for them, tried his best to ease their sorrow. On days when Fiona found it difficult even to get out of bed, he would take her hand and tell her, "One foot in front of the other, lass, that's the only way." And that was how she existed, numbly plodding along, unable to tell from one minute to the next if she wanted to live or die.

For most of her seventeen years, Fiona had embraced life. Despite all of its struggles, there had always been something to look forward to – evenings by the fire with her family, walks with Joe, the life they'd planned together. But now her love of life and the hope with which she greeted her future were gone. Now she lived in a drab netherworld, adrift in a limbo. Unable to walk away from life because of her little brother's dependence on her, but unable to engage in it because of the crushing losses that weighed so heavily upon her, she merely endured.

She no longer found any purpose in her life, no longer

carried any dreams in her heart. Her father's words, words that had kept her going through many a hard time, held no meaning for her now. "Got to have your dreams, lass. Day you lose them, you might as well take yourself down to the undertaker's, for you're as good as dead." She looked around herself now at all the graves, thought about her still-born dreams, and knew she *was* as good as dead.

A chill wind whipped through the cemetery, rattling the bare-branched trees. Fall had given way to winter. Christmas and New Year's had come and gone; she'd been oblivious to them. It was already the middle of January, 1889. The papers all had a new story now – Jack the Ripper was dead, they said. He'd committed suicide. A body had been pulled from the river at the end of December. His name was Montague Druitt, a young London barrister. Druitt had a family history of mental instability and those close to him said they'd seen signs of erratic behavior. He'd left a note saying it would be better for him to die. His landlady had told police he kept strange hours, that he was often absent at night, only coming home after dawn. The press speculated that Druitt, plagued by horror and remorse after the Adams Court murders, drowned himself. His death gave Fiona no joy. She only wished he'd taken his life before he killed her mother.

The winter wind brought snowflakes with it. She stood up. The air was turning bitter. A thaw had enabled the undertakers to bury her brother. She thought about him, so full of mischief, now buried in the hard ground, and felt tears threaten again. She searched her mind for some small comfort, some reason why she had lost her family, Joe, everything she had, as she did a hundred times a day, every day. As always, she found none. She walked out of the graveyard and headed for Roddy's flat, a sad, pale figure against the bleak winter sky.

20

During the early months of 1889, Seamie Finnegan shot up like a weed. His legs grew long and stalky and his body lost some of its puppy fat. He'd turned five in December and was fast leaving babyhood behind. He had the astonishing resilience of the very young and this, coupled with Fiona's loving presence, helped him cope with the loss of his mother, his beloved brother, and his baby sister. He was a bright, sensitive child, almost always cheerful, and he was devoted to his sister, very finely tuned to her moods. When he sensed she was slipping away from him into that dark, quiet place inside herself where she sometimes went, he would clown for her until he got her to smile, or, if she was beyond smiling, he would climb into her lap and let her wrap her arms around him until she was better.

And Fiona was every bit as devoted to him. He was all she had and she was fiercely protective of him, unwilling to let him out of her sight, only surrendering him to Roddy or Roddy's fiancée, Grace Emmett. His freckled face, his sweet, childish voice, were her only comforts.

She looked at him now as she prepared his tea. He sat at the table, a fork in his fist, eager for his meal. She put his food before him and he tucked into it hungrily. Bread, boiled potatoes, and a small kipper. It's not enough for a growing child, she thought; he should have milk and meat and green vegetables. But it was all Roddy could do. He was supporting the two of them and his wages were stretched thin. He'd bought Seamie a warm sweater just the other day to protect him against the cold March weather, and he'd even made her a birthday present of a new shawl last week, when she'd turned eighteen.

Fiona felt grateful to him for all he'd done for them. She also felt guilty. She saw the way he and Grace looked at each other. She knew they would be married by now and living under the same roof if it weren't for her and Seamie. They'd been living with him since November. In recent weeks, she'd gained a bit of weight and lost the sunken, hollow-eyed look she'd had. She could manage the marketing, the cleaning, and the laundry now. It was time for her to go back to work and find a room for herself and Seamie. Roddy couldn't take care of them forever.

But the very idea of finding her own place overwhelmed her. She had no money. What was left of the twenty pounds from Joe had gone to pay for caskets and funerals. The landlord had sold the contents of their flat – their few bits of furniture, their dishes, her mother's clothing, even the navy gloves Charlie had brought for her, and kept the proceeds in lieu of the rent that was owed him. Roddy had managed to salvage one thing from the sale – a cigar box with her parents' wedding rings, photos, and documents in it. She had no job, either. She'd seen a friend from Burton Tea on the street who told her that her place there had been filled. Ralph Jackson had found someone new, too. She could start hunting, but it might take weeks to find something, and even when she did, it would be another month before she would have enough money to rent a room.

She had hoped for help from her Uncle Michael. Her mother had written him after her father's funeral, but received no reply. Maybe he hadn't gotten the letter. Mail often went astray from one end of London to the other, never mind from London to New York. She would write again.

A shout from downstairs took her out of her worries. It was Mrs. Norman, the landlady. She went to the landing. Mrs. Norman was standing at the bottom of the stairs, a letter in her hand. "For you, luv. Just came," she said, waving the envelope impatiently.

Fiona went downstairs for the letter, thanked her, then disappointed her by returning to Roddy's flat to read it in privacy. The letter was from Burton Tea. It was addressed to her mother. She could see from the crossed-out writing on the front that it had been sent to Montague Street, then Adams Court, and now here. She opened it. Meticulous copperplate regretfully informed Mrs. Patrick Finnegan that her application to the Burton Tea Company for compensatory monies had been denied. Because her husband's death was due to the negligence of a fellow worker, David O'Neill, and not the Burton Tea Company per se, no award would be made. She was advised to contact a Mr. J. Dawson, Labor Clerk, with any further inquiries.

Fiona folded the letter back into its envelope. She'd forgotten all about her mother's trip to Burton's. She tried to recall how much she'd asked for. Ten pounds? Twenty? That was nothing to a company the size of Burton Tea. That William Burton wouldn't even give a few quid to the family of a man who'd died on his premises seemed very unfair. Something flared briefly inside of her, but was doused just as quickly. Unfair or not, she told herself, there's nothing you can do about it. Resigned, she placed the letter in her cigar box and sat down to her tea.

She watched her brother as he pushed his crust of bread around his plate, sweeping up the last bits of his fish. Me and Seamie, she thought, we wouldn't even be where we are right now if it wasn't for William Burton and his bloody warehouse. Me da would still be alive, we'd all be back on Montague Street. I wonder what he ate for his tea today? Roast beef maybe, a nice chop? I bet it wasn't a bleeding penny kipper.

Like embers fanned by a breath, the smoldering indignation she'd felt sparked and struggled into a flame. Slowly, so slowly that she was barely aware of it happening, her resignation flared into anger. That money could've helped them so much when they'd moved to Adams Court, when they didn't have enough for good food or warm clothes.

When she didn't even have the pennies needed to buy paper to write to Joe. And it could help Seamie and her now. It could provide the boost they needed to move out of Roddy's flat. To make a new start. The bastard, she fumed. She was furious for the first time in a long time and she relished it. It made a change from grief. It strengthened her and brought back a little of her old determination.

"Finish your tea, Seamie," she said suddenly, getting up from the table.

He gave her a puzzled look.

"Come on, finish up. You're going to see your Auntie Grace for a little while."

Seamie obeyed his sister, stuffing the rest of his bread into his mouth. She bundled him up, put her own jacket on, and took him to Grace's. She told her she had an errand, that she'd be gone for an hour or two and asked if she'd mind watching Seamie. Grace, surprised at Fiona's sudden animation, said of course not. And then she was off, heading west toward the City. She wasn't entirely certain where she was going, but she would ask until she found Mincing Lane. It was late in the day, nearly five-thirty. Burton might be gone by the time she got there, but he might not.

That money's ours, she thought, striding briskly through the dark streets, her skirts swishing around her legs. Mine and Seamie's. If William Burton thinks my da's life isn't even worth ten pounds, he's got another thing coming.

After forty minutes' walk and a few wrong turns, Fiona found 20 Mincing Lane, home of Burton Tea. The offices occupied a magnificent limestone building enclosed by an iron fence. Just inside was a small glassed-in office where the porter was enjoying a mug of hot tea and a pork pie.

"We're closed, miss," he said. "See the sign? Visitors' hours from nine to six."

"I 'ave to see Mr. Burton, sir," Fiona said, leveling her chin. "It's urgent."

"Do you 'ave an appointment?"

"No, I don't, but –"

"What's your name?"

"Fiona Finnegan."

"What do you want to see the guv about?"

"About a claim my mother made," she replied, pulling the envelope from her skirt pocket. "I 'ave a letter here saying that it's null and . . . and . . . void. 'Ere . . . see? But that's not fair, sir. Me da was killed at Mr. Burton's wharf. There's got to be a mistake."

The porter sighed, as if he were used to this sort of thing. "You'll 'ave to see Mr. Dawson. Come by tomorrow and 'is secretary will give you an appointment."

"But, sir, that won't do me any good. If I could just see Mr. Burton –"

"Listen, dearie, the guv's own mother couldn't get in to see 'im. 'E's a very busy man. Now be a good lass and do like I told you. Come back tomorrow." He returned to his pork pie.

Fiona opened her mouth to speak, then shut it again. Arguing with this man was a waste of time. He was not going to let her in. She walked down the steps. Outside the gate, she turned to cast one last reproachful glance at him and saw that he was getting up from his chair. He left his office and walked down the hallway.

He's going to the loo, she thought. She stood at the gate biting her lip. She didn't want to see a clerk. She had to see Burton himself. She needed that money. On an impulse, she dashed back up the steps, sped past the porter's desk, and made for the stairway ahead of her. She ran upstairs to the first floor. The vestibule was dark. She pushed through the glass doors that led off it and found herself in an even darker hallway. Her footsteps echoed on the polished wood floor. Frosted glass doors lined both sides of the hallway. They all looked the same. She tried a doorknob; it was locked. This can't be where Burton works, she reasoned. It's not grand enough.

She headed for the second floor. This looked more promising. On the left side of the hallway were four doors, solid wood with brass nameplates, all closed. On the right was one massive double door. It was open. She tiptoed up to it and peered inside. She saw a large room with an enormous desk in the middle of it. Behind the desk, from floor to ceiling, were rows of wooden filing cabinets. Three of the files, instead of being pull-out drawers, opened on a hinge, like a door. Behind the fake file door was a wall safe. On the desk was a brass lamp with a green glass shade. The light it provided was scant, but enough to illuminate the banded piles of notes on top of the desk. Fiona's breath caught; she had never seen so much money. Surely Burton wouldn't refuse her ten pounds.

To the right of the desk was another door. It was halfway open. Someone was in there; there was a light on. She took a hesitant step forward, wondering if she was out of her mind. She was trespassing. If he came out right now and saw her, he'd assume she was trying to steal his money and have her arrested. Glancing at the piles again, she almost lost her nerve.

Just as she passed the desk, she heard voices coming from the inner office. Burton was not alone. Should she still knock on the door? She heard two men laughing, heard them resume their conversation, then heard one of them mention a name she recognized: Davey O'Neill. Curious, she took a step closer.

"O'Neill? 'E's be'aving 'imself. Giving me names. Just like you told 'im to."

"Good, Bowler; I'm glad to hear it. That lad's been invaluable. Here's another five pounds for him. What has he told you about Tillet?"

Bowler. Bowler Sheehan. Fiona's blood ran cold. Her curiosity about Davey O'Neill was forgotten, along with her desire to plead for ten pounds. She had to get out of there. Now. Sheehan was a bad bloke. A very bad bloke. Whatever he was doing here, he wasn't collecting for charity. She'd made a huge mistake sneaking into Burton's office and if she got caught she'd pay for it. Dearly. She took a step back, then another. Quiet, be quiet, she told herself. Nice and slow. Don't rush. She kept her eyes on the inner office door. She could still hear them speaking.

"Tillet's trying to cobble them together again, but 'e's only got a few. A ragtag bunch at best."

"Yes, but knowing him, he won't give up until he has a full, functioning union again. If only we could get him the way we got that bastard Finnegan."

Fiona froze.

"Aye, that was a good job, wasn't it?" Sheehan said, chuckling. "Fucking flawless! Snuck up there and put the grease down meself, I did. Un'ooked the door, banged it a few times, then 'id be'ind a tea chest and watched Mr. Union Organizer slip and fall five stories. And O'Neill got the blame!" He laughed loudly.

Fiona bit her lip to keep from screaming. Images and snatches of conversation flew through her mind in a blinding rush. Her father's funeral. Mr. Farrell and Mr. Dolan saying how strange it was that Paddy had fallen when he was so careful. The fact that the accident happened soon after her da had taken on leadership of the local. Davey O'Neill following her down Barrow Street.

Her breath came in short little gasps. She couldn't get her mind around it. Her da, murdered. Because Burton didn't want his workers to go union. Murdered by Bowler Sheehan, who was sitting only yards away from her, laughing about it. Disoriented, no longer aware of where she was in the room, she took a clumsy step backward. Her heel hit the desk with a loud thud. She lost her balance, stumbled, and righted herself. Her hand came down on a pile of notes.

Inside the office, the talking stopped.

"Fred? Is that you?" The door was jerked open and William Burton emerged. His eyes widened at the sight of Fiona. His gaze traveled to the top of his secretary's desk, where her hand was resting on his money. "What are you doing in here? Who let you in?"

Fiona didn't answer; her fingers tightened around the notes. In an instant her fear vanished and a white-hot rage surged through her. She threw the stack of money at Burton; it sailed over his shoulder. He advanced on her and she heaved the desk lamp. It hit the floor in front of him and exploded in a shower of glass and oil. "You murdering bastard!" she shrieked. "You killed 'im! You killed my father!" She threw a letter tray; it hit him in the chest. She threw an inkwell, another stack of money.

"Sheehan!" he bellowed. "Get out here!"

At the sound of that name, she bolted. Her fear had come back full force. She ran out of the office, slamming the door after herself. Out the double doors, down the hallway, and down the staircase she flew, clutching an unthrown pile of notes in one hand, her skirts in the other. She was halfway to the first floor when she heard feet pounding after her.

"Stop her, Fred!" Burton shouted down the staircase. "Stop the girl!"

She was at the top of the last staircase when the footsteps started to gain on her. It was Sheehan; she knew it without looking. She hurtled down the stairs at breakneck speed, running for her life. The porter's office came into view. If he'd heard Burton yelling, he'd be outside of it waiting to block her and she'd have just one chance to dodge him. She cleared the last of the steps, bracing herself for a confrontation, but he wasn't in his office. She shot through the entrance doors, down the steps and toward the gate, with Sheehan only yards behind her. It was then that she saw the porter. He was standing by the gate, fiddling with the lock. His back was toward her. Sheehan bellowed for him from behind her. He turned; he had an oil can in his hands. "What the devil . . ." he started to say. Fiona put on a final, desperate burst of speed, ran past him and through the gate before he knew what was happening. As she cleared it, she reached back for one of the bars and jerked it toward her. The gate locked shut. And that's what saved her.

She took off down Mincing Lane. Behind her, she heard Sheehan screaming at the porter to get the bloody gate open. She risked a glance back. The man fumbled the key and dropped it. Enraged, Bowler kicked him, then kicked the gate. Next to them, William Burton watched her run. Their eyes locked for a split second, and looking into them, she knew that if the two men got hold of her now, he, not Sheehan, would be the one who would beat the life out of her.

She ran into Tower Street. There she saw an eastbound bus pulling away from its stop, caught up with it and jumped on the back. She hunkered down in a seat, gasping for breath, and looked out the window. They could be right behind her; she was certain they saw her turn off Mincing Lane. They might've seen her get on the bus. What if they got into a cab and followed her? Fear shrieked at her. She was too visible. The bus trundled down Tower Hill. She jumped off when it stopped to pick up passengers.

She scurried across to the north side of the street and ducked inside the entry of a public house. From there, she watched the traffic. It was sparse because of the hour – nearly seven – and she could see every vehicle. She watched a westbound bus go by, two growlers, a horse and cart, and three hansoms. And then, not three minutes after she'd got inside the pub, she saw a private carriage, sleek and black, traveling east at a fast clip. She stepped back into the shadows as it passed, watching as one of its occupants shouted at the driver. It was Sheehan. The carriage picked up speed and veered off to East Smithfield Street and the Highway, following the route of the bus she'd been on. She closed her eyes, leaned against the wall, and started to shake.

"You all right, miss?"

Her eyes snapped open. She looked into the face of a rheumy-eyed old gentleman on his way out of the pub.

"If it's a drink you're after, and if you don't mind my saying so, you look like you could use one, the ladies' parlor's across the taproom, through that door."

A drink. Yes, that was a good idea. She had never ordered herself a drink in a pub in her entire life, but now seemed like a good time to start. She could sit down for a few minutes and try to still her trembling legs. She could figure out what to do next.

She entered the pub, moved through the crowded, smoky taproom, and pushed open a door marked LADIES. She found herself alone in a dingy, gaslit room that had a few wooden tables, velvet-covered stools, mirrors, and flocked wallpaper. The publican bustled in behind her, took her order, and disappeared again. By the time she'd sat down and smoothed her hair back, he'd returned with her half-pint of beer. She reached into her pocket for the coins she knew she had and felt paper crinkling instead. What's this? she wondered, peering into her pocket. She saw the notes and her heart skipped a beat. Quickly, she fished out a half-shilling and handed it to the publican, who gave her change and left.

She peered into her pocket again. How the hell did the notes get in there? She thought back to the scene in Burton's office. She'd been throwing things, everything she could find. She must've had the money in her hand when he called for Sheehan and stuffed it into her pocket as she ran. She pulled the bundle out. It was a stack of twenty-pound notes. She counted them. When she finished, she refolded the stack and put it back in her pocket. She had five hundred pounds of William Burton's money.

She lifted her glass to her mouth, drained it in one go, and licked the foam from her lips. Then she caught sight of her reflection in a mirror, blinked at it, and said, "You're dead."

*　　*　　*

"Lord, child, where 'ave you been? I was worried sick," Grace said.

Fiona had arrived at her door just after eight, flushed and out of breath.

"I'm so sorry, Grace. I was at Burton Tea. I went to collect the compensation money from my father's death. They kept me waiting for ages! I ran all the way back 'ere; I didn't want to keep you up too late," she said, forcing herself to smile.

"And somebody was there this late? They must work awfully long hours at Burton's."

"Aye, they do. The man's a slave driver." She saw her brother sitting at the table looking at a book of nursery rhymes. "Come on, Seamie, luv," she said. "We've got to go." She buttoned his jacket, then turned to Grace to thank her. She knew she might never see her again. Her throat tightened. Grace and Roddy were the only people she had in the world, and after tonight they, too, would be out of her life. "Thank you, Grace," she said.

She laughed. "Don't be silly. It's nothing. 'E's an angel."

"I don't just mean tonight. I mean for everything you've done."

"Oh, go on," she said, embarrassed now. "I 'aven't done a thing."

"You 'ave and I'll never forget it," Fiona said, hugging her tightly.

When she got to White Lion Street, where Roddy lived, she looked down it to make sure no one was loitering. Then she hurried into his building and ran upstairs. She let herself into the flat, hustling Seamie ahead of her, locked the door, and wedged a chair against it. She began to pack. There wasn't much time. Sheehan was looking for her at this very moment. By now he and Burton had undoubtedly pieced everything together with the help of the porter, to whom she'd given her name. They knew who she was, why she'd come, and what she'd overheard. It might take him a day or two to find her, but she wasn't taking any chances. They had to leave Whitechapel. Tonight.

She had no idea where to go, but she'd decided that they'd get on a train. Any train. It didn't matter where they went as long as it was far away from London. She hoped that when she wasn't seen for weeks, Burton would assume she'd gone to ground and forget about her.

She had no valise, so she got an old flour sack from under the sink and put her and Seamie's clothing in it. What else should she take? She got her father's cigar box down from the mantel and dumped its contents on the table. Birth certificates, she would take those. A lock of red hair – Charlie's baby hair – keep that. Her parents' wedding photograph . . . she looked at it, at the young woman in it, so pretty, so full of life, of hope. Thank God her mother would never know that the handsome man by her side had been murdered. At least she'd been spared that.

Overcome by a fit of trembling, Fiona closed her eyes and leaned against the table. Though she was thinking and functioning, she was still in shock. She'd heard it with her own ears, yet she couldn't comprehend it. Her da . . . murdered. Because William Burton did not wish to pay his dock workers sixpence an hour instead of five. Rage boiled up inside her again. I *won't* run away, she thought wildly; I'll stay here and go to the police. They'll help me. They will. They'll listen to me . . . and I'll tell them what Burton's done and they'll . . .

. . . laugh in my face. How outrageous it would look. Her accusing William Burton of murdering her father. The police would never trouble the likes of him based on her accusation, and even if they did, he'd never confess. He'd tell them that she'd broken into his office, destroyed his property, and stolen his money. He'd say he'd caught her red-handed and had witnesses. And then she would go to prison. Seamie would be alone; Roddy and Grace would have to raise him. It was hopeless! Burton had murdered her father and there was nothing she could do about it.

And not only would there be no justice for his death, if she didn't get out of London, she'd surely have an accident of her own. Searing tears of impotence rolled down her cheeks and splashed onto her parents' picture.

"You all right, Fee?" Seamie asked.

She hadn't realized he was watching her. "I'm fine, Seamie, luv," she said, wiping her eyes.

"Are we going somewhere?" he asked, eyeing the sack.

"Aye, we're taking a trip, you and me."

His eyes widened. "A trip? Where?"

She didn't know. "Where? Well, it's . . . um . . . a surprise. We'll ride on a train and it'll be lots of fun."

While Seamie entertained himself by making train noises, Fiona continued to sort through the contents of the cigar box. Her parents' wedding rings . . . she would take those. Her father's clasp knife . . . keep that. Rent receipts . . . those could go in the fire. At the very bottom of the box she found a pile of letters from her Uncle Michael.

She held one up. The return address said: "M. Finnegan, 164 Eighth Avenue, New York City, New York, U.S.A." She was wrong. Dead wrong. Roddy and Grace weren't the only people she had. She had an uncle in New York. Michael Finnegan would take them in. He would look after them until they got on their feet and she would repay him by working in his shop. "New York," she whispered, as if saying the place's name might make it real. It was so far away. All the way across the Atlantic Ocean. They'd be safe there.

In an instant, she made her decision. They'd take a train to Southampton and a boat to America. Burton's money would buy their passage. Working quickly, she got another flour sack and cut a square out of it. She unbuttoned her blouse, untied her camisole, and with a needle and thread stitched three sides of the fabric to the inside of the garment to make a pocket. She took the notes out of her skirt and slid them into it, all but one. She planned to go to the Commercial Road, where she could hire a cab to the station, but she wanted to stop at the pawnbroker's first, to see if she could find a traveling bag. She couldn't go to New York with a flour sack.

"We going yet, Fee?" Seamie asked, all wound up now.

"In one minute. I just 'ave to write Uncle Roddy a note."

"Why?"

"To tell 'im about our trip," she said. To tell him good-bye, she thought. "Be a good lad and put your jacket on."

Fiona hunted for a sheet of paper and tried to figure out what to write. She wanted to tell Roddy the truth, but she didn't want him worrying, and most of all, she didn't want to put him in any danger. Sheehan would certainly come calling at his flat when he learned she had been living here. She doubted he was stupid enough to mess about with a police officer, but he might break in hoping to find something that would tell him where she was. She found a pencil and started to write.

Dear Uncle Roddy,

My money came from Burton Tea. It was more than I thought we would get and I am going to use it to take Seamie and myself off to start a new life. Please don't worry about us, we'll be fine. I'm sorry to go so suddenly, but it's easier for me this way. There have been too many hard good-byes of late and I want to go tonight, before I lose my nerve. Thank you for taking care of us. We would never have made it if it wasn't for you. You've been like a father to us and we'll miss you more than I can say. I will write when I can. Seamie

There . . . no names, no addresses. She put the note on the table. She felt terrible about running away like this, but there was nothing she could do. Roddy wouldn't be able to save her when Sheehan found her. Casting one last glance around the flat, she gathered her brother and her sack, opened the door, locked it behind them and pushed the key under it.

She was just about to start down the staircase when she heard the front door open. There were heavy footsteps in the entry and male voices. Three of them. She felt a tug on her skirt. "Fee . . ." Seamie started to say. She clapped a hand over his mouth and told him to be quiet. The voices were low; the words indistinct, but as one of the men moved closer to the stairs, she heard him quite clearly. "This is where the copper lives," he said. "She's bound to be 'ere, too."

It was Sheehan.

She dug frantically in her pocket for the key to Roddy's flat. She had to get inside; she had to hide Seamie. Where was the bloody key? She turned her pocket out, then she remembered that she'd pushed it under the door. Way under, so no one could get it. Panic-stricken, she knocked on the neighbor's door as softly as she could. "Mrs. Ferris?" she whispered. "Mrs. Ferris . . . are you there? Please, Mrs. Ferris . . ." There was no answer. She tried the other door. "Mrs. Dean? Danny? Are you there?" No one answered. Either they weren't home, or they couldn't hear her.

She listened at the banister again. Snatches of conversation drifted up. ". . . on the second floor . . . need to take care of it . . . not 'ere . . . too much noise . . ." Suddenly, there were feet on the stairs. They'd be on the first landing in seconds, and then it was only one short flight of stairs to the second. Her fear turned into terror. She picked Seamie up, grabbed the flour sack, and dashed upstairs to the third landing, hoping that their heavy steps covered the sound of her own. She heard them stop at Roddy's door, then she heard scrabbling.

"Come on, 'urry it up," Sheehan said. "My granny can pick a lock faster."

When she heard the door open and the men go inside, she started up the last flight of stairs. If she could get out onto the roof, they could walk across to the neighboring building and hide behind the chimneys until Sheehan left. She reached the landing; it was piled high with rubbish – crates, buckets, burlap bags. A moldy old mattress, full of holes, was propped against the wall. She tried the door; it was locked. "Come on, come on . . ." she pleaded, twisting and tugging at the knob, but it wouldn't budge. They were trapped. If Sheehan thought to look up here, they were done for.

She rooted in the flour sack for her father's clasp knife and opened it with trembling fingers. She glanced at her brother, standing by the mattress wide-eyed and frightened. She held her finger to her lips and he did the same back to her, then she leaned over the banister to listen. She heard nothing; they must still be inside the flat. She leaned over farther, straining for some sound, some indication of what they were up to, when she suddenly heard Seamie utter a cry.

Only inches from his leg, a huge brown rat was wriggling out of a hole in the mattress. It sniffed at him and bared its teeth. Fiona ran over and jabbed at the animal with her knife. It snapped at her. She kicked the mattress and it withdrew. She quickly stuffed a rag into the hole, then returned to the railing. They were just coming out of the flat.

"Maybe O'Meara does know more than she put in the note, Bowler, but you'll 'ave to work 'im over if you want to find out," she heard one of them say. " 'E's not going to volunteer the information, is 'e?"

"I don't touch coppers," Sheehan replied. "They're like bloody bees. Swat at one and the whole damn 'ive comes after you."

There was some mumbling – Fiona couldn't make it out – and then she heard Sheehan tell his men to check the roof.

"Oh, God," she gasped, "oh, no." He'd see them. They had to hide. Quick! But where? There was only the mattress. She lunged across the landing, stuffed her flour sack into the space behind it, then reached for her brother. "Come on, Seamie," she whispered. But he wouldn't. He stood away from it, shaking his head. She could hear feet coming up the stairs. "It's all right, luv, it's all right . . . the rat's gone. *Please*, Seamie . . . come on!" He turned fearfully toward the sound of the footsteps, then bolted toward her. She pushed him in, then wedged in next to him, her back against the wall, her knees straining into the mattress. She felt for him in the dark. "Sshhh . . ." she whispered. The stench of rats was suffocating. There's more than one, she thought, there must be dozens. Just then, the ticking bulged against her leg. She bit her lip to keep from screaming.

"You see anyone?" she heard Sheehan shout.

"No!" The man was on the landing now. She heard him try the knob. "Door's locked," he shouted. "There's nothing up 'ere but rubbish."

"Look around, Reg. Make sure."

The man, Reg, was kicking at things and swearing. He was coming closer. Terror bound Fiona's chest tightly; she could barely breathe. Greasy beads of sweat rolled down her skin. She tightened her grip on the knife, desperate to protect Seamie. Please, please, don't come any closer, she begged silently. Go away, just go away . . .

Something brushed her foot. She dug her nails into her palm. Then she felt a fat, oily body slither over her ankle and her control broke. She plunged the knife into it. There was a horrible, high-pitched squealing. Again and again she stabbed the rat. Its cries alerted the others. The mattress came alive with warm, squirming bodies.

There was shouting, then stamping. "Fuck! Get off! Fucking bastards . . . Jesus!"

"Reg . . . what is it?" There were more feet on the stairs.

"Bloody rats! A whole fucking nest of them!"

Fiona heard the others laugh, heard Reg run down the steps. There was the sound of scuffling, then a loud thump, like someone getting knocked against a wall.

"It's not fucking funny, Stan! One crawled up me trouser leg. Big as a bloody cat, it was!"

"Shut up. Both of you. You see any signs of 'er up there?"

"There's nobody up there. Go 'ave a gander yourself if you don't believe me."

Bowler let out of a string of curses. "She can't 'ave gone far," he said. "Reg, you take the Whitechapel Road. Stan, take Commercial Street. I'll take Stepney. We'll meet at the Blind Beggar. The thieving bitch! When I find 'er, I'm going to bash 'er bloody skull in."

Fiona heard them go. She waited until she heard the downstairs door slam, then scrambled out from behind the mattress, stamping her feet. Seamie was teary and trembling. She held him close and told him he was very, very brave.

"Who were they, Fee?" he asked.

"Very bad men."

"Why did they come after us?"

She couldn't tell him the truth. "They wanted to steal our money," she said.

"Can we still go on our train ride?"

"Of course we can. We'll go right now."

"Will they come after us again?"

"No. Never again. I won't let them." She picked up the flour sack, took her brother by the hand, and started down the steps.

The idea that William Burton was certifiably insane had crossed Bowler Sheehan's mind before. As the man paced back and forth in his study, crazed by anger, it crossed his mind again. He'd arrived at Burton's home half an hour ago to tell him that Fiona Finnegan had fled Whitechapel. He thought Burton would be relieved, but he wasn't. He was furious, enraged beyond reason. He screamed abuse at Sheehan for letting her slip through his fingers, screamed until the veins stood out in his neck and the spit flew from his lips and his icy black eyes blazed.

He was no longer shouting now, but he was still pacing. "She's dangerous," he said. "I can't have this. I've just begun negotiations with Albion Bank to take Burton Tea public.

They're leery as it is with all the talk of a dock strike. They're not going to care much for a murder accusation leveled against me, either. She can do me harm, Bowler. She knows what I did to her father."

"It doesn't *matter* what she knows," Sheehan said, picking his nails with a knife blade. "She can't touch you. Even if she told the police, they'd never believe 'er, she 'as no proof. The *last* place she'd go right now is to the coppers. She's got a lot more to worry about than you do. She stole a large sum of money and there are witnesses to the fact."

But Burton would have none of it. He kept going on and on about how she was a sneaking, meddling bitch and how this was going to destroy his public offering, and how he needed the money the shares would raise to finance his expansion.

Sheehan closed his knife, thinking how blokes like Burton made the getting of money so fucking complicated with all their stocks and shares. It was so much easier to just *take* it. He'd had just about enough for one night. It was late. He needed a good meal and a glass of whiskey. He did not need to sit here, listening to this barmy cunt rant.

"What exactly would you like me to do? Knock on every bleeding door in London?"

Burton stopped pacing. He turned his bottomless black eyes on him. And Bowler, a ruthless individual who could kill a man with his bare hands when warranted, was surprised to feel a chill go down his spine.

"What I would like," he said, "is for you to find the girl as quickly as you can and then dispose of her, as I asked you to do earlier."

"I told you. I've tried —"

Burton brought his fist crashing down on his desk. "Try harder!"

Sheehan stood and left. Outside, he spat disgustedly, then informed Reg and Stan that he would be going to Quinn's alone and they would be spending the night on White Lion Street watching Roddy O'Meara's flat. They started complaining immediately. They wanted a pint . . . they were hungry . . . they had a couple of girls waiting for them. Bowler told them to shut up. First he had to listen to Burton, now to these two. If Burton didn't pay so well, he would've cut him loose long ago. The fucker was far more trouble than he was worth.

21

The nightmare was always the same. The dark man was gaining on her. He'd chased her into an alley that ended in a brick wall. There was no escape. She threw herself at the wall, tried to scrabble up it. The footsteps grew louder, a hand closed on her shoulder, and –

"Half an hour to Southampton, miss."

Fiona jerked awake, wild-eyed. The conductor was shaking her.

"Sorry to startle you, but we'll be pulling in shortly."

"Th-thank you," she stammered. She took a deep breath, trying to calm herself. It was always so real, that awful dream, so bloody real. She looked over at Seamie. He was sleeping. He'd dozed off just after they'd boarded the train at seven that morning. As soon as the conductor had taken their tickets, she'd fallen asleep, too, worn out from her ordeal. They'd been on the move ever since they'd left Roddy's nearly ten hours ago. Their first stop had been the pawnbroker's, where she'd found a carpet-bag. As she'd pulled a twenty-pound note from her pocket to pay for it, the blue stone Joe had given her had fallen out on the counter. The pawnbroker had looked it over and asked if it was for sale. Fiona wondered why she was keeping it. Joe was gone; why hang on to a painful reminder of him?

" 'Ow much?" she said.

"One pound, six shillings."

She was astonished at the amount. She didn't answer, trying to decide whether to part with it. The pawnbroker mistook her indecision for unhappiness with the price.

"All right, two pounds, plus the carpetbag thrown in, and that's me final offer."

She blinked at the man. Two whole pounds for a stone, and the bag for free? He must be barmy. She quickly accepted his offer before he could change his mind.

" 'Ave you got any more like this?" he asked, pocketing the stone.

"No, but I 'ave this." She slid Joe's ring off her finger and handed it to him.

"It's not worth much. Give you three shillings for it."

"Done," she said, pleased to be two pounds, three shillings, and a carpetbag richer.

She repacked their belongings and headed to the Commercial Road. She was very jumpy. Every step of the way she expected to hear Sheehan's voice, to feel a rough hand come down on her shoulder. She'd felt safer when they finally got into a cab. The driver took them to Waterloo Station, where they made their way to the ticket counter. To her dismay, they'd missed the last train by twenty minutes. She purchased two tickets for the morning train, then bought herself and Seamie hot tea and thick bacon sandwiches. They holed up in the ladies' waiting room for the night. Away from the windows. Just in case.

Now, as she stretched in her seat, Fiona tried to anticipate what would come next. They had to find their way from the train station to wherever the passenger ships docked. A cab would be the best idea. It would cost money, but it would save them from getting lost. Seamie woke up a few minutes outside of Southampton and she had just enough time to get his boots and jacket on him before the train pulled into the station. The second they got off, he had to go to the bathroom.

"You'll 'ave to 'old it for a second," she told him. "I don't know where the loo is."

As they walked down the platform, she saw a billboard for Burton Tea and shuddered. She had no idea how far

William Burton's reach extended. The sooner she got herself and Seamie on a boat, the better.

She finally spotted the ladies' room and whisked her brother in. When he was finished, she marched him to the sink, where she washed his hands and his grubby face. Then she took care of her own needs, took another twenty pounds out of her camisole and put it in her pocket. Back in the station, they followed signs directing them to the cabs. They passed the platform and she instinctively cast a glance up it, just to make sure Sheehan wasn't standing at the other end. It was empty except for a man so burdened with baggage that he could barely walk. He was staggering under the weight of his suitcases, and he didn't see the stack of newspapers directly in his path.

"Look out!" Fiona yelled to him.

Too late. He caught his foot and stumbled. He landed with a bang, his cases flying everywhere. She ran to him. "Blimey!" she cried, hooking her hands under his arm and helping him up. "Are you all right? That was some fall."

"I-I think so," he replied, getting to his feet. He inspected himself. "Nothing seems broken. Useless porters, never around when you want them." He smiled at her, pushing his hair out of his eyes. "Nicholas Soames," he said, offering her his hand. "Most obliged."

Fiona was about to take it when she noticed it was bleeding. "You're 'urt!" she said.

"Oh, dear. I hate the sight of blood. Especially my own. Makes me feel . . . quite . . . lightheaded . . ."

"Oh, no! Don't! I won't be able to pick you up if you faint!"

She led him to a bench. He sat down and put his head between his knees. "Terribly sorry."

"Sshhh. Just sit still till you feel better. I'll see to your bags."

"Too good of you," he mumbled.

Fiona turned back to the platform to survey the damage. A hatbox had rolled away. She sent Seamie after it. One

228

suitcase had landed intact. The other two had sprung open, scattering clothes. A large portfolio lay open, revealing two paintings. They were bright and odd, almost childish. It would take a bit of doing to get everything back in the cases. She sighed impatiently; she didn't want to be fooling with somebody else's belongings. She wanted to be on her way to the boat. But she couldn't just leave the man. He needed help. She started gathering his things.

"Are the paintings all right?" he asked, picking his head up. "They're not damaged, are they?"

"They're fine," she said. "Nothing's damaged as far as I can tell."

"Thank goodness. They're my stock. I'm going to sell them."

"What?" she asked irritably, trying to wrestle all the clobber back into the suitcase.

"I'm going to sell them in New York."

"Oh, aye?" she said, closing the case. She had no clue what Mr. Nicholas Soames was on about. He's babbling, she thought. Must be dizzy. Nobody could sell those paintings; they looked as if Seamie had made them. As soon as she got the one suitcase closed, she scrambled over to the other and put his clothes neatly back inside of it. Seamie reappeared, dragging the hatbox behind him.

"Thank you, my good man," Nicholas said, making room on the bench for him.

Fiona carried one suitcase over, then the other. "Are you feeling any better?" she asked, anxious to be going.

"Much, thank you. You've been too kind. Don't let me keep you, I'll be fine."

"But 'ow will you carry all these bags?" she asked, concerned.

"Oh, I imagine a porter will be along any minute. They're probably madly busy with people arriving for the New York ship."

"You wouldn't know 'ow to get to the ship, would you?"

"Not exactly, but I'm headed to the docks myself. To

the White Star Terminal. Are you? Would you like to share a cab?"

"Yes," she said eagerly, relieved not to have to find her way alone.

"Right, then. Let's go, shall we?" he suggested. Fiona nodded and they set off down the platform together, Nicholas with only three suitcases this time. Fiona carried his portfolio and her carpetbag, and Seamie brought up the rear with a hatbox.

In the hackney, Fiona, Nicholas, and Seamie had the chance to make introductions properly, and Fiona was better able to study her strange new companion.

Tall and angular, Nicholas Soames looked very boyish. She guessed he wasn't much older than she was – early twenties at the most. He had straight blond hair, cut long in front, which he was constantly sweeping off his brow. His features were finely sculpted, his nose perfectly straight. He had a handsome smile, but his eyes were his most remarkable feature. They were turquoise-blue and framed by long curling lashes that any woman would've envied. From the way he spoke, and from his elegant clothes and leather suitcases, she guessed he was a gentleman. He told them he was bound for New York and Fiona said she was, too.

"Going first class, are you?" he asked. She shook her head no, thinking that Nicholas Soames was very polite. It was painfully obvious that they, with their poor clothes and worn carpetbag, were going steerage.

"I am. Got stuck with a frightfully pricey room. By the time I booked, they had no more single cabins available and I had to take a double."

Fiona was suddenly worried. What does "book" mean? she wondered. Did you have to make arrangements in advance to get on a ship? This was something she hadn't counted on. She thought getting on a ship would be like getting on the train. You bought your ticket and got on.

What if it wasn't? "Do you 'ave to . . . book . . . to get on the ship?" she asked, afraid of the answer.

"Oh, my, yes. It's a big, complicated business getting a boat from here to America. Lots of people to be situated. But you must've known that. Otherwise you wouldn't be getting on today's boat, would you?" Her anxious expression told him she had not known. "Um . . . well, look," he said, "perhaps the boat's not sold out. You never know. Maybe somebody had to cancel. Go to the ticket office as soon as we arrive and see if they've anything left. I'll watch Master Seamie while you inquire."

"Would you?"

"It's the least I can do."

The cab ride didn't take long. Nicholas paid the driver, having inquired the price before they left the station, and Fiona gave him back half the fare. Together they went inside the White Star Terminal to the ticket office. It was bedlam. Hundreds of people were milling about, carrying bags and dragging trunks, crates, and overstuffed suitcases.

"First class!" a uniformed man shouted. "First class to board. This way, please."

Nicholas ushered Fiona into the queue, then sat down to wait with Seamie.

"Yes?" the agent barked.

"Yes, please . . . two for New York."

"I can't hear you, luv!"

She cleared her throat. "Can I get two steerage tickets, please? For today's ship?"

"Today's ship sold out two weeks ago. And next week's is fully booked, too. We're selling tickets for the one that leaves in a fortnight, the *Republic*."

"A fortnight?" Her heart sank. They couldn't wait a fortnight. It would mean staying in a hotel in Southampton for two weeks. It would cost the earth. She wanted to leave now, today. She thought again of William Burton and the look in his eyes. Had they given up looking for her? What if Sheehan found out where she'd gone? Was Burton angry enough to have her tracked down? The thought terrified her.

"Yes, a fortnight. Steerage, is it?"

"I can't wait that long. Are you sure there's nothing left on today's ship?"

"I said so, didn't I? If you don't want the next available passage, then step aside. You're holding up the queue."

That was it, then. She and Seamie were not getting on the ship. They were stuck in Southampton. She didn't know the city; she had no idea where to find a reasonable, clean lodging house. She had a lot of money, but she also knew she had to be careful with it; it was the only thing that allowed them to escape. It would buy them tickets to New York and give them a start there and she had to make it last.

She walked over to Nicholas to gather Seamie and their belongings. She was tired and confused. She had no idea where to go or what to do next. Maybe she could find a cheap tuckshop, get a cup of tea, and sit down for a minute. Then she could figure out her next step.

"How did it go?" Nicholas asked hopefully.

She shook her head. "They've nothing left. We'll go in a fortnight."

"That's deuced bad luck. I'm very sorry to hear it. Will you be all right in Southampton? Have you a place to stay?"

"We do," she said, not wanting to be any more trouble. "Thank you for watching Seamie, Mr. Soames. And good luck to you in New York."

"And to you, Miss Finnegan."

Nicholas Soames watched his new acquaintances walk away, unsettled by the look on the girl's face. It wasn't just disappointment or frustration, it was fear. She looked frantic. He should help her somehow. The little boy was tired. Maybe he could . . . no, it wouldn't work, it was a long trip and they were strangers. Who knew how they would behave?

Oh, what the devil. He had a weakness for strays. Maybe he'd regret his action, maybe not. He'd knew he'd certainly feel miserable if he didn't help them. They looked as if they had nobody and it was hard to be all alone in the world. He knew that well enough.

"Miss Finnegan!" he shouted. "Miss Finnegan!" She couldn't hear him; she was too far away. "Bugger these suitcases," he groaned, picking them up and stumbling after her. "Miss Finnegan!" he hollered again, closer this time.

Fiona turned around. "Mr. Soames, what's wrong? Are you dizzy again?"

"No, I'm fine," he said, putting his things down. "Look, please don't think me forward or indecent; I'm not trying to suggest anything untoward . . ."

Fiona looked perplexed.

". . . but as I told you, I have a double room on board the ship and I don't need all the space. If you went as my wife . . . if we posed as a family, they'd let us on together. You could share my room. It'll have two single beds and probably a cot stowed somewhere. I promise you you'll be perfectly safe in my company."

Relief flooded her face. She didn't hesitate. "Oh, Mr. Soames, thank you! Thank you so much! We couldn't 'ave waited another two weeks. We'll be as quiet as mice, you won't even know we're there. We'll pay our share. 'Ow much is it?"

Nicholas watched as she reached into her camisole and pulled out a wad of twenty-pound notes. She seemed to be a very poor person with a great deal of money. Oh my God, he thought, horrified, she's a thief!

She extricated one note. "I want to pay more than 'alf," she said, "because Seamie and I are two people." Her face was so full of gratitude and relief, so honest and open, that he felt ashamed of his momentary suspicions. She wasn't a thief. She was an East London girl. Rough, but decent. Maybe she'd saved up the money.

"Put that away," he said. "We'll settle up later. Now

233

listen, this is what we'll do . . . I'll go get our boarding passes. When they hand me only one, I'll say they made a mistake, that I made a family booking – that's why I booked a double room. They'll accept it; I'm sure they will." He frowned.

"What is it?" Fiona asked anxiously.

"We'll have to get round the lack of wedding rings somehow. If they think we're trying to save money by all going in one room, they might question us or look for signs that we're not really married. For now, just put your gloves on."

"I 'aven't got any gloves," she said. "But I do 'ave these." She rooted in her carpetbag for a moment and produced two thin gold wedding bands. "They were me parents'."

"Brilliant!" he exclaimed, slipping the larger one on. "We'll fool them for sure now. Just remember, you're Mrs. Soames and I'm Seamie's father." He went after the boarding passes. In a few minutes he was back, triumphant. "Got them," he said. "I'd better hold on to them. That's what the head of the family would do, don't you think?"

She nodded.

"Isn't this jolly!" he exclaimed, grinning like a child who just pulled off a prank. "We really did fool them. I hear first class is excellent on this line. The rooms are supposed to be quite comfortable and the food very good."

"Is it very dear, Mr. Soames, the dinners and such?" Fiona asked.

"It's Nicholas. And no, it's not expensive, it's paid for in your ticket. Didn't you know?"

"No, I didn't. All paid for? That's wonderful!" she said, smiling.

"We'll have loads of fun," he continued, his spirits high. "There's music and dancing. You can play games and cards. There will be plenty of people to talk to. We'll see and be seen."

Fiona's smile faded. "Mr. Soames . . . Nicholas . . . you've been very kind to us, but I don't think we can go after all. I'm afraid you won't want to see or be seen with us."

"What? Why ever not?"

She gestured at her clothes. "First class is grand, isn't it? And we've got no nice clothes. This is it."

"Really?" he asked, incredulous. He'd never met anyone who could honestly say that all she owned was the shirt on her back. He frowned, looking them up and down. She was right. It would be a problem. They'd have to have new clothes. "You know, I'm sure we could get to a shop and back in time," he said.

"Do you think so?"

"If we hurry. First class will take another hour to board, and then they'll give second class an hour, and then there's steerage. Let's give it a try."

As they scrambled to check their bags, Nicholas said, "Is that jacket all you've got? How do you stay warm? You'll need a proper coat and so will Seamie, and good warm gloves and scarves. It's only March, you know. The air will be brisk on board." As they left the porters to struggle with their things, he began ticking items off on his fingers. "You should have two or three skirts and a few shirtwaists. A coat, a dress or two for evening, and a couple of hats, don't you agree?"

He looked at Fiona. She nodded. "Whatever you think," she said.

Her expression – a trusting mixture of hope and uncertainty – touched him. He offered her his arm. "All right, then. Come along, Mrs. Soames. We haven't got all day!"

Fiona stood on the *Britannic*'s first-class aft deck, port side, gripping the railing tightly. The wind was bitterly cold, but she barely felt it as it snatched at her hair and tore at her skirts. She looked in disbelief at her hands, encased in leather gloves, at her new skirt, her boots.

In the space of two hours, in a crowded department store, Nicholas had transformed her, in appearance at least, from a London dock rat to a proper young lady. She now owned a new wool coat, good leather boots, three woolen skirts, four shirtwaists, two dresses, two hats, and a leather belt. Not to mention new nightclothes, underwear, stockings, tortoiseshell hairpins, and a second big carpetbag to hold it all.

He had made all the clothing decisions, pulling together outfits, deciding which coat, which hat. Fiona had acquiesced to everything; after all, he knew what one wore traveling, she didn't. When he finished, he picked out an outfit for her to wear to the ship and suggested she have her old things packed. She ducked back into the fitting room and put on her new coffee-colored skirt with a beige-and-cream-striped shirtwaist, a soft brown leather belt, and new tobacco-colored boots. A navy coat that grazed the floor went over the outfit, which was topped off by a broad-brimmed hat. When she looked in the mirror, she saw a stranger staring back at her. A tall, slender woman, elegantly dressed. She had touched the glass, her fingers meeting the stranger's. Is this really me? she'd wondered.

Two days ago she hadn't enough money to rent a one-room flat in Whitechapel. Now she was traveling to New York first class, sharing a room with a soft bed and its own modern loo, a room more luxurious than anything she'd imagined. They'd had tea and biscuits in the cabin an hour ago. Supper was at eight, with a concert to follow. Yesterday, she'd only been able to scrounge a kipper for Seamie's tea; tonight her little brother, napping in his cot now, would dress in a new flannel jacket and matching short pants, then dine on delicacies. It all felt absolutely unreal to her, like moving in a dream.

Everything had changed. Her old life was gone, literally swept away overnight, and she was on the threshold of a new one. She looked different; she felt different. As surely as Nicholas had transformed the outside, pain and loss and bitterness had worked on the inside, effecting changes that she herself sensed, but barely comprehended.

Gone was the coltish girl who'd sat by the river, dreaming of her future with the boy she loved. In her place was a sober young woman, hardened by grief and disillusionment. A woman who no longer thought of courting and kisses and a little shop in Whitechapel. A woman who no longer carried dreams in her heart, only nightmares.

As she stood on the deck, William Burton's words came back to her. ". . . if only we could get Tillet the way we got that bastard Finnegan." And Bowler Sheehan's response, his obscene laughter. ". . . that was a good job, wasn't it . . . put the grease down myself . . . watched Mr. Union Organizer slip and fall five stories . . ."

Fiona wanted to scream until she couldn't hear those voices anymore. But she knew that as long as she lived, she would never forget them. The truth was branded on her heart. Everything that had happened to her, to those she loved, had happened because of William Burton. There would be no justice, not now, not ever, for she would never be able to prove what he had done. But there would be revenge. In New York, somehow, she would make something of herself. Poor people could become rich in America. Weren't the streets paved with gold? She would see how people made money, and she would figure out how to make it, too.

"It's not over, Burton," she whispered to the ocean, its waters black in the winter twilight. "It 'asn't even begun."

On the horizon, England slipped out of sight. Her homeland. The ground in which her family was buried. The streets where she and Joe had walked. All gone. She could see nothing now but water. The ocean unnerved her; she couldn't see across it to the other side as she could see across the Thames. She felt unbearably alone and frightened of what was to come. She closed her eyes, wishing for something, someone to hang on to.

"You look troubled, my child," said a voice at her elbow. Startled, she turned toward it. A kindly-looking man in a black cassock, a priest, was standing beside her. "At prayer, were you? That's good. It eases the soul. You can tell the Almighty your troubles and He will hear them. God will provide."

Really? she thought, stifling a bitter laugh. He's done a terrible job of it so far.

"Here, let us pray together now and ask His help in easing your burdens," the priest said, handing her a rosary.

She shook her head. "No, thank you, Father."

The priest regarded her, nonplussed. "But surely you believe in the power of the Almighty to help you in your time of need? Surely you believe . . ."

Believe in what? she wondered. She had once believed with all her heart in the strength of love, the permanence of home and family; she'd believed that her dreams would come true and her prayers would be answered.

Now she believed in one thing only – the money stitched up in her camisole. Those pounds had saved her life – not Joe, not God, not her poor dead parents, not a union, not mumbled prayers or rosaries or penny candles.

Fiona thought of her father, of a conversation they'd had once in front of the fire. It seemed like years ago. His words had confused her at the time; she had mulled them over in the months after his death, never fully understanding them, but now their meaning was perfectly clear.

"What I believe, Father," she said, handing him back his rosary, "is that three pounds of meat makes a very good stew."

PART TWO

22

"Move it, would ya? Move yer goddamned ass, goddammit!" the cabdriver shouted. Ahead of him, a wagon laden with bricks was moving too slowly for his liking. He pulled up hard on his horse's reins, forcing the animal to swerve sharply. The cab's wheel caught the curb as it skirted the wagon, tossing Fiona and Seamie around on the seat like dice in a cup.

They'd only gone two blocks from the terminal and already their glimpses of the city and its people had confirmed what they'd heard aboard the *Britannic* – that New York was beastly loud and beastly fast. All around them, people moved as quickly and heedlessly as the traffic. Men darted across intersections, dodging oncoming carriages. One, in a bowler hat, read a newspaper as he walked, turning the pages and a corner without missing a beat. Another ate a sandwich as he hung off a trolley. A woman wearing a straight skirt and cutaway jacket strode briskly toward her destination, shoulders thrown back, chin lifted, the plumes on her hat trembling with every step.

As the hansom cab nosed its way up Tenth Avenue, Fiona and Seamie took in the vast freight yards and factories that lined it and the frenetic activity that attended them. Teams of horses drew huge rolls of paper to printers' shops or bales of cotton and wool to textile mills. Men lowered newly woven carpets, crates of twine, china cabinets, and pianos from factory loopholes to delivery wagons. They heard them shouting orders to one another in brash

241

American voices. They saw laundries billowing steam into the crisp air, glimpsed red-faced women inside their open doors twisting water out of sheets. They smelled coffee roasting, biscuits baking, and less savory odors from soap factories and slaughterhouses.

New York, Fiona sensed, was nothing like London. It was young, an upstart. A new city whose every street and building spoke of speed and modernity. She remembered how Nick had reacted when the boat docked, how he'd held up the entire first-class section when he stopped on the gangplank, enraptured by the very sight of the place.

"New York!" he'd exclaimed. "Just *look* at it, Fee! The city of commerce, of industry. The city of the future. Look at all the buildings! The thrusting architecture, the soaring lines. They're artistic ideals realized. Temples of ambition. Paeans to power and progress!"

She smiled to herself now. That was Nick all over. Nattering on about artistic ideals when all she – and a thousand others – wanted was to get off the bloody boat.

Seamie, sitting on the edge of the seat, turned to her and said, "Will they like us, Fee? Auntie Molly and Uncle Michael?"

"Of course they will, luv," she replied, wishing she felt as confident as she sounded. A little voice inside her reminded her that her aunt and uncle had no idea that she and Seamie were about to show up on their doorstep. What if they *don't* want you? the voice asked.

She silenced it. Of course they would. Michael was their father's brother. They were his family and he would do right by them. Oh, he might be a bit surprised at first – who wouldn't be? But they would be welcomed and made much of. She had dressed herself in a navy skirt and white shirt-waist and Seamie in the tweed jacket and short pants she'd bought in Southampton so they would be sure to make a good impression. She told herself how very lucky they were to have family to go to, unlike poor Nick, who had none.

Nick, she had learned over the course of their journey,

had had a falling-out with his father; that's why he'd left London. His father owned a bank and expected him to run it one day, but Nick had other ideas. He was passionate about what he called the new art – the work of a group of painters who lived in Paris. He'd worked as an art dealer for a time in that city and now he was going to open a gallery of his own in New York. He would represent these new painters exclusively. Impressionists, he called them. He'd shown her the half dozen canvases he'd brought with him. At first, she'd thought them very odd. They looked nothing like the paintings she had seen in windows of shops and pubs – ones of children and dogs, or courting couples, or hunting scenes. But the more he told her about the ideas behind the paintings, and the painters themselves, the more she grew to like them.

Nick kept one of the canvases – a small still life of white roses, apples, bread, and wine – on the night table that separated their two beds, where he could always see it. It was signed "H. Besson," and Fiona had found herself strangely drawn to it. It made her think of Joe. Of how much she still missed him, longed for him. She had wondered how this simple little painting could stir up such feelings. Nick said it was because the artist had painted it with his heart.

Though they'd been apart for only half an hour at the most, Fiona missed Nick already. Horribly. Today was Thursday. They'd promised to meet the following Thursday at his hotel. It was only a week away, but it seemed like forever. She missed his enthusiasm and his optimism, his irrepressible sense of adventure, his funny, impractical ways. She remembered their first supper together. As they were walking to the dining room, she'd been seized by panic. She had no idea how to act or what to say. How would she ever pass as his wife, as one of the quality?

"It's simple," he'd told her. "Always be rude to the help. Sneer at every new idea the world presents. And never stop talking about your dogs."

She would have preferred a bit of *useful* advice – like which glass was for water and which for wine. That first dinner had been a disaster. She'd been confused by the profusion of cutlery, crystal, and china. By the time she'd figured out which was the soup spoon, Seamie was drinking his consommé right out of the bowl. He'd lowered it, made a face, and said, "This tea is 'orrible!" She'd made him put it down and use his spoon and tear pieces off his roll and butter each piece – as Nick did – instead of slathering the whole roll. She couldn't get him to do much else. He was balky and cranky and couldn't understand why he suddenly had to call his sister Mother and a strange man Father. He didn't like the lobster salad and refused to eat his quail because it still had its head on.

To make conversation, Nick had asked her about her family. While she'd been busy formulating a reply to that difficult question, Seamie answered it for her. "Our mam's dead," he'd said plainly. "She was stabbed by a man called Jack. Our da's dead, too. 'E fell at the docks. They cut 'is leg off. Charlie and Eileen are dead, too. Bad men chased us. They wanted our money. We 'id be'ind a mattress. It 'ad rats in it. I was scared. I don't like rats."

When Seamie finished, Nick's mouth was hanging open. After a few seconds of excruciating silence, he asked if it was true. She told him it was. Looking at her plate, she explained what had happened to her family, leaving out William Burton's involvement. Seamie knew nothing about it. Nobody did and she wanted to keep it that way. It was a black, horrible thing – a thing for herself alone. When she'd finished, she'd raised her eyes to Nick's, expecting to see an expression of distaste on his fine, patrician face. Instead, she'd seen tears in his eyes.

During the nearly three weeks they'd shared a room, meals, and a life, she'd grown incredibly close to this charming, impossible, good-hearted man. She still wasn't quite sure how it had happened. Perhaps it was because they were both so alone in the world. She had lost her family and been forced to leave her home, and so – in his own way – had he. She never expected them to become good friends; she'd assumed their backgrounds were too different, the class divide too great, to permit it. But that was before the two of them, with Seamie nestled in his cot, had spent stormy nights huddled in their cabin, sipping tea as the ship pitched and rolled, telling each other their hopes and dreams. It was before Nick made both her and her brother practice the phrase "Hello, Harold, I hear Havana's hellishly hot," over and over until they stopped dropping their aitches. Before she'd brought him ginger tea and read to him from his volumes of Byron and the Brownings during the strange spells of fatigue he was prone to. Before he'd sat on the edge of her bed, soothing her, after she'd screamed herself awake from yet another nightmare.

It was before she'd discovered the photograph. The one she was sure she wasn't meant to see.

One morning, after Nick had left for his customary walk on deck, Fiona saw that he'd left his watch open on the night table. It was gold, beautifully worked, and undoubtedly valuable. Not wanting anything to happen to it, she'd picked it up to tuck it away. As she did, a small photograph fluttered out. She retrieved it and saw a handsome, dark-haired man smiling back at her. His face was full of love for the person who'd taken the picture. She'd known then that the photographer had been Nick and that this man was his lover.

Who else would he be? People didn't keep pictures of friends in a watch case. It would certainly explain why Nick never talked of a sweetheart, even when she'd told him about Joe. Or why he'd never shown interest in her or any other woman on the ship. She'd been afraid of that when they first settled into their room. She'd been so eager to get on the ship, she'd never even considered that he might be motivated by something other than a kind heart. That first night, tucked under her covers, afraid to fall asleep with a strange man just feet away, she asked herself what she would do if he made a move. She could hardly complain to the captain – they were supposed to be married. But he'd never given her one second's cause for concern. She had stared at the handsome man for a few more seconds, wondering what he was like, if he would ever come to America, wondering what on earth two men did together. She'd never met a man who liked other men. Then she'd chided herself for being nosy and put the watch away.

The cab stopped short, jouncing Fiona into the hard wooden door, making her forget all about Nick and their journey. There was more cursing and yelling as the driver fought his way through the intersection of Eighth Avenue and Fourteenth Street, bouncing over ruts and bumps on his badly sprung wheels. Fiona could see that the factories had given way to neat, well-kept houses and shops. The cab picked up speed again, then stopped four blocks later in front of a squat, three-story brick house on the east side of the avenue between Eighteenth and Nineteenth streets.

Fiona, her hands shaking with anticipation, scrambled out of the cab, then lifted Seamie and their things down. She paid the fare and the carriage lurched off, its wheels spraying dust and gravel. Holding her carpetbags in one hand and Seamie in the other, she looked up at number 164.

It was not what she expected.

The sign over the shop read: M. FINNEGAN – GROCERIES and listed the opening hours, but the shop was closed. The door was secured with a padlock; the large shop window was streaked with dust. Inside of it, dead bugs and mouse droppings littered a display of goods, their wrappers bleached and wrinkled by the sun.

In the bottom right-hand corner of the window was a sign. It read:

> To be offered at Public Auction by First Merchants
>   Bank:
> 164 Eighth Avenue: 25'-wide three-story building
>   on a 100' lot.

Operated as a retail establishment and residence.
Date of auction: Saturday, April 14, 1889
For further details, please contact
Mr. Joseph Brennan, Real Estate Agent
21 Water Street, New York

Fiona blinked at the sign. She put her bags down, made blinders of her hands, and peered into the window. She could see a white apron balled up on the counter, a large wall clock behind it – its hands indicating the wrong time, a brass cash register, gas lamps, and shelves still stocked with goods. What happened? she wondered anxiously. Where is everyone?

"Come on, Fee. Let's go see Uncle Michael."

"In a minute, Seamie."

She took a step back and looked up at the second floor. There were no signs of life. She tried the door to the upper floors; it was locked. She told her brother to stay put, then went to knock on the door of number 166, but that, too, was empty. From the dress forms inside, the bolts of cloth and spools of thread scattered about, she guessed it had been a dressmaker's. She tried number 162, after picking her way through a pile of empty paint buckets and old brushes stacked outside of it. Again there was no answer. She was biting her bottom lip, and starting to panic, when a teenage boy passed her on the sidewalk.

"Excuse me . . ." she said. "Do you know Michael Finnegan? Do you know where he is?"

The boy, hands in his pockets, said, "Whelan's Ale House, most likely."

"Sorry?"

"Whelan's. One block north." He started to move off.

"Wait, please! Doesn't he live here anymore?"

"He sleeps here, miss, but he lives at Whelan's." Smirking, he pantomimed a drunk upending a bottle. Fiona's confused expression told him she hadn't understood. The boy rolled his eyes. "Do I gotta spell it out? He drinks. Spends his days at the boozer, then staggers back here. My dad does the same, but only on Saturdays. Mr. Finnegan, he's there all the time."

"That can't be," Fiona said. Her uncle was no drunkard. He was a hardworking shopkeeper. She had his picture, his letters, to prove it. "Do you know why his shop's closed?"

A piercing whistle came from the end of the block. "Coming!" the boy yelled. He turned back to Fiona, impatient to join his friends. "Didn't pay his bills. Went crazy when his wife died."

"Died!" she repeated, stricken. "Molly Finnegan is *dead?*"

"Yeah. Cholera. Last fall. It took a lot of people. I gotta go," he said, trotting off. "Whelan's Ale House. On Twentieth," he shouted over his shoulder.

He left Fiona standing on the pavement, her hands pressed to her cheeks, trying to take in this latest disaster. This can't be happening, she told herself. It can't be. The boy must be mistaken. She had to find Michael. He would explain everything and then they'd have a laugh over the silly misunderstanding. "Come on, Seamie," she said, picking up their bags.

"Where are we going now, Fee?" he whined. "I'm tired. I want something to drink."

Fiona tried to sound cheerful and sure of herself so her brother wouldn't hear the anxiety in her voice. "We're going to find Uncle Michael, Seamie. He's not at home right now. We have to see where he is. He'll be very happy to see us, I'm sure. Then we'll all have a nice drink and something to eat, all right?"

"All right," he said, taking her hand.

Whelan's Ale House did not look like the sort of place where respectable workingmen went for a well-earned jar. Dingy and run-down, it was the type of place gutter drunks crawled into after they'd scraped up four cents for a shot of gin or whiskey. Taking a deep breath, Fiona pushed the door open and stepped inside. It was quiet, at least. Three men were playing a game of billiards; two more sat slumped at the bar.

"Ladies drink in the back," the bartender said, wiping a glass with a dirty rag.

"I don't want a drink," she said to him. "I'm looking for my uncle. Michael Finnegan."

"Hey, Michael!" he yelled. "Someone here to see you!"

"Tell 'em to fuck off," a figure at the end of the bar said, not bothering to turn around.

"Stay here," Fiona instructed Seamie, leaving him by the door. She'd seen belligerent drunks before and she wanted to be able to grab her brother and make a quick exit if things turned ugly. She approached the man who'd spoken. He was wearing a worn tweed jacket with holes at the elbows. His black hair was long and unkempt.

"Excuse me, are you Michael Finnegan?"

The man turned to her. She gasped. He was the spitting image of her father. Same chin, same cheekbones, same startlingly blue eyes. He was a few years younger than her da and not as broad-shouldered. He was clean-shaven. His face was softer, not weathered from years at the docks, but still, she knew it as well as she knew her own.

"I t'ought I told you –" he snarled, then, seeing he was addressing a woman, he apologized. "Sorry, lassie, t'ought you was one of them vultures after me for money. Didn't mean to . . . ." His words trailed off. He squinted at her, staring into her eyes as intently as she was staring into his. "Do I know you?" he asked.

"I'm your niece, Fiona."

He was silent for a few seconds. "Me niece?" he finally said. "Paddy's lass?"

Fiona nodded. She pointed to Seamie. "That's my brother, Seamus."

"Me niece!" he repeated wonderingly, his face softening into a smile. "Let me look at you! Jaysus, if you don't look just like me brother! Just like him! Me niece!" He lumbered off his barstool and enveloped her in a bear hug, nearly suffocating her with whiskey fumes.

"Can I get you something, miss?" the bartender asked as Michael released her.

"No, thank you. I don't –" she started to say.

"Tim!" Michael bellowed. "Get a drink for me niece, Finona!"

"Fiona . . ."

"Here, sit down," he insisted, giving her his stool and pulling up another one. She demurred. "No, sit," he said, pushing her down onto the stool. "Sit and tell me how you got here. Tim! A drink for me niece! A shot of your best whiskey!"

"A soda water will do," she said quickly.

"And somet'ing for the nipper," he said, beckoning Seamie to join them. "Come on, Seamus lad, come sit next to your Uncle Michael." He pulled up another stool and Seamie, wide-eyed and uncertain, climbed onto it. "Give the lad a whiskey, too, Tim." He went to sit down, missed the barstool, and landed on the floor. Fiona jumped up to help him.

"What are you doing here? Have you come for a visit?" he asked, brushing himself off.

"More than a visit," she said, settling him back on his stool. "We're in New York for good. We've emigrated."

"Just youse? Where's Paddy? Isn't he with you? And Kate?"

Fiona dreaded having to tell him. The man had lost his wife and from the looks of things, wasn't handling it well. "Uncle Michael . . ." she began, pausing to hand Seamie one of the two soda waters the bartender had brought, ". . . my father is dead. He fell from a loophole down the docks." Michael said nothing, he just swallowed hard. "My mother's dead, too. Murdered."

"Murdered?" he cried. "When? How?"

Fiona told him about Jack. She told him about Charlie

250

and the baby and how she and Seamie had only survived it all because of the kindness of Roddy O'Meara.

"I can't believe it. All of them gone," he said, dazed. "Me brother . . . so many years went by, but I always t'ought I'd see him again." He looked at Fiona with eyes full of pain. "Did . . . did he suffer?"

She thought about her father's last moments. She remembered the way he had looked in the hospital bed, his body broken. She remembered overhearing Burton and Sheehan talking about his death, laughing about it. Michael didn't have to know his brother had been murdered over a penny-an-hour wage hike. She could at least spare him that. "It was a bad accident. He didn't live long," she said.

He nodded, then ordered another shot. The bartender placed it in front of him. He tossed it back as if it were water.

"Uncle Michael," Fiona said. "Seamie and I, we were just at your house. What happened? To Molly and the baby? To the shop?"

"Another round, Timothy. Make it a double."

Another one, on top of the one he'd just downed. He was already pissed. Fiona watched him wait agitatedly for the fresh glass, drumming his fingers on the bar. He was desperate for it. The boy she'd met was right; he was a drunkard. The glass arrived. She watched as he downed that in one swallow, too. His gaze was becoming detached and unfocused.

"Aunt Molly . . ." she pressed.

"She's dead. Cholera."

"I'm sorry."

"She was weak after the baby. Might've licked it if she'd been stronger."

"The baby was born?"

"Aye. Two weeks after the outbreak."

"What happened? Did it . . . is it . . . ?"

"She lived."

"Lived! Where is she?" Fiona asked, alarmed. "She's not

in the flat, is she?" She couldn't bear to think of a little baby all alone in a dark, empty flat.

"No, she's with Mary . . . a friend . . ." He heaved a sigh; talking was growing more difficult for him. ". . . friend of Molly's . . . took her after the funeral." He held up a finger for the bartender.

Blimey, not another one, Fiona thought. He can hardly speak as it is.

"Where does Mary live?" she asked. "Where's the baby?"

"With me . . . at home . . . with Mary . . ."

He was becoming incoherent. She had to get answers out of him quickly, before he couldn't talk at all. "Uncle Michael, the shop, it's to be auctioned, isn't it? Can the auction be stopped? How much do you owe?"

"I hate that fucking shop!" he shouted, banging his fist on the bar. Frightened, Seamie slid off his barstool and hid behind his sister. "I won't set foot in it! Fucking bank can have it! It was our shop, mine and Molly's. She made it pretty. Made it t'rive." He paused to slug down another mouthful of whiskey from yet another glass the bartender had put in front of him. His eyes were bright with unshed tears. "My Molly!" he cried brokenly. "I wish He'd taken me when He took her. I can't go on without her . . . I can't . . ." He picked up his glass again. His hands shook.

"The shop, Michael," Fiona persisted. "How much do you owe?"

"T'ree hundred-odd dollars. That's the bank. Another hundred or so to me vendors . . . haven't got it . . . only got a few dollars to me name, see?" He put his hand in his pocket and pulled out two bills, scattering coins as he did. "Fucking t'ings . . ." he muttered, as pennies and nickels rolled and spun over the dirty plank floor.

Fiona leaned her elbows on the bar and rested her head in her hands; it ached unbearably. This was not how it was supposed to happen. Not at all. She had imagined a warm welcome. Hugs from her aunt. Sandwiches and tea, and a fat, jolly baby to hold. She hadn't imagined this. After a minute, she stood up. She had to get out of Whelan's. Coming to New York had been a mistake. There was no family here to help her. She was on her own.

Michael·looked at her, terrified. "No," he begged, clutching her hand. "You're not going, are you? Don't go!"

"We're tired," she said, pulling her hand free. "Seamie's hungry. We need a place to stay."

"My flat . . . you can stay there . . . please, I've got nobody," he said, maudlin now. The liquor was making him surly one minute, sloppy the next. "It's a little messy, but I'll clean it."

Fiona laughed mirthlessly. Clean a flat? He hadn't even managed to pick his coins up.

He took her hand again. "Please?" he asked.

Not wanting to, she looked into her uncle's eyes. The misery she saw there was so abject, so deep, that the No she'd planned to say died in her throat. The day was growing long. In another hour, dusk would be coming down. She had no idea where to look for another place to stay. "All right. We'll stay," she said. "For tonight, anyway."

Michael fumbled in his pocket, produced a key, and gave it to her. "You go on. Sure, I'll come right after," he said. "I'll clean it up . . ." He belched. ". . . it'll be spotless. Tim, give us one more . . ."

Back at 164 Eighth Avenue, Fiona unlocked the door, and herding Seamie before her, walked upstairs to the second floor. As they stepped inside their uncle's flat, the stench of sour milk and rotted food greeted them. It was dark in the foyer; they could barely see ahead of themselves. Telling Seamie to stay put, Fiona walked down the narrow hallway, feeling her way along the wall until she came to the kitchen. A tattered lace curtain hung in the window. She pulled on the shade under it and it snapped up noisily, startling her. She heard the sounds of scurrying rodent feet and loudly stamped her own to roust any stragglers. Sunlight streamed into the kitchen. Its rays pierced the swirling dust raised by her movements and illuminated the biggest, most breathtaking mess she'd ever seen.

Dirty dishes clogged the sink. They covered the table and littered the floor. Here and there, bugs dined on the crusty remnants of food left to them by the mice. Glasses contained slicks of old beer and rancid coffee. The floor was crunchy underfoot in places, sticky in others. The stink made her nauseous. She opened the window, desperate for fresh air.

"Fee?" Seamie called from the hallway.

"Stay there, Seamie," she told him, moving from the kitchen to the parlor. She opened windows there, too, throwing light on similar chaos. Empty whiskey bottles and dirty clothes were strewn about. Mail was heaped on the floor. Fiona picked up a sealed envelope. It was addressed to Michael Finnegan from First Merchants Bank and was marked URGENT. She picked up a folded piece of paper. It was from a butcher and demanded immediate payment of monies owed. An unopened envelope – heavily postmarked – caught her eye. It was the letter her mother had sent after her father's death.

It was quiet in the parlor. The only sound was the rhythmic ticking of the mantel clock. Fiona, reeling from the reception she'd received, didn't hear it. All she heard was the sound of a million problems shrieking at her. Her aunt was dead. Her uncle was a raving drunk. Her cousin was somewhere in this godforsaken city, but where? The shop was closed; the job she'd counted on did not exist. The building was going to be auctioned. Where would they go when it was? What would they do? How would she find a place to live? A job?

She moved through the flat; everywhere she went, there was another mess. The bathroom was vile. Michael's bedroom, like the parlor, was littered with empty bottles. Tangled sheets hung off the bed onto the floor. On one of the pillows rested a framed photograph. Fiona picked it up. A pretty woman with merry eyes smiled back at her.

"Feeeee!" Seamie wailed. "Come on! I'm scared!"

"Coming, Seamie!" she shouted, running to him.

"I don't like it here. I want to go home," he fretted.

Fiona could see the worry in his face and the exhaustion. She couldn't let him see how upset she was; she had to be strong. "Ssshhh, pet. It'll be all right, you'll see. We'll get something to eat and I'll tidy up a bit and things will look a lot better."

"Is that Auntie Molly?" he asked, pointing at the photograph she was still holding.

"Yes, luv."

"She's dead, isn't she, Fee? That's what Uncle Michael said."

"Yes, I'm afraid she is," Fiona said. She wanted to change the subject. "Come on, Seamie, let's find a shop and get some bread and bacon for sandwiches. You'd like a bacon sandwich, wouldn't you?" She reached for his hand, but he whipped it away.

"Dead! Dead! Dead!" he shouted angrily. "Just like Mam and Da and Charlie and Eileen! Everyone's dead! I hate dead! Father's dead, too, isn't he? Isn't he, Fee?"

"No, Seamie," Fiona said gently, kneeling down in front of him. "Nick's not dead. He's in a hotel. You know that. We're going to see him in a week."

"No, we aren't. He's dead," Seamie insisted, delivering a savage kick to one of their bags.

"No, he isn't! Now you stop this!"

"He is! And you'll die, too! And then I'll be all alone!"

Seamie's eyes filled with tears. His face crumpled. The sight split Fiona's heart in two. He's just a tyke, she thought. He's lost all his family except me. Lost his home, his friends, everything. She pulled him to her. "Nick isn't dead, luv. And I'm not going to die, either. Not for a long, long time. I'm going to stick around and look after you and keep you safe, all right?"

He snuffled into her shoulder. "Promise, Fee?"

"I promise," she said. She released him and made an X on her chest. "Cross my heart and hope to die –"

"No!" he howled.

"Sorry! Just . . . just cross my heart. How's that?"

He wiped his eyes with the back of his hand, then said, "Granddad O'Rourke's dead and Nana O'Rourke, too. And Moggs the cat. And Bridget Byrne's puppy that wouldn't eat and Mrs. Flynn's baby and . . ."

Fiona groaned. She took a handkerchief from her pocket and wiped his nose. She wanted her mother. Her mam would know what to say to Seamie to soothe his fears. She'd always known what to say to her when she was frightened. Fiona didn't know how to be a mother. She didn't even know where to buy their dinner or where they would sleep in all this mess. She didn't know what tomorrow would bring, where to look for a room, or what they would do for an income. Most of all, she didn't know what had possessed her to come to this bloody city. She wished now that she'd taken her chances and stayed in England. They could've gone to Leeds, Liverpool, or way up north to Scotland. West to Devon or Cornwall. They would have been better off in some grotty mill town, a mining town, some dung heap of a one-horse country town. As long as they were somewhere in England and anywhere but here.

23

Nicholas Soames flinched as the doctor placed a stethoscope against his bare chest. "I say! Where do you keep that thing? The icebox?"

The doctor, a stern, well-fed German, was not amused. "Breathe, please," he commanded. "In and out, in and out . . ."

"Yes. Right. I do know how it's done. Been at it for twenty-two years," Nick grumbled. He took a deep breath and let it out. He didn't want to be here, in Dr. Werner Eckhardt's examination room, with its nasty smell of carbolic and its sinister metal devices for prying and poking, but he had no choice. The fatigue had taken a turn for the worse aboard the boat. Fiona had wanted to send for the ship's surgeon on more than one occasion, but he wouldn't let her. *Couldn't* let her, or he might have found himself turned back to London.

He'd written to Eckhardt, whom he knew to be one of the best in his field, just after he'd arrived at his hotel yesterday to request an appointment. The doctor had written back telling him he'd had a cancellation and could fit him in today.

As Nick continued to take deep breaths, Dr. Eckhardt moved the stethoscope from his chest to his back, listening intently. Then he straightened, removed the instrument from his ears, and said, "It's in your heart. There are lesions. I can hear them. There's a hissing in the blood."

Well, isn't that just like a German? Nick thought. No platitudes to soften the blow. No hand on the shoulder. Just

257

a nice hard conk on the head. And then his glibness, which he used as a shield against the world and its ugliness, failed him and he thought, Oh, God. It's in my heart. My *heart*.

"Your illness is progressing, Mr. Soames," the doctor continued. "The disease is an opportunist. If you want to slow its progress, you must take better care of yourself. You need rest. A good diet. And no exertions of any kind."

Nick nodded, dazed. First his heart. What next? His lungs? His brain? He could picture it, invading his skull like some barbarian army, eating away at his faculties bit by bit until he was reduced to picking dandelions and singing nursery rhymes. He wouldn't allow it. He'd hang himself first.

As the doctor droned on, he found himself wishing that Fiona were here. She was so loving, so loyal, so good. She would take his hand and tell him it would be all right, just as she had on the ship. Or would she? he wondered anxiously. Even a heart as kind as hers had its limits. If she found out what was really wrong with him, he would surely lose her, his dearest Fee, his only friend. Just as he'd lost everyone else.

"Are you listening to me, Mr. Soames?" Eckhardt asked, giving him a close look. "This is no joke. It is critical that you take plenty of sleep. Ten hours at night. And naps during the day."

"Look, Dr. Eck, I'll take more rest," he said, "but I can't become an invalid. I've a gallery to open, you see, and I can't do it from a reclining position. What about a course of mercury?"

Eckhardt waved a hand dismissively. "Useless. It blackens the teeth. Makes you drool."

"Charming! What else have you got?"

"A tonic of my own devising. Makes the system more robust, more resistant."

"Let's try that, then," Nick said. As he started to dress, Eckhardt decanted a dark, viscous solution into a glass vial, stoppered it, and instructed him on the dosage. The doctor told him to return in a month's time, then excused himself to attend another patient. Nick looped his silk tie into a soft Windsor knot, inspecting his face in a wall mirror as he did. At least I still *look* healthy, he thought. Maybe a little pale, but that's all. Eckhardt's exaggerating. All doctors do. It's how they keep their patients. He put his jacket on and slipped the bottle into his pocket. On his way out he asked the receptionist to send the bill to his hotel.

Outside, the sunny March morning was bracing. Nick cut a fashionable figure in his gray three-piece suit and rather forward choice of a brown tie, brogues, and great-coat, instead of black. He walked down Park Avenue – hoping for a hackney – with his hands jammed into his pockets. His gait was loping and oddly graceful. The brisk air brought color to his pale face, with its high cheekbones and stunning turquoise eyes. He attracted many admiring glances, though he was aware of none of them, lost as he was in his own thoughts.

He finally secured a cab and instructed the driver to take him to Gramercy Park. On its way, the carriage passed an art gallery on Fortieth Street. With its white gilt-edged awning, its polished brass doors and its bronze urns flanking them, it looked extremely prosperous. As he stared at it, his expression became determined. He would have his gallery, and it, too, would be prosperous. He would not allow his illness to defeat him. He was made of tougher stuff and he would prove it. To Eckhardt. To himself. Most of all, to his father, who had called him an abomination and advised him to die quickly and spare the family any further disgrace. An image of the man came unbidden. Portly, brisk, unsmiling. Wealthy beyond belief. Powerful. Monstrous.

He shuddered, willing the image away, but it persisted and he saw his father as he'd looked the night he'd learned of Nick's illness, fury twisting his face as he'd slammed him into a wall. He lay on the floor afterward, gasping for breath, watching the black toe caps of his father's oxfords as he paced the room. The shoes, from Lobb's, were polished to a harsh gleam. The trousers, from Poole's, were sharply creased. Appearance was everything to the man. Speak and dress like a gentleman and you were one, regardless of whether you beat your horses, your servants, or your son.

Shaking the memory off, Nick reached for his watch. He was supposed to meet with an estate agent at eleven to view sites for his gallery. By mistake, he opened the back of the case. A small photograph, neatly trimmed, fluttered into his lap. He picked it up. His heart clenched as he regarded the young man smiling back at him. On the wall beside him were the words "Chat Noir." Nick remembered the place so well. He could almost taste the absinthe and smell the night air – a rich mix of cigarette smoke, perfume, garlic, and oil paint. He could see his friends – their faces, their shabby clothes and stained hands. He pressed his hand to his heart and felt it beating. Lesions? If the shattering loss he'd endured last autumn hadn't stopped it dead, what could a few spots do? He continued to stare at the photograph and suddenly he was no longer in New York, he was in Paris again. Henri was sitting across from him at the café wearing his favorite wine-red jacket. It wasn't March, it was May, the very night they met. He was there again, in Montmartre . . .

". . . two hundred fifty francs for that . . . that *poster*?" Paul Gauguin shouted in thick, wine-slurred French. "Why, it looks like something from a lamppost, a billboard!"

"Better a poster than a child's cartoon . . . like your Bretons!" Henri Toulouse-Lautrec shot back, eliciting shrieks of laughter from the rest of the company.

Earlier that day, Nick had sold one of Toulouse-Lautrec's paintings, a colorful portrait of Louise Weber, a music hall performer known as La Goulue. His employer, the renowned art dealer Paul Durand-Ruel, had been uncertain about representing Toulouse-Lautrec, but Nick pressed him and he'd agreed to let him show a few canvases. Nick had garnered only a small commission from the sale, but he'd earned something else – a victory for the new art.

It was no mean feat, selling the new generation. Moving a Manet, Renoir, or Morisot – the ones who'd started it all – was hard enough. But Nick had faith. In 1874, when the vanguard first exhibited, they couldn't sell anything either. A critic, taking his cue from the name of Monet's canvas *Impression, Sunrise*, had dismissed them all as impressionists, mere dabblers. Rebelling against what society deemed acceptable – historical and genre paintings – they sought to present the real, not the ideal. The seamstress bent over her work was as valid a subject to them as an emperor or a god. Their techniques were loose and unstudied, the better to evoke emotion. The public had reviled them, but Nick adored them. The realism with which they portrayed life spoke to his hunger for some small degree of honesty in his own existence.

At Cambridge, he'd read economics because his father made him – he wanted him well-prepared to take over Albion, the family bank – but he'd spent his spare time studying art. The first time he'd seen work by the Impressionists, at the National Gallery, he'd been nineteen years old, working at Albion over the summer and hating every second of it. Afterward, he'd walked out of the museum, flagged down a cab, and instructed the man to drive around the city for an hour – anywhere he liked – so that he could weep in privacy. By the time he'd arrived home that evening, he knew he couldn't stay at Albion or return to Cambridge. He would defy his father and leave for Paris. He hated his life – the suffocating days; the family dinners at which his father drilled him with questions on finance, then berated him for not knowing the answers; the unbearable parties where his mother's friends pushed their daughters on him like whoremongers, for he, as his titled father's only son, was considered a catch. His whole life was a pretense. Who he was – what he was – was unacceptable. But in the canvases of Monet, Pissarro, Degas, he'd glimpsed the world as it *was*, not as some would have it appear, and he'd embraced that vision.

Nick downed another mouthful of wine as Gauguin and Toulouse-Lautrec continued to taunt each other. He was enjoying himself immensely. Spirits were high, the mood triumphant. La Goulue herself arrived amid hoots and applause. Nick looked around and saw Paul Signac and Georges Seurat arguing heatedly. Émile Bernard was teasing a handsome young man with long, dark brown hair, a painter Nick didn't know, because the waitress was in love with him. Some of his colleagues from the gallery had come. The Van Gogh brothers, too. Vincent, rumpled and cross, and solemn Theo, director of the Montmartre Goupil's – a rival gallery. It was a wonderful party, a wonderful night – and then disaster struck.

Nick had been stuffing himself with steamed mussels, sopping up their garlicky broth with hunks of crusty bread. He'd just reached across Gauguin for the remains of a loaf when, out of nowhere, a large, putrid cabbage came sailing through the air and hit him in the head. He sat there in shock, speechless, blinking slime out of his eyes. A cry went up and members of the party were dispatched to apprehend the sniper. The man was collared and marched back to the scene of the crime. He turned out to be a postal clerk infuriated by Gauguin's paintings. And not only did the rotter refuse to apologize, he berated Nick for sticking his fat head in the way, causing him to miss his target.

The stink was unbearable. Nick stood up, announcing he had to go home and change, when one of the party – the young man the waitress fancied – offered to take him to his flat where he could wash and borrow a clean shirt.

"My name is Henri . . . Henri Besson," he said. "My place is nearby, only a street away."

"Let's go," Nick said.

They ran all the way up the five flights of stairs to Henri's tiny room, with Nick pulling off his shirt on the way. Once inside, he bent over a small paint-stained sink and poured a pitcher of water over his head. Henri gave him soap and a towel, and when he'd dressed, a glass of red wine. Nick had been in such a hurry to wash that he hadn't taken in Henri's room, but once he was clean, he did. And to his astonishment, everywhere he looked – hung on the walls, propped against the empty fireplace, leaning on the few bits of furniture – were some of the most vibrant, light-infused paintings he'd ever seen. A young girl at a dance, the spreading blush on her ivory cheeks subtle and perfect. A laundress, her skirts kilted up above her meaty knees. Bloodstained porters at Les Halles. And then he saw one that floored him – a portrait of two men at breakfast. One sat at a table with toast and a newspaper, the other sipped coffee at a window. They were dressed, not even looking at one another, but an attitude of familiarity marked them as lovers. It was at once innocent and incendiary. Nick swallowed. "Bloody hell, Henri . . . have you shown this?"

Henri came over to see what he was looking at, then shook his head. "Our friends paint the truth, Nicholas, and they are hit by cabbages." He laughed. "Or rather, their representatives are." His smile faded as he touched his fingers to the canvas. "They reveal us to ourselves and people cannot bear it. Who would accept the truth of my life?"

They hadn't rejoined the others. They'd finished one bottle of wine, then opened another, talking late into the night about their painter friends, the writers Zola, Rimbaud, and Wilde, the composers Mahler and Debussy, and themselves. And the next morning, as the first rays of the sun caressed Henri's sleeping form, Nick lay awake just watching him breathe, barely able to breathe himself because of the strange new fullness in his heart . . .

A police officer rapped harshly on the cab, startling him out of his thoughts. "There's an overturned cart ahead," he yelled to the driver. "No one's moving. Turn off on Fifth."

Nick looked down at the photo still in his palm. The jacket Henri wore made him smile; he remembered buying it for him. He slid the photo back inside the watch case. Henri had thought he was too good to him, too generous. It wasn't so. The gifts Henri gave – love, laughter, courage – had mattered so much more. He was the one who'd convinced him to stand up to his father, to live his life as he chose. It had taken some doing, a few fights, including a rather loud scene in the Louvre. It was in English, at least – Henri insisted on speaking it so he could improve – so most of the museum's patrons hadn't understood them, but still, it had been quite embarrassing.

"Henri, please! Lower your voice –"

"Say to me I am right! Admit it!"

"I wish I could, but –"

"But? But what? You don't need his money. You make excellent money at the gallery –"

"Hardly excellent."

"No, very excellent! It pays the rent, buys us food and wine, gives us a good life –"

"Bloody hell, Henri, you're making a scene! People are staring –"

"Let them! *Qu'est-ce-que vous regardez, eh? Mêlez-vous de vos affaires!*" he barked at a pair of nosy matrons. He looked Nick in the eye. "Tell him to go to hell, Nicholas. Let him cut you off. You can make your own success. You are Durand-Ruel's best salesman. Every gallery in Paris wants to fire you –"

"*Hire* me –"

"You can open your own gallery and make offices in London, Amsterdam, Rome –"

"Henri, you don't understand, it's not that simple –"

"*Messieurs, s'il vous plaît . . .*" the guard cautioned.

A stony silence followed. Henri feigned interest in a Vermeer. Nick regarded him as he stood scowling, arms crossed, his dark hair cascading down his back. Such a beautiful man, he thought, so good-hearted and warm. Talented. Smart. Stubborn as hell. And I love him more than I've ever loved anyone. Beyond all reason.

Henri cast a baleful glance in the guard's direction, then hissed at Nick, "You *want* to go home. You miss the ugly London. The rain. The clouds. You cold English, you don't love me."

"English*man*, Henri. And I do love you. Madly. But, I –"

Henri cut him off. "Then you do not love yourself. If you go back, it will be your death, you know that, don't you? You don't owe him your happiness, Nicholas. You don't owe him your life."

"I feel I do."

"*Mon Dieu . . .* why?"

"Duty, I suppose. I'm his only son. Our ancestors started Albion over two hundred years ago. Six generations have run it; I'm supposed to be the seventh."

"But you despise banks, Nicholas! You don't balance your accounts . . . you don't even go to deposit your commissions. I have to do it."

"I know, I know . . ."

"And you could leave Paris for a *bank*? Your life here? Your work? You could leave me?"

"But that's the whole bloody problem, isn't it, Henri? I can't leave you."

Nick had fallen in love with Henri the night he met him and Henri returned his feelings. He had made love before – furtive, closeted fumblings that left him feeling soiled and ashamed, but he'd never been in love. Now he was. The wonder of it! Suddenly, the most banal activity was imbued with magic. Buying a chicken was an indescribable delight because he would bring it to Henri, who would cook it with herbs and wine for their supper. Finding white roses in the market was his day's greatest achievement – never mind that he'd sold six paintings – because they were Henri's favorite flower. And to go to Tasset & Lhote on a Saturday and select the best paints, the finest brushes – things Henri couldn't hope to afford – and quietly leave them by his easel gave him an unspeakable joy. Within a month, they had taken a flat together and what followed was a year of perfect happiness. Nick was promoted twice. Durand-Ruel said he had never seen such sure instincts in one so young. And every night, there was Henri to come home to. To talk to and laugh with and rehash the day with.

But there had been a black cloud on the horizon – his father. He'd been furious when Nick left for Paris. He'd left him alone at first, hoping that his interest in art was merely a phase. But now he wanted him home. He'd turned twenty-one, he'd written, and it was time to take up his responsibilities. His father wanted to expand the bank's influence, to open branches throughout England and Europe. The world of business was changing, he said. He wanted to take Albion public and he wanted his son by his side helping to engineer its growth.

When Nick refused to return, he cut off his allowance. That hadn't worked, so now he was threatening to disinherit him. If this happened, he stood to lose a staggering legacy: millions of pounds in cash, trusts, and investments; a London town house; an Oxfordshire estate; holdings in Devon and Cornwall; a seat in the House of Lords. He'd written his father with a proposition: If he gave him a little more time, just the summer, he'd come to London in September to talk. The man had agreed. It was the beginning of July now. He and Henri would leave Paris for Arles in two days' time, and over the coming weeks, he would try and figure out what to do.

A chill wind blew in through the hackney's window. Still lost in his reverie, Nick didn't feel it. He and Henri had rented a beautiful old stone house in Arles. They went for hikes across the countryside, slept soundly at night, woke rested, and swore they'd never go back to noisy, dirty Paris. Henri painted during the day and Nick corresponded with artists and clients, or read. Sometimes they walked to town to take supper in a café, but mostly Henri cooked. The night he'd told him of his decision, Henri had made an onion tart. Nick hadn't been able to eat a bite . . .

"I'm very worried about Vincent, Nicholas. He's not

right," Henri said, pouring himself a glass of white wine. They were having supper in the garden.

"None of you is," Nick replied.

"Do not make jokes. This is serious." Henri went on to describe the trouble with Vincent Van Gogh, who was also in Arles for the summer, but Nick hardly heard him. All summer they'd talked about art, their friends, food, wine – everything but the one thing that weighed most heavily upon them. Tonight, however, they would have to talk about it. Nick had made his choice. That afternoon, while Henri was out painting, he'd walked to the post office and mailed a letter to his father informing him of his decision. Then he'd sat down on a bench nearby and waited until the post office closed and the postmaster came out with a sack of mail and took it to the railway station and put it on the Paris-bound train, so he knew he couldn't get it back. When he got home, he'd found Henri pulling the tart out of the oven. He'd tried to tell him then, but Henri had thrust cutlery at him and told him to set the table.

"I saw Vincent in town this afternoon," Henri continued. "He is so thin, I barely knew him. He had on an old jacket and threadbare trousers. I thought he was a vagrant. He invited me in to look at his work."

"How is it?"

"Astonishing. He has a still life with a coffeepot that you must see, and a portrait of a Zouave boy . . . the colors! So strong, so completely original."

"In other words, it'll never sell."

"Well . . . " he said, giving Nick a hopeful look, ". . . maybe in the hands of a good salesman, the best in Paris . . ."

Nick swallowed a mouthful of wine and gave him a long look in return.

"Would you at least try?"

"Yes." Nick put his wineglass down, but his hand was shaking so, he knocked it over.

Henri jumped up to wipe up the spill. "Nicholas, you

are clumsy . . . look, it's all in your plate." Nick had not touched his food, Henri noticed. "Why aren't you eating? Don't you like the tart?"

He didn't answer. He chest felt compressed, as if all the breath had been squeezed out of him.

"Nicholas, what is it?"

"Henri, I . . ." He couldn't get the words out. "Oh, God . . ." he moaned.

"Tell me what's wrong! Are you ill?"

He looked at Henri, reached for his hand. "I . . . I wrote my father today . . ." He saw Henri's face go white and rushed to finish, ". . . I told him I would not . . . I would not be coming home."

Henri knelt by Nick's chair and touched his cheek. Nick pulled him close and held him tightly, until he felt him sobbing. "Henri, why are you crying?" he asked. "I thought you'd be *happy*."

"I am happy, you idiot. Happy for myself. I'm crying for you . . . for all that you've lost. Your home, your family . . . so much."

"Sshhh, it's all right. You're my home now. And my family."

They had shed more tears that night and they had laughed, too. Nick had known he would grieve over his decision for some time yet. But it was the right decision. They returned to Paris halfway through August. Nick dived back into his work, determined to provide his artist friends with the money and validation that a sale brought. Henri's work began to sell. Two canvases at Durand-Ruel, three at Goupil. When August turned into September and Nick had had no word from home, he decided his father had made good on his threat and that there would be no further contact. It pained him deeply, but he could bear it. He had found an abiding love with Henri and that was what he needed most. At the time he'd thought their happiness would last forever . . .

*   *   *

The cab jerked to a stop on the east side of Irving Place, wrenching Nick out of his memories for good. He climbed out, fumbled for his wallet, and paid the driver. Genteel, he thought, taking in the aspect of the neighborhood. Old money. He smiled, wondering how old could old money possibly be in New York? A generation? Two? Old or new, he didn't care, as long as New Yorkers bought his paintings.

And they would. Durand-Ruel had come to New York in '86 with three hundred Impressionist canvases and the response had been overwhelming. There were many wealthy people here with the requisite sophistication to appreciate the new art. And he would have plenty to sell to them. Before he'd left for America, he'd wired thousands of pounds to the gallery – almost all the money he had – along with a telegram telling his former colleagues what he wanted and instructing them to send the paintings to a bonded warehouse in New York. They would arrive within the week. And when they did, seeing each canvas would be like seeing the face of an old friend. Each contained a little piece of the artist's life, his soul. Something of his life was in those canvases, too. His and Henri's. If he succeeded with his venture, if he opened up markets for the new painters, provided them with income so they could keep working, then something good would come from all he'd suffered.

Still smiling, he set off for the realtor's. Eckhardt can stuff all his gloom and doom, he thought. He had no plans for an imminent departure. Not today. Not tomorrow, either. He had important work to do and he intended to see it done.

24

"Uncle Michael?" Fiona called from the doorway of her uncle's bedroom. "Uncle Michael, can you hear me? You have to wake up now."

There was no response from the sleeping man. He was lying on his back in his bed, tangled in his sheets. He wore a grimy union suit and socks that were full of holes.

"Maybe he's dead," Seamie ventured.

"Don't start that again, Seamie. He's *not* dead. Dead men don't snore."

She called her uncle's name again. When he still didn't answer, she gave him a shake. He snored on, oblivious. She slapped his cheeks lightly, then grabbed his arms and pulled him up. He flopped back down. Fed up, she gave him a shove, then marched off to the bathroom.

Over the course of her first, sleepless night in New York, Fiona had come to realize that Michael must not lose his shop. His livelihood and hers depended on it. Yesterday, after she had put Seamie down for a nap, she'd gone out to buy groceries. She'd had to walk seven blocks before she found a decent shop. The shopkeeper there was a chatty sort who asked her who she was, then said he knew her uncle, knew how hard he'd worked to save up to buy the building. "He made a good living out of that shop. He could again if he'd just stop the boozing," he added.

After she'd returned, she rolled up her sleeves, knotted her skirts, and got busy cleaning. She discovered that under all the rubbish was a roomy, well-appointed flat. In addition to Michael's room there was a second bedroom that she'd slept in and a nursery that Seamie used. There was a real indoor bathroom with a flush toilet and a porcelain sink and tub. Plus a parlor, and a kitchen with a new oven, a double sink, and a big round oak table. As she'd dusted and swept, she saw many pretty touches. A green glass vase with the words "Souvenir from Coney Island" painted on it. A pair of pressed-glass candlesticks next to a trinket box embellished with seashells. Framed pictures of flowers. There was a tufted three-piece suite covered in plum velveteen in the parlor, and a wool rug in shades of moss and light green. None of these was first quality, but they'd been carefully chosen and spoke of a solid working-class prosperity.

Obviously, her uncle had made a good living and he could do so again. She herself was not going to work in a tea factory or clean pubs for a pittance; she was going to work for him, just as she'd planned. She was going to learn the business and then she was going to open her own shop with Burton's money. She'd only spent forty pounds so far of the five hundred she'd taken from him. She'd changed fifty on board the ship and they'd brought her two hundred fifty American dollars. Her remaining four hundred and ten pounds would bring her over two thousand more. It was a fortune, this money, but it was also her and Seamie's future and she had to preserve it. She knew from experience that factory wages barely covered the rent on a shabby room and meager meals. If she wasn't careful, she'd end up using the money to make ends meet, eventually whittling it away to nothing. And then she'd end up as poor as she was in Whitechapel. And she was determined she was not going to be poor ever again. She was going to be rich. She had promises to keep regarding William Burton and Bowler Sheehan, and though she had no idea yet what form her revenge would take, she knew she would need money – piles of it – to effect it. She was going to go up in the world, not down, and that snoring wreck in the next room was going to help her.

In the bathroom she took a glass she found resting on the sink and filled it with cold water. Then she returned to the bedroom and poured it on her uncle's head.

He gasped, sputtered, and sat up. He blinked at her and said, "Who the divil are you? And why are you trying to drown me?"

She stared at him, incredulous. "Don't you remember us? We're your niece and nephew. Fiona and Seamie. We talked to you in Whelan's yesterday. You told us we could stay here."

"I t'ought I dreamed that," he said, reaching down to pick his trousers up off the floor.

"Well, *t'ink* again," she said angrily. "You didn't dream it. No more than you dreamed that the flat was clean or your bed was made or that there was a pork chop on a plate in the kitchen. Who do you think cooked it? Fairies?"

"Divils, more like. It was burned to shite." He got out of bed and hunted for his shoes.

"Why, thank you," Fiona said, her voice growing louder. "Thank you very much!"

Michael pressed his palms to his ears, grimacing. "Me head hurts. Don't talk so much."

Fiona was furious now. "I *will* talk, and you'll listen. You've got to stop drinking, Uncle Michael. I'm sorry Molly died, I know it must be hard for you, but you're going to lose your shop."

"It's already lost," he said. "I owe hundreds of dollars. Money I haven't got." He opened the top drawer in his bureau as he spoke.

"But I do."

He laughed. "Not that kind of money," he said, rooting around in the drawer.

"Yes, I do. I have a . . . a settlement. From my father's employer. For his accident. I'd loan you what you need. You could pay off the bank and all your creditors."

"Ah!" Michael said, having found what he was looking for. He pulled out a flask, opened it, and took a long pull.

"No, stop that!" Fiona cried, dismayed. "Uncle Michael, please! Listen to me –"

"No, you listen to me," he said, frightening her with the sudden ferocity of his anger. "I don't want your money. I don't want your help. What I do want is to be left alone." He took another swallow of whiskey, shrugged on a shirt, and left the bedroom.

Fiona trailed after him and Seamie after her. "But don't you care about the shop?" she asked. "Don't you care about yourself? Your baby? Don't you care about us?"

Michael snorted. "Care about you? Lass, I don't even bloody know you."

Fiona recoiled as if she'd been slapped. You bastard, she thought. If it had been the other way around, if his children had come to her parents for help, her da wouldn't have treated them so poorly.

"You're going to end up on the streets, you know," she said, her temper flaring like the fuse on a stick of dynamite. "A dosser with nowhere to go. Sleeping in alleys. Eating out of rubbish bins. Just because you won't get hold of yourself. Do you think other people haven't suffered losses? Do you think you're the only one? I almost lost my mind when I lost my parents, but I pulled through. Seamie, too. Truth of it is, a five-year-old boy has more . . . more *balls* than you do!"

That stopped him. "You don't give up, do you?" he said, reaching into his pocket. Fiona flinched as he chucked something at her. It landed with a clunk at her feet. "There!" he shouted. "Take it! Take the fucking shop! It's yours. Just leave me alone, ya banshee!"

He left, slamming the door behind him. Fiona felt tears welling. She looked down at the floor so Seamie wouldn't see them. As she did, the object Michael had thrown caught her eye. It was silvery and shone brightly against the dark boards. It was a key. Michael's words echoed in her ears. *Take it. It's yours.* She bent down and touched it, then quickly pulled her hand away.

273

What was she thinking? Was she mad? A person needed to know a lot to manage a shop – how to order the right amount of supplies, how to keep track of inventory and read a balance sheet. She didn't have that kind of knowledge, Joe did. But Joe isn't here, is he? a voice said. The voice deep inside her that always pointed out things she'd rather not have pointed out. He's in London, it continued, with Millie Peterson. And you're in New York with no job, living in a building that's going to be sold right out from under you if you don't stop moaning and whining and find a way to prevent it.

She reached out her hand again and curled her fingers around the key. As she did, she heard footsteps on the stairs outside, then a tentative knocking. The door swung open on squeaky hinges. "Hello? Michael?" a voice called. "Are you there?"

She snatched the key off the floor, put it in her pocket, and stood up.

"Hello?" A woman poked her head in. "Michael? Oh!" she exclaimed, startled. "My goodness! You made me jump." She came inside, one red, sodden hand pressed to her chest. She was small and sturdily built, with thick chestnut hair pinned back in a bun, a sweet round face and large brown eyes. Her sleeves were rolled up, her forearms were flecked with soap suds. "I'm Mary Munro, Michael's tenant. I live upstairs," she said.

"I'm Fiona Finnegan and this is my brother Seamie. We're Michael's niece and nephew. I'm sorry for startling you. I didn't mean to."

Mary's eyes took in Fiona's tear-streaked face. "I heard shouting. That's why I came down," she said in a soft Scots burr. "Looks like quite a welcome he's given you."

Fiona managed a weak smile. "Not quite the welcome we were expecting," she said.

Mary shook her head. "Come upstairs. You look like you could use a cup of tea." She chattered away as she led them to the third floor. Fiona learned that she'd emigrated

274

from Scotland ten years ago and had lived here for three years with her son and father-in-law. Her husband was dead. He had been killed in a train accident at the freight yards. At the door, they were greeted by a tall boy, about fourteen, whom Mary introduced as her son.

"Get the nice cups and saucers out, Ian, and put the kettle on," she said, settling them at her kitchen table. "Let me get this lot rinsed and hung and then we'll all have a nice hot drink."

Mary's kitchen smelled of good things – bread and cinnamon and bacon. The sink gleamed. The stove was freshly blacked. The linoleum floor was worn and cracked in places, but it shone with a new coat of wax. White tatted curtains hung in the windows. Humble but immaculate, it reminded Fiona of her mother's kitchen and being in it soothed her.

"Would you like to take a peek at your cousin?" Mary asked, wringing out diapers.

"The baby? Is she here?"

"Aye, she's in the parlor. She's a bonny bairn, she is. I've had her ever since the funeral."

"Oh, I'm so relieved she's all right," Fiona said. "Michael told me she was with a friend, but he didn't tell me where. He didn't even tell me her name."

Mary shook her head. "Doesn't know his own name anymore, that one. Eleanor's her name, after Molly's mother. We call her Nell. Go on, go see her. I won't be much longer."

Fiona walked into the parlor and saw a pudgy fist waving around inside a laundry basket and heard a tiny voice burbling cheerfully. She peeked inside. The little girl was a vision. She had the black hair and blue eyes of her father and the plump, round-faced prettiness of her mother. When Fiona took her little hand and cooed to her, she was rewarded with a big gummy grin. She lifted the baby out of her basket and carried her into the kitchen, so glad that she was all right.

"There we are!" Mary said, getting the last of Nell's diapers hung on the line outside her window. She smiled when she saw Fiona and Nell making goo-goo noises at each other. "A little princess, she is. Tell me, Fiona, would you be Patrick Finnegan's lass? From London?"

"Yes, I would."

"Thought so. The accent gave you away. Molly told me about Michael's brother. I think she had hopes of luring your brother . . . Charlie, is it? . . . to New York to work in the shop."

"He would've loved that."

"Would have? He's not here with you?"

"No, he isn't. He died several months ago."

"I'm so sorry!" Mary said, putting down the teapot she'd just picked up. "How terrible for you and your parents to lose him so young."

"Actually, we lost them before we lost Charlie," Fiona said. As Mary abandoned the teapot altogether and sat down, Fiona told her an abbreviated version of all that had happened to herself and Seamie over the past few months.

"Lord, Fiona, after all that, then you travel to America and find your uncle in a state. What a shock you've had!"

"Aye. I'm not sure I'm over it yet," she said, a hint of bitterness in her voice. "From what my parents told me, from the letters we had from him, I thought he was a good man. I never thought he'd be so unkind."

Mary shook her head. "Oh, but he isn't. You mustn't think so. At least . . . he wasn't. He was the kindest man. Always smiling, always ready to help. It's the drink that makes him this way. He never drank before Molly died. Maybe a pint or two at his local, but he wasn't a drunkard. He was a good man, a good husband. Hardworking. He fixed up their flat and was going to fix up mine. And he wanted to expand the shop, too. He had so many plans, did Michael. If Molly could see him now, she'd be heartbroken. I don't know what to do. I've tried soft words and threats. I've taken Nell away from him. Nothing works.

Soon he'll be out on the street. And then what? Molly was my best friend. I love Nell like my own. What will I tell her when she's grown? That her own father abandoned her?" Her voice caught. "Oh dear, here I go . . ." She wiped her eyes. "I'm sorry. I can't stand what he's doing to himself. It's the grief. I know it is. He's never cried, Fiona. Not once. Keeps it all bottled up. Drinks and shouts when what he needs to do is weep."

Mary poured the tea. She sliced into a thick dark ginger-bread and served generous pieces. Fiona sampled hers. It was very good and she complimented Mary on it. She sipped her tea. It was terrible. As bad as the tea she'd bought yesterday. "Delicate" was how the shopkeeper had described it. "Dishwater" would be more accurate. It was a third-rate congou, a black China tea as flat and lifeless as an old straw mattress. Stuart Bryce, a man she and Nick had befriended on the ship, a tea and coffee importer who was opening a New York office for his firm, had warned her about the tea in America. She made a mental note to find herself some Indian leaves. Like all Londoners, Fiona found life's trials easier to bear with a strong cup of tea in hand.

Mary stirred sugar into her own cup, then said, "I don't know if you know this, but he's going to lose the shop. It's bad for him and it's bad for us, too. The new owners may not let us stay. I don't know where we'll go. Michael didn't charge us a lot. And I don't know where we'll find a place with a backyard for Alec and his plants. That's my father-in-law. He's a gardener. He doesn't get much work anymore, he's too old, but he still makes a few dollars here and there." Her bright eyes were worried.

"That's what we were shouting about just now," Fiona said, still smarting at the memory of her row with Michael. "I'd hoped to work for him. I want to have a shop of my own one day. I hoped he could teach me what I need to know."

"If only I had the money," Mary said, "I'd pay the bloody

bank off myself. But he owes a fortune . . . hundreds of dollars . . ."

"It wouldn't do any good," Fiona said, staring into her teacup. "I've already tried. I have a bit of money on me and I offered to pay back what he owes, but he refused." She swirled the liquid, then slowly said, "But he did give me his key. And he told me to take the shop."

There was a beat of silence. Mary said, "He gave you the key?"

Fiona looked up at her. Mary's eyes were no longer anxious. She was leaning forward, sitting on the edge of her chair, her expression intense and excited.

"Well, sort of. He threw it at me."

"My goodness, lass! You have the key and the money . . . you can open the shop again!"

Ever since her uncle had stormed out, Fiona had been thinking the exact same thing. Now Mary had spoken her thoughts aloud. "Do you really think I could?" she asked softly.

Mary leaned across the table and took Fiona's hands in hers. "Aye! You just said you wanted a shop, didn't you? Take your uncle's!"

"But I don't know the first thing about shopkeeping, Mary. What if I make a big cock-up of it?" She was eager at the prospect one second, terrified the next.

"You wouldn't, Fiona. I just know you wouldn't! I can tell you're a capable lass. You'll learn what you don't know. Michael didn't know everything when he began. He had to learn, too."

The whole idea was madness – pure and simple – and it was a huge risk to take with her money. But ever since she'd touched that key, she'd wanted to have a go. What if it worked? What if it just bloody well worked? She'd be able to save the shop, keep Mary and her family here, keep her uncle off the streets, and save herself from a factory job, too.

"I – I guess I'd have to go to the bank and talk to someone in charge there," she said hesitantly. "I've never even set foot in one. I wouldn't know what to tell them. And even if I did, they might not listen to me."

"I bet they would. They're bound to take a loss at an auction. They'll never get all their money back. I'm sure they'd rather the mortgage payments were continued. We'll do what we can, won't we, Ian?" Ian nodded vigorously. "We'll help you clean it up. I'll keep an eye on Seamie and wash the curtains for you. We don't want to leave our flat, do we, Ian?" Ian shook his head. They heard the door open and close. "Oh, that'll be Alec," Mary said. "He'll help you, too. He could make flower boxes for the windows. Molly was going to have them. She wanted them done in time for the spring. Oh, say yes, Fiona, do! Give it a go!"

Fiona grinned. "All right, Mary, I will!"

Mary jumped up and hugged her and told her over and over again that she wouldn't fail. She'd make a success out of the shop, she would. As she sat back down, a man who looked to be in his sixties came into the kitchen. His clothes were worn but clean, pressed, and neatly patched. He had gray hair underneath a tweed cap, a gray beard, and gentle gray-green eyes.

"Got me fish meal, Mary," he announced gleefully in such a thick Scots accent, Fiona barely understood him. "It's first-rate."

"Dad," Mary scolded, "don't be stinking up the place when we have guests."

Mary introduced Fiona and Seamie to her father-in-law and told him about their plans. He promised to make Fiona beautiful window boxes full of hyacinths, daffodils, tulips, and pansies. He said he was going outside to prepare his flower beds and asked his grandson to help him.

"Coming, Granddad," Ian replied, popping his last bite of gingerbread into his mouth. He took the buckets from his grandfather, watched by a wistful Seamie.

"Would you like to help, too, laddie?" Mary asked. "I'm sure they could use another pair of hands." Seamie nodded eagerly. "Off with you, then."

Fiona smiled as her brother, a bucket in his hands, followed Alec and Ian out of the flat. It would be good for him to be outside with companions and not dwelling on who died. She helped Mary clear the tea-things and they decided it would be best to start cleaning the shop right away.

As Mary dug in her broom closet for soap and rags and scrub brushes, Fiona went to the window to check on her brother. The kitchen overlooked the backyard and she had a clear view of him; he was using a hoe to mix dirt and fertilizer in a wheelbarrow. He was awkward with the large tool, but Alec didn't seem to mind. She could hear the older man encouraging him, telling him if he gripped the handle a little farther down, it would be easier to manage.

A gentle breeze blew in. Monday would be the first day of April, and spring – from the feel of the breeze – wasn't far away. She was glad. Warm weather would mean she wouldn't have to put a lot of money into heating the building. Her stomach fluttered as she thought about the shop, but she reminded herself that she'd survived losing her family, eluded murderers, and had gotten herself and her brother to safety. She could bloody well handle a grocery shop.

"Here we are," Mary said, taking the baby from her and handing her a mop, a metal bucket, and a cake of soap. "I'll just get Nell's basket and we'll go downstairs."

Outside, as Fiona turned the key in the shop's lock, Mary said, "Just think, lass. You're only in New York a day and already you have a shop. Makes a body think all those sayings about America being the promised land and the streets being paved with gold might be true, doesn't it?"

The lock tumbled. Fiona turned the knob and the door swung open. A stench strong enough to bend nails hit her. She gagged, then covered her nose with one of Mary's cleaning rags. As her eyes adjusted to the darkness inside the shop, she spotted the source of the stink – a meat cooler. Its contents appeared to be moving. Maggots, she realized.

Thousands of them. Plump and white and squirmy. She swallowed hard, trying to keep the gingerbread she'd just eaten down.

"Makes me think a saying my father once heard from a Chinese sailor might be true," she said, overwhelmed by the mess before her.

"What was it?" Mary asked, her eyes tearing, a handkerchief pressed to her nose.

"Be careful what you wish for; you might just get it."

25

"Hush now, Nell, there's a good girl . . ." Mary crooned to the squalling baby. It did no good. The child's shrieks were ear-splitting.

"Fee? Can I have money for some doughnuts? Can I have a nickel?"

"No, Seamie, you can't eat doughnuts for dinner."

"It's lunch, Fee. Ian says it's called lunch here, not dinner. Supper is dinner. I want a nickel."

"No."

"Charlie always gave me a nickel."

"Charlie never gave you a nickel. We didn't have nickels in London."

"Well, a penny then. Can I have a penny? Can I have five pennies?"

From the cellar came a tremendous crash, then shouting, "Aw, crikey, Ian! Look what you did! I'm covered in it now . . ."

"*You* did it, Robbie! I told you to hold on to your end!"

Fiona dropped the rag she'd been using to polish the cash register and ran to the door. "Ian! Robbie! Are you all right?" she yelled above Nell's din.

Ian was halfway up the stairs holding a piece of a wooden crate in his hands. Below him stood Robbie, his friend, covered in brown mush, holding another piece.

"We were trying to bring some bad apples up. The crate fell apart," he said.

Fiona felt a tug at her skirt. "Fee, I want a *nickel*!"

Mary shouted that Nell, wailing like a fire siren now,

must be wet and that she was going to take her upstairs. Fiona told the boys to go upstairs, too, and wash. She reached in her skirt pocket with grimy hands and fished out two quarters. "Go and buy dinner . . . I mean *lunch* . . . for everyone when you're finished, Ian," she said. "And take Seamie with you. Please."

When they had left, and the shop was quiet, Fiona sat down on the stool behind the counter and leaned against the wall. She was sweaty and dirty, tired and sore. The optimism she'd felt at Mary's kitchen table on Friday had drained away, leaving her feeling certain she'd bitten off far more than she could chew. She, together with Mary, Ian, and Robbie, had been cleaning nonstop for days and there was still a mountain of work ahead of her. She'd thought Michael's flat had been a wreck; it was nothing compared to the shop.

Vermin and neglect had wreaked havoc. When they'd made it past the ungodly smell of rotted meat, she and Mary had discovered rats nesting in a chest of tea. Others had chewed through pickle barrels, leaving them to leak all over the floor, and had gnawed through cigar boxes to get at the tobacco. Weevils were in the flour and oatmeal. Dead flies rimmed the honey and molasses jars. Fruits and vegetables had shriveled in their bins.

It had taken them two days just to haul the rotten goods to the curb. The meat cooler had to go; it was ruined. Mary, Ian, and Robbie had worked like dray horses. She had wanted to pay them, but Mary refused to take any money. Nonetheless Fiona had managed to slip the boys a dollar each when she wasn't looking. Alec was pitching in, too. He was out back constructing window boxes. Seamie was also doing his share, dusting whatever he could reach. Only Michael was nowhere to be seen. He hadn't lifted a finger to help. Not even when she'd accosted him at Whelan's that morning to ask him about the cash register.

"I can't open the till, Uncle Michael," she'd said tightly, angry at seeing him blind drunk yet again. "Is there a key for it?"

"Aye."

"Can I have it?"

"No. It's not your cash register. It's not your shop," he declared loudly, so inebriated he had to hold on to the bar to keep from falling off his stool.

"But you said to take it."

"Changed me mind. Don't want it opened."

"You bloody man! Give me the sodding key!" she shouted, exasperated.

"Give me a dollar first," he said.

"What?"

"Give me a dollar and I'll give you the key."

"I can't believe this. You're going to *sell* me the key? Have you no shame?"

"Shame I've plenty of, me darlin' girl. It's cash I'm low on."

Fiona stood fuming. She didn't want any more money going from Michael's hand to Tim Whelan's till, but she needed the key. She pulled a bill out of her pocket and traded it for the key. "One dollar," she said. "That's all you're getting, so you'd better make it last."

Casting black looks first at her uncle and then at Tim Whelan, she'd turned on her heel and headed for the door. Her hand on the knob, she looked back at Michael and said, "She's beautiful, you know." He stared at her uncomprehendingly. "Your daughter. Nell. She has blue eyes and black hair like you and the rest is all Molly."

Pain sliced across his face at his wife's name. "Nell they call her?" he asked. He ordered another.

"Stupid sod," she muttered now, resuming her polishing. She needed his help desperately. Cleaning, as hard as it was, she was perfectly capable of. But talking to banks and creditors called for skills she didn't have. Two of Michael's suppliers – the miller and the fishmonger – had already paid a call. They'd seen the shop open and had come in to demand their money. She had paid them, hoping to ingratiate herself, hoping they'd restore her uncle's credit, but they refused. How would she find new suppliers? And when she did find them, how would she know if they were overcharging her? She didn't even know what things cost yet. Or what Americans ate. How would she know what quantities to order? Did a shop of this size go through a forty-pound bag of porridge oats in a week? Or two bags? Or ten? How much milk should she buy for one day? How many chops and sausages? This wasn't going to work. She was too bloody green. She wouldn't get any farther than the bank. She'd gone there yesterday, Monday, and made an appointment to see the president at the end of the week. He'd see she didn't know anything about running a shop and toss her right out the door.

Instinctively, she reached into her pocket for the blue stone Joe had given her, just as she'd always done when she was worried or scared, but it was gone. Of course it was, she'd pawned it. A feeling of bereftness swept over her. She longed for him, needed him so. If only he were here. He'd know exactly what to do. This wouldn't be so hard if they were in it together. When she got upset, he'd tease and kiss her until he made her laugh, just as he'd always done. It was so painful to think of him. It was like touching her fingers to a big, ugly bruise to see if it still hurt and wincing when she found out it always, always did. Why couldn't she just forget about him, as he'd forgotten about her on Guy Fawkes night?

The clock on the wall struck noon. It'll be five o'clock in London, she thought. Teatime on a Tuesday. He'd be leaving his office for his home, wherever that was. She wondered what his life was like now. Did he live in a fancy house? Did he wear fine clothes and go about in a carriage? Was he an important man at Peterson's now? Was he happy? It tore her up to think that every day Millie got to look into his eyes, see him smile, touch him. And she? She would never set eyes on him again. Maybe he was home having a hot meal, or maybe he was at a fancy restaurant somewhere, or . . .

Wherever he is, he isn't standing arse-deep in a mess of

a shop, covered in polish and pickle brine, the bastard, her inner voice said indignantly. Fiona tried to take her cue from the voice. She tried to feel angry instead of sad; it was easier. She tried to tell herself that she didn't care where he was or what he was doing, because she hated him. But she didn't. She loved him. Still. Despite everything. And what she wanted most in the world was for him to come through the door, take her in his arms, and tell her it had all been a terrible mistake.

Fat bloody chance, she thought. With effort, she pushed thoughts of Joe out of her mind. She had work to do and no time to stand around feeling sorry for herself. The walls needed painting. She had no idea where to go to buy paint, but she remembered seeing paint buckets by the curb of the neighboring building when she first arrived. Whoever lived there had had the place freshly painted. Maybe he or she would know where to go. As she stepped outside, a carriage pulled up. The door opened and a tall blond man jumped out, a picnic hamper in his hand.

"Nicholas!" she cried happily. "What on earth are you doing here?"

"I missed you! I know we were supposed to meet on Thursday, but I couldn't wait."

Fiona was delighted to see him. His smile alone lifted her spirits. "You look wonderful," she said. And he did – as ever, handsome and stylish. But perhaps a little too pale.

"And you look like a filthy little ragpicker!" he replied, rubbing at a streak of polish on her chin. "What on earth are you doing?" His eyes roved over her, taking in her rolled-up sleeves, her kilted-up skirts. He looked at the pile of rubbish on the curb, the empty shop, the auction sign still in the window, and frowned. "Hmmm, things not going according to plan, old trout?"

"No, not quite," she said, smiling at his odd term of endearment. He called her the most horrible names. Old shoe. Old baggage. Old mole. Old stick.

"What happened?"

She sighed. "Well . . . my aunt's dead and my uncle's a drunkard who hasn't worked in months. The bank's foreclosed on his shop and plans to auction it. I've got an appointment with the bank president to see if he'll let me take over. I've already spent too much of my own money paying off creditors. And it might all be for nothing. The bank could easily turn me down."

"I see."

"How are things with you?"

"Smashing!" he said brightly. "I can't find anywhere to live. And I can't find a place for my gallery. Everything's too small, too dingy, or too dear. And just an hour ago I received a telegram that all the paintings I bought – my entire stock – were put on the wrong boat out of Le Havre and sent to Johannesburg. Bloody Africa! It'll be yonks before they get here. My hotel is noisy. The food is dreadful. And the tea is unspeakable. I can't understand anyone in this bloody city. They don't speak English. And they're beastly rude, too."

Fiona grinned at him. "I hate New York," she said.

"I do, too. Despise the blasted place," he replied, grinning back.

"But when we got off the boat you said –"

"Never mind what I said. I was delirious." He put an arm around her shoulders.

"Oh, Nick," she sighed, leaning her head against him. "What a cock-up."

"A thumping great one."

She looked up at him. "What will we do?"

"Guzzle champagne. Immediately. It's the only thing for it."

Fiona took his things, put them inside the shop, and told him she had to go next door to see if she could find out where to buy paint. He said he'd go with her. As they stood at the door, they heard raised voices – a man's with a New York accent and a woman's with an Italian one. It sounded as if they were fighting. Fiona, her hand raised to knock, drew back, but she'd been seen and within seconds a cheerful young man wearing paisley suspenders and a matching tie was ushering them in.

"Come in, come in! I'm Nate. Nate Feldman. And this is my wife, Maddalena." A striking dark-eyed woman with masses of thick black hair piled up on her head waved to them from behind a drafting table. She wore a paint-stained white blouse and a slate-gray skirt.

Fiona introduced herself and Nick, then said, "I . . . I was hoping you could tell me where to buy some paint. House paint. I'm working on the shop next door . . . my uncle's shop, and I noticed paint buckets outside a few days ago . . . I hope we're not interrupting . . ."

"Oh, you heard the yelling?" Nate said, laughing. "Don't worry, it's just the way we work. We yell and scream, then the knives and guns come out, and whoever's left standing wins." He looked at Fiona's uncertain expression, then Nick's. "I'm joking, you two! It's a joke. You know . . . ha ha ha? Now, listen to this idea and tell me what you think . . ." With his hands, he shaped the outline of a large poster in the air. "There's a picture of a wagon, and over it, the words: HUDSON'S SELTZER, and there's a driver, he's leaning out of his seat and talking to you, the customer. He's saying, 'For stomach trouble, try our bubbles, we deliver on the double!' Look, here's the picture, show them, Maddie . . . see? What do you think? Do you think it works?"

"Yes. Yes, I do," Nick said. "The illustration is very engaging."

"What about the words? Do you like —"

"Nate, for goodness' sake! Invite them to sit!" Maddalena scolded.

"Sorry! Please . . . have a seat," he said, gesturing to a settee covered with prints and posters. Fiona picked up a poster and moved it aside.

"Excuse the mess," Nate said. "This is our office as well as our home. We just went into business for ourselves. Opened our own advertising agency. It's chaos."

"This is wonderful, Mr. Feldman," Fiona said, admiring the poster in her hands.

"Nate, please."

"Nate," she said. "What a beautiful picture!" The poster read, WHEATON'S ANIMAL CRACKERS – AN ADVENTURE IN EVERY BOX! The illustration showed children in a nursery who had just opened a Wheaton's box. The crackers had leaped out, changed into real zebras, tigers, and giraffes, and were cavorting around the room with the children on their backs. Fiona knew Seamie would be pestering for a box the second he saw it. "Wheaton's must be selling animal crackers hand over fist with an ad like this," she said.

"Um . . . well," Nate said sheepishly, "that one hasn't run yet."

"None of these have," Maddie said, coming out from behind her table. "We've only been open a week. We're too new to have clients yet."

"All of these were done on spec," Nate explained. "We approached a bunch of companies and offered to do the first ad for free. If it pulls the customers in, they'll pay us for a second one."

"Sounds like a hard way to start out," Nick said.

"It is. But we'll get real accounts soon," Nate said optimistically. "We have tons of contacts. Me from Pettingill. That's the firm where I worked. And Maddie from J. Walter Thompson. It's just a matter of proving ourselves first, isn't it, Mad?"

Maddie nodded and smiled at her husband and Fiona saw a hopeful look, but one tinged with worry, pass between the two. Nate turned back to his guests. "I've really forgotten my manners today. Can I offer you a drink, some lunch?" he asked.

"Oh! Nate, *caro,* I . . . I haven't been shopping yet today," Maddie said awkwardly. She turned to Fiona. Her cheeks were flaming. "We've been so busy, you see, that I forgot to go."

Fiona realized that Maddie and Nate were broke. "Oh,

that's all right. We can't stay anyway," she said hastily. "We . . . I . . . there's the shop and . . ."

Nick, ever gracious, stepped in. "Look, I wouldn't hear of you serving us anything, not when I've just arrived on Fee's doorstep with a whopping great hamper of food and two bottles of the widow Clicquot's finest. Won't you come share a bite with us instead? I insist. Really. I bought too much and I can't bear for it to be wasted. Not when there are all those starving children in . . . um" – he waved a hand – "oh, wherever the starving children are these days."

Fiona urged them to say yes, and finally they did. Back in the shop, Nick opened his hamper and pulled out caviar, lobster salad, chicken in aspic, smoked salmon, bread, fruit, and pretty little cakes. The hamper contained china plates, silverware, and crystal glasses for four, but there was food enough for twice that number. They used the counter for a table and as they ate, they talked. Nate and Maddie wanted to know all about Nick and Fiona and what they planned to do in the city. Then Nate lectured Fiona on the new science of advertising, on its power, its importance, and the necessity of getting one's name embedded in the public's consciousness. He told her she must advertise when she got the shop open again. She told him she would be their first paying customer and Nick said he would be their second.

As they were eating, the boys came back with a huge bag of doughnuts, which Fiona took away from them until they'd eaten some proper food. Ian raced upstairs for more plates. Seamie hugged Nick and told him how glad he was that he wasn't dead. "Don't ask," Fiona said at Nick's horrified expression. Seamie called him Father and Fiona had to explain to Nate and Maddie that it wasn't what it looked like. Mary came down, having fed Nell and put her down for a nap, and made Nick's acquaintance as he handed her a glass of champagne. Alec came in from the garden with a finished window box and marveled at how good the shop looked.

"Thank you, Alec," Fiona said fretfully, fixing him a plate. "I hope I'm not just cleaning it for the next owner."

Mary shushed her worries and Maddie, finished with her lunch, looked at the walls and said a creamy beige would look a lot nicer than the stark white that was on them now. She gave Fiona the address of a local paint shop and the name of the color she had in mind and Ian and Robbie volunteered to get it. She said the walls would have to be washed before they could be painted. She took a bucket Fiona had filled with soapy water, rolled up her sleeves, and started in. Fiona, touched, told her she didn't have to do that, but she shrugged and said if she didn't, she'd have to go back to work with her husband, and frankly, she'd rather wash walls. Feigning offense, Nate picked up a rag and began to polish the door handle. Nick, enthusiastically incompetent, grabbed the mop and started pushing it around, but only managed to make the floor dirtier.

As they laughed at him, Fiona felt the burdens she carried on her slender shoulders lighten a bit, and for the first time since she had arrived in New York she felt happy, truly happy. Maybe things hadn't worked out quite as planned, and maybe she didn't have an uncle to help her, but she had the wonderful Munros, especially Mary, who was so encouraging. And having her dearest Nick with her and her new friends – all of them following their own dreams – cheered and inspired her and made her take heart. If Maddie and Nate could risk everything on their business, if Nick could try and make a go of a gallery, then she could make a go of this shop.

26

"Good afternoon, Mr. Ellis, I'm Fiona Finnegan . . ." Too mealy-mouthed, Fiona thought. She paced nervously, her boot heels echoing on the marble floor of the bank president's antechamber. There was cold, shiny marble everywhere she looked – underfoot, on the ceiling, everywhere but on the walls; they were covered with murals of old Dutch merchants. One group was unloading a ship. Another was setting up a shop. A third was buying Manhattan from the Indians for what looked like two bracelets and a necklace. She tried again. "I'm Fiona Finnegan. Good afternoon, Mr. Ellis . . ." Still not right. "Mr. Ellis, I presume. I'm Fiona Finnegan. Good afternoon . . ."

"Are you quite sure you wouldn't like to sit down, Miss Finnegan?" Mr. Ellis's secretary, a Miss A. S. Miles, according to her nameplate, asked. "He may be a minute."

Fiona jumped at the sound of her voice. "No. No, thank you," she said, giving her a jittery smile. "I'll stand." Her hands were cold and her throat felt tight.

She was wearing her best clothes – a chocolate skirt and a pinstriped shirtwaist – waiting for them to make her feel confident. That's what Nick said good clothing did. She wore her long navy coat over the outfit, with a rose-patterned silk scarf tucked into the collar. Her hair was twisted up in an approximation of a style Nick had invented for her one afternoon on the boat when he was bored. The twist wasn't perfect – she'd been too anxious to fuss – but it would do.

Over the past week, she'd put nearly three hundred

dollars of her own money into her uncle's shop. Some of it had gone for things like a new meat cooler, paint, and new shelves. Some had gone to pay off the rest of his creditors. She hoped that clearing his debts would impress First Merchants and show them she was serious and capable.

She was staring out the window into the busy thoroughfare known as Wall Street when she heard Miss Miles say, "Miss Finnegan? Mr. Ellis will see you now."

Her stomach writhed like an eel. She walked into Franklin Ellis's office, a room appointed with dark wood paneling, Hudson Valley landscapes, and massive mahogany furniture. He was standing at his credenza. His back was to her, but his black suit, macassared hair, and the way he held an index finger up while he finished reading a document, gave her the impression of a severe and humorless man.

If only Michael were here, she thought, already intimidated. If only she didn't have to do this alone. She'd asked him to come with her last night – begged him – but he'd refused, the tosser. Even if he didn't want to set foot in the shop, he could've come to the bank with her. What did she know about any of this? Nothing! All she was sure of – because she'd looked at his payment book – was that her uncle's building had cost $15,000. Four years ago, he'd put $3,000 down and taken out a thirty year mortgage at six percent for the remainder. His payments were $72 a month. He'd stopped paying in November and now owed the bank $360, plus $25 in penalties. If Ellis asked about profits and percentages, if he wanted to know how much of her anticipated income the mortgage represented, or what her operating expenses were, she was sunk. I am going to make the biggest bloody hash of this, she told herself. He won't listen to me. He won't take me seriously. He won't . . .

Franklin Ellis turned around. Fiona smiled, extended her hand, and said, "Good afternoon, Mr. Fiona. I'm Finnegan Ellis." Oh, bloody hell! she thought. "No, I – I mean – I'm –"

"Have a seat, Miss Finnegan," Ellis said in clipped tones, gesturing to a chair in front of his desk. He ignored her outstretched hand. "I understand you're here to discuss one hundred sixty-four Eighth Avenue."

"Yes, sir," she said, trying to recover. "I have enough cash to pay you the three hundred eighty-five dollars my uncle owes. And I'd like you to consider letting me take over the responsibility for running his shop."

With effort, she calmed herself, focused her mind, and methodically began to make her case. Opening a small leather portfolio she'd borrowed from Maddie, she took out all the receipts from her uncle's vendors showing his balances paid and presented them for Ellis's inspection. Next she sketched out her plans for modest advertising: a half page in the local newspaper to run for three consecutive Sundays, because Sunday's edition was cheaper to advertise in than Saturday's. She showed him the ad – a fetching pen-and-ink sketch of the shop done by Maddie and Nate extolling its superior selection and service. The sketch would serve a double purpose; in addition to using it as an ad, she planned to have flyers made out of it with a coupon good for a free quarter pound of tea with any purchase of a dollar or more.

As she talked about her plans for the shop, Fiona completely forgot her nerves. She didn't see Ellis's eyes flicker to his watch. She didn't see them travel over her bosom. She didn't know that he wasn't even listening to her; he was thinking about his dinner plans. She didn't correctly read the expression on his face. She saw interest where there was only mild amusement – the sort one would feel while watching a performing dog bark out answers to sums.

Believing she had his attention emboldened Fiona. She talked on about the improvements she'd made: the new paint, the window boxes, the pretty lace valance for the window. She told him all about her ideas to trump the competition by offering home-baked goods, better-quality produce, and fresh flowers. She had even planned for a delivery service, figuring that if she could save the neighborhood women a bit of time at no extra charge, they'd shop at Finnegan's exclusively.

"So you see, Mr. Ellis," she concluded eagerly, her cheeks flushed, "I believe I can run my uncle's shop profitably and make the required payments in full every month."

Ellis nodded. "How old did you say you were, Miss Finnegan?"

"I didn't, but I'm eighteen."

"And have you ever run a shop before?"

"Well . . . I . . . not exactly . . . no, sir, I haven't."

"I appreciate your efforts on behalf of your uncle, Miss Finnegan, but I'm afraid you're a bit too young and inexperienced to take on the responsibility of a business. I'm sure you'll understand that I have the bank's interests to consider and I feel that the safest course of action in light of the present circumstances is still an auction."

"Begging your pardon, sir, but that doesn't make sense," she argued. "You're going to *lose* money on the auction. I'm offering to make up the back payments and continue to meet the terms of the loan. That's a six-percent profit. Surely, you'd rather make money than lose it. . . ."

"Our interview is concluded, Miss Finnegan. Good day," Ellis said icily, not pleased to have his business explained to him by an eighteen-year-old girl.

"But, Mr. Ellis –"

"Good day, Miss Finnegan."

Fiona gathered her papers and put them back in her portfolio. With dignity befitting a queen instead of a crushed young woman, she rose and extended her hand again, waiting this time until Ellis took it. Then she left his office, hoping her tears wouldn't fall until she was outside of it.

She was beaten. All her work of the last week was wasted. And the money she'd spent! Christ, she'd as good as thrown it away. How could she have been so stupid to think a bank would actually listen to her? She dreaded going home. She knew Mary would be waiting for her, hoping it had gone well. What would she tell her? She was counting on her. They all were. And after she broke the bad news, then she could begin what she'd dreaded the most – looking for a place to live, a job. Watching as the building was sold. Watching as her uncle became homeless, lost to the streets, a wild, muttering gutter drunk.

She fastened the clasp on her portfolio. Her head was down and she was unaware of the elegantly dressed man sitting in the leather chair just outside Ellis's door, his ankle resting on his knee. Tall, fortyish, and remarkably good-looking, he eyed her with interest and appreciation. He stubbed out the cigar he was holding, rose, and walked over to her.

"Ellis turned you down?"

Fiona, still having difficulty holding her tears in, nodded quickly.

"He's a bit of an old woman. Have a seat."

"I beg your pardon?"

"Sit. I overheard you. Your ideas are good. You're on target with the differentiation."

"The what?"

"Differentiation." He smiled. "Like the word? I coined it myself. It means setting yourself apart from the competition. Offering things they don't. I'll see what I can do."

He disappeared into Ellis's office, slamming the door behind him. Fiona, stunned, continued to stand exactly where he'd left her until Miss Miles told her to sit down.

"Who is that?" Fiona asked her.

"William McClane," she said reverently.

"Who?"

"McClane? Of McClane Mining and McClane Lumber and McClane Subterranean. Only one of the richest men in New York," she replied, in a tone that suggested Fiona must be a bumpkin not to know such a thing. "He made his first fortune in silver," she said in a hushed, girlish voice. "Then he went into logging. Now he's working on plans for New York's first underground railway. Rumor has it he's going into electricity and telephones, too."

Fiona had only the vaguest idea what a telephone was and no idea at all what electricity was, but she nodded, pretending she did.

"He owns First Merchants, too. And" – she leaned in closer to Fiona – "he's a widower. His wife died two years ago. Every society lady in town is after him."

Mr. Ellis's door opened again, silencing their conversation. Mr. McClane came out.

"You've got your shop," he briskly informed Fiona. "See Ellis about the details. And spend a little more on the advertising. Take a whole page if you can and run the ad on Saturdays, not Sundays, even if it costs more. That's when most of the men in your neighborhood get paid. You want your name fresh in people's minds when the money's there, not after it's gone."

Before Fiona could get a word out, he had tipped his hat to her and Miss Miles and left, leaving her standing there in his wake, staring after him, whispering the words, "Thank you."

27

All of the large terraced limestone houses on Albemarle Street in newly fashionable Pimlico were flawlessly maintained, their shutters and doors painted an identical glossy black, brass postboxes polished to a gleam, and flowers allotted suitable space in terra-cotta planters or ceramic urns. Each dwelling had a black gas lamp in front of it that now, at nine o'clock on a drizzly April evening, glowed brightly.

The houses spoke of a solid, commendable sameness that, if somewhat uninspired, was at least above reproach, a quality much desired by their occupants – newly minted members of a middle class keen to prove itself every bit as refined and respectable as its established old money neighbors in Belgravia and Knightsbridge. There was nothing brash, nothing out of place, nothing unseemly. There was no litter on the street, there were no vagrants or stray dogs. It was as quiet as a graveyard, as stifling as a coffin, and Joe Bristow despised the very sight of it.

He longed for the color and life of Montague Street. He missed coming home at night to the excited shrieks of his siblings, the taunting jokes of his mates, an impromptu football game played on the rough cobbles. Most of all, he missed walking up to number eight, to the black-haired girl who sat on her step playing with her brother or ignoring a pile of sewing. He missed calling her name, watching as she lifted her head, as her whole face broke into a smile. For him.

His carriage, a black calèche pulled by a handsome roan, both wedding gifts from his father-in-law, pulled up to the portico at the front of the house. His steps did not quicken as he neared his door, nor did his heart warm with anticipation at seeing his wife. His only hope was that she would already be asleep and the servants, too, whose presence in his home and his life he could not get used to. The sight of his agitated housekeeper pacing at the top of the steps told him this was not to be.

"Oh, Mr. Bristow! Thank God you're finally home, sir!" she cried.

"What is it, Mrs. Parrish? What are you doing out 'ere? Where's Mathison?"

"Gone to his pantry, sir, to look for a second key for your study."

"Why would he —"

Joe's words were cut off by the sound of glass shattering.

"It's Mrs. Bristow, sir. She's locked herself in your study and she won't come out," Mrs. Parrish said breathlessly. "I thought she was in bed. I had just gone up to my own room when I heard a crash. I ran back down . . . I . . . I don't know what happened . . . she just went mad! She was throwing your papers and smashing things. I couldn't stop her. I tried, but she pushed me out. Oh, please go up to her, sir! Hurry, before she does something to hurt the baby!"

Joe bolted up to the second floor. Millie was poorly and had been ever since they'd gotten back from their honeymoon over two months ago. Her pregnancy was a difficult one. She'd started to bleed last month and had nearly lost the baby. Her doctor had ordered her to stay in bed.

As he fumbled in his pocket for the key, he heard sobs coming from the other side of the door and a series of loud thumps, as if a pile of books had fallen over. He got the key in the door, opened it, and saw that his entire study had been ripped apart. Papers were all over the floor. A bookcase had gone over. The panes of his secretary were smashed. In the middle of the devastation stood Millie, her face streaked with tears, her blond hair loose, her belly protruding under her nightclothes. She held a sheaf of papers in her hand. He recognized them. They were reports from the private investigator he'd hired to find Fiona.

"Go back to bed, Millie. You know you're not supposed to be up."

"I couldn't sleep," she said tearfully, "so I got up and came in here to see if you were home. I found these. I saw them on your desk. You're looking for her, aren't you? She moved or . . . or left London or something and you're trying to find her."

Joe didn't answer her. She hadn't seen them on his desk because he'd locked them inside his secretary. He didn't think it wise to argue that point now, though. He knew very well what she was like when she was angry. "Come on, Millie, you know what the doctor –"

"Answer me, damn you!" she shrieked, throwing the papers at him.

"I'm not going to talk about this now," he said forcefully. "You're too upset. You've got to calm down or you'll 'urt the baby."

"You're sleeping with her, aren't you? You must be, you don't sleep with me. Not once in five months! All this time you've been telling me work's the reason you're home late every night, but it's not, is it? It's that filthy little whore!" She flew at Joe and beat her fists against his chest. "You stop it!" she cried. "You stop seeing her!"

Joe grabbed her by her wrists. "That's enough!" he shouted.

She writhed and twisted, trying to break free of his grasp, cursing at him. Then, all of a sudden, she did stop. She winced, then stood perfectly still.

"What is it?" he asked her.

She looked at him with large, frightened eyes. Her hands went to her belly. A whimper rose from her throat and she doubled over. Joe put his arm around her. He tried to get her to straighten but she wouldn't. She cried out twice, digging her nails into his arm.

300

"Shhh, it's all right," he said, trying to soothe her. "Just take a deep breath, there's a girl. It's going to be fine. It's just a cramp. The doctor said you might get them, remember? 'E said not to worry about them."

But it wasn't just a cramp. As she took a few steps forward, still trying to straighten, he saw glistening ruby droplets soaking into the carpet beneath her feet.

"Millie, listen to me," he said, trying to keep his voice calm. "I'm going to call the doctor. 'E'll come see you and everything will be fine. Let's get you back in bed now, all right?"

She nodded and started to walk toward the door. Another pain gripped her, bending her double again. It was then that she saw the crimson stains on the toes of her white slippers. "Oh, no," she cried. "Oh, God . . . please, no . . ." Within seconds her cries had turned to shrieks.

Joe picked her up and carried her out of the study. A frightened Mrs. Parrish was standing in the corridor, a candle in her hand. "Get Dr. Lyons!" he barked at her. " 'Urry!"

Joe sat on the wooden bench outside Millie's hospital room, his head in his hands. He'd listened to her cries – and her screams – throughout the small dark hours until they'd finally, mercifully, stopped just as the dawn was breaking.

Dr. Lyons was with her now, and two nurses, and her father. She had not wanted him near her and he didn't blame her. This was all his fault. He should have come home early yesterday, brought her flowers, had dinner with her. That's what husbands were supposed to do. He never should have fought with her. And he never should have looked for Fiona.

The morning after their wedding night – when he'd walked out of their hotel suite to drink himself silly – he'd woken to a vicious hangover, a sobbing wife, and the knowledge that he could not live this way. He did not love Millie and could not bring himself to sleep with her, but he could at least behave in a kind and considerate manner toward her. They'd left for France that afternoon and he'd endured his endless honeymoon – Millie's face, her voice, her mindless chatter, and her constant entreaties to make love – as best he could. He was polite and solicitous of her during the day, escorting her to shops, museums, cafés, the theater – wherever she wanted to go. But at night he would retreat to the separate room he'd insisted upon at every hotel in every city they visited, for peace, relief, and the space to grieve for what he'd done and all that he'd lost.

At first, she was merely wounded by his lack of attention. As time went on, she became incensed. His rejection hurt her vanity. She wanted him and she was not used to being denied. A week after they'd left London, they'd had the first of many horrible fights. At the Crillon in Paris, in the hallway outside their rooms. They were retiring for the night after dining at the Café de la Paix. Millie wanted him to come to her room. He refused. Again. She accused him of being cold to her. She stormed and wept and told him that this wasn't how married people were with each other. He bore her tirade silently, keeping the truth of his feelings to himself, not wanting to be cruel. She raged on, reminding him that he had not been cold with her on Guy Fawkes night and demanded to know why he had changed.

"You didn't mind my kisses then," she'd said reproachfully. "And you couldn't wait to put your hands on me. You told me you wanted me that night, Joe. You told me you loved me."

"I never told you I loved you, Millie," he'd quietly replied. "We both know that."

By the time they'd returned home, relations between them had deteriorated into constant arguments. Joe left at dawn most mornings and came home after dark to avoid her, throwing himself into his work. Buckingham Palace had awarded Peterson's a Royal Warrant. The business grew, nearly doubling its volume. Tommy was ecstatic. He was as happy with Joe as Millie was furious with him. But

Joe found only distraction in his work, not solace.

His mother wrote him repeatedly after he returned home. She wanted him to come and see her, she needed to talk to him. There were things she had to tell him. But he would not go. He didn't want to visit his family; they'd only see how miserable he was. He couldn't bear the thought of going back to Montague Street, of seeing Fiona's house and the places where they used to walk. Places where they'd talked of their dreams, their future. Places where he'd taken her in his arms and kissed her. His mum came to the house a few times, and to his office, but he was always out.

All he wanted was to see Fiona. Just see her. To look into her eyes again. To see himself there, no one else, and know she still loved him. To hear her say his name. But he knew he had no right and he'd promised her he would not, and for a long time he was able to honor that promise. Until one March evening when his need for her had overwhelmed him and he'd gone back to Whitechapel. His heart ached at the memory of it now. If only he'd known what happened, if only he'd known what she'd been through. He remembered it so clearly, the sickening shock of it . . .

"Joe, lad, are you still here? It's four clock!" Tommy Peterson said. "I thought I told you to go home early. Spend some time with your wife."

"I just wanted to finish up these accounts . . ." he began.

"They can wait. Go home and enjoy your evening. That's an order."

Joe forced a smile, thanked Tommy, and said he would. As soon as his father-in-law left, he let the smile drop. Going home was the last thing he wanted to do. He'd come home late last night to find Millie sitting at the dining room table with platters of cold, congealed food in front of her. He was supposed to have joined her for dinner. He'd said he would and he'd forgotten. She'd picked up a platter of salmon and heaved it at his head. God only knew what tonight would bring.

He gathered his papers and called for his carriage. As he was riding west, he envisioned the long evening in store for him. He slumped back in his seat, pressing the heels of his hands against his eyes. He felt like a prisoner in his own life. He couldn't face Albemarle Street, that house, Millie. He groaned, wishing he could shout and yell until he was hoarse. Wishing he could kick the shit out of the carriage. Wishing he could run away and disappear into the streets of London. He opened his eyes, loosened his tie, and unbuttoned his collar. It was stuffy in the carriage, hard to breathe. He needed to get out. He needed to get some air. He needed Fiona.

Before he could talk himself out of it, he shouted at his driver to pull over. When the man stopped, he said, "I'm getting out 'ere. Take my things 'ome. Tell Mrs. Bristow I'll be late."

"Very good, sir."

He hailed a hackney, told the driver to take him to Whitechapel, and gave him the address of Burton's. If he was lucky, he'd make it there before quitting time and he could catch her coming out. She would be angry with him – he had to be prepared for that – but maybe, just maybe, she'd talk to him.

He arrived at the factory just before six. He waited by the doors, pacing and fidgeting. Finally the whistle blew, the doors opened, and the tea girls came streaming out. He searched the faces, but hers wasn't among them. He waited until the last girl had gone and then he waited some more, in case she was sweeping up or gathering her things. But then the foreman came out and locked the doors behind him and there was no more point in waiting.

He began to feel uneasy but decided there must be some explanation. He would try Jackson's. Maybe she'd left Burton's to work at the pub full-time. But she wasn't there. And neither the man behind the bar nor the girl cleaning tables had heard of her. The girl told him the Jacksons were out right now visiting Mrs. Jackson's poorly mum, but they'd be back in an hour or so if he cared to wait. He did not.

He was more than uneasy now. He knew Fiona had been sick on the day of his wedding. A fever, his mum had told him. What if she hadn't recovered? What if she was poorly and unable to work? Panicking, he broke into a run and headed for Adams Court. Mrs. Finnegan would have at him and Charlie would want to kick his arse. They might not let him see her. He didn't care. They'd tell him if she was all right. He had to know she was all right. She has the money, our savings, he told himself. It would've been enough to see her family through. Oh, please, please, let her be all right, he prayed. He shot through the brick passageway that led from Varden Street to Adams Court, down the narrow walkway, and was just about to knock on number twelve when the door opened and a startled young woman with a baby in her arms asked him what he wanted.

"I need to see the Finnegans," he said, panting. "Fiona. Is she 'ome?"

The woman looked at him as if he were mad. "The Finnegans?"

"Aye. Can you get Fiona for me, missus?"

"Who are you, lad?"

"My name's Joe Bristow. I'm Fiona's . . . I'm a friend of 'ers."

"I . . . I don't know 'ow to tell you this, but the Finnegans . . . they don't live 'ere anymore."

Joe's heart filled with dread. "Where did they go? Did something 'appen? Something 'appened, didn't it? Is Fiona all right?"

"You'd better come inside."

"No, tell me what 'appened!" he shouted, wild-eyed with fear.

"It's better if you come in," the woman said. "Please." She grabbed his sleeve and led him down a short hallway to a room at the back of the house. She bade him sit on the only chair in the room and she sat down on the bed, her baby on her lap. "I'm Lucy Brady," she said. "I used to be Kate's neighbor, before –" She shook her head, upset. "I can't believe you didn't 'ear about it or read about it. It was in all the papers."

" 'Ear about what? You've got to tell me, Mrs. Brady, please."

Lucy swallowed. "There was a murder. It was the Ripper," she began. " 'E killed a woman at number ten, Frances Sawyer. It was very late at night, but the police think Kate saw 'im. She was on 'er way to the doctor's, 'er baby was ill. Jack . . . 'e . . . 'e killed 'er, too. Oh, Lord, I'm sorry to be the one telling you this."

Joe's whole body began to shake. He felt a terror like he had never known. One that turned his blood, his bones, his very heart, to sand. "Did 'e . . . did Fiona . . ."

"She was the one that found 'er mother." Lucy closed her eyes. "The poor lass, I'll never forget that night as long as I live."

"Where is she now?" he asked, weak with relief.

"Last I 'eard, she went to live with a friend of the family. 'E's a police constable."

"Roddy. Roddy O'Meara."

"Aye, that sounds right. 'E was looking after 'er and 'er little brother."

"What about Charlie? And the baby?"

"Dead, both of them. The baby right after 'er mother. And the lad soon after. 'E came 'ome from a fight, saw 'is mother, and ran off. They found 'is body in the river."

Joe covered his face with his hands. "My God," he whispered. "What 'ave I done to 'er? I left 'er 'ere in this shit'ole. Left 'er to this . . ."

"Are you all right, Mr. Bristow?" Lucy asked.

Joe didn't hear her. He stood up, dazed, barely able to breathe. "I've got to find 'er . . ." he said. He took a step toward the door. His vision faded. His legs buckled and he collapsed.

*   *   *

"You've a visitor, Mr. O'Meara. A lad. 'E's waiting for you upstairs."

From where he was sitting, two steps above the landing to Roddy's flat, Joe heard Roddy and his landlady talking in the downstairs hallway. He heard Roddy's heavy tramp on the steps and then the man was on the landing. He was wearing his constable's uniform and carrying groceries. He seemed to have aged since Joe'd last seen him. The loss of Paddy and the rest of the Finnegans must have grieved him deeply. Joe knew that they had been more than friends to him. They were his family. The only one he had. Feelings of sorrow, guilt, and remorse, his constant companions now, rose up inside him. He hadn't eaten or slept since he'd seen Lucy Brady yesterday. This was all his fault. All of it.

" 'Ello, Roddy."

"Evening," Roddy said. His expression told Joe he was not pleased to see him. "You look like shite, lad, I don't mind telling you," he said. "That wife of yours feed you?" He opened the door to his flat and ushered him in. He motioned for him to sit, but Joe remained standing.

"Roddy, I . . . I need to see Fiona. Is she 'ere?"

"No," Roddy replied, taking off his jacket and hanging it on the back of a chair.

"Do you know where she is?"

"No."

Joe didn't believe him. "Come on, Roddy."

"I said I don't bloody know where she is!"

"You don't know? You looked after 'er, took care of 'er."

Roddy turned, skewering him with the anger in his eyes. "Aye, I did. And that's more than I can say for some!"

Joe looked at the floor. "Look, Roddy . . . I know I'm a bastard. I don't need you to tell me. I just need to know she's all right. I just want to see 'er. Tell me where she is. Please."

"Lad, I'm telling you the truth. I don't know where she is."

Joe was about to argue further when he saw that the anger had left Roddy's face and a worried look had taken its place. Something was wrong.

"What is it?" he asked. "What's going on?"

"I wish I knew." Roddy sat down at his table and poured himself a glass of ale from a stoneware jug. "I have to say, lad, I'm very disappointed to see you. And not only because I don't care for you." He tipped the jug toward him, but Joe shook his head. "You waiting for a bus? Sit down." Joe did as he was told and Roddy continued. "Fiona was here. She and Seamie both."

Joe nodded. "I saw Lucy Brady yesterday. She told me what 'appened."

"She stayed with me after her mother was killed. It took a while till she was back on her feet, but after a few weeks she was managing again. She was talking about looking for work and a room of her own, and then I get home one night and there's a note on the table saying she's left. Right out of the blue. It said she got some money from Burton's – compensation money for Paddy's death – and that she wanted to leave quick-like, with no long good-byes. She didn't say where she was going."

"That doesn't sound like 'er. Why wouldn't she want you to know where she'd gone?"

"At first I reckoned it was because she'd taken off to be with you and didn't want me to find out, knowing full well I'd stop her. But you sitting here puts paid to that theory."

"What do you think now?"

Roddy took a swallow of his beer and set the glass down. "I don't know. None of it makes any bloody sense."

"Roddy, she's all alone somewhere," Joe said anxiously. "We've got to find 'er."

"I've tried! I've got all the men at my station looking. I managed to get a description of her and Seamie to practically every station in the city, but I've heard not'ing. Nobody's seen hide nor hair of them."

"What about a private detective?"

"I t'ought about that but I haven't got the money."

"I do. Give me a name. I'll 'ire 'im tonight. She 'as to be in London. It's not like she would've taken a train somewhere, she wouldn't know where to go. She'd never even been on a bus before I took 'er to Covent Garden. She can't 'ave gone far."

Roddy wrote down a name and address on a slip of paper and handed it to Joe, telling him to make sure he told the man that P. C. O'Meara sent him. He told him to come see him the minute he heard anything. He walked Joe to the door and though he didn't take his hand, he wished him luck. And for the briefest of seconds, Joe thought he saw something besides anger and worry in Roddy's brown eyes. He thought he saw an expression of sadness. For him.

At ten o'clock at night, the outlying stalls of the Covent Garden market were eerily silent. The round willow baskets the porters used to carry produce were piled high; a few carts stood empty. Here and there, broken flowers and crushed fruit littered the streets and the air was pungent with the smell of rotted vegetables. It always amazed Joe, who was walking back to his office after a late dinner with a client, that a place as hellishly noisy as the market was in the morning could ever be so still, so deserted. As he crossed a narrow lane and walked through an open arcade into a large cobbled piazza, he could smell the scent of horses from a nearby stable. He heard one whinny and kick against its stall. A rat in its hay, he thought. Wynne, his father's horse, hated them.

"Joe. Joe Bristow," a voice suddenly called from the darkness.

Joe stopped. He hadn't seen a soul when he entered the square.

"Over 'ere."

He turned around and saw a man leaning against one of the arcade's iron columns. The figure pushed itself off and walked out of the shadows. Joe recognized him. It was Stan Christie. A lad from Whitechapel. They'd been in the same class as youngsters until the day their teacher decided to discipline Stan with a cane, and Stan, at the tender age of twelve, had ripped it out of the man's hand and beaten him unconscious with it.

" 'Ow's things?" Stan asked, sauntering toward him.

"Smashing. You're a little far afield tonight, aren't you?"

"Aye. I came all this way just to see you."

"I'm touched, mate. I didn't know you cared."

Stan walked with his arms clasped behind his back like a professor or a priest. Since he was neither, Joe was certain he was concealing something. A club. A knife. Explosives. One never knew with Stan.

"Making some inquiries, I am. For the guv'nor," he said. His right hand came out from behind his back. He touched his finger to the side of his nose and gave Joe a knowing look.

"Oh, aye? Which guv'nor would that be? The prime minister? The Prince of Wales?"

"You want to watch your mouth, lad. Mr. Sheehan don't take no gyp."

Sheehan. Bowler Sheehan. Jesus. He had no idea Stan worked for him.

"What does Sheehan want with me?" he asked, keeping his voice even.

" 'E wants to know where the Finnegan girl is. Everyone knows you were sweet on 'er before you put Peterson's daughter up the pole, so I was thinking you might know."

"What's Fiona to 'im?" Joe asked angrily, his apprehension gone. He didn't like Sheehan's interest in Fiona. Not one bit. Stan was closer now and Joe wished to God he had his clasp knife on him. Or the pry bar he used on fruit crates. A razor. A bunch of keys he could thread through his fingers. Christ, he'd take a fucking corkscrew.

"Mr. Sheehan asks the questions, Joe. 'E don't answer them."

"Oh, aye? Well, 'ere's 'is answer: Tell 'im 'e can go shit in 'is big black bowler 'at. 'Ow's that?"

Stan chuckled, then, a split second later, swung the cosh he'd been hiding behind his back. Joe had been expecting it; he ducked the blow. The club missed his head and clipped his shoulder. Swearing at the pain, he drove his head into Stan's face and was gratified to hear a sickening crack as his nose shattered. Stan shrieked. His hands flew up to his nose, leaving his body open. Joe landed a savage kidney punch. Stan dropped the cosh. Joe picked it up, slid it under his throat, and jerked it hard.

"You move and I'll choke the life out of you, I swear I will . . ."

"All right, all right . . ." he rasped, holding up his bloodied hands.

"What does Sheehan want with Fiona?"

Stan didn't answer. Joe pulled the cosh tighter. Stan's hands scrabbled at it; he dropped to his knees. He was choking. Joe eased the pressure. That was a mistake; Stan had been faking. He grabbed Joe's arms and flipped him over his head. Joe landed hard, smacking his head against a cobble. The bright lights in his eyes blinded him for a few seconds; he tried to get up but faltered. Stan was standing over him now, threatening to cave his skull in if he didn't tell him where Fiona was. Joe, lying on his left side, still had the cosh in his hand. He knew he had about two seconds to make use of it or they'd find him here in the morning, his head crushed like a melon. With a yell, he sat up and slammed the club into Stan's kneecap, eliciting a bloodcurdling scream. Stan had had enough. Promising Joe he'd kill him the next time he saw him, he staggered off.

Joe got to his feet. He wanted to give chase, but his legs were too shaky. His head was throbbing. He touched it, wincing as his fingers found a goose egg. He had to get to Roddy and tell him what happened. This was bad news. If Stan was ready to beat the life out of him on the mere suspicion that he knew where Fiona was, what would he do to her when he found her? How the hell had she gotten tangled up with Sheehan, of all people? And why? He'd have to get to Henry Benjamin, too, the private detective he'd hired, and tell him to speed up the search. He'd met with him two days ago. Benjamin said it was unlikely Fiona had gone far. He was confident he'd be able to find her in a week or two. That was too long. Joe wanted her found tomorrow. Fiona was smart, she was tough; but Bowler Sheehan was a damn sight tougher.

"That's the hardest thing, you know," Millie said. "Finding a good baby nurse. I've seen ten already and I wouldn't let any of them mind a cat, never mind a baby. You can't be too careful. I liked the last woman, but Mrs. Parrish saw her put biscuits in her pocket when I went out of the room. She didn't know she was watching. You can't have a sneaky nurse. God knows what she'd do if my back was turned. Sally Ennis said she caught her nurse putting gin in her baby's milk. Can you imagine?"

Joe lifted his head from the balance sheet he was reading. "No, I can't," he said, trying his best to sound interested.

"I don't know what I'm going to do," she said anxiously, putting her needlework down. "The agency said they'd send more women over, but what if I don't find someone in time? What if the baby comes and I haven't got a nurse?"

"Millie, you'll find someone. You've got plenty of time. Your aunt will come and stay and she'll 'elp, too. She'll find you a nurse if need be. Don't fret over it. What you need to do is finish that christening gown. The baby can't be christened in 'is nappies, can 'e?" Joe tried to sound positive. He knew what was really bothering her and he didn't want her dwelling on it.

"You're right," she said. She smiled bravely and he was relieved to see it.

Four days ago, after lifting a heavy vase down from a high shelf, she had suddenly started to bleed. Her doctor had been sent for. He managed to stanch the bleeding and

312

save the baby, but he said the risk of a miscarriage still existed. He'd confined her to bed and instructed that she was to have no physical strain or emotional upsets whatsoever. Looking at her now, in the waning light of a Sunday afternoon, Joe saw how drawn she looked. There were dark circles under her eyes. She was far too pale. He felt sorry for her. It pained him to see her suffer.

She had felt uncomfortable earlier and had sent Olive, her maid, to his study to ask him if he might sit with her and keep her company until she fell asleep. He had agreed, bringing the ledgers he was working on with him and pulling up a chair next to her bed. He was trying hard to be a better husband to her, to be a comfort.

She chattered on about the christening gown and other clothing she was making for the baby. He tried his best to pay attention and take part in the conversation, but it was hard. He was so distracted. Last night he'd met with Benjamin again. The man had walked into the pub where Joe was waiting. "Recognize this?" he'd asked, dropping something into his hand. It was the blue stone from the river. The one he'd given Fiona.

Benjamin said he'd gotten it at a pawnshop near Roddy's flat. Not only had the pawnbroker remembered a girl matching Fiona's description, he remembered that she'd traded the stone for cash and a traveling bag, and that she'd had a young boy with her. He said she'd also pawned a gold ring with a tiny sapphire, but he'd already sold that. Benjamin had to pay five quid to get the stone. The pawnbroker knew what he had – an ancient scarab, probably dropped from the ring of a conquering Roman noble as he brought his fleet up the Thames.

Joe had paid Benjamin for the stone. He'd closed his fingers around it as the detective finished speaking, knowing for certain then that Fiona was no longer in London. That she was truly gone. But where? Benjamin also felt she had left the city. He would, too, he said, if Sheehan were after him.

That was going to make it a lot harder to find her. She had no family, no friends outside of London, which meant there was no single, logical destination for her. She could be anywhere. Benjamin told him not to give up hope. He was sure someone besides the pawnbroker had seen her leaving Whitechapel. He was going to talk to the hackney drivers who plied the Commercial Road to see if one of them remembered her and, if they were really lucky, where he'd taken her.

Joe knew Benjamin was doing his best, but the waiting was killing him. The knowledge that the person he loved most was alone in the world, with no one to turn to, maybe in terrible trouble, occupied his every waking hour.

He looked at Millie, propped up in a confection of lacy pillows and bolsters, working her needle in and out of the white silk of the christening gown, and was once again seized by the unreality of his life. None of this was supposed to be happening. He wasn't supposed to be here in this house, married to this woman. He was supposed to be in Whitechapel, married to Fiona. They would have just opened their first shop and they'd be working every minute of every day to make it a success. It would be hard, a constant struggle, but it would be everything he'd ever wanted. Just to sit across the table from her at night as they talked about the day. To sleep in the same bed with her, make love to her in the dark, slowly and sweetly. To hear someone call her Mrs. Bristow. To dandle their baby on his knee and listen to his mother and hers argue about whose side of the family the child favored.

"Joe, dear? Which do you like better? Annabelle or Lucy?"

Millie's voice shattered his lovely daydream and brought him back to reality. "What, Millie? I'm sorry, I was thinking about work."

"I asked which name you like better if the baby's a girl. If it's a boy, I'd like to call him Thomas, after my father. Thomas Bristow. I think it has a nice ring to it. I'm *sure*

314

it's a boy. I just have this feeling. I –" Millie stopped talking and pressed her hands to her belly.

Joe shot forward in his chair; the ledger slid off his lap. "Millie, what is it? Is something wrong? Should I get the doctor?" he asked, alarmed.

She looked at him. "No . . ." she said slowly, a smile of wonder and joy breaking across her face. "I'm fine. The baby kicked, Joe. I felt it. I *felt* it." She reached for his hand and pressed it against herself. He felt nothing. She was looking at him, but her gaze was inward. "There!" she whispered excitedly. "Did you feel it?" He hadn't. She pressed his hand in harder and suddenly he *did* feel it. An impossibly small elbow. Or a knee, or maybe a heel. A tiny, defiant flutter. The baby – his baby – was suddenly *real*.

Strong, roiling emotions ripped through him – fatherly feelings, fierce and protective, and feelings of utter desolation. He knew with an awful and ancient certainty that he would love this child. And he knew that he wished it had never come into being. His future – as this baby's father, as Millie's husband – rose up in front of him. Tears came to his eyes, tears of love and grief for this baby that was his, but not his and Fiona's, for this hopeless, empty life. He tried to blink them away. He heard Millie, her silk nightgown rustling, move toward him.

"Ssshhh," she whispered, kissing him. "It's all right. You'll love the baby, Joe. You will. And the baby will love you. He does already. And maybe, when he comes, you'll love me. And then we'll be a family and everything will be all right."

"Mr. Bristow?"

The sound of the doctor's voice pulled Joe out of the past and into the present. His head snapped up. " 'Ow is she?" he asked.

"She's had a very hard time of it, but she'll be fine."

He felt relief wash over him. "And the baby?"

315

"I'm afraid the baby was stillborn. We couldn't stop the contractions. It was a mercy he went as he did."

"It was a boy," Joe said dully.

The doctor nodded. He put a hand on Joe's shoulder. "It was too early in the term for an infant to survive outside the womb. He would only have suffered. There will be others for her. In time."

"Should I go in to 'er?" Joe asked. He started to get to his feet.

Dr. Lyons kept a steady pressure on his shoulder, forcing him to stay seated. "No, no," he said quickly. "That's not a good idea. Not just yet. Mr. Peterson will be out momentarily. He'll advise you." The doctor went off in search of some breakfast, saying he would be back to check on Millie in an hour or so.

Joe slumped back on the bench, too empty to weep. The baby was stillborn. Like everything else in his life, all his dreams, his hopes. Like everything he'd always wanted to be – good, kind, upstanding. A loving husband and father. Ever since he had felt the little thing kick, he had hoped to hold it and care for it and love it. Its tiny, questing movements had seemed like a promise that something good would come out of all the misery. But now the baby was dead. Because of him.

The door to Millie's room opened and his father-in-law came out.

Joe stood and faced him. "Does she want to see me?" he asked.

Tommy stood motionless, his fists clenched at his side, his face frozen in an expression of cold fury. "The only reason I'm not going to kill you right here is because of Millie," he finally said. "She told everything. How it's been between you two. About the girl. Fiona. I don't know if she meant to. She was delirious from the pain and the chloroform. She told me about Guy Fawkes night . . . and her part in it. A hard thing to hear." He looked at the floor, his jaw working, then at Joe again. "I want you out of the

316

house. Out of our lives. Take what's yours and go. There will be a divorce on the grounds of adultery. Yours. If you contest it, I'll –"

"I won't," Joe said. Divorce, he thought. He would have his freedom. Should he feel glad of that? He didn't. He felt sorry and ashamed. No one got divorced. It was a drastic, ugly, scandalous thing and the fact that Tommy had demanded it only indicated how much he despised him. He, Tommy Peterson, the man whose approval had once meant the world to him. Joe picked up his jacket. He glanced at the door. "I'd like to tell 'er I'm sorry," he said.

Tommy shook his head. "Leave her be."

As Joe walked down the corridor, Tommy shouted at him. "Why? Why, you stupid sod? You had it made. You had it all – everything you could ever want."

Joe turned and gave him a sad, bitter smile. "Everything, Tommy, and nothing at all."

28

"And I want two lamb chops . . . those there, the big ones, yes . . . a pound of pearl onions, a bunch of parsley, and half a pound of sweet butter. You got the porridge oats, didn't you?"

"Yes, Mrs. Owens," Fiona said, scrambling after her customer as she moved through the crowded shop. "Seamie, luv, bring up some more apples," she shouted at her brother. He dumped the lemons he was carrying into a bin and hurried back down the cellar stairs.

She felt someone take her elbow. "I want some of your tea, luv. I have the coupon from your flyer . . . the one for a quarter pound? You won't run out, will you?" It was Julie Reynolds, who lived across the street.

"Miss! Miss!" another voice called. "I want some of the Madeira cake before it's gone!"

"Right away, ma'am," Fiona shouted back. She turned back to Mrs. Reynolds. "Not to worry, Mrs. Reynolds. I've two more chests in the basement. Just give me one minute."

Fiona heard a sharp rapping. "Young man, can you get me some flour, please!" It was an elderly woman knocking the handle of her cane against the counter.

"Right away, my lovely," Nick said, careening toward Fiona. He weighed out a pound of apples as she dug in a basket for pearl onions. They traded quick, harried smiles. "Lord, the place is crawling! I've a wad of coupons in my pocket from your flyer and reams more in the till. We're going to need another tea chest up from the basement soon. How many ads did you run?"

"Just the one in the little neighborhood paper!"

"All this business from one little ad? Nate's right. Advertising *does* work!"

He shot off to ring up the apples and Fiona blessed him for being here to help. She would've been lost without him. He was so charming and chatty. The ladies loved him and he loved playing shopkeeper. It was another game, a prank, and Nick, an overgrown child, delighted in it.

She weighed and wrapped the lamb chops, the butter and the pearl onions, stacked them next to the bag of porridge oats, and tossed a bunch of parsley on top of it all. "Have you tried our ginger biscuits?" she asked Mrs. Owens, handing her one. "They're very nice. I can't keep Seamie out of them," she added, knowing from Mary that Mrs. Owens was a fond mother to her five children, hoping to add a little more to her bill.

"Homemade, are they?" the woman asked, savoring the bite she'd taken.

"Just this morning. Mary Munro did them. She made all the baked goods."

"Oh, I know Mary! She's a wonderful baker. Give me half a dozen. They'll keep the kiddies quiet. I need a quart of milk and two pounds of flour, too. And don't forget my tea, Fiona! Here's my coupon. It is good? I don't want any rubbish."

"It's an excellent tea, Mrs. Owens. It's T-G-F-O-P," she said, with a meaningful nod. "Tippy Golden Flowery Orange Pekoe." She'd seen Joe do that. Drop some rarefied term into the conversation. It implied a shared, superior understanding of the product, made a customer feel in the know.

"I saw that on the chest. What does it mean?"

"It's the tea's grade. It tells you you've got nice large leaves with lots of bud. It means it's all new growth, plucked from the top of the bush, not a lot of tough, old leaves from down the branches." She lowered her voice. "There's some who wouldn't know the difference," she said, glancing around, "but those who do, insist on the better grade."

Mrs. Owens nodded knowingly. "Give us our quarter pound, lass. Lord knows how long it's been since I had good tea – years!"

Fiona smiled at Mrs. Owens's enthusiasm. She shared it. If there was one thing she could not abide, it was bad tea. Frustrated by the offerings of her uncle's supplier, she'd closed their account with him and trekked down to South Street, to Millard's, her friend Stuart's importing firm, and had him devise a custom blend of Indian tea. She told him what she wanted, and using Assam leaves from three estates, Stuart had concocted a blend that was full-bodied and brisk, with a bright, malty character. He was glad to do it. He was having difficulty moving his Indian tea. His American customers only wanted to buy what they knew, which was China tea. His Indian tea was better, but he hadn't been able to sway them. Fiona, however, would have nothing else. She immediately recognized its quality. She'd known that her customers would like it, too. Thanks to Mary, she'd met many of them before today. Young workingwomen, or wives of dockers and factory men – almost all immigrants – they were partial to good tea. It was the one small luxury their workaday lives afforded them.

Fiona weighed Mrs. Owens's tea and plunked the bag on the counter with the rest of her things. Then she wrapped her ginger biscuits, weighed out two pounds of flour, and ladled milk from a large two-handled dairy can into the quart-size jug Mrs. Owens had handed her. "Will that be all?" she asked, starting to total her purchases.

The woman was casting a longing glance at the shop window. "Oh, those new potatoes look so good. Let me have two pounds and a bunch of asparagus, too. Mr. Owens is partial to it. I think that'll do for now. I'll barely be able to carry what I've got."

"Would you like this delivered?"

"Delivered? Finnegan's delivers now?"

"Yes, ma'am. All day Saturday and afternoons during the week when my delivery boys get out of school."

"How much?"

"No charge for *you,* Mrs. Owens." There was no charge for anyone, but why mention it?

"Well, yes, then!" the woman said, flattered and delighted. "And give me a bunch of those pretty daffodils, too. I'll take them with me since I don't have anything else to carry. And see that those boys mind my milk jug!"

Mrs. Owens paid for her goods and left. Without missing a beat, Fiona turned to her next customer. "Now then, Mrs. Reynolds, thank you so much for waiting. What can I get for you?" And after Mrs. Reynolds was taken care of, there was still a steady stream of women to attend to. Fiona was being run off her feet and she was ecstatic. People were buying! They purchased milk and bread and flour – the staples – but they also bought the more expensive items: bunches of fresh-cut flowers, Mary's biscuits, and new spring vegetables right out of the window!

Fiona had agonized over that window. She'd left it to the last minute, only completing it at six that morning. She'd never arranged a window before and hadn't known where to start, but she knew it had to be beautiful and so eye-catching that it pulled people in off the street. Standing alone in the middle of the shop, she'd looked around at all the goods that had been delivered – oats, pickles, milk, flour – wondering how on earth to create a display from them. As she saw the sun's first rays brighten the street, she started to panic. Then she heard Joe's voice in her head, saying, "It's all in the presentation, Fee. That's what makes punters want to buy." Her eyes came to rest on a crate of asparagus – she hadn't planned to buy it, it was dear – but the veg man convinced her, saying that people craved fresh vegetables after the long winter and would pay extra for them. Her gaze moved to the new potatoes, so little and rosy in their tender jackets . . . the golden loaves of bread delivered by the baker's boy . . . the daffodils that Alec had procured . . . and the duck eggs, brown and speckled in their hay-lined crate . . . and then she had a brainstorm.

Tearing upstairs, she took a white tablecloth from Molly's linen closet. She grabbed a green vase from the sitting room and a blue-and-white-spattered enamel bowl from the kitchen and ran back downstairs. In the shop's cellar, she dug up an empty fruit crate, a big round biscuit tin, and a few baskets, climbed in the window and got to work. When she had finished, she went outside to view the result.

What she had wrought was a perfect picture of spring. A burst of bright yellow daffodils in the green vase stood in the center of the window atop the biscuit tin, which she'd covered with the white linen cloth. Behind them, standing in a tall wicker basket, were long golden loaves of bread. Next to them, on top of the wooden crate, was another basket, piled high with new potatoes. Next to that, asparagus bundles tied with twine stood in the blue-and-white bowl. And in front, in a small hay nest she'd made, were six perfect duck eggs. Rustic and inviting, Fiona's display was utterly unlike any other shop window, stuffed as they were with tins of boot black, faded packets of soap, and tired-looking boxes of sweets. Her little tableau spoke of the warm, green days to come. Of tulips poking up through the moist earth and tiny buds on trees. It was heartening and cheerful and delighted passersby fed up with winter fruit and old potatoes.

The window illustrated for Fiona the first and most important rule of retailing, one she had learned from Joe, from the markets and shop windows of Whitechapel, and one she understood instinctively: Create a desire for something and people will buy it.

A woman staring at the window came in, followed by a breathless Ian. Fiona pointed at Mrs. Owens's order and gave him the address. He quickly packed the groceries in a crate and was off. Robbie came in as he was leaving and Fiona gave him Mrs. Reynolds's order to deliver. She thought, with irritation, how very helpful it would have been to have her uncle working alongside her as well, instead of pickling himself at Whelan's. She'd dragged him in yesterday, and made him fix the sticky till drawer and show her how to unroll the awning. It had cost her another dollar. And while he was in the shop, he'd criticized many of her purchases.

Some of the vendors had sold her double what he would've ordered for the week, taking advantage of her inexperience. She heard about that until her ears burned. Then he cracked an egg on a plate, poked the flat yoke, and told her it was old. He stuck his hand into the flour barrel, sifted some between his fingers, and found weevils. He saw the three chests of tea from Millard's and told her she'd bought way too much and that it would go stale before she sold it all. He prodded a fish, examined its gills, and told her it was off. She angrily retorted that none of it would've happened if he'd been there to help her with the buying. Grumbling, he'd moved the chests of tea and coffee, along with rusks, oatmeal, and a few other necessities that women came in for often, closer to the counter, and the glass jars of cocoa, nutmeg, and cinnamon sticks out of the sun; then he told her to get the matches off the meat cooler, lest they take the damp.

For just a moment, he was the knowledgeable, competent shopkeeper she knew he could be, but just as she thought he might stay and help her, he left, saddened by the place. On his way out, he belittled her pretty touches – the lace valance, the glass plates for Mary's pastries, the window boxes, and the hand-painted OPEN sign Maddie had made for her. This was a working-class neighborhood, he'd said. People were interested in value for money, not frippery.

He was wrong, Fiona knew he was. Working people loved beauty as much as wealthy people. Maybe more so, since they had so little of it in their lives. But his words had upset her and Nick, who had come over to help her get ready, had to restore her shaken confidence. He'd told her her missteps were only beginner's mistakes and she had

323

time to put them right. He told her what mattered most were talent and ability, and she had plenty of both. He'd taken her face in his hands and ordered her to march to the fishmonger and tell him to shove that old cod he'd sold her straight up his bum, fins and all. She had, and she'd gotten a beautiful, fresh fish to bring back with her. Then she'd made the miller replace the flour and the poultry man give her new eggs.

As she wrapped the last of the ginger biscuits for a customer – all gone and it wasn't even ten o'clock yet! – Fiona realized that she'd done it: she'd reopened the shop. She had customers – dozens of them! So many that she was running out of things left and right. She would have to restock, and quickly. "You can't sell off an empty cart," Joe used to say. She was so relieved it had all gone well, but more than that, she was happy. And proud. The tea, the pastries, the pretty window – they were all her ideas and they'd all worked. It was an amazing feeling, to succeed at something. It was a new feeling for her – part happiness, part pride – and she relished it. With a painful twinge of regret, she remembered sitting on the Old Stairs with Joe as he tried to tell her about his successes at Peterson's and what they meant to him. She'd been too jealous, too threatened, to listen. If only she *had* listened to him. If only she'd tried to understand him, instead of fighting with him. If only, if only.

As she held the door open for a customer who wanted to take her purchases with her, Fiona saw a van pull up outside the shop. The driver came up to the door, asked her name, then handed her a box.

"What is it?" she asked him.

"With him, you never know," he said, already back in his van and snapping the reins.

Fiona looked at the box. It was a shimmering blue rectangle, about twelve inches by fourteen, with a hinged lid inlaid with pieces of iridescent glass. She turned it over. The words "Tiffany Studios" were etched on the bottom. Puzzled, she opened it. She was surprised to find a newspaper inside –

a copy of the *New York World*. The words "Turn to page 5" were written on the front page. She did, and saw that her ad, the one Nate and Maddie had done, the one she'd run in the *Chelsea Crier*, took up the entire page. She was stunned. How had this happened? She hadn't run this. She couldn't afford to. The *World* was a huge city paper, not some little neighborhood rag. Maybe that explained why the shop was so full of people.

A small white card slid out from between the pages and fluttered to the ground. She picked it up. The writing was large and masculine. It said:

> My Dear Miss Finnegan,
>   *I hope this small gift contributes to your success.*
> *Best wishes,*
>
>   *William R. McClane*

William McClane wondered if he was losing his mind. He was late for a supper at Delmonico's and he could not afford to be. It was a private supper hosted by the mayor. Many of the city's leading financiers were attending. It would be the perfect forum to talk up his plans for a city-wide subterranean railway, to generate interest and excitement among the very people whose support would be crucial to his success.

And what was he doing? Sitting in his parked carriage on the godforsaken West Side across from a small grocery, waiting, hoping, for a glimpse of a young woman whose face he had not been able to put from his mind since he'd first seen her a week ago in the offices of his bank. A face that was full of contradictions – at once anxious and determined, open yet guarded, strong yet heartbreakingly vulnerable. A face that was the most compelling he had ever seen.

On an impulse, on the way up Fifth to dinner, he'd told Martin, his driver, to turn left. He said he wanted to make a stop before Del's. Martin had raised an eyebrow at the location. "Are you sure of the address, sir?" he'd asked.

When Will assured him that he was, Martin shook his head as if to say he didn't understand him anymore. Will knew the feeling; he didn't understand himself. He didn't understand why he had risked his bank's money on a girl with good ideas but no experience. Or why he'd made his secretary Jeanne go across town every day for four days running to search the newsstands until she found a copy of the *Chelsea Crier* with Fiona's ad in it so he could run it in the *World*.

He didn't understand why he thought about a girl he didn't even know a hundred times a day. Or why – with a full life, with the demands of his business and the pleasures of friends and family – he should suddenly find himself feeling unbearably lonely.

Forty-five years old, William McClane had had a long time to live with himself, to know his own mind. He understood his motivations, knew his goals. He was a shrewd and rational man, one who had used his formidable intelligence and brilliant business sense to parlay a modest family fortune into a staggering sum of money. He was a highly disciplined man who prided himself on his adherence to fact and logic, and on his inability to be swayed by emotion or flights of fancy.

So what on earth was he doing here? Lurking like some masher?

On the way over, he'd told himself he was merely attending to business. Looking out for his bank's assets. He was just making sure Miss Finnegan got off on the right foot. After all, a shop was a lot for a young woman to handle. But as the minutes ticked by, bringing the hour hand of his watch closer and closer to seven and still she did not emerge from the shop, the disconsolate feeling that suffused him forced him to admit that his visit had nothing to do with his assets and everything to do with the stricken look in her eyes after Ellis had turned her down, the touchingly brave way in which she'd held her head up and her tears back as he addressed her, and the relief in her face, real

326

and palpable, when he'd told her she could have the shop.

He had to know that she was all right. That things had gone well for her. And if they hadn't, he wanted to be the one to put them right. She had sparked feelings in him. Feelings of concern and protectiveness, and deeper, unfamiliar ones, too. Feelings he did not understand and could not name.

Will checked his watch. It was exactly seven o'clock; he really should be leaving. Not only was he late for Del's; he was attracting attention. His brougham, custom-made in England, easily cost twice what any of the surrounding buildings did, and people were stopping to stare at it. And, to his horror, at him in his evening attire. At Del's or the opera house, no one would've glanced twice, but there, in this working-class neighborhood, he was making a spectacle of himself. And that was something a man of his background and breeding did not do.

He was about to rap for Martin to drive off when the door to the shop opened and a young woman wearing a long white apron came out. His heart leaped at the sight of her. Fiona. She slipped the hooked end of the long pole she was carrying into a metal eye over the doorway and began to roll up the awning. And then, before he even knew what he was doing, he was out of his carriage and striding across the street. As he stepped onto the sidewalk, the shop door opened again and a young man came out. He took the pole from her, finished rolling up the awning, then suddenly picked her up and twirled her around, both of them whooping and laughing. When he put her down, she kissed his cheek.

Will stopped in his tracks. The man was her husband, of course. For some reason, he hadn't pictured her married. She'd seemed so alone to him that day at the bank, as if she had no one to fight her battles, no one in her corner. Watching the two of them, he marveled at their excitement, their giddy emotion. They must've had a good day, made some money. That a few dollars could make anyone so happy amazed him. Anna, his late wife, had never embraced him like that, not even when he'd made his first million. He suddenly wished he were back in his carriage. He was an interloper barging in upon their happy scene. He felt awkward and, to his bewilderment, achingly disappointed. He turned to go, hoping he hadn't been noticed, but in that instant Fiona saw him. Her face, already glowing with happiness, became incandescent.

"Mr. McClane! Look, Nick, it's Mr. McClane, the man I told you about! The one from the bank! Oh, Mr. McClane, you wouldn't believe the day we had! There were so many people! Rivers of them! Oceans! We're out of everything! We've nothing left to sell, nothing at all! And it's all because of you!"

And then she flew across the few feet between them, flung her arms around his neck, and hugged him so hard she nearly choked him. He was so shocked, and so delighted, that he was absolutely lost for words. His hands came up to her back. He could feel the heat of her body through her blouse. Her hair tickled the side of his face and her cheek felt like satin against his own. She smelled like butter and tea and apples and a warm, sweetly sweaty woman.

And then, as if remembering herself, she pulled away and took a flustered step backward and his whole body keenly felt the loss of her touch. "You've done so much for us! First saving the shop for me and then the ad!" she said. "How did you get it into the *World?* Did I leave a copy with Mr. Ellis?" She didn't wait for an answer, but kept talking breathlessly, sparing him an explanation. "You don't know what this means for us . . . for my family." She was smiling still, but he saw a bright film of tears in her eyes. "We won't have to move and I won't have to find work and the Munros can stay and . . . oh, no! Oh, look what I've done!" Will followed her horrified gaze to the front of his jacket and saw that it was covered in flour. "I'm so sorry! Let me get a cloth!" She disappeared into the shop, leaving him standing next to her companion.

"Excitable old thing, isn't she?" he said, looking after her and laughing. He extended his hand. "I'm Nicholas Soames, a friend of Fiona's. I'm very pleased to meet you."

Only a friend? Will brightened and shook his hand. "The pleasure is mine, sir."

Fiona came out and fussed with his jacket, rubbing at the flour and generally making things worse, until he assured her it was fine and would surely come out with a good shake. Privately, he was glad that Charlie Delmonico kept spare jackets and trousers closeted away for his best customers in case of spills or splashes. As she gave up, stuffing the cloth into her pocket, Nick turned out the gas lamps, locked the shop's door, and handed her the key.

"I'm going to go upstairs and see if Mary needs help with the supper, Fee. What should I do with this?" He held out the Tiffany box Will had sent her earlier in the day.

"Let's have another look!" she said eagerly. Nick opened it. The box was stuffed with bills and coins. They looked at the money, then at each other, then burst into laughter like two children with a box of candy. Will couldn't recall ever having had so much fun making money. Maybe he ought to give up mining and lumber and subterranean railways and try shopkeeping.

"Hide it somewhere, Nick. Put it under my bed. That's next month's mortgage payment. If Michael finds it, he'll drink every saloon in the city dry." She looked at Will. "My uncle has a bit of a problem with whiskey. I'm sure Mr. Ellis told you."

Will nodded. Ellis had, using some very choice words. He was a bit taken aback by Fiona's directness. No one talked openly about such things in his circle. They went on all right – drinking and gambling and worse. But the rule was what you didn't talk about didn't exist.

"Nice to have met you, Mr. McClane," Nick said, heading inside.

"And you, Mr. Soames."

"Can you join us for supper, Mr. McClane? Or is it dinner? I get mixed up. I'd love to have you. We all would. It's meant to be a bit of a celebration. At least it is now! This morning I was so worried, I thought no one would come. Do join us! Nick brought champagne."

"It's Will, I insist. And I'd love to join you, but I'm due at a business supper shortly."

Fiona nodded. She looked at the ground, then up at him again, her lovely smile gone. "Probably a nice quiet supper, I imagine. You'll have to forgive me. I don't usually rattle on so. I'm too wound up. I don't know how I'll ever get to sleep tonight."

Will realized she thought he was declining her offer because she'd put him off with her boisterous behavior. Nothing could be further from the truth. "Miss Finnegan, you didn't . . . please don't think . . . I like that you're excited about your shop. I'm the same way. Give me half a chance and I'll talk your ears off about my subway. Look, I still have a little while before I need to be uptown. I find a walk often helps greatly when I'm wound up. Shall we take a short stroll?"

"I'd love to! Mary won't have the supper ready for a while, not with Nick up there meddling. But I'm not keeping you, am I?"

He flapped a hand at her. "Not at all. I have plenty of time," he said. He didn't. He was good and goddamned late. And he didn't care.

She smiled again – a broad, generous smile that was genuine and unselfconscious and utterly disarming. He had put the smile there and the realization of it made him happy. She took off her apron and laid it on a step inside the doorway to her flat. "I'm ready," she said. "Let's go."

"Hold on," he said, pulling a handkerchief from his pocket. He gently rubbed at her cheek with it. "Cinnamon. A long streak of it. Looks like you're leading a war party." She laughed. Her skin was as silken as a rose petal. He kept rubbing even though the cinnamon was gone, then

330

stopped before she thought he was only trying to touch her. Which he was.

They set off and she told him if she was to call him Will, then he must call her Fiona. He agreed, suppressing a smile at her appearance. Strands of hair had sprung loose from her twist and her clothes were grubby and rumpled. But her face was flushed with color and her magnificent cobalt eyes were sparkling. Will thought she was the most beautiful woman he had ever seen.

As they headed east on Eighteenth Street, he asked her about the shop, what her customers had bought, and where she'd gotten her good ideas. Her answers were smart and insightful. And then she started asking him questions. Peppering him, really. On how wealthy New Yorkers had made their fortunes. What did they make? What did they sell?

"Well, Carnegie made his fortune in steel," he began. "And Rockefeller in oil. Morgan in railroads and finance and . . . why do you want to know all this anyway, Fiona?"

"Because I want to be rich. I want to be a millionaire, Will."

"Do you?" he asked, smiling at yet another taboo broken. Another social rule blithely tossed over her shoulder and smashed like an old milk bottle. She obviously didn't know that women weren't supposed to talk about money. At least the women of his class. He had a feeling she wouldn't have given a damn if she did know.

"Yes, I do. How do you go about it? How did you do it?"

Smash went another milk bottle. Never inquire too closely about a friend's finances, he'd been taught. But he found her directness refreshing and her appeals for advice flattering and he had no hesitation in answering her. "With a small family fortune to prime the pump, timber lands I'd inherited in Colorado, and the foresight to buy more land there with plenty of silver in it."

Her brow wrinkled as she frowned. "I haven't got any

of those things," she said. "But I was thinking – if the shop does well, I could take out another loan and open a second. Maybe ten or fifteen streets north of the current one . . ."

"In Hell's Kitchen? I think not."

"Well, south then," she ventured. "Or a few blocks east. Maybe in Union Square. I've been there, it's very busy. And then I could open another and before long I'd have my own chain . . ."

Will gave her a long look. "Don't you think it might be wise to walk for a bit before you run? You've been open one day. And a very good day it was, but you still need to learn a few things before you open a second shop."

"Like what?"

"Like the nature of your clientele. Open a shop like yours in Hell's Kitchen and your window will go in in ten seconds flat. They'll rob you blind. It's a rough neighborhood. And yes, you're right – Union Square is very busy, but it caters to a well-heeled crowd looking for luxury goods, not groceries. Take some advice my father gave me when I was starting out, Fiona: Use what you know to grow. Right now, you don't know enough about the city's neighborhoods to make major investments in any of them. Don't get ahead of yourself. Start small."

"How? With what?"

Will thought for a few seconds. "You said that all your cakes and biscuits sold out, right?"

Fiona nodded.

"You know sweet pastries sell, so now try savories. Meat pies . . . chicken pies . . . those sorts of things. It's a risk – you may not sell them – but it's a calculated one. Odds are you will. Try a selection of good candy. If people are buying biscuits, chances are they'll buy chocolate. What else? The asparagus sold out, right? I had the most delicious braised lettuces at Rector's the other night. They were new, not full-grown. Maybe people who like fresh vegetables would buy those, too. Maybe not, but you should investigate every possibility. Anticipate every need. Be the first to give your customers what they want, even if they don't yet know they want it."

A window opened above their heads. A woman leaned her thick forearms on the sill and in a heavy Irish brogue shouted, "Sean! Jimmy! Where the divil are yehs, yeh bollocks? Yer pork chops are gettin' cold. Get in here now or I'll whale yeh both!"

"Pork chops, Will," Fiona said wryly, gesturing up at the window. "That's what my customers want. I'm not going to get rich selling those."

Will laughed. "Maybe not. At least, not right away. But you'll learn. You'll find out what sells and what doesn't and why. And you'll build on that knowledge. You'll get *smart*, Fiona. And that's the first step to getting rich."

"Is it?"

"Yes. I never would've known to buy my silver mines if I hadn't been in Colorado already because of my lumber interests there. I wouldn't be trying to sell the city on my subway plan if I didn't have a thorough knowledge of underground engineering from my mines. Trust me on this. Use what you know to grow."

They continued to walk and talk, heedless of time passing, and not once was there an awkward silence, a second when one of them couldn't think of anything to say. Will was utterly enchanted by Fiona; he'd never met anyone like her – a woman so passionate, so direct and honest, so completely without guile. She fascinated and intrigued him and he wanted to know more about her. He asked about her family, and when she told him what had happened to them he stopped dead in the middle of the sidewalk on Eighteenth between Fifth and Broadway, unable to believe what she had endured. It explained everything about her, answered all his questions. Why she was here. Why she was struggling to make the shop successful, why she was determined to make herself wealthy. He admired her courage, her fortitude, but his heart ached for her, too. Without thinking, he took her hands in his and told her to come to him if she ever needed anything – help, advice, anything at all. He hadn't meant to do it; it was a forward gesture, but the impulse overtook him. She simply squeezed his hands back, thanked him, and said she would.

When they reached Union Square, Fiona exclaimed at how far they'd walked and said she would have to get back. Supper was bound to be ready. Before they did, however, she spotted a flower seller – a thin, grubby girl of no more than twelve – hawking her wares. The girl had crimson roses. Fiona looked at them longingly, then suddenly said she would have some even though they were dear. As a treat for a good opening day. He tried to buy them for her, but she wouldn't allow it. He noticed that she gave the little girl more than the price of the flowers. She loved red roses, she told him, and gave him one for his buttonhole.

When they finally arrived back at the shop, a little redheaded boy – her brother, he learned – was hanging out of the window. He bellowed at her to hurry up. Everyone was starving, he said. Will kissed her hand, held it for longer than he should have, then finally told her good-bye. He looked back once as his carriage pulled away and saw her standing on the sidewalk holding her roses, looking after him. And never in his life was he sorrier at the imminent prospect of a bottle of Château Lafite and a seven-course meal.

29

Stan Christie and Reg Smith were only yards from Roddy O'Meara's back. He couldn't see them, but he heard their footsteps, heard one slap a cosh against his palm.

"Go ahead, Bowler, give the word," Roddy said, sitting himself down at Sheehan's table. "Just be bloody certain they can get to me before I get to you."

Sheehan leaned back in his chair. He worked a bit of food from his teeth with his tongue, then nodded curtly. Reg and Stan fell back to their places at the Taj Mahal's bar. Bowler pushed his plate, with most of a thick, juicy steak still left on it, toward Roddy. " 'Ere. I was going to give it to my bitch, Vicky . . ." – he nodded at the ugly, fearsome terrier lying at his feet – ". . . but on your wages, you probably need it more."

"Didn't know you were married, Bowler," Roddy said, picking up the half-eaten steak and tossing it to the dog. "Your wife's quite a looker." The animal swallowed the chunk of meat whole, then let out a loud, rumbling fart. Roddy heard snickering from behind him.

"Shut it!" Bowler barked. He glared at Roddy. "What do you want?"

"Your man at the bar had a tussle with a lad by the name of Joe Bristow the other night."

"You're joking, right? Don't tell me you're 'ere over two lads scrapping."

"I'm here over a lass. Fiona Finnegan. Bristow says your gorilla wanted to know her whereabouts. I want to know why."

"I don't know what you're talking about, Constable," Bowler said, in a highly aggrieved tone. "And what's more, I think you've quite a nerve barging in 'ere, ruining a man's dinner, accusing 'im of crimes 'e didn't commit . . ."

Roddy sighed, then steeled himself to listen as Bowler ranted on, feigning ignorance, innocence, outrage – the usual. When he finally ran out of steam, Roddy said, "If that's the way you want it, Bowler, fine. You know I've always believed in live and let live. A criminal like you wants to take money off another criminal like Denny Quinn, that's all right by me. As long as you're not bothering good working people, I couldn't give a tinker's piss. But I'm warning you, that'll change. Tell me what I want to know or I'll make t'ings hard for you. You leave your house in the morning, I'll be there. You go to a pub, a whorehouse, a dog fight, cock fight, rat fight – I'll be right behind you, stuck to your arse like a shitty nappy. You even try to –"

"All right! All right!" Bowler said. "Christ, I'm sorry the Ripper murders ever stopped. I liked it better when Jack 'ad you lot running about with your skirts over your 'eads playing blindman's buff. Kept you out of me 'air."

"What about Fiona?" Roddy demanded.

Bowler took a swallow of beer, then said, "Your Miss Finnegan stole five 'undred quid from an associate of mine. 'E wants it back. 'E doesn't want no trouble. 'E just wants me to find 'er and get it back."

"And who might this associate be, Bowler?"

"That I can't tell you. Suffice it to say 'e's a toff and 'e don't want 'is business known."

Roddy nodded. "Fine," he said, standing up, "we'll do it the hard way. When you're tired of lying to me, you let me know."

"Aw, for God's sake, O'Meara, I can't bloody win with you! You want the truth, I tell you the truth. And then you don't believe me!"

"Bowler, you wouldn't know the truth if it bent you over

and fucked you up the arse. I've known that girl me whole life. Helped raise her, I did. And I know she's as likely to steal five hundred pounds as you are to be knighted for good works. I'll be seeing you."

Roddy left Bowler muttering about the fact that England was still a free country the last time he checked. No one could push him around. He had rights, by Christ.

When Roddy reached the door, he turned and said, "Wherever she is, Bowler, not'ing better happen to her. Something does, it's you I'm coming after."

"That's bloody great! I don't know where the 'ell she is any more than you do! Anything else you want to 'old me responsible for? The Trafalgar Riots? The 'Undred Years' War?"

Outside the Taj, Roddy took his cap off and ran a hand through his hair. He was frustrated and worried. Always worried. He was no wiser now as to Fiona's whereabouts than before his interview with Sheehan. He'd fix that bleeder, though, for telling him tales and wasting his time. He'd gone to see him on his own time today, but the next time he paid him a call, it would be on the force's time. He shivered, chilled by a cold wind blowing in off the river.

He hoped Fiona was warm enough, wherever she was. Seamie, too. The nipper's mittens were worn out. He'd bought him a new pair the night they'd left. He wondered if he'd ever get the chance to give them to him. He pulled his collar up around his neck, jammed his hands in his pockets, and started for home.

30

Fiona lowered her head and wept. She was standing at the entrance to the cemetery where her mother, father, brother, and sister lay. The gate was padlocked. She'd tried to get in, rattling the bars until their hinges squealed and her palms were raw, but to no avail. She wanted to sit with her family. She wanted to tell them her troubles and know they were listening even if they couldn't reply. She lifted the padlock and crashed it down against the lock's face-plate, over and over, fighting back tears.

A voice called her name, a voice with a soft Irish lilt. "Fiona, lass . . ."

She dropped the padlock; it clattered against the gate. Her father was standing on the other side, only inches away. He had his jacket and cap on, and his grappling hook slung over his shoulder, just as if he were coming home from the docks. "Da!" she cried, unable to believe her eyes. "Oh, Da . . ." She thrust her hand through the bars. He caught it in his own and held it to his cheek.

"Da, where have you been? I missed you so." She was crying now. "You'll come out of there now, won't you? You'll come home and bring Mam and Charlie and the baby . . ."

He shook his head. "I can't, luv. You know I can't."

"But why? I need you, Da." She tugged on his hand. "Please . . ."

"Take this, Fiona," he said, and she felt him put something into her hand. "You have to use what you know."

She looked down at what he'd given her. It was a tiny

plant. No more than four inches high. A slender, fragile stalk with a few glossy green leaves on it. She raised her eyes to his, confused. "What is this?" she asked him.

"What you know."

"What I know? Da, that doesn't make any sense . . . I've never seen a plant like this . . ."

He released her hand and took a step backward.

"Where are you going? Da, wait!" She cradled the little plant to her chest with one hand, the other clutched at her father. "No, don't go. Please, don't go. Come back . . ."

"Care for it and it'll grow, lass. So big, you can't imagine." He waved at her, a bittersweet smile on his face, then walked away, fading into the gloom of the cemetery.

"No!" she sobbed. "Come back! Please, please, come back!" She shook the gate with all her might, but it held fast. She crumpled against it and gave over to her grief.

As she wept, she heard the sound of horses galloping. She looked up and saw a carriage approaching. It was sleek and black, polished to a glossy sheen. Flames flickered crazily in the lanterns on its sides. Two stallions, each the color of night, pulled it. Blue sparks flew from their hooves as they crashed over the cobbles. It looked as the devil's carriage might look if he decided to go for a midnight ride. What she saw next convinced her that it was.

Frances Sawyer, or what was left of her, held the reins. Her face was gone; Jack had cut it away. Her skull gleamed whitely in the gaslight, the scraped bone slick with blood. Her tattered dress hung about her mutilated body in blood-soaked shreds. Fiona could see her ribs fold and crease, accordion-like, and the flayed bones of her arms work as she brought the horses up sharply. She turned her head, the edges of her severed throat sliding wetly over each other, and stared from empty black eye sockets. " 'E's 'ere," she said, her voice thick and gurgling.

Flattened against the gate, unable to move or scream, Fiona forced her eyes from the coach's driver to its occupant. The window was open, but she could only see his silhouette – top-hatted, hands crossed on his walking stick. Still . . . she knew who it was. Jack. The dark man. His fingers curled around the sill. The door was flung open and tea leaves poured forth in a torrent. He stepped out, touched the brim of his hat in a mock salute, and grinned, revealing pointed white teeth clotted with blood. It wasn't Jack. It was William Burton. And he was holding a knife.

He lunged at her, his right arm raised. The blade made a loud, sucking *thuk* as it sank hilt-deep into her chest. She screamed at the pain. He pulled the knife out, licked the wet crimson dripping from it, and said, "An Assam. Has to be. Too strong for a Darjeeling. Too rich for a Dooars." He raised the knife again, but her paralysis had broken. She flailed at him madly.

"Stop that, Fiona!" he cried, fending off her hands. "Jaysus!"

"I'll kill you!" she shrieked, tearing at his face.

"Ow! You little . . . that hurt!" He took her by the wrists and shook her. "Wake up, you daft lass! It's me, Michael! Not the bloody bogeyman!"

Fiona woke with a start. She opened her eyes. An angry, sleep-swollen face was staring back at her. Her uncle's. Not Burton's. She looked around, her heart still hammering. She was sitting in a chair in Michael's parlor. The shop's ledger and a copy of the London *Times* were at her feet. She was in New York, not London. She was safe, she *was,* she told herself. But she had to look down at her chest to make sure there was no knife sticking out of it before she believed it.

"Uncle Michael . . . I'm sorry . . . I was dreaming . . ." she stammered.

He released her. "What the hell's the matter with you?" he muttered. "Screeching and carrying on . . . scared the bejaysus out of me. T'ought someone was killing you."

"So did I."

"What are you doing out here anyway? Why aren't you in bed?"

"I was going over the books. For the shop. I guess I fell asleep."

He nodded. "Well . . . as long as you're all right now," he said gruffly.

"I am," she said, but then a violent fit of trembling overtook her. He saw it and told her to stay put. Still grumbling, he padded off to the kitchen. Fiona heard water running. Blimey, what a nightmare, she thought. The worst one yet. She covered her face and moaned softly at the memory of Jack. Of Burton. They had melded in the nightmare, become one and the same man, a hellish amalgamation of her greatest fears. A bogeyman, all right. The King of the Bogeymen.

She leaned forward in her chair to collect her papers, determined to throw the dream off. As she reached for the *Times,* lying open on the floor, her eyes came to rest on the article she'd been reading. "Lucrative Public Offering Engineered for Tea Merchant," the headline said, and under it, "Burton Tea Embraces Ambitious Plans for Expansion."

That's what's done it, she realized. She'd bought a copy of the paper earlier in the day, as she often did, hoping for some news of the docker's union, and instead she'd seen the Burton article. Although she didn't completely understand what the stock market was, or how it worked, she remembered her father talking about the offering, citing it as one of the reasons Burton would never willingly consent to a raise for his workers. She knew that the offering represented a huge triumph for him, and indeed the article detailed how interest in the shares had surpassed his expectations. It went on to say that Burton planned to use the monies raised to modernize his London operation and purchase his own tea garden in India – moves that would allow him to land and package tea more efficiently. "It is my aim, over the next two years, to both reduce the cost of my tea to the public and provide a handsome return on my shareholders' investments," he was quoted as saying.

And though, as the reporter noted, he would now have to answer to shareholders, control of the company remained with him, as he had retained fifty-one percent of the one and a half million shares issued.

Knowing that William Burton prospered when her father, her entire family save for Seamie, lay in the cold ground, cut Fiona as deeply and painfully as the knife in her nightmare had. Before reading the article, she'd gone over the shop's ledger and had been pleased to find that its earnings were higher than she'd thought, high enough to allow her to begin to pay herself back the money she'd used to cover her uncle's debt. That knowledge had given her a wonderful sense of security. But now, in the aftermath of the nightmare, the shop's earnings seemed paltry. Laughable, even. They were nothing compared to Burton's wealth.

As the *Britannic* had left the shores of England, she had vowed revenge on Burton. Fine words, she thought. And words were all they were. It was now the first week of May; she had been in New York for over a month and still had no idea how she would carry out that revenge. Or finance it. She knew she would need a lot of money to strike at someone as powerful as Burton. But as yet she had no idea of how to make that money. Will had told her she should build on what she knew. The trouble was, nothing she knew would make her rich. Oats and biscuits and apples were not silver or oil. She needed to find something, something that would make her fortune . . . but what?

Michael came into the parlor carrying a cup of tea. "Here, drink this," he said. His gesture surprised Fiona. She wasn't used to displays of concern from him, but she accepted it gratefully. He sat with her for a few more minutes, yawning and rubbing his face. Looking at him, she was again amazed by his resemblance to her father. An image, blurry and fleeting, flashed into her mind – her father as he'd looked in her nightmare. He was trying to give her something, trying to tell her something, but she couldn't remember what. And then Michael said he was going to bed and that he hoped that the bogeyman had made his one and only appearance for the night, and as quickly as the image had come, it was gone again. He advised her to get some rest, too.

"I don't think I could sleep if I tried, Uncle Michael," she said, standing. She knew if she did go to bed, she'd only lie awake reliving her nightmare. Work was the only antidote to her fears, the only thing in which she could lose herself. She reached for the apron she'd thrown over the back of her chair earlier and tied it around her waist.

"It's midnight," Michael said. "Where the divil are you going?"

"Downstairs. To get a jump on the day."

"Wait till sunup at least. You shouldn't be down there alone."

Fiona gave him a tired smile. Alone? With all those ghosts and memories? "I won't be, Uncle Michael," she said. "I've got the bogeyman for company. And all his friends, too."

Often, on nights when he couldn't sleep, Nicholas Soames liked to walk Manhattan's streets. There was a calm, peaceful feeling to be had after dark. A sense of the monster at rest. The city seemed to belong to him and him alone at such times. The sidewalks were empty. Shops were shuttered. Only the pubs and restaurants were lit up. He could actually stop and look at things, if he liked. There were few people about to jostle him, and no one to mutter if he paused to investigate an interesting building or peer into a pretty courtyard.

He had walked quite a distance tonight. All the way from his hotel on Fifth and Twenty-third, down past Washington Square to Bleecker Street. It was late, just after midnight and, finally tired, he decided he would find his way to Broadway and see if he could scare up a cab.

He was about to cross Bleecker when he saw them. Two

men. They were walking side by side. Not holding hands, not touching, but he knew all the same. From the way one inclined his head toward the other. From their easy laughter. He knew.

He watched as one of them opened the door to a saloon and they both disappeared inside. He stood there as motionless as a lamppost. Two more entered the saloon. And then one on his own. And then a foursome. When he got up enough nerve to cross the street, he saw a small sign next to the door. THE SLIDE, it said. A hand passed in front of him. Fingers curled around the door handle. "Coming in?" said the hand's owner, a man with curly blond hair.

"Me? No . . . I . . . no, thank you. No."

"Suit yourself," he said.

In the second before the door closed, he heard laughter, smelled cigarettes and wine. He bit his lip. He wanted to go in. He wanted to be with his own kind for an evening. To share a bottle of claret with a handsome man. To let the mask drop. Just for a bit.

He grasped the handle, then let it go. It was too dangerous. He wasn't free to be what he was. Hadn't he learned that by now? With all the grief and pain he'd brought upon himself, his family, Henri? He walked away from the door, retreated to the shadows of a large sheltering elm.

Go back, he told himself. Turn around. Now. This was too risky. What if someone saw him? Someone he knew? He cast one last glance at The Slide and saw a man walking toward it. He was tall and beautiful with long dark hair that fell to his shoulders in thick waves. From a distance he looked like Henri. The man paused, squinted into the shadows at Nick, then shook his head and laughed. "Are you going to hide under that tree all night, Chicken Little?" he asked. He was still laughing as the door closed behind him.

Nick stared at the door. He raked a hand through his hair. All he wanted in the world right now was behind it. Companionship. Laughter. Warmth. Understanding. His longing was overwhelming. I'll only go for a short while, he told himself. Just an hour. I'll just have a drink or two. Maybe chat for a while. It's harmless, really. Just one drink and then I'll leave. Just this once.

31

"How about some more pie, Seamie luv?" Mary asked, getting up from the table.

Seamie nodded eagerly and held his plate out.

"The bottomless pit," Fiona observed.

"Oh, rubbish. He's got a good healthy appetite. Like a growing lad should."

"I'll have some more, too, Mum," Ian said, standing up to help his mother.

"Me, too," Fiona said.

"Fiona, that's your third piece!" Mary said, laughing. "Who's the bottomless pit?"

Fiona, giggling sheepishly, handed her plate to Ian. Mary's cooking was delicious. Her pie crust was golden and flaky, the steak pieces tender in their rich gravy. Her mashed potatoes were fluffy and her peas cooked perfectly.

Mary piled the plates high again. She'd made a lot of food and Fiona was glad of it. She was starving. It had been another busy Saturday and she'd been on her feet all day. They ate in Michael's kitchen instead of Mary's, as it was roomier and had a big table they could all fit around. When it came to cooking, Fiona had little ability and even less interest, but it was important to her that Seamie had good hot meals. She and Mary had made a deal weeks ago: she would supply the food for the evening meal and Mary would cook it. It was an arrangement that suited them both. Fiona enjoyed supper with the Munros. She'd come to think of them as her family. She and Seamie were a part of their lives, and they of hers, in a way that her

346

uncle – who still spent most of his time at Whelan's – was not.

"Everybody have what they need now?" Mary asked, setting plates on the table before she sat down again.

"Yes, plenty," Fiona said.

"I'll have them window boxes replanted for you by Wednesday, lassie," Alec said.

"Will you really?" she asked, delighted. "All of them?"

"Aye, the new plants are ready. I just have to take out the old ones and build up the soil a bit before I put them in. They'll be bonny."

Fiona had never known anyone like Alec. He lived to garden. He needed to put his hands in the earth, to touch and cultivate green things as other people needed air. He loved his plants like children, fussing and laboring over them always, worrying if the leaves on one of his beloved rosebushes showed a spot of rust or mildew. Seamie adored him. They spent hours out in the backyard – the elderly man in his cap and tweed jacket, the little boy in short pants and a sweater – clearing weeds, turning manure into the flower beds, staking the rose canes, coddling the peonies.

Once, as she was bustling past the shop's rear door, which opened out onto the backyard, Fiona had glimpsed Seamie, his sweet freckled face luminous with wonder, observing a large iridescent butterfly that had perched on the back of his hand. The butterfly had suddenly flown off, leaving him to look longingly after it, stung by its defection. Fiona had wanted to run out and hug him and tell him to never mind, the butterfly would come back, but before she could, Alec went to him. He put a hand on Seamie's shoulder and watched the beautiful creature fly away, explaining all the while how butterflies lived and migrated, how they helped pollinate flowers, how this one had taken pollen from their strong healthy lilac tree and would bring it to other lilacs to help them grow. Seamie had accepted his words without tears or anger, without asking if the butterfly would die. As they resumed their digging, Fiona had silently thanked Alec, a gardener who, it seemed, could cultivate all sorts of seedlings.

As Seamie was telling Fiona the names of the plants that he and Alec had potted today, she heard the flat door open and close, followed by the sound of heavy shuffling foot-steps in the hallway. It was Michael. Fiona felt a flash of anger, certain he was going to ask her for money. He didn't usually come home from Whelan's this early. He must be skint again.

Mary flashed Fiona a look. "Do you think he'd join us?" she whispered.

Fiona snorted. "Not unless you're serving whiskey as well as steak pie," she said. She had all but given up hope that her uncle would ever stop drinking.

"How long has it been since he had a good meal? He should eat some proper food."

"I know it, Mary. I try. I always leave him a plate of leftovers. Sometimes he eats them, sometimes he doesn't."

"You should ask him to come in."

"He won't listen to me. He never does. You try."

"All right, I will. I'll ask him."

"In this century or the next?" Alec grumbled.

"Keep talking, normal-like," Mary said. "He won't come if he thinks we're talking about him."

"Which we are," Alec said.

Fiona started talking again as if nothing unusual were going on. "I think new flowers will really freshen the windows," she babbled. The heavy footsteps came closer. Michael hurried by the kitchen and passed into the parlor. "Can you imagine how pretty they'll look with the lace curtains hanging above them? I hope you've got a lot of pink in the mix, Alec, and some nice sunny yellow ones and –"

"Michael?" Mary called lightly. "Is that you?"

After a few seconds of silence a gruff "Aye" was heard.

"Are you hungry? I've made a steak-and-onion pie. There's plenty here."

Fiona nodded her approval. Mary was doing well. She was coaxing a wary, wounded animal, one that was more likely to turn tail and run than lick the hand outstretched.

Silence again. Then, "Steak and onion?"

"Yes; come have a bit."

Fiona's eyes widened in disbelief as she heard her uncle walk toward the kitchen. He appeared in the doorway, his cap in hand, and she struggled to keep her expression neutral. She felt both sorrow and anger when she looked at him. He was as skinny as a stray dog, at least thirty pounds thinner than in the picture Molly had sent them, yet his face looked as bloated as a drowned man's. His hair was long and scraggly. His clothes were dirty. He was unshaven and smelled like a pub.

"Hello, Michael," Mary said, smiling. "Fancy a cup of tea with your pie?"

"Aye," he said quietly. "I would."

"Well, sit down. Here, between myself and Fiona. Ian, shove over a bit."

"That's all right," he said. "I'll eat in the other room."

"Don't be silly. You can't balance a plate and a cup of tea on your knees. Sit down."

Michael sat, not looking at any of them. Mary put a plate of food in front of him, along with a knife, fork, and napkin. Fiona poured him a cup of tea.

"Thank you," he said. He picked up his teacup with shaking hands and drank from it. "That's a good cup of tea," he added.

"It's the new one I bought from Millard's," Fiona said. "It's from India."

Michael nodded. He looked at Fiona, lifted his chin slightly, and said, "I drink tea with me supper, not whiskey. Regardless of what some might think."

You've got a damn good pair of ears on you, Fiona thought. "Good for you," she said. "Whiskey ruins the taste of food and Mary's pie is so delicious. I've never had better."

"Oh, go on with you," Mary laughed, feigning modesty.

"It's true, Mum," Ian said. "Are there any more potatoes?"

"Here you are."

"Pass me the gravy, too?"

They were all playing a game. Acting nonchalant. Trying to pay Michael no mind. Ian put the gravy boat down and asked for the peas. Alec asked for another cup of tea. Seamie burped and Fiona told him to excuse himself. It was as if they were all following some prearranged cue, acting as if nothing were out of the ordinary, as if they all – Michael included – had been eating dinner together every night for the past twenty years. There would be no recrimination, no pleading, no censure. Both Mary and Fiona had tried those and failed. Just acceptance. A good meal. Company and conversation. Head down, painfully self-conscious, Michael looked as if that was more than he could hope for.

Hoping to draw him into the conversation, Fiona asked him a question. "I was thinking it would be a good idea to put window guards in, Uncle Michael. Do you know where to go for them? I think we should have them in both flats."

"Window guards? What for?"

"For Nell. She'll be walking before long and you can't be too careful."

As if hearing her cue, Nell piped up from her basket tucked beneath the kitchen window. Michael stiffened and put his fork down.

Oh, Lord, he's going to bolt, Fiona thought. She got up quickly, hoping to prevent it. "There's our girl!" she said brightly, picking up her cousin. "Must've just woken up. How she can sleep through the commotion around here, I do not know." She sat down again with the baby on her lap. "Can she have some potato?" she asked Mary.

"Yes. And a little bread with gravy. Just make sure she doesn't get any onion. She's not fond of it."

Alec asked if Mary had saved the potato peelings for his

350

compost pile. Ian and Seamie made faces at each other. Fiona spooned potato into Nell. And Michael sat as still as death, his meal forgotten, his eyes rooted on his child.

"Can I hold her?" he suddenly asked, his voice barely a whisper.

Fiona passed the baby to him. He pushed his chair back and took his daughter. Fiona saw the emotion on his face and knew he was thinking of Molly. Don't run away, she pleaded silently. Stay with her.

"Eleanor Grace," he said, his voice quavering. "What a pretty lass you are."

Nell sat cradled in her father's gaunt arms, her enormous blueberry eyes intent upon his face. Her forehead puckered. "Bah, bah, dah!" she suddenly declared.

Michael looked up, incredulous. "She said Da!" he exclaimed. "She said Da! She knows me!"

"Yes, she did. She does know you," Fiona said, knowing full well Nell said bah or dah to everything.

"Dah! Dah!" the baby crowed, bouncing in his lap.

Good girl, Nell, keep it up, Fiona silently urged her. She glanced at Mary, who was nearly beside herself. With a trembling hand, Michael touched his daughter's cheek. Nell latched on to his thumb and gummed it.

"Looks so like her mother," he said. "So like Molly." And then he put his hand over his face and started to weep. Great tears rolled down his cheeks and dropped onto Nell's dress. Sobs wrenched themselves out of his chest. His grief came out of him fast and hard, like summer rains in a desert, flooding the defenses he'd erected to keep it back. His anger and bitterness crumbled; he had only his sorrow now and it overwhelmed him.

"Lord God, what a lot of fuss over a bairn," Alec muttered.

Mary shot her father-in-law a look. "That's right, Michael lad," she soothed, "you have a good cry. It's high time you did. There's no shame in crying over a woman like Molly. You just let it out. It'll do you a world of good."

"I wish she was here, Mary," he said, his voice hitching. "I wish she could see Nell."

Mary nodded. She took his hand and squeezed it. "She is, Michael. She can."

32

"You checked the back door?" Ed Akers asked as Joe shuttered and padlocked his pitch.

"Aye."

"And the peaches? They're up 'igh where the mice can't get at them?"

"Aye. Cherries, too. I've seen to it all, Ed."

"Good lad," Ed said, patting Joe on the back. " 'Ere, 'ere's something extra for you." Joe thanked him. "Don't mention it. Stall's doing better than ever since you started. Could sell sand on a beach, you. Well, I guess that's it, then. Avoided the missus and 'er pack of demons all day, but I'll 'ave to go 'ome sometime, won't I?"

Joe smiled. "There's no 'elp for it," he said. Ed was in his forties and had twelve children. He loved to complain about his wife and kids – Mrs. Akers and all her pains, he called them. He loved to go on about the racket they made, the hell they raised, what a plague they were, how they took all his money, but every night when he went home, he always had a parcel tucked under his arm filled with cherries, strawberries, or broken biscuits he'd got cheap from the baker's stall. It was an act, his complaining, but Joe pretended to go along with it for form's sake.

"Aye, no 'elp at all," Ed repeated, nodding. Joe waited for him to go, but Ed was stalling. He rattled the padlock, looked up at the night sky, predicted a clear and mild June Sunday, then awkwardly said, "Listen, it's none of my business, but why don't you take some of the brass I gave you and go down the pub? Enjoy yourself a bit? You shouldn't be alone so much, a young lad like yourself."

"Maybe some other time. I'm knackered tonight," Joe said. "I'm going to feed Baxter, give 'im a good brushing, and turn in early."

Ed sighed. "Suit yourself, then."

"I will. Night, Ed. See you Monday."

"Night, lad."

Joe walked west. Three streets away was a row of stables that some of the stall owners used to house their horses and carts. One of these belonged to Ed, who allowed Joe to sleep in the hayloft. Ed liked that he was there to keep an eye on things and Joe liked that he didn't have to pay to sleep with strangers in a verminous lodging house.

Ever since he'd left his and Millie's home, six weeks ago, he'd been living rough, barely eating, doing odd jobs around Covent Garden as he could find them. One day, hungry and weak, he'd stumbled and fallen outside a pub. A friendly pair of hands had helped him up. To his surprise, and his shame, it was Matt Byrne, a lad from Montague Street who worked in Covent Garden now. Matt recognized him and asked what had happened to him. Over the pub meal Matt insisted on buying for him, Joe told him his marriage was over and he was on his own. He was having difficulty finding a proper job, he said, because Tommy Peterson had put the word out not to hire him. Bristling, Matt told him to go see his friend Ed Akers, who was looking for help. Ed was his own man, he said. Peterson didn't own everyone in Covent Garden. Not yet he didn't.

It wasn't much, his new job – just selling and delivering produce to costers and small shops – and it was quite a comedown from his former position at Peterson's, but it was better than starving and he was grateful for it. He'd bought two blankets from a secondhand stall and made a bed for himself in the hayloft. He got his meals from tuckshops and bathed once a week in the public baths. It was a grim arrangement, but it suited him. It gave him the means to keep himself and it allowed him to be alone at night, and solitude was something he craved now.

A group of loud, boisterous factory girls in their Saturday-night finery passed him. One smiled at him. He looked away. Behind them, a young couple strolled, holding hands. He hurried his pace. Joe hadn't been honest with Ed. He wasn't tired. He just couldn't stand to be around people anymore. It hurt him to see a happy courting couple, to hear the laughter of factory girls. He had been like them once – merry, optimistic, eager for whatever the day brought. Now, everyone he touched, he hurt. Everything he touched turned to shit.

He ducked into a tuckshop and bought a sausage roll. The place was only a hole in the wall, but it did have two grotty tables and the girl behind the counter, a pretty brunette with a sweet smile, invited him to sit and eat for once instead of always rushing out. He tersely declined and left, eager to get to the stable where he knew there wouldn't be a soul but himself – only Baxter and an old black tomcat who liked to curl up next to him as he slept.

There was no moon out, only stars, and it took him a minute to fumble his key into the lock. Once inside, he felt for the lantern he knew to be hanging to the left of the door and the box of matches next to it. " 'Ello, Baxter!" he called. "Who's a lovely boy, then?"

Baxter, a chestnut gelding, whinnied from his stall. Joe hung the lantern from a peg on a wooden post and walked over to scratch the horse's ears. Baxter mumbled at Joe's jacket pocket with his soft, whiskered lips.

"No sausage rolls for you, old son. They say it's pork, but I 'ave me doubts. Could be one of yours in there and that would make you a cannibal. That's a capital offense, Bax. You'd be 'anged for certain and then where would we be? 'Ere, 'ave these instead." He pulled two carrots out of his trouser pocket and fed them to the horse. Then he led the animal out of his stall and let him stand where he liked.

There was no need to tie him; Baxter was a gentleman.

As the horse stood blinking his large black eyes, Joe brushed him, using firm, rhythmic strokes, moving from his neck over his back to his haunches. When his coat was gleaming, he teased the knots out of his mane with his fingers. Baxter would've been fine without the carrots or the brushing, but Joe told himself the horse needed the pampering to stay good-tempered and tractable. In fact, it was he who needed this nightly routine. He needed to care for a living creature, to nurture something as a way of filling up the empty aching void within himself, as a way of taking his mind off all the pain he'd caused.

With Baxter out of his stall, Joe cleaned out the soiled hay, put fresh hay down, then poured oats into the trough. The horse, smelling his supper, trotted back into his pen without complaint. Joe bade him good night, then took his lantern and made his way upstairs to the hayloft and his own bed.

The loft was nothing but a plank floor under a pitched roof, but it was well-built, with loophole doors at the front that shut tightly, and it kept both wind and water off him. He took his jacket off and laid it neatly on top of the hay bale that served as his bureau. Then he pulled a flask from his back pocket, unscrewed the cap, and poured it contents – rich, creamy milk – into a chipped bowl at the top of the stairs. The tom kept late hours – Joe had never seen him come in – but he was always there in the morning, nestled in the crook of his knees. Joe made sure he always had milk for him and the cat repaid his kindness by keeping the mice down.

After he'd eaten, he stripped down to his underwear, fluffed the hay under his horse blanket, then bedded down to read his newspaper. When he finished, he snuffed the lantern and pulled his other blanket over him. He lay quietly, knowing it would be ages before he slept. Distant sounds of laughter and singing carried up from a nearby pub. He felt so alone, so utterly isolated. The knowledge that a short walk could bring him to a bright, jovial taproom full of weekend merrymakers only served to reinforce his loneliness. He could no longer laugh or smile. He was too haunted by what he'd done. Broken by remorse.

Once, when he was little, perhaps ten or so, two of his mates had had to go in early from a game of football on a Saturday evening to go to confession. He asked what that meant and they told him they had to tell the priest their sins and say they're sorry for them, and then they could go to heaven. Joe had wanted to go with them. He wanted to go to heaven, too, but they said he couldn't. Only Catholics could and he was a Methodist. He'd run into his house, upset. His Granny Wilton, who had minded him and his siblings while his parents worked the Saturday-night market, asked what was wrong.

"I'm going to 'ell for my sins because I can't tell God I'm sorry," he said.

"Who told you that?" she'd asked.

"Terry Fallon and Mickey Grogan."

"Don't pay them no mind," she said. "It's nothing but a lot of mumbo jumbo. Them Papists can mumble 'ail Marys till the cows come 'ome. Won't make one bit of difference. We're not punished for our sins, lad. We're punished by them."

She'd made him feel better, mainly because she'd hugged him and given him a biscuit. He'd been too little to understand her words then, but he knew what they meant now. Once, when he had Fiona and they had all their dreams and hopes, he'd known heaven right here on earth. Now he only knew despair. His gran was right. God didn't have to punish him; he'd created his own hell. By himself and for himself.

Miserable, he turned onto his back and tucked his hands behind his head. From where he lay, he could see the dark, starry sky through the loft's window. One star twinkled more brightly than the others. He remembered looking at this star . . . it seemed like a million years ago now . . . and telling it that he loved his girl, Fiona. Telling it they'd be together soon. He wondered where in the big wide world she was. The private detective he'd hired had not found her and was no longer looking now that he no longer had the money to pay him. Roddy had had no luck, either – though he had warned Sheehan to stay away from her. Joe prayed that wherever she was, she was safe and out of harm's way. He wondered if she ever thought about him, if she ever missed him. He mocked himself for even harboring such hopes. After what he'd done to her? He was certain she hated him, as Millie hated him and Tommy hated him. As he hated himself.

He closed his eyes, sick with loneliness and grief, longing for the black abyss of unconsciousness. Finally, after he'd tossed and turned for the better part of an hour, he fell into a fitful, shallow sleep, one full of demons and frights that made him flail and cry out. Shortly after one such cry, there came a soft padding of feet on the steps and an avid lapping at the milk bowl. After the tom finished drinking, he circled Joe. He paused once, baring his teeth at something in the darkness, then settled himself into the hay. The cat's presence did not disturb Joe. Instead, it gentled him. His breathing evened out and deepened. He surrendered to sleep. And all night long, the tom stayed up. Blinking its yellow eyes in the darkness. Awake. Abiding. Keeping watch.

33

"Oh, you should see it, Fee! It's absolutely perfect! The window runs the whole length of the front wall. The place is *filled* with light. And it's huge. Did I tell you that? I can easily get thirty canvases on the walls and another ten on easels in the middle of the room. I'm going to have the floor refinished, and then I'll have the walls repainted and then . . ."

Nick was striding around the shop as he talked, too excited to stand still. He'd just rented a shopfront in Gramercy Park, which he was going to turn into a gallery, and the flat above it, where he was going to live. It was a pretty four-story building with another tenant above him and the landlady and her two sons on the top floor. He'd given the woman a security deposit and the first month's rent, then dashed over to Eighth Avenue to tell Fiona.

She'd been polishing the counter as he burst into the shop and she'd been alarmed at the sight of him – he was thinner than ever and as pale as milk – but he wouldn't stop talking long enough for her to ask him if he was all right.

". . . and the ceiling is so high, Fiona! Fifteen feet! Oh, it's going to be the most wonderful gallery in New York!" He leaned over the counter and kissed her smack on the lips.

"Mind yourself!" she scolded, laughing. "You'll get wax all over your jacket."

"You'll come see it, won't you, Fee?"

"Of course I will. As soon as you like. Nick, are you feeling –"

He cut her off. "Can you come tonight?" He held up his hands like a traffic cop. "No, not tonight, not yet! Not till it's all fixed up and the paintings are here and" – he paused to cough, covering his mouth – "I've got them all hung and everything's pretty and" – he coughed again, even harder. Then he reached for his handkerchief and turned away until the harsh, racking spasm stopped. When he turned back to her, his eyes watery, she was no longer smiling.

"You didn't go to the doctor's like you promised, did you?" she asked.

"I did."

She crossed her arms. "Really? What did he say it was, then?"

"He said ... uh ... that it was ... um ... some kind of ... chesty thing."

"A chesty thing? Oh, *that* sounds like something a doctor would say, you lying little –"

"I did go, Fiona! I swear it! Dr. Werner Eckhardt. On Park Avenue. He even gave me medicine. I've been taking it and I feel much better, I do."

Fiona's tone softened. "But you don't *look* well," she fretted, her brow knit with worry. "You're too pale and thin and you've got shadows under your eyes. Are you eating properly, Nick?" She ran her finger around the inside of his shirt collar. "You're swimming in your clothes. And now you've got a cough. I'm worried about you."

Nick groaned. "Oh, don't be such a badger, old mole. I'm fine, really I am. I'll admit I'm a bit tired, but it's only the gallery. I've been working dreadfully hard trying to locate a good place. I've been seeing ten, twelve shopfronts a day at least. And now I've found it! Did I tell you how beautiful the neighborhood is? And that there's a wisteria vine in front that hangs above the window? Did I tell you about the window? How huge it is?"

"Three times at least. You're trying to change the subject."

"Am I?"

"Promise me you'll eat properly, Nick. Not just champagne and those horrible fish eggs."

"All right, I promise. Now tell me what's new with you, Fee. I've been blathering away and haven't even asked how you've been."

There wasn't much to tell. She'd had a busy week at the shop. Michael still hadn't returned to Whelan's and she and Mary were starting to think that maybe he wouldn't. He'd been pulling his weight in the shop and was talking about fixing up Mary's kitchen. She'd taken Seamie shopping for new clothes because he'd shot up again and Nell had started teething.

"Mmm-hmm," Nick said impatiently when she'd finished. "What else?"

"What do you mean, what else?"

He smiled knowingly. "Has William McClane come calling again?"

Fiona colored. "Of course not."

"I still can't believe it. Only in New York for a few months and already you've hooked yourself a millionaire."

"Will you stop? We took a stroll together, that's all. I'm sure I'll never see him again."

"He's beastly wealthy, you know. I remember my father mentioning him. I think they dined together once or twice. I saw how he looked at you. I'm sure he fancies you."

"Don't be ridiculous! I'm half his age and I'm not wealthy like he is or from the right circles."

"Fiona, you're a beautiful, captivating young woman. What man wouldn't be after you? Admit it . . . you fancy him, don't you? You can tell me."

Fiona gave him a sidelong glance. "A little, maybe," she allowed. "He's a wonderful man. He's charming and kind. Incredibly smart. He knows everything. And he's a gentleman, but . . ."

"But what? How can there possibly be a 'but' at the end of all that?"

Fiona shrugged.

"Fee?"

She frowned, rubbed her polishing rag over an imaginary dull spot.

"Ahh, I think I know. It's that chap from London you told me about, isn't it? Joe."

She polished harder.

"Still?"

She put the rag down. "Still," she admitted. "It's daft, I know. I try to forget him, but I can't." She raised her eyes to Nick's. "I once heard a docker, a man who'd lost his hand in an accident, tell my father that he still felt the hand. He said he felt the joints ache in the damp or the skin prickle in the heat. That's what it's like with Joe. He's gone, but he isn't. He's still inside me. I can see him. Hear him. I still talk to him in my head. When will these feelings stop, Nick?"

"When you fall in love again."

"But what if I don't?"

"Of course you will. You're just not over him yet. My advice is to spend more time with McClane. An Astor or a Vanderbilt would make a nice companion, too. That's just what you need, Fee. A nice New York millionaire. That'll make you forget that barrow boy of yours. What did you and McClane talk about during your stroll anyway? You never told me."

"The shop. And subterranean railways."

Nick made a face. "How romantic."

"He's trying to help me, Nick. I told him I wanted to become a millionaire. I told him I needed to find the thing that would make me rich."

"And what did he say? Did he give you the secret behind all his millions?"

"He said to be patient, to watch and learn and see what sold and figure out ways to build on my sales. And if I did that, something would come of it. Small things at first. And then bigger things, like offering prepared foods, or maybe

362

even opening a second shop. He had a funny way of putting it; he said to use what I know to grow."

"Did it work? Have you made your fortune yet?"

Fiona frowned. "No. We're making more than we were, though. Mary's savories are selling out every day and we're going to start offering prepared salads, too. We're actually going to have to get a new cooler to accommodate it all. But I'm not a millionaire yet. Not even close."

"Not to worry, Fee," Nick said, patting her hand. "I'll tell you how to become a millionaire."

"How?"

"Marry one."

She took a swipe at him, but he ducked. "I'm not marrying anyone. Ever. Men are far too much trouble."

"Not me."

"Especially you."

The shop door opened. Michael came in frowning. He was holding a piece of paper.

"Speaking of trouble . . ." Fiona said under her breath.

"Fiona, this invoice can't be right," he said.

"Which invoice, and why not?"

"The one from the tea supplier. Millard's. What did they bill you for the last time?"

"There wasn't a last time. This is the first bill. What's wrong?"

"It says we've had nineteen chests from them since you opened the shop again."

"That sounds right. I can check the delivery receipts to confirm it, but I'm sure Stuart wouldn't cheat us."

"This is the Indian tea?" Michael asked, setting the invoice down on the counter.

"Yes."

He shook his head. "I'll be damned. I was lucky if I moved a chest of the old stuff."

"A week?"

"A month!"

Fiona looked at the invoice, her eyes following her finger

down the column. Nineteen chests had been sold to Finnegan's in a two-month period. She was down to her last two. That meant she'd been selling just over two chests a week, against her uncle's one chest a month. She got to the bottom of the invoice, mentally checking Millard's arithmetic, and found that the total corresponded to the number of chests sold, plus the two in the shop's basement.

And then she saw it.

Embossed at the bottom of the invoice was the name "R. T. Millard" over a drawing of three species of fauna identified as a coffee bush, a cacao tree . . . and a tea plant.

As Fiona stared at the tea plant, a slender little stalk with bladelike leaves, the fine downy hairs on her neck began to prickle. She didn't hear her uncle anymore, though he was still talking. She recognized the plant. She'd seen one before. In a nightmare. Her father had given it to her, passed it to her through the bars of a cemetery gate. "What is it, Da?" she'd asked him. His answer echoed in her head now. "It's what you know."

It had been right there in front of her all along. Bloody tea, of all things! "Use what you know," Will had said. Blimey, if there was one thing she knew, it was tea! She could tell a Keemun from a Sichuan, a Dooars from an Assam by the smell alone. She'd known that her Indian tea sold, but she hadn't known how well. That little plant, so delicate, so fragile was the very thing she'd been searching for. It would be *her* oil . . . and steel . . . and lumber. Her fortune!

"Fiona, lass? Did you hear me?" Michael said, snapping his fingers in her face.

She hadn't. A humming had started in her blood. It surged through her, taking hold of her, making her heart pound. She was on fire with the power, the possibilities, of her new idea – an exclusive blend, wholesale accounts, an expanded selection of teas in the grocery shop, maybe even a tearoom. A beautiful, enchanted place like the one in Fortnum & Mason's.

"I said we've got to reorder. We're down to two chests. We'll be through them by next Wednesday at the rate we're going. I'm guessing we'll need at least eight more to get us t'rough the coming month," Michael said.

"No."

"No? Why not?"

"Because we're going to order more than eight. We're going to buy up every chest of Indian tea Millard's has and swear them to secrecy on the blend! No one else must have it!"

Michael looked from Fiona to Nick, as if he might know what his crazy niece was on about, but Nick just shrugged. "Why would we do that?" Michael asked. "It's mad! No shopkeeper orders more than he can sell."

Fiona cut him off. "We're not just shopkeepers anymore."

"No?" Michael said, raising an eyebrow. "What are we then?"

"Tea merchants."

"The usual, Mr. McClane?"

"Yes, Henry. Have Mr. Carnegie and Mr. Frick arrived yet?"

"I haven't seen them, sir. Here you are."

"Thank you, Henry."

"My pleasure, sir."

Will took a healthy swallow of his Scotch, then scanned the Union Club's bar for signs of his guests. Andrew Carnegie and Henry Frick, partners in the largest steel concern in the country, were dining with him tonight to discuss his plans for the subterranean railway. They were interested in supplying him with steel and he was interested in wooing them as investors. Their support, and the support of other leading industrialists, was more crucial than ever now, for there was a new obstacle to his goal to build the city's first subway – one that threatened to derail all his careful planning and politicking.

The door to the bar room opened. Will turned, hoping to see at least one of his guests, but instead saw a petite brunette in a blue plaid jacket and skirt. She clutched a pad and pencil in one hand, her purse in the other. Her sharp, quick eyes fastened on his; she made a beeline for him.

"Hello, Will," she said.

He smiled at her. "Always a pleasure, Nellie. What are you drinking?"

"Scotch. Rocks. Make it quick, will you?" she said, glancing at the bartender. "I figure I've got five, maybe ten minutes before the gargoyle catches me."

The bartender hesitated. "Mr. McClane . . . I can't, sir. The rules say —"

"I know what the rules say. *I* say give Miss Bly a glass of Scotch with ice. Now." Will didn't raise his voice, he didn't have to.

"Right away, sir."

Will handed Nellie her drink. She knocked back half of it in one gulp, wiped her lips with the back of her hand, and went for the jugular. "I hear August Belmont's thrown his hat in the ring. My source at City Hall says he submitted his own plan for the subterranean railway."

"Why don't you ask him yourself? He's sitting in the corner with John Rockefeller. Disparaging my plan, I'm sure."

"Because he's a stiff and he never tells me anything. Come on, Will. I've got a nine-o'clock deadline."

Will drained his glass and motioned for another. "It's true," he said. "He's got his own team of engineers. They mapped out a completely different route from mine and gave the plans to the mayor two days ago. They're telling him their plan is more economical."

Nellie put her glass down and started writing. "Is it?"

"On paper. In reality, their plan would cost the city more. A lot more."

"Why?"

"Belmont's route runs through ground that's swampy in

some places, pure shale in others. In some locations, he's put down lines that go right through underground streams. His routes are more direct than mine – that's how he's selling the mayor on his economics – but because of the natural obstacles, the whole operation will cost more – in time, man-hours, and material."

"What are you going to do?"

"Tell the mayor to get his head out of his ass and go with my plan."

"You know I can't use that. Much as I'd like to. Give me a real quote."

Will pondered, then said, "I have every confidence that our esteemed mayor and his learned councilors will consider Manhattan's topography, geography, and transportation requirements when weighing the merits of each plan. And I am equally confident that when they do, they will not fail to see the egregious flaws, errors, miscalculations, and outright misrepresentations of the Belmont plan. Not only would such a scheme bankrupt the city, but the faulty engineering principles used to implement it would jeopardize the very integrity of Manhattan's streets and structures – not to mention the safety of its citizens . . . how's that?"

"Perfect," she said, scribbling furiously. "Thanks, Will, you're a peach." She finished writing, closed her notebook, and took another swallow of whiskey, emptying her glass. Will got her another. She looked at him closely as he handed it to her.

"You all right? You look a little peaky."

"Me? I'm fine."

"You sure?"

He nodded, shrinking a bit under her gaze. He liked Nellie – very much, in fact – but he was always mindful of her profession. Giving a reporter business information was a good thing if you played it right, giving her personal information could be downright dangerous. He saw she was still looking at him, expecting an answer. He decided to admit to fatigue in hopes it would throw her off. "Maybe it's the work," he said. "I have been a bit tired these last few days."

"I'm not buying that. You thrive on competition. Something's wrong. Are you ill?"

Will sighed irritably. "Nothing's wrong! I'm fine, I just . . ."

She raised her glass to her lips, then stopped midway. "It's a woman, isn't it?"

"Anyone ever tell you you're too damn nosy, Nellie?"

"Everyone. Who is she?"

"Nobody! There is no woman! It's the subway. All right?"

Nellie raised an eyebrow, but she let the topic drop. Will was relieved, though he was angry with himself for allowing his emotions to show so blatantly. Fiona was on his mind constantly now, and try as he might, he couldn't make sense of his feelings for her. He'd tried to tell William Whitney, one of his oldest friends, about her, but Whitney only asked him why he was making such a fuss. "Just buy the girl a bauble and take her to bed," he'd advised.

He thought about telling his sister Lydia, but didn't think she'd react well; she was forever trying to interest him in a friend of hers, a widow from Saratoga. He'd finally decided on his younger brother Robert. They'd had drinks here a week ago, on the eve of yet another one of Robert's jaunts to Alaska, where he was prospecting for gold. Robert was thirty-six and had never married. He'd lost his fiancée, Elizabeth, to tuberculosis when they were both twenty-four. They had been deeply in love. Her death had broken his heart and he'd never gotten over it.

"Why all the agony, Will?" Robert had asked. "Bed her and be done with it."

"You sound just like Whitney. It's not like that," Will had said.

"We're speaking of a potential wife? Forgive me. I thought you meant a mistress."

"We're speaking of a woman. The most beautiful, smartest, funniest woman I've ever met," Will said.

"Does she know your feelings?"

"Maybe. I don't know. I haven't told her."

"Why not? It's been what . . . two years since Anna passed? Your mourning's over. You're free to marry again if you like. What's stopping you?"

"Complications, Robert. She's not . . . we don't share the same background."

"Ah," Robert said, taking a long swallow of his drink.

"She's a shopkeeper. I don't think my sons would accept her. Liddy, either. I don't know how her family would feel about me. And, of course, I'm a good deal older than she is."

"That *is* a difficult situation, my boy," Robert said. He paused for a moment, then said, "Do you love her?"

"I can't stop thinking about her. I've never met anyone I could talk to so easily . . ."

"Will . . . do you *love* her?"

He blinked, confused. "I don't know."

"You don't *know*? Will, you've been in love before, haven't you? I mean, with Anna, of course . . . and your various . . . well, you *have*, haven't you?"

Will looked into his glass. "No. No, I haven't." He swallowed selfconsciously. "Is this what it's like? This feeling . . . this sense of longing? It's horrible!"

Robert had laughed, amazed. "Yes, that's what it's like," he said, signaling to the waiter. "I'm going to get you another drink. Maybe the whole damn bottle. You look like you need it." He shook his head. "Didn't you ever wonder what you were missing?"

"No. I didn't believe in it. I thought it was something lady novelists invented." He shrugged helplessly. "Don't misunderstand me, Robert, I did feel something for Anna. She was a wonderful mother, a helpmate, a gracious person. But it was nothing like this."

"Christ, Will, that really does take the cake. In love for

the first time." He laughed. "I guess you *can* teach an old dog new tricks."

He grimaced. "Did you have to say *old* dog?"

Robert flapped a hand at him. "Why don't you let her decide if she'd like to see you? If you're worth it, she'll put up with the hardships."

"*If* I'm worth it?"

"Yes. If. And if she's half the woman you say she is, she's more than up to the task. Her family will come around. Yours, too." He smiled. "I already have. Liddy will. And you can disinherit your children if they refuse to."

A hand suddenly waved in front of his face. "Will? Will, are you listening to me?"

"Sorry, Nellie."

"Gee whiz, you've got it bad," she said. "You can say, or not say, whatever you like, but someone's stolen your heart." She leaned in closely. "You do have one, don't you?"

As Will was laughing, Cameron Eames, a young city judge and a friend of Will's eldest son, Will Junior, breezed through the door. "Evening, Mr. McClane," he said.

"Hello, Cameron," Will said.

"You have a guest, I see. I wasn't aware the club admitted ladies. Oh, it's *you*, Nellie."

"Gee, that's a fresh one, Eames. Hey, you lock up any kids lately? I saw some boys playing stickball a few streets over. You know what they say – stickball leads to stickups. You can't be too careful. Better call out the paddy wagons. Maybe the army while you're at it."

There were chuckles from two gentlemen standing nearby. Will heard them, so did Cameron. His face darkened. "That was a hysterical piece of reporting. From a hysterical lady reporter led more by her heart than her wits," he said.

"The kid was ten years old, Eames."

"He was a criminal."

"He was hungry."

Eames, fuming, turned to Will and said, "If Will Junior

arrives, would you let him know I'm in the dining room, Mr. McClane?"

"Of course, Cameron."

"Enjoy your meal, sir." He stalked off.

"That wasn't smart, Nell. Now he's going to tell the maître d' and get you thrown out."

"I'm sure he will. Why should his club be any different from his courtroom? He throws me out of *that* all the time, the smug little shit," she said. "Sorry. I know he's Will Junior's friend."

Will shrugged. "He's still a smug little shit." He felt a hand on his shoulder. "Hello, Dad. Nellie," a voice said. Will turned and smiled at the solidly built wheat-blond man of twenty-five standing at his side. It was his eldest son. As Will greeted him, always happy to see him, to see any of his children, he was struck by how much he favored his late mother. The older he got, the more he reminded him of Anna and her Dutch ancestors, with their fair coloring and their grounded, no-nonsense ways.

"I'm meeting Cameron. Any sign of him?" Will Junior asked. Cameron and Will Junior had grown up together in Hyde Park on the Hudson and attended Princeton together, joining all the same clubs and the same fraternity. Married now, they both kept homes in the Hudson Valley where their young families were ensconced, and apartments in the city where they stayed during the work week.

"He's in the dining room," Will replied.

"Good," Will Junior said. He turned to Nellie. "Scorcher of an article."

"I'll take that as a compliment."

"You could ruin a man's career with stories like that."

"Cameron can do that by himself. He doesn't need my help."

Since last January, when he'd been appointed a justice of the city's criminal courts, Cameron Eames had been on a highly publicized campaign to clean up New York. Contrary to the unending praise heaped upon him by the majority of the city papers, Nellie, a reporter for the *World*, had written a piece about a young Polish boy from the Lower East Side whom Cameron had remanded to the Tombs, Manhattan's jail, after he'd been caught stealing a loaf of bread. Though the theft was the child's first offense, he was locked up with a group of seasoned criminals. The next morning, the guards found his body stuffed under a mattress at the back of the cell. He'd been assaulted – a polite word for raped – and choked to death. Will's stomach turned when he'd read the article. He'd wondered how Cameron could've been so stupid.

"Cameron had a moral choice to make and he made it," Will Junior said, defending his friend.

Nellie laughed. "Please, McClane. The more so-called criminals he locks up, the more press he gets. We both know that. It's not morality that's driving Cameron, it's ambition."

"All right then, Nellie, Cam's ambitious. So am I and so are you. There's nothing wrong with that," Will Junior said hotly. "He wants to be the youngest justice ever named to the state supreme court. He'll do it, too, despite your attempts to slander him. His campaign's a success. He's put more criminals behind bars in a year than his predecessor did in the last three."

Will gave his son a long look. "All small-timers from what I hear. Cameron needs to go after the root of the problem if he's going to make a difference, son – the gaming-hall owners, the madams, the gang bosses. And the police officers who take bribes from them."

Will Junior snorted. "I said Cameron was ambitious, Dad, not crazy. The important thing is that he's locking up the lowlife. Making the streets safer for the rest of us."

"A wise judge understands the difference between stealing for gain and stealing to eat."

"You're too soft-hearted, Dad," Will Junior said irritably, ever impatient at subtleties, always one for the black-and-white view. "Stealing is stealing. The immigrant classes are overrunning the city. They have to be taught that their contempt for the law won't be tolerated here."

"Easy to say when you've never been hungry," Nellie said.

"How about the baker he stole from? What about him? Hasn't he got a family to feed?" Will Junior asked, his voice rising.

"For God's sake! It was a loaf of bread, not the contents of the man's cash register . . ."

Will gritted his teeth as Will Junior and Nellie continued their debate. He loved his son, but he found him – and many members of his generation – ruthless in their pursuit of money and standing and harsh toward the less fortunate. He had reminded him on many occasions that both the McClanes and their mother's family – the Van der Leydens – had at one time been immigrants. As had members of all the city's wealthy families. But Will's lectures made no difference to his son. He was an American. And those getting off the boat at Castle Garden were not. Italian, Irish, Chinese, Polish – nationality made no difference. They were lazy, stupid, and dirty. Their numbers spelled ruin for the country. The boy's intolerance was something he'd learned for himself, not from his parents. And it was the one thing Will did not like about him.

As he regarded Will Junior, gesturing at Nellie now, he wondered what he would make of Fiona. He knew the answer: he'd be appalled at the idea of his father seeing a woman who worked for her living, one who was a member of the very immigrant class he despised.

"No, Nellie! You're wrong!" he exclaimed, his voice too high for his father's liking. Will was just about to admonish him when they were interrupted by a loud, pushy "Hello, darlings!" Will stifled a groan. This would not help matters. The voice belonged to Peter Hylton, editor of "Peter's Patter," a feature in the *World* that was part of a new phenomenon in publishing known as the society pages. Designed to amuse readers with reports of the affairs and amusements of wealthy New Yorkers, "Peter's Patter" had become the newspaper's most popular feature, helping to push its already huge circulation through the roof. No one admitted to reading it, but everyone did. When the column praised a play, the theater's box office was swamped. If it panned a restaurant, it closed within a week.

Will thought the column an appalling and irresponsible misuse of the press, little better than rank gossip-mongering. Hylton did not respect the codes of public decency. He thought nothing of mentioning that a certain coal baron had been seen at the opera in the company of a woman not his wife. Or that the recent sale of a Fifth Avenue mansion was due to the owner's losses at the racetrack. The papers had recently begun to print photographs, and Hylton often had his photographers lurking outside of restaurants and theaters with their infernal cameras and flashes. Will had been blinded by them on more than one occasion. He did not like the man, and Will Junior despised him. Three years ago, when Will Junior had made his first bid for a seat in Congress, Hylton had written about his fondness for chorus girls. He was unmarried at the time, but such behavior did not sit well with the public. He lost the election. He tried to sue Hylton, but had no case. Hylton had described him, but had never actually referred to him by name. When pressed by Will Junior's attorney, he denied he'd been talking about him. He said his subject was another young businessman from a prominent family. Will Junior had had to drop his complaint.

"Hylton!" his son hissed now. "What the hell are you doing here?"

"I'm about to dine, dear boy. I'm a member now. Didn't you know? Just got voted in."

"Then I'm damn well resigning! I won't patronize a club that allows the likes of muckrakers like you and her" – he hooked a thumb in Nellie's direction – "in it."

"I'm the muckraker," Nellie said primly. "Peter doesn't deserve the title."

Will Junior ignored her. "You both think you can just go around sticking your noses into other people's business and splashing it all over the place, don't you? Anything goes, as long as you get fodder for your damned rag!"

Peter, a short, fat man given to bright clothing and gold jewelry, recoiled, pulling his stubby-fingered hands to his chest like a chipmunk. "My word! Hopefully the dining room's a little more civilized," he said, moving off.

Nellie watched him disappear into the dining room – a room whose occupants together were worth more than the gross national product of many countries. Whose power and influence shaped political and financial policy at the national and international levels. The envy in her eyes was palpable. "How come Hylton can get into this club and I can't?" she asked Will.

"Because he comes from a prominent family, believe it or not, and he's a man," he said.

"That's debatable," Will Junior fumed. "He's as swishy as a silk dress."

"He's got a wife and children. They live in New Jersey," Nellie said.

"I don't blame them," Will Junior said. "Will you join us for dinner, Dad?"

"I'm afraid I can't. I'm expecting guests. Carnegie and Frick."

"I'll be eager to hear how it went. I'll stop by your office first thing tomorrow. Bye, Dad," he said. He turned to Nellie. "Miss Bly," he said icily.

As he departed, the maître d', looking thunderous, advanced on them. "Miss Bly, I've told you a hundred times, ladies are not allowed in the Union Club," he said, taking her elbow.

She jerked it out of his grip, finished her drink, and placed the glass on the bar. "Thanks for the Scotch, Will. Looks like your ghoul here's throwing me out of this mausoleum."

"Miss Bly! I insist you depart the premises this instant!"

"All right, chuckles, keep your hair on. I can see when I'm not wanted."

"Hardly, Nell," Will said, smiling. He watched her leave, grousing at the hapless maître d' every step of the way. When she was gone, he looked around at the interior of his club. Mausoleum! He'd never thought of the Union in quite that way before, but Nellie had a point. Two elderly men shuffled by in dinner jackets, shouting at one another because they were both hard of hearing. Am I going to be here when I'm seventy? he wondered. Creaking around, gumming my dinner, haunting the place like some ghostly old fart?

He glanced at the other men around him – friends and colleagues – as they clustered by the bar or moved into the dining room. They spent their evenings here, not at their homes. Because there was no reason to. There was no love, no passion in their marriages, no warmth in their beds. He knew this; there had been none in his, either. They gave their hearts to their businesses, not their wives; that's why they were all so damned rich.

If it was that sort of arrangement he wanted, Will knew he could easily have it. His sister and his late wife's friends had taken it upon themselves to matchmake. If he went along with their designs, he'd find himself married to the same sort of woman his wife had been – socially eminent, old money, well-bred – with the same dull, unsatisfying marriage he'd had. His new wife would be his social equal. A partner. At best, a friend. She'd endure his sexual demands uncomplainingly, as Anna had, but she'd never demonstrate an ounce of desire or pleasure, because it wasn't proper. Sex was coarse and vulgar and only for making children. If he wanted a romp with a woman who enjoyed love-making, he'd take up with a mistress, as he had done many times in the past. He and his wife would have separate lives, separate bedrooms.

But, by God, if Fiona were his, he wouldn't stay in a separate bedroom. He'd make love to her every night, then fall asleep beside her, breathing in the sweet smell of her. He'd kiss her awake every morning and watch the life come back into those amazing eyes, watch her face crinkle into a broad, beautiful smile just for him. What would that be like? he wondered. To spend your life with a woman you were madly, passionately in love with? He'd never known. He was forty-five years old and he had never known what it was like to be in love. But he did now. Nothing, no one had ever touched his heart as she had.

The door to the bar opened again and Will saw Carnegie and Frick walk through it, their long robber-baron faces somber enough to knock the romance out of Cupid. And suddenly he had no wish to discuss subways.

"Robert, would you do it again?" he had asked his brother. A week ago. In this very room.

"Do what?"

"Ask Elizabeth to marry you. Even though . . . I mean, with all that happened."

"Even though she died?" Robert said gently. "Even though the love I felt for her seems to have ruined me for any other woman? Yes, I would. Without hesitation." Then he'd leaned forward and covered Will's hand with his own, a rare gesture between them. "You've followed your head your entire life, Will. It's time to follow your heart. You deserve that. At least once in your life. Everybody does."

34

Fiona, hands on her hips, stared at the mountain of wooden chests piling up on the sidewalk. A deliveryman handed her a piece of paper. She read it and signed it. Then she closed her eyes and inhaled. She could smell it, even through the lead-lined wood. Tea. Warm, rich, and beguiling. There was nothing like it.

"You're mad, you know that?" Michael said, suddenly appearing from behind Millard's wagon. "That's fifty bloody chests of tea! *Fifty!* Where the devil are you going to put it all?"

"In one sixty-six. Right next door. It's clean and dry in there. There's nothing to scent the tea, since it was only a fabric shop, not a stable or some other smelly thing. You *know* all this. I *told* you I spoke with Mr. Simmons and that he gave me a good deal on the rent," she added impatiently.

"I thought it was just talk! I didn't think you were serious."

"Could you help the men move it inside, do you think? Instead of standing here carrying on?" She glimpsed her brother scrambling up the chests. "Seamie! Come down before you fall!"

"Aw, Fee!"

"Fiona, that's five thousand pounds of tea sitting there," Michael said, following her as she went to yank her brother off the chests. "Five thousand pounds! You've spent a bleeding fortune! Who do you think you are? An Astor? A Vanderbilt? Well, you're not –"

"Not *yet*," she corrected him. "Seamie! I said come down!"

"Catch me, Uncle Michael!" Seamie yelled, launching himself straight at his uncle.

"Who the hell . . . ooof!" he grunted, stumbling backward with an armful of five-year-old. "Jaysus, lad! Almost knocked me straight on me arse, you did!"

"Might've shut you up for five minutes," Fiona said under her breath. To her brother she said, "Go inside and wash up for supper."

Brushing dust from his shirt, Michael resumed his rant. "What I want to know is who is going to pay for all of this?"

"We are. Millard's gave us ninety days instead of thirty. That's plenty of time."

Michael shook his head. "Hardly! Why did you have to buy fifty crates all at once?"

"I wanted to buy out Millard's entire stock of Indian tea. So no one else could get their hands on it. I told you that already, too. You don't listen to me."

"Two months from now we'll still be sitting on this, owing Millard's hundreds of dollars –"

Fiona cut him off. "No, we won't! Between the shop and my tearoom and the wholesale accounts –"

"What tearoom?"

"The one I'm going to have. I've already started hunting for a location."

"And what wholesale accounts?"

"Macy's. Crawford's. Child's Restaurants . . ."

"They've ordered from you?"

"Well, not yet." Michael rolled his eyes. "But they will!" she insisted. "I've got appointments with their buyers next week. I *know* they'll buy the tea as soon as they taste it. I just need a name for it. And some packaging I can show them. If you'd just help with the chests and let me go in to Nate and Maddie . . ."

"Too many bloody big ideas," Michael groused, pulling

a pair of work gloves from his pocket. "It's that William McClane who put them in your head. Next thing you'll go and buy us a whole bleeding tea plantation."

Fiona ignored the comment. She wished he hadn't mentioned Will. She had enjoyed his company so much and the fact that he hadn't called on her again saddened her, though she scolded herself for even having expectations. She told herself it was daft to think someone of his stature would be interested in her; she wasn't even good enough for a Whitechapel costermonger. Losing Joe had done more than break her heart – it had shattered her confidence, making her feel unattractive and unworthy. Feelings that Will's apparent lack of interest only served to confirm.

Michael, finally tired of haranguing her, grabbed a dolly from the delivery wagon and wheeled it over to the tea chests. Fiona returned to the shop, where her friends were waiting. Nate was chewing on the end of a pencil, his brow furrowed, as he contemplated the drawing Maddie had spread out on top of the oak counter.

Fiona took a look at it. "Oh, Maddie!" she cried, delighted. "It's beautiful!"

"Do you like it?" Maddie asked, flushing with pleasure.

"I love it!"

"I'm so glad. I was uncertain about the background. I wanted to ask Nick his opinion. He has such a good eye. He's coming soon, no? For supper, you said?"

"Yes, he is," she replied, turning around to look at the clock. She frowned when she saw it was already six-thirty. "He was supposed to be here by now. I wonder what's keeping him," she said. She was worried. He hadn't looked good the last time she saw him, but he'd said he felt fine. He'd told her not to fuss. She fretted too much, she knew she did. About Nick, Seamie, everyone. It drove them mad, but she couldn't help it. She'd lost too many people not to worry about coughs and colds and little brothers climbing too high.

"Maybe it's the painters," Maddie said. "He said he was having them in this week. To do the walls. Remember? Maybe they're keeping him."

"You're right. He did say that. He'll probably be along any minute." Relieved, Fiona turned her attention back to her friend's illustration.

Maddie had created a captivating scene of an Indian procession. Bejeweled maharajas on white elephants led the parade, followed by sari-clad women bearing baskets of tea leaves and children cavorting with parrots and monkeys. The maharajas held a banner aloft. It was blank.

"Will something go here?" Fiona asked, pointing to it.

"The tea's name," Nate said. "We need to give it one. We need to create a brand."

"A brand?"

"Yes. We have to teach the public to ask for your tea the same way they ask for a root beer, say, by ordering a Hires, or for soap by asking for a bar of Ivory. We have to convince them that your tea is better than the stuff sitting in a crate at their grocer's."

"How do we do that?"

"By brainstorming, to start with. Here, take some paper, and here's a pencil. Here, Mad, here's one for you. Let's start by writing down everything good about your tea, all of its qualities, to see if there's something there that would make a good name or a catchy slogan."

The three started scribbling, tossing words and descriptions at each other.

"Brisk . . . malty . . . biscuity . . ." Fiona said.

"Biscuity?" Nate echoed.

"It means a good aroma from a properly fired leaf."

"Too specialized. Keep going."

"Um . . . soothing . . . invigorating . . ." Fiona said.

"Well . . . which one?" Nate asked.

"Both."

"How can it be both?"

"I don't know, but it is."

"Coppery . . . strong . . . bold . . ." Maddie said.

"Refreshing . . . restorative . . ." Nate said.

The three friends kept on this way for a while, calling out anything they thought might be good, until they'd filled up their sheets of paper with words, but they still didn't have anything they liked. Stumped, Nate sighed, tapping his pencil against the counter. His eyes roved over Maddie's paper, looking for something they'd missed, then he looked at Fiona's notes.

"Hey!" he said. "What's this you've written, Fee?"

"Nothing, just scribbles."

"No, it's good. As a matter of fact, it's great! Look, Maddie."

In the lower left corner, she had written the words "delicious" and "tasty." Then she'd scribbled out "tasty" and had written "tasty tea," then "tastea," then she'd played around substituting the "tea" for "ty" on a few other words, like "raritea" and "qualitea."

"I think we've got something here," he said excitedly. "How about this . . . TasTea – a qualitea . . . with great affordabilitea . . . no, that's wrong, the last part. Um . . . what else could we do? Propertea, subtletea, personalitea, honestea, hostilitea . . ."

"Hostilitea?" Fiona said. "Oh, that's appealing, Nate."

"No . . . no, specialtea!" Maddie shouted.

"That's it, *cara*!" Nate yelled, kissing his wife. "Let's see . . . TasTea . . . TasTea . . . a qualitea . . ."

". . . an honestea, a most refreshing specialtea!" Fiona shouted.

"Yes! Yes! Perfect! Can you fit it all in the banner, Mad?"

"*Sì, sì,* I have room for it," Maddie said.

"There, Fiona, you have your ad! You can put it in newspapers, on billboards and buses, and you can use the design for your packaging, too."

"Thank you both! This is so exciting!" Fiona exclaimed, squeezing Nate's arm. "Imagine, my own brand of tea! Oh, blimey, I hope it sells! It has to, I have five thousand pounds of it sitting outside the door and an uncle who's ready to string me up."

"Of course it will," Nate said. "With an agency like Brandolini Feldman behind it, it can't fail. And the thing is, Fiona," he added eagerly. "A brand's just the *beginning*, only the tip of the iceberg. There are more kinds of tea than this one blend, right?"

"Yes. Dozens of different kinds."

"Well, just imagine a score of teas all sold under the TasTea name. Imagine the little tearoom you want to open turning into a fashionable destination, then growing into a chain! Imagine tearooms throughout New York and Brooklyn and Boston and Philadelphia . . ."

". . . up and down the whole East Coast, throughout the whole country!" Fiona exclaimed.

"And you'll have wholesale accounts with hotels," Nate said.

"And department stores," Fiona crowed.

"And railways and passenger ships," Maddie added.

"And you two will be doing nothing but TasTea ads and campaigns and packaging and . . ."

"It will be a huge success," Maddie said, beaming. "For all of us!"

Laughing, Fiona took her friend's hands and started to waltz around the store with her, whirling giddily until they were both so dizzy that Nate had to steady them. The three of them were making so much noise that no one saw the boy step into the doorway, his cap in his hands. He was about ten years old. He stood for a while, watching them anxiously, hoping he'd be noticed, then finally came up behind Nate and tugged on his jacket.

"Excuse me, sir," he said.

"I'm sorry, son," Nate said. "I didn't see you there. What can I do for you?"

"Is this where Fiona Finnegan lives?"

"Yes, that's me," Fiona said, leaning on the counter, trying to catch her breath.

"You have to come with me, miss. Quick. You have to," he said, starting for the door.

"I'm Stevie Mackie. My ma said to get you. She says our lodger, Mr. Soames, is dying."

Fiona took the stairs at 24 Sixteenth Street two at a time. All thoughts of tea and tearooms were gone from her mind. She had only one thought now, only one fear – that she was going to lose her best friend in all the world.

In the cab they'd taken, Stevie told her that his mother had learned of Nick's illness just this afternoon. The rent was past due and she'd gone to see him about it. When no one answered the door, she'd let herself in. She'd found him in his bedroom. He was very sick.

"With what, Stevie?" Fiona had asked, terrified of his answer.

"I don't know. My ma didn't say. She wouldn't let me go into his rooms. She's awful scared of the cholera. She found a notebook on his table, though. Your address was in it and his doctor's. She sent me after you and my brother after the doctor."

I should never have listened to him, Fiona thought, racing up the last few steps. He wasn't well. I knew he wasn't. I should never have believed his rubbishy explanations. She got to the door, Stevie on her heels, and tried the knob. It didn't budge, the door was locked. "The key, Stevie," she said, her voice trembling. "Where's the key?"

"Ma!" he shouted up the stairwell. "Ma, I've got Miss Finnegan. She needs the key."

Fiona heard footsteps on the landing above her, and then a tall woman in her forties, plain and rawboned and wearing a faded calico dress, came down the stairs toward her.

"Have you got the key?" Fiona asked her urgently.

"You're Miss Finnegan?"

"Yes."

"I'm Mrs. Mackie . . ."

"I need the key," Fiona said, her voice rising.

"Yes, yes, of course," Mrs. Mackie said, flustered. She dug in one pocket, then the other. "He was calling for you. I don't know how long he's been like this. Some days, I think –"

"The key!" Fiona shouted.

"Here," she said, holding it out. Fiona snatched it, then jammed it into the lock. "He's very bad, miss." Mrs. Mackie said, agitated. "I wouldn't go in there if I were you. It's not a sight for a young lady and God only knows what it is he has."

Fiona opened the door and ran inside, leaving Mrs. Mackie in the hallway. The flat was dark, the curtains were drawn, but she knew the way. She'd been there before. "Nick?" she shouted, running through the foyer, down the hallway, past the kitchen, into a double parlor and out again, down another hallway past a bathroom to his bedroom. "Nick?" she called again, but there was still no answer. "Please, God, please let him be all right," she whispered. "Please."

A powerful, wrenching stench hit her as she opened the door to his room – the smell of sweat and sickness and something else, something low and black and fearfully familiar – the smell of despair. "Nick?" she whispered, rushing to him. "It's me, Fiona."

He was lying in his bed, a large ebony four-poster, wearing only his trousers, which were wet with urine. He was still and looked as white and bloodless as the sweat-soaked sheets underneath him. The beautiful man she had met in Southampton was gone; an emaciated wraith had taken his place. She pressed her palms against his cheeks, found that he was clammy but warm, and sobbed with relief. She pushed a lock of damp hair off his forehead and kissed him. "Nick, it's me, Fiona," she said. "Can you hear me? Answer me, Nick, please answer me."

His eyelids fluttered. He swallowed. "Fee," he croaked, "go away." His lips were cracked; his mouth was dry. She ran into the bathroom, found a glass, and filled it with water. Back at his side, she held his head up and pressed the glass to his lips. He clutched at it, gulping the water greedily. He coughed, then vomited a good deal of it back up. Fiona turned him over on his side until he was done retching so he wouldn't choke, then helped him to drink more, a bit at a time. "Easy," she said. "There's plenty here. Go slowly . . . that's it."

When he'd drained the glass, she laid his head gently down on his pillows.

"Please go, Fiona," he whispered. "I don't want you here . . . can take care of myself." He began to shiver. His hands scrabbled futilely at the sheets. Fiona grabbed the quilt he'd kicked down to the bottom of his bed and covered him with it.

"Yes, I can see that. You've done a bang-up job of it so far," she said. His teeth started to chatter. She got in the bed next to him, put her arms around him, and held him, trying to warm him. "I swear, Nick, as soon as you're better, I'm going to kill you for this."

"Not going to get better."

"Yes, you *are*! Tell me what's wrong!"

He shook his head. She was about to badger him when a loud, booming "Hallo?" was heard from the hallway.

"In here!" she shouted.

A bald, bespectacled man with a silver beard entered the room. "Dr. Werner Eckhardt, ja?" he said. "Excuse me, please." He shooed Fiona away and began to examine Nick.

Fiona watched anxiously from the bottom of the bed, her elbows cupped in her palms as the doctor questioned Nick, stared into his eyes, massaged his neck, and listened to his chest. "What's that for?" she asked, when he produced a syringe.

"To steady the heartbeat," he replied. "How long has he been like this?"

"I . . . I don't know. I saw him last Sunday. It's Saturday now . . ."

The doctor uttered an expression of disgust. "I told him

this would happen. I instructed rest and a proper diet." He produced a second syringe. "To undo the dehydration," he said. "I need a basin of hot water and some soap. Washcloths and towels, too. He will have bedsores from lying in the damp. They must be cleaned before they become septic."

Fiona did as she was told. She collected everything the doctor required and then, over Nick's feeble protests, helped Eckhardt strip off his clothes, wash him, change his dirty bedding, and put him into clean pajamas. She prided herself on a strong stomach and did not flinch at the raw, angry sores that mottled his thighs and backside, but the sight of his hipbones jutting through his flesh, his bony kneecaps, and the hollows between his ribs made her chin quiver. She'd seen that he'd lost weight. She'd known he was unwell on the ship. Something had been wrong all along. Why, oh why hadn't she pressed him?

"There, that's better. We let him lie still for a few minutes, no? Give the drugs time to take effect. We talk outside. Come."

As soon as they were out of Nick's earshot, Fiona grabbed the doctor's arm. "Is he all right? He's not going to die, is he?"

"Are you related to Mr. Soames?" Eckhardt asked.

"Yes. I'm . . . I'm his cousin," she lied. "He's dying, isn't he?" she asked tearfully.

The doctor shook his head. "No, but he is very ill. He will make it through this, but if he doesn't begin to take care of himself, he will deteriorate. Rapidly. I will tell you, as I have told him, that the spirochete is an opportunist. Good diet and plenty of rest are essential to forestalling it. As far as treatment goes –"

"Please, Dr. Eckhardt," Fiona said, worried to death about Nicholas and confused by the man's long-winded explanation. "What's wrong with him? What does he have?"

Eckhardt peered at her over the top of his spectacles

with an expression of surprise. "Why, syphilis, of course. Forgive me, I thought you knew."

"Miss Finnegan, you take him out of here right now!" Mrs. Mackie shrilled. "It's shameful! A disgrace! I won't have the likes of him under my roof!"

Fiona sat on Nick's settee. "Mrs. Mackie," she said, trying to keep her voice steady, her anger under control, "I'm not sure he can be moved right now."

"Either you move him or I'll move him. And all his goods, too. Right into the street!"

Fiona took a deep breath, trying desperately to figure out a way to deal with her very sick friend, his flat, his things. She didn't want to move him, he was too ill, but it appeared she had no choice. Mrs. Mackie had been standing in the next room while she and Dr. Eckhardt were talking. She'd heard everything.

Fiona watched the woman as she continued to rant. Fiona's terrible temper reared at the sight of her, kicking inside of her skull like a wild horse. This woman had come in here to get her rent money. She had seen Nick, seen the condition he was in, and she had returned to her flat, leaving him to suffer – soaked in his own piss, shivering in his sweat. She hadn't even given him a glass of water. Now she was throwing him out. Fiona felt her hands ball into fists. She wanted nothing more at this very second than to knock Mrs. Mackie on her righteous arse. But she couldn't; she needed her cooperation.

"Look, Mrs. Mackie," she finally said. "I'll take Mr. Soames with me right now, but please allow me to keep his things here for the next two weeks. We'll pay you an extra month's rent for the inconvenience."

Mrs. Mackie pursed her lips, mulling her offer. "Plus I keep the security deposit," she finally said. "All of it."

Fiona agreed, relieved. Nick's paintings, mistakenly routed to Johannesburg instead of New York, had finally arrived and were downstairs in crates. She couldn't let this shrew put them out on the street. She had no idea where she herself would put them, but she'd deal with that problem later. Right now she had to take care of Nick.

When she walked back into his room, she found him propped up against his pillows. His eyes were closed, but his breathing sounded better and his skin didn't have quite the same pallor. He still looked heartbreakingly frail, though, and she wondered how on earth she was going to get him dressed and into a cab.

"He told you," he said weakly.

"Yes."

He turned his face away. "I expect you'll be leaving now. I quite understand."

His words were like a match to the fuse of her anger – anger at Mrs. Mackie, at Dr. Eckhardt and the matter-of-fact way he'd told her about Nick's illness, and anger at Nick for letting himself get so sick. The fuse caught and her fury exploded. "You stupid, stupid man!" she shouted. "Is that what you think? That I want to leave you just because you're ill? Is that why I pleaded with a God I don't even believe in to save your sorry arse? So I can walk out on you?"

Nicholas said nothing.

"You answer me, Nick! Why did you lie to me?"

"I had to!"

"Not to *me*!"

"I . . . I thought I'd lose you, Fiona. For God's sake, it's *syphilis*!"

"I don't care if it's the plague; don't you ever lie to me again! I knew something was wrong and you told me there wasn't! You could've died!"

"Please don't be so mad at me," he said quietly.

Fiona realized she was yelling at a very sick man. She walked around to the other side of the bed so she could see his face. "I'm not mad at you. But no more fibs, all right? We're in this together. You're coming home with me and you're going to get well."

Nick shook his head. "I can't burden you like that."

"It's not a burden," she said, sitting on the bed. "You can sleep in my room. Mary and I can take turns looking after you, and –"

"Fiona, there's something I need to tell you. There are things you don't know about me. I didn't get this disease from . . . from a woman."

She nodded and Nick pressed on, awkwardly trying to explain his sexual predilections, until she stopped him.

"Nicholas . . . I know. I saw the photo. It fell out one day as I was putting your watch away. He looked so happy, the man in the picture. I thought you must've taken it and that he must be your lover."

"He was," Nick said sadly.

"Was? Where is he now?" she asked.

Nick closed his eyes for a few seconds. When he opened them again, they were bright with tears. "In Paris. In the Père Lachaise cemetery. He died last autumn."

"Oh, Nick, I'm so sorry. How? What happened?"

Over the course of the next hour, with pauses for water or a rest, Nick told Fiona all about Henri. He told her how they met and how much Henri had meant to him. So much, in fact, that he'd turned his back on his family to stay in Paris with him. He had been happy, he told her, and he hadn't regretted his choice, but one September evening his happiness was taken away.

He and Henri were walking by the Seine, he explained. Henri hadn't felt well. He had chills and aches. Nick felt his head, then put a comforting arm around him. Normally, he didn't touch Henri in public – it was too dangerous – but he was so concerned, he'd done it without thinking. The gesture was seen by a group of louts walking behind them. They were set upon and thrown into the river. Henri went under, but Nick was able to pull him out. "He was conscious when I got him to the street," he said. "But by the time help arrived, he'd passed out."

He himself had been roughed up; he'd suffered cuts and

bruises, a black eye, nothing too serious. Henri, however, had a fractured skull. He never regained consciousness and died two days later.

"I was devastated," Nick said. "I couldn't eat or sleep. I didn't show up for work for over a month and lost my job."

The hospital notified Henri's parents – a proper bourgeois couple who lived outside Paris. They hadn't approved of their son's painting, or his companions, and refused to allow any of them to attend his funeral.

"I grieved alone," Nick said. "I thought I would go mad with sorrow. I couldn't bear the sight of our flat, the streets we'd walked down, the cafés where we'd eaten."

Then, two weeks later, he'd received a letter from his mother, begging him one last to time to reconsider, to come home. Her words caught him at a weak moment. Distraught, in need of the comfort of his family – even though he knew he could never tell them about Henri – he decided to go back. There was nothing left in Paris for him.

When he arrived home his mother and sisters were happy to see him, but his father was hateful; he berated him constantly for ignoring his responsibilities. Nick tried his best to please the man. He took up his duties, worked hard, oversaw the opening of new bank branches, even undertook the grinding preparatory work on a string of public offerings that Albion was underwriting by poring over countless balance sheets, deeds, and payrolls; by visiting factories and dockyards, mines and mills – but nothing he did was good enough. He became severely depressed, started to drink, and even contemplated suicide. He went out every night just to avoid his father. Sorrowing, bitter, desperate for distraction from his pain, he allowed himself to fall in with a group of upper-class wastrels – spoiled, decadent young men, most of whom were of the same persuasion as he was. One drunken, out-of-control evening, they ended up at a male brothel in Cleveland Street and he slept with one of the rent boys. It was human contact, a way to lose himself. He'd regretted it the next morning, but he'd done it again, many times. He continued to drink and woke up many mornings unable to remember where he'd been the night before or how he'd gotten home.

His health began to suffer. He felt weak, lethargic. His mother noticed and made him see the family physician, Dr. Hadley. He assumed the man would treat his case with discretion, but he was wrong. Dr. Hadley diagnosed syphilis and promptly reported it to his father, who beat him bloody. He threw him against a wall in his study, called him an abomination, and cursed God for giving him such a son. He told him to get out of his house. He gave him a choice: Go to America and die there quietly and he'd establish an investment fund for him, one that would provide a generous income. Or stay in London and die penniless in the streets.

"I was lying on the floor, Fee, trying to catch my breath. My father was walking out of his study when he suddenly came back, leaned over me, and told me he knew what I was. He said he knew about Paris and Arles, and Henri, too. I felt my blood go cold. He told me what the house I lived in looked like and the names of the cafés I frequented. 'If you know all that, then you know about Henri's death, don't you?' I said to him. And as I said it, hatred flooded me. I'd always known he was a monster, but to think he'd known of my loss and said nothing! And then, Fiona, he smiled and said, 'Knew about it? Nicholas, I paid for it!' "

Fiona was weeping as Nick finished his story. Her heart was breaking for him. That a father could do to a child what his father had done to Nick was inconceivable to her. To have his son's lover murdered. To throw his own flesh and blood into the streets like a dog.

Nick wiped his eyes. The small reserve of strength he'd built up after Eckhardt's visit was ebbing away again. Fiona realized she had to get him home fast, before it was gone completely.

As she was hunting for clean clothes to put on him, he

said, "At least now it won't be long before I join Henri."

"Don't you talk that way," she told him, her voice fierce. "Henri is just going to have to wait. You're in my hands now. And you're going to get better. I'm going to make you."

35

"Their numbers are growing," Davey O'Neill said. "Scores more are joining every week. They're not afraid. They're bloody angry and they're not going to back down. They'll strike before the year is out. My guess is autumn at the latest."

O'Neill watched as William Burton's face darkened. He saw him slide his hand into his pocket, saw his fingers curl around something inside of it.

"Careful now, guv. Cut the other one off and we'll 'ave to get someone else to do your earwigging," Bowler Sheehan said, snickering.

Davey didn't flinch. He didn't budge. It was better not to. Burton reminded him of a savage animal – a wolf or a jackal – the sort of animal that watched and waited and never chased until you ran. Burton had cut him once, here on Oliver's Wharf, and Davey did not want to feel his knife again, though the physical pain, as bad as it was, had been short-lived. It was the other kind, the kind that came from inside, from the scabbed place where his soul used to be, that drove him mad. A pain that made him want to cut his own throat every time he sat in a union meeting, memorizing names and dates and plans. Or listened to one of his fellow dockers wonder aloud how it was that the owners and foremen always seemed to know the union's next move before they themselves did. He would have topped himself, too, if it weren't for his wife and children. They would be destitute without him. As it was, Burton's money had given them the only security they'd ever known. He could afford a doctor for Lizzie now and the right medicine. Seeing the color come back into her cheeks and watching her frail matchstick limbs fill out were the only things that brought him any joy.

Sarah, his wife, had never questioned the story he'd told her about his ear or the sudden change in their fortunes. She just took the extra money he handed her every week without comment, grateful to have it. There was meat for everyone at teatime now. There were warm woolen underthings and new boots for the children. She'd asked for a new jacket and skirt for herself, too, but he'd said no. And she'd wanted to move the family to a better house a few streets over but he would not allow that, either. She'd protested and he'd told her she was to mind what he said and not question him for he had good reasons.

But one day, fed up with his tightfistedness, she'd bought herself a new hat – a pretty straw boater with red cherries on it. She'd come home wearing it, pleased and proud of the only new thing she'd ever had. He'd ripped it off her head and thrown it into the fire. Then he'd slapped her so hard he knocked her down. He'd never hit her before. Never. She'd cowered and cried and he'd felt sick to his stomach, but he'd warned her that if she ever disobeyed him again, she'd get far worse.

Dockers weren't stupid. If a man's wife suddenly flaunted a flashy hat, if his kids had new clothes, it was noticed and remarked upon. Though Tillet and the other leaders expressly forbade violence, Davey knew there were rank-and-file members who would rip him limb from limb if they ever found out he was spying.

Sarah hadn't bought herself anything new after that. She didn't smile much anymore, either. She turned away from him when he came to bed, and her eyes, when she could bring herself to look at him, were cold. He'd overheard her once talking to her mother, telling her she thought the money had come from thieving. Oh, Sarah, he'd thought, if only it were that noble!

Burton took his hand out of his pocket and cracked his knuckles. "What are the exact numbers? What have they got in their war chest?"

"Impossible to say exactly," Davey replied, hoping he could bluff.

"Try, Mr. O'Neill, try. Or my colleague here will walk into your flat and snap your daughter's neck as if she were nothing more than an unwanted kitten."

Sickened yet again by his utter powerlessness, Davey talked. "The Tea Operatives and General Laborers' 'ave about eight hundred members," he said.

"And the money?"

"Nothing to speak of."

Sheehan laughed at that and asked Burton what he was worrying about. But then Davey told them that the stevedores' union was nearly five thousand strong and had three thousand pounds in their coffers. And they had pledged their support. If the dockers walked off the river, the stevedores would be right behind them. So would the lightermen and watermen. Burton raised an eyebrow at that, but Sheehan flapped a hand at Davey's words.

"The more the merrier, they'll all starve," he said. "Three thousand quid won't feed the whole riverside. Not for long. Even if they do call a strike, they'll come crawling back in two, maybe three days. Soon as their beer money runs out."

"I hope you're right, Mr. Sheehan," Burton said quietly. His calm, low tone unnerved Davey. "I can't afford a strike. Not now. My capital's spread far too thin."

"It'll never 'appen," Sheehan said. "You're worrying over nothing, guv'nor. Just like that Finnegan girl. I told you she'd disappear and she 'as. Probably dead by now."

Burton reached into his breast pocket and handed Davey an envelope. Their gaze locked for a few seconds as he took it from him, and Davey saw that Burton's eyes were as flat and impassive as a shark's. They were devoid of fury and that should've comforted him, but it did not. He would've preferred anger to what he saw in them now –

a black, yawning emptiness. Bottomless and terrifying.

"There are river rats below us. I can hear them scrabbling," Burton said.

Davey didn't hear anything. "I . . . I beg your pardon, sir?"

"Rats will eat anything if they're hungry. Even human flesh. Did you know that?"

"N-no, sir. I didn't."

"Go home, O'Neill," he said. "Go home and keep the rats away." Then he turned and walked to the edge of the dock.

Confused, Davey looked at Sheehan, but Sheehan only shrugged. Davey left then. He went back through the dark warehouse, just as he always did, walking at first, then suddenly he broke into a panicked run, stumbling once, righting himself, and running even faster until he reached the street door. As he grasped the handle, he looked back over his shoulder, expecting to see Burton right behind him, his knife raised, his awful dead eyes boring into him. He hurriedly let himself out and ran down the Wapping High Street, more afraid than he'd been the night Burton cut him, more afraid than he'd ever been in his life.

36

"Keep them up for one more second, duck, whilst I get this on you. Just one more second . . . there!" Mary said, threading Nick's arms through the sleeves of a fresh pajama top. She tugged the opening over his head, buttoned the neck, then leaned him back against his pillows. "That was very good! You couldn't do that last week; I had to hold your arms up for you."

"I'll be running the hundred-yard dash in a week," Nick said, smiling. "Just you wait."

"I doubt that, but you *are* making progress. Your color's improved and you've more strength than you had. If only we could get some meat on those bones. All right, now for the bottom half." Mary slid his pants off, dipped her sponge in warm water, and washed him down.

Nick had been mortified the first time she bathed him. No one had ever done that except his Nanny Allen and he'd been a child then. He'd protested, saying he could take a proper bath, in a tub, by himself, but Mary paid him no attention. She'd bustled him out of his clothes, kidding him until he got over his modesty. "I've seen one before, you know," she'd said. "Mr. Munro, God rest him, had some fine equipment on him. How do you think I got Ian?"

Nick had laughed despite himself. "I'm sure mine will be a disappointment to you, Mary. I can't compete with a strapping Scotsman. They build their men big over there."

"Indeed they do, lad," she'd said, with such a note of lusty desire in her voice, she made him laugh even more.

398

He looked at his night table as Mary dipped her sponge and wrung it out again. There was a vase of roses on it from Alec, a book of verse by Walt Whitman from Nate and Maddie, and a self-portrait that Seamie had made. They had all been so good to him. He was astonished by their kindness. He felt Mary's gentle hands kneading his calves, chafing his ankles. To keep the blood moving, she'd explained. His own mother had never touched him so.

And Fiona . . . a lump rose in his throat at the thought of her. She'd saved him. He was only alive because of her, his lionheart. She'd begged and bullied him into pulling through. Her devotion amazed and humbled him. She'd given up her bed and had been sleeping on the floor next to him on a mattress. The first few nights, when he'd been afraid, she'd talked to him in the dark. When the pain got very bad, she'd reached up and taken hold of his hand. The strength in that hand . . . he knew it was a mad notion now, but then he'd felt as if her fierceness, her formidable will, flowed out of her and into him, giving him courage.

He was still not fully recovered, but because of Fiona and her family and the Munros, he was better than he had a right to be, and had even begun thinking that he might soon be up and about. Eckhardt, that angel of darkness, was supposed to visit him that afternoon and tell him when he could get out of bed.

Mary finished his sponge bath, slid fresh bottoms on him, and pulled the sheets up to his chest. He tried to thank her, but she shushed him. She went to dump the bathwater, then came back with the baby in her arms. "I've got to get the supper started," she said. "Could I leave Nell with you for a bit? Are you up to it?"

Nick said he was. She tucked the baby into the crook of his arm, gave him a rusk for her, and bustled off to the kitchen, humming as she went. As the baby gummed her biscuit, Seamie came bounding into his room, crawled up on the bed, and demanded a story.

"Where have you been? You're black as a sweep!" Nick said to him.

"Trapping slugs. They're eating the flowers."

"Did you dig a bunker to do it? Look at your ears!"

"There you are!" Michael said, striding into the room. "Come on. It's time for a bath."

"Noooo!" Seamie howled, carrying on as if his uncle had threatened him with the guillotine instead of the tub.

"Mary said you're to have one. You're too dirty to sit at the table."

"But, I don't *want* one!"

"It's very simple, laddie – no bath, no supper."

Seamie looked to Nick for a reprieve. He shook his head sorrowfully. "I'm afraid there's no help for it, old man. She made me have one, too."

Seamie capitulated. He followed his uncle out of Nick's room, his head hanging down, a condemned man. Nick was trying to stop Nell from mashing the soggy rusk into her dress when he heard a soft knock at the door.

"*Signora!*" he exclaimed, delighted to see Maddie standing there. "*Ciao, mia bella!*"

"*Ciao, bello.* Do you have a moment? I want to show you the drawing for Fiona's tea boxes. It's almost complete, but I think the background needs work. See where it folds to make the lid? What do you think?"

"Bring it closer, Maddie . . . here, why don't you pull up a chair?"

She sat down near the bed and held the illustration up. "I see what you mean," Nick said. "Once the box is cut and folded, the bungalow's going to disappear. Get rid of it. You don't need it. The parade's busy enough. Just extend the greenery over the top and . . ."

As they were talking, a terrible caterwauling started in the bathroom.

> *"I'm a rambler, I'm a gambler, I'm a long way*
> * from home,*

And if you don't like me, then leave me alone.
I'll eat when I'm hungry, I'll drink when I'm dry,
And if whiskey don't kill me, I'll live till I die. . . ."

"What *is* that?" Maddie asked, alarmed.

"Seamie and Michael singing," Nick said, laughing. "Isn't it awful?"

He was about to resume his critique of Maddie's work when they both heard the door to the flat bang open, then slam shut. Sharp, determined footsteps came down the hallway.

"Michael!" Fiona bellowed, stalking by Nick's door with a large metal scoop in her hand.

Nick and Maddie made uh-oh faces at each other.

"What do you want? I'm busy!" he shouted back.

"Did you leave a bag of cinnamon on top of the tea chest in the shop? The whole bloody thing stinks! Smell it! That's a good fifty pounds of tea ruined!"

"Don't come in, Fee, I'm naked!" Seamie yelled. "You'll see my willie!"

"Oh, Seamie, nobody's interested in your willie. And I don't want to hear you singing that daft drinking song!"

"Is it always this noisy here?" Maddie asked, giggling.

"This is nothing," Nick said. "You should've been here two nights ago when Seamie bounced on the settee and went right through it. There were some fireworks then."

Mary came into the room with a cup of beef broth. Maddie took the baby from Nick so he could drink it. "You're to get it all down you, Nick," Mary said. "Every drop. And I want you to try a little solid food later. A bit of mash and gravy."

She left. A few seconds later a wet, naked Seamie went whizzing by the door, with Michael in hot pursuit. A few more minutes passed, then Fiona came in with a tea tray.

"Hi, Maddie, how's the tea box coming? Hi, Nick, how are you feeling?" she asked them. Before either could answer, she said, "Taste this for me, would you? Tell me if you like

401

it. Michael left a big bag of cinnamon sticks on top of the tea. I thought he'd wrecked it, but now I think he might just have invented a whole new product – scented teas! Just imagine – we could do the same thing with vanilla beans. And cloves. And maybe some dried orange peel."

"I think it's awfully good," Nick said.

"It's wonderful!" Maddie chimed in, taking another sip.

The doorbell rang. "Coming!" they heard Mary call. Fiona sat down on the end of Nick's bed. She took her boots off and tucked her feet up under her. As they sat discussing other ideas for other flavors, Nate poked his head in.

"How's the patient?" he asked cheerfully.

"Very well," Nick said.

"I passed a newsstand on my way back from a client's office. Thought you might like a paper. Hi, Fee. Hi, Mad." He crossed the room, bent over, and kissed his wife. "What smells so good?"

Fiona, all charged up by her latest idea, launched into a breathless explanation. Nate loved the idea and he and Maddie immediately started tossing out ideas for names. Seamie, wearing clean clothes, his wet hair combed back, ran in with a picture book and crawled into his sister's lap. The doorbell went again. Michael walked by, grumbling that his flat was turning into Grand Central Station.

They were all chattering away, sipping cinnamon tea, when suddenly Dr. Eckhardt appeared in the doorway, his black bag in hand. He took a look around the room, then said, "If I recall correctly, I instructed rest and quiet."

There were sheepish expressions all around.

"Come on, Seamie, we have to go now," Fiona said, pushing him off her lap.

"Why? I want a story!"

"Later. The doctor has to examine Nick so he can make him better."

"Is he going to kiss his boo-boo?"

Fiona snorted laughter. So did Nate, Maddie, and Nick.

A withering look from Eckhardt sent them scurrying. The doctor shut the door after them, then proceeded to examine his patient, spending a long time listening to his heart, feeling his abdomen, inspecting his fingers and toes. When he was finished, he told Nick he was doing better than he expected.

"That's good news," Nick said happily. "What's done it? The medicine?"

Eckhardt shrugged. "I doubt it. Laughter, comfort, good care . . . these are far more potent medicines than I can offer. But you must continue to take bed rest. You may walk around the apartment a few times a day, in fact I advise it, but no more than that. If you feel like eating some real food, do so. As for everything else" – he inclined his head toward the doorway – "the specialists in the other room seem to have it well in hand. Your family, I presume?"

"No, they're my . . ." Nick paused. He thought of his father, who'd thrown him against a wall. He thought of his mother and sisters, who had not written to him in all the weeks he'd been here. He thought of Mary, touching him so tenderly. Of Seamie and Michael and Ian and Alec. And he thought of the person he loved most in all the world, Fiona. Then he smiled broadly and said, "Yes, Dr. Eck. My family."

37

"Bloody hell, Mary! Where did they all come from?" Fiona asked, trying to take in the scores of red roses – in vases on end tables; in canning jars on the windowsill, the mantel, the secretary; in buckets on the floor.

"I don't know! They came an hour ago. I tried to get your attention, but you and Michael were busy, so I had the deliveryman bring them up and I put them in water. There must be two hundred of them. Oh, I almost forgot! There's a card . . ."

Fiona looked at the name on the front. "It's for . . . *Michael?*" she said in disbelief. "Who'd be sending him all these roses?" She was miffed and more than a little jealous. No one had ever sent her two hundred roses.

"Hothouse flowers." Alec sniffed dismissively, inspecting the blooms.

Seamie was holding one long stem like a wand, tickling Nell's nose with the petals, making her giggle.

"Fiona?" Michael yelled from the doorway.

"In here," she shouted back.

"Do you have the shop key? I can't find . . . Jaysus! What's with all the flowers? Your horse win the derby?"

"No. Is there something you want to tell us?"

"Tell you?"

"Here." She handed him the card. "They're for you."

"What?" He snatched the card, saw his name on the envelope, and ripped it open. "That figures," he said derisively. "A typical eejit with far too much money. Has to send four thousand roses when a bunch of tulips would do."

"Who sent them?" Fiona asked.

"Who's an eejit?" Seamie asked.

"Never mind, Seamie. Uncle Michael, who sent them?"

"William McClane."

Fiona arched an eyebrow. "Really? I had no idea it was like that between you two."

"That's very funny, Fiona, but he didn't send them to me. They're for you . . ."

Fiona's eyes widened.

". . . the card's for me. He wants to take you to Delmonico's on Saturday, but he wants my permission first. He says the flowers are a small token of his esteem. He says —"

"Give me that!" she demanded, grabbing the card.

"What's it say, lass? What's it say?" Mary asked excitedly, slipping her arm through Fiona's.

Fiona read it aloud.

"Dear Mr. Finnegan,

"With your consent, I would like to invite your niece to supper at Delmonico's on Saturday evening. I would call for her at seven o'clock. Reservations would be for eight o'clock. I would have her home by midnight. Please ask your niece to accept these roses as a small token of my esteem. I await your reply.

"Respectfully,
"William Robertson McClane."

She hugged the card to her chest.

"Oh, Fiona, how exciting!" Mary squealed. "William McClane, no less!"

He wanted to see her again. And she wanted to see him. And the notion that he'd been thinking about her, that he'd gone to a florist and picked out red roses – far too many of them – and sent them to her just because he knew she liked them made her indescribably happy. It felt so nice that somebody – that a *man* – wanted to please her.

"Delmonico's is a fancy place, isn't it, Mary?" she said, her eyes shining. "What will I wear?"

"We'll go shopping, Fiona. One afternoon when the shop is quiet and you can steal away, I'll leave Nell with Alec and we'll go to Sixth Avenue and find you a dress."

Michael glowered at Mary, visibly unhappy with her enthusiasm. "What's so exciting about Will McClane, anyway?" he groused. "I've seen him. He's not so much. He's the wrong church, you know. Wrong party, too. He's a Republican," he said darkly, as if informing them all that Will was a mass murderer. "And besides, I haven't made up me mind yet."

"Don't you even think of saying no," Fiona warned him.

"How can I say yes? I can't play chaperon to someone ten years older than me."

"Chaperon? I don't need a chaperon, Uncle Michael. I'm eighteen years old!"

"And he's forty-odd and too damned rich! No niece of mine is gadding about the city at night on the arm of a –"

"What's going on?" Nick asked groggily. He'd stumbled out from the bedroom and was knotting the belt on his silk dressing gown. "I heard voices. I thought I was dreaming." He blinked at the sea of roses before him. "My word, look at all the flowers! Did somebody die?" he asked, alarmed. He put his hand over his heart and checked for a beat. "Good God! I hope it wasn't me!"

38

"Bugger off, Baxter, you noisy sod," Joe muttered. He pulled his blanket over his head and burrowed down deeper into the hay. The rapping continued, forcing him out of sleep and into consciousness. He groaned loudly. He didn't want to be awake. Awake meant the return of all the demons sleep had banished. He tried not to hear the noise, tried to will himself back into sleep, but it persisted. "Baxter!" he shouted. "Pipe down!"

The rapping stopped. Joe listened, hoping that was the end of it, but then it started up again, more furiously than before. He realized it wasn't the horse. Baxter stamped when he wanted something. This was knocking – loud and insistent.

"Joe! Joe Bristow!"

That ruled out Baxter for certain.

"Joe! Are you in there? Open the door! Right now!"

Joe sat up. He knew that voice. Better than he knew his own. He got up and quickly pulled on his clothing. He ran down the steps from the hayloft, buttoning his shirt as he went, unlocked the door and yanked it open.

"Mum."

"Ah, so you do remember me?" Rose Bristow said tightly. Her face was flushed from pounding on the door and her straw hat was askew. She carried a large, heavy-looking basket.

" 'Ow'd you know I was 'ere?"

"Meg Byrne's Matt told me 'e saw you," she said, her eyes bright with anger. "Said 'e 'elped you get a job. 'E also told me that you'd left 'ome. That Millie lost the baby. That you're getting divorced. Tiny things, I guess, but it would've been nice of *you* to let us know. Bloody 'ell, lad, I've been worried sick about you! Didn't know what 'ad 'appened to you. Still wouldn't if it 'adn't been for Matt. Ashamed I was, to 'ear it all from 'im. Not knowing what 'appened to me own son!"

"I'm sorry, Mum. I didn't mean to make you worry."

"Didn't mean to make me worry? What else would I be doing? Not 'earing from you, never seeing you, not even knowing where you'd gone . . ."

Joe looked down at the floor. Now he could add his mother to the list of people he'd hurt and disappointed. It grew longer by the day.

Rose kept up her tirade for a few more minutes, then her angry expression softened. "Oh, never mind," she said, hugging him tightly. "At least I've found you now. And not before time, from the looks of things." She released him. "What's ailing you? Why 'aven't you come round? You should be at 'ome with your own, not living in a stable like the mule you are. Are you going to invite me in or not?"

"Aye, come in, Mum. It's not much. 'Old on, I'll get you something to sit on."

Rose bustled inside and seated herself on a wobbly milking stool that Joe produced. He sat on the third step of the wooden stairs.

"Where do you sleep?" she asked, looking around the stable.

"In the 'ayloft."

"What do you eat? You're thin as a rail. Your clothes are 'anging off you."

"There's a tuckshop nearby."

"Oh, luv, this is 'orrible. What are you doing 'ere? What 'appened?"

Joe told her everything. From his awful wedding night to his discovery of what had befallen Fiona to Millie's miscarriage.

Rose sighed as he finished, her face weary, angry, and sorrowful all at once. "That is one glorious mess you've made of things, I must say."

He nodded miserably.

"Come 'ome," she said. "You should be with your family now."

"I can't, Mum. After everything I've done, I just want to be alone. I can't be with people. I 'urt everyone I touch. I've ruined Fiona's life. Millie's, too. I killed me own child." He covered his face with his hands, trying to hold back his tears. He felt so guilty for what he'd done – so corrosively guilty – and so achingly sad.

Rose stroked her son's head. "Listen to me, Joe. Look at me . . ." He lowered his hands. His eyes were filled with such pain, such suffering that his mother's eyes filled with tears as she looked into them. "I don't give a damn what 'appened to Millie," she said. "She's a selfish, scheming girl. Always was, always will be. She chased you, got you to bed, and got what she wanted. Not that you're innocent, mind you, not by a long shot, but there will be another 'usband for Millie, and children, too. She'll do all right and maybe she'll learn not to take what isn't 'ers. As for the baby, I think 'e's far better off going back to God. I do. There's nothing worse for a child than being born to parents who don't love each other. The poor little thing got the lie of the land. 'E 'eard the rowing, felt the coldness, and decided to turn back and wait, that's all."

Joe closed his eyes and wept. He'd been trying hard to hold back his tears, he didn't want to cry in front of his mother, but he couldn't help it, they were pouring out of him like blood from a deep wound. He knew Fiona hated him. Millie hated him. Tommy hated him, too. He hated himself. He had expected his mother to hate him, but she didn't, and her words, her kindness, felt like redemption.

Rose wiped his eyes, shushing him, soothing him with her touch, her voice, just as she'd done when he was a child. "You're paying for your mistakes, lad. And you'll continue to. You lost the one you loved, lost a child. That's an 'igh price. Damned 'igh. But you've got to bear up. You can't let yourself sink. I won't 'ave it. You're made of tougher stuff than that. Everyone makes mistakes and everyone 'as to live with what they've done. You're no exception."

Joe nodded and blew his nose.

" 'Ere, look what I brought you," she said. She reached into her basket and pulled out a steak-and-kidney pie, a bowl of mashed potatoes, a jug of gravy, plates and cutlery.

Joe managed a smile. That was his mum all over, thinking whatever ailed him could be fixed with pie and mash. He loved her for it.

"Go find us something to drink like a good lad. Didn't you say there was a tuckshop nearby?"

"Aye, I did."

He took two cracked mugs he kept on the window ledge and went off after some hot tea. When he got back, Rose had piled a plate high for him. He dug into it, ravenous for good food.

"Like that, do you?" she asked, smiling at him.

He smiled back. "I do."

39

Fiona stepped out of William McClane's carriage and stared up at the imposingly grand façade of Delmonico's restaurant at Twenty-sixth Street and Fifth Avenue. A couple walked ahead of them, up the stairs, through the door, and into the darkly paneled foyer. The man was distinguished looking in a crisp dinner jacket, the woman elegant in a burgundy silk dress, a black aigrette in her hair.

Those are Will's people in there, not mine, she thought. Impossibly wealthy people who know the right things to do, how to pronounce the names of French wines and which damn fork is the fish fork. Nick had taught her some of these things on the ship, but she'd promptly forgotten them. Why did anyone need so many forks anyway? she fretted. You could only get one in your mouth at a time. She felt her confidence crumbling, and for a second she wanted nothing more than to get back into the carriage. Then Will took her arm and Mary's and said, "You are both so stunning tonight, you're going to make me the envy of every man in the place." Then he leaned in close and whispered, "And that's coming from *me* . . . the typical eejit with far too much money."

Fiona and Mary burst into laughter, and Will did too, and then he pulled them up the steps after him and Fiona was laughing so hard when they reached the door, she forgot to be nervous.

"Oh, Will, I'm so sorry. He's completely out of control. The worst-behaved child in all of New York," she said, once they were inside.

"You're speaking of your uncle, I assume."

"No!" She giggled. "Well . . . yes! Him, too. But I meant Seamie."

"I think it's the funniest thing I ever heard," Mary said. "Did you see Michael's face when Seamie said it? I thought he would choke."

"No, I was busy wondering if it's illegal to sell children to the circus," Fiona replied.

Will's reception at Fiona's home had been an unmitigated disaster from the second he'd walked through the door. He'd shaken hands with a gruff Michael; then Mary; then Alec, whom he could barely understand because of his accent; then Nick, who'd been sitting on the settee in his crimson dressing gown, swathed in a paisley throw and propped up between two pillows like a pasha; then Ian; and finally Seamie – who'd taken his hand, pumped it heartily, and said, "Are you the typical eejit with far too much money?"

Michael, mortified, told him to apologize, but Seamie defiantly reminded him he'd said it first. Mary ushered everyone into the parlor, hoping to salvage things, and reminded Michael to serve drinks. Ian, who'd been allowed a glass of sherry, swallowed too much at once and almost choked. Alec got tipsy and told an off-color joke. Finally Nick, always her savior, introduced the topic of the subterranean railway into the conversation and everyone warmed to it. Michael, who'd worked as a navvy when he first arrived, was curious about the engineering aspects. Mary wanted assurances it would be safe. Ian wanted to know how fast the trains would go. Then Fiona had looked at the clock, exclaimed that it was nearly eight already, and said they'd better be going. Luckily, she'd been able to talk her uncle into allowing Mary to chaperon her instead of himself.

They were barely inside the restaurant before they were descended upon. One man took Will's coat and hat; another, Fiona's wrap. Patrons, coming and going, stopped to chat with Will. He seemed to know everyone. Within the space of a few minutes, Fiona and Mary had met the mayor, the diva Adelina Patti, Mark Twain, William Vanderbilt, the architect Stanford White, and the scandalous free-love advocate Victoria Woodhull. Delmonico's was a melting pot where social pedigree meant nothing. Whether your money was earned two hundred years ago or two days ago made no difference. Politician, actor, showgirl, blueblood – as long as you could pay for your dinner, you were welcome. Fiona had begun to wonder if all of New York was in the restaurant when Will suddenly said, "You ladies know how to curtsy?"

"Curtsy? Why? Is the Queen here?" Fiona asked jokingly.

"No, but her son is."

Seconds later, he made a curt bow, then warmly took the hand of a portly, balding man with pale, protruding eyes and a pointed gray beard. As Fiona waited for Will to introduce her, she suddenly realized she was staring at the Prince of Wales, Albert Edward, and heir to England's throne. She and Mary exchanged panicked glances. Mary made a passable curtsy and Fiona quickly mustered an approximation. It was neither graceful nor elegant, but the prince didn't seem to notice. He took her hand and kissed it, and said he was sorry he'd already dined, he would've liked to invite them to his table. He drew closer to Fiona, said he detected London in her voice, and asked why such a lovely English rose had been transplanted. Fiona replied that she'd come to New York to make her fortune and was pursuing her own tea business.

"Are you?" the prince asked. "How unusual! But young women get up to all sorts of things nowadays, don't they? I hope you can teach the Yanks a thing or two about tea. I find the offerings in this country simply appalling."

"Only because you haven't tried my tea, sir. I'll send you some tomorrow. Along with a basket of currant scones and homemade raspberry jam and double cream and fruitcake that Mrs. Munro makes so you can have a proper afternoon tea and not the rubbish that passes for it here."

Although Fiona did not know it, her words were terribly bold. Merchants did not press their wares upon the future monarch. But she had no idea that such royal protocols even existed, much less an awareness that she was violating them. She was only being friendly. And the prince, not one to stand on ceremony where a pretty face was involved, was charmed.

"I would like that very much, Miss Finnegan," he replied. "I'm at the Fifth Avenue Hotel."

"It's as good as done."

Then the prince took his leave, patting Will on the shoulder. "Keep an eye on that one, old boy," he advised. "You just might learn something."

After the prince was gone, Will shook his head. "You're unbelievable," he said, laughing.

"Am I? Why?"

"I bet if I looked up 'merchant' in the dictionary, I would see your picture there."

"No, I think it's under bold-as-brass," Mary said.

Fiona jutted her chin. "The prince needed some decent tea. It was the least I could do."

"I just hope you have a lot of it on hand," Will said. "If it gets out that the Prince of Wales drinks TasTea, you're going to be swamped with orders. And I do mean swamped."

"Get out to where? And how? Only you and Mary heard me."

"To the papers. At least two reporters – two that I know by sight, maybe more – were edging in to listen to your conversation. One of them was Peter Hylton – the city's biggest gossipmonger. I'm just advising you to be prepared, that's all."

"Your table is ready, Mr. McClane, if you care to be seated," the maître d' said.

Will motioned for Fiona and Mary to precede him. Once inside the dining room, Fiona tried to keep her eyes trained on the maître d's back to keep from gawking, but it was impossible. The room enveloped her the second she set foot in it, seducing her with its grandeur. It was opulently decorated with crystal chandeliers, hand-blocked crimson wallpaper, and voluminous silk curtains. Gaslight illuminated it, reflecting in the enormous gilt mirrors, glinting off a silver fork, a crystal wineglass, a circlet of diamonds adorning a pale neck. A warm thrum of conversation and laughter washed over her, punctuated by the sounds of cutlery against china, glasses clinking.

She felt eyes upon her – men's admiring, women's appraising – and was certain that her hair wasn't correct, her dress wasn't up to snuff. Modest, ignorant of her beauty and of its effect upon others, she imagined their interest could only be critical. She felt she was no match for these people in their expensive clothing, just as she'd been no match for Millie Peterson in hers. She stole shy glances at the women around her, women in yards of richly colored satins and taffetas that were ruched, pleated, beaded, embroidered, flounced, gathered, draped, wrapped, and tucked. Gems the size of coins dangled from dainty earlobes, and ropes of pearls cascaded down cream-cloud bosoms molded by fine French batiste and buttressed by whalebone.

Her own ensemble, at Nick's insistence, was simple and uncluttered. She wore a dress of ivory silk georgette with capped sleeves, an amethyst sash, and a cascade of purple lilacs embroidered on the skirt. The fluid material skimmed her body becomingly, making her look willowy and fey in contrast to many of the women in the room who looked positively upholstered.

She wore no corset; she never had. Mary made her try one on in Macy's lingerie department, after she'd bought her dress, but it dug and itched and squeezed the life out of her and she left it right where she'd found it. A good cotton camisole and drawers had served her well so far and would continue to do so. And besides, she liked her bosom where bosoms belonged, not jammed up under her chin.

Her only jewels were a pair of pearl eardrops borrowed from her late aunt's jewelry box. She wore no plumes or diamond sprays in her hair, just a cluster of mauve roses that Alec had clipped from one of his bushes. As she walked through the room, her stride alternately bold and coltish, her bright, curious face as fresh and open as a pansy, every head turned. She made women suddenly feel that they were wearing too many jewels, that their hair was overdone, their dresses too fussy. Men whispered to one another, "Who *is* that with McClane?" She was like a flawless diamond, one whose beauty would only have been diminished by an overwrought setting.

Fiona's interest in the room and its occupants was soon replaced by curiosity as to the maître d's intentions. The man was nearly across the room, and seemed, as yet, to have no inclination to seat them. Puzzled, she turned to Will.

"I asked for a private room," he explained. "This one's a fishbowl. I hope you don't mind." They continued to the end of the room and up a set of stairs, and then their escort stopped at a set of double doors, opened them and stepped back, to allow them to enter first. "After you," Will said, his hand on the small of her back.

Fiona gasped as she stepped into the room. "Oh, Will!" she whispered, walking into the center of the room, turning around and around in it.

"My lord!" Mary exclaimed, too stunned to move out of the doorway.

Will shrugged, trying for nonchalance, but too obviously pleased with Fiona's reaction to pull if off. "You told me you liked roses," he said.

The room had been converted into a lush, bloom-filled bower. Roses were everywhere – hanging in garlands, standing in vases. Peonies and hydrangeas hid the fireplace. Ferns stood tall in the corners. Even the floor was hidden, carpeted with lush green grass. A table, set up in the middle of the room, was covered in white linen and decorated with more

416

roses. They were twined into the branches of two tall silver candelabra. Across the room, two sets of French doors were open, letting in the warm summer air and the moonlight. Fiona could barely believe what she was seeing, couldn't imagine how anyone had done this. She was seized by a sense of unreality so strong, it was dizzying. She had stepped out of her world – where people worked with their hands and drank beer and ate sausages – into Will's, where they had gardens built in restaurants on a whim. For one night. It seemed like a dream, or the work of fairies, but it wasn't. It was Will.

She turned away and bent her head over a cluster of moss roses, inhaling their scent, not wanting him to see her emotion. Joe had given her a rose. On the Old Stairs. A single red rose. She had given him her heart, her dreams, her life. They hadn't mattered to him. He'd crushed them all. She had given Will nothing of importance – a conversation, laughter, a pleasant hour together. And he had done this. For her. Just because she liked roses.

"Do you like it, Fiona?" he asked softly.

She turned to him smiling, her face luminous in the candlelight. "Like it? Will, it's wonderful! I . . . I don't even know what to say. I've never seen anything so beautiful."

"If you'll excuse me," Mary said tactfully, "I'm going to find the lounge."

Will waited until she had left the room, then he handed Fiona a rose. He was standing very close to her, and before she knew what was happening, he had folded her into his arms and kissed her. And the feeling of his lips, gentle yet insistent, erased all thoughts of Joe from her mind, took away all the sadness, all the longing. She had just begun to kiss him back, warming to the taste and feel of him, when a voice at the door said, "Some champagne before dinner, sir? Ah! Pardon me."

Will released her. Embarrassed, she moved away from him, smoothing her skirts for something to do. "A bottle of Heidsieck, please," he said.

"Very good, sir."

He left. Will was just about to pull her to him once more when they heard Mary's footsteps.

"Good God! I feel like I'm sixteen years old again," he growled.

After Mary returned, the waiter came with champagne and they sat down. As she had the evening they'd first walked together, Fiona found Will not at all intimidating, but incredibly easy to talk to. Mary was her sweet, merry self, and all three got along very well. They talked nonstop all through dinner, starting with the sweet bluepoint oysters and progressing on to the terrapin soup, the poussins in a truffled cream sauce with duchesse potatoes and haricots verts, to the lobster Newburg and the baked Alaska, Delmonico's signature dessert.

And during the long, leisurely meal an entirely new feeling, one she'd never experienced, descended upon Fiona – a wonderful sense of being cared for, of being protected from the world and all its worries. She looked at Will now, as he was advising her on her tea shop, and thought how very handsome he was. He was the most graceful, elegant man she'd ever seen. Her eyes swept over him, taking in his thick shock of brown hair, his broad smile and strong jaw. He even sat beautifully, tall and straight-shouldered. His collar was snow-white and crisp, his tie expertly knotted. His black dinner jacket hung perfectly from his frame. She thought of her father in his patched secondhand jacket. And Charlie's with the elbows gone, and Joe's, a tweed with flecks of blue in it that matched his eyes . . .

Joe again, damn him. She'd made a pact with herself not to think of him anymore, and now here he was, intruding on this perfect evening like a boorish, uninvited guest. It was as if he were sitting at the table in a fourth chair, watching, listening, smirking. She could all but see him smile cheekily as he turned and asked her how Will's kiss tasted, if it felt as good as his.

"It doesn't, does it?" he asked her.

"It does. Even better," she silently shot back at him.

He shook his head. "No, it's all this" – he gestured at the garden, the lavish dinner. "That's what feels good, not the kiss. Nobody kissed you like I did. Nobody ever will."

"I think a tearoom's an excellent idea, Fiona," Will said, breaking in upon her thoughts. "With the tea resource already in place and Mary's baking talents, I'm sure it would be a success. Have you started thinking about a location?"

"I have," she said. "I've looked around Union Square, but the rents are too dear, and Madison Square as well . . ."

Will nodded as she spoke, listening, questioning, encouraging her. She noticed how warm his eyes were, how they crinkled at the corners when he smiled. She decided brown eyes were much nicer than blue ones. Will's mouth was nice, too. Thanks to the waiter, she'd barely had time to enjoy his kiss. But she might have another chance. The night was still young.

I'll show you what feels good, Joe Bristow, she promised silently. Just you wait.

"The park is beautiful in the moonlight, isn't it? I've never been here this late," Fiona said.

"Nowhere near as beautiful as you are," Will said, squeezing her hand.

They were walking along Bethesda Terrace toward the lake, Will having suggested a stroll after their dinner. Mary had begged off, saying she was tired and would prefer to sit in the carriage. She had the driver for company if she got bored, she told them.

"Thank you, Will, for everything," Fiona said. "For the garden, the dinner . . . for putting up with my overbearing uncle. I had the most wonderful time."

"I'm glad, Fiona. I did, too. I'd like to see you again. Soon."

"I'd like that, too."

Will took a gold watch from his pocket and squinted

at it in the darkness. "I think we should probably turn back now. It's nearly eleven-thirty."

"Not yet," Fiona said. She glanced behind herself, checking that there were no people nearby. She tugged on Will's hand, leading him off the path into the shelter of some maple trees. Then she pulled him close and kissed him. He pulled away and looked at her, surprised.

"I thought I'd been too forward in the restaurant," he said. "I thought maybe you didn't want me to –"

"Kiss me back, Will. I *do* want you to," she whispered. And she did. Desperately. She wanted his lips on her, his hands on her. She wanted the warmth and smell and feel of him to erase every kiss, every touch, every promise Joe Bristow had ever given her. She wanted to fill her senses with him, fill her memory with him, so that there was no room left for Joe inside her.

Will took her in his arms, crushing her to him, and kissed her deeply. And then it was her turn to be surprised. This was a man, she realized, not a boy. She could feel the heat of his strong hands on her back, the warmth of his broad chest under her palms. He kissed her cheek, behind her ear, her throat. He cupped her breasts, kissed the tops of them. It felt good, so good that she closed her eyes and sighed. It'll be all right, she thought. I'll forget Joe. I will. And then he suddenly took her face in his hands and kissed her forehead. She opened her eyes, puzzled. He took a few steps away from her.

"Either I take you home, now, Miss Finnegan, or I don't take you home at all. And then your uncle will come after me with a shotgun."

Fiona giggled and blushed, understanding his meaning. She smoothed her hair, then cheekily offered him her elbow. He shook his head.

"What's wrong?" she asked him.

"I need a minute," he said awkwardly, adjusting his trousers.

Fiona looked in the direction of his fly. Even in the

420

darkness she could see that the fabric appeared to be elevated. She giggled harder.

"Really, Fiona! I wish you wouldn't laugh," he said, feigning outrage. "This is a rather humiliating position for a forty-five-year-old man of some worth and standing to be in." He glanced down at himself, then whistled, full of admiration. "Lord! I haven't had a hard-on like this since I was a schoolboy."

"Will!"

"What? You did it!"

Fiona, giddy with laughter now, kissed him again over his protests. He told her if she didn't stop it they wouldn't get home until morning. She felt happy, hopeful, and excited. She was going to fall in love with Will. She was certain of it. She couldn't quite remember what falling in love felt like; she had always just *been* in love with Joe, but it must feel like this.

As she and Will walked back to the carriage, arm in arm, Fiona told herself that she had found someone new, just as Rose Bristow said she would. Someone kind and smart and funny and wonderful. Someone who built gardens for her, even though she wasn't rich and didn't have a father in the produce business. Someone who would make her forget Joe. He hovered at the edges of her consciousness now, like a ghost in the gloom of a forest, but she was positive she would soon forget him entirely. He would be gone from her life, her mind, her memory. Really gone. Forever.

40

Fiona looked at the address scribbled on the slip of paper she held in her hands, then looked at the number on the brick building in front of her. This was it: twenty-one Nassau Street. Hurst, Brady, and Gifford – Stockbrokers. During their dinner at Delmonico's, Will had insisted she go to his broker's for a lesson on the stock market.

"Do you know the difference between the rich and the poor?" he'd asked her.

"Yes. The rich have all the money," she'd replied.

"No, my dear," he said. "The rich understand that money begets money. Take a portion of your profits, invest it wisely, and before you know it you'll have the money you need to open your tearoom."

And today, three weeks after their dinner, she had a little more money to invest than when they'd first spoken of it, for Will's prediction had come true. The papers had gotten hold of her impromptu audience with the Prince of Wales. Peter Hylton wrote that the future king of England could take tea in the grandest salons the city had to offer, but he preferred the wares of a pretty little tea merchant from Chelsea. And so did the dashing William McClane.

Will had bristled at the fact that his name had been bandied about in gossip columns, and in such a salacious manner, but Fiona had no time to be offended; she'd been promptly deluged with customers. Young, fashionable types came in carriages, thrilled to pieces with themselves for daring to go slumming on the West Side. Maids and house-keepers came for their mistresses. And inquiries came from restaurants, hotels, and stores. Panicked, Fiona had run to the printer to order more boxes and then to Stuart to tell him to get her more tea. She'd had to hire two full-time girls to ring up purchases and one more to pack TasTea boxes. Fiona often joined them, shaking her head at the fact that she'd come all this way only to find herself packing tea again.

Will was supposed to have accompanied her this afternoon, but he'd gotten tied up in a meeting. He'd sent his carriage with a note explaining his absence and telling her to go without him. Fiona hadn't wanted to go today; she was too busy. But when he stopped by last night to say hello and had seen her stuffing bills she couldn't fit into the night box into a jar, he'd put his foot down. "My broker's. Tomorrow. No arguments," he'd said.

She walked up the steps, pushed the door open, and entered what looked like hell on a bad day. There was a great wooden desk at the front of the room. Its owner was standing on his chair, his back turned to her, yelling. Behind it, a wooden railing ran the breadth of the room, separating the reception area from the clerks' desks. Visored men in vests and shirtsleeves sat at the desks, wiping sweat from their faces and rapidly dipping their pens in ink pots, scribbling furiously. Brokers ran back and forth, shouting at the clerks. Their noise, plus the sound of telegraphs and ticker tape machines, was deafening. She heard language more appropriate to the waterfront than a place of business.

One of the clerks, fed up, shouted, "But I just wrote that jackass's purchase at ten!"

"And he wants to sell it before it drops to five! Hurry up!"

"Barnes!" a man yelled from the back of the room. "Hobson's on the line. He wants your head for telling him to buy Sullivan. Says you've ruined him."

"Oh, yeah? Did I know this was going to happen? Tell him to go to hell!"

Fiona walked up to the wooden railing, thinking how it

reminded her of a fence, and the men inside it of wild bulls snorting and charging, penned up for other people's safety. She approached the man standing on his chair. "Excuse me, sir," she ventured.

He ignored her. He was listening to a flushed, breathless lad who was standing in a huddle of men. "I was just down the exchange," the boy said. "It's a mess! People are screaming and yelling. I saw three fights break out –"

"What about the Sullivan brothers?" somebody asked.

"One's in the hospital. Heart attack. The other one's dead. Shot himself."

His news prompted loud expressions of anger and disgust.

Fiona tried again. "Pardon me, is Mr. Hurst available?" She might as well have been invisible. The men paid her no mind. She was beginning to despair of ever getting anyone to listen to her when she felt a hand on her back. "Will!" she exclaimed, happy to see him. "I thought you couldn't make it."

"I managed to break away. I haven't got long," he said. "My secretary's got meetings scheduled back-to-back for me today. I don't know if I'm coming or going." He winced at a shouted obscenity. "What the devil's going on here? Where's Hurst?"

"I don't know. I've been trying to get someone's attention, but I haven't been successful."

"Mr. Martin," Will barked at the man standing on the chair. The man turned around. "There is a lady present. I expect you to behave accordingly."

"Sorry, Mr. McClane. Didn't see you there, miss." He turned, put his fingers in his mouth, and blew a piercing whistle.

He had seen her. She hadn't had Will with her at the time, though.

"Lady in the house, gents!" Martin yelled. The clerks and traders craned their necks, saw Fiona and Will, and immediately quieted down. Mr. Martin picked up his telephone and informed Mr. Hurst that William McClane was here to see him. Half a second later, a tubby man came flying down the stairs to the upper floors, his hand extended. He welcomed them, then shouted at the office boy to bring refreshments for Mr. McClane and his guest.

Fiona was getting used to this now, to the way the waters parted before Will. In the three weeks he'd been calling on her, he'd taken her picnicking on the New Jersey palisades with Seamie, to Rector's for dinner, and to the opera. Her uncle had allowed her to go on the picnic without a chaperon – feeling that Seamie was enough of a third wheel – but he'd insisted that Nick, who was up and about now, accompany her to the opera. He'd heard untoward things went on in the private boxes there. And he made Mary go to Rector's with them, for he'd been told it was nothing but a lobster palace, and fast. Wherever they went, people fell over themselves to please Will. Fiona had had to train herself to expect service when she was with him, and not to hand the waiter her plate, remove her own wrap, or pour the wine. She realized again, as she saw Peter Hurst scramble to attend to him, what an immensely powerful man he was.

"Peter, what's all the commotion about?" he asked.

"A takeover."

"Whose company?"

"A shipbuilder's in Brooklyn. Sullivan Brothers. Three of the major shareholders have been buying up stock, it appears. They consolidated today and ousted the family. Nobody saw it coming. It's a dreadful business."

"They can do that?" Fiona asked, following the two men into Hurst's office. "Someone can just take away another person's company?"

"I'm afraid so," Hurst replied. "It's a very ungentlemanly way of doing business, but it's perfectly legal –" He was interrupted by the sound of a phone ringing. He excused himself, answered it, then handed it to Will. "It's for you."

"What is it, Jeanne? Right now?" He sighed. "All right,

yes. Tell him I'll be there." He handed the phone back. "I'm sorry," he said to Fiona. "I've got to go. The mayor. The subway. The usual nonsense. I'm going to take a cab and leave you the carriage."

"We'll take excellent care of her, Mr. McClane," Hurst said.

"Good. I'll see you this evening, darling," Will said, standing up to leave.

Fiona followed him into the hallway. "Will, you look tired. Are you all right?"

"I'm fine, it's just that blasted man. I'm eager for the whole thing to be resolved." He smiled. "As long as it's resolved in my favor, of course."

"You'll get the contract. I know you will."

He kissed her cheek, said he wished he had her confidence, and left.

Fiona returned to Hurst's office and listened as he explained the basics to her. Though none of it was hard to grasp, he talked slowly, as if he were conversing with an imbecile. Her mind wandered as he told her the difference between stocks, bonds, and commodities futures for the second time. She couldn't help thinking about the commotion downstairs, about the two men who'd lost their company and the shareholders who'd taken it from them. It gnawed at her. There was something in it, something she was missing.

"One moment, Mr. Hurst," she said, interrupting him. "About the Sullivans . . . you said they never saw this coming. Didn't they realize what was happening?"

"No. But then, I'm sure they weren't looking for it, either. It's a rare occurrence."

"But it *does* happen . . ." she said, more to herself than to Mr. Hurst. The pieces were clicking into place now. A clear picture emerged in her mind: investing was a financial tool, a way to make money. But it could also be a tool of aggression – a weapon. Buy enough pieces of a company and one day you'd own it.

"Oh, yes," Hurst said. "Owners become incautious. Too trusting. Or too arrogant. They think they're invulnerable." He smiled sympathetically. "I see all this has you worried, Miss Finnegan. What a terrible introduction to the market. Please don't let it distress you. The majority of transactions we handle are very secure. Let's move on to better topics."

But Fiona wasn't worried. Or distressed. Just the opposite. A new possibility was sparking in her mind, the very beginnings of a plan.

Hurst droned on, telling her how her account would work, how to buy and sell, all about fees and commissions. He explained the newly devised Dow Jones Industrial Average in *The Wall Street Journal*. She let him rattle. Her mind was going a hundred miles an hour, alive with the possibilities of her plan – a plan that had eluded her for so long.

"So, you see," he said ploddingly, finally wrapping up his lesson, "you can follow your stock's progress very easily just by looking in the newspaper. Let's say you'd bought five thousand shares of McClane Subterranean yesterday at fifteen dollars a share. We see here that it closed today at sixteen and a quarter." He picked up a pencil. "Now, that gives us . . ."

". . . one dollar and twenty-five cents per share multiplied by five thousand, which would give me a profit of six thousand two hundred and fifty dollars. Goodness, Mr. Hurst, Mr. McClane is absolutely right. This *is* a good way to make money!"

Hurst blinked. "Yes, it is. Now, if there's anything else I can do for you . . ."

"There is," she said, sitting forward in her chair. "I'd like to buy some shares of Burton Tea. An English company."

Hurst frowned. "Are you certain that's wise, Miss Finnegan? A transaction so soon? Mr. McClane led me to believe you were quite new to the market."

"I was. Thanks to your excellent instruction, Mr. Hurst,

I no longer am. Now, about those Burton shares?"

"One moment. I'll need to look up the price."

Hurst disappeared into the hallway. Fiona picked up a stock certificate from his desk. It was for ten thousand shares of Carnegie Steel. It was only paper, yet it was a piece of a company. Soon, she would hold a piece of Burton's company in her hands. Only a tiny piece, but she would make that piece bigger – even if it took her twenty years to do it. And when it was big enough, she would ruin him.

"There we are, Miss Finnegan," he said, returning to his desk. He glanced at her, then paused. "Are you all right? You look flushed. Is it too warm? I can open another window."

Fiona assured him she was fine. He told her that Burton Tea was currently trading at around twenty dollars a share. She asked for ten shares. It was a huge amount of money, and such a small beginning, but it was a beginning all the same. He pushed some papers across his desk toward her. Her hands shook with emotion as she filled them out. She could feel his eyes on her. Can he see it? she wondered. Can he see the rage inside? The sorrow? All the black, ugly things Burton put there? She finished with the papers, catching his gaze as she handed them back. She held it for a heartbeat, watching his eyes widen before he glanced away. He looked as if he'd seen something he would've preferred not to.

Fiona thanked him for his help. Then she told him she would like to make a standing appointment with him every Friday to purchase additional shares of Burton Tea.

"Every Friday? You must have tremendous faith in the stock. Do you know the chairman?"

Fiona nodded. "All too well, Mr. Hurst. All too well."

41

"It's going to be a boy, I just know it," Isabelle, Will's daughter-in-law, said.

"How do you know?" his daughter Emily asked, looking up from her needlepoint.

"He's troublesome. Always kicking. Never stays still."

"What will you name him?" Edmund, Will's youngest son, asked.

"William Robertson McClane the Third," Will Junior, Isabelle's husband, said, putting a golf ball into an overturned vase.

"That's original," Edmund snorted. He was sitting in a wing chair, one leg hanging over the side. He was home from Princeton for the summer and working in the city on the subway project with Will Junior. "I have a better name, Izzie!"

"What?"

"Edmund!"

His brother threw a golf ball at him, missed and dented a side table.

"Boys . . ." Will said absently, making them all laugh.

"He thinks we're still five," James, the second eldest, said.

"When you throw golf balls in the house I do," Will replied, looking out the French doors of the large sunny sitting room where they were gathered to the rolling hills of his estate, the horses in the distance, and the Hudson beyond. He'd go for a walk if only he didn't feel so indolent after his enormous dinner. Maybe in a minute, with one of his sons, or Richard, his son-in-law. The women would stay behind. Isabelle was in the last weeks of her confinement. As befitted a woman of her station, she no longer went out in public and saw only family and female friends.

Will looked at his family and felt a deep glow of paternal pride. Emily had written asking him to come home to Hyde Park for the weekend. They wanted to see him, she'd said, he'd been away too long. He suspected they thought he was lonely without their mother. He appreciated their thoughtfulness, but he would have preferred to be in the city with Fiona. He wanted to take her to Saratoga or Newport, someplace where they could spend a long, lazy July weekend together – even if it meant he had to invite Mary or Nick along. But then Emily's letter had arrived, and Fiona, when she learned of it, told him to go see his family. She was so busy with the tea shop, she couldn't have gotten away for an entire weekend. And besides, she'd promised to take Seamie to Coney Island on Saturday evening. The Munros were going, Nick and Michael, too. If he changed his mind about Hyde Park and wanted to eat hot dogs, shoot the chutes, and see the bearded lady, he was welcome to join them, she'd said.

Will had shuddered at the very notion. There were times when he was reminded of the great differences in their backgrounds, a difference that sometimes made him feel self-conscious when he was in her element, but never seemed to affect her when she was in his. She carried herself with grace always and charmed everyone she met.

He had begun to introduce her into society, just dipping her toes in the water, and she'd done so well. Two nights ago, he'd taken her and Nick to a party at the Metropolitan Museum of Art in honor of the famed landscape painter Albert Bierstadt. She'd looked so beautiful. She'd worn a dress of teal green and a pair of earrings that looked like diamonds but were really paste and were borrowed from her friend, Maddie. The dress's lines were spare, almost Grecian. She had a way, he'd noticed, of wearing the simplest of things to the greatest effect.

She'd told him Nick had gone with her to pick the dress out. He was a bit jealous of the lad, though he tried not to be. He had asked her once if he was competing with Nick and she had surprised him by bursting into laughter. If anything, she'd said, *she* was competing with Nick. Usually he could tell, but with Nick he'd had no idea. The lad was not effeminate. There was his interest in art, and his sartorial excesses – the Liberty of London vests, the white linen suits, the heliotrope cravats, but Will had ascribed those eccentricities to his nationality. He was English, after all, and that explained a lot. Fiona and Nick were very close, inseparable even, and he knew from the tenderness they showed each other that he wouldn't have had a chance with her if young Soames fancied women. To please her, he'd taken Nick up and was trying to further his career. At the Bierstadt party, he'd introduced him to William Whitney, Anthony Drexel, and J. P. Morgan, art collectors all.

And he'd introduced Fiona to Caroline Astor, the imperious queen of New York society. Most women would've been quaking. Not Fiona. She'd merely grinned, shook Caroline's hand, and said, "Smashing party, isn't it?" Caroline had been curt and icy to her, but could not resist inquiring where she'd bought her lovely dress. "Paris?" she asked. "London?"

"No, Macy's," Fiona had replied.

Caroline's eyes had widened, then she'd laughed warmly. Fiona had that effect on people. She was utterly unpretentious. She charmed frosty socialites and stuffy businessmen just by being her lovely, irreverent self. She'd even dazzled Morgan – the richest man in the country when Will introduced them – by meeting his imperious gaze, smiling, and shaking his hand just like a man. Later, Morgan had good-naturedly groused to Will that she was not intimidated by him in the least and should've had the good grace to show a bit of awe.

Will was head over heels in love with her and he wanted nothing more than to tell her. He'd almost done so once, in the carriage on the way back from a supper, but he'd felt a tension in her as he broached the topic. He thought perhaps she doubted his sincerity. Maybe she feared, as he once had, that things would not work out between them and was afraid to get her heart broken. He had a feeling someone had done that before. She had a passionate nature – he felt it in the way she touched him, the way she kissed him, but there was a wariness, too. He would introduce her to his family soon. That would show he was serious. He would do it for his children's sake as well. Eventually he and Fiona would run into Will Junior or James at a restaurant, or someone would mention having seen him with her. Luckily none of them read "Peter's Patter." Hylton had taken quite a shine to Fiona. She was mentioned in his column nearly every week. He always described what she wore and noted that she was always on the arm of either the dashing young Englishman, Nick Soames, or Will, and that it was anyone's guess who would win her. Obviously, Nick's sexual orientation and his role as chaperon had escaped him, too.

"Dad?" Will Junior said. "I asked you a question. Didn't you hear me?"

"No, sorry. I was miles away." He saw Emily glance at him, then drop her eyes back to her needlework.

"I asked if the engineering reports on the Brooklyn line had come in yet."

"Not yet. I expect them tomorrow."

Silence fell again. James took a turn with the putter. Edmund tossed a golf ball into the air. Emily pulled her needle through her canvas. Will's eyes lingered on his daughter's hands. They were so delicate and white. Nothing like Fiona's; her hands were always work-roughened. At Rector's the other night, he noticed a scratch across the back of one as she'd reached for her wineglass. The sight of it – such a tough little fighter's hand – had made his heart melt. Fiona's were not pretty hands, not like Emily's, but to him they were beautiful.

James coughed. Will looked up and was distinctly aware of tension in the air. He saw Will Junior give Emily a nod, and then she stood suddenly and asked Isabelle to come with her for a walk. Just a short one around the grounds, she said. It would do her good. Isabelle raised herself with her husband's help and lumbered off after Emily. Will was left with his three sons and his son-in-law. Edmund had gotten hold of two more golf balls and was juggling them now, oblivious to the strained vibrations. Richard was skulking in the background. Will Junior and James were standing at the mantel, no longer playing with the putter. Something was going on. They'd asked him to come here today for a reason. He eyed Will Junior and James, making them squirm, then said, "Well, what is it?"

"What's what?" Edmund said, catching the balls and regarding his father.

"Dad . . ." Will Junior began, ". . . we wanted to talk with you."

"You couldn't talk in New York?"

"No, it's too personal," Will Junior said. He shifted his weight from one foot to the other, clearly uncomfortable.

"We've heard things," James continued. "People have seen you out with a young woman."

"It's none of our business," Will Junior said, "but there's been quite a bit of talk. We just . . . we just think it's not right to squire a mistress about so openly."

Will smiled at his sons' sense of propriety. "The woman you speak of is not my mistress. Her name is Fiona Finnegan. I'm courting her. In a very respectable fashion, I might add. I'm sorry, I should've realized you'd hear about it. I should have told you about her earlier."

"Courting!" Will Junior echoed, a shocked expression on his face. "With an intent to marry?"

Will shrugged, becoming irritated by this inquisition. "It's a bit soon for that, but since you ask, yes . . . it's a possibility."

"Dad!" Edmund exclaimed, smiling warmly. "That's great! What's she like? Is she pretty?"

Will laughed. "Very."

Will Junior said nothing. He simply stared at his father in disbelief.

"I've met her family," Will continued. "In due time, I'll introduce her to all of you."

"Dad, we don't . . . you can't . . . this won't do," James said coldly.

"I've heard she's not even twenty years old. And a *shop-keeper*," Will Junior said, spitting out the word as if it left a bad taste in his mouth. "Have you gone mad?"

"I beg your pardon?" Will said, affronted by both the question and his son's tone.

"She's no one we know," James said. "And the age difference alone –"

"I'm forty-five, not eighty-five, thank you," he snapped.

Will Junior paced the length of the room, then turned back to his father, visibly upset. "Think of how this will look to subway investors. We can't afford a scandal now, we can't afford any ill will whatsoever. Not with Belmont in the game. Not with all we've got riding on this."

"A scandal?" Will repeated, looking at his son as if he were crazy. "Don't be ridiculous."

"I'm not being ridiculous!" Will Junior said, his voice rising. "Can't you see –"

"I know what your real objection is," Will said, cutting him off. "Why don't you come out with it? It's that she's working-class and Irish, isn't it?"

"My objection is that this . . . this *fling* of yours will ruin all we've worked for."

"Will, leave Dad alone," Edmund said, rushing to his father's defense. "He knows what he's doing. He's allowed to date a girl if he wants to."

"To *date*? Edmund, shut up, will you?" Will Junior shouted. "You don't know what you're talking about. What do you think this is? A college social? This is *business*, the real world, not school. We can't allow ourselves to be compromised."

"Son, that's *enough*," Will said sharply. He let a few seconds elapse, time enough for Will Junior to cool off, then, in a conciliatory tone, he said, "Wait until you meet her. You'll see what a wonderful person she is. You'll change your mind."

"I have no intention of meeting her. Not now. Not ever," Will Junior said angrily. He stormed out of the room, James and Richard trailing in his wake.

Edmund stayed behind. "Don't mind them, Dad," he said quietly.

Will sighed heavily. He'd gotten to his feet in the middle of the argument. Now he sat back down. "Maybe it's too soon. Too close to your mother's death."

"Oh, please, Dad. It's been two years since our mother died. His problem is that it's too close to his run for Congress. He's worried how your romance with a younger woman will sit with his conservative voters."

"That's uncharitable of you, Edmund. Will Junior's ambitious, but he's not that harsh."

Edmund shrugged. "If you say so. I think he's as harsh as sandpaper myself."

"Maybe he really is worried about the subway deal. He's put his heart into it and he's done a very fine job. Maybe he really is nervous about the competition. If we could just nail that contract," Will said. "Then I could prove to him he's wrong. If I had the papers signed he couldn't object anymore. He'd have nothing to object to."

"So what if he objects, Dad? Let him! What can he do? Cut off your allowance?"

Will gave his son a weary smile. "No," he said, "but he can create the sort of scene he just did. You all matter too much to me for that. I don't want to see any of you angry

435

or unhappy. I'm going to have to redouble my efforts on the subway. As soon as we get that contract, he'll come around, Edmund. I know he will."

42

To Joe, the sight of eight Montague Street was like a knife in his heart. He stood in front of it, wishing to God that the door would open and she would be there, smiling, her blue eyes shining, just as she had been the day he took her to the West End. Last year at this time he still lived on this street, still sat out on the step at night with his mates, still dreamed of a shop, a life with Fiona. Only a year ago. It seemed like a lifetime.

He pulled himself away, walked to number four and knocked. His father answered it. "Well, well. The prodigal returns," he said.

"Nice to see you, too, Dad."

Peter Bristow looked at the bundle of pink carnations his son was holding and scowled. "Could 'ave at least sprung for roses. 'Ad 'er worried sick, you did. Didn't know where you was. Neighbors whispering. Lads talking down the market, saying Peterson kicked your sorry arse out. All the crying and carrying on I 'ad to listen to on your account . . ."

"I'm sorry, Dad. I'm sorry. All right?"

Peter shook his head. "I'll say you are. Come inside. I'm not in the 'abit of 'aving me Sunday dinner on the step."

Joe rolled his eyes and followed his father in, glad he'd decided not to move back home. He was boisterously greeted by his brother Jimmy, who was sixteen; thirteen-year-old Ellen, who was taller and prettier than he remembered; and eight-year-old Cathy in pigtails and a pinafore. He kissed his mother, who was lifting a big leg of lamb out of the oven. He nearly scolded her when he saw it – he knew how dear lamb was – but she was proud of the joint, pleased it had turned out well, and so he said nothing. She saw the carnations in his hand, fussed over them, and had Ellen put them in a vase. Joe carried the lamb to the table while his sisters saw to the potatoes and Brussels sprouts. There was an awkward silence as they sat down to eat, then Cathy said, "Mum said Millie lost the baby, Joe. 'Ow did she lose it? Did it wander off? 'As she found it yet?"

"Be quiet, Cathy!" Ellen scolded.

Joe stopped cutting his lamb. "The baby's not lost, luv," he said quietly. " 'E's in 'eaven."

"But why? Why is 'e there?"

"Oi! Eat your supper and mind your business, you," her father barked. "We'll 'ave no more talk of babies or Millie or any of it."

"Stupid!" Ellen hissed, elbowing her.

"Am not!" Cathy said sulkily. "I only said –"

"Pass me the gravy, please, Cathy, there's a good girl," Rose said. "Tell us about your new job, then, Joe."

Joe did, grateful to his mother for changing the subject. When he'd finished, his father said, "Seems to me you could do a bit better with all your experience."

Rose shot her husband a look.

"I tried. Tommy's blackballed me. I was lucky to get what I've got," Joe said. He chewed a piece of lamb and swallowed it. "It's not forever, though. I'm putting most of me money away." He hesitated for a second, then said, "I've got an idea for a new business."

"What is it, luv?" Rose asked excitedly.

"As soon as I've got enough saved up, I'm going to get me own barrow, fill it with the best produce, and take it door-to-door in one of the better neighbor'oods. Mayfair, maybe. If I make enough money, I'll buy an 'orse and cart so I can go farther afield. To Knightsbridge, say, and I'll 'ire another man to take the barrow on the Mayfair route.

Then I'll keep adding carts and routes till I 'ave a good deal of the West End covered." He was animated now. A little of his old spirit was back. "This way, the cook or the 'ousekeeper gets the finest produce brought right to 'er on a daily basis. She can pick and choose and not 'ave to go shopping 'erself or take whatever old rubbish the corner shop delivers, see? I'm thinking of calling it 'Montague's – Where Quality and Convenience Meet.' After the street, like. What do you think?"

"I think it's a grand idea," Rose said.

"I'd work for you," Jimmy said. "I could 'elp you in the morning and get back in time to 'elp Dad in the afternoon."

"I think it's the daftest idea I ever 'eard," his father said. " 'Ow are you going to get the cooks to buy from you? They already 'ave their favorite shops . . ."

"Peter . . ." Rose said. He didn't hear her.

". . . and 'ow will you know what to put on the barrow? And 'ow much of it? You'll be running out of one thing while you 'ave too much of another. You'd do well to stay in the job you've got and be thankful for it."

"You just told me I could do better!" Joe said, frustrated by his father's constant criticism, his refusal even to consider a new idea.

"Just keep your 'ead down for now and don't make another cock-up of things," Peter said.

Joe balled up his napkin. "I don't know why I came back 'ere," he said, standing up to go. "I'm sorry, Mum. Thanks for the dinner."

"Sit down!" Rose snapped. "You're not going anywhere. You're going to finish the food I cooked for you!"

She turned to her husband angrily and Joe saw that his father, who had a good eighty pounds on his mother and stood a foot taller, flinched. "And you, Peter, you'd do well to get be'ind your son for once, instead of telling 'im 'e's daft for coming up with a new idea. A *good* idea! If 'e'd gotten a little more encouragement round 'ere in the first place, 'e might never 'ave left for Covent Garden. And 'e wouldn't 'ave gotten tangled up with the likes of bloody Tommy Peterson and 'is bloody daughter!"

The whole family was silent. Meekly, they all resumed eating. Ellen dished out more meat. Cathy ate her sprouts without a peep even though she hated them. Joe poured gravy on his potatoes. Peter stabbed at a piece of lamb, then grudgingly said he might know of a barrow for sale. Maybe he could put a deposit on it and Joe could pay the balance out of his weekly wages. Rose patted her husband's hand and gave her eldest a hopeful look.

The rest of dinner proceeded uneventfully. When it was over, Peter sat in front of the hearth with his paper and pipe and dozed off. Jimmy went out to meet his friends, as did Ellen and Cathy after they'd helped their mother with the washing up. Rose asked Joe if he fancied a stroll before he headed back to Covent Garden. He said he did.

As they walked down Montague Street, his eyes were drawn back to Fiona's house. His mother noticed. "There are two families in there now. One upstairs, one down. Lord, I miss them. Kate was like a sister to me," she said.

Joe nodded. He missed them, too. So much that it hurt. He turned to his mother and asked, "Do you think she'd ever forgive me, Mum? Not that she'd ever love me again. I know that's too much to ask, but maybe she could just forgive me."

Rose hesitated. "I don't know, luv. It's amazing what the 'eart can bear. People say it breaks, but it doesn't. It would be easier if it did. If it just stopped beating, stopped feeling." They turned the corner. "I suppose she might. It 'appens. I once forgave your father."

"For what? Being a miserable old sod?"

Rose shook her head and Joe noticed his mother suddenly looked faraway and sad.

"For what, Mum?"

"When you were only six and Jimmy three and Ellen just born, your dad left. 'E took up with a widow who worked at the Spitalfields market. She was no beauty, but

440

'er kids were grown and she 'ad a room all to 'erself."

"Me own dad?" Joe said, floored.

Rose nodded. " 'E couldn't cope with marriage and fatherhood and another new baby. We 'ad no money whatsoever. We lived with me parents. 'E worked for 'is father. It was an awful time."

"But you coped, Mum."

"Of course I did, my children needed me. I could cope. 'E couldn't."

Joe looked at her, still in a state of shock.

Rose laughed at his expression. "Men are the weak ones, luv. Didn't you know? Oh, you make a lot of noise, but it's the women who are strong. Where it counts. In 'ere," she said, touching her fingers to her heart. Pain flickered across her face at the memories. "A brand-new baby. Colicky. Wouldn't feed. Never let me sleep. Jimmy and you only sprogs. Barely enough money for food. And then me 'usband ups and leaves me." She laughed bitterly. "And me dad asks me what *I'd* done to drive 'im out. Thank God I 'ad me mum. I wouldn't 'ave made it without 'er."

"What 'appened? 'E came back? You let 'im?"

"Aye. 'E was back within the month. Tail between 'is legs."

"Why'd you take 'im back?"

"I needed me 'usband. You kids needed your dad. And I loved the blighter. It took a while, but I forgave 'im. 'E was sorry and 'e tried so 'ard afterward. And even though what 'e'd done 'urt, I could understand it. The way you lot cried and carried on, I wanted to leave meself."

"Blimey, me own dad," Joe said. "I never knew."

"Maybe that explains your father, luv. Why 'e is like 'e is. So careful and cautious. Afraid to put a foot wrong and mess things up again. Maybe that's why 'e's angry with you. You made the same mistake 'e did." Joe nodded. "What all this means is, I don't know if Fiona can forgive you. It's not for me to say. But I do know 'ow much she loved you, and 'ow much you loved her. And you shouldn't go through the rest of your life without at least trying to see if she will."

"I want to, Mum. I would. If only I could find 'er."

Rose frowned. "You weren't able to find out anything? Not even with that detective?"

"Only that she'd pawned some things in a shop near Roddy's flat. That's it."

"Fiona's a capable girl, I'm sure she's all right wherever she is. And I'm sure she 'ad 'er reasons for leaving the way she did, but still, it's very strange."

Joe said it worried him too. He told his mother something he hadn't told her before because he hadn't wanted to alarm her – he told her about his run-in with Stan Christie.

"Oh, Joe, I don't like the sound of that at all," she said anxiously. "What on earth does Bowler Sheehan want with Fiona?"

"According to Roddy, Sheehan says she stole some money and 'e wants it back."

"What? That makes no sense! Nothing about this does. Fiona wouldn't steal. And it's so unlike 'er not to tell Roddy where she went. Of all people! 'E was like a father to 'er. More family than 'er own uncle, who didn't even write to Kate or send money after Paddy died."

Joe stopped walking. He took his mother by the shoulders. " 'Er uncle . . ." he said slowly.

"Aye. 'E lives in New York City. 'E's a shopkeeper, I think. I remember Kate telling me that Charlie wanted to go there and work for 'im."

"Mum, that's it!" he shouted. "That's where she is, I'm sure of it! Where else would she 'ave gone? Especially with Seamie to look after. Do you know 'is name? 'Is address?"

"I don't. It would be Finnegan, of course, but I don't know 'is first name. Roddy would, though. Maybe 'e knows the address, too."

"Mum, I'm going to go," Joe said excitedly. "To New York. She's there, I just know it. As soon as I can get the money together. I'll need quite a bit, I would think. Enough

442

to get over there and to pay for room and board while I look for 'er. I've got to get my business going. I can make more working for meself than I can working for Ed."

"Let's go back and ask your dad about the barrow 'e mentioned. I've got a bit of pin money put aside, I could 'elp with the deposit," Rose said.

Joe kissed her. "Thanks, Mum. Let's go to Roddy's first, though, before we go 'ome. See if 'e knows the address. If 'e does, I could write 'er right away."

"All right," Rose said. "Let's go." She started off in the wrong direction.

"No, it's this way," Joe said, tugging on her arm. "Come on, Mum, 'urry!"

43

Fiona thumbed the pages of the leather-bound book she was holding.

"What have you got there?" Will asked her.

"The *Collected Poems* of Alfred, Lord Tennyson."

He glanced over at it. "A first edition. Very rare. Printed in Venice," he said, wiping dust off a bottle of wine he was holding. "Do you like Tennyson?"

"I might if I hadn't been forced to memorize him in school," she replied. She closed her eyes, hugged the book to her chest, and recited "Crossing the Bar" perfectly, opening her eyes again on the very last line.

"Well done!" Will remarked, putting the bottle down to applaud. He'd taken off his jacket and tie and had draped them over a leather settee. He was wearing a crisp white shirt – its cuffs held together with monogrammed gold rectangles – a silk vest, and trousers of fine, light wool.

Fiona flushed at his praise. She returned the book to its place at the bottom of an oak bookshelf that was at least twenty feet high. Dozens more lined the walls of Will's enormous library. Ladders positioned on rails allowed access to the upper shelves. The library was twice as big as Michael's entire flat, but it was only one room in a mansion that took up an entire city block – the corner of Fifth Avenue at Sixty-second Street. This was her first visit to Will's home. He'd taken her to dinner at Delmonico's, accompanied by Nick. As soon as they were done, they journeyed uptown and Nick headed downtown where, he said, he was going to meet a painter friend. They would all rendezvous back at Del's just before midnight, then continue on to Eighth Avenue and Michael would never be the wiser. They'd done this twice before and he hadn't caught on yet. It was the only way she could ever have any time alone with Will. The first time they'd gone walking in the Park, and the second time riding in the carriage. They'd been able to talk to each other without a third person always listening, and steal a few kisses, too.

When they'd arrived at the house – just over an hour ago – he'd given her the grand tour. It had taken that long just to walk through it. It was impossibly huge and stupefyingly opulent. It had a receiving room, two drawing rooms, three parlors, a dining room, endless hallways, a sitting room, a games room, several studies, a gallery, a conservatory, huge kitchens, a ballroom that could hold three hundred, several rooms that appeared to serve no purpose whatsoever, and Will's enormous library, plus various bedrooms, bathrooms, and quarters for the servants. Fiona thought it more a palace than a house and nearly tripped several times trying to take in all the carved marble, the gilding, the painted panels, the tapestries, silk curtains, crystal chandeliers, the paintings and sculpture. Overwhelmed, she was glad when they finally reached the library, with its spare decor. Just the orderly shelves, two desks, and two leather bergères and a settee grouped in front of the fireplace. It was a chilly night, even though it was summer, and the butler had built a fire for them. Its light, plus the glow from several candelabra, illuminated the room.

"Will . . ." she said now, turning in a slow circle to take in the thousands of titles before her. "Just how many books do you have?"

He thought for a few seconds as he struggled with an uncooperative corkscrew. "About a hundred thousand, give or take a few."

"Blimey!" she whispered, walking the length of one wall, her boot heels clicking on the polished stone floor. She heard a cork pop.

"Ah! There we go. Do you like Margaux, Fiona? This is a '69. Older than you are."

Fiona shrugged. "I don't know. I've never had it. I never had wine at all until you took me to Delmonico's. Only champagne. It was all Nick would drink on the ship, so I drank it, too."

Will blinked at her. "Really? What did you drink in London?"

"Tea."

"I mean with your luncheon. And your dinner."

Fiona tapped her chin. "Hmmm . . . with my luncheon. And my dinner. Let me think. Ah, yes, I remember now . . . tea. And then there was tea. Oh, and we also had tea. A rather run-of-the-mill Assam from the corner shop most days, but occasionally a *divine*" – she fluttered her lashes on the word – "Darjeeling if a crate broke at the docks and my father and his mates could get to it before the foreman found out."

Will gave her a look. "Making fun of me?"

She grinned. "What do you think we drank on a docker's wages?"

"What were they?"

"Twenty-odd shillings. About five dollars."

Will grimaced. "I guess you wouldn't be drinking wine on that, would you? But you are now. Here, come and try this."

He had settled himself on the settee. Fiona joined him. She liked it here in his library. She felt safe sitting close to him. She always felt safe with him, wherever they went. Safe and cared for. Those were good feelings. Not as good as the breathless, desperate, longing feelings of being in love. Those feelings still eluded her no matter how much she wished they would come. But they *would* come. In time. She was certain of it. It was still too soon. She barely knew Will, after all. She hadn't been seeing him long enough to be *in* love yet. She was still *falling* in love. And that was a different thing entirely.

He poured two glasses of wine. She reached for one but he drew it away.

"Not so fast. A lesson first, before you drink one of the best wines the world has to offer."

"Do I spit it out? They had a wine-appreciation lesson on the ship. I watched them. They swirled it in their mouths then spat it in a bucket. I guess they weren't too appreciative."

"You spit this out, my girl, and I'll string you up."

"Is it good, then?"

"Very. Close your eyes."

She did. "Now what do I do?"

"Close your mouth. Just for a few seconds. Can you manage that?"

Fiona giggled.

"Inhale it first," Will said, holding the glass under her nose. "Take a nice deep breath." Fiona did as she was told. She could feel him near her, feel his warmth, the resonance of his voice. "What do you smell?"

"Um . . . grapes?"

"What *else*?"

She inhaled again. "Currants, I think. Yes, currants. And . . . and pepper? And a bit of something else . . . I know – vanilla!" She opened her eyes.

"Very good. You've an excellent nose. I'm impressed."

He handed her the glass. It was lead crystal, as heavy as a brick. She took a mouthful and swallowed it. It was like drinking velvet. She took another mouthful and felt its warmth spread through her body. She noticed that Will was sitting very close to her. She could see the flecks of copper in his warm brown eyes, a small freckle above his top lip, a lick of gray in his hair. He smelled of starched laundry and leather and clean skin. It was wonderful, his scent, much nicer than an old glass of wine. It brought blood to her cheeks and made them glow. She held his gaze for a few seconds, certain he was going to kiss her, wanting him to. And then he did.

"You've got an excellent mouth, too," he said, taking the wineglass from her hand and placing it on the table. He kissed her neck, and behind her ear, making her shiver. He stroked her breast through the fabric of her dress firmly but gently, making her sigh. He was sure of himself. Confident in the way he touched her, and she was reminded again that he was no boy. He'd had a wife once, and if her uncle was to be believed, mistresses, too. He knew what he was doing, which was more than she could say. As she felt his hands on her back, undoing the buttons there, felt him sliding her camisole straps over her shoulders, she suddenly knew why he had brought her here tonight, why they had come to his home instead of walking in the park.

"Will, don't . . ." she said breathlessly, not ready for this. But he didn't stop. As the candles flickered, casting a warm glow over the shelves of books, the wine, the leather settee, her skin, he kept on stroking her bare breasts, kissing her lips, moving his fingers in just the right way under her skirts. He was skilled. He knew just where to touch her and how. His hands and lips made her feel weak, made the place between her legs ache, made her feel as if she wanted to peel his clothes off and pull him down to her. Entranced by desire, she no longer wanted him to stop. She wanted to feel the heat of his skin against hers, to feel him inside of her.

He kissed her again, then said, "Come to bed with me, Fiona. I want you . . . I want to make love to you."

She froze. Only seconds ago, there had been fire in her veins, now there was ice. She broke their embrace. "No, Will," she said sharply. "I don't want to . . . I . . . I can't."

Will sat back against the settee and closed his eyes. "What is it? What's wrong?" he asked.

"I . . . I could get pregnant."

He opened one eye and looked at her. "There are devices, you know. I would've taken precautions."

"Well . . . it's not just that . . . I can't . . . I'm not . . ."

"It's all right, Fiona," he said, taking her hand. "You're

448

not ready. That's all I need to know. You don't have to explain. I understand. I was too pushy."

"No, Will, you weren't," she started to say, "I . . . I want you, too, I do . . . I just . . ."

"Shhh," he said, stopping her mouth with a kiss. He pulled her camisole together. "At least put those away, will you? There's only so much a man can stand."

Fiona buttoned herself up. Her cheeks were burning, but not from modesty.

She had lied. To Will. To herself. She let him believe her reticence was due to a fear of pregnancy when she knew the real reason, knew it and refused to admit it. His words, *I want you . . . I want to make love to you* – they were Joe's words, the very words he'd said to her that afternoon in Covent Garden when he'd made love to her in his narrow bed, when he told her he loved her and he always would. The second Will had uttered them, images of Joe had filled her mind. The way he'd looked when he'd dumped out their cocoa tin in her lap, when he'd given her the tiny sapphire ring, when he'd scooped her up in his arms. She remembered his touch, the way he'd opened her up to him, opened himself to her, until they'd become one – one body, one heart, one soul.

These images tortured her. She wanted to be with Will, to think only of him, to be in love with him. She wanted to move on, to put Joe behind her. So very much. And she'd been trying, but it never worked. He always came back. She might hear a voice that sounded like his, or glimpse a pair of eyes nearly as blue as his, or see a lad walk with the same cocky swagger, and suddenly he was with her again – in her mind, her heart.

"Fiona?" Will said gently. "Are those tears?"

She quickly brushed her cheeks, embarrassed. She didn't know she'd been crying.

He pulled out his handkerchief and dabbed at her eyes. "I've upset you, I'm sorry. I shouldn't have been so demanding. I'm a clod. Truly. Don't cry, darling. It breaks my

449

heart." He held her close, whispering to her. "I'd never take advantage of you. Never. I'd rather die than hurt you. I just got carried away, that's all. My feelings for you are that strong." He released her, looked into her eyes, and said, "I'm bad at these things, Fiona. I can talk your ears off about business, as I'm sure you know by now, but I'm at a loss when it comes to matters of the heart. Always have been." He paused for a second, then said, "I've never told you this before . . ."

Her hands clenched. No, Will, she thought. Not now. Please, please, not now.

". . . I've wanted to say it to you for a long time, but I've been, well . . . afraid to, I guess. In case you didn't return my feelings. I . . . I love you, Fiona."

Why had he said it? Why now? Why not on some perfect night when they were walking arm in arm from a dinner and laughing and thoughts of Joe were a million miles away. They'd had such nights. They'd given her hope, made her believe that she could forget him.

Will kissed her lips tenderly, lovingly. He looked into her eyes, waiting for her answer.

She would tell him that this wasn't going to work. She would say she loved another man and always would. That she'd tried to get him out of her heart, but couldn't. That she'd grow old loving him. That she hated herself for loving him.

Instead she said, "Oh, Will . . . I . . . I love you, too."

44

"I shouldn't have let you do this. It's too soon for all this walking," Fiona fretted.

"Oh, don't fuss so! I'm fine," Nick huffed. "Everyone treats me like I'm some delicate, wilting flower. As if I'm going to fall over if a strong breeze comes up. I've been out already, you know. Parties and suppers and such. I'm not an invalid anymore!"

"No, but you certainly are bad-tempered."

"Sorry," he said, trying to look contrite. "But I'm fine, Fee. Really."

"No fibs?"

"No fibs. I feel good. I'm just discouraged by the rubbish we've been shown, that's all."

About ten yards ahead of them, at the corner of Irving Place and Eighteenth Street, the real estate agent turned and said, "Everything all right, Mr. Soames? Not tiring, are you? I'm sure you'll like the next property. It's a gem."

"I'm sure it is. As dogholes go," Nick muttered. He was desperate to find a new site for his gallery. It had been two months since his collapse and he was eager to return to work.

"All this walking's made me awfully thirsty. I wish there was someplace to sit for a second and have something to drink," he said, threading his arm through Fiona's. "There should be a tearoom in the neighborhood. Have you looked here yet?"

"No, but I should. I'm having no luck elsewhere. Though I can't imagine I'd be any more successful than you've been

451

today. It seems there's nothing available. Everything's too small or too expensive."

Nick nodded. "I don't think I'm ever going to find an arrangement like the one I had. It was so perfect. Will doesn't know of anything, does he?"

"No, I asked him."

"How is the dashing Mr. McClane?"

"Very well. I . . . I'm in love with him, Nick."

Nick stopped dead, taken aback by her declaration. "So soon? Are you sure?"

"Positive," she said brightly.

Too brightly. This is all very sudden, he thought.

"Remember when you told me I'd fall in love again? That I'd forget all about Joe? Well, I have. I didn't believe you, but you were right. I really have."

He gave her an uncertain smile. "That's wonderful," he started to say. "He's a very . . ."

"He's a very wonderful man," she said forcefully. "He's smart and good and kind. And he loves me. He told me he did."

Whom are you trying to convince, old trout? Me or yourself? Nick wondered. She was looking away from him and her face seemed so closed. Her forehead was furrowed into a frown. Her eyes looked hard and tense.

"Have you met his family yet?" he asked.

"No, I haven't. They're being rather difficult right now. Apparently Will's eldest son doesn't like the idea of his father seeing me. I guess I don't have the right pedigree."

"Oh, really? And just who the hell does the little rotter think he is?" Nick said angrily. "He'd be damned lucky to have someone like you in his family. Bloody Americans and their bloody social pretensions! Two generations of lumber money and they think they're aristocrats."

Fiona smiled at his gallantry. She looked like herself again. "And who are you, then, you toff?" she teased, taking his arm. "The Duke of Dour? The Crown Prince of Cranky?"

"Something like that," he said, suddenly self-conscious.

Her nonsense titles sounded oddly familiar to his ears. It had been a long time since anyone had called him by his rightful title. He doubted anyone ever would again. That was fine by him. His own particular pedigree had brought him nothing but grief. He'd shed it when he left England and wanted no further part of it.

"Look, Prince Fusspot, there's that house again," Fiona said.

"Hmmm?" he said, glad of a new subject.

"The derelict house. Right there. We've passed it twice. How can someone just leave a house to rot?" She released his arm and walked up to it, squinting at it in the sunshine. Nick looked at it, trying to see what interested her so much. It was nothing but a tumbledown wreck, though it did have a pretty rosebush in the front, a crimson climber that hung over the doorway.

"Mr. Soames?" the realtor called.

"Come on, Fee," Nick said. "We're being summoned. Time to see yet another space that's too dark, too pokey, and too dreary."

The realtor showed them four more properties, none of which suited him, then left them back on the corner of Irving and Eighteenth, with the promise to notify him if any more properties became available.

"Shall we get a bit to eat, Fee?" Nick asked, weighing the merits of the Fifth Avenue Hotel versus one of the new Child's Restaurants with their spotless white-tiled floors and brisk, efficient waitresses. "Tea and scones? Or an ice cream soda? Or maybe one of those sundaes with whipped cream and nuts and . . . Fee?"

He'd thought she was right beside him, but she wasn't. She was standing a few yards away – in front of the derelict house again. Her hands were resting atop the iron fence that separated the front yard from the sidewalk. She was staring up at the tall boarded-up windows dreamily.

"What on earth are you looking at?" he asked, joining her.

"It must've been stunning once, this house."

"Not anymore. Come away before the cornice falls off and kills us both."

But she wouldn't be budged. "Someone must've loved it once. That rose didn't get there by itself, and look at these . . ." She leaned over the fence and touched a tall blue spike of delphinium. "Someone just left it, Nick. Just walked away from it. How could a person do that?"

Nick sighed impatiently. He wanted to leave. He was tired and hungry, but it was more than that. He was uneasy; he had the unpleasant feeling that they were being watched. He looked around, telling himself he was being silly. But he wasn't. There was a man sweeping the sidewalk two houses down and he was eyeing them unhappily.

"Hey! What are you doing there? There's no loitering on this street," he shouted.

"We're not loitering," Fiona said. She released the fence and took a few steps toward him. "We're admiring the building."

"Speak for yourself," Nick grumbled.

"Do you know why it's boarded up?" she asked the man.

"Of course I do. I'm the caretaker, aren't I?"

Fiona walked over to him and introduced herself. Nick had no choice but to follow. The caretaker told them his name – Fred Wilcox – and that he looked after the building for its owner, an elderly woman named Esperanza Nicholson.

"Why has she abandoned it?"

"What's it to you?" Wilcox asked.

"It makes me sad seeing such a beautiful house falling to ruin."

"It is sad," Wilcox said less gruffly, softened a bit by Fiona's honest admission. "Fifty-odd years ago, Miss Nicholson's father gave her the house as a wedding present. She was going to live in it with her husband when they got back from their honeymoon. She had the place all done up – furniture, carpets, wallpaper – everything. And all of it the very best quality, mind you, no rubbish. Then, a day before the wedding, her intended jilted her. It destroyed her. She lived with her father, became a recluse. The old man's gone, died years ago, but she still lives in his house. She had this one boarded up and left it to crumble. Won't live in it. Refuses to rent it or sell it."

"It's as if she's punishing the house for what happened," Fiona said. "Mr. Wilcox, is there any way we could see the house? Can we go inside?"

"No, I can't let you do that," Wilcox said, shaking his head. "You might get hurt in there."

Nick despaired of ever getting a cup of tea. He was feeling put out because he hadn't found a site for his gallery. He wanted to leave Gramercy Park and the unproductive afternoon behind him. He knew better than to suggest they not go into the house, though. Once Fiona got a bee in her bonnet there was no stopping her. He dug in his pocket, pulled out a dollar, and handed it to Wilcox, hoping it would speed the process up. It did.

"All right then, here's the key for the garden floor," the caretaker said, handing Fiona an ancient, blackened skeleton key. "If anything happens to you, if you break your fool necks in there, I don't know nothing about it. You got in through a loose board, right?"

"Righto," Nick said. He turned and trotted off after Fiona, who was already charging through the gate. He kicked his way through the wildflowers and weeds to the door, which she was struggling to open. "If we so much as *glimpse* a rat, I'm off," he said.

"Here, help me turn this key. I can't budge it. I think the lock's rusty."

Nick used all his strength. "It's stuck. Wait . . . there it goes."

Fiona nudged him out of the way in her eagerness to get inside. She pushed the door open and rushed in. Crumbling bits of rotted wood and rusted metal fell on her head. Nick brushed the debris away, laughing at her as he did. Inside, the inner door had rotted off its hinges and was lying inside the foyer. They gingerly walked across it and into the house.

"Oh, this is beautiful, Fiona! Really!" he said sarcastically, looking around. The ceiling was mostly gone. The lath was exposed where big chunks of plaster had fallen. The wallpaper was hanging down in strips. A chandelier lay on the floor, smashed to bits. Mildew had blackened the once white sheets covering the furniture. "Come on, let's go."

But Fiona wasn't leaving. She advanced from the first room through a set of sticky pocket doors into the second. He followed, thinking she was mad, not understanding her obsession with this place. Halfway there, his foot went straight through a floorboard. He pulled it out, cursing.

"Nick! Isn't this something?" she called from the other room.

"Yes, if you're a termite," he said, stumbling through the doors. As he wiped splinters off his cuff, Fiona marveled at the ornate pier mirrors, their silver now peeling from the glass. He opened his mouth to complain that the dust was making him wheeze, when something in her expression made him close it again. He hadn't been able to comprehend her obsession with this moldering house, but watching her now, seeing the emotion in her face as she wiped cobwebs off a mantel, he suddenly did. She identified with the house. It was a creature that someone had abandoned. As someone had once abandoned her.

She bent to examine the carvings on the mantel, then squealed with fright as a family of stray cats shot out of the grate. They scrambled past her toward the back of the house and squeezed out of an empty pane in a grime-caked window. Laughing shakily, one hand pressed to her chest, she followed them. "I think there's a yard out there," she said. "Let's go see."

The door was stuck. The lock worked, but its hinges were rusted. Working together, they managed to pull it back

456

eighteen inches or so from the jamb. Fiona squeezed through first. Once she was out, he heard her gasp. "Oh, Nick! Hurry! Oh, look at them all!"

He squeezed out, wondering what she could be exclaiming about. And then he saw them. Tea roses. Hundreds and hundreds of them. The entire backyard – and it was a large one – was full of them. They were sprawling over walls, pathways, a rusted iron settee, each other, basking and preening in the sunshine. He recognized them instantly. His father had favored them and had kept scores of bushes on his Oxfordshire estate. Aristocratic old girls, tea roses. He remembered the gardener telling him how their ancestors had been smuggled out of China a hundred years ago by Englishmen in love with the lush flowers and intoxicating tea scent. They could be tricky to grow, tough to get a repeat bloom out of, but these were blooming in the heat of summer!

"Smell them, Nick, they smell like tea!" Fiona said. "Look at these . . . have you ever seen a pink like that? Look at that pale yellow one . . ." She was running from bush to bush, burying her face in the blooms like a demented bumblebee.

Nick pulled a blossom to his nose, closed his eyes, and inhaled. For a second he was back in Oxford on a perfect summer day. He opened his eyes again in time to see Fiona rush up to him. She giddily tucked a rose behind his ear, threw her arms around his neck, and hugged him tightly.

"My goodness, old shoe! I never knew roses had such an effect on you!"

"They do!" she said, taking his hands in hers. "And beautiful, big old houses in Gramercy Park. And tea. Oh, Nick, this is it! Don't you see? This house will be your gallery . . . and my tearoom!"

45

"Couldn't I have just five minutes of her time?" Fiona pleaded. "I promise I won't overstay my welcome."

"You already have. Miss Nicholson does not receive visitors."

"But I only want to ask her about her property . . . the Gramercy Park house . . ."

"Then I suggest you contact her attorney, Mr. Raymond Guilfoyle, forty-eight Lexington Avenue." Miss Nicholson's butler moved to close the door. Fiona blocked it with her foot.

"I've already done that. He told me she doesn't wish to rent the property."

"Then you have your answer."

"But –"

"Kindly remove your foot, Miss Finnegan. Good day."

As the door swung closed, Fiona heard a woman's voice, high and querulous, call, "Harris, who's there? What is it?"

"A nuisance call, madam." The door closed. Fiona was left standing on Miss Nicholson's stoop. Well, that's the end of that, she thought, crestfallen. Both Wilcox and Guilfoyle had told her Miss Nicholson would not rent the house, but she'd foolishly thought that if she could see the woman in person, she could change her mind. She'd gotten her hopes up; now they were dashed.

A breeze grabbed at her hat. She caught it, held it down, and repinned it. "Damn it all!" she cursed. She wanted that house. Desperately. Ever since she'd seen it – over a week ago – it was all she thought about. It looked a wreck, yes,

458

but with a bit of work it could be gorgeous. Wilcox said the plumbing was fine. It had been put in new when Miss Nicholson's father bought the house and he regularly ran the water to keep the pipes and drains clear. The bricks needed repointing and the roof needed work. The walls, floors, and woodwork needed refurbishing, and the kitchen was antiquated, but structurally, the house was sound. Although Miss Nicholson didn't give a toss what happened to it, Wilcox admitted he couldn't bear to see it just fall to ruin, so he'd tried, in small ways, to keep it up over the years.

She and Nick had talked about how to make it work. She would take the garden and parlor floors, and he the top two floors – the third floor for his gallery and the fourth for his flat. They would split the rent and apply to First Merchants for a loan to finance the repairs. They both would've preferred that their plan not hinge on borrowing money, but it couldn't be helped. They were both currently suffering from an acute cash shortage.

Fiona had poured money into TasTea. In the last month alone, she'd hired two more girls to work in the shop, bought her own wagon and a team of horses for deliveries, and hired a man to drive it. She'd also spent a small fortune to develop and advertise her new scented teas. She and Stuart had experimented for weeks – testing and rejecting blend after blend – before they'd come up with a mixture that was strong enough to stand up to the flavors she'd devised, but not so strong it overpowered them.

She'd also spent heavily on Burton Tea stock. The London dockers had finally walked out. After months of agitating for better wages and an eight-hour day, the union had given the word to strike after a group of men had been denied their plus money. The men had united – preferred men, casuals, stevedores – and they'd shut down the river. All the waterfront businesses were suffering. The price of Burton stock had fallen to nearly half its original value and Fiona was using every dollar of her profits to buy as much as she possibly could. She had also wired five hundred dollars to the dockers' union, anonymously. Michael had been furious when he found out how much she'd sent, but she didn't care. It was for her father and her mother and Charlie and Eileen and she would've sent a million if she'd had it.

Nick, too, was pinched for money. He was expecting the first of what would be quarterly checks from his investment account in London, but it had not yet arrived. Nick said his father was undoubtedly holding onto it in hopes that he'd die and save the bank the postage. Although he had left London with two thousand pounds, he had spent most of it already – on the customs tax assessed on his shipment of paintings, on renovations to the space he'd rented from Mrs. Mackie, and on scores of canvases from young painters he'd recently met in New York – Childe Hassam, William Merritt Chase, and Frank Benson among them. He was down to three hundred dollars.

Nick, Fiona had discovered, was hopeless with money. It was August now. They'd been in New York for nearly five months and he still hadn't opened a bank account. When she moved him into her uncle's flat, she discovered he kept his cash in a pair of brown brogues – bills in the right, coins in the left. He told her he despised banks and refused to go near one. She told him she was opening an account for him at First Merchants. What was he going to do when he sold a painting? Take a client's bank draft, stuff it in his shoe, and hope it magically turned into cash?

He handled money like a child who believes there will always be more. Making do was a foreign concept to him. A week after arriving at her uncle's he'd given Ian some cash and asked him to go get a few things for him. Ian, unable to decipher his handwriting, had come into the shop to ask Fiona to interpret. Upon reading the list, she'd marched into his room to take him in hand, telling him he only had so much money left, and perhaps he ought to tighten his belt a bit until more arrived from London. He'd sulked. He *needed* those things, he told her. He couldn't do without leather-bound books. He hated nasty, shabby books with cardboard covers. He also needed a new pair of silk pajamas. And a bottle of scent. And good paper. And a silver fountain pen from Tiffany's. Was that really so much to ask for? She wouldn't drink bad tea, would she?

"A pot of tea costs a damn sight less than Mark Twain's complete works bound in red moroccan, Nicholas," she'd scolded.

He did not understand that one could go a day without Beluga or French champagne and live to tell the tale. Chastened by his collapse, he agreed to follow Dr. Eckhardt's instructions to the letter – every one, that was, except the no-champagne edict. Weak, sick, he had nonetheless sat up in his bed and defiantly declared he was a man, not a barbarian, and if this was how he was expected to live, he would rather die. Eckhardt had finally given in, convinced the mental anguish he was inflicting upon his patient would do him more harm than a few glasses of sparkling wine.

Readying herself for the walk back to Chelsea, Fiona tried to accept the situation. She and Nick would have to start looking at more properties, that was all there was to it. But her heart kept reminding her of the graceful lines of the cast-iron balconies, the soaring windows that let in so much light, the lovely gilded mirrors, and the roses . . . oh, the roses! She could just see the backyard full of women in white dresses and broad-brimmed hats taking tea. A tearoom in that house would be a success, she knew it would. It couldn't possibly fail.

But it already has, she told herself. Sighing, she decided she'd better get going before the butler called the police on her – a task she was sure he would relish. When she was halfway down the steps, the door opened again. She turned. "I'm *going*," she said. "No need to get shirty."

"Miss Nicholson will see you," the butler said.

"What?" she asked, confused. "Why?"

"I am not in the habit of discussing my employer's business on the stoop," he replied frostily.

"Sorry," she said, bounding back up the stairs.

The butler closed the door behind them and ushered her into a dark foyer wallpapered in a morbid shade of burgundy. "Follow me," he instructed. He led her down a long hallway, hung with portraits of forbidding-looking men and women, through a set of massive wooden doors and into a parlor every bit as gloomy as the foyer. "Miss Finnegan to see you, madam," he said, then disappeared, closing the doors after him.

The curtains were drawn. It was dark and it took Fiona's eyes, used to the bright sunshine, a few seconds to adjust. Then she saw her . . . sitting across the room on a straight-backed divan. One jeweled, blue-veined hand rested atop an ebony walking stick. The other stroked a spaniel that was lying in her lap. She wore a crisp black silk dress with a ruff of white lace at her throat. Fiona had been expecting a doddery old dear, but the pair of gray eyes now assessing her were piercing. And the expression on the lined face, crowned by a sweep of silver hair drawn back into a neat bun, was sharp.

"Good afternoon, Miss Nicholson," Fiona began nervously. "I'm Fiona –"

"I know who you are. You have an inquiry concerning my property?" she said, gesturing to a chair with her walking stick.

"Yes, ma'am," Fiona said, sitting down. "I should like to rent the property. I want to open a tearoom on the bottom two floors – I own a tea business, you see – and my friend would like to rent the top floors. He's going to open an art gallery." Fiona explained her and Nick's plans to Miss Nicholson in detail.

The woman frowned. "My building's in terrible condition. Can't you rent another?"

"I've been looking, but I haven't found anything as

462

wonderful as your place. It's a shame to let a lovely house like that just die, Miss Nicholson. It's a bit of a wreck, but it has good bones. And the roses . . . oh, you should see them! Hundreds and hundreds of blooms. In ivory and pink and yellow. They would absolutely make the place. No one else in New York would have a tearoom with tea roses in the backyard. I just know people would come."

The woman's face softened at the mention of the roses. "Had them sent from England," she said. "Fifty years ago. Planted them myself. My father's gardener wanted to do it, but I wouldn't let him."

Fiona was just beginning to take heart, just beginning to think she was making progress, when Miss Nicholson's eyes narrowed. "How do you know about those roses?" she asked.

Fiona looked at the floor. "I went inside," she said sheepishly.

"You trespassed."

"I did," she admitted. "There was a loose board and —"

"Wilcox," Miss Nicholson said contemptuously. "He must be rich from that loose board by now. Not a week goes by that some fool doesn't offer to take the house off my hands. Usually for a pittance. How much money do you have behind you, Miss Finnegan?"

"Not much, I'm afraid. Only about a thousand dollars. I've just plowed a fortune back into my business. I'm trying to make a go of a new kind of tea, a scented tea, and it's costing me. But it's doing well," she quickly added. "And profits from my original line are strong. I just know I could make a bundle with this tearoom, too, Miss Nicholson. I've already got the cook in place, all I would need is a wait staff. After the renovations are done, of course. I'm prepared to pay for them myself, but I was hoping the rent might reflect the building's current condition and . . ."

As she talked on, Fiona noticed Miss Nicholson was listening intently. She hasn't thrown me out yet, she thought. Maybe I'm winning her over. Maybe she'll give me a chance.

But before she had even finished speaking, Miss Nicholson abruptly cut her off, saying she had no interest in renting the building and bid her good day.

Fiona was sorely disappointed, and angry, too. She felt the woman had toyed with her, had allowed her to build her hopes back up, only to dash them again. She stood stiffly, drew a calling card from her purse and placed it on a marble-topped table. "If you should change your mind, you can reach me at this address," she said, forcing herself to smile. "Thank you for your time." She had no idea if the woman had heard her. Her gaze was directed at a painting hanging over her fireplace.

Fiona walked to the parlor doors, but before she reached them, Miss Nicholson suddenly said, "Why are you putting so much effort into a business, Miss Finnegan? Why don't you marry? A woman as beautiful as you are must have many admirers. Haven't you a sweetheart? Someone you love?"

"I have."

"Why don't you marry him?"

Her gray eyes held Fiona's. It was as if she could see inside her.

"I can't. He married someone else," she said quickly, mortified at admitting this to a stranger. A bitter old woman, at that. "I'm sorry to have intruded, Miss Nicholson. Good day."

"Good day," the old woman said, a ruminative expression on her face.

"What cheek!" Fiona fumed as she stalked off down the sidewalk. "Prying into my affairs. Asking me about Will and why haven't I married him. It's none of her bloody business."

Then she stopped short, realizing with a sense of despair that it was not Will she had been thinking about when she answered Miss Nicholson's question. It was Joe.

46

The single window of Kevin Burdick's office was grimed with soot. The walls were covered in paint that might've been white once but was now yellow from age and tobacco smoke. It was a still, hot summer day and the air inside the room stank of grease and sweat.

"I want you to offer her money, Mr. Burdick," William McClane Junior said. "Five thousand . . . ten . . . whatever it takes. Just get her to drop my father."

Burdick, a private detective, shook his head. "Not a good move. What if she doesn't take the bait? What if she takes offense instead and runs right to your father? It won't take him long to figure out who's behind the offer."

"You have a better idea?"

"Indeed I do," he said. His wooden chair creaked loudly as he leaned back in it. "The best way to handle this would be for me to get something on this girl . . . this" – he consulted his notes – "Miss Finnegan. Something of an unsavory nature. Then you go to your father with the information under the pretext of concern. He breaks it off, grateful to you for telling him, and no one's the wiser as to the true nature of your involvement."

Will Junior smiled. The man was right; his way was much safer than trying to buy the girl off.

Burdick clasped his hands and put them behind his head, exposing saucer-sized sweat stains under his arms. "I'll need some time, of course. And half of my fee up front."

"That won't be a problem," Will Junior said, reaching into his breast pocket. As he pulled out his wallet, he saw a fly crawl over the remains of Burdick's lunch – a rank corned-beef sandwich and a wilted pickle. He felt his stomach lurch.

"How's the subway plan going?" Burdick asked.

"The mayor still hasn't decided. Our plan is clearly the better of the two, but how often have you known the city fathers to make a smart choice? It's anyone's guess as to what will happen." He pushed the money across the desk. Burdick counted it, then stuffed it in his pocket.

"You really think your father's relationship with this woman will hurt your chances?"

Will Junior snorted. "Of course not. It's just what I tell him."

"Then why wreck his romance? What do you care who he's fucking? Eventually he'll finish with her and move on. Am I right? From what you've told me, she's not his sort of people. It's not like he's going to marry her."

"That's the problem, Mr. Burdick. He might. He seems to have lost his mind."

Burdick nodded. "I follow you," he said. "You don't want any stepbrothers. Or sisters."

"Exactly. She's young. She'll have babies. Probably quite a few. She's Irish, after all. She'll outlive my father. He'll leave all his money to her and her brats and I'll never see a penny of it. And that just won't do. Congressmen don't make the kind of money industrialists do."

Will Junior already had an expensive existence to finance – the Hyde Park house, the apartment in the city, all the servants, his growing family, Isabelle's insatiable appetite for new clothes, his own appetite for pretty actresses. And it would only get worse.

"I need my father's money to get to the White House, Mr. Burdick. I'm not going to stand by while some gold-digging bitch gets her hands on it," he said, standing up to leave.

"She won't," Burdick assured him.

"I hope you're right."

Burdick belched. "Trust me."

*   *   *

Fiona was so excited, she was practically dancing down the sidewalk.

"Come on! Hurry up, would you?" she urged her uncle, tugging at his arm. "Nick, Alec, you get behind him and push and I'll pull. Maybe that will get him moving."

"Leave off! I'm walking as fast as I can," Michael said, shaking himself free of his niece's grasp. "Acting like a lunatic, you are."

"I'm going to call it The Tea Rose. After the roses. Just wait until you see them! Now, don't forget what I told you, Uncle Michael. You have to use a little imagination . . ."

"Jaysus, I heard you the first five times! Calm down, Fiona!"

But she couldn't calm down. Two days ago, Raymond Guilfoyle, Esperanza Nicholson's lawyer, had walked into the shop and changed her life. Fiona's heart had raced at the sight of him; she'd hoped he had come to tell her Miss Nicholson would rent her the shop after all. He had not. Instead, he informed her that his client wanted to sell her building. For two thousand dollars. A mere fraction of what it was worth.

"I beg your pardon?" she'd said.

"I was as surprised as you are, Miss Finnegan," Guilfoyle said. "And I don't mind telling you that I strenuously advised against this. The house is worth ten times the price, even in its current condition, but Miss Nicholson doesn't listen to me. Or anyone else. She is her own counsel."

He'd left a contract for her to sign and advised her to have a lawyer of her own read it.

Fiona had immediately gone to First Merchants to arrange for a loan, one large enough to cover the purchase price and renovations, only to be told by Franklin Ellis that he could not sanction it. "It's highly unusual to lend this amount to a young unmarried woman, Miss Finnegan," he said, adding that if her uncle was willing to act as guarantor and put up his shop as collateral, he would reconsider.

Fiona had been ready to burst with anger. She had proved herself to this man. She had rescued her uncle's shop, made it more profitable than it had been, and opened her own tea shop. Why did he need anyone's signature on a loan but her own? For a second she'd been tempted to go to Will, but he was away on business, and besides, that's probably just what the man expected her to do – go crying to Will. His pride had been bruised when Will overruled him on her account. Now he had a chance to injure her pride. Well, she wouldn't let him. She could fight her own battles. Michael would guarantee the loan. All she had to do was show him the house.

Finally they rounded the corner and the house came into view; thirty-two Irving Place.

"There it is!" Nick said gleefully. "The big one. Right across the street."

Michael stared at it. "Bloody hell!" he finally said. "*That's* it?" His tone was one of horror, but Fiona, lovestruck at the very sight of the place, didn't notice.

"Isn't it wonderful?" she said. "Let's go in. Be careful, Alec, there's a lot to trip over."

"It looks like someone tossed a bomb in here," Michael grumbled as he entered the foyer. "I thought you'd done well to get a house in Gramercy Park for two thousand, but now I wonder if it's not Miss Nicholson who got the better end of the deal."

He walked around, inspecting the rooms, an unhappy look on his face. Alec went into the backyard. He'd come to see the roses. Nick went upstairs to measure his rooms.

"Just who were you planning to serve tea to here, lass?" Michael asked, brushing dust off a mantel. "The dead? They're about the only ones who'd appreciate the decor."

Fiona glowered at him. "You have no sense of possibility," she said. "Just imagine the walls painted cream, soft chairs, and tables covered with china and silver."

Michael still looked skeptical.

"Come on," she said, taking his hand and leading him

out into the garden, where Alec was examining the roses. "Now . . . just imagine coming into the yard in June with the roses in bloom and white lace tablecloths and pretty teapots and fancy cakes and lovely women in summer hats . . ."

Michael looked at the roses. He also looked at the crumbling brick walls, the rusted iron sundial, the tangle of weeds clotting the path. "Who's going to clear all this out?" he asked.

"Alec. With two or three lads."

"And the renovations? You'll need more than two or three lads for that."

"I know that," she said impatiently. "I've already got a carpenter in mind, as well as a plasterer and painter. They'll bring the men they need with them."

"And I suppose you're going to come down here every day and oversee a dozen workmen? Maybe put on a pair of overalls while you're at it and pick up a hammer?"

"I *am* going to come down here every day, but no, Uncle Michael, I'm not going to put on overalls. They don't suit me. I thought Frank Pryor, the carpenter, would make a good foreman," she said through gritted teeth. Why was her uncle always so difficult? Why was he never agreeable to her plans? Never behind her? Why was everything a bloody fight with him?

"What about the money? The four thousand dollars you want to borrow will cover the price of the building plus your renovations, right? What about everything else? Like the silverware and the china you'll need. And tablecloths and trays and the waitresses' wages and God knows what else."

"I can use some of my own money for that. Remember the shop? And TasTea?" she asked sarcastically. "They do produce income, you know. And Nick will help, too."

"With what? His good looks? He's broke, lass! You told me so."

"His money's due from his father's bank soon. He told

me his fund's worth over one hundred thousand pounds and he expects at least two thousand pounds every quarter. It's just a matter of another week or two. He's going to pay me rent for the upper two floors and help with the cost of their renovation. As for the things I need, I don't have to buy them new. Nick says I can get china and silver at auction houses and secondhand shops cheap. He's going to take me."

Michael scowled. "This is a waste of time and money," he said. "You've got one of the richest men in New York after you and all you can think of is peddling tea. What's wrong with you? McClane'll marry you soon and this'll all be for naught. That's what you ought to be doing – figuring out how to get a ring on your finger. Not messing about in this shit heap!"

Fiona's eyes sparked with anger. "For your information, Will hasn't asked me to marry him," she said hotly. "Nor has anyone else. I've got myself to look after and a brother to raise and nobody's paying my bills but me."

Michael flapped his hand at her. "Why don't you fix up the house and rent out the floors? It would be a decent income without all the bother of a tearoom."

"No!" Fiona thundered. "Have you listened to anything I've said, you bloody man? A tearoom will help build my tea business. I've already explained all this!"

They were shouting now. Michael told her he wasn't risking any shop of his over such a foolish venture. Fiona said he wouldn't have his shop if it weren't for her. Telling her she couldn't hold that over his head forever, he stalked back into the house. She was on his heels, badgering. She wanted this building, needed it, felt she nearly had it in her hands, and now he was going to take it away from her. Alec, who'd heard the whole fracas, stood in the doorway behind them, puffing on his pipe. He motioned Michael over.

"Alec, can't it wait?" he asked testily.

"It cannot."

470

Michael followed him into the backyard. Fiona hung back in the doorway, listening, waiting for her chance to go at her uncle again as soon as Alec finished with him.

"What is it?" he asked, exasperated.

The old gardener pulled the pipe from his teeth and gestured at the rosebushes. "Tea roses, them are," he said.

Michael gave them a quick glance. "Aye, so they are."

"As hale and hearty as a highland lass," Alec said, fingering a strong green cane. "Surprising, that is, for a tea rose. You're not likely to find them so vigorous this far north. Teas like the warmer climes. Yet look at these, coming up out of the weeds and cat shit and growing right up to the skies. Almost as if the wee buggers wanted to make something of themselves."

Alec released the cane and looked at Michael. "Funny things, roses. Folks tend to think they're delicate, fragile. But some of them are right tough little bastards. Give them bad soil, bad conditions, they still grow. Insects, spot, drought – doesn't stop them. Prune them down and they'll come back at you twice as hard. Some roses are real fighters. Roses like that ought to be encouraged, I'd say."

Alec shuffled off. Michael was left staring at the roses, half-cursing, half-blessing the old Scotsman. After a minute or so, he turned back to the house. Fiona was still standing in the doorway, her face anxious and hopeful all at once. He looked at her, shook his head, and said, "Come on, then. Let's go to the bank."

47

"Peaches 'ere! Lovely English peaches. None of your French rubbish. Sweet Dorset peaches! Who'll buy? Who'll buy?"

Joe's voice rang out clear and strong down Bruton Street in fashionable Mayfair. It was nearly noon. The sun was high and the temperature was inching above eighty, roasting for London. He was dripping with sweat. His shirt was stuck to his back. The blue kingsman around his neck was soaked. He'd set off from Covent Garden just before dawn and his muscles were aching now with the effort of pushing his barrow. He was tired and sore and happy.

He had seven pounds in his pocket, two of which were pure profit. And he had two more hidden under a loose board in Baxter's stall. Though he had quit Ed Akers's job to start his own business, Ed still allowed him to sleep in his hayloft as long as he continued to feed and groom Baxter. Joe was glad of it; he didn't want to pay for a room. He didn't want to spend one penny he didn't have to. He was saving for a passage to New York. He figured he'd need about six pounds for the boat fare, and another six to live on while he was there and six more for two extra one-way tickets.

Eighteen quid was a lot, but he'd have to pay for food and accommodations while he looked for Fiona and he didn't know how long it would take to find her. Maybe only a few days, but maybe weeks. And when he did find her, if by some miracle she didn't send him packing, if her poor bruised heart still had even just a tiny flicker of love left for him, maybe he could convince her to give him a second chance and to come home with him. If he could, he wanted to know he had enough money to pay her and Seamie's way back to London.

"Coo-eee! Joe! Joe Bristow, over here!"

Joe turned in the direction of the voice. It was Emma Hurley from number twenty, a kitchen maid, a girl of fourteen up from Devon to work in London and thinking the whole thing was one great adventure. She was standing by the gate to the servants' entrance, wearing a gray dress with a white pinafore, cuffs, and collar. Joe smiled at her as he wheeled his barrow over. He liked Emma. She was rosy-cheeked and full of the devil. He'd only met her two weeks ago, and already he knew all the goings on in number twenty. His lordship was dotty, her ladyship was fierce, the cook and the butler fought constantly, and the new valet was ever so handsome. Emma prattled to everyone about everything – himself included. She'd told her friends – maids and nannies in the neighboring homes – about him and they'd told their cooks and now he had a dozen new customers on Bruton Street alone, thanks to her.

"The new girl's just ruined Cook's cauliflower gratin," she told him, giggling. "Burned it to a crisp! Cook boxed her ears. You never *heard* such a carry-on, Joe. Give us two heads, would you? And a bunch of parsley. Oh, and some peaches. Five pounds, please. Her ladyship just informed us that she would like fresh peach ice cream after supper this evening. Good of her to tell us now, wasn't it? Be a miracle if it freezes in time. Cook was *livid* about the cauliflower. Thought she'd have to send one of us down the shops. But I told her you'd be along any minute. Saved that poor girl's life, you did!"

Joe assembled Emma's order. After she paid him, and he gave her her change, he placed a generous bag of strawberries in her hand. "Those are for you, Em. Don't tell Cook." He grinned at her. "I was thinking you could share them with a certain valet."

"I'm finished with him, Joe. Caught him snogging with

473

the parlormaid. I'll share them with Sarah, the new girl. Cook's got her scrubbing the pantry floor for a penance. She'll be in need of a treat by this evening, if she lives to see it!"

"Emma! Where are you, girl? Hurry up!" a voice shrilled from inside.

"I'd better get going. You too, Joe. There's Elsie, from number twenty-two, waving for you. See you tomorrow. Ta-ra! And thanks for the berries!"

Joe shoved off. He made seven more stops on Bruton Street before turning off and heading for Berkeley Square. The piles of fruits and vegetables on his red barrow, with the words MONTAGUE'S – WHERE QUALITY AND CONVENIENCE MEET painted on the side, had diminished considerably. He was worried he might run out of stock before he finished the route. Sales had been good this morning.

It was starting to take off, this plan of his. He'd been discouraged at first; his idea hadn't caught on right away. It had taken the cooks and their scullery maids a little while to understand that he wasn't a delivery boy from some shop, that he was bringing the goods – the very best goods, mind you, no tired old lettuces the shop owner wanted to get shut of – directly to them. Saving them the trip. Helping them out if they were short of something.

Now he was expected at many places and often got impatient looks, foot-tapping, or the sharp edge of some harried woman's tongue if he was late. His prices were slightly higher than the nearby shops – because he only bought first-rate stock – but none of his customers complained. They knew quality goods when they saw them.

At the top of Berkeley Square, he stopped the barrow for a few seconds to wipe his brow. It was a balky heavy thing, about five feet long and three feet wide, with two wheels in front, two in back, and a pair of handles jutting from the end. A brake kept it from rolling away on a hill. It was tricky to maneuver, especially when it was piled high with goods. A pony and cart would be such an improvement. He could carry more goods and move faster, too. He'd get a rig eventually, but not until he got back from America. And when he had it, he'd hire his brother Jimmy to push the barrow on a second route. He'd add carts and routes as he could afford to, and then, one day – a shop. The shop he'd always wanted. And maybe, just maybe, he'd be able to share it with the girl he'd always wanted.

The barrow felt even heavier as he resumed his route, but he didn't mind. He felt hopeful for the first time in a long time. And that hope gave him strength. He felt as if he could push it all around Mayfair, all around London, for that matter, across the whole country, up to Scotland even, if that's what it took to win Fiona back.

"Strawberries, sweet and red!" he cried. "Put 'em in a pudding, put 'em in a pie, see 'em for yourselves, ladies, don't be shy!"

He had four pounds to his name. In a few more weeks, if he was lucky and business continued to be good, he would have the eighteen he needed to get to New York. He would find Fiona there. He would talk to her and he would make her listen to him. He would make her understand how deeply sorry he was for all that he'd done. He would tell her how he wanted to spend the rest of his life making it up to her, if only she'd let him. He would tell her how much he loved her and somehow, some way, he would make her love him again. He had to. She was the one thing he wanted most in all the world, the only thing that mattered to him. He'd lost sight of that once and he'd lost her. Maybe he would have a chance to get her back – a chance he knew he didn't deserve, but one he'd reach for with both hands if only it would come his way.

48

"Martin!" Will shouted to his driver from the steps of City Hall. "My office! As fast as you can! There's a ten-dollar bill in it for you if you get me there before the hour!"

He jumped into his carriage and closed the door. Martin cracked the whip; he had ten minutes to go thirty blocks. As soon as he'd pulled away from the curb, Will pounded on the seat and let out a huge, exultant yell. It was his! He'd done it! He'd won the contract for New York City's first subterranean railway.

After years of planning and months of trying to prove that his plan was better than August Belmont's, he finally swayed the mayor. He'd just concluded a meeting with the mayor and his aldermen to finalize everything. He had the document – signed and sealed – in his breast pocket. Ground could be broken in as little as a month's time. After all the time and effort he'd put into this project, all the money he'd spent, he finally had the go-ahead.

He couldn't wait to tell his sons that the contract was theirs. They'd be ecstatic. Winning it meant the world to Will Junior. He'd worked so hard on it. Will imagined his expression, his shouts of delight when he told him the news. And right after he told them, he would tell Fiona. He hadn't seen her in days. Two weeks, actually. Tying up the subway contract had taken every minute of every day. And she'd been so busy with her new purchase – that building down on Irving Place – that she'd had no free time either. He'd see her tonight, though. And he'd take her out for supper no matter how much she protested, no matter how busy she said she was. They would celebrate tonight. Just the two of them. Hopefully Nick would be available to chaperon her. He was easier to get rid of than Mary. He couldn't wait to be with her, to sit across a table from her and gaze into those astonishing sapphire eyes, to take her in his arms later, even if she wouldn't let him take her into his bed.

He leaned back in his seat and closed his eyes, remembering the night at his house when he wanted to make love to her. He thought of it constantly. He ached with desire at the mere memory of her soft lips, her bare skin, her beautiful body. Just picturing her as she'd looked then, half-naked, her hair coming down, made him feel weak. He had wanted her as he'd never wanted a woman in his entire life. And he'd come on too strong. He'd frightened her. What an oaf he was. Pawing her like a dog, asking her to sleep with him before he'd even told her how he felt about her, before he'd told her he loved her. She wasn't one of his mistresses, a worldly, sophisticated woman embarking on an affair. She was a girl of eighteen. Inexperienced and uncertain of herself. Uncertain, no doubt, of him as well.

The thing that bothered him the most was that she had wanted him, too. He'd felt it in her kiss, in the way she'd clung to him. He had made her want him and then he'd ruined everything by demonstrating all the finesse, all the sensitivity, of a rutting bull.

Christ! How many women had he slept with that he didn't love. Now he was in love with one – head over heels in love – and she'd never sleep with him. Not after the way he'd behaved. Not until he married her, most likely. And that wouldn't happen for a while because he still had to introduce her to his family. He still had to wait for Will Junior to come around to the idea of his courting a woman from a different class. The boy was overcautious, so worried about the possibility of a scandal, so worried about its effect on the subway contract . . .

. . . the subway contract.

Will, leaning back in his seat, sat up straight.

The subway contract was his now. He'd not only proved Belmont wrong, he'd proved his son wrong, too. Will Junior's objections to Fiona were entirely unfounded. Their relationship hadn't caused a scandal. It hadn't shied the mayor or potential investors. Surely once he handed his son the contract, he would see that. And he would stop his truculent behavior and consent to meet Fiona. It had taken him forty-five years to find someone he loved. Who knew how much time he had left on this earth? He'd satisfied his family's demands, won his sons the means for more income and greater prestige with the subway project; now it was time for him to have what he wanted.

He rapped on the window that separated him from his driver.

"Yes, sir? What is it?" Martin asked, after sliding the window open.

"I need to make a stop first, before we go to my office," Will said. Martin scowled. "You'll still get your ten dollars, Martin, don't worry! Take me to Union Square!"

"Where, sir?"

"Union Square!"

"To what address, sir?"

"Tiffany's, Martin. And hurry!"

"Peter Hylton thinks we're a couple, you know," Nick said to Fiona from atop a wooden ladder. He was trying different colors on a wall in the tearoom and he'd managed to get more paint on himself than on the plaster. "I read his column today. He wrote about us being business partners, your plans for a tearoom and mine for a gallery, and said we'd be partners in love before much longer. I hope Will's jealous. Do you think he might be? Then we could have a duel over you, Fee! Pistols at dawn. Wouldn't that be exciting?"

"Peter Hylton is a horse's ass and so are you," Fiona said, lifting a sterling wine cooler out of a crate. She was sweaty and dirty. Her sleeves were rolled up and her skirts were knotted behind her. Her feet were sore and swollen from being on them all day and she'd taken off her boots and stockings hours ago. The cooler was heavy and ornate, covered with repoussé flowers and animals, and sporting two Bacchus heads for handles. "What's this doing here?" she asked Nick, putting it on the floor. "I thought we decided not to buy it."

"We decided *to* buy it."

"We? Or you? This is supposed to be a tearoom, Nick. I have no use for this."

"But just imagine it on the gilt sideboard we found. Polished and piled high with fresh strawberries in the summer. Or at Christmastime, brimming with sugar-frosted grapes and pomegranates. It'll be stunning, Fee. And besides, it's not American and 1850s, as the antique dealer said. It's English. George the Third and a steal at twice what we paid."

Fiona sighed, put the wine cooler on the floor, and began digging in the bottom of the crate. The purchases they'd made in an East Side antique store had arrived earlier in the day. She was just unpacking them now. She pulled out a set of silver serving pieces that had been tucked underneath the cooler. Nick had insisted she buy them. They'd been poking around in the newly arrived contents of a Madison Avenue mansion whose owner had passed away. While Nick had piled up china and linen, she had gone through the silver. She'd found three partial sets of sterling and a full set of silverplate and decided she'd take the silverplate. It wasn't as nice as the sterling, but at least it all matched. "Don't be banal," Nick had scolded. "Matching silver is for maître d's and the nouveau riche. Buy the sterling."

Over the past two weeks, as builders worked on the house, Fiona and Nick had scoured antique and secondhand shops for the things they needed. They'd found gorgeous pieces of furniture – two ebony desks and matching chairs for Nick, and damask settees for his clients to rest themselves on. And for her a Louis Quinze-style gilt sideboard to hold cakes and pastries, ladies' chairs with needlepointed seats, Queen Anne tea tables, cast-iron furniture for the garden, Limoges china, Frette linens, and four pairs of almost new watered-silk curtains in a gorgeous shade of light green – all at a fraction of what she would've have paid for them new.

The work at thirty-two Irving Place was proceeding apace, though not without the occasional unforeseen disaster – like a rusted waste pipe, a roof that leaked, and joists that termites had destroyed. The house was rapidly eating through the money she'd borrowed from First Merchants, which made her anxious. Managing workmen – making them do exactly what she wanted done, and making them do it over sometimes, too – made her short-tempered. And running back and forth between Eighth Avenue and Irving Place exhausted her. But even so, she was incredibly happy. She fell asleep every night and woke up every morning excited, thinking about the tearoom, her Tea Rose, and how beautiful it would be. And when she arrived there each day, quickly walking through the rooms to see what had been accomplished since the previous day, her heart filled with pride and happiness. The Tea Rose was her baby. She had conceived of the idea, nurtured it, and soon she would watch it bloom. Unlike the grocery shop, it was hers, all hers.

"What do you think about this color, Fee?" Nick called from his perch. Earlier that day, they'd gone to the paint man and Nick had made him mix up batch after batch of color for her rooms and his. "I want a soft white for my gallery. And a fresh spring green for the trim," he'd instructed the man. "Not too green and not too yellow. Light, but not so light it disappears. A celery color, really, but with some beige to tone it down. And for the tearoom I need a cream just tinged with pink. The color of a woman's blush. Don't make it too pink, and don't make it too orangy, either. I'm thinking of a rose petal, not an apricot." Fiona thought the man would kill him.

She looked at the colors on the wall and picked the lightest of them, a warm beige with just a hint of pink in it. "That's my favorite, too," he said. She looked at him and saw that he had circles under his eyes. It was nearly nine o'clock. They'd been going at it for over twelve hours.

"Come down from there. Now. You're going to bed."

"But I'm not finished," he protested.

"In the morning. You're tired. I can see it in your face. I won't have you exhausting yourself, Nick. I mean it. You know what happened the last time."

"But I feel fine —"

"Nicholas Soames, you can't open a gallery if you're dead!" she said sharply.

He gave up and climbed down the ladder. He covered his paint pots and put his brushes in a jar of turpentine. "What about you? You need rest, too," he said.

"I won't be much longer. I want to do a bit more unpacking and then I'll go home."

Nick kissed her good night, getting paint on her as he did, then went upstairs to his flat. Fiona stretched her tired limbs after he'd gone, trying to ease the stiffness. She was about to resume her unpacking when a movement from the garden caught her eye. It was the roses. She could see them swaying in the night breeze through the new windows she'd had installed. Unable to resist them, she went outside. They were her creatures, these flowers, and she was theirs. As she walked into the garden, she fancied they were bobbing their lush heads in greeting.

The night sky was clear and filled with stars. The air was cool and the grass felt soft beneath her bare feet. The scent of a nearby rose drew her. She was nuzzling the pale yellow bloom, enjoying the feeling of its petals against her cheek, when she heard the footsteps crunching on the graveled path behind her. She didn't turn around. She knew who it was.

"I told you to go to bed and I meant it. What are you doing back down here?"

"That's not a very nice greeting, is it?"

Fiona spun around. "Will!" she exclaimed. It had been days since she'd seen him.

"Nick let me in. I rang the wrong doorbell. Look at you!" he exclaimed, laughing, looking for a clean place on her face to kiss her. "You're filthy! And I wanted to take you to dinner, too. To celebrate. But they'll never let you in Del's looking like that. I don't even think they'd let you in a Bowery dive. What on earth have you been doing?"

"Working in here all day. It's dusty. And Nick just smeared paint on me. What are we celebrating?"

Will grinned. "McClane Subterranean. We got the contract!"

Fiona whooped for joy, genuinely happy for him. She knew how hard he'd worked for this and what it meant to him. "Oh, Will, congratulations! I'm so excited for you!" He picked her up, over her protests that she'd get him dirty, and spun her around. When he put her down, she took his hand and led him to an iron settee she'd bought. "Tell me all about it. I want to hear everything!"

He described the last two weeks, all the work, all the meetings and arguing and cajoling. He told her about today, about how good it felt when the mayor had finally told him the project was his. And how elated his sons had been when he broke the news to them. How his eldest had insisted they all go out to the Union Club for drinks. And how they'd all gotten tipsy together, a little too tipsy. He was still a bit lightheaded. And how Will Junior had apologized for his bad behavior and told him that he wanted to meet Fiona and suggested he bring her to the country so she could meet the entire family.

Fiona was surprised and pleased to hear of his change of heart. It meant he had finally accepted their relationship. She knew that his refusal to meet her had pained his father greatly. It hadn't made her feel very good, either.

"Come upstate next weekend," Will said. "Bring Nick and Mary and a whole squad of policemen as chaperons if that's what it takes to make your uncle happy."

"I'd love to, Will, but I've painters scheduled to start on Saturday. Maybe the following weekend?"

"No, this weekend. I insist." He took her hand in his, rubbed at the paint on it with his handkerchief. "You work too hard, Fiona. Far too hard. I don't want you to. Not anymore. I don't want you to ever have to work like this again. I want to take care of you and spoil you and take every worry, every care, away from you."

Fiona looked at him as if he were mad. "Will, what on earth are you going on about?"

But instead of answering her, he took her in his arms and kissed her hard, so hard he took her breath away. "I've missed you so much. I never want to be apart from you for so long again."

"We won't be, Will," she said, touching his cheek, wondering if it was the drinks he had with his sons that were making him so strange. "You've got your contract now, and my tearoom is coming along. Before long it will open and I won't be putting in such long hours. I'll have my evenings free again and –"

"I want more than your evenings, Fiona. I want to kiss you awake in the morning in our bed. I want to eat every meal with you and look at you across my table. I want to come home to you at the end of the day and see your pretty smile, see our children come running to me."

He reached into his pocket and pulled out a small box. And though the night was warm, Fiona suddenly felt very, very cold. He opened it, took out a magnificent diamond ring, slid it onto her finger, and said, "Fiona, will you marry me?"

"Jaysus Christ! Look at the size of it! It's as big as an egg!" Michael exclaimed.

"Stop exaggerating," Fiona said.

He lifted the enormous emerald-cut diamond out of its box and showed it to Mary. "It's beautiful, Fiona! Why are you keeping it in the box? Why aren't you wearing it?" she asked.

"I didn't think I should."

"Why not?" Michael asked. "It's yours, isn't it?"

"Not really. Not yet, anyway. I . . . I didn't say yes."

Michael looked at her aghast. "You turned him down?"

"No . . ."

"What *did* you do then?"

"I told him I needed time to think."

"About what?"

"About whether I want to spend the rest of my life as Mrs. William McClane," she said testily. "I'm choosing a husband, not a new coat. It's a marriage, you know. Vows, a commitment. I want to be sure. I want to know in my heart that he's the one."

"If he isn't, who is? The King of Siam? Sure, if you don't marry Will McClane, I'll marry him meself. He'll keep you like a princess, he will. No more flogging tea and pork chops. You'll be farting through silk the rest of your days."

"Michael, mind your language!" Mary scolded. "This is a delicate matter. Fiona's right to take her time. It's the biggest decision she'll ever make."

"But he's a good man and he's mad about her! What more could she want?"

Fiona sighed. Why couldn't they have been asleep? She thought the whole house would be in bed when she came in, but Michael and Mary had been sitting in the parlor sipping sherry together. The late hour and her flushed face had told them that something was up. She wanted to keep Will's proposal to herself, to mull it over in privacy, but they'd pressed her and she'd told them what had happened. Michael put the ring back in its box now and handed it to her.

"My advice to you is get that ring on your finger and tell him yes before *he* has second t'oughts," he said. "Before

484

he realizes just how headstrong and ornery you are."

"Thank you very much."

"I'm only trying to look out for you. What'll I tell me brother when I see him in heaven?"

"What makes you think you'll get in?" Fiona asked.

Michael ignored the barb. "He'll knock me head off, he will. 'Michael,' he'll say to me, 'why didn't you look out for her? Why did you let her waste her life fooling with tearooms?' "

"I'm not wasting my life! I love The Tea Rose! And TasTea and the grocery, too."

"Aw, lass, that's not women's work. Having babies and making a home, that's women's work. That's what makes lasses happy and pleasant, not willful and shrewish like you. You've done it now, sure you have. If you lose McClane, you'll not find another like him so soon."

"I'm going to bed," Fiona declared, upset.

Mary caught up to her in the hallway. "Don't pay him any mind," she said gently. "He just wants to see you happily settled, that's all. Do what your heart tells you. It's all that matters." She gave her a motherly kiss and told her she ought to get some sleep. Fiona suddenly missed her own mother terribly. Her mam would have soothed her and said all the right things. How had she been able to do that? How had she known what the right things were?

Mary was halfway down the hall when Fiona called to her.

"What is it, luv?"

"What did your heart tell you? When your husband asked you to marry him?"

Mary smiled. "It told me that the sun rose and set because of him, the birds sang for him alone, that I couldn't live a day without him. Do you know what that feels like?"

"Yes," Fiona said. "I do."

In her bedroom, she put the ring box on top of her bureau, lit her lamp, and pulled her shade. She was weary and looked forward to sleep. She unbuttoned her blouse, slipped her skirt off, and laid them over the back of her chair. As she finished, her eyes fell on the ring box again. She pressed the catch and slid the ring onto her finger. The diamond twinkled as if someone had caught a star and set it. It was perfect, absolutely flawless, and it looked so very out of place on her hand, with its cuts and scratches, its large, reddened knuckles. She took it off, placed it back in its box, and put the box in a bureau drawer to keep it safe.

As she crossed the floor to get her nightgown, she caught sight of herself in her mirror. Standing before the glass in her camisole and petticoat, she unpinned her long, black hair and let it fall to her shoulders. Will had told her she was beautiful. Am I? she wondered.

She looked at herself appraisingly, trying to see whatever it was he saw that made him want to kiss her, to make love to her. She circled her waist with her hands, then cupped her breasts, pushing them up and together. She stepped out of her knickers, unbuttoned her camisole, then shyly looked at her own naked body. Her skin was smooth and supple, kissed with the soft glow of youth. Her limbs were strong and slender. She ran a hand over her flat belly, trying to imagine it full and round. Will had said he wanted children with her. Right away. She would be nineteen next spring. Many girls were married by her age; some were mothers. If she married him, she herself soon would be. It would be nice to have a husband. A tiny baby to hold.

She closed her eyes and tried to imagine being in bed with Will, tried to picture his face, to feel his hands and lips on her body, caressing her. But the brown eyes she tried to picture were sky-blue. The hair, tousled and too long, was blond. The lips whispering her name weren't Will's. "I love you, Fee," they said. "I always will." He was the one whom the sun rose and set for, whom the birds sang for. The one she couldn't live without.

"No," she whispered frantically. "Go away. Please go away."

It had been weeks since she'd thought of him, since she'd

allowed herself to remember his face, his voice. She tried to push them down now, these images, but she'd dammed them back too long. They burst their confinements and flooded out, unbidden and unwanted, a million memories of Joe: the way he looked at the river, squinting at her in the sunshine; the sound of his laughter; the smell of him, sweaty from the market or clean from his Sunday bath; the feeling of his heart beating under her hand. Their power, their force and clarity staggered her. It was as if he were here in the room with her, as if she could reach out and touch him. But she knew the minute she opened her eyes there would be nothing there, no one. She would be alone. Tears seeped out from under her dark lashes. She cried out softly with the pain of her longing.

She made herself think of Will, of all his wonderful qualities, trying to convince herself that it was he, not Joe, she loved now. But her heart wasn't listening. It was walled up and closed off. It had made its choice long ago and had been denied. And now it ached inside of her, broken and empty and as cold as a stone.

She opened her eyes and looked at her reflection again. She saw a face that was tear-stained, riven by sadness and anger. She saw a body that was supple now, but would someday shrivel. She saw a young woman who would one day become an old one – stiff, brittle, and alone. And she knew that if she did not banish Joe once and for all from her heart, if she did not accept the love Will was offering her, she would end up just like Miss Nicholson – her life wasted, spent mourning for something that never was.

She quickly put her clothes back on, then lifted the ring box out of her bureau drawer. She opened it and slid the ring onto her finger. She paused for a second at her bedroom door, listening. There was no sound. Mary had gone upstairs. Michael had gone to bed. She reached for her purse, then quietly left her room, and her home, determined to bury her past forever and embrace her future.

* * *

"You can't tunnel there, I've told you this already, Hugh," Will said. He was standing in the sitting room off his bedroom, squeezing the neck of his tall black telephone as if he'd like to throttle it. "How are you going to blast? You'll blow Grand Central right into the East River! We're going to use the cut-and-cover method. Open a hole, lay the tracks, close the hole . . . what? I can't hear you . . . hold on . . ."

Will banged the earpiece on his desk, vowing that someday soon the newly formed McClane Communications would give American Bell a sound ass-kicking. When the line cleared, he resumed his conversation with the mayor, wondering why the man had nothing better than the subway to occupy his time at midnight on a Saturday. He himself was in his night robe and had been ready to retire with a glass of wine and a book when the phone rang.

Now he was embroiled in a discussion on underground engineering when all he wanted to do was lie down and nurse his wounded pride. Earlier in the evening, he had asked Fiona to marry him. He had hoped she would leap into his arms and say yes. Instead, she had asked for time to think. She'd kissed him and told him how honored she was. She'd told him she loved him, and he believed her. But as he'd held her, he felt a stiffness in her, a guardedness he was very familiar with. She had drawn back from him as she always did when he got too close.

"Can you hear me now? Good. Disruptive? Yes, of course it will be. Laying an entire railway under the city is bound to be disruptive."

The butler's sudden appearance in the doorway startled him. He thought the man had gone to bed. "There's someone here to see you, sir," he whispered.

"Who is it?" Will mouthed. First the mayor's call and now a visitor. At this time of night? What was wrong with people?

"Miss Finnegan, sir."

Will held a finger up, staying the man. Sometimes Bell's

488

lousy service came in handy. "Hugh?" he shouted. "Hugh, I'm losing you . . . the line's going again. What? I can't hear you . . ." He slammed the earpiece into its holder. "If it rings, don't answer it," he said, dashing out the door, down the hall and then down the stairway to the foyer. Fiona was standing there. She was disheveled. Her hair was unpinned. Her face was pink with perspiration.

"What is it?" he asked, alarmed. "What's wrong? You're all out of breath!"

"I . . . ran," she said, her chest still heaving.

"Ran? From where?"

"Home."

"*You what?* All the way from Eighth Avenue? Fiona, are you crazy? There are all sorts of characters out at this hour. Something could've happened to you!"

"Don't scold me, Will; I couldn't find a cab. I had to come . . . I . . ." She was so out of breath, she couldn't finish her sentence. "Oh, Will . . ." she gasped. She buried her hands in his hair, pulled his face to hers, and kissed him. ". . . I wanted to tell you yes! Yes, I'll marry you!"

Will was surprised to see Fiona in his home and taken aback by this sudden turn of events. "Fiona, I . . . I don't know what to say. I'm delighted . . . but are you certain? I thought you wanted some time."

"I don't. I've made up my mind. I want to be your wife. If you still want me to."

"Of course I do. More than anything in the world." He held her close, moved that she had run all the way here to tell him she wanted to be his. When she had asked him for time, he was certain she had wanted it only to figure out how to tell him good-bye gracefully. Now she was here, in his arms, making his fondest wish come true.

"Come sit down," he said, ashamed to find his voice a little hoarse suddenly. "You're panting like a racehorse. Would you like a glass of wine? I just opened a bottle. It's in my bedroom. Go sit in the study. I'll bring it. Or maybe you'd like something cold?"

"What I would like is a bath," she said, ignoring Will's invitation to wait for him in the study. She followed him up the stairs.

"A *bath*?" He turned and looked at her on his way into his bedroom, wondering if all that running had addled her mind. "I was thinking I would get you a drink and then get you home. It's terribly late."

"I'm not going home," she said quietly. "I'm staying here tonight. With you."

Will, who'd picked up the wine bottle, put it back down with a thump. "I see," he said. "Are you quite sure about this?"

"Yes." She crossed the room and kissed him again. Sweetly. Deeply. Then she unbuttoned her blouse and shrugged it off, stepped out of her skirt and boots and stood before him in her white underthings. Her camisole, moist with sweat, stuck to her skin. He could see the shape of her breasts through the fabric, the darker shade of her nipples. He wanted to carry her to his bed and make love to her. Now. This very second. Without even stopping to get out of his robe. But he wouldn't. He'd take his time. Somehow he would find the self-control not to take her where she stood.

"Will, I've just run for blocks and blocks. I'm sweaty as a navvy. Do you think I might have a bath? Does this palace of yours have bathtubs? Or do I need to get the washtub out and boil some water?"

"No, of course not," he said, laughing. "It's in here."

He led her through his bedroom – a masculine affair – into his bathroom, an enormous room, all done in white Carrara marble, with an oriental carpet on the floor, two sinks, huge framed mirrors on the wall, and a large marble tub in the center.

He turned the taps on, then rooted around in his cabinets for something to scent the water. All he had, besides lime and bay rum, was sandalwood. Nothing flowery or sweet. The sandalwood would have to do. He poured some into the water, watched it foam, then found some towels and left her to her devices. After a few minutes, worried he had forgotten something, he knocked on the door and said, "Are you all right in there? Do you need anything?"

"I'm fine. Just a little lonely."

"Would you like company? I won't look."

Fiona laughed. "You wouldn't see anything anyway. There are so many bubbles, I feel like I'm sitting in a meringue. How much bath oil did you put in?"

"Too much, I guess," he said sheepishly, coming in. "Sorry, the valet usually does that sort of thing. Here, would you like a sip of wine?" He pulled a chair over to the side of the tub, sat, and handed her his glass.

She took a sip, closed her eyes and sighed with pleasure. Will found a washcloth and scrubbed her neck and shoulders. "That feels good," she said. He rubbed the cloth over her face, teasing her, telling her she cleaned up nicely.

She took another sip of his wine, then said, "I feel like I'm in a castle here, Will. Just like a princess. So safe from the world. And everyone in it."

"You'll always be safe with me, Fiona. Nothing will ever hurt you. Ever. I swear it." He leaned forward and kissed her wet mouth. She shivered as he did. The water was cooling.

"You're cold. I'll get you a towel."

He walked to the back of the room where a wide walnut armoire ran the length of one wall. He opened and closed various doors, wondering where the hell the towels were kept.

"Ah! Here they are," he said. Fiona stood up, her back to him. Water sheeted off her skin. He saw the long, graceful line of her spine, the narrow curve of her waist, her round bottom, pink from the bath. "Control, Will," he whispered to himself. "Control."

He came around to the other side of the tub and held the towel out for her. Her arms were crossed in front of her chest. Her wet hair was stuck to her skin. Water ran down her smooth belly, over her hips, and down her ivory thighs. It dripped from the patch of black hair between her legs. He tried not to stare, but he couldn't help it. "My God, just look at you. You are so lovely, Fiona. So very lovely."

"Am I?" she asked in a voice that was so small, so vulnerable it made his heart bleed. He looked into her eyes; they were huge and liquid and heartbreakingly unsure.

"Yes, you are. And I'm going to make love to you right in the tub if you don't come out."

She laughed and stepped out and he folded a huge Turkish towel around her shoulders and sat her on his stool. He wrapped another around her hair and rubbed. When she was dry, she stood up. He held out a robe for her.

"I don't want it," she said, shrugging her towels off. There was no uncertainty in her eyes anymore. She reached for his sash, undid it, and pushed the robe off his shoulders. He was naked underneath it. She pressed herself to him and the feeling of her bare flesh against his made him swiftly hard. She ran her fingers through the brush of curly hair on his chest. Kissed him there. "I want you, Will," she whispered. "Make love to me."

He led her to his large four-poster bed. The bedspread and curtains were made of a thick midnight-blue silk and she looked like a Venus carved from alabaster against them.

Her hands were tentative and shy at first. She brushed her fingers over his chest, his back, down to his bottom. It was more than he could stand. He took her hands away, sat up, and rustled in his night table. He stretched out beside her again, held her, and kissed her, stroking her body for as long as he could bear it. Her desire for him, the smell and taste of her made him crazy. He couldn't control himself any longer. He tried to hold back, tried to be gentle, but the feeling of being inside her overwhelmed him and it was over all too quickly.

"Will," she said after a few seconds. "Didn't you take it out?"

"Take what out?"

"What do you think?" Her voice was panicky in the darkness.

"It's all right, Fiona," he said soothingly. "I took care of it." She obviously wasn't a virgin, but she wasn't experienced, either. He wondered who had made love to her before – some dumb kid? He'd show her what real lovemaking was.

"Took care of it? How?" she asked.

"A French letter," he said, sitting up to remove the spent condom. He dug a fresh one out of his drawer and explained how it worked. Then he said, "I'm sorry about that, darling. I couldn't hold back, I tried." He put the new condom on. "It was just a practice run anyway. It'll be better the second time. I promise." He took her face in his hands, kissed her, then moved his hand between her legs.

"We're going to do it again?"

"Mmm-hmm. And again and again. Until I have you begging for mercy."

She laughed, and her laughter soon became sweet, surprised sighs as he gently pushed one finger and then another inside her – stroking her until he felt her breath quicken, felt her start to writhe against him. And then he took his hand away.

"Oh, Will, no . . ." she murmured. "Don't stop, please . . ."

"Ssshh," he said, quieting her protests with kisses. Already hard again, he slipped inside her. He moved slowly, luxuriously, with no urgency this time, as if he had a hundred years to kiss her and touch her and be inside of her. He kissed her mouth, then whispered to her how beautiful she was. He cupped her breasts and used his teeth and lips on them, sucking them, flicking his tongue over them. Then he put his hand under the small of her back and pressed her hips tightly against his own and thrust himself deeper inside of her. She gasped. He felt a change come over her as her body responded to his in a way she clearly hadn't expected. She stiffened, twisted against him as if she wanted to push him away, then moved with him, surrendering to him. Her eyes locked on his, and for an instant he thought he glimpsed something unsettling in them, something wild and bereft. And then as quickly as it had come, it was gone – and her eyelids fluttered closed and her whole body arched against his and shuddered. She came in quick, hard little spasms and he knew that he'd taught her this intimate new knowledge. It thrilled him and excited him beyond belief. He wanted to come, but he held back, wanting her pleasure more than his own. Wanting to love her over and over again. To make her his own.

49

"You know a Joe Bristow?" Roddy asked a man who was loading apples onto his barrow.

The man eyed his uniform. "Never 'eard of 'im, mate."

Roddy asked another man who was adjusting the blinders on his donkey. "Who wants to know?" he said, suspicious. "Is 'e in trouble?" Like most costers, he harbored a deep mistrust of police and a fierce protectiveness of his own.

"He's not in any trouble," Roddy said. "I'm a friend of his. I need to see him."

"Try Fynmore's pitch. Fynmore's 'igh Quality Produce, see it? Just down the street on the left? 'E buys 'is goods there."

Roddy thanked the man and hurried off. He hoped he wasn't too late. It was only four-thirty. The gas lamps were still lit and the sun wouldn't be up for another hour, but costers started their days with the larks. Roddy had knocked off half an hour early from his shift in order to catch a bus and get to Covent Garden early. He wanted to catch Joe before he set off on his morning rounds. He'd been mulling over an idea ever since Joe and his mother had come to his flat a few weeks ago to tell him they knew where Fiona was. He'd needed Grace's consent to implement it, however, and he'd been hesitant to ask her. She was a patient woman, but patience had its limits. Then, last night – right out of the blue – she'd come to him with the same idea. He'd kissed her and told her she was a woman in a million.

Roddy was certain that Joe was right about Fiona's

whereabouts and he was furious with himself for not thinking of it. He had been so sure she hadn't gone far; he'd never dreamed she might've gone to America. Joe and Rose had been sorely disappointed when he told them he didn't have Michael's address, but Fiona had taken her family's belongings, including the letters from her uncle. He was certain Michael lived in New York, though, and that he was a shopkeeper of some sort.

He was also certain that Joe should get himself to America as soon as possible. He had a feeling about it. He didn't know *why* exactly – the feeling made no sense at all. Joe had hurt her and she had made it very plain that she never wanted to see him again. But deep in his gut, Roddy felt she needed him. Right now. He put a lot of stock in gut feelings; he always had. People said police officers – the good ones – had a sixth sense about things. As to who was telling the truth and who wasn't. What a fugitive's next move might be. Roddy's sixth sense had never let him down. As he neared Fynmore's, he spotted Joe. He was just pushing off. He had another lad with him.

"Joe!" he yelled. "Joe Bristow!"

Joe turned around and set the barrow down. "What are you doing 'ere, Roddy?" he asked. "Got the Covent Garden beat now?"

"No, I'm here to see you."

"Something wrong?" he asked, suddenly worried. "It's not me mum, is it?"

"No, lad. Calm down. Not'ing's wrong. I bumped into your mother yesterday. She told me you were out on your own now and putting aside money to go after Fiona."

"Aye."

"How much will you need?"

"About eighteen quid, I think. For the fare, plus room and board and –"

Roddy cut him off. "How much have you got?"

"About six quid. Give or take a few shillings."

"Here . . ." Roddy reached into his trouser pocket and

pulled out a wad of bills. "It's me savings. Grace's, too. There's fifteen quid there."

Joe looked at the money in his hand and shook his head. "Roddy, I can't take this."

"Grace wants you to have it as much as I do. We want you to find Fiona. Go on, lad, take it. Get your arse on the boat."

Joe nodded decisively, then pocketed the bills. "Thank you, Roddy. I'll pay you back every penny. I swear it."

"Bloody right you will!"

Joe took his brother by the shoulders. "Jimmy, you're in charge now," he told him. "For the next few weeks, till I get back, you're the guv'nor."

"Jaysus! Are you going right now?" Roddy asked.

"I am," Joe said.

"What? Going where? Wait a minute! It's only me second day, Joe!" Jimmy protested.

"You're a smart lad, Jimmy. You'll do fine. Just follow the route I showed you. Tell our mum I went to find Fiona. Tell 'er I'll write as soon as I get there. Do a good job, Jimmy. You 'ear me? A good job. Don't bollix it up!" He took off trotting.

"Wait a minute! Joe, wait! Aw, fuck!" Jimmy cried, watching his brother disappear down the street. He cupped his hands around his mouth. Joe!" he yelled after him. "Where the 'ell are you going?"

"America, Jimmy!" he shouted over his shoulder. "New York!"

50

"Have a seat, Mr. McClane. Relax," Kevin Burdick said in his most soothing voice.

"Don't tell me to relax, goddammit!" Will Junior shouted, pacing the confines of the tiny airless office. "He's going to *marry* the girl in a month's time!"

"You're kidding me."

"I wish I were. He's proposed to her. She's walking around with a diamond the size of a baseball on her hand. It cost a fucking fortune. *My* fucking fortune! Whatever you've got on her, it better be good. What *have* you got?"

Burdick cleared his throat. "Nothing."

Will stopped pacing. "What?"

Burdick squirmed in his chair. "I tried to dig up something, but she's the straightest arrow I've ever seen. There's no man on the side. She doesn't frequent saloons or opium dens or sell orphans on the black market. The worst thing I've seen her do is gamble on the ring toss at Coney Island. She does nothing but work, sleep, and see your father."

Will was white with anger. "What are you telling me? That I can't stop this wedding? Is that what I paid you for?"

"Let me finish, Mr. McClane. I think I can still help you. Though I haven't been able to find anything on Miss Finnegan, I have got something on her friend, Nicholas Soames. It seems he has a habit of frequenting queer bars. He's become a regular at The Slide on Bleecker Street."

"So what?" Will shouted. "My father isn't marrying Nicholas Soames!"

"I realize that. What I hope to do is to use Mr. Soames's sexual preferences to engineer a scandal. It's a long shot, but I think it could work."

"How does that help me? I don't give a shit what happens to Soames."

Burdick leaned forward. "You're going to have to wise up before you get to Washington, Mr. McClane, or the folks there will eat you alive. There's going to be a raid. We're going to enlist the help of your good friend the judge."

Understanding broke across Will Junior's face. "Eames," he said.

Burdick nodded. "Hizzoner hisself. Take a seat, Mr. McClane. Take a load off. Here's what we're going to do . . ."

51

Joe blinked against the bright light of the sunny New York morning. He put his duffel bag down by his feet. "Blimey, Brendan, we made it! I thought when that doctor started poking around, you were done for," he said, laughing. "You should've seen 'im, Bren. Looking in your ear and squinting. Probably blinded by the light coming in the other side."

"Very feckin' funny, ya English gobshite, ya. I saw him looking down your drawers and squinting. Speaking of gobshites, where's Alfie? And Fred? They make it t'rough?"

Joe and Brendan looked around anxiously for their cabin mates, Alphonse and Frederico Ferrara. The four of them had traveled steerage together from Southampton to New York. Joe spotted them – two black-haired, almond-eyed lads – fighting their way toward them through the throng of people getting off the boat. "There they are," he said, waving them over, relieved that they, too, had made it through Castle Garden Immigration unscathed. "Just look at all these people," he added, taking in the crowds. "The 'ackneys can't even move. I think we're better off walking. Any idea which way it is from 'ere?"

"North, definitely. And east, I t'ink," Brendan said. "We'll have to ask someone."

Joe and Brendan had decided to take a room together. Brendan, a big, bluff redheaded Irishman of twenty-one, had come from a farm outside of Connemara to seek his fortune. He planned to navvy in New York until he had enough money for his fare out west, then prospect for gold in California. He'd heard that the Bowery was the place to go for cheap lodging houses. Joe'd grown close to him in the weeks they'd spent together. He'd told him about Fiona and how he hoped to find her.

Alfie and Fred, who'd emigrated from a poor village in Sicily to London, where they'd worked for a cousin who had an ice cream business until they'd made enough money for the fare to New York, would join their mother, father, and extended family in a tenement one of their uncles owned on Mulberry Street. Joe would be sorry to say good-bye to the Ferraras. They'd had a lot of fun together, the four of them – playing cards, drinking beer, and dancing at the impromptu parties on the steerage deck. Teaching one another some choice phrases in Italian and English. Teasing Brendan about his country brogue and the way he said "feck" for "fuck." Laughing and joking and talking on into the night from their bunks.

"Which way do you go?" Alfie asked, as he and his brother joined Joe and Brendan.

"We're not sure," Brendan began. "We were going to head up toward –" His words were cut off by a blood-curdling shriek. He jumped back in terror, pulling Joe with him as a plump, dark-haired woman came hurtling toward them.

"*I miei bambini, i miei bambini!*" she wailed, throwing herself at Alfie and Fred, showering them with kisses. "*Oh, Dio mio, grazie, grazie!*"

She was followed by half a dozen children and then a tiny wizened old lady who was kissing her rosary. A few younger women, some holding babies, crowded around. Half a dozen men, old and young, stood well away from the melee, grinning and slapping each other.

"Jaysus, what a racket," Brendan said to Joe. "If that's how they carry on when they're happy, I'd hate to see them at a wake."

Joe laughed, watching as Alfie and Fred hugged the

sobbing woman. Then they went to the old woman, who took each of their faces in her gnarled hands and kissed them in turn. They hugged and were hugged – violently – by everyone else present, and then the introductions began. Joe and Brendan met Mr. and Mrs. Ferrara, the grandmother, both grandfathers, Uncle Franco, Aunt Rosa, brothers, sisters, cousins, nieces and nephews. Still teary, the boys' mother kissed Joe and Brendan, too, and then she started rattling at her sons in Italian, smacking their chests with the back of her hand.

"*Sì, Mamma, sì . . . i nostri amici . . .*" Alfie said. He turned to his shipmates. "My mother want you to come. To our house. To eat." Under his breath he added, "Bloody hell, say yes! She cook for a week!"

Joe and Brendan said they'd be happy to, which earned them another shower of kisses. They hoisted their bags up onto their shoulders and set off, following the chattering gaggle of Ferraras, taking in the sights as they walked. Joe could hardly believe the size and noise of the place. He was so taken with all the buildings, with the loud, boisterous people, that he forgot to look where he was going and collided with a lad wearing a sandwich board.

"Sorry, mate," he apologized.

The boy smiled at him. TasTea – a qualitea, an honestea, a most refreshing specialtea! his board read. "Think nothing of it, sir. Here, enjoy a free sample," he said, handing him a small box of tea.

Joe thanked him and turned to show his gift to Brendan, but Brendan had moved off ahead and was busy winking at a pretty doe-eyed blonde waiting for a trolley.

"Be'ave yourself," Joe said. "You'll get us arrested and we've only just got 'ere."

"Aye, and I'll be staying, too, if all the lasses look like that one. Just look at this place, will you? A big blue sky. Not one feckin' rain cloud in sight. Warm, too. No potato fields far as I can see. Maybe no potatoes if I'm really lucky. Not here two seconds and we've already got ourselves invited to dinner. I like this place, Joe. Bet a man could do well for himself here."

"It's huge, Bren. Bloody enormous! You could get lost 'ere and never find yourself again," he said, peering down a bustling street.

Brendan gave him a long look. "Worried about your lass, are you?"

"Aye."

"Don't be. You'll find her. I know you will. From all that you told me, she's bound to be here somewhere. You've only got one problem that I can see."

"What's that?"

"If she's as pretty as you say, you'd sure as shite better hope I don't find her first."

Joe rolled his eyes. Brendan shifted his heavy duffel from his right shoulder to his left. As they crossed Broadway, they saw an elegant carriage roll by. "I'm going to have one just like that when I'm rich," he said. "And I'll have an Englishman to drive it. Maybe you, if you're lucky."

"Kiss my arse, Brendan," Joe said absently, still looking around, searching the sidewalks, the shopfronts, the faces of the people who passed him, hoping against hope for a glimpse of Fiona.

Brendan, in high spirits, started to whistle. He soon tired of that and began to sing.

> "Good-bye, Mrs. Durkin, I'm sick and tired of
> workin',
> No more I'll dig the praties, no longer I'll be poor.
> As sure as me name is Barney, I'm off to
> Californey,
> Instead of diggin' praties, I'll be diggin' lumps of
> gold . . ."

A few of the young Italian women looked back at him, giggling. He grinned, doffed his cap, and launched into the next verse.

"In the days that I was courtin', I was never tired resortin'
to the alehouse and the playhouse and the other house besides . . ."

"Brendan, they're Alfie and Fred's sisters," Joe warned.

"Aw, they don't even know what I'm saying."

"But I told me brother Seamus, I'll be off now and grow famous,
and before that I return again, I'll roam the whole world wide. . . ."

Joe laughed at his irrepressible friend. His high spirits were contagious. And he was right. Fiona was here. Somewhere in this city. All he had to do was find her.

Nick stared at Fiona as if she were mad. He shook his head as if he wanted to clear his ears, as if he hadn't heard her correctly. He could not believe what she had just said.

"Nick?" she said hesitantly. "What's wrong? I thought you'd like the idea. I thought you'd be happy. It'll mean so much more space for you and –"

"What's *wrong*?" he finally said. "*What's wrong?* Fiona, you've just told me you're giving me the whole building! You've just told me you're not going to open The Tea Rose. *That's* what's bloody wrong!"

"Please don't yell."

"I just don't understand this," he said, pacing the confines of his parlor. "You *love* this house. You fought so hard to get it. You convinced that batty old dear to sell it to you for a song, convinced the bank to lend you money, and you've been working like a dog for weeks to turn it into something beautiful. Now you're almost there and you're just going to abandon the whole thing? For God's sake, *why*?"

Fiona, pale and fragile-looking against the high back of a crimson wing chair, fidgeted with the clasp on her purse. "It's just that I'm so busy with the wedding . . . and then there's the honeymoon . . . we'll be gone for two whole months and . . ."

"Busy? Busy with what? Getting a dress fitted? Ordering a cake? That's nothing! I've seen you juggle five hundred things at one time. As for the honeymoon . . . can't you simply postpone opening the tearoom until you return?"

"No, I can't." She looked down at her purse again. "Will wants to have children, Nick. Right away. He says he wants to be here to see them grow up."

"Yes, well, that's usually what happens when people get married. So what?"

"He wants to raise them upstate. In Hyde Park. He wants me to live up there. Permanently. He doesn't want me to work anymore. He says women of my . . . of my future station don't. It's unheard of. It would reflect badly on him and he won't allow it."

Nick nodded. It made sense now. What Will had found charming in Fiona when she was his sweetheart – her ambition, her devotion to her work – would not be so charming in a wife. After all, his wife should be devoted to him, not her own interests. To his home. His children.

"I knew this would happen," he said. "I'd hoped otherwise, but I was fooling myself. I knew it the second you told me you were engaged."

"It's just an old tearoom, Nick," she said, a pleading note in her voice. "And a little shop in Chelsea. What are they compared to Will's businesses? Nothing, really."

"Listen to yourself! That's rubbish and you know it. The Tea Rose . . . TasTea . . . they're more than nothing. A lot more. They're you. You made them."

"He's not doing it to be mean, Nick. He says he wants me to stop working so hard. He wants to take care of me, to provide for me."

"But this was your *dream*, Fiona. Learning the business

at your uncle's. Having something of your own one day. Remember? Remember how we talked about it on the boat? How can you just turn your back on your dream?"

"You don't like Will. That's why you're saying these things."

"Of course I like Will. He's a perfectly nice man. But a typical man. He wants to subdue the very thing that captivates him – your spirit, your fire. He'll do it, too. He's already begun. This isn't you. This isn't the Fiona I know. Giving up everything she's worked for, everything she loves, simply because someone tells her to. Not at all."

"I don't know why you're being so mean to me," she said sorrowfully.

"And I don't know why you're lying. When I was sick, you made me promise never to lie to you again. About anything. And now you're lying to me."

"Lying?" she cried. "Nick, I'm not. I never would."

"Yes, you are!" he shouted, making her flinch. "To yourself as well as me."

He walked over to the window and looked down at the street below. He was furious. He remembered what it was like to do what you had to do instead of what you wanted to do. He remembered Paris, and how it felt to see a new painter's work – all the passion, the excitement. And then he remembered returning to London and working on his first project – a printing company's public offering. He'd spent weeks and weeks in Albion's offices, going through ledger after ledger, reviewing endless columns of figures, valuing assets, assessing revenues and liabilities . . . feeling as if he were slowly suffocating.

Did she really think this would be enough? Marriage, a nice house, security? Enough to compensate her for all she was giving up? It wouldn't be. Maybe for some women, but not for Fiona. He knew her. Knew that she needed to be in love – truly, deeply in love. And she wasn't. No matter what she said, he knew she wasn't. He waited until he was calmer, then he pulled an ottoman over to her and sat down. Their knees were touching.

"Would you like to hear what I think?" he asked.

She lifted her eyes to his. "Do I have a choice?"

"I think you don't love Will at all. You've just convinced yourself you do because you're so bloody scared you'll never fall in love again, that you'll never love anyone the way you loved Joe. So you jump at the first man who falls in love with you. Oh, you like him a lot . . . what woman wouldn't? He's handsome and dashing and all that, but you don't love him. Not really."

Fiona shook her head. "I can't believe you're saying these things. You're the one who told me I would forget Joe. You told me I would fall in love again."

"And I still say you're going to. I just don't believe you have."

"Oh, is that what you believe? Well, you don't know anything about it," she said defensively. "You don't know how he feels about me. Or how I feel about him. You don't know how good he is to me. What we talk about. How he makes me laugh. You don't know how nice it is when we're alone together, how happy he makes me."

"Don't mistake making love for being in love," he said curtly.

Fiona dropped her gaze. Her cheeks were blazing. He was being rude and cruel, he knew he was, but he couldn't stop himself. He wanted to wound her. He wanted to get through to her and make her see the truth.

"That's not what I was talking about," she said at length. "That's not it at all."

"Then what is it? Is it money?" he asked harshly, raising her face to his. "Is it? If that's what you're after, I can give you money. My check arrived from my father's bank. For nearly three thousand pounds. I'll give it to you. All of it. You don't have to do this."

Fiona sat motionless, a stricken look on her face, and Nick knew he'd gone too far.

"I don't want Will's money," she said quietly. "I want

Will. I want a man who loves me. One who won't break my heart."

Nick gave her an icy smile. "Of course he won't. How can he? You haven't given it to him."

He waited for a reply, but he didn't get one. She held his gaze for a few more seconds, tears of anger and hurt in her eyes, then ran out of his flat, slamming the door behind her.

52

Joe, his chin in his hand, his elbow on the table of a greasy Bowery chophouse, watched as his waitress, a frowzy, unsmiling woman in a grimy dress and stained apron, slammed two plates of the day's special – pork chops, boiled potatoes, and green beans – onto the table.

"That'll be twenty-five cents apiece," she said.

Joe and Brendan each paid her a quarter. She pocketed the money without thanks, refilled their glasses with weak, foamy beer, then marched off to the kitchen, bawling orders at a hapless busboy. She was like most of the people Joe had encountered during his first week on New York's teeming Lower East Side – harsh, hard-bitten, worn down by the constant struggle of making ends meet.

Brendan sawed away at his pork chop. Joe picked at his halfheartedly.

"What's wrong with you? Why aren't you eating?" Brendan asked, glancing at him.

He shrugged. "Not 'ungry, I guess."

"You'll find her. It's only been a few days."

"It's been a week," he said, sighing. "A whole week and no luck. A copper I talked to said to knock on doors in the Sixth Ward, south of Walker Street. 'E said it was 'eavily Irish there. I've combed the whole damn area – nothing. A dozen Finnegans – and two Michaels – but neither of them the right Michael. Another cop I met told me to try the West Side, a neighborhood called Chelsea and one called 'Ell's Kitchen. But 'e said it was rough and to watch myself above the thirties. I'm worried about 'er. I can't 'elp it.

What if it didn't work out with 'er uncle? What if she's on 'er own somewhere? She doesn't know 'ow to cope in a big city. She'd never been out of Whitechapel before I took 'er to the West End. She's just a lass with a young child to look after. Maybe living in some poxy room in a place with a name like 'Ell's Kitchen. Christ, Brendan, they'll eat 'er alive. And what if I'm dead wrong and she never came to New York at all?"

"You've got your drawers in a twist over not'ing," Brendan said. "Sure, she's with her uncle and safe as can be. From what you told me, it's the only t'ing she could've done. Keep looking. Don't give up. All you've got to do is find the man and you've found her. Did you look in that directory? The one the porter on the boat told you about?"

"I did, but it's only for professionals. Doctors and lawyers and the like. But I wrote down all the Finnegans listed anyway. Even if they're not Michael, they might know of 'im."

"What about the Irish missions? Or charitable societies? Me mam told me to go to the Sons of Saint Patrick if I got into trouble."

"Bloke I met at our boardinghouse told me about the Gaelic Society. Says 'e 'eard they're gathering names and addresses of Irish people in New York so that new immigrants can find their relations. I'm going there this afternoon. Right after I check out a few names in the East Twenties. I figure I'll keep on with the East Side before I 'ead west."

"That's a good idea," Brendan said, still sawing furiously at his chop. As he spoke, his knife snapped in two. The handle hit the edge of his plate and flipped it over, dumping his lunch on the table. "Feckin' t'ing!" he swore. "It's not a pork chop . . . it's a feckin' shingle!"

Joe laughed, despite his poor mood. "You're in New York now, you big Irish mug. It's fuck, not feck."

"Oh yeah? Well, fuck you. And feck you, too!" Disgusted, he wiped his spilled lunch onto his plate with his napkin.

" 'Ere," Joe said, pushing his plate across the table.
" 'Ave mine. 'Ow was your morning? You 'ave any luck?"

"Maybe," Brendan said through a mouthful of food.
"Met a lad in a bar last night. He says some boyo by the
name of McClane is building a subterranean railway.
They're hiring two hundred men to start. Another two
hundred in a month's time. Says they're looking for men
with mining experience to set the dynamite, brace the
tunnels and such. I've never done any of that, but I can
swing a pickax and hoist a shovel with the best of them."

"Think you'll get it?"

"I t'ink so. Foreman said he liked the look of me. Told
me to come back tomorrow morning. I hope I do. Every
building site I've gone to it's, 'We've not'ing for you, Paddy,'
or ''Tis men we want, not donkeys, Mickey.' Real feckin'
comedians."

"Mister, you need any errands run? Cigarettes fetched?
Shoes shined?" A boy of about ten, wearing a tattered shirt,
patched overalls, and no boots, had appeared at their table.

Joe absently reached into his pocket for a nickel and
held it out, hoping the boy would go away. Instead, he gave
him a withering look. "I ain't no bum. Ain't ya got a job
for me?"

Joe was trying to think of something when Brendan said,
"Why don't you have him look for Fiona?"

"Brendan, 'e's only a kid. What's 'e going to do? Comb
the West Side by 'imself?"

"I can find people, mister!" the boy piped up. "My old
man runs off with the rent money every week no matter
how well my ma hides it. I always find him. Tracked him
across the river to Weehawken once. What's her name? I'll
find her for you."

Joe looked at the lad. He was thin. Probably hungry. He
reminded Joe of himself at that age. Eager to work, to prove
himself. "All right, then –" he started to say. His words
were cut off by the waitress.

"Why, you little sewer rat!" she shrilled. "I told you not

to come in here!" She took the boy by his ear. "I'm going to get the cook after you. He'll beat you silly. Maybe that'll teach you!"

" 'Old on a minute, missus," Joe said, snatching the boy's arm. "We're negotiating a business transaction 'ere."

"The only people allowed in here is paying customers," the woman said. "No loiterers. Cook's orders."

" 'E's our guest," Joe said. "We were just about to buy him a meal. Terms of the deal."

The waitress shook her head, much put out, but she released the boy and he quickly sat down. "Another special?" she asked.

"No, t'anks," Brendan said. "We want to hire him, not kill him. Bring him a sandwich. What kind do you want, laddie?"

"I want a couple of Coney Islands. With mustard, onions, and sauerkraut," the boy said. "And baked beans on the side."

"Jaysus, I'm glad I'm not sleeping next to you tonight," Brendan said.

"What do you want to drink?" the woman asked.

"A pint of Schaefer's in a frosty mug."

"Don't push your luck, sonny."

"A lime rickey, then."

As they waited for the boy's meal to appear, Joe and Brendan learned that his name was Eddie and he lived in one room on Delancey Street with his factory-worker mother, his unemployed father, and four siblings. Joe told him he needed to find a man named Michael Finnegan, a shopkeeper, and his niece, Fiona. He gave him a quarter and the boy promised he would find them. As soon as he was finished eating, he asked Joe where he was staying, then took off on his errand.

"He might just surprise you," Brendan said, looking after him.

" 'E couldn't do any worse than I 'ave," Joe said.

Brendan leaned back in his chair and wiped his mouth.

He belched, then said, "Well, I'm off, too. Have to buy meself a good pair of leather boots for me new job. And a new hat."

"What's the 'at for?"

Brendan smiled smugly. "I'm going to see the Ferraras tonight."

"You need a new 'at to visit Alfie and Fred?"

"No, you daft bollocks, I'm only pretending to visit those two. It's Angelina I'm really going to see."

"In your dreams, lad. Alfie and Fred lived with you, remember? They know what you're like. They'll never let you near their sister."

"We'll see about that."

They bid each other good-bye, with Brendan heading downtown and Joe heading up. As he walked along, Joe's mood improved. As the tenements of the Lower East Side gave way to the genteel brownstones of Gramercy Park, he felt less worried, even a little optimistic. Some parts of the city were very pretty, and this was one of them. Yes, New York had its hard side, but it was also an exciting place. And one – seen through the eyes of Brendan, Alfie, and Fred – that was full of promise and hope. It was a place to start over, to carve out a whole new life. A place for second chances. Maybe even for him.

As he walked up Irving Place, an altercation between some workmen and their foreman caught his attention. "What the hell is wrong with you two? Haven't you got ears? I told you, take the first sign down, and put the other one – the one for the art gallery – in its place."

"I thought they was both supposed to be up, one under the other," one of the men said.

Joe looked at the cause of the argument. It was a pretty, hand-painted sign attached to the front of a brick town house. THE TEA ROSE, it said.

"She's upstairs," the boss said. "She'll be down in a minute. She told me to get the sign down right away. When she sees what you've done, she's going to hand me my balls.

And then I'm going to hand you yours. You know what she's like. Fix it."

Joe shook his head, laughing. Whoever she was, the woman who owned the place must be a harridan. She'd certainly put the fear of God in those men. He moved off toward Twenty-third Street where, he hoped, one M. R. Finnegan, notions dealer, a man he'd heard about from his landlady, might be the very man he was looking for.

53

Fiona stood in a plush mirrored dressing room, scowling at the corset she'd been laced into. "I don't want one. I don't like them. They pinch," she said.

Madame Eugénie, the city's most exclusive couturier, paid her no attention. "It is not about what you want, but what the dress requires," she declared. Lips pursed, she circled Fiona, appraising the corset's effect, then shook her head unhappily. "Simone!" she barked.

A harried young woman wearing a pin cushion on her wrist appeared. "Yes, madame?"

"Pull it tighter. Stop when I say."

Fiona could feel the girl's nimble fingers undoing the knot in the back, taking up the slack in the strings. Then she felt her dig her knee into her rump for leverage and pull. "Stop!" she protested. "It's too tight! I won't be able to sit, or eat . . . or even think!"

Madame Eugénie was unmoved. "On your wedding day, you don't sit or you'll wrinkle the dress. You don't eat or you'll stain the dress. And you certainly don't think! You'll ruin your pretty face with wrinkles and frowns. You have only one job – to look beautiful. A little more, Simone . . ." she said, patting the sides of the corset.

Simone gave one last mighty tug. As she did, Madame reached down the front of the garment, grabbed Fiona's breasts and hiked them up. "Now!" she ordered. Simone knotted the laces and Fiona suddenly found herself with a full, high, molded blancmange of a bosom.

"Blimey, it's twice as big as when I came in!" she said,

turning to Mary and Maddie, seated on slipper chairs behind her.

"Look at you!" Maddie exclaimed. "It's wonderful! I'm going to get one just like it."

Madame and Simone left to get the wedding gown. Fiona turned back to the mirror, frowning at herself. The damned corset was squeezing her to death, restricting her movements, confining her. She couldn't breathe. With a cry of frustration, she untied the strings, ripped it off and threw it on the floor. She buried her face in her hands and tried to hold back her tears.

Mary was at her side in an instant. "Fiona, what's wrong?" she asked.

Fiona looked at her through brimming eyes. "Nothing," she said.

"Nothing? Is that why you're crying?"

"Nick is supposed to be here, Mary," she said, completely overwrought. "To help me with the dress. He was supposed to come. He even wrote it down in his calendar the last time we were here. He promised he would. How will I know if it looks right without him?"

"If he said he'd come, he will," Mary said. "I'm sure he's just running late."

"No, that's not it. He's not late. He's not coming. I haven't seen him since we rowed. That was a week ago. He's not coming today and he's not coming to the wedding, either."

Mary and Maddie exchanged worried glances. Fiona had told them about her horrible fight with Nick. They were very sympathetic. They'd taken her side and agreed that Nick was awful to say the things he'd said. She herself was still angry at the way he'd treated her. At the way he'd badgered her. Most of all, she was angry because he was right – though she couldn't bear to admit it. She didn't want to walk away from The Tea Rose. But she didn't have any choice.

After her fight with Nick, she'd gone back to Will to

question the necessity of a confinement and of raising their children upstate. She'd told him she'd much prefer to keep on as she was. Even after the babies came. He'd said it was out of the question. He'd explained, again, that women of his class were not seen in public with big bellies. Besides, if she wasn't careful, she would exhaust herself and that's how women lost babies. And really, how could she mother small children and run a business at the same time? He understood her drive to work, he'd said, understood what was behind it, but insisted that that part of her life was over. He was a wealthy man, more than able to look after her needs. He was adamant and she had not dared to bring up the subject again.

Confinement – how she hated the word. It sounded like a prison sentence. The women where she'd grown up hadn't been confined during their pregnancies. Big bellies were nothing unusual in a neighborhood of large families. Where was the shame in a lovely big stomach, one as full and round as a billowing sail? People knew what was in there, and how it got there, too. A woman could be as coy as she liked; the evidence, squalling and undeniable, would appear in nine months regardless. Babies were everywhere on Montague Street – nursing in their mothers' arms, lugged about by sisters, dandled on their fathers' knees. They were a part of things, not an encumbrance. And no Whitechapel woman stopped working just because she was pregnant. They cleaned and cooked. They hawked goods from market stalls or mopped pub floors until their pains forced them to bed. And after, they returned to their work without a lot of fuss.

As she stood in Madame's fitting room, she was suddenly furiously jealous of Nick and Nate and Maddie. They'd all followed their dreams and started their own businesses – just as she had. But they got to keep theirs. And she didn't.

Madame Eugénie had provided tea and coffee and cakes. Mary poured a cup of tea for Fiona and handed it to her. After Fiona had sipped from it and put it down, Mary wiped her face tenderly, as she might've wiped Nell's or Seamie's. Then she took her hands in hers and said, "Nick will come to the wedding, Fiona. I know he will. He just needs to cool off."

"He hates me," Fiona said disconsolately.

"Oh, shush! He does not hate you. He adores you. Maybe you should just give him a little time. Did you ever think that maybe this is hard on him? Maybe he's a little jealous?"

"Jealous? Mary, that's ridiculous! You know he's not interested in me in that way."

"I meant jealous of losing you. You're his dearest friend, Fiona."

"His family," Maddie added.

"And now you're marrying and moving away and starting a whole new life. Maybe he thinks he's losing you. Maybe that's why he's been so prickly."

Fiona thought about this. "Do you think that's it?"

"It might be. Just be patient. Give him a little time."

Madame Eugénie bustled back into the room with a box in her hands. Simone followed with Fiona's gown. Madame stopped in her tracks. She looked at the corset lying on the floor, at Fiona's tear-stained face, and then at Mary.

"Nerves," Mary whispered.

Madame gave her a knowing look, then turned to Fiona. "Look, *chérie*, what your future husband sent," she said. She opened the jewel box she was carrying and held up a breathtaking pearl choker with a diamond medallion in its center. Fiona's eyes widened. Mary and Maddie gasped. "From Paris. Cartier. To go with your dress," Madame said. "It is exquisite, no? Try it." She fastened the choker on Fiona. "A man who sends such things . . ." She shrugged, at a loss for words. "Well, a woman who has such a man has nothing to cry about."

Fiona looked at the choker in the mirror. She touched it, entranced. Never in her life had she seen anything so beautiful. Will was so outrageously good to her, so kind, so thoughtful. She had admired Emily's pearls when she'd met her and her brothers a few weeks ago at Hyde Park. He'd overheard her and now he'd given her her own pearls. He was sweet to her, Emily had been sweet to her, his whole family had been. Even Will Junior had gone out of his way to make her feel welcome. Madame was right. Most women would not be crying days away from marrying a man like Will. What was a stupid little tearoom compared to his love for her? To her love for him? And I *do* love him. I do, she insisted to herself. No matter what Nick thinks.

She turned to Madame, who was holding the dreaded corset, and dutifully held her arms out. When it was laced up again, Simone carefully removed her gown – also a gift from Will – from its hanger and helped her into it. It had been fitted once already. She was there today to make sure it needed no further alterations. Madame fastened the long row of buttons running up her back, smoothed the bodice, tugged on the skirt, then stepped back and smiled. "Perfect!" she declared. "I've always said it – the prettier the girl, the plainer the dress. It's the homely ones who need all the decoration," she added with Gallic bluntness. "For distraction."

Fiona turned in the mirror. Since she'd met Will, she'd bought herself a handful of pretty dresses. They were rags in comparison to this gown. It was ivory and made of Belgian lace painstakingly stitched onto a silk sheath and embellished with thousands of tiny pearls. Madame had guided her away from the exaggerated leg-o'mutton sleeves, high neck, and fussy ornamentation currently in vogue toward a plainer silhouette just beginning to become fashionable. The dress had a squared décolletage that showed off her graceful neck, three-quarter sleeves, an ivory satin sash with a closure made of silk roses, and a train that swept prettily from the waist to the floor. She would wear an ivory tulle veil that stopped at her hem. Looking at herself in the gown and the jewelry, her hair piled on top of her head, Fiona saw a woman looking back at her, soon a wife. A girl no longer.

"My word, but you're a looker, old shoe. I barely recognize you."

She spun toward the doorway. "Nick!" she cried, smiling, truly smiling, for the first time in weeks. He was leaning against the door, hat in his hands, a wistful look in his eyes. She grabbed her skirts and ran to him, then stopped a few steps away. "I thought you weren't coming . . . I thought . . ."

"Silly old toad. Of course I'd come," he said.

They stood that way for a few more seconds, Fiona twisting the ring on her finger. Nick inspecting the rim of his hat.

"I didn't mean . . ." he started to say.

"It's all right," she said, finishing the discussion.

Nick looked into her eyes. "Friends?" he asked hopefully.

"Always," she said, hugging him tightly. They held each other for a long time before letting go.

Madame turned to Mary and Maddie. "Is this the husband? He should not see her yet!"

"No, he's the jealous boyfriend," Maddie said.

"I heard that, Maddie!" Nick scolded.

"Quel dommage," Madame said. "Such a handsome man. The wedding pictures would be stunning. And the children, too."

54

Joe woke with a start to see a small freckled face hanging over him. "I found her. I told you I would, didn't I?" Eddie crowed, perched on the edge of his bed. "I said I would and I did!"

"Are you going to kill him or will I?" Brendan grumbled from across the room. It was six o'clock in the evening and he'd been napping, exhausted from swinging a pickax all day. Joe had been lying down, too, worn out from tramping the streets. He propped himself up on one elbow now, to hear what the boy had to say.

"Michael Charles Finnegan. Fifty-four Duane Street. He's a flour merchant," Eddie began. "I asked around down by the docks and a wagonman who moves goods from the river to warehouses told me about him. He's Irish, but he came to New York from England just like you said. He has a niece, too! I asked the man was her name Fiona and he said it sounded right."

Joe sat up instantly. "Eddie, where'd you say this man lives?"

"Duane Street. Number fifty-four. Off Broadway."

"Good work, lad." Joe reached under his bed for his boots.

"It's her, isn't it?" Brendan asked, blinking at him.

"It's got to be," Joe said.

"You going down there?"

"Aye."

"Good luck, mate."

"I've got another name, too," Eddie said, as Joe was

tying his laces. "In Chelsea. A beat cop who walks my street says he knows a Michael Finnegan from the Emerald Society. Says he had a grocery up there. He's not sure he's still there, though. Says the bank took his shop. I could go up there for you. See if he's still around."

"Won't need 'im. I'm sure this Duane Street address is it," Joe said. But then he saw Eddie's eager face fall and realized the lad had been hopeful of another job. He flipped him a quarter and told him to go check it out. Eddie was off like a shot. He slammed the door on his way out, provoking a string of curses from Brendan.

Joe was only seconds behind Eddie, on fire with anticipation, certain that Michael Charles Finnegan was his man. Certain that within a matter of a half hour or so, he'd see her again. His lass.

His hands shook as he headed west on Canal Street, threading his way through a surge of people heading home for the evening. He was nervous. Scared, even. How would she react to seeing him? She wouldn't expect him to be here, that's for sure. What if she sent him away? Refused to talk to him? He had hurt her badly and he knew it. Would she even give him the time of day . . . much less forgive him?

If he could just see her, talk to her, he could make it right. He knew he could. This was his second chance. He'd fought for it and he was not going to lose it. If she sent him away, he'd come back. If she told him to go home, he'd stay. He'd write Jimmy to take over the business and he'd stay here and find a job and not give up until he'd convinced her he was sorry and he loved her. Until he'd convinced her to take him back.

At the top of Duane Street he stopped, clenched his fingers into fists, released them again, and started for number fifty-four.

Fiona read the headline of the London *Times* for the third time, hugged it to her chest, then read it again: "Dock

Laborers Declare Victory," it read. "Employers Concede Defeat."

Happy tears rolled down her cheeks and splashed onto the paper. She let them fall. It was late in the evening and there was no one around to see her. She was alone in her uncle's parlor, relishing the wonderful news.

It was a complete – and completely wonderful – surprise. The dock strike had delayed the arrival of the *Times* for weeks on end. It had been so long since she'd had a copy of the paper, she'd had no idea the strike was even near a resolution, much less a victory. Earlier in the day, she'd asked Michael, who was headed to the bank, to see if there were any copies at the newsstand. He'd come back with one and had tried to give it to her, but she'd been busy in the shop and had asked him to put it upstairs. She hadn't even glanced at it until a few minutes ago. And now, after reading about the negotiations, the concessions, the declaration of victory, about labor leaders Ben Tillet and John Burns having their carriage unhooked from its horses and pulled through the streets by euphoric strikers, about the wild celebrations and marches, the women coming out onto the Commercial Road by the thousands to cheer their husbands and sons, she still couldn't believe what had happened.

They'd done it. The dockers had won.

Against all odds, the rough-and-tumble men of the London river had banded together, held fast against poverty, and hunger and triumphed over those who would exploit them. Poor, often illiterate, unsophisticated in the ways of politics, they'd stood together and bloody well won.

Fiona's heart was full of love for her father. He'd been a part of this strike, too, and its victory would've meant the world to him. "You should've been there, Da," she whispered. "This was your fight. You should've been there to see it won." She wiped her eyes. Mixed with her happiness she felt sorrow, too. And bitterness. As she always did when she thought of what had happened to her father . . . and why.

But now, about a year after his death, the complex mixture of emotion she felt had shifted and changed. Her feelings of pride and loss and grief were undiminished, her rage toward William Burton was still immense, but the fear she had felt the night she'd fled Whitechapel, the desperation, and the scalding impotence had faded.

She pictured Burton as he must've looked when he found out about the victory. Sitting at his desk in his office. Silent. Enraged. For once, powerless. He was no longer the omnipotent figure, the master of men, he thought he was. He had murdered to stop the union, he had destroyed her family for his own ends. But he had been shown that he could no more stop the forces of trade unionism than a child could stop the sea from washing away his sand castle. Justice would prevail. The dockers had theirs. And one day, she would have hers.

She felt it was a sign – a good omen – this victory. Her life had changed. And it would continue to change. For the better. She could feel it. She was no longer a frightened girl alone in the world with no one to turn to. She had her family. Her friends. And a week from now, she would have Will. He would be her husband, her protector, and he would keep her forever safe from the likes of Burton and Sheehan.

To think that the wedding was only a week away! Though it was going to be a small affair – only family and close friends – there was still so much to do. She was glad of an evening to herself. It was rare that the house was so quiet. Michael and Mary had gone to a show. Alec, Ian, and Nell were upstairs. Seamie was asleep. Even Will was away in Pittsburgh on subway business – his last trip before the wedding. Laying her newspaper down, she went to the kitchen and put the kettle on. She cut herself a slice of Mary's lemon cake, brewed a pot of vanilla tea and carried it into the parlor on a tray. While the tea was steeping, she rummaged for a piece of paper and a pen, so she could make herself a list of all the things she still needed to do.

An hour later, she had finished her cake and her list,

and was drowsing on the settee. A crisp autumn breeze blew in through the window, bringing with it a hint of falling leaves and coal smoke. The weather was turning. She pulled her shawl around her shoulders and snuggled down into the couch. Just as she was about to nod off completely, she heard a loud pounding on the downstairs door, and her name being shouted from the street. She sat up groggily.

"Helloooo! Is this the Finnegans? Is anybody home?"

A peaceful evening around here is just too much to ask for, she thought, going to the window. She raised the sash and stuck her head out. A boy was battering on the door.

"What is it?" she shouted, irritated.

He looked up. "Are you Fiona Finnegan?"

"Yes. What do you want?"

"Boy, am I glad I found you, miss! Can you come downstairs?"

"Not till you tell me what this is about."

"It's real important, miss. I've got an urgent message for you. From a fella."

55

At eight in the morning, in a courthouse in lower Manhattan, an exhausted Fiona sat on a hard wooden bench. Her face was swollen from crying, her clothes were rumpled from the night she'd spent at the Tombs, the city jail on Centre Street. Next to her sat her attorney, Teddy Sissons, the man who'd handled her purchase of Miss Nicholson's property, and Stephen Ambrose, a criminal lawyer Teddy had recommended. A few other people were scattered about the courtroom, sitting quietly, waiting for the judge to arrive and begin the day's proceedings.

"This can't be happening," she said. "I knew he was in trouble when the boy came, but I thought it was his health."

"It *is* happening," Teddy said. "And he's in serious trouble. What the hell was he doing at The Slide? It's a den of vice. He shouldn't have been within a mile of the place."

"Well, he was!" Fiona snapped. "And he got himself arrested and now you have to get him out. You have to . . ." Her voice caught. She started to weep again. "Oh, Teddy, do something! What if they keep him in jail?"

"Most likely that won't happen," Stephen Ambrose said. "As long as the charges are misdemeanors, he'll probably just have to pay a fine."

"What if they're not?" Fiona asked. "Will he go to prison?"

"No," Teddy said grimly, rubbing his eyes under the horn-rimmed spectacles he wore. "He's foreign. They'll deport him."

Fiona cried harder. Teddy gave her his handkerchief.

Ambrose, well-dressed, well-groomed, and wearing a diamond ring, said, "The trouble is the judge who's going to preside at the arraignment . . . Cameron Eames. He's a hard man. He's been running a campaign to clean up the city – closing down gaming dens, brothels, places like The Slide. One of the cops I talked to says Eames leaned on Malloy, the police captain, to carry out the raid. He's tough on offenders. And the fact that he wouldn't set bail doesn't bode well."

Fiona closed her eyes and sat back against the bench. This was a nightmare, one she'd been wishing she could wake up from ever since the boy, a messenger Nick sent from the Tombs last night, had arrived at Michael's. She'd rushed to the jail hoping to get him out, to at least see him, but the desk sergeant wouldn't permit it. Captain's orders, he said.

She hoped he was all right. Hoped he'd had something to eat and drink, and someplace to sleep. She heard Teddy's words echoing in her head, ". . . he's foreign . . . they'll deport him." If that happened, it would destroy him. He'd lose his gallery and everything he'd worked for. He'd be forcibly taken back to London. To his hateful father who'd threatened to cut him off without a penny if he returned. He'd be all alone. How long could he possibly survive like that?

She felt a hand on her back. "Darling! What on earth is going on?" Her heart lurched. It was Peter Hylton.

"Say *nothing*," Teddy hissed in her ear.

"I heard Nick was arrested last night. And in The Slide, too! Slumming, was he?"

"I . . . I don't know, Peter . . . I don't know what happened. There's been a terrible mistake." Her emotion overtook her again and tears slipped down her cheeks.

"Oh, dear! It's him, isn't it? Nick's the one. Look at you, you've been crying buckets. No woman cries like that over a man she doesn't love. I always knew McClane didn't have a chance."

"Peter," Fiona began wearily. "We're not . . ." Teddy's elbow in her side silenced her. She turned around.

Peter knew nothing about her engagement to Will. Only members of their immediate circle, her lawyers, and the discreet Madame Eugénie knew. If anyone admired her ring, she told them it was only glass and that she'd bought it herself for fun. Will had wanted the match kept quiet. He knew people would talk about it plenty after the fact; he didn't want Hylton getting a head start. The man was relentless. He'd know about the dress, the cake, and what Fiona planned to wear to bed on her wedding night. And he'd make sure all of New York knew, too. She heard him flip open his notebook, heard his pen nib scratching over the paper.

She turned around. More people had come into the courtroom. Quite a few had notebooks. She recognized Nellie Bly, a friend of Will's. A woman she quite liked. A woman who, with a few paragraphs, could ruin Nick. She realized that even if he wasn't convicted, the press would hang him anyway. All they needed was to mention the sort of clientele The Slide catered to and he was finished. There would be a scandal. An ugly one. The society people who patronized his gallery would drop him like a hot coal. His business would be destroyed and that would kill him as surely as the privations of jail and deportation.

Panic set in. Her chest felt tight. She told Teddy she needed air and was going outside for a few minutes. On the steps of the courthouse she hugged herself against the chilly morning and wondered what she was going to do. If only Will were here, he'd know. But he wasn't. He was in Pittsburgh and wouldn't be back for days. As she stood there, feeling hopeless and lost, she looked through the window of an office across the street, a law firm, and the receptionist talking on a telephone. In a flash, she was across the street and through the doorway. She would call Will at his hotel. He might not be there, but it was worth a try.

"Excuse me," she said. "I have an emergency and I need to use your phone. I'll pay you."

"I'm sorry, miss, but I can't."

"Please. I wouldn't ask you, but my friend's life depends on it."

The woman hesitated. "All right," she finally said. "Do you know the number?"

Fiona told her the name of the hotel in Pittsburgh, and after a minute or so the girl had the place on the line. She handed the telephone to Fiona, who asked the clerk for William McClane. To her relief he was there, breakfasting in the dining room. The clerk would get him, he said. Fiona nearly sobbed when she heard his voice on the other end.

"Fiona? Darling, what is it? Is everything all right?"

"No, Will, it's not." With tears in her voice, she told him what had happened.

His response was harsh and immediate. "Fiona, listen to me. I want you to get out of there as quickly as you can."

"Will, I can't. Nick needs —"

"I don't care what Nick needs!" he snapped. "The Tombs, the courthouse, they're no place for you. You've got to distance yourself from him. From all of this. Immediately. This is going to be a goddamned mess when the press gets hold of it. And not just for Nick. I want you to go upstate. Take Seamie with you. And Mary. I'll call Emily and tell her you're coming. Fiona? Are you still there?"

There was a beat of silence, then, "Yes . . . yes, I'm here."

"I'll try and cut this trip short. I'll get home by tomorrow night if I can. Do not talk to anyone about this. Do you understand me?"

"Yes. Quite."

"Good. I've got to go now. Do what I said and everything will be all right. Take care, darling. I love you."

"I love you, too," she said. The words tasted like acid in her mouth.

"Good-bye."

"Good-bye, Will."

The line went dead. She listened to it click for a few seconds. Then she placed the earpiece back into its cradle, handed the receptionist a dollar bill, and thanked her. She walked to the door stiffly. Her limbs felt as cold as ice. Will had told her to abandon Nick. Her best friend. The man who had rescued her when she had no one. Now he had no one and she could no more abandon him than she could cut out her own heart. She returned to the courtroom and sat beside Teddy. More people had arrived. The benches were filling. Just then, the door to the judge's chamber opened. A court officer emerged. "All rise!" he boomed.

Fiona stood, along with the rest of the courtroom. Cameron Eames entered dressed in a flowing black robe. He glanced around the room, then sat down to read his docket. She was amazed at how young he looked. And how hard. There was no compassion in that fair, boyish face. No mercy. When he'd finished with his docket, he called for the prisoners to be brought in. A door opened at the front of the courtroom and a line of men was marched in. They were cuffed. Fiona craned her neck, searching frantically for Nick. When she finally spotted him, she gasped. His left eye was purple. There was a gash on his cheek and dried blood under his nose. He was limping. His jacket was torn.

"Nick!" she sobbed, rising in her seat.

"Hush!" Teddy hissed, pushing her down.

Nick hadn't heard her, but Eames had. He cast an irritated glance in her direction. "Criminal Court of the City of New York is now in session," he intoned. He apprised the men of the charges leveled against them. "Loitering, disorderly conduct . . ." he read.

"Both misdemeanors," Ambrose whispered, hopeful.

". . . public lewdness, solicitation . . . and sodomy."

"He's cooked. That last one's a felony. They won't let

530

him off with a fine. If he doesn't plead guilty, they'll go to trial. For some reason, Eames wants an example made of these men."

"Stephen, isn't there anything we can do? Anything at all?" Fiona asked, pale with fright.

"I've got one idea," Stephen said. "Not a very good one."

"Anything. Try anything."

"You said Nick walks the streets at night?"

"Yes. Often."

"Why?"

"To tire himself. Sometimes he can't sleep."

Ambrose nodded.

Eames called the first prisoner, an unsavory-looking fellow who pleaded guilty to all the charges. Two respectable-looking men were called after him. Both were asked if they had counsel. Neither did. Guilty pleas were entered for both. It was Nick's turn next. When the judge asked if he had a lawyer, Stephen Ambrose stood and approached the bench. Nick, who'd been sitting with his head down, looked up in surprise. His eyes traveled from Ambrose across the benches, searching. And then he saw her. Their eyes locked and she saw the fear in his. He tried to give her a quick smile, but winced instead. It was all she could do to stay in her seat and not run to him and throw her arms around him.

Eames asked Ambrose how his client pleaded.

"Not guilty, Your Honor," Ambrose replied.

"Counselor, I'm in no mood for antics. Mr. Soames was apprehended at The Slide. There are eyewitness accounts, testimonies from the arresting officers," Eames warned.

Ambrose held up his manicured hands. "I do not dispute my client's presence at The Slide. Nonetheless, I maintain he is innocent of all charges. There's been a terrible mistake, Your Honor."

"There always is," Eames sighed, eliciting titters from the courtroom.

"My client, Mr. Soames, wandered into the said premises quite innocently. He was simply looking for something to drink and did not recognize the establishment for what it is. My client suffers from insomnia and has a habit of walking the streets at night to tire himself. Being a foreigner, he is not entirely familiar with all the parts of our city, or the nature of some of its denizens. He was unaware that he was patronizing a place of ill repute."

Fiona held her breath. Stephen's ploy was risky. What if Nick had indeed visited The Slide before last night? What if one of the other prisoners said so? She looked at them. Several were smirking but nobody said a word.

"Mr. Soames is a respectable and upstanding member of society," Stephen continued. "These charges are spurious. A law-abiding man has been wrongfully arrested –"

"Counselor –"

"And badly treated, too. I would like the record to reflect that."

"Counselor Ambrose, I am not impressed by this cock-and-bull story," Eames said. "I've seen all sorts of ploys to avoid punishment and this one is as old as the hills."

Fiona started to cry again. It really was hopeless.

"Oh, don't cry, darling. I can't stand it," a voice whispered emotionally from behind her. It was Peter Hylton. "Your Honor! Your Honor!" he shouted, standing up.

Oh, no, Fiona thought. "Mr. Hylton, don't –" she started to say, but he was already in the aisle.

Eames banged his gavel. "Order! Do not shout at me, sir. Approach the bench."

"Sorry." Peter scurried to the front of the courtroom.

"What is it? Mr.–" Eames asked.

"Hylton. Peter Randall Hylton. I write a column for the *World* – 'Peter's Patter' – and –"

"What is it, Mr. Hylton?"

"I just wanted to tell you that Mr. Ambrose is telling you the truth! There has been a mistake. A dreadful mistake. Nick Soames isn't . . . you know," he said, waving his hand.

"No, sir. I do not."

"A pansy!"

The courtroom erupted in laughter. Eames crashed his gavel down again.

"Well, he isn't," Peter insisted. "He has a sweetheart, you know. A female one. I won't name names here – it wouldn't be right – but it's true."

Fiona saw her chance. She stood up and asked for permission to approach the bench. Eames granted it and she walked up to him, her legs shaking. To think that Ambrose had called his ploy a long shot. Hers was about a million to one. Will would be furious with her, but it couldn't be helped. It was all she had – all Nick had. She cleared her throat and said, "Your Honor, what Mr. Hylton said is true. Mr. Soames is my fiancé. We've been engaged for two months." Gasps, followed by mad chatter, filled the courtroom. Eames banged his gavel and threatened the occupants with ejection. "What Mr. Ambrose said is also true," she continued. "Nicholas does not sleep well and walks at night to tire himself. I don't quite know how he got himself into a place like The Slide, but I'm sure he didn't mean to. And I'm sure he regrets his mistake terribly."

Ambrose shot Fiona a horrified look. "Your Honor . . ." he hastily began. The rest of his words were drowned out by the noise of the people in the benches. Reporters, sensing a good story in the making, were crawling over one another, trying to get Fiona's full name, the proper spelling of Soames, the address of Nick's gallery.

Eames, infuriated, banged his gavel as if he meant to break it in half. "Sit down, Counselor!" he shouted. His voice effected the silence his gavel could not. He gathered his papers together and stood. "Counselor Ambrose, I am growing very, very tired of you and your sideshow. I'm going to call a short recess and when I return I want to see everyone back in his or her seat. And I want to be able to hear a pin drop. Do I make myself clear?"

No one dared speak; everyone nodded. Eames turned on his heel and left the courtroom for his chambers, slamming the door behind himself. The boom echoed hollowly.

Fiona returned to her seat and sat down next to Teddy. Stephen Ambrose wedged in beside her. "That took balls," he said quietly.

She nodded miserably. She had hoped to save Nick. Now, it appeared, she had only made things worse.

Ambrose noticed her broken expression. "Cheer up," he told her. "You never know, if Eames doesn't send Nick to the gallows after that, he just might set him free."

Will Junior took a large swallow of Scotch, grimaced cheerfully as it went down, and said, "Cameron, you're a genius, you know that? A goddamned genius!"

Cameron, sitting in his chambers with his feet up on his desk, grinned at his friend. "It *is* going rather well. Even if I do say so myself."

"Going *well*? Cam, it couldn't possibly go any better. I can't believe she's here!" he exclaimed, leaning back in his chair and smiling up at the ceiling. "That she actually spent the night at the Tombs and is sitting in a courtroom with faggots and criminals! My father's going to be furious! What happened after Ambrose pleaded?"

Cameron laughed. "Then Hylton put his two cents in. God, I wish you could've seen it, Will. He actually stood up and told the whole courtroom that Nick Soames isn't a pansy. I thought I was going to fall out of my chair."

Cameron went on to describe Peter Hylton's performance and Will listened raptly, shaking his head in disbelief over his good fortune. This was all going off perfectly, better than he'd dared to hope. Cameron had told him that the courtroom was packed with reporters. A few photographers had shown up, too. There would be a huge scandal. By tonight – maybe even by lunchtime! – the shit would be flying. And Fiona Finnegan was going to get *covered* with it! His father would surely finish with her now. He'd have to. Marrying a respectable woman from another class was one thing, but marrying a woman who consorted with deviants was quite another.

"... and then, Will ... oh, you won't believe this ... she gets up and tells me she's engaged to Soames. Since two months!"

"What?"

"She said they were engaged, and that Soames stumbled into The Slide by accident, because of insomnia or some such horseshit." He waved his hand dismissively. "They really do think I was born yesterday."

This is the luckiest day of my life, Will Junior thought as Cameron finished his tale. She has played into my hands completely. "Cameron . . ." he said slowly.

"Hmm?" he replied, refreshing Will's drink.

"What if I'm wrong? What if my father were to actually forgive this mess?"

"Then all our hard work and the favor I called in with Malloy will have been for nothing. But surely he wouldn't, Will. Not after it makes the papers."

"In his present unhinged state, anything's possible," Will Junior said. He drained his glass and regarded his friend. "I think, Justice Eames, that what we have in front of us is nothing less than a way to get Miss Finnegan out of the picture permanently. And I think we must avail ourselves of this extraordinary opportunity."

Cameron returned his gaze, then nodded, and Will Junior knew that he'd taken his meaning. They'd always been good at reading each other's thoughts. It had served them well when they'd needed to cook up stories as youngsters and again when they'd been caught cheating on their exams at school. They had come far together, he and Cameron, and they would go farther still.

"If your father ever learns what happened, he'll string me up."

"He won't. How could he? I'm surely not going to tell him."

"What am I going to say when he finds out I was the officiating justice?"

"What can he say? Technically, you don't even know who she is. Have you ever seen them together?"

"No."

"Has he ever introduced you?"

"No."

"Did he tell you they were engaged?"

"Of course not."

"Then how can you be blamed? You simply didn't know. You were only doing your job. When the time comes – if it ever does – that he asks you about it, you'll tell him if only you'd known who she was, you would never, ever have insisted on this condition."

"All right. But you'd better go now. Out the back way. Same way you came in. Don't let anyone see you, Will. Not anyone."

"I won't. Stop worrying, Cam. Make this happen for me."

Cameron stood up and put his robe back on. The two men made plans to meet at the Union Club for dinner, then Will made his exit. He felt an enormous sense of relief wash over him. Soon this would be over. Seamlessly, perfectly over. His father would never suspect that Cameron had done what he was about to do on purpose. And he'd never expect that he himself had engineered it. He'd done too fine an acting job for that – apologizing for his bad behavior, welcoming the girl into the family – and his father had bought it all. As he headed down the dark hallway used by court officers to whisk the infamous and condemned in and out of the building, Will Junior told himself that he really owed Cameron one for this. He knew of a good way to pay him back, too. As soon as he got his seat in Congress, he'd set about working to get Cam the state supreme court seat he wanted so badly. And one day, when he got to the White House, the very first thing he would do would be to nominate Cameron Eames for Federal Supreme Court justice. Every president needed a judge in his pocket.

Fiona looked around at the courtroom's stark white walls, at the dour portraits of the great men that hung on them. She looked at the American flag in the corner, the gilt seal of the City of New York. She looked everywhere, hoping for some indication that there was kindness in this room, an understanding of human foibles. She looked for a sign that the men who wielded so much power over others' lives tempered that power with wisdom and tolerance. But she saw only the hard, impassive faces of the court officers and the imposing emptiness of the judge's chair.

Eames would never accept her story. Stephen had angered him. Hylton had made things worse, and she had added the final straw. He would insist on a trial, and then send Nick away.

The door to the judge's chambers suddenly opened, startling her. Eames reemerged and took his seat. All around her, Fiona heard shifting and shuffling as spectators and reporters sat at attention, ready to see what sort of developments the next round would bring. Eames was not going to keep them waiting. As soon as he had settled himself, he called for Stephen Ambrose and Fiona to approach.

He cleared his throat, casting a glance over his courtroom as he did. "Contrary to the way I am sometimes portrayed in various of the city's lesser newspapers," he began, looking pointedly at Nellie Bly, "I am not without understanding. Or compassion."

Fiona's heart leaped with hope.

"I am also willing to admit that a mistake may have been made in the case of Mr. Soames."

Her legs went weak with relief. It's going to be all right, she thought. He's going to let Nick go.

"Miss Finnegan, you say that Mr. Soames is your fiancé, and that you are certain he happened into The Slide by accident . . . is that true?"

"Yes, Your Honor."

Eames turned toward the prisoners. "Is that true, Mr. Soames?"

Nick looked at Fiona, a panicked expression on his face. She gave him a nod. And a look that warned him not to wreck this, his one and only chance.

"Yes, Your Honor," he said quietly.

"Very well, then. I am prepared to release Mr. Soames into your custody, Miss Finnegan. On one condition . . ."

"Yes, Your Honor, anything," she said, beaming with relief and the happy knowledge that her plan had worked. She'd saved Nick! Soon this whole horrible nightmare would be over.

"I insist that you marry Mr. Soames today. In my courtroom. As proof of your sincerity."

For a second, there was absolute silence in the courtroom, and then the place erupted. Stephen, joined by Teddy now, harangued the judge, telling him that this was unheard of and completely out of line. Eames shouted back, telling them he knew bullshit when he smelled it, telling them he wouldn't be made a fool of in his own courtroom. Reporters shouted questions at her, at Nick, at Eames. Spectators chattered merrily among themselves, remarking that this was better than Tony Pastor's theater. And Fiona stood silent and alone, dazed by the choice that Eames had just given her.

As she stood, a sudden movement caught her eye. It was Nick. He was waving at her as best as his handcuffs would allow, trying to get her attention. She walked over to him. There was no one to stop her. Eames was embroiled in his argument. Two of the court officers were wrestling an unruly prisoner who'd stood up and cheered back into his seat. Two more were trying to quiet the crowd.

"Stop this. Right now," he said. "I won't go through with it."

"Yes, you will."

"Are you mad?" he hissed. "You're throwing your life

away! And for no reason! This isn't a hanging offense, Fiona. They'll charge me, I'll pay a fine, they'll let me go."

"No, they won't. Teddy says the judge will put you in jail, keep you there for weeks, then have you deported after a trial. Deported. To England. Do you understand what that means?"

"Do *you* understand what it means, you stupid girl? You can't marry Will if you've already married me! They allow that sort of thing in some places – Arabia, Africa, the South Sea Islands – but not in New York!"

"I don't want to marry Will."

Nicholas lowered his head into his hands. "Please, Fiona. Please. I've had enough insanity over the last twelve hours. I don't need yours now."

"Nicholas . . . you married *me* once. Now I'm marrying you."

"That was a pretend marriage and you know it. This won't be."

"You saved me."

"Hardly."

"You did. Me and Seamie both. Believe me when I tell you that. Now I'm saving you."

Nick raised his head and looked into her eyes. "Why?"

Fiona shrugged helplessly. "Because I love you."

An officer appeared at her elbow. "I'm sorry, miss, I can't allow access to the prisoners," he said brusquely, leading her back to the judge's bench.

Eames, fed up with the noise level, started banging his gavel again.

"Order! Order!" he shouted. "One more outburst and I'll clear the courtroom!"

When quiet was restored, he began again. "I'm prepared to show faith in Miss Finnegan's story. All I require in return is proof of her word, Counselor. If Mr. Soames is truly innocent I should like to release him, but I will not have the authority of this court mocked."

"Your Honor," Fiona said, trying to make herself heard,

but she was drowned out by Stephen's vociferous denouncement of the judge and his courtroom. He said that his cruel condition would ruin the church ceremony his client had planned. He was grasping at straws, trying to come up with anything he could to change Eames's mind.

"A civil ceremony does not preclude a religious one," Eames countered. "They can still have their church wedding. I don't wish to prevent it."

"Your Honor, please!" Fiona shouted.

"What is it, Miss Finnegan?"

"I accept your condition. We both do."

Eames nodded. "Very well. I'll give you two hours to assemble the requisite papers while I finish the court's business. Bring the next prisoner, please. How do you plead?"

Fiona, dizzy with exhaustion and shock, sat down. Three reporters, wolfish and ravening, tried to push their way through to her, but Teddy and Stephen saw them off. A fourth persisted. It was Nellie Bly.

"I need to talk to her, Teddy," Fiona heard her say. "Not as a reporter, as a friend."

"It's all right, Teddy," Fiona said. He let her by.

Nellie sat down next to her and leaned in close so no one could hear their conversation. "Fiona, what are you doing?" she asked quietly. "Will loves you, I know he does. I knew it before he did. I saw him mooning over you one night in the Union Club, though he wouldn't admit it. I've seen you together, seen how he looks at you. Why would you hurt him like this?"

"Because they're going to kill Nick if I don't."

"Fiona, this is America. They're not going to *kill* him. He'll do a bit of time. At worst he'll be deported –"

Fiona cut her off. "Do a bit of time?" she said angrily. "Like breaking rocks with a pickax he can't even lift? Or trudging along in a chain gang until he collapses?" The very thought of Nick chained and forced into hard labor made her sick with fear. "He has a weak heart, Nellie," she said, choking back a sob. "He can barely lift one of his paintings, never mind a shovelful of dirt . . . or . . . or a barrow filled with rocks. He wouldn't last a week . . ." Her voice faltered, then broke. Tears coursed down her face. It was too much for her. Nearly losing Nick. And now losing Will for sure.

"I'm sorry, Fiona. I didn't know. Christ, what a choice to have to make . . . ssshhh, I'm so sorry . . ." Nellie comforted her, and when Fiona had herself under control again, she straightened and looked at the judge. "Goddamn you, Eames, you son of a bitch!" she shouted.

Eames had been speaking to a prisoner; he stopped. Color flooded his face. "What did you say?" he asked.

"You heard me! Is this an arraignment or the Spanish Inquisition?"

"How dare you –"

"I'll tell you what it is – it's a travesty! Forcing someone into marriage like this. You know it, and so does everyone in this courtroom!"

"That's enough!" Eames thundered, getting to his feet. "I'll thank you to show due respect to my office, if not myself, when you address me in my courtroom!" he shouted. "Bailiff! Remove Miss Bly and all press from the courtroom. This instant!"

The court was cleared. Order was finally restored and Eames was able to get on with the business of processing the arrested men. Fiona, with Teddy's help, was able to exit the courthouse via the back entrance, thus avoiding the reporters on her way uptown to get her and Nick's documents. He tried to dissuade her. What Eames had done was illegal, he said, the man had no right to demand or enforce such a condition. He and Stephen would sort it out, he promised. It would only take a few days. A week.

Fiona, one arm held out to flag down a hackney, turned to him. "A week? You want me to leave him in the Tombs for a week? Did you see his face? God knows if that's all they've done to him." A cab slowed and she ran for it. "I'll be back in two hours," she called. "Stay with him. Stop him from doing anything stupid."

"It's too late for him," Teddy sighed, as the cab pulled away. "I was trying to stop you."

"Elgin? I thought your last name was Soames," Cameron Eames said, looking at Nick's birth certificate.

"It's Elgin. I go by my mother's name, however – Soames."

Fiona regarded Nick. This was news to her. Very shortly her last name would become Elgin, too. Or would they use Soames? She felt a wave of dizziness wash over her. For a few seconds she thought she might faint. It wasn't surprising. She'd had no sleep, nothing to eat, and then, of course, there was this slight matter of marrying Nick.

"What is this?" Eames asked, pointing at an abbreviation before Nick's name.

"It . . . um . . . it stands for viscount."

Oh, what is he doing now? Fiona wondered wearily. It was far too late in the game for any more stunts. They'd tried them all already. Did he really think pretending to be royalty was going to intimidate a judge?

"Viscount?" Eames asked.

"Yes."

"What is a viscount, exactly?"

"A duke's eldest son."

"Your father is a duke?"

"The Sixth Duke of Winchester."

Fiona shot him a dirty look. "Stop it, you fool," she mouthed. The Duke of Winchester's son. Really! Next he'd be telling them she was the Princess Royal.

He gave her a sheepish glance in return. At least she thought it was sheepish. It was hard to tell with one of his eyes swollen. He looked better than he had, though. The judge had allowed him to wash his face. He'd also smoothed his hair back and changed into the fresh clothes she'd brought. He looked presentable. Like a young man of good standing at least, and not a criminal.

Fiona had managed to change her clothes too. She'd

sneaked into Michael's flat unnoticed. Luckily Mary had gone out somewhere with the children. In her room, she'd torn off her crumpled things and put on a white lace blouse and a turquoise sateen suit. Then she'd quickly combed her hair and snatched a hat from her closet. As she was digging in a drawer for her birth certificate, she came across her parents' wedding rings and stuffed them into her pocket. She'd had a scare as she was on her way out. Just as she'd stepped into the parlor, the front door opened and Michael came in. She ducked back inside her room just as he came down the hallway toward the loo. She couldn't let him know what she was doing. If he found out, he'd try to prevent it. She'd crept out while he was still in the bathroom, then ran to Seventh Avenue, where she'd been able to get a cab to Gramercy Park. It had taken some searching to locate the little leather portfolio Nick kept his papers in, but she'd finally found it under his bed. She'd snatched a fresh shirt and jacket from his closet, and then dashed back to the courthouse. If Peter Hylton and his crew wanted pictures they would have them, but not of her and Nick looking dirty and disheveled. At the very least, they would wear clean clothes on their wedding day.

Their wedding day.

Her hands started shaking at the very thought. She was marrying Nick. She would promise herself to him, and he to her. Forever. The light-headed feeling came back with a vengeance. She closed her eyes and dug her nails into her palms, concentrating on the pain. Don't, don't, don't, she told herself. Don't think about this. Don't think about anything. Just get it over with.

When Eames had finished with Nick's certificate, he verified the information on Fiona's, had them fill out their marriage license. Fiona gave Teddy her parents' rings to hold. The courtroom was empty now except for her, Nick, Teddy, Stephen, and Eames. She was grateful for that. The morning had been a circus and all the clowns were still waiting for them outside on the courthouse steps. At least they wouldn't have to say their vows in front of a throng.

With little ado, Eames began. There were no pleasantries, no romantic sentiments, simply the ceremony, the exchange of rings, and the vows. And then the thing was done. And they were standing there facing each other with thin yellow bands on their fingers. Nicholas and Fiona Soames . . . or was it Elgin? Husband and wife. Till death do them part.

Eames had them sign their marriage certificate, then had their lawyers sign it. Then he bid them good day, telling Nick he was free to go and advising him, with a tight little smile, to steer clear of The Slide and all such establishments on any future peregrinations.

The four of them stood there awkwardly, not knowing quite what to do, until Stephen broke the silence by clapping his hands together and announcing that there was a gauntlet of press outside, and if they wanted to pull this off and make people believe Nick's arrest was a mistake, if they wanted to prevent a scandal, they'd better look the part of the happy newlyweds. They gathered their things and followed him out.

On the steps of the courthouse, Stephen Ambrose informed those present that Cameron Eames had an outrageous sense of justice and owed his clients an apology. Mr. Soames's arrest had been an egregious mistake. He had suffered terribly at the hands of the police and the court system, and then he'd been intimidated into marrying his fiancée, the former Miss Fiona Finnegan, much sooner than either of them intended. "This is 1889," he bellowed, slapping his fist into his palm for effect, "not the Dark Ages! No man should be forced to marry in a courthouse among criminals just to clear his good name!" He added that although all charges against his client had been dropped, Mr. Soames was considering suing the city for unlawful imprisonment and the violation of his civil rights.

Pictures were taken, including one of Nicholas kissing his new bride's cheek, and one of Fiona holding a bouquet of roses a reporter had bought from a flower seller.

Questions were asked and answered, names spelled and spelled again, best wishes and congratulations were heaped upon the couple, and then, finally, the crowd dispersed. Teddy and Stephen said their farewells – both men commented that the day had easily been the most interesting one of their careers – and then they left. And Fiona and Nick were alone.

Fiona was the first to speak. "Nick . . . I . . . I think I'm going to faint."

"No, don't! There's a bench over there, under that tree. Come on."

He took her elbow and led her away from the courthouse. She sat down and rested her head on her knees. Her skin was clammy. Her heart was racing. She felt as if she was going to be sick. "What have we done?" she moaned. "What will I tell Will?"

Nick rubbed her back gently. "I'm sorry, Fiona," he said. "I'm so, so sorry." And then he burst into tears. He cried so hard she could barely understand him. ". . . ruined your life . . . Will . . . you . . . loved him . . ."

Fiona thought about what he was saying. She looked at the buildings around them, the trees, the sun high in the noon sky. Then she turned back to him. "No, I didn't. Not really," she said in a voice that was oddly calm.

"What?" he said, sniffling.

"You were right. Remember that night at your flat? When we argued? You said I didn't really love Will. Not the way I loved Joe. I loved many things about Will. His good heart. His intelligence. I loved the glamour of his life, and I loved being wanted by someone again, being held and cared for. But I don't love *him*. Not like I should. I'm only sorry, deeply sorry, that I'm about to cause him so much pain. Joe was my true love, Nick. Like Henri was for you. You only get one of those in a lifetime. Hard as it is, I think it's time I accepted it."

"Do you love me?"

She smiled at him. "You know I do."

"I love you, too. And I'll take good care of you, Fee. And Seamie, too. I promise I will. I'll be the best husband ever. I know it won't be the most conventional marriage . . . I . . . I can't give you children . . . but I'll give you everything else. A good home. Clothing. Nice suppers out. Whatever you like. I haven't as much money as Will, but I have quite a bit. About ten thousand pounds a year. And the gallery's almost open. My prospects are really quite excellent, you know."

Fiona gave him a sidelong look. "Nicholas Soames . . . are you proposing to me?"

"I guess I am. A bit after the fact."

"I accept."

"Do you?"

"Absolutely." She leaned her head on his shoulder. "I'd marry you again in a second, Nick. I'd have done anything to keep you here. You're the most important person in the world to me. You and Seamie."

She heard him sniffle again. After a few seconds, he said, "Are you certain it's what you want? It's just that, if you wanted to I suppose we could get a divorce."

"No, we couldn't. It would cause as much of a scandal as the one we just barely avoided, and I've had enough excitement for a while."

"What about your lovely dress, Fee? And the jewels Will gave you?"

"Someone else can wear the dress. As for this . . ." She pulled the enormous diamond off her finger and put it in her purse. "It never did look right on me."

"And your trip. You were looking forward to it and now you can't get on that boat and sail off to France next week."

"No," she said, smiling up at him joyously as she realized what she could do instead. "But I can go to my beautiful Tea Rose, Nick! I can put my apron on and get to work." She laughed. "I won't have to give it up! How could I have ever even *imagined* it? You know something? I can't wait! I can't wait to be back there, to see my roses and open the place and be up to my neck in tea and scones."

Nick took her hand. "*I'll* take you on a honeymoon, Fee."

"Will you? Where?"

"Coney Island."

Fiona laughed. "With Seamie and Michael and the Munros tagging along. Now that would be romantic!"

Fiona and Nick sat on the bench holding hands and talking until the clock struck one, and Fiona realized how late it was, and realized, too, how anxious everyone at home would be. She had run out of the house last night as fast as she could, only taking a few seconds to tell Alec that something had happened to Nick.

"We'd better go home, don't you think?" she said. "They'll be beside themselves with worry. We've got to tell Michael what happened."

Nick groaned. "I think I'd rather be deported."

They stood to go and Fiona noticed that the cut on his cheek was bleeding again. She dabbed at it with Teddy's handkerchief, which was still balled up in her hand. "By the way," she said, "that was a daft stunt you tried to pull. Passing yourself off as a viscount – have you no shame?"

He caught her hand. "Fiona, that was no stunt," he said quietly.

She looked at him, assessing his expression. "You . . . you're not joking, are you?"

He shook his head. Then he took her hand, kissed it, and, with a rueful smile, said, "Let me be the first to congratulate you on your nuptials, Viscountess."

56

Joe, freshly washed from a morning bath, the one bath he was allowed per week by his landlady, pulled a clean shirt over his head and tucked it into his trousers. He looked at his face in the small square of a mirror hanging over the one bureau in his room, then ran a comb through his hair. Today he would start hunting in Chelsea. He'd been in the city for three weeks already and had found no sign of Fiona. It was getting harder and harder to maintain his optimism.

Michael Charles Finnegan had turned out to be another dead end. He had a niece, all right – her name was Frances and she was ten years old. Eddie's luck had been no better. He'd found the address on Eighth Avenue – it was a grocery shop – and knocked on the door. An old man had answered and said that a Michael Finnegan did indeed live there, but that he was out for the evening. He told Eddie to come back in the morning. Eddie tried to ask whether Michael had a niece, but the man cut him off, saying there had been enough commotion for one night and that he wasn't going to answer any more questions from street urchins. Then he slammed the door on him.

That had been the day before yesterday. Eddie had gotten work handing out flyers yesterday and couldn't return to Eighth Avenue, but he'd given Joe the address. He would go there himself this morning. He needed to find Fiona. Soon. He was being extremely careful with his money, but it was dwindling nonetheless. "Where are you, lass?" he sighed aloud to the empty bedroom. "Where the devil are you?" A crushing feeling of despair overtook him. He sat down on his bed for a few minutes, his elbows on his knees, convinced that he would never find her, that all his hopes, all his efforts, would be for nothing.

He shook the feeling off, determined to keep hunting. He couldn't allow himself to give up now. She was here. He felt it; he knew it. All he had to do was find the right Finnegan. As he reached for his boots, there was a sudden pounding on his door that was so loud it made him jump.

"Mister!" a small voice piped through the door, "open up! I found her! This time I really found her!"

Joe was across the room in two quick strides. He yanked open the door. Eddie was standing on the threshold with a newspaper in his hands. "Look! It's her, ain't it? Fiona Finnegan! She's the one, ain't she?"

He took the paper. And there, on the second page, was a picture of Fiona, but not the Fiona he'd known. This Fiona was smiling. She wore a stylish suit and a pretty hat. She looked beautiful. Absolutely radiant. A man was kissing her cheek. The headline said, "New York's Most Glamorous Couple Wed in Courthouse Ceremony." The article, written by a Mr. Peter Hylton, read:

> No column in this edition, dear readers. There's only one story worth reporting today – and that's the dramatic courthouse wedding of the handsome young art dealer, Nicholas Soames, to Fiona Finnegan, the lovely proprietress of TasTea and the soon-to-be-open Tea Rose salon. Hearts are breaking all over the city this morning at the news and a certain well-known millionaire-about-town, Mr. Soames's rival for Miss Finnegan's hand, has retreated to the country. All's fair in love and war, darlings, but I digress! Back to Tuesday night and the wrongful arrest that led to a wedding . . .

The article detailed Nicholas Soames's arrest, his lawyer's defense, Hylton's own heroic testimony on Mr. Soames's behalf, and Miss Finnegan's tearful plea to the judge. In addition to the article, there were sidebars on Nicholas Soames's gallery and on Fiona's burgeoning tea business.

Joe was stunned. This wasn't real. It couldn't be. He kept reading. Fiona lived in Chelsea, the article said. Above her uncle's – Michael Finnegan's – grocery shop. The very place Eddie had visited. If only *he'd* gone there, to Eighth Avenue, instead of to Duane Street. Oh, God, if only he had . . .

"Mister? Are you all right? You don't look so good," Eddie said. "You want a cup of coffee? Some whiskey? Maybe you should sit down."

"I'm fine," Joe said woodenly. He reached into his pocket, pulled out the first thing he touched, and handed it to Eddie.

"A whole dollar? Gee, thanks!"

Joe ushered him out. He picked up the paper again and stared at the picture, hoping that somehow it wasn't Fiona. But it was. Her face, her smile, they were unmistakable. He felt empty. Hollowed out. There was nothing inside him anymore. No heart, no hope, no life. They were gone. Ripped out in an instant.

As he looked at her, a bitter laugh escaped him. What a fool he was. She was hardly the poor, bereft figure he imagined she would be. She wasn't in trouble, she wasn't lost or frightened, either. How presumptuous he'd been to assume she was miserable and alone without him. She was a beautiful, successful woman, no longer the girl whose heart he'd shattered on the Old Stairs. She'd moved on and made an entirely new life for herself. A good life. She looked as happy as a new bride should with her dashing groom – a man who, from all appearances, was a bit of a step up from a Whitechapel costermonger.

Joe looked at him – roughed up, but still handsome – kissing her cheek, and felt sick with jealousy at the thought of her in his arms. What did you expect? he asked himself angrily. You left her and she found someone new. Just as she should've done.

For a split second, he considered going to see her. Just to lay eyes on her one last time. But he knew it would be selfish and unfair and would only upset her. This was all his fault, not hers. It was a fitting turn of events, really. A just punishment for what he'd done to her. He heard his grandmum's voice again, "We're not punished for our sins, but by them."

He would not go to see her. He would let her get on with her life. As he would get on with his. Without her. She was not coming back to him. She was not coming back to London. He felt a pain rise up in him, a deep crushing feeling of loss that terrified him. He needed to stay ahead of it; he couldn't let it catch up to him. If he did, it would break him into pieces.

He pulled his duffel bag out from under his bed. He would leave today. He had his return ticket. He'd go find Brendan on his work site, say good-bye, then head over to the piers to see if there was a White Star boat leaving tonight and if it had any berths left. He opened the top drawer of the bureau, grabbed his things and shoved them into his bag. His map of New York was in there, too. It lay folded open to the West Side of the city. To Chelsea. Where she lived. Where he'd planned to go today. He'd missed her by a day. One bloody day.

Without warning, the pain slammed into him. It pulled him down into its fathomless depths, engulfing him, drowning him. Filling him with its suffocating grief, its sorrow, its madness. And he knew that this was how it would be for him. Now and forever more.

PART THREE

57

"'Ere, Stan, use more kerosene," Bowler Sheehan ordered. "Fucker's got to burn, not fizzle."

"All right, all right," Stan Christie grumbled. "Give us a mo', would you? Christ, you've got your knickers in a twist."

Bowler would've gobsmacked Stan for that if only he could see him. But it was so bloody dark in William Burton's old tea-packing factory, he could barely see his hand in front of his face. The only light came from a pale crescent moon. Its weak rays struggled in through high, paneless windows, illuminating rotted tea chests and snaking gas lines. Everything else – doorknobs, hinges, gas lamps, and sconces – was long gone. Carried off by scavengers.

There was a thud. "Oh, me shin! Fuck this! I can't see a fucking thing!" Reg Smith yelled.

There was a snort of laughter. "Light a match," Stan said.

"You're a real fucking comedian, Stan, you are."

"Oi! Shut it. Want someone to 'ear us?" Bowler growled.

"I 'ate this, guv," Reg complained. "I've splashed kerosene all over me shoes. It'll stink for days. Why are we doing this dogsbody job anyway?"

"Burton wants to collect on 'is insurance policy," Bowler replied. " 'E's 'ad this place on the market for years. Can't find any takers. If it burns down, the blokes at the insurance company 'ave to pay 'im. Long as it looks like an accident."

"What's 'e need with insurance money? 'E's richer than Midas," Stan said.

"Not anymore. Burton's fortunes have taken a turn, lads," Bowler said. "Got 'is arse 'anded to 'im when 'e tried to break into the American tea market a few years back. And 'is estate in India went bust just last year. Bloke 'e 'ired to manage it ran off with the money. 'E's got big debts to pay and needs a bit of cash to pay them."

"It's arson what we're doing," Stan said knowledgeably. "We've never done arson before."

"Put it on your curriculum vitae, lads," Bowler said sarcastically. His tone was lost on them.

"We could, you know," Stan said thoughtfully. "It's not every bloke 'as as much experience as we do, Reg. Pickpocketing, robbing, breaking and entering, extortion . . ."

"Fixing sporting events . . ." Reg said.

"Breaking arms, kneecapping . . ."

"Topping blokes, don't forget that. That's a big one."

"We could teach a course, us. For lads coming up in the business."

"Aye, we could!" Reg said excitedly. "But what would we call it?"

"The Stan Christie and Reg Smith School of Mayhem and Murder," Bowler said.

" 'As a nice ring to it, don't it?" Reg said. Stan agreed.

As they tossed ideas for classes back and forth, Bowler sat down on a tea chest and rubbed his face. That it should come to this. A man of his stature mucking about in a shit-hole at midnight with the likes of these two. And for a madman like Burton, who'd only become more unpredictable and violent over the years as his money troubles increased. He'd seen him attack his own foreman, and he'd even gone for Stan once when the lad had laughed inappropriately. Once he wouldn't have considered doing a job like this. He'd have left it for the small fish, the amateurs. But paying jobs were harder and harder to come by.

It was all different now. Not like the good old days – 1888 B. J., Bowler liked to call them – Before Jack. That grandstanding bastard had ruined it for everyone. In the wake of the murders, the legal and moral authorities of London had made the East End their top priority. They had assigned more constables to the streets. There were more preachers. More missions and do-gooders. And that flipping Roddy O'Meara, good to the promise he'd made, *had* stuck to his arse all these years. Tailing him, talking to him in public as if he were some filthy informer, raiding the gaming dens and whorehouses he controlled. A bit of relief had come three years ago, after O'Meara made sergeant and had to spend most of his time behind a desk, but if his duties now kept the man from harassing him personally, he made certain his officers took up the slack.

And while the forces of right were pressing down on him, his own marks were growing more and more lawless. Some had stopped paying him altogether, like Denny Quinn down the Taj. Quinn was always pleading poverty, but he'd made pots of money out of the Taj. Bowler knew the real reason he wasn't paying – that bloody Sid Malone.

Bowler spat, feeling bilious at the mere thought of his rival. Malone was young. An upstart. He'd come out of nowhere. A few years ago, he'd been just another wide boy – breaking heads, doing the odd robbery, moving stolen goods. There were hundreds of them. Minor criminals who thieved to eat or pay for a bed in some poxy lodging house. Malone hadn't remained in the ranks for long, though. Brains and balls, combined with a reputation for ruthlessness, had ensured a swift rise to the top.

Like Bowler himself, Sid Malone controlled scores of illicit establishments and collected protection money. Unlike Bowler, he operated south of the river, in Lambeth, Southwark, Bermondsey, and Rotherhithe. Live and let live, had been Bowler's policy. As long as Malone stayed put on his side of the river, he would stay on his. Only Malone wasn't staying put. Over the last few months, he'd used his influence with wharfingers and shipowners to further some very bold, and very lucrative, activities – running guns to Dublin, opium to New York, high-end swag to Paris. His success with these pursuits had sharpened his ambition. Rumors had been circulating that he was about to make a play for the north bank of the river – Bowler's own back-yard. And yesterday, they'd been confirmed. Malone had made an appearance at the Taj. Reg and Stan had seen him. He'd had a meal, bet on a fight, and fucked one of Quinn's whores.

The cheek. The bloody cheek, Bowler thought. He didn't know whose neck he wanted to break more: Malone's for pissing in his territory or Quinn's for letting him.

Bowler would've killed Malone without a second's regret if only he could get the chance, but the man was well protected. To get to him, you'd have to plow through half a dozen lads first, each of whom was built like a brick shit-house. But Bowler knew what to do – he'd get to Denny Quinn instead. A message was going to be sent. A warning. It was too bad – he quite liked Denny – but if he permitted that sort of behavior, where would he be? Floating arse-up in the Thames, that's where. Malone's Thames.

Kerosene fumes hit him, making him cough. "Are you two finished yet?"

"Aye, guv. We are," Stan said.

" 'Ow's our vagabond friend?"

"A bit cold at the moment, but we'll soon warm 'im up."

Bowler's eyes had adjusted to the darkness and he had no trouble picking out the lifeless body on the floor or the tobacco tin sticking out of its pocket. They'd found him dozing in an alley. He'd put up quite a fight. A shame, really, but there was no help for it – the old gent would hardly have consented to being burned alive. When the flames were put out, it would look like a dosser had had himself a smoke and accidentally set the place on fire. "Got the bottle?" he asked.

"Right 'ere," Reg said, holding up an empty gin bottle.

"Matches?"

"Aye."

They quietly left the building the way they'd come in, through a side door, locking it with the key Burton had provided, leaving everything just as they'd found it. Outside, Reg poured kerosene into the bottle, then soaked a length of sacking, twisted it, and stuffed it into the neck, leaving a few inches at the top for a fuse. Then he lit a match and touched it to the rag. It caught, flaring violently.

"Now, lad!" Bowler hissed.

Reg sent the bottle whizzing through an empty window. Already running, Bowler glanced back to make sure his lads were following. Stan was right behind him, but Reg was standing still, waiting to see if the flames took. Bowler heard an enormous, sucking *whoosh*, followed by an ear-splitting explosion. The gas lines are still live, he thought before the force of the blast knocked him arse over tit. Windows in the neighboring factories and houses shattered. Shards of glass rained down around him. As he struggled to his feet, he felt Stan at his elbow. "Let's go!" he shouted.

"What about Reggie?"

"Forget 'im! 'E's done for!"

In the space of mere seconds, flames had engulfed the building. The street had filled with smoke. Just then, Reg came loping out of the thick gray billows. His face was streaked black, there were cuts on his cheeks. " 'Ard way to make a living, this," he said wearily. "From 'ere on out, guv, let's stick to the rackets."

58

"Put the bottle down, Lizzie!" Roddy O'Meara thundered. "Right now! You put one mark on her and it's t'ree months in the nick. Hear me, lass! I said put it down!"

"Stinking little bitch tried to steal me punter!" the woman shouted. "I'll cut 'er face off! Like to see 'er steal anyone then!"

Lizzie Lydon, a prostitute, had knocked another street-walker named Maggie Riggs to the ground in front of a pub called The Bells. She was now sitting astride her, attempting to jam a broken bottle into her cheek. Maggie's hands were wrapped around Lizzie's wrist, desperately trying to stay it. Roddy was only five yards away from them and could easily overpower Lizzie if he got to her in time. If he didn't, Maggie would pay the price.

"Come on, Liz, put it down. You don't want the kind of trouble you'll get if you cut her."

Lizzie looked up at him. Her face was twisted by anger, but her eyes were brimming with tears. "But I saw 'im *first*, guv," she said. " 'E was *my* punter! Went to the loo and when I got back she was 'alfway out the door with 'im!"

Roddy took a few steps toward her. "Give me the bottle, luv."

"I've been sleeping rough for a week!" she cried. "I just want a bed for the night, that's all." Her gaze fell upon Maggie again. "And I 'ad it, too! Till *she* thieved me customer!"

"Let her up. Sleeping rough's still better than the nick."

Lizzie laughed mirthlessly. "You're wrong there, guv. At

least you get a bowl of skilly in the nick. At least it's warm."

Roddy was squatting beside Lizzie now. He reached out for the bottle. "Come on, now," he coaxed. "We're all t'rough carrying on." She handed it over. He helped her up, then Maggie, eyeing their worn skirts and grimy hands as he did. Lizzie's own cheek was horribly scarred, torn in some long-ago fight. Maggie's wrists, sticking out past the cuffs of her threadbare purple jacket, were nothing but skin over bone.

Roddy was well aware that he should arrest them for being drunk and disorderly, but he wouldn't. They weren't criminals, these women, they were just desperate. Desperate and hungry and spent. He told them what mission would allow them a bowl of soup without making them choke down too much religion with it and warned them that he wouldn't be so lenient the next time. Then he advised the half dozen onlookers who had gathered to be on their way and resumed his walk, heading east toward Christ Church.

As a sergeant, Roddy was no longer required to patrol the streets, but it was a long-standing habit with him, one he indulged in nightly for an hour or so on his way home to his family and his two-story row house in safe, respectable Bow. It kept him in contact with the people he was paid to protect. It also let the bad element know that he was out there on their turf, watching them.

"Evening, sir," came a voice from the gloom.

Roddy squinted into the fog and saw a squat, bulky figure approaching – helmeted, a row of brass buttons on his blue jacket. He smiled. It was McPherson. Twenty-five years on the force and still walking the streets. Not because he wasn't good enough to move up. He was one of the smartest, toughest officers Roddy had ever known and he'd been offered advancement many times, but he'd always turned it down. The man wanted nothing to do with the headaches and frustrations of rank.

"Quiet night, Constable?" he asked.

"For the most part. Yourself?"

"Stopped one lass tearing off another's face," Roddy said nonchalantly.

"That so?"

"Aye."

McPherson laughed. "You're a rum one, Sergeant. Most of the brass can't wait to get off the streets, you can't wait to get back on 'em. 'Eaded 'ome, are you?"

"Aye. T'ought I'd walk a bit first. See what I can see."

"I just saw something interesting meself."

"Oh, aye?"

"Sid Malone and Denny Quinn. Coming out of the Taj." Roddy frowned. "Malone? The bloke from Lambeth?"

"The very one."

"Whitechapel's pretty far afield for him. Wonder what he's up to?"

"No good, I'm sure."

"What's he look like?"

McPherson shrugged. "Like every other criminal in London. Big. Tough. Just as soon kill you as look at you. You've never seen 'im?"

"If I did, it was some years ago." Roddy remembered that Charlie Finnegan had worked with a lad called Sid Malone at the brewery, and that this lad had tried to manhandle Fiona. He had paid him a call shortly thereafter, advising him never to trouble her again. The Sid Malone he remembered had been a bully, and bullies picked fights with people weaker than themselves. The Sid Malone who had visited the Taj was picking a fight with someone stronger. A lot stronger.

"I 'ear 'e's very busy on the south bank," McPherson said. "Maybe 'e's thinking of setting up shop in our neighbor'ood."

"Could be. Keep your ear to the ground."

"I will. You heading north, Sergeant? Go take a gander at the tea factory. Fire nearly burned the whole street down. Forty-odd families 'omeless. Official word is a dosser was in there smoking. Fell asleep and set the place alight."

Roddy spat. A bad taste had crept into his mouth. "Unofficial word is Bowler Sheehan. Sure, we'll never pin it on him. It's all 'Hear no evil, see no evil.' As usual."

"Sheehan's a firebug now?"

"He does the odd job for the man who owns the place. William Burton. Estate agent I talked to says Burton's had the building on the market for years. My guess is he hired Sheehan to help him collect a big fat insurance check."

"Well, 'e picked a good night for a fire. Nice and dry. Not like tonight." He rubbed his hands together. "This is Ripper weather."

"Aye, it is. Don't talk about him much anymore. He's a forbidden topic in my home."

"Mine, too."

It was a forbidden topic in the homes of all the officers who had worked on the case. Wives had heard the stories over and over again and were tired of their husbands' obsession with a madman.

"It's over with, Roddy. It's done!" Grace had shouted at him shortly after they were married, after he'd thrashed himself awake from yet another nightmare. "They found that body in the Thames and everyone says it was Jack. Nothing you can do will bring those women back. Or Kate Finnegan. For God's sake, why can't you let it go?"

Why indeed? He wanted to. He didn't want to see Annie Chapman's dead eyes in his nightmares. He didn't want to wake up with the scent of blood in his nostrils. He didn't want to hear Fiona's sobs as they lowered her poor murdered mother into the ground. He wished he could just believe what he was supposed to – that Montague Druitt, the young barrister whose body police had pulled from the Thames in '88, was the murderer.

As if reading his thoughts, McPherson said, "It's a load of tripe, the Yard saying Druitt was the Ripper. I never believed it."

Roddy gave him a long look. "Nor I. Not'ing fits. The poor lad was as mad as a hatter, but he wasn't a murderer.

No history of violence. And he didn't know Whitechapel."

"Not like Jack knew Whitechapel."

"Or still does," Roddy said softly.

It was a thought both men shared, but rarely voiced – the idea that Jack was still out there somewhere. Biding his time. Each had seen a body or two over the years – street-walkers who'd been strangled or stabbed – and each had wondered if it was Jack's work. Had he learned to control his compulsions? Indulging them less frequently? Had he learned to vary his method? The top brass did its best to keep these deaths quiet. The case was closed, they said. The Ripper was dead.

"Should let it rest, I guess," McPherson said. "We'll never know for sure, will we? 'Ave to file it under unfin-ished business."

Roddy nodded. Unfinished business. That was part of the job no one had told him about. Subduing a man, what to do when you were outnumbered – these were things that could be learned. But no training could prepare you for the unsolved cases. The dead ends. The failure. As a young man, he'd refused to accept it, believing if he just worked harder, he'd solve every case. He'd find the clue, the one overlooked detail, that would help him catch the thief, the child molester, the murderer. He'd learned differently over the years. He'd learned that sometimes there were no clues. Sometimes criminals were smart. Or lucky. He'd learned, after many years, how to kiss his wife at the end of the day and put his children to bed, knowing full well that robbers prowled as he did so, women were beaten, murder-ers walked free. He'd had many teachers, but none better than Jack.

"I'm off, then," McPherson said. "Going to take a stroll round Brick Lane. The scenic route. Night, Sergeant. Safe 'ome."

"And you, McPherson. Take care."

Roddy continued east. He twirled his nightstick as he walked, sunk deep in the memories of '88. The past wasn't gone on a night like this. It was as real as the solid cobbles under his feet, the bitter air he breathed. He consoled himself with the one good thing that had come out of all that misery – Fiona's and Seamie's escape from this place. Their new life in America.

He'd just had a Christmas card from Fiona with a likeness of herself, her husband Nicholas, and Seamie enclosed. She'd grown into such a beautiful woman. But then again, she'd always been a bonny lass. And Seamie was a young man now. Handsome and tall. Roddy had been so happy to get the card. He was always happy when her letters and photographs arrived. It pleased him to think what she'd made of herself. A tea merchant! The biggest one in all of America, no less.

Her husband was a toff, Roddy could see it from the photographs, but she said he was very good to her and that she loved him very much. From the looks of things, she'd done a damn sight better for herself with this bloke than she would have with Joe Bristow. The thought of how Joe had treated her still rankled at times, but Roddy's feelings toward him had long since softened.

He could still see the lad as he looked when he'd returned from New York. Hollow. As if his very heart had been torn out. He'd given Roddy four pounds that he had left over, a promise to pay back the remainder, and a newspaper that showed photographs of Fiona and her new husband and told all about their wedding. Roddy had made him come in and drink a glass of whiskey. He hadn't had the heart to tell him he'd received a letter from Fiona two days after he'd left. He hadn't seen much of him after that. He'd come on two or three occasions to pay off his debt and that was it.

In all the letters he'd had from Fiona over the years, she'd never asked about Joe. And Roddy had never mentioned him. Why stir up old hurts? He'd never mentioned Bowler Sheehan, either, or his claim that she'd stolen money from William Burton. The whole thing still puzzled him, but after he'd learned she was in New York, he'd stopped worrying that Sheehan would harm her. He'd never known her to be anything less than honest, but maybe she'd been so desperate to get away from here, from her grief, that she'd relieved Burton of a few quid to do it. So what? He'd had plenty to spare.

In every letter he'd written to her, he asked her to come back to visit. He would so love to see her and Seamie again and meet her husband. She'd always declined, however, citing Nicholas's poor health. She had invited him and his family to New York, too. Countless times. He wanted to go, but he couldn't face the long sea voyage. His weak stomach would make the two weeks a misery. The only time he'd been on a boat was when he'd traveled from Dublin to Liverpool with Michael and Paddy. He'd spent the entire journey with his head over the railing and the Finnegans laughing at him. His eyes crinkled with merriment at the memory.

Paddy . . . Christ, how I miss him, he thought. His smile faded. If only he hadn't taken the watchman's shift that night . . . things would have been so different. They'd all still be here . . . Paddy, Kate, the children. That was all Paddy had wanted – his family and the means to provide for them. It wasn't a lot to ask for. Not much at all.

His memories were interrupted as he nearly crashed into a woman walking past him. Her head was down. "Sorry, guv," she mumbled as she shuffled past. "Didn't see you in the fog."

He caught a glimpse of red hair. He knew her. "Alice? That you?"

She turned around. "Aye, it's me. Is that you, Sergeant? I can't see too well this evening."

Roddy drew a sharp breath. "Who did this?" he asked.

"Punter."

"Just now?"

"Last night."

He steered her over to a street lamp and inspected her

face. Her eyes were swollen to slits. There was dried blood in the corner of one, more in her nostrils. Her cheek was mottled like bad fruit.

"Jaysus, Alice. You know him?"

She shook her head. "Never seen 'im before. Wouldn't 'ave gone with 'im, but 'e offered me a shilling. Looked like a toff, 'e did. When we got back to my room, 'e went barmy. Kept saying, 'I found you, I found you.' Beat me silly. Went on and on about rats, then pulled a knife on me. Thought I was done for, I don't mind saying, but I made 'im see that there weren't no rats and 'e calmed down."

"You should have those eyes looked at."

"Chance would be a fine thing, guv. I'm skint. Going to see your man down the Bells. 'Oping 'e'll give me a glass on the never. That'll take the pain away."

Roddy reached into his pocket and handed her sixpence. "Get somet'ing to eat first."

Alice tried to smile but winced instead. "You're all right, Sergeant."

"Mind what I said. Get yourself some soup."

"I will. Ta, guv."

The hell you will, Roddy thought, watching her go. You'll run right down to the Bells and drink it all. As the fog closed around her, he realized that even if Jack was dead, his spirit lived on in these mean streets. In the bastard who'd beaten Alice. In the barman who would note her swollen eyes and shortchange her. In the lads who'd taunt her and rob her of any remaining coins she had as she staggered home. In the hunger and misery of all the Alices and Lizzies and Maggies who shivered on street corners selling themselves for fourpence. In the callous brutality of someone like Bowler Sheehan who'd burned forty families out of their homes for a few quid. In the cold ambition of up-and-comers like Sid Malone who were only too eager to outdo him.

Roddy shivered, chilled by more than the fog. Suddenly

he wanted to be in his bright, cheerful house. With Grace fussing over him and his supper warm from the oven. He turned and headed north. For home. And a brief night's escape from all of the unfinished business.

59

Nicholas Soames, New York's most celebrated art dealer and a darling of city society, leaned on his silver-topped walking stick and regarded his wife of ten years with a grin. Though she had asked him to come to the riverside that morning, to the cavernous brick building that housed TasTea's operations to see her latest project, she was now so caught up in her work she was completely unaware he'd arrived.

"The new machine is beautiful, Nick," she'd told him over breakfast. "Just breathtaking! You've got to see it. Come after lunch. Promise you will!"

And he had, though he shouldn't have. These days, the smallest exertions brought on the pain. He felt it now – tiny slivers of glass stabbing at his heart. Over the last two years his condition had worsened dramatically, but he'd managed to hide a good deal of his decline from Fiona. He knew that the truth would upset her, and more than anything in the world he wanted to shield her from unhappiness. She'd already had so much more than her share.

She stood about twenty yards away from him, utterly absorbed by the huge noisy contraption in front of her. Nick shook his head. Only his Fee could find this heap of clanking metal appealing. He had absolutely no idea what it was or what it did; he only knew that she'd had it made in Pittsburgh for the astronomical sum of fifty thousand dollars and that she intended for it to do nothing less than revolutionize the tea trade. As he watched her, his smile – one made up of equal parts love, pride, and amusement – broadened, warming his pallid complexion. "Just look at you!" he clucked. She had looked so polished, so elegant, when she'd left the house earlier. Now she looked an absolute fright.

She had thrown her jacket over a stool as if it were an old dish towel. The sleeves of her white blouse were rolled up; there was a smear of black grease across one. Her hair was wild; strands had come undone from the neat twist she always wore. She was snapping her fingers unconsciously, talking to someone hidden by the machine. He could see her face in profile; her expression was lively and intense. How he adored that face.

As Nick continued to gaze at his wife, the machine suddenly rumbled to life, startling him. He followed Fiona's gaze to its maw and saw that red TasTea tins were emerging from it in an orderly procession along a conveyor belt. Fiona grabbed the first tin and tore its lid off. She pulled out what looked like a tiny white bag and examined it.

"Goddammit!" she shouted, her voice more American now than English. She pulled out another bag, and another. Then she put her thumb and forefinger in her mouth and gave a piercing whistle. There was the sound of metal grinding and then the machine stopped. "Stuart!" she yelled. "They're still tearing! Every bloody one of them!"

Nick blinked in surprise as a head suddenly popped out from under a devilishly complex conglomeration of gears, plates, and tracks. It was Stuart Bryce, Fiona's second-in-command. She had hired him away from Millard's eight years ago.

"What?" he hollered. "I can't hear you! This sodding thing's made me deaf!"

"It's the tension on the rollers, it has to be," she shouted, handing him one of the bags.

Another voice was heard from under the machine. Nick assumed it belonged to the pair of feet next to Stuart's head. "It can't be! We've adjusted the roller three times!"

"Then adjust them a fourth time, Dunne! You're the mechanic, aren't you?"

Nick heard a snort of disgust, then: "It's *not* the rollers, Mrs. Soames. It's the stapling mechanism. The staple edges are tearing the fabric as the bags pass through."

Fiona shook her head. "The edges are too raggedy. The cut would be clean if a staple made it. It's the *tension*, Dunne. The muslin's being pulled apart, not sliced. Now are you going to fix it, or am I?"

"I'd like to see you try."

Oh dear, Mr. Dunne, Nick thought, wrong move altogether. He took Fiona's jacket off the stool, folded it, and sat down to watch the fireworks.

Fiona stood there for a few more seconds, glaring at Dunne's feet, then picked up a wrench, crawled under the conveyor belt, and made for the center of the machine. Her skirt caught on a nail jutting from a floorboard. She yanked it. It tore. Nick flinched. Hand-woven Venetian silk. Fashioned in Paris by Worth. Oh, well.

There was a good deal of grunting and cursing. A yelp. A few minutes of silence. A cry of triumph, then: "Start it up!" The monster rumbled back to life. Fiona came crawling back out of the maze of pipes and shafts. Nick saw that she'd managed to get grease on her cheek and that one of her hands was bleeding. Tins rolled out again. She dropped her wrench and grabbed the first one, hurriedly inspecting its contents. A grin lit up her face.

"Yes!" she cried, throwing it high into the air and laughing. "Yes! Yes! Yes! We did it!" As a hundred little bags rained down, she spotted Nick. With a squeal of delight, she picked one up and ran to him. She sat down on a tea chest and dangled the muslin bag – which he now saw was filled with tea – in front of him. The bag had a string attached to it by a tiny metal staple, and attached to the string's other end was a red paper tag printed with the words "TasTea Quick Cup."

"It's fabulous, my love. Just smashing. What on *earth* is it?" he asked, wiping the blood off her hand with his handkerchief. It had dripped over her fingers, onto her diamond wedding band and the stunning ten-carat emerald-cut diamond he'd given her for their first anniversary. He frowned at her hand. Rough, grimy, scarred in places, it belonged to a charwoman, a laundress, not the richest woman in New York. A woman who owned the largest, most lucrative tea concern in the country, as well as thirty-five Tea Rose salons and over a hundred high-end groceries.

Fiona pulled her hand out of his grasp, impatient with his ministrations. "It's a *tea bag*, Nick!" she said excitedly. "It's going to modernize the entire industry! You just put one of these into a cup, add boiling water, steep, and you're done. No mess, no waste. No cleaning teapots or making more than you need."

"Sounds very efficient," Nick said approvingly. "Very American."

"Exactly!" Fiona crowed, leaping to her feet. "It's all to do with saving time and effort, you see. 'A new tea for a new century!' Like that? Nate came up with it. He wants to target young people – modern types who think tea is fuddy-duddy – and create a whole new market. Nick, you should see Maddie's sketches! One shows an actress in her dressing room having a Quick Cup. And there's a typist making herself a Quick Cup at work, and a student having one while he's studying, and a bachelor having one as he's shaving. And Nick, Nick . . . listen to this: Nate's hired the composer Scott Joplin to write us a song. It's called 'The Hasty TasTea Tea Bag Rag'! A month from now, everyone will be humming it and dancing to it. Oh, Nick luv, can't you just see it?"

Fiona's incomparable eyes sparkled with blue fire. Her face was flushed. Nick thought then, as he had on so many occasions, that she was the most beautiful woman he had ever seen. Her passion made her so. He found himself every bit as thrilled as she was about her latest invention. She's always had that gift, he thought, an astonishing ability to make other people feel as excited about her ideas and projects as she was. It explained, in large part, her enormous success.

He remembered how, years ago, she'd convinced the Southern states to drink TasTea. Her sales in that region had been dismal. She'd tried ads, discounts, and contests, but nothing seemed to spark interest. Her fellow tea merchants said the South was an impossible market to crack. People drank lemonade and punch and mint juleps. Few people drank tea; it was too damn hot for it. Fiona had mulled these gloomy statements for weeks, racking her brain for a way to prove her competitors wrong. And then, one morning at breakfast, she'd impetuously poured the remains of her teapot over a glass of ice. "If we can't get them to drink TasTea hot, we'll get them to drink it cold," she'd declared.

She'd tinkered and experimented until she'd perfected a technique for brewing a crisp, clear glass of iced tea, then she, Stuart, and a half dozen of her salesmen had marched on the South. They set up booths in cities and towns, flying banners that said, THIRSTEA? TRY A NICE COLD, ICE COLD TASTEA! They tirelessly handed out glass after glass of ice tea and coupons good for a nickel off a half-pound tin. Fiona charmed, cajoled, and strong-armed people into trying her tea and they found it every bit as bracing and refreshing as they found her. By the time she and her troops limped home three months later, they'd won the South handily. Nick didn't doubt for a second that she'd convince the whole country to buy her new tea bags, either.

Fiona was humming a ragtime tune now. Laughing, she grabbed his hands, pulled him up, and commenced a giddy quickstep. Nick followed her light steps, keeping up with her perfectly, then stopped and twirled her around. As he did, a vicious pain shot through his heart, making him gasp. With a great effort, he managed not to clutch his chest.

Fiona stopped dead. Her smile was gone. "What is it?" she asked. "Nick, are you all right? Tell me what's wrong. Is it your heart?"

He waved off her concern. "No, darling, not at all. It's my back, actually. A muscle cramp, I think. I'm getting so old and creaky, I must've pulled something."

Fiona's expression told him she didn't believe him. She made him sit down and started to fuss over him, but he reassured her that he was perfectly fine. He made a good show of massaging the muscles in the small of his back, confident the pain in his chest would subside in a minute or two. Fiona, unconvinced, was asking him whether she thought it might be a good idea to call Dr. Eckhardt when Stuart came over to say hello, accompanied by the mechanic, Dunne, a grizzled and cantankerous man, who – Nick learned – had come from Pittsburgh with the machine to make certain it worked properly once installed in its new home.

The discussion turned to the machine's capabilities and Stuart, giddy with plans for world domination, babbled on about output and distribution. Nick tried to steady his breathing, hoping it would quiet his heart. He had to get out of there. Quickly.

A sudden crunch of gears hurried Stuart and Dunne back to the machine. Feeling as if a giant hand were squeezing his heart, Nick stood and lightly told Fiona that he had to go, too. He said he was expecting Hermione, the manager-ess of his gallery, to stop by with the weekly report. Hermione Melton was a young Englishwoman he'd poached from the Metropolitan Museum two years ago, after Eckhardt had told him he could no longer work. To his relief, he saw his hale-and-hearty act was working. The worry had receded from Fiona's face. He asked her if she would be home for supper. She said she would. He kissed her good-bye and sent her back to work.

The pain in his chest was paralyzing now. Slowly, he walked toward his carriage. He climbed in, leaned against the seat, and closed his eyes. When he could, he reached into his breast pocket, took out a small bottle, and extracted a white pill. It would calm the struggling organ that was heaving and flopping inside him like a beached fish. "Come on," he groaned, "do something."

After what seemed like an eternity, his carriage pulled up outside the palatial Fifth Avenue mansion that he and Fiona shared. He climbed out and steadied himself against the balustrade that flanked the front steps, his trembling hand blue against the white marble. The door opened. He looked up and saw Foster, his butler. He heard the man's customary welcome turn into a cry of alarm. "Sir! My goodness . . . let me help you . . ."

Nick felt his legs go weak as the pain in his chest exploded, engulfing him in a burning blaze of light. "Foster, get Eckhardt . . ." he managed to gasp in the instant before he crumpled.

Fiona Finnegan Soames, her skirts gathered in her hand, picked her way carefully over the lattice of train tracks that separated her tea factory from West Street. A young night watchman, perhaps eighteen years of age, trailed after her.

"Can't I hail you a carriage, Mrs. Soames?" he asked. "You shouldn't be out by yourself. It's dark and there's all types about at this hour."

"I'll be fine, Tom," Fiona said, striding ahead of him, suppressing a smile at his concern. "I'm in need of a walk tonight. Too wound up about the new machine."

"She's a beauty, ain't she, Mrs. Soames? One hundred bags a minute, Mr. Bryce told me. I ain't never seen anything like her."

"Indeed she is," Fiona said. She stopped suddenly and turned to face the lad. "Why is it a *she*, Tom?" she asked.

"Beg your pardon, ma'am?"

"The new machine. Why is it a *she*, not a *he*?"

Tom shrugged. "Same reason a boat's a she, I guess. You never know what it's gonna do. Sweet one minute, meaner than an old sewer rat the next. Just like a woman."

Fiona arched an eyebrow. "Is that so?"

Too late, Tom realized his mistake. "I . . . I'm sorry, Mrs.

Soames," he stammered. "I didn't mean nuthin' by it. I always forget you're a woman."

"Thank you very much!"

"I . . . I didn't meant it like *that*," Tom said, hopelessly flustered now. "You're awful pretty and all, Mrs. Soames, it's just that you . . . you know what you want. You're not all silly and fluttery. Batting your lashes and making like you don't know how to cross the street on your own. You know what I mean?" He took his cap off. "Aw, geez, Mrs. Soames, please don't fire me."

"Don't be silly," Fiona said. "Speaking one's mind isn't a firing offense here."

She expected the boy to be relieved, instead he looked pained. "See?" he said. "You never know where you stand with a woman. If you were a man, you'd have tossed me out on my ear."

"Then I'd be a fool."

Tom's confusion deepened. "For what? Being a man?"

Fiona laughed. "That, too. But mostly for firing one of my best workers."

The lad grinned. "Thanks, Mrs. Soames. You . . . you're all right."

"For an old sewer rat," Fiona added with a mischievous wink.

"Yeah! I mean, no! I mean –"

"Good night, Tom," Fiona called, stepping into the street.

As she crossed West Street, deftly dodging carriages, trolleys, and the odd automobile, she walked at her usual brisk pace with her head held high, her shoulders thrown back, her gaze direct and unshrinking. That directness – not just in her gaze, but in her speech, her demands and expectations, her entire manner – had become her trademark. She was known for her ability to see through the bluster and condescension of bankers and businessmen and cut through the false numbers and padded invoices of suppliers and distributors. The coltish uncertainty of her teenage years had vanished, replaced by an indelible, unshakable confidence, the kind earned from hard work and achievement, from battles waged and won.

As she reached the east side of the street, she turned to take one last look at her factory, pleased by what ten years of her labor had wrought – the huge red freight cars, each with the white TasTea logo emblazoned on its sides, and the massive building rising above them. Behind the building were TasTea's docks, port to a fleet of moored barges standing ready to depart at dawn's high tide. Some would travel across the river to New Jersey, others northward to bustling Hudson towns: Rhinebeck, Albany, and Troy. Still others would sail farther yet, up the Erie Canal to Lake Ontario, where huge freighters waited to take TasTea to the bustling cities that lined the Great Lakes, ports of entry to the burgeoning northwestern states.

Most women would not find enchantment in a riverside factory, but to Fiona it was beauty itself. Worry wrinkled her brow as she thought about her new machine and what she hoped it would do. She had spent a fortune on it, and she would spend more still. On local and national ad campaigns, on packaging and promotions and new means of distribution. On every plan, scheme, and stunt she, Stuart, and Nate could dream up. Over the coming year, she would be shoveling money at this new venture. It had better work.

She took a deep breath and blew it out again. The frogs were on the move. She'd long ago decided that "butterflies" was too delicate a term to describe the feeling she got in the pit of her stomach when she undertook a new project. These weren't butterflies she was feeling; they were big, heavy bullfrogs. She knew them well. They'd visited her when she'd first unlocked the door to her uncle's abandoned shop. And the day she'd ordered her first fifty chests of tea from Millard's. They were there when Miss Nicholson, long dead now, had sold her the building that would become The Tea Rose. They'd worried her when she and Michael opened the second Finnegan's grocery, on Seventh Avenue and Fourteenth Street, and every time she'd opened a new Tea Rose, be it in Brooklyn Heights, Baltimore, or Boston.

Nick could tell when she had them. He would fix her a pot of tea, steeped until it could strip paint. Just how she liked it. "Douse the little bastards with this," he'd say. "Frogs hate tea."

At this stage of her life, she recognized the frogs as necessary evils, little green demons whose presence forced her to rethink obsessively all her assumptions and expectations, to streamline plans and expenditures, and in so doing, minimize the margins for error. She knew by now that she ought to worry only if the frogs didn't plague her.

They jumped and bounced now, but even their acrobatics couldn't dampen her enthusiasm for Quick Cup. Oh, the promise that new machine held! If Quick Cup did well in the United States, she would launch it in Canada and eventually England and France, too – markets ripe for a new approach to tea – and conceivably triple, even quadruple, her sales.

She continued north past Jane Street, lost in her thoughts, unconsciously walking faster in an effort to burn off the jittery excitement coursing through her. I really should hail a cab, she thought, I don't want to keep Nick waiting. But she didn't. She was still anxious and couldn't bear the thought of riding in a stuffy carriage. And there was something else disturbing her. Underneath the jostling of the frogs lay a deeper dread – a fear for Nick's well-being.

That pain he'd had at the factory today – had it really been his back, or his heart? His hand hadn't gone to his chest. And he always rubbed his chest when he had pains. And he would've taken the medicine Eckhardt had given him. He'd been ordered to take it right away at the very first sign of discomfort and he was very good about doing so. Fiona's brow smoothed a little, her shoulders relaxed. He had looked a little pale, and tired, but that was to be expected. After all, he had a serious illness and there were bound to be effects. "But he's really all right," she said aloud. "He is."

Over the last ten years, Fiona had taken every precaution to ensure Nick's health. She had seen to it that he ate well – not his champagne-and-caviar diet of old. She made sure he had plenty of rest and the necessary exercise. And once, in a misguided burst of conviction that someone somewhere must be able to cure syphilis, not just treat it, she'd dismissed Eckhardt and engaged a series of doctors from both America and Europe to examine him.

Nick had acquiesced, patiently tolerating the poking and prodding of the first half dozen physicians she'd inflicted upon him. He put up with stinking poultices and vile medicines. He endured therapeutic baths – sitz baths, steam baths, air baths. Massages. A shaved head. Open windows in December, long underwear in July. But when the seventh doctor put him on a diet of nothing but boiled cauliflower and celery juice and tried to bar him from listening to his new gramophone – too stressful to the nerves, the doctor had declared – his patience snapped. He told Fiona her quacks were only hastening his demise and demanded Eckhardt's immediate reinstatement.

Chastened, she had gone to the German to apologize and to beg him to come back. And without fuss or recrimination, he'd agreed. When she thanked him for his graciousness, saying it was more than she deserved, he'd waved her words away. An expert on the physical workings of the human heart, Werner Eckhardt also had a deep understanding of its emotional motivations. "Be careful of too much hoping, ja?" he'd warned her. "It is hope, not despair, that undoes us all."

Eckhardt could say what he liked. She would continue to hope. And he would continue to take good care of her precious Nicholas. If he hadn't been able to arrest the disease, he'd at least managed to slow its effects. It had not attacked Nick's brain or nervous system, as Eckhardt had originally feared. It had settled in his heart and stayed there.

And as far as she could tell, it had not gained a great deal of ground since the day she'd found him deathly ill at Mrs. Mackie's. Nothing will happen to him, she assured herself. He was fine and he was going to stay fine. He had to, because she could not bear losing her best friend, her husband.

She smiled to herself now, remembering the first years of their madcap marriage. They'd lived in Nick's flat above his art gallery and The Tea Rose. She had spent all her time opening more tearooms, more groceries, and building her TasTea business, and Nick had worked to establish himself as the city's preeminent dealer of Impressionist art. Both of them were out of the flat all day, chasing business, making money, utterly devoted to their work. They limped home at night after Seamie had been retrieved from Mary's, opened a bottle of wine, and ate whatever they could scrounge up from The Tea Rose's kitchen, hearing Seamie's lessons, sharing the events of their day, advising and encouraging each other.

Neither Fiona nor Nick had any interest in domestic duties and it became a joke between them that nobody in their marriage wanted to be the wife. Now, poor Foster was stuck with the job. It fell to him to decide what they would eat for supper, what kind of flowers were required for the dining room, and if the laundress was getting the sheets white enough.

"Carriage, missus?" a cabdriver bellowed at her, jarring her out of her thoughts. She was about to accept his offer when she realized where she was: Gansevoort Street, with its Friday-night market. Dozens of braziers glowed brightly. Their hot orange flames beckoned to the evening shoppers, drawing them close for a handful of chestnuts, a roasted potato, hot soup. Fiona could hear two women chatting, their mittened hands wrapped around fat brown mugs, their breath and the vapor from the hot liquid mingling in the cold night air. She saw a butcher hold up a rope of sausages, smelled doughnuts frying. "No, thank you," she told the driver, waving him on. Within seconds she had turned off West onto Gansevoort, indescribably happy – as always – to be at a market.

She allowed herself to be swept along by the flow of people, delighted simply to watch and listen. She took in the wooden barrows – pushcarts, they were called in New York – piled high with all manner of goods, from winter fruits and vegetables to secondhand clothing, pots and pans, penny candy, stain removers, and tonics. Peddlers shouted their wares and she listened to them, entranced.

She was wandering contentedly, her merchant's heart excited and curious, poking her nose into every stall, examining the contents of every pushcart, when she saw him. A tall, blond lad, good-looking with a devilish grin. He was turned away from her, but she could see the side of his face. He wore a threadbare jacket, a dark cap, and a red neckerchief. His fingers poked through the ends of his gloves. It hurt her to see that they were blue from the cold. As she continued to stare, he winked at a customer, then handed the woman – with a flourish – a paper cone filled with hot chestnuts.

The lad turned toward her and she instantly saw he wasn't who she'd thought he was. The smile wasn't right, nor the cheekbones exactly, nor the shape of his nose. His eyes were brown, not blue. And he was only a boy, maybe seventeen years old. The lad she was thinking of would be almost thirty by now. And he'd be running Peterson's of Covent Garden, not peddling chestnuts. "You're seeing things now, you daft cow," she told herself. A combination of the darkness and not having eaten all day. She looked away, feigned interest in a used copy of *Wuthering Heights* at a nearby bookstall, and tried to chuckle at her own silliness. But the laughter didn't come.

The day she'd married Nick she'd realized, with an awful certainty, that she would never stop loving Joe Bristow. She had tried to make herself believe otherwise once with disastrous consequences. And though it was a hard thing to

581

admit, she had done her best to accept it and go on with her life. She tried never to think of him. And when she did, she told herself that she'd made peace with what he'd done. It was mostly true. With the passage of time and the immense distance between her old life and her new one, understanding had finally replaced her anger. And her sorrow.

Joe had been young and he'd made a terrible mistake, one that had hurt him, too. She imagined he was happy now, but that night on the Old Stairs, the night he'd told her what he'd done, his own grief had been genuine. He'd been a bright and eager lad, one who'd been held down by his father and his circumstances, and he'd let his first taste of success go to his head. The way she saw it now, he'd been seduced by more than Millie – he'd been seduced by Tommy Peterson's power and money, by his own enormous ambition.

Ease and wealth – these things could be hard, almost impossible, to resist. Fiona knew this to be true, for she had allowed herself to be seduced, too – by William McClane and the life of privilege he had offered her. In the weeks and months after her wedding to Nick, it had become increasingly important to her that she find it in herself to forgive Joe, for she had discovered how very painful it was to hurt someone and be so very sorry for it, and yet not be forgiven. For Will had not forgiven her.

She winced now at the memory of their last meeting. It had occurred at Will's apartment the day after her wedding. He'd rushed back from his trip only to find that the woman he loved, the woman who'd promised to marry him, had married someone else. He was destroyed by her betrayal and had ranted at her furiously, telling her she'd ruined his life and her own. Then, spent, he'd sat down and covered his face with his hands. Weeping with remorse, Fiona had knelt by him, trying to explain how she'd had no choice. She told him that Nick had faced prison and deportation and that she knew he'd never survive it. Will had raised his head then and said, "Obviously, Nicholas Soames means a lot more to you than I do."

Fiona had met his gaze. "Yes. Yes, he does," she'd said softly. Then she'd stood up, for there was nothing more to say, and left Will's home. It was the last time she'd seen him alone. They'd glimpsed each other in passing at theaters and restaurants and exchanged at most a curt nod, a few polite words, nothing more. Five years ago, he had married again – a woman from his circle, a widow close to his own age. From what Fiona heard, he spent more time in the country these days and left the running of his businesses to his sons, James and Edmund. Gossip columnists reported on his and his wife's frequent trips to Washington to visit his eldest son, Will Junior, who'd become first a congressman and then a senator, and who, many said, would one day run for president.

Fiona had suffered for hurting Will, but she knew that had she to do it all over again, she would. Nick was everything to her and she could not have borne losing him. And though theirs was not a conventional marriage, no woman ever had a more devoted husband. He gave her everything she could want from a man – kindness, humor, intelligence, respect, wise counsel. Well, she thought ruefully, paging past an illustration of Heathcliff on the wild Yorkshire moors, almost everything.

There were nights when she tossed and turned in her huge empty bed, fretting about her business, or Seamie's terrible grades in Latin, or Nick's health, when she physically ached with longing for someone to hold her and make love to her. And, as she'd grown older, she found she was prone to another sort of ache, too – a sad tug deep down inside that came whenever she saw a tiny baby. She'd felt it just two weeks ago when she'd held perfect, beautiful Clara – Maddie's new baby. Her and Nate's fourth. She had so wanted children of her own. She and Nick had talked about it once, years ago, and he'd confessed that he desired a family with her and would've done his damnedest to make her pregnant if only it weren't for his illness and his grave fear of passing it on to her.

Early in their marriage, aware that she might be pining for the sort of physical contact he couldn't provide, he'd encouraged her to take a lover. "Find someone, Fee," he'd told her. "Someone you can share a romantic dinner with and a bottle of wine and your bed. You can't spend the rest of your life like a nun. You're far too young."

When, after several months, she'd produced no lover, Nick told her that according to an article on the new science of psychology he'd been reading, she was sublimating her desires. She told him she had no idea what he was talking about and doubted whether he did. He proceeded to tell her all about Sigmund Freud, a brilliant doctor from Vienna, and his startling theories on the human mind. Sublimation, he said, was when a person had desires, but couldn't or wouldn't act on them. The energy of these desires was then diverted to another area of the person's life. Work, for example. Fiona had rolled her eyes at him, but he insisted that the theory explained her extraordinary success. She put all the energy she should be expending in bed into minding her business.

"Why don't you try that, Nick? Minding *your* business, that is," she'd suggested.

"Oh, don't be a such a prude, Fee. If you can't talk about sex with your own husband, then who can you talk about it with?" he'd chided.

A pillow flung at his head finally silenced him. And despite what he might think, Fiona knew her reluctance to begin an affair with someone had nothing to do with prudery. She didn't want a *lover*. She wanted to be in love. She'd had a lover in Will, a skillful one, and though her body had responded warmly to his, her heart had remained aloof. She remembered lying next to him in bed after they'd first made love, listening to him breathe as he slept, feeling more alone than she'd ever felt in her life. She wanted what she'd had with Joe. She'd met hundreds of men over the past ten years – many of whom were smart, accomplished, and handsome – many of whom had fallen in love with her. She had tried to warm to a few of them, searching their eyes for a flicker of what she'd found in Joe's. But she'd never found it.

"That's a good story you've got there, darlin'. That Brontë lass could turn a phrase."

Startled, Fiona looked up to see the bookseller, a plump and none-too-clean Irishwoman, regarding her from the other side of the pushcart.

"If I could charge for that story itself, why, I wouldn't let it go for under a t'ousand dollars," the woman said, tapping the book with a grimy forefinger. "You heard me right! A t'ousand dollars! And I'd call it a bargain, too, for the two lives you got there. Why, you can't find a man who wants to open a door for you these days, never mind one who wants to dig you up when you're dead just to hold you again. Cathy and Heathcliff, now them was two people who knew what was what. They knew what love is. It's a disease, sure it is! Worse than the typhoid and it'll kill you just as quick. Best keep clear of it, I say."

Fiona laughed. "I couldn't agree more."

The woman smiled, emboldened by her response. "There's a few more lives in there, too – Edgar and Isabella and Hindley, but they're pretty small ones and I'd throw them in for free . . . if I was selling the *story*, mind. But that's the beauty of it, darlin', it's only the book I'm selling! A few sheets of paper, some scraps of leather to hold them together. So I can sell it cheap, you see. Dirt-cheap! For you, half a dollar."

Fiona squashed her inborn instinct to haggle, one that had been nurtured by her mother at the Whitechapel markets, and paid the woman her price. She herself made a very good living, and though it was expected, she would not barter with one who worked so hard for hers. She slipped the book into the briefcase she carried and turned to go home. It was after seven now and she didn't want to keep Nick waiting any longer.

As she started back toward West Street, her eyes were again drawn to the blond chestnut seller. He was trying to convince a group of dockers to buy his wares, but they were headed home to their suppers and had no interest. He tried to entice a pair of factory girls, and after that, a priest – all to no avail. Raggedy children clustered around him, begging for the hot nuts. Fiona noticed he slipped them one now and again, saw how a little girl held it in her bare hands to soak up its warmth before she ate it. Then, turning to search for new customers, the lad spotted her. Instantly, he turned his patter on her, smiling and flirting and telling her more than she wanted to know about chestnuts in general and his fine specimens in particular.

"Go on, missus, try one," he urged, tossing one chestnut and then another at her, forcing her to catch them. "There y'are, ladies and gents," he added approvingly. "Never met a woman yet who'd didn't want to get her hands on a hot pair of nuts."

The ragamuffins giggled. An older woman, her basket on her arm, winked at her. Fiona, blushing, dug in her briefcase for her wallet, scolding herself for succumbing to the charms of a handsome barrow boy yet again.

"Will it be one batch, missus, or two?"

"I'll take everything you have," she said, fishing out a bill.

That shut him up for a few seconds. "What? All of 'em?" he finally asked.

"Yes, all of them," she said, eyeing his blue fingers, thinking he ought to have a proper pair of gloves.

"Right away," he said, picking up his scoop. He shoveled chestnuts until he had nearly a dozen paper cones filled. Fiona paid him, then handed the cones to the urchins who'd been watching the transaction longingly. "Thank you, missus!" they cried, stunned at her generosity. She smiled as they raced off with their prizes.

When the lad turned from his till – an old cigar box – to give Fiona change from her five dollars, she was gone.

He scanned the crowd for her and glimpsed her heading toward West Street. He shouted for her, but she didn't turn around. He asked his neighbor to watch his stall, then bolted after her. She'd left nearly four dollars' worth of change. He reached the curb just in time to see the cab she'd flagged pull into the stream of traffic. He shouted again. She looked at him from the cab's rear window. He waved the bills at her. She turned away. The carriage picked up speed.

The lad stared after her, puzzled as to how any woman with such a beautiful face and nice clothes and so much money to throw around could have such incredibly sad eyes.

60

"Darling? What on earth are you doing?" came a voice from inside. Its languid, molded tones pulled Joe Bristow from his reverie. His memories rose like mist over a lake and vanished.

He turned away from an open window. Across the room, a black-haired woman watched him, propped up on one elbow in her carved ebony bed.

"Stargazing," he replied.

She laughed. "How whimsical. Close the window, won't you? I'm freezing to death." She lit a cigarette and took a deep drag, her green cat's eyes fixed hungrily on him. She was naked except for a pair of jeweled Indian earrings. Her flawless skin, always pale, looked even whiter set against the red-and-magenta embroideries that canopied her bed. Her body was taut and lean with small breasts and slim hips. Her straight black hair just grazed her jawline. She'd had it cut – a daring move, even for her. "Come back to bed," she purred, exhaling a plume of smoke.

"I can't," Joe said, pulling the doors closed behind him. "I've got an early day ahead of me. Going to Camden Town to suss out the market. See if the area would support a Montague's." He walked across the room, gathering his clothes off the floor. He was talking too quickly. He knew he was. And the excuse he'd offered was a lame one. But he couldn't stay. He had to get away from her before she saw it – the sadness, profound and racking – that always descended upon him after he slept with a woman he did not love.

"Camden Town?" she asked, her eyes narrowing. "But Camden's closer to my house than yours. It's going to be a trip from Belgravia to Greenwich tonight and back to Camden in the morning." She sat up. "What possesses you to live in Greenwich anyway?"

"I like my 'ouse," he said, slipping out of his borrowed robe. "I like my orchards. I like being near the river."

"No, that's not it," she said, her eyes roving over his body, taking in his long, muscular legs, lightly furred with blond hair; his perfect bum; the graceful flare of his back.

"It isn't?"

"No. It's because you can keep the world at arm's length out there. And your lovers."

Joe started to say something placatory, but she waved his words away. He hoped she was not going to be difficult.

Maud Selwyn Jones had invited him to her home for a late supper. To discuss business, she'd said. She was a decorator – the best in London – and he'd hired her to unify the look of his forty-five Montague's shops and work on the interior of the new Knightsbridge flagship. She didn't need to work – not with her money – but she said it kept her amused and angered her father, which was always fun. As well-known as she was for her decorating, she was even better known for her outrageous exploits. Trekking in Nepal. Riding a camel across Morocco. Camping with Bedouins in Arabia. Her former husband, a drunken boor by all accounts, was killed during a trip to Cairo. He'd insulted the owner of a restaurant after a meal had disappointed him and had been found in an alley two days later, stabbed. Robbers, the police had said, but no one believed them. Maud, already rich from her father's Welsh coal money, had inherited his millions, too. She was a restless soul who loved any country as long as it wasn't England. She especially loved the East, and – rumor had it – when she couldn't go there, she settled for the East End. For the dark streets of Limehouse and its notorious opium dens.

She and Joe had drunk a good deal of wine during dinner and had followed it with brandy in her drawing room. After the bottle had been emptied, she'd walked over to his chair, knelt down between his knees, and kissed his mouth. He'd enjoyed the kiss, but when it was finished, he'd tried – fumblingly – to explain that he wasn't a very romantic bloke . . . that he wasn't . . .

"What?" she'd asked mockingly. "Not the marrying type? Don't flatter yourself, darling, it's not your heart I'm after." Then she'd proceeded to undo his trousers and use her full, rouged lips to make him forget himself. Just for a bit. To forget the constant pain of living without Fiona. They'd gone to her bedroom and he'd tried to lose himself completely in her lovely, eager body. And he'd succeeded . . . for a little while. He'd even fooled himself into believing that he'd escaped the sadness completely this time. But he hadn't. When it was over, the pain came back twice as hard. As it always did after his lust had cooled and his body had been sated but his heart found itself cheated – found itself still broken, still empty, still full of a longing that could never be satisfied.

"Are you certain you'd rather not stay?" Maud asked. "You can have one of the guest rooms. You don't have to spend the night here." After he declined again, she said, "You are the most alone man I've ever met, Joe. As wary and damaged as a wounded tiger."

He didn't answer. Dressed now, he walked over to her bed and kissed her forehead. Then he pulled the covers over her and told her to sleep.

"I don't sleep, darling," she said, leaning over her night table to light her lamp and the hookah next to it.

Maud's servants had all gone to bed, so Joe let himself out. As he walked toward Eccleston Street, hoping to find a hackney, the familiar sadness descended upon him like a great black bat, enveloping him in its leathery wings. He was thankful for the icy winter night, thankful to be alone. This evening had been a mistake. One he'd made before, and one he would undoubtedly make again. He'd been with women like Maud on other occasions. Women who didn't ask for what he couldn't give. Who made demands on his body, his time, but never his heart. Women who were walled off in some way. Guarded. Damaged.

Damaged. How funny, he thought. That's exactly what Maud called me.

He smiled bitterly. He was beyond damaged. He was broken. Smashed to bloody pieces. He was alone in the world without the one person who could make him whole. And he always would be.

61

"Nothing, Peter? Nothing at all?" Fiona said, staring at her stockbroker. "That's impossible!"

"No, not impossible," Peter Hurst said, leaning back in his chair. "Just unusual. They've been getting harder to find, as you know. I was only able to get you two thousand last week. Five hundred a fortnight ago. This week they've dried up completely."

"Why?"

"Because no one's selling! Everyone who was willing to sell has done so – to you. Because of you, Burton Tea has become an extremely illiquid stock."

Fiona, who'd been pacing her office as Peter was speaking, found herself by the riverside windows. The gray sky, sodden with spring rain, cast a pall over her. She looked out at the broad river below, but didn't see the Hudson. She saw another river. Another wharf. She saw gray fog swirling around it, and a dark figure waiting there. For her. She closed her eyes against the image, against the rage and pain the sight of the dark man stirred in her. Still.

Once a week for the last ten years, she had met with Peter to buy shares of Burton Tea. At first, when the stock was trading between fifteen and twenty dollars a share, she'd struggled to buy even minuscule amounts – ten shares one week, twenty the next. As her fortune had grown, she doggedly acquired as many as she could. Now, owing to the company's troubles in India and America, the stock – when it could be found – could be bought for around five dollars a share. But price wasn't the issue for Fiona; it was finding a seller.

To date, she'd accumulated twenty-two percent of Burton Tea under a score of different corporate names, not one of which – thanks to the shrewdness of her attorney, Teddy Sissons – was traceable to her.

Her stake in Burton Tea was huge, but it wasn't enough. She would not stop buying shares until she had fifty-one percent – and the company. Ten years had done nothing to diminish her hatred of William Burton, and no matter what it cost, she would ruin him. It wasn't justice – she knew she would never have that – but it was retribution. The only flaw in her plan, as ever, was that it made no provision for Bowler Sheehan. She had spent entire nights pacing her bedroom by candlelight, racking her brain for a way to ensure that he, too, paid for what he'd done. But she'd never been able to figure out how. The only way was to make Burton name him as a co-conspirator in her father's murder. But to do so, Burton would first have to confess his own guilt – something he would never do. No matter how many times she gnawed at the problem, she could not find a solution. She'd lived with the terrible knowledge of what Burton and Sheehan had done to her father – to her whole family – for a decade. And here she was, still waiting. Still impotent. Hobbled by her broker's inability to find more shares and by her own inability to conceive of a way to destroy Sheehan. How much longer would she have to wait?

Hurst shuffled his papers together on his lap. "I'll do my best, Fiona, but I doubt I'll get more shares before the month's end."

She turned on her heel. "Peter, I need them *now,* not next month! Send someone to London. Find the shareholders and shake the stock out of them!"

"I understand your frustration," he said, taken aback by the sharpness in her voice, "but you have to realize that you own twenty-two percent and the owner himself retains fifty-one percent. That doesn't leave a great deal in circulation."

"I can't believe he still holds fifty-one percent. He'll have to sell some soon."

"He's held them this long, Fiona, he's not going to sell now."

"But he's up to his neck in debt," Fiona said, sitting on the corner of her desk. "He's borrowed nearly three hundred thousand pounds from Albion Bank. His Indian estate went bust and his venture into the American market failed miserably." She smiled grimly at the memory. She herself had single-handedly engineered that disaster by undercutting his prices fiercely – even at a loss to her own bottom line. Burton's agents had set up shop on Water Street in June of '94. They were closed by January of the following year. "He needs to raise cash, Peter. He's going to sell some of his own shares. He has to."

Hurst shook his head. "Fiona, I must tell you – not just as your broker, but as your friend – that I don't understand your obsession with this stock. I never have. The company, as you pointed out, is not financially sound. You're right about the debt. It's too heavy. One more disaster and his ability to meet his loan repayments could be jeopardized. You have an astronomical amount of money invested in Burton Tea. These stocks are nothing but liabilities. You don't need any more of them. What you need is –"

"Peter, you don't know what I need!" Fiona shouted. "Just get me the goddamned shares!"

Peter blanched. Not once, in all the years they'd known each other, had she ever spoken to him so harshly. He stood up, tucked his papers into his briefcase, and said he hoped to have something for her next week.

Ashamed of herself, Fiona laid a hand on his arm. "I'm sorry. I didn't mean to snap at you. I just . . . I'm not myself today . . ."

He looked up from his bulging briefcase, concern mixing with the hurt in his eyes. "I knew something was wrong the minute I walked in here. You look terrible."

And she did. She wore a charcoal waistcoat with black

594

passementerie closures, a crisp white blouse with a gray-and-black-striped silk cravat tucked into the collar, and a slim black skirt. The dark colors emphasized the newly deepened hollows of her face and the fact that she'd lost a good deal of weight. Her irrepressible vitality was diminished. She seemed small somehow. Fragile.

"It's Nick, isn't it?" he asked, his eyes darting to the photograph she kept on the credenza behind her desk.

"Yes," she admitted, angry at herself for losing control, for letting fear and emotion get the better of her. This was something she didn't want to talk about. Talking about it made it real.

"I thought it had to be family. The only other time I've ever seen you as upset as you are now was when Seamie had appendicitis. Is Nick's health not good?"

Fiona shook her head. Her face crumpled. She swore, then covered her eyes with her hands, as if trying to press her tears back in.

"Fiona, what happened? Is he all right?"

She was unable to answer. She felt his arm around her, heard him awkwardly murmuring comforts. When she finally lowered her hands, he pulled a crisp white handkerchief from his pocket and handed it to her.

"How bad is he?"

She took a deep breath. "I'm making more out of it than it deserves," she said. "He's weak, mainly. And he doesn't have much appetite. He has to stay in bed most of the day, but just yesterday, he walked around the garden. He told me so when I got home."

"How long has he been like this?"

"Since February."

Peter's eyes widened at that. Fiona saw them and wished she hadn't told him. She wished he would leave. Now. She didn't want to see his fear. She didn't want to have to reassure him. It was all she could do to keep reassuring herself.

Two months ago – the very day her new machinery had arrived at the factory – she had come home from work eager to have supper with Nick, only to learn that he'd had a "spell," as Foster had put it. She'd raced upstairs to see him and found him tucked up in bed, white and frail and working to draw breath. She'd kissed him and pressed his face between her hands, nearly hysterical with worry, until Eckhardt, who'd been sitting by his side, led her away. He explained that Nick had overtaxed his heart and needed to rest.

"He'll be all right, though, won't he? Won't he, Dr. Eckhardt?" she'd asked, her voice breaking, her fingers digging into the doctor's forearm.

"He is resting comfortably, Mrs. Soames. Look at him . . . see? A little difficulty with the breath, a little weakness. It will ease."

Fiona had nodded then and let the doctor's calm voice soothe her. She briefly wondered if he might be withholding the truth, but dismissed the thought. An unflinching realist in most areas of her life, she continued to remain willfully blind to the truth where Nick was concerned. She wanted him to get better, and therefore he *would*. Signs to the contrary frightened her, but she refused to see them as a pattern of decline and explained them away as mere potholes on the road to recovery.

"What does Eckhardt say?" Peter asked.

"That his symptoms will ease," she replied. A voice inside reminded her that Eckhardt had said that two months ago, and since then Nick had shown little improvement. She silenced it.

"It's just a setback, then. A temporary condition."

Fiona nodded. "That's right. He'll be up and about again shortly."

Peter smiled. "I'm glad to hear it." He gave her a peck on the cheek and told her to call on him if she needed anything.

After he left, Fiona looked at the clock. It was six. She thought about packing up her things and going home early. She could catch up on her unfinished work in her study, after supper.

She'd always loved coming home at night to windows lit up against the darkness and Nick waiting for her in the drawing room, eager to hear about her day, but now she found herself feeling anxious as evening approached. There was only Foster to welcome her. Nick was always upstairs in bed. Sometimes he was awake, and sometimes he wasn't. She would stand outside his bedroom door when he wasn't, wishing she could go in to him, sit on his bed, and talk to him. Needing to lay eyes on him, to see for herself that he hadn't lost any ground during the day. She tried to be optimistic. Maybe tonight he'd feel like coming downstairs and sitting in the drawing room. They could share a bottle of claret and chat in front of the fire, just as they'd always done.

The Fifth Avenue mansion was stolid and imposing from the outside, but warm and welcoming inside. They'd built it when Nick had first begun to slow down. He'd wanted to be able to get to the Park and the Met without traveling. He'd decorated the place beautifully – all four floors of it, with its grand entrance, huge dining room, library, study, double parlor, conservatory, huge kitchens, and countless bedrooms. No fusty antiques were allowed, only pieces commissioned from the new guard. Windows, mirrors, and lamps from Louis Comfort Tiffany. Silver from Archibald Knox. Furniture and chandeliers from Émile Galle. Paintings from Nick's beloved French artists and from the new cadre of American painters he championed.

Fiona smiled now, thinking about the wonderful times they'd had there. So many parties and dances. She was rarely there during the day, but at night she often returned to find an impromptu dinner for friends in full swing. Or maybe an anniversary celebration for Michael and Mary, who'd married back in '91, or a birthday party for one of their children. In the summer there were always picnics in the backyard complete with lanterns in the trees, music, an assortment of starving artists, plus Seamie home from boarding school, sneaking champagne and dancing with pretty art students. Nick loved to entertain, loved an evening filled with friends, food and wine, noise and laughter, gossip and drama.

Fiona's smile faded. It had been weeks and weeks since laughter had filled the house. Friends had come to see Nick, of course, but Eckhardt permitted no long visits, no boisterous behavior, nothing that would tire his patient. She felt a small tremor shake the foundation of her hope, her insistent optimism, and a sadness, thick and choking, move from her throat to her eyes. Tears brimmed again. She wiped them away angrily. "Stop. Just stop it," she told herself. "Right now."

She gathered her papers and shoved them into her briefcase, then grabbed her coat and hurried out, not even stopping to wish her secretary a good evening. She wanted to go home. To her house with its massive marble walls, it solid front door, its iron gate. It was a fortress, that house. It had kept her and Nick and Seamie warm and safe all these years. They'd wanted for nothing inside it, feared nothing. Until now. Now a dark thing stalked, circling, sniffing the air, waiting for its chance.

She knew this beast; it had visited her before. But she had learned to be vigilant. She would lock the doors against it. She would stand guard. And this time, it would not get in.

62

"God, Nick, I can hear your teeth chattering from here," Teddy Sissons said. "I'm going to put another log on the fire."

"Thank you, Teddy," Nick said, drawing a cashmere throw around his shoulders. Since his collapse he was always cold. He leaned forward, refreshed his and Teddy's teacups, then sat back again, tired from even so small an effort. His condition was grave. Eckhardt had told him that he didn't have long, and he was eager to put his affairs in order. He knew he should be in his bed, not in the drawing room, but his bedroom, with all of Eckhardt's medicines and liniments lined up on his night table, felt oppressive.

Out of all the rooms in his house, he loved this one best. It wasn't the most fashionable, but it was the most comfortable. It was filled with squashy, down-filled settees and armchairs, fat silk cushions, and ottomans, and it had a huge fireplace, perfect for roasting oneself. Most of all he loved this room because it contained so many memories of happy times with Fiona. They had spent countless nights and lazy Sunday afternoons here, curled up on the settee in their stocking feet, Seamie between them, planning and scheming and dreaming.

"There!" Teddy said, clapping soot off his hands. "Now that's a fire!"

"Fire? It's a blast furnace! Could you have stuffed any more wood in there?"

"You need the warmth, your hands are blue." Teddy seated himself again, pushed his glasses up on his nose, and returned his attention to the thick document on the table before him, Nick's will. "As I was saying, I think you're overly concerned. Even without a will, state law mandates that all your possessions, all your holdings and assets, go directly to your spouse. No one can contest that."

"You don't know my father. The second I've departed this vale of tears, I know for a fact that the odious man will – at the very least – try to prevent my trust fund from passing to Fiona. It's worth a great deal of money. Well over a million pounds the last time I checked."

"A *million* pounds? Your Albion fund?" Teddy asked, jotting down notes.

"Yes."

"When you and Fiona were married, that fund was only worth about a hundred thousand pounds. What on earth did you invest in?"

Nick waved a hand. "God knows."

"You don't keep tabs on your own trust fund?"

"Not really. I know that the original stocks my father bought appreciated in value over the last ten years. And that he bought a very large block of shares from some company or other three or four years ago and plunked them in my account. I have no idea why he did this. They don't produce income. In fact, they've lost a good deal of their value."

"Does your estimate of a million pounds reflect those losses?"

"Oh, Teddy, I don't bloody know," Nick sighed. "Ask Hermione. She keeps track of the statements and deposits the checks. I haven't touched a penny of my father's money for years. As soon as the gallery started to make money, I gave all the income generated from the trust away."

"All of it?"

Nick nodded. "My father has been supporting New York's artists for years. He also helped fund the Met's expansion and provided them with a comprehensive collection of work from new American painters." He grinned.

"Wasn't that generous of him? When I'm gone, I want Fiona to have the fund. Every penny. She'll put it to good use."

"Have you discussed this with her?"

"I've tried. She refuses to talk about it."

"Is she here? We should apprise her of your wishes and your father's likely reaction to them."

"No, she's not. She's been hovering for days. Bringing me all my meals and every pot of tea herself." He laughed. "I can't even go to the loo without her following me. She hasn't gone to work for over a week, but the minute she heard you were coming over she found a reason to go out. She's afraid, I guess. I've tried my best to keep the truth from her and I succeeded for quite a while. But it's rather undeniable these days. I mean, look at me, I'm a ghost."

"Not yet, you aren't. And don't get any ideas while I'm sitting here, either."

Nick smiled. "Undertaking not in your line of work?"

"No, it damn well isn't." He started writing again. "All right, what else besides the fund? Go slowly, one thing at a time. We need to be specific."

Nick proceeded to itemize his assets and possessions for Teddy and his instructions for how they were to be apportioned. Nick's share of the house would go to Fiona, as would all of its furnishings, his art gallery and all his paintings, and his personal possessions. In addition, he specified a generous legacy for Seamie, whom he'd always thought of as his son, and who, in fact, still called him Father, not Nick. He also made monetary bequests to Ian Munro and Nell Finnegan, and Sean, Pat, and Jenny Finnegan – Michael's and Mary's children – and Stephen Foster, his butler.

"Spell it out clearly, Teddy," Nick said. "Make it airtight. I don't put it past the man to try and take everything from Fiona, from the house right down to my cuff links."

"Nick, don't worry about it. I want you to rest –"

". . . in peace?" Nick smiled wickedly. He couldn't say such things in front of Fiona, they upset her, but he could in front of Teddy and he was glad. Steady Teddy, he and Fiona called him. Always smooth and unruffled, always capable. He'd saved them both from a scandal when Nick was arrested at The Slide, and he'd guided them through the minefields of rules and regulations involved with the growth of their businesses. Teddy was a counselor in every sense of the word, a rock. He never got emotional or teary and Nick needed that now. He needed someone tough and unsentimental whom he could joke with, for he was determined to face death the same way he'd faced life, with a healthy measure of flippant disregard.

"I was going to say *easy*. I assure you, as long as your marriage is legal – and yours is – your father cannot claim your legacy. You were married in a court of law, and again at Trinity Church . . ."

Nick nodded. A few months after his courthouse wedding, when he was certain Fiona truly did not want a divorce, he insisted they marry in the Anglican faith – his family's faith – to make certain his father could never question the legitimacy of their union.

"The documents for both ceremonies were duly recorded and filed. Everything's fine. Are you certain your father doesn't know you're married?"

"I can't imagine he does. I'm sure he would've made trouble by now if he did. I don't believe he knows anything about me at all."

"He never communicates with you?"

"No."

"But surely he must inquire about you. Perhaps through other parties?"

"My father hates me, Teddy."

"I'm sorry. I didn't know it was daggers drawn."

Nick shrugged. "Don't be. One can't pick one's relatives, unfortunately. Only one's friends." He leaned back into the cushions, tired from all the talking, and closed his eyes for a few seconds while Teddy organized his notes. When he opened them again, he looked at a portrait of Fiona and said, "Teddy, it's as a friend that I need to ask you to do something else for me."

Teddy looked at Nick over the top of his glasses. "Anything. You know that."

"Take care of Fiona," he said, his glibness gone, tears glistening in his eyes. "She needs people to look after her, you know. She may not look like she does, but she does. She rushes around all the time and she doesn't eat properly and she works far too hard and . . ." His voice cracked. He couldn't finish. He swore at himself under his breath, not wanting to get all damp and emotional in front of his smooth, unflappable friend.

Teddy gave him a minute to collect himself, then said, "You know you don't need to worry on that score, either. I'll take care of her. And so will Seamie and Michael and Mary and Alec and Maddie and Nate and Stuart and Peter and everyone who loves her."

"I want her to marry again. She's still young. She could have children, a proper family. It's what I want most of all and it's the one thing I can't put in any will. I want you to be a matchmaker for her."

"It's not one of the firm's specialties, but I'll try," Teddy said, trying for levity. "Who do you have in mind?"

"Who indeed? That's just the problem. She's richer than most of the men in this city and smarter than all of them."

Teddy laughed and Nick did, too. But it was forced. Exhausted now, Nick said his good-byes and rang for Foster to help him back to his bed. As they heard the butler's footsteps in the hallway, he turned to his friend and counselor, his Steady Teddy, one last time. "Look out for her," he said. "Promise me."

"I promise," Teddy said, awkwardly wiping his eyes on his sleeve.

63

Joe scooped up a handful of freshly shelled peas and inspected them. They were unblemished, smooth, a clutch of perfect, tiny green jewels. He held them to his nose and inhaled. They smelled so good – of rich Kentish dirt, of spring. He chewed a few. They were deliciously crisp.

Bristow's of Covent Garden imported the finest fruits and vegetables from around the world year-long to satisfy the desires of its wealthy and demanding clientele. Joe had only to send a clerk from his office downstairs to the warehouse to enjoy the luxury of a ripe, sweet peach in the winter, but even with the bounty of the globe at his fingertips, he loved nothing better than the first gifts of spring from the good English soil.

As he continued to sample his produce, he suddenly heard a voice at his ear. "How do you expect to make a profit, monsieur, if you eat up all your wares?"

Joe laughed, pleased to see his friend and customer Olivier Reynaud, head chef at the Connaught. He took the man's huge mitt of a hand, pink and thick-fingered, and trickled a stream of peas into it – all the while telling him how good they were, how fresh – the first crop! – how beautiful they'd look framing a salmon steak or pureed into a soup with mint and cream.

Olivier nibbled, nodded, and ordered six bushels of peas, one hundred pounds of new potatoes, two crates of asparagus, three of spinach, two dozen vanilla beans, four crates of oranges, and three crates each of mangoes, pineapples, and bananas. "Did they finally throw you out of your office?" he asked, eyeing Joe's rolled-up shirtsleeves and his vest, already smudged with soil.

"Oh, I'm just pitching in," he replied. "The 'ead seller came up at five to tell me two of 'is men were out sick today and could I send a clerk down to 'elp out. Only one lad was in and 'e was busy writing up orders, so I came down. Didn't want to overwork the poor sod."

"You mean you didn't want him to have all the fun."

Joe laughed, caught in a fib. "Aye, that, too. 'Ere, 'ave a look at these." He pulled a length of cotton sacking off a small willow basket and Olivier smiled with delight. Inside, carefully nestled in a bed of white rice, were fresh truffles, coal-black and pungent.

"Dug from French soil two days ago," Joe said proudly. "Look at that . . . feel it," he urged, handing the man a particularly large specimen. "Firm, plump, and spotless. The very best the Perigord 'as to offer. Shall I put you down for two dozen?"

"Two dozen? Are you mad? Twelve! I have a budget." Olivier lifted the truffle to his nose, then regarded it with a soft and dreamy expression. "The perfume . . . it's indescribable, no? The very scent of fucking."

Joe shook his head. "You frogs. Can't keep the kitchen and bedroom separate, can you?"

"And why should we? Both are the stuff of life. But how can I expect a man who eats this . . . *merde*," – he pointed to Joe's half-finished sausage roll sitting in a wad of crumpled paper atop a crate – "to know it?"

"What's wrong with it?" Joe asked. He loved to wind Olivier up. "It's sturdy fare for a sturdy English belly!" Despite a weakness for sausage rolls, fish and chips, and various other foods of his childhood, Joe's culinary tastes were as refined as his friend's.

"Pah! You English have no belly! No tongue! I come to London not just to cook, my friend, but to educate. To teach you Saxon mules what is real food. And what do I get? Fillet returned because it's too rare. No one to eat my calves' brains. Requests for that damned Worcestershire sauce with *everything*! I could serve them rocks and they would never know the difference!"

"Rocks in onion gravy, maybe," Joe admitted.

"Come to my kitchen tonight and I show you what real food is," Olivier ordered, jabbing a finger into Joe's chest. "And bring a woman, for God's sake! You eat like a barbarian and live like a monk. Give me those." He pointed at the truffles.

"Twelve, you said?"

"No! All of them!" Olivier shouted, in a lather now. "What? Shall I leave this treasure to be ignored? Or, worse yet, mistreated by some English bungler!"

"Would you like this delivered, Olivier?"

"All but the truffles. I take them now. And I see you tonight. Nine o'clock sharp!"

Joe smiled as his hotheaded friend marched off. He was pleased with himself. None of the young bucks he'd hired to sell could move a wagon load of fruits and vegetables, plus an entire basket of pricey truffles *and* get themselves a personal invitation from the finest chef in London. But whom to bring? Jimmy was busy with wedding plans these days. Maybe Cathy.

He picked up a grapefruit and smelled it. To him, its scent was sweeter than the most expensive French perfume. He turned to survey his huge warehouse, bustling with porters loading orders onto wagons, with sellers moving goods, with chefs from the best restaurants, hotels, and clubs making their selections, and felt a flush of pride. Then he looked at his watch – it was now seven o'clock – and felt a twinge of guilt. He wasn't supposed to be down here in the warehouse. He was supposed to be upstairs making his way through a mountain of paperwork. He'd meant to. He'd even come in early to get a head start, but when the head seller had come upstairs saying he needed another pair of hands, he hadn't been able to resist. He had to go sell, just for a while. He promised himself he'd only stay an hour, and he'd already been here two. But how could he tear himself away? He never got to work the floor anymore; he was always going over numbers with accountants, or arguing over plans for new shops with architects and builders. He missed the warehouse. Nothing excited him like the challenge of selling.

"There he is!" he heard someone shout. He was caught.

He turned around, the grapefruit still in his hand, and smiled at his brother Jimmy, his second-in-command, and Cathy, his pretty, blond sister, who worked for him at his largest shop, the Chelsea branch of Montague's.

"We pay blokes to do this, you know," Jimmy said.

"Just keeping me 'and in," Joe said defensively.

"We should get 'im a barrow, Jimmy. Put 'im back on the 'Igh Street flogging apples and oranges, that's where 'e belongs," Cathy teased. "If you can bring yourself to put that grapefruit down, maybe you could take me to see the new shop I'm supposed to run. We were supposed to meet there 'alf an hour ago."

"Bloody 'ell! I completely forgot! Sorry, luv. I'll just grab me coat and we'll go."

Joe placed the fruit back in its crate while Jimmy and Cathy headed upstairs. As he bounded up after them, he heard them excitedly discussing the Knightsbridge shop. All three siblings had huge hopes for what was going to become Montague's new flagship. Cathy was going to manage it. She was a smart girl – all of eighteen now – quick, outspoken, a little brash. She could be a handful at times, but she was family and the only person Joe trusted with something as important as the flagship. Jimmy, twenty-six years old, and a fruit and veg man through and through, wanted to distinguish it as the premiere destination for the best, most exotic produce in London. It would have all the usual goods, of course, but it would have things many Londoners had never even seen before: blueberries, okra, and pumpkins from the States; giant gooseberries, litchis, and kumquats from China; guavas, papayas, and star fruit from the tropics; fiery hot peppers and giant watermelons from Mexico; tamarinds and coconuts from India. And Joe, he simply wanted it to be the best, most modern, most comprehensive grocer's in the world – the very pinnacle of his ambitions.

". . . but lettuce and endive and spinach, those are delicate goods," he heard his sister say. "If it's too warm they wilt; too cold and they'll be black in no time. 'Ow are you going to 'old them properly? From what you've described, you 'aven't got enough space to –"

"Just listen, would you? You never let me get a bloody word in! We've got a misting system installed. Joe thought it up. It keeps all the delicate stuff crisp. Like you just picked it."

"A misting system?" Cathy repeated, giving her brother a shove. "You're 'aving me on!"

"I swear, Cat."

"Crikey, Jimmy, really?" she asked, excited now instead of skeptical. "Do the blokes from 'Arrods know? They'll be fit to be tied!"

"Nobody knows and you can't tell anyone, either. It's going to make 'Arrods –"

"It's going to make 'Arrods look like a tatty 'ole-in-the-wall," Joe said, twisting both their ears as he raced past them through the foyer. "Come see the plans!"

Inside his office, spread across a huge oak table, lay the blueprints for the flagship. Joe and Jimmy took Cathy through it. The first floor was open, its ceiling supported by large columns. It would contain all of the fresh foodstuff and produce. In the back a wide marble staircase led to the second floor, where the flower shop was located, as well as fine chocolates and candies, coffee and tea counters, a tobacco counter, and a section for fine wines. On the third floor there was a restaurant where shoppers could partake of a light meal or afternoon tea.

"Oh, Joe, it's wonderful!" Cathy exclaimed. "What's the decor like? What are the colors?"

"Well, it's dramatic, I can say that much. London won't 'ave seen anything like it."

"Maud?" Cathy asked.

"Um . . . not entirely."

"Joe, what 'ave you done?"

"Bought murals of the four seasons for each of the ground-floor walls. Thumping great paintings! Maud's in agreement. She thinks they're brilliant. They give the place a very distinctive look. Of luxury. Exclusivity."

"Blimey, Joe, it's a *shop*, not a museum."

Joe held his hands up. "I know, I know . . . just don't say anything until you see them, Cathy. They're very spectacular and unexpected and just the thing to set us apart from the competition."

"What about white? What's wrong with white tiles on the walls?" Cathy asked.

"They're awful. They'd make the place look like an abattoir."

"And the floors?"

"All tile. Not white, though, blue and green. With hidden drains. You'll be able to 'ave your girls wash things down. Slosh soap around and all," Joe said. Cathy looked relieved. She was a stickler for cleanliness and was known to sack people on the spot over streaky windows or dirty floors.

"And for the second floor? And the restaurant?" she asked.

"Peacocks," Jimmy said.

"*Peacocks!* Shitting all over the place? 'Ave you two gone mad?"

"Not real birds, just paintings," Jimmy said hastily.

Cathy looked from Jimmy to Joe. "I can't wait to see this place, I think. It is finished?"

"Nearly," Joe said. "Maud's working round the clock to get everything done before 'er trip. She goes to China next month."

"I know. She stopped by the Chelsea shop last week to shout at the painters. They got the color wrong on the window trim." She grabbed a pencil and held it like a cigarette. "Aubergine, darling," she said in a dramatic voice.

"I told them aubergine and they've given me bright fucking purple!" She touched the back of her hand to her forehead and sank to the floor in a pretend faint.

"Get up, you silly git. She's nothing like that," Joe said.

"She is! You should've seen 'er 'air! She cut it off!"

"I've seen 'er 'air. Are we ready?"

"Is that all you've seen?" Cathy asked, smiling cheekily at him from the floor.

Joe blinked at his sister. "I beg your pardon?"

Cathy shrugged. "Just wondering," she said, hopping up. "Maud said she can't wait to go to China. Seems she wants to get shut of a certain blue-eyed devil. Didn't give any names. I was wondering if you might know who 'e is?" She looked directly at Joe.

"I wouldn't," he said brusquely, reaching for his jacket. "Come on, let's go."

"Good! I'm glad," Cathy said, stopping her brother to straighten his tie. "Because I 'ave someone else in mind for you. She's going to be at Jimmy's wedding. A nice girl from Stepney –"

Joe took his sister by her chin. "Stop. Right now," he said sternly. "I'm not looking for a wife. I'm married to my work and that's the way I like it, all right?"

"All right, all right," Cathy said, slapping his hand away. "I'll keep quiet."

"I doubt that," Jimmy said.

"Just for *now*. Come on, 'urry up. I want to see the shop. Time is money and you two are wasting both." She strode out of Joe's office breaking into the first verse of "Bow Bells."

Joe looked at Jimmy. Jimmy looked at Joe. He shrugged. "It was your idea to put 'er in charge of the flagship," he said. "Good luck, old son."

64

Nick lay in his bed watching the moonlight stream in through the window. Agitated, unable to sleep, he felt as if a ten-ton weight were sitting on his chest. It was difficult to breathe. It was such work to pull the air in and push it out again. It tired him immensely.

He rolled over and propped himself up on his pillows, trying to alleviate the pressure on his straining lungs. It didn't work. Instead, a paralyzing spasm of pain shot through his chest and down his left arm, making it go numb.

Nick knew he was dying and he was afraid.

All that he loved best was here in this world – Fiona, her family, all their friends. Paintings and music. Cold champagne. White roses. Who knew what the next world held, if there even was one. A stern God who would surely disapprove of him. Mopey angels like the ones Giotto painted. Pious saints. A lot of sanctimonious old farts floating around on clouds. That was no place for him and he didn't want to go there.

Another pain gripped him. He moaned softly. The disease was torturing him. He wished for a release from it, and yet he was terrified to let go. He struggled to draw air, to bear the pain in his chest, to keep the fragile embers of his life burning.

The pain softened its grip slightly and a comforting image came to him – the face of his old love. Seeing Henri soothed him. Wherever he was headed, maybe Henri would be there waiting for him. And maybe it wouldn't be as awful as he imagined. Maybe it would be a wonderful place. A sunny Italian villa, perhaps, where he could meet Leonardo and ask him who his Mona Lisa was. Where he'd share a bottle of wine with Michelangelo and find out who that gorgeous David was. Or maybe it was Paris, where he'd have supper with Vincent in a café by the Seine and Vincent would be jolly and well-fed for a change because everyone in heaven bought his paintings. A place where it was always June and always warm and roses were always in bloom. A place were he could live happily with Henri.

He lay back against his pillows now, feeling more peaceful, less afraid. But then another troubling thought disturbed him. If he left now to be with Henri, what would happen to Fiona?

He turned his head and looked at her. She was asleep in the big armchair she'd had Foster pull close to the bed, a book open in her lap. For the past few nights, he'd been able to make her go to her own bed around midnight or so, but tonight she'd refused to leave him. She'd sat up as he drifted in and out of sleep until exhaustion had finally overtaken her.

How he loved that face with its determined chin, full mouth, and honest blue eyes. She could be such a hard, bossy piece of work when it came to her business, but with those she loved she was kind, generous, and utterly devoted. She had given him so much happiness. He smiled, thinking about the surprises life holds in store. When he'd left London, banished by his father, he'd been alone, with no friends, no one to care for him. And then he'd found her. He remembered how she looked on the train platform in Southampton as she picked up his things – her worried face, her shabby clothes, and that accent! He would never have imagined then that he'd marry this Cockney girl, live with her in a New York mansion, and be happy and loved.

He wanted so much for her – success and security, but

mostly he wanted her to find someone to whom she could give her heart completely. Someone who understood who she was and would never try to change her, someone like the boy she'd loved in London. That foolish lad had lost a jewel when he lost her.

But would she? he wondered anxiously.

And then he saw Henri again. He was walking away from him, toward a beautiful stone house set amid fields of lavender. He was wearing an old blue smock; his hands were covered with paint. He turned, beckoning, and suddenly Nick could smell the sweet summer air and feel the sunshine on his face. Arles, that's where he was going. To their house in the south of France. Of course! Hadn't Henri always said that's where they should live?

"I can't," he whispered tearfully. "I can't leave her."

In the moon-washed darkness of his bedroom, he cocked his head as if listening to a distant voice. He nodded, then turned to the sleeping Fiona.

"You'll be all right, Fee," he whispered. "I know you will."

Fiona jerked awake. "What's wrong, Nick? Are you all right? Do you need Dr. Eckhardt?"

"I'm fine."

She blinked at him groggily. "What is it, then?"

"I just wanted to tell you that I love you."

She smiled with relief. "Oh, Nicholas, I love you, too," she said, stroking his cheek. "Now go back to sleep. You need to sleep."

"All right," he said, knowing he wouldn't but closing his eyes anyway to make her happy.

Fiona settled back in her chair and picked up her book. Within minutes, she had slipped back into sleep.

Nick now felt as light and insubstantial as the night air. He had the oddest fancy that he *was* the air, and the night and all the green living things just outside his window. He felt one last, brief, agonizing pain as the weak and swollen artery at the base of his heart burst, filling his chest with blood. Taking quick, shallow breaths, he closed his eyes. The pain eased. A trace of a smile danced on his lips.

A few seconds passed, then Nicholas Soames sighed softly. His large and generous heart faltered and was still.

65

In the verdant, tranquil grounds of Trinity Church's uptown cemetery at Broadway and 155th Street, the Reverend Walter Robbins committed Nick's body to the ground and his soul to God.

Fiona stood by the grave as she'd sat in the church, staring ahead, her expression blank, utterly detached from the service. The minister's words were babble, his prayer book and cross, props. Nick was dead and nothing he had to say could give her comfort.

". . . our brother Nicholas is in heaven now, at rest in the bosom of Abraham. He has joined our Savior Jesus Christ in the promise of life eternal . . ."

Fiona wished she had the man's smug confidence. How the hell did he know where Nick was? She wished she could put a stop to this pretense of knowledge and authority on his part, and to the farce of manners and decorum on the part of the mourners. She looked around now at the people, all in proper attire. Black gowns and suits; black kid gloves; jet stickpins and brooches. Sniffles here, a sob – quickly stifled – there. Dainty handkerchiefs pressed to moist eyes. No loud or unseemly displays.

Fiona wanted to be both loud and unseemly; she wanted to howl. She wanted to push the lid off Nick's coffin, pull him out, let him see the sky and the clouds and the new green leaves one last time before the lurking undertaker packed him into the sodden ground. She wanted to hold him tightly and kiss his cheek and ask him if he'd had any idea how happy he'd made her, how much she had loved him. She wanted to scream her grief to the skies and wail like an animal, but she couldn't.

This wasn't a Whitechapel wake, it was a New York society funeral, and all of society was in attendance. People from the museum. Artists Nick had represented. Her own colleagues and clients from the tea trade. Many of her employees. Seamie. Her Uncle Michael and Aunt Mary. Ian, who was grown now and a banker. Ten-year-old Nell. Sean and Pat, the six-year-old twins. Baby Jenny, nestled in Mary's arms. And Alec, still sprightly at seventy-five. Fiona knew she would have to keep herself in check in front of them all, to keep her emotions tightly contained, twisted up inside her in a neat, hard little knot. She stood perfectly still, her fists balled at her sides, alone with her sadness and anger, wishing that the minister would just shut up. That he would stop his fatuous pronouncements, slap his prayer book closed and admit that he didn't have one damn clue where Nick was. And while he was at it, he could acknowledge that he, too, found God's general level of incompetence absolutely intolerable.

Fiona had decided long ago, after she'd lost her family and nearly lost her life, that God was little more than an absentee landlord. Careless, uninterested, busy elsewhere. Nothing had happened since then to cause her to reevaluate her conclusion. She found it hard to believe in a Supreme Being who allowed her mother and father to die cruel deaths, while permitting murderers to flourish. She had often heard priests and ministers, when flummoxed by a hard question, respond by saying, "God works in mysterious ways." As if that explained everything. It didn't. In fact, it made Him sound like some cheap magician. A banco tout, a sleight-of-hand man, a con.

". . . never doubt that God gives us the strength to bear our grief . . ." the minister continued.

Fiona looked at him closely. He was little more than a boy. Blond, pink-cheeked, pudgy. Maybe twenty-two years old. Probably fresh out of divinity school. The apple of his mama's eye, no doubt. His robes were new and of excellent quality. She looked at his feet. Family money, she thought. Hand-stitched calf was not purchased on a young minister's salary. He wore a thick gold wedding band that was still shiny. Newly married. Maybe a baby on the way.

What can you tell me of grief, reverend sir? she wondered, searching his benignly somber face. She herself was well acquainted with it and knew there was no bearing the unbearable. The best you could hope for was to survive it.

She watched as Nick's coffin was lowered into the ground. The minister sprinkled earth over it, reminding everyone present that they were but dust and to dust they would return. And then it was done. People started to leave the gravesite. Fiona stayed put. There would be a supper at Michael's now. How on earth would she get through it? She felt a strong arm around her shoulders. It was Seamie. He kissed the top of her head. He could do that now. At fifteen, he was already two inches taller than she was and the very image of their brother Charlie. He was taller than Charlie had been at that age, and not as muscular, and he was a proper little American gentleman, not a swaggering East London lad, but his mischievous green eyes and ready laugh, his good heart and manly disposition were exactly the same as his older brother's.

Charlie would have been twenty-six now, she thought. A grown man. She wondered what he would have made of his rough London life had he been allowed to live it, the same as she wondered what Seamie, with private schooling, summer hiking trips, winter skiing trips, and so many other privileges and opportunities, would make of his.

For years she had cherished hopes that Seamie would return to the city to share both her house and her business after he graduated. But as he'd gotten older, she'd begun to have doubts. The boy lived for the outdoors. He spent his school holidays hiking and canoeing in the Catskills and the Adirondacks, and was burning to explore the Rockies and the Grand Canyon. Nothing excited him more than discovering a new plant, insect, or animal. His grades reflected his passions – he was at the top of his class in the natural sciences, mathematics, geography, and history. And at the bottom in English, Latin, and French.

"That lad has the soul of a tinker," Michael often said. "Same as your da before he met your mam. Sure, you'll not get him to settle down and sell tea. He'll be off for parts unknown."

Fiona knew her uncle was right. Seamie would travel the world. Nick's legacy plus the trust fund she had established for him would enable him to do so. He'd write her from Cairo and Calcutta and Katmandu and descend upon her between adventures, but he would not work in the tea trade or live on Fifth Avenue. She would grow old in her large and beautiful house alone.

"Come on, Fee," Seamie whispered, giving her a squeeze. "It's time to go."

She leaned her head on his shoulder, allowing herself to be led. He'd come home from his school, Groton, two days ago for the funeral and she was glad of it. His presence comforted her in a way no one else's could. They'd come through the worst together, crossed an ocean, started life anew, and their bond was deep. Fiona knew how much she would need him in the days to come. After the drama of death was over, after all the commotion of a funeral – that's when the hard part began. When you sat alone with your sorrow. Seamie always knew exactly what to say to her when she was at her lowest, always sensed when she needed to feel the warmth of his hand in hers.

Teddy Sissons and his wife came up to her and asked her to please call on them for anything she needed. They were followed by other people saying variations of the same thing. Good, kind people. People who meant well, who loved her and whom she loved. Yet now, she couldn't bear the sight of them. She went through the motions, nodding, thanking them, trying to smile, and was relieved as they drifted away from her toward their carriages.

"You're staying with us tonight, Fiona. You and Seamie," Michael said from behind her. Fiona turned around. Her family was assembled, ready to depart.

She shook her head. "I couldn't, Uncle Michael, I –"

"Don't argue, Fiona," Mary said. "This is one fight you won't win. We've plenty of room and I won't have you two rattling around in that big house all by yourselves."

She managed a smile. "Thank you," she said, embracing her aunt.

"I'm going to plant a white rose, a climber, right by the headstone. He'd like that, would Nick," Alec said. His chin quivered. He turned away, wiping at his eyes. "I'd best tell them diggers not to roll the sod right up to it," he added, walking off toward the grave.

"Seamie, Ian, go with him, would you?" Mary asked. "He doesn't see as well as he used to. I'm afraid he'll fall in."

Ian trotted after his grandfather, followed by Seamie. Mary shepherded her brood toward the family's carriage. Michael told her he'd be along in a minute.

"How are you holding up, lass?" he asked Fiona when they were alone.

"I'm fine," she said. "Really."

She looked at her uncle and saw that he did not believe her. "I miss him, Uncle Michael. I miss him so much."

"I know you do. We all do." He took her hand and held it, awkward in his emotion. "It'll be all right, Fiona, you'll see. It's only the body that's gone. Only the body. There's a part that doesn't go in the ground, a part that stays inside you forever."

Fiona kissed her uncle's cheek. She appreciated his kind words and only wished she could believe them. She didn't feel Nick inside her. All she felt was a vast, aching emptiness.

"It's time we were going," Michael said. "Do you want to ride with us?"

"No, I need a few minutes to collect myself. I'll go alone. Will you take Seamie?"

Michael said he would and Fiona walked toward her carriage, desperate to be by herself, if only for a short while. As she neared it, she saw a tall man, expensively attired, standing by it, his back toward her. He turned at the sound of her steps and removed his hat. His hair was silver now, but he was still handsome, still elegant.

"Will," she said falteringly. She didn't offer him her hand for fear he would not take it. She barely knew what to say. They hadn't spoken to each other in any meaningful way since they'd parted company a decade ago.

"Hello, Fiona," he said. "I'm sorry . . . I wanted to . . . how are you?"

"Not very well," she replied, looking at the ground.

"No, I can't imagine you would be. What a stupid thing to ask." He was silent for a few seconds, then said, "I heard that Nicholas . . . that he passed. I wanted to come to the funeral, but I didn't know if you would want me there. I came here instead. To offer my condolences."

Fiona raised her eyes to his. "Why?"

He smiled sadly. "Because I, of all people, know how much he meant to you."

Fiona dropped her gaze again. A sob shuddered through her body. And then another. Will's words, his unspoken forgiveness, touched her deeply. The tight knot of emotion in her chest loosened, releasing all the sorrow and anger inside her.

She started to cry. Will took her in his arms and let her.

66

Fiona sat in her office, her elbows propped up on her desk, her fingers pressed to her temples, trying to massage away her splitting headache. In front of her was a memo from Stuart, a sales report on her newly launched Quick Cup. She had tried to read it four times already, but couldn't get beyond the third sentence. Under it lay a pile of letters and invoices that needed her attention. Her secretary was waiting for them. She knew that if she didn't make a start, a proper one, she'd never get through it all.

A gust of May air blew in through an open window, rustling her papers and caressing her face. She shuddered. Spring mocked her. Outside, green things struggled to life. Tulips, freesia, and daffodils showed their bright faces to the sun. Dogwood, magnolia, and cherry trees burst into bloom. And children ran shrieking with delight through the park, arms outstretched, welcoming the world back to life.

But spring's beauty did not lighten her grieving heart, it only made it heavier. She shrank from the warm sunshine that fell on her shoulders and winced at the happy twittering of the birds. Everything and everyone was giddy with the promise of spring, and she? She felt dead inside. Nothing gave her joy – not the opening of a new tearoom, nor a successful ad campaign. Not even the flowering of her beloved tea roses. It was all she could do to drag herself to work every morning. She could barely muster the energy to harangue Peter Hurst for more Burton shares, or to try and learn if she'd sold ten tins of Quick Cup or ten thousand.

Her wall clock chimed the hour. Two o'clock. She groaned. Teddy Sissons was due any minute to go over Nick's will. She wasn't looking forward to his visit. She couldn't bear to be near anyone lately. Merely talking to people was a strain. Sighing, she returned her attention to Stuart's memo, determined to make headway. When she was halfway through the first page, a knock on the door interrupted her.

"Fiona?" a voice called.

"Hello, Teddy," she said, forcing a smile. "Come in. Can I get you a cup of tea?"

"No, thanks," he said, setting his briefcase down on her desk. "I'd prefer to get right down to it. I have to be at the courthouse by four."

Fiona cleared room for him. He pulled a sheaf of papers out of his case and sat down. As he sorted them into order, laying them neatly on the desk, his glasses slid down his nose. She leaned across the desk and pushed them back up.

"Thanks," he said absently. He looked up at her. "How are you doing?"

"Fine. Better, much better."

"You're a terrible liar."

She gave a weary laugh. "Bloody awful, then. How's that?"

"It's truthful, at least. All right . . . here we are." He handed her a copy of the will. "Most of it's routine, but there are a few things I'm going to need your instructions on."

He began rattling off the points of the will, detailing all of Nick's non-monetary bequests. He apologized for the lengthy, technical language, but explained that Nick had insisted everything be strictly by the book. Fiona tried her best to follow along, but the words swam in front of her eyes. By the time he got to Nick's various bank accounts and how they were to be disposed of, her headache was excruciating. Just as she thought she couldn't last another second, he turned the final page of the document.

"That's it, Fiona," he said. "Except for one last thing."

"What?" she said, wincing from the pain.

"As I'm sure you know, Nick had a private investment fund at Albion Bank in London. His father settled a sum of money upon him when he left England, a sum that was invested in various stocks and which, in turn, produced income."

She nodded.

"This fund, too, was left to you. Its value currently stands at nearly seven hundred thousand pounds."

"Teddy, that can't be right. That's over three million dollars!"

"Yes, I know. It was worth even more at one point. A lot more."

"But *how?* That account was only worth about a hundred thousand pounds when we married."

"There was an additional purchase of stock."

"By whom? Nick? He refused to go near a broker. Or a bank."

"No, by Lord Elgin. His father. Shortly before he died, Nick told me his father had added shares to the account. He also said that he didn't expect him to relinquish the money without a fight. Although the fund clearly belongs to you, Randolph Elgin could try to block its transfer, and in my opinion, he will. I've yet to see someone turn over what amounts to more than three million dollars without a fight."

"So fight him, Teddy. Do whatever it takes. I'll pay for it. Nick's father is a horrible man. I'd be delighted to deprive him of the money. I rather relish the idea of using it for some positive end. Something Nick would approve of. Maybe scholarships for art students or a bequest to the Met."

"All right," Teddy said, riffling through more papers until he found the documents he wanted. "You'll need to tell me whether you want the fund as it is, with its current investments intact, or whether you want to liquefy it and have the sterling wired to your bank."

"Liquefy it," Fiona said, massaging her temples again. She was irritable and impatient to be done.

"Are you certain? It may be easier to get Elgin to give up shares rather than a lump sum of cash. As I recall, there are some good earners here and one rather large dud. Let's see . . . Abingdon Publishers . . . Amalgamated Steel, that's a good one . . . Beaton, Wickes Manufacturers . . . Brighton Mills . . . Oh, here's the bad apple! It's a tea company, Fiona. Burton Tea. Christ, why did Elgin buy so much of it? And why did he hang on to it? It's lost two-thirds of its purchase value."

Fiona stopped rubbing her temples. "Teddy, what did you say?" she whispered.

"Um . . . Burton Tea?"

"How many shares exactly?" she asked, scrabbling for a pen and paper.

Teddy ran his finger down a column. "Quite a lot, actually."

"Teddy, *how many*?"

"Four hundred and fifty thousand."

Fiona caught her breath. Teddy looked up at her. She looked back at him with eyes as wide as saucers. "That's how he did it," she said. "The lying, cheating bastard! I never understood how he retained fifty-one percent of his shares when he was so deep in debt. That's *exactly* how he did it."

"Did what, Fiona?"

She didn't answer him. Instead, she yanked open a desk drawer and pulled out a folder. She opened it, consulted the documents inside, and scribbled figures. "Fifty-two percent!" she said, her voice quavering. "I've got fifty-bloody-two percent!"

"Of *what*?"

"Of Burton Tea, Teddy. Let me see those," Fiona said, reaching for the statements.

He handed them to her. The most recent records were on top. She paged backward quarter by quarter until she found what she was looking for: the Burton Tea purchase. It had been added to Nick's fund in March of 1894. Elgin had paid nearly three pounds – about fifteen dollars – per share. The total of Burton Tea stock, plus Nick's other stocks – which had appreciated by then to just over one hundred and sixty thousand pounds – made the account worth about one and half million pounds, a staggering sum of money. She quickly fished out her own statements for the same quarter and found that she had paid between eighteen and twenty-one dollars a share for Burton Tea. Nick's shares had been acquired at a discount.

Next, she compared Nick's March '94 statement to his most recent statement – March of '98. Teddy was right: Everything but Burton Tea had made gains, and the Burton Tea losses had been so severe, that even with the other stocks' growth, the account had lost over half its '94 value. Nick's four hundred and fifty thousand shares of Burton Tea were currently worth just under five hundred thousand pounds.

The dates, the difference in share prices, the losses – they were all clicking into place.

"Teddy, get me Nick's fund. Intact," Fiona said, looking up from the statements. "No matter what it takes, do you understand me? I *must* have those stocks. Start tonight. Send a letter to Albion . . . no, a telegram . . ." Panic suddenly gripped her. "Elgin can't sell the stocks, can he?" she asked anxiously.

"Of course not. Nick's assets were frozen while the will went through probate here in New York. Now they legally belong to his next of kin. That's you."

"Good. Good. Inform Elgin of my wishes immediately." She stood up and started pacing. "Get the telegram out tonight, Teddy. Tonight. Can someone in your office do that? I want him to know first thing tomorrow morning. Go on, Teddy, leave now. My driver will take you. You'll just have time to stop by your office before you have to be at the courthouse."

Wearing an expression of utter confusion, Teddy was hustled out of Fiona's office and into her carriage. She made him swear that he would get the telegram fired off, then barked at her driver to take him to his office posthaste.

Back in her own office, Fiona sat down in her chair again, dumbfounded. She didn't know whether to laugh or cry. The Burton Tea shares she'd so desperately needed had been in her own husband's investment account all along. Thirty percent of the one and a half million issued. Right in Nick's hands.

It all made perfect sense. Burton would have needed money in '94 to finance his entry into the American market. He'd already borrowed three hundred thousand pounds from Albion by then. His shareholders knew it and – according to various newspaper articles Fiona had read – were uneasy about it.

In order to obtain the additional funds he needed without his investors finding out, Burton had probably offered to sell Elgin himself – not the bank – a chunk of his personal shares. And he'd offered them at a significantly discounted price, as Fiona had seen in the statements. Burton knew Elgin would keep the shares safe, for he'd undoubtedly convinced him that as Burton Tea established itself in America – a huge country with a growing population – their value would increase. When that happened, Burton would use his American-made profits to buy his shares back at the higher price and Elgin would make a killing.

Since the sale was to be kept quiet, Elgin would not have been able to use Albion's money. Albion was now a publicly held bank and its records were subject to its shareholders' scrutiny. So Elgin had used his own money and tucked the shares into a private account, Nick's account. He likely had his personal secretary or some trusted senior clerk administer it. They would have been the only two people in the bank who even knew the account existed. Elgin would naturally assume that the shares would be safe and that no explanations to Nick would be needed. As he well knew, his son hated everything to do with Albion. He would never seek to claim the shares; he had no interest in his investments, only the income they produced. And Nick had been gravely ill. When he died – unmarried and heirless – the fund would simply revert back to his family.

Both men must have thought it a perfect arrangement: Burton would have the loan he needed, Elgin would eventually make a tidy sum of money, and no one would ever be the wiser.

But there were two things Elgin had not wagered on: first, that Burton's expansion into America would fail, and that that disaster would render him incapable of buying his stock back; and second, that Nick wouldn't die – that he'd marry and leave everything he owned, including his investment fund, to his wife.

Fiona took a deep breath and blew it out again. She stood up, unable to sit still from the shock of what she had learned. Her eyes fell on the photograph of Nick she kept on her credenza. If only she'd known, but how could she have? He never told her what was in that account. He didn't know himself. He never even knew what he had in his wallet.

She picked up the photograph. For the first time since Nick had died, she felt him here with her. He was still protecting her, still watching over her. Though his body was gone, his spirit lived on in her heart. He was a part of her and always would be. Just as Michael had said.

A breeze blew into the room again and this time she didn't shudder. This time she smiled, imagining that the breeze's soft caress was Nick touching his hand to her cheek. She hugged the photograph to her chest, closed her eyes, and whispered "Thank you" to him, for this, his final gift.

67

"And so, to my brother James, I offer my sincere congratulations," Joe said, toasting at his brother's wedding breakfast. "And to my new sister-in-law, Margaret . . ." He paused, feigned a look of regret, then said, ". . . my 'eartfelt condolences."

There were whoops and catcalls from the guests, laughter from the bride and her sisters.

"That's very funny, Joe," Jimmy shouted over the din. " 'Ope the fruit you sell is fresher than your jokes. Can we eat now?"

"To Jimmy and Meg!" Joe said, raising his glass. "Long life, 'ealth, wealth, and 'appiness!"

"To Jimmy and Meg!" the company responded. Glasses were clinked, there were calls for the groom to kiss his bride and more catcalling as he did. As Joe looked around to make sure the waiters had started to serve, he felt a tug on his sleeve. It was his grandfather, who was seated next to him.

"There's something wrong with this," the old man said, pointing to his glass. "It's the queerest lager I've ever tasted."

"It's champagne, Granddad. From France."

"Frenchy beer? Too fancy by 'alf, if you ask me. What's wrong with Fuller's, lad?"

Joe stopped a waiter and instructed him to get his grandfather a pint of bitter from the kitchen. He told another one to open more champagne and get it poured. His guests had drained their glasses and were clamoring for more. He badgered a third to bring more bread. Then, for the first time that day, he sat down.

Joe was hosting his brother's wedding breakfast at his home in Greenwich and he wanted everything to be perfect. It was his gift to the couple. He adored his new sister-in-law, a girl from a Whitechapel costering family, one without much money, and he wanted to give her a lovely day. The caterers and florist had arrived at dawn to decorate the ballroom of his Georgian mansion, but as soon as the sun was up and he saw that the day would be fair, he changed his mind and had them bring everything outside. The ballroom was nice, but nothing could top the beauty of his grounds.

Joe's home was an old manor house whose softly rolling hills and fertile fruit orchards ended at the Thames's south bank. Ancient oak trees dotted the landscape, as well as cherry trees, dogwoods, and climbing roses. Formal flower gardens were laid out behind the house. Joe had had the tables set up just beyond them. From where they were seated, his guests could see his flowering apple, pear, and quince trees in the distance, and beyond them, the river.

As he looked around, mindless of the food that had been put in front of him, concerned only with his guests' enjoyment, he had to smile. His father was eating a piece of lovely coral-colored salmon and talking to his neighbor, a fishmonger, about the merits of Scottish smoking methods versus Norwegian. His sister Ellen, whose husband was a wholesaler at the Smithfield meat market, was nodding approvingly at the bacon. Another neighbor from Montague Street, a Mrs. Walsh who made her living selling flowers outside the West End theaters, was admiring the table arrangements. Joe's Cockney family and their friends were more demanding at table, more exacting in their tastes, than any earl or duke could ever hope to be. Costers all, every man and woman present had strong opinions as to who grew a better potato – Jersey or

Kentish farmers – what type of feed made for a better gammon steak, and who produced the superior strawberry – the English or the French. They argued as vociferously over which butcher turned out a better banger and who fried up a better piece of cod as their titled counterparts did over whose club served the best beef Wellington.

"Uncle Joe! Uncle Joe!"

Joe turned around. Ellen's children, three tow-headed moppets, descended upon him.

"Mum says there's a cake," Emma, the youngest, said. "A pretty one with flowers on it!"

"There is, pet. Would you like to see it?" All three children nodded. "It's in the pantry. Go take a peek." They started off. "And, Robbie . . ."

"Yes, Uncle Joe?" the eldest said, turning back.

"I'll take that fork, thank you."

Robbie marched back and surrendered the fork he'd tucked into his back pocket, then dashed off giggling.

" 'Ooligans, them three," his grandfather said. "Aren't you going to eat your breakfast?"

"I will, Granddad; I 'ave a bit of business to attend to first, though. Be right back."

Joe walked over to Jimmy and Meg. "Everything all right?" he asked them.

"Joe, luv, everything's wonderful!" Meg said, taking his hand. "Thank you!" A freckle-faced redhead, she had chosen a high-necked organdy dress in a warm off-white. Jimmy had given her a pair of pearl eardrops for a wedding gift and her mother had tucked white roses into the neat coiled braid at the nape of her neck. Joe had always thought her a pretty girl, but the flush in her cheeks, and the radiant softness in her eyes every time she looked at her new husband, made her beautiful.

"I'm glad you're enjoying yourself. Do you think I could borrow your 'usband? I'll only keep 'im a minute."

Meg said she wouldn't mind and Jimmy followed Joe toward the house.

"What's up?" he asked.

"Got a wedding gift for you."

"Another one? Joe, it's too much –"

"No, it isn't. Come on." He took his brother into his study, closed the door behind them, and motioned to a large flat box on his desk. "Open it," he said.

Jimmy lifted the top off and pulled back a piece of soft green flannel. A large rectangle of brass flashed back at him. He read the inscription: BRISTOW'S OF COVENT GARDEN WHOLESALE PRODUCE, JOS. AND JAS. BRISTOW, PROPRIETORS, then looked at his brother, stunned.

"Jesus, Joe . . ."

Joe took his hand and shook it. "Partners," he said.

"I never expected this. Why did you do it? It's your business, you started it . . ."

"And I never could've made a success out of it without you. It's your business, too. Just thought we ought to formalize things. The solicitors are doing the paperwork. Ought to be finished next week. Between your new salary and 'alf of the assets of London's biggest produce wholesaler, you shouldn't 'ave any trouble buying Meg that 'ouse in Islington she likes."

"I . . . I don't even know what to say. Thank you." Overcome, he grabbed his brother and pounded him on the back. Then he picked up the plaque and tore out of the study to tell his bride of their good fortune.

Back outside, Joe watched them – Jimmy beaming as Meg traced the letters of his name – with a wistful smile. Jimmy had done well for himself. He'd married a wonderful girl, a girl he truly loved. They'd have a family soon. And now, with the partnership, he'd have the means to keep his new wife and their future children comfortably.

Joe himself was a millionaire several times over. Even with giving half the wholesaling business to Jimmy, he still owned all the Montague shops and Montague's lucrative door-to-door delivery business. And yet, watching his brother, he felt like a pauper. Out of the two of them, only Jimmy had what was really valuable.

Standing with his hands on his hips, Joe suddenly felt someone hook an arm through his.

"That was a nice thing you did, luv," his mother said.

"No more than 'e deserved," Joe said. "I should 'ave done it long ago."

Rose was wearing a russet silk dress he'd bought her and a paisley shawl. Older, grayer now, she still looked pretty to him. Years ago, he had insisted that she and his father move out of the damp, drafty Montague Street house to a nice new terraced house in Finsbury. They stayed for a week, then, lonely for Whitechapel and their friends, they went back to the old place and refused to budge. Joe, conceding defeat, bought the house for them and had it fixed up. Though he'd settled a large amount of money on them, his father still sold at the market every day but Monday with his mother by his side. Their big splurges were a new barrow and frequent attendance at the music hall.

Rose looked at her son's face. She followed his gaze to Jimmy and Meg. "Thinking about 'er, were you?"

"Who?"

Rose gave him a look. "It's been ten years, luv."

"I know how long it's been, Mum, so stop before you start. I wasn't thinking about anyone."

"All right, I won't say a word. It's just that I worry, that's all," Rose said gently. "You're nearly thirty years old. You should 'ave a wife. A family. 'Andsome, successful man like yourself. I know ten lasses who'd give their eyeteeth for one like you."

Joe groaned, but there was no stopping his mother.

"All I want is for you to be 'appy, luv."

"I am 'appy, Mum. Perfectly 'appy. My work keeps me very, very 'appy."

"Oh, rubbish. You work as 'ard as you do so you

never 'ave to stop and think about 'ow un'appy you really are."

"Mum, I think Granddad needs some 'elp with 'is kipper. Why don't you —"

"There you are!" a bright female voice exclaimed. It was Cathy. "Why on earth are you standing 'ere skulking, Joe, when you should be talking with your guests? Sally's 'ere. She's sweet on you. Thinks you're a smasher."

Joe laughed. "Sally Gordon? Your little school friend? She's what . . . ten years old? She needs a nursemaid, not an 'usband. Is she even out of braids yet?"

"Yes, she is. You might actually notice 'ow pretty she's become if you could bring yourself to stop mooning after a ghost."

Joe looked away. That hurt. Cathy had gone right to the bone. As usual.

"That's enough, lass," Rose cautioned.

"Someone 'as to tell 'im 'e's wasting 'is life, Mum," she said defiantly. "Might as well be me." She looked at her brother, lifting her chin as she spoke. "Fiona Finnegan's a million miles away and she's married to a toff and she's not coming back and that's that. Sally Gordon's right 'ere and she's in love with you. She can 'ave 'er pick of lads, but you're all she talks about. God knows why. She'd change 'er mind right quick if she knew what a mopey old pickle you are!"

"I said that's enough!" Rose snapped. Cathy flounced off.

"A mopey old pickle?" Joe said, laughing despite himself.

"That's the one child out of all of you I could never control," Rose fretted, scowling after her youngest. "I 'ope you know what you're doing 'iring 'er to run the new shop."

"I do. I wouldn't 'ave anyone else."

"She is a smart lass, I'll give 'er that," Rose said. "And good'earted in 'er way. And mad about you. She loves you, Joe. Wants the best for you, like we all do." She squeezed his arm. "You know, you really should be talking to your guests. And it wouldn't 'urt you to say 'ello to Sally. Just to be polite."

Joe covered his mother's hand with his own. "Let's go find Sally, then. But no matchmaking, Mum. I don't need a wife. I've got you and Cathy to 'enpeck me and that's all one man can stand."

68

"He's going to fight, Fiona," Teddy Sissons said, slapping a thick bundle of documents down on her desk. "These arrived at my office this morning. His lawyers are good. They've thrown up every obstacle I anticipated and a few more besides."

As Fiona started reading the papers, Teddy sat down. He took a handkerchief from his pocket, removed his glasses, and mopped his brow. It was an unseasonably hot June day.

"This is outrageous!" Fiona exclaimed. "He's offering me a third of the shares' value in cash if I withdraw my claim immediately. A bloody third! And the offer expires in sixty days, after which time I will receive nothing! This is completely illegal. Can you believe the man's cheek?"

"I can," Teddy said, tucking his handkerchief away. "And as your attorney, I advise you to accept his offer."

"What?"

Teddy put his glasses back on. "I advise you to accept."

"But, Teddy, you know how much I want those shares," she said angrily, perplexed by his turncoat behavior.

"Let me finish, Fiona. You must understand something. This whole business is about to turn ugly. You're a very wealthy woman. You don't need these shares. You don't need this fight. Let it go."

Fiona tilted her head as if she hadn't heard him correctly. "I'm not afraid of a fight. What in the world makes you think I'd settle?"

"There's going to be a tremendous cost involved."

"I said I'd pay whatever it took –"

"In time as well as money," Teddy said brusquely, cutting her off. "Before the suit ever goes before a judge, they'll waste a year or two of your time and thousands of your dollars sending for original documents – your birth certificate, marriage license, Nick's will, his death certificate – all to establish your identity, to confirm Nick's, to verify that a wedding indeed took place. They'll tie up the proceedings forever."

"Perhaps someone from the firm could go to London with the documents in hand. It might be a good idea to have a man there keeping the pressure on," Fiona said.

"That wouldn't work. No one in my firm is licensed to practice in England."

"Surely you have affiliates there. What do you do if an American client dies and has assets in England?" Fiona felt she was stating the obvious and wondered why Teddy, who was usually such a bulldog, hadn't brought it up.

"Well, yes. There is a group of London barristers we work with."

"Then arrange a meeting for me. I'll go to London myself next week if I have to."

"What about your businesses? You can't just leave them."

"Stuart Bryce is more than capable of running TasTea in my absence and Michael can handle the tearooms and the grocery shops," she said.

Teddy shifted in his chair. Then he said, "When you have time to study the papers, you'll see that Elgin's lawyers got their hands on Nick's medical records. Not Eckhardt's – he wouldn't surrender them – but records from a Dr. Hadley. As I understand it, it was he who first diagnosed Nick's syphilis."

Fiona nodded. "Yes, that's true. Hadley was Nick's family's doctor."

"According to Hadley's notes, Nicholas contracted his illness from another man."

"How did the lawyers get these notes? That's all confidential information."

"If Hadley's a friend to Elgin, he probably handed them over."

"Why are you bringing it up, Teddy? What does it have to do with my claim?"

"A great deal. Elgin's lawyers intend to use Nick's syphilis and his . . . er . . . alleged sexual proclivities to argue that your marriage was a sham, that Nick was mentally incompetent from his illness when he entered into it, that it was never consummated, and that you've no rights to his estate."

Fiona shook her head, her eyes wide with disbelief. "They wouldn't dare."

"With this much money at stake, they certainly would."

"It makes no difference," she said hotly. "I'm still going to fight them."

"Will you?"

"Yes! You know I will," she said impatiently. "I've told you so again and again. Why are you even asking?"

Teddy looked away. After a few seconds, he cleared his throat and said, "Fiona, whether a marriage has been consummated is a terribly difficult thing to prove or disprove. But that doesn't stop lawyers from trying. Do you understand me?"

"No, Teddy, I bloody well don't! Stop being so delicate. Are you saying they're going to ask me whether Nick and I made love? I'll tell them we did."

Teddy turned his gaze on her. "You know, I've always admired your rather formidable will, your refusal to back away from difficulties. But sometimes strength isn't about perseverance. Sometimes it's about knowing when to quit."

"Teddy, listen to me –"

"No. You listen to me," he said sharply. "You have no idea what trial lawyers are capable of. What if Elgin's men insist that a doctor – one of their choosing – examines you? What if they come to New York to depose your household staff?"

"It'll never happen," Fiona said.

"Won't it? Compare the cost of sending a couple of lawyers across the Atlantic to losing over *three million dollars*! Of course it will! They'll ask your own maid if you and Nick ever shared a bed. They'll ask about stains on the sheets, Fiona. They'll subpoena your doctor and ask if you were ever pregnant. If you ever miscarried. If there's any reason why, in ten years of marriage, you failed to conceive."

Fiona swallowed, sickened by the very idea.

"Ugly enough?" Teddy asked. "Just wait. If they find things aren't going their way, they'll get themselves a London rent boy – some poor syphilitic who's sick and destitute. They'll pay him to say he had intercourse with Nick on several occasions. He'll give dates, times, locations. He'll know whether Nick had a mole on his backside or a scar on his thigh. They'll get an old school friend of his, someone with heavy gambling debts, to swear that he couldn't function with women."

"They can't do that!" Fiona cried, slamming her hands down on the desk.

"Don't be so damned naive! They can and they will! Randolph Elgin is not playing games. He wants to hold on to those shares every bit as much as you want to take them. He'll stop at nothing." Upset to find himself yelling, Teddy leaned back in his chair and took a breath.

There was silence in the room as Fiona got up from her desk and poured two cups of tea from the pot on her credenza. She put one in front of Teddy and took hers over to a window. As she sipped it, she gazed at the Hudson's gray waters. She had expected underhanded behavior from Elgin and he had not disappointed her. Yet she still found herself shocked that he would drag his dead son's past into a courtroom. Randolph Elgin, it appeared, was as ruthless as his associate William Burton when it came to matters of money.

Teddy wanted her to settle. To walk away from what promised to be a vicious fight. She knew his advice was prompted by a desire to protect her and she appreciated it. But it seemed to her that Teddy was missing something important. He'd read the letter from Elgin's lawyers and saw only a vile court battle brewing, but she saw something else. Something written between the lines. Fear. Randolph Elgin was afraid.

Clearly, he hoped that his threat to pry into her private life and expose the most intimate details of her marriage would scare her off. He must be worried, she reasoned, to stoop to such measures. He must think I can win. His lawyers have told him my claim is good and that he stands to lose Nick's fund. He's dreading the prospect of telling Burton he lost his shares. If he can intimidate me into dropping my claim, he'll never have to.

The knowledge that Elgin feared her gave Fiona courage. She would not back down. "Teddy, this is what I want done," she said, sitting down next to him. "Write Elgin's lawyers and tell them that one third is an insult. Tell them —"

"Fiona, I urge you to accept his offer. If you persist in your claim, I can no longer represent you. I gave Nick my word that I would look after you. I would be breaking my promise if I encouraged you in this."

"I'm going back to London."

Teddy heaved a great, defeated sigh. "When?"

"Within the week."

"Fiona," he said wearily. "I'm begging . . . *begging* you not to. They'll tear you to shreds. They'll make sure every sordid accusation makes the New York papers. There will be a scandal and this time I won't be able to stop it. You'll be ruined. You can close the doors to TasTea today. We all knew about Nick and it didn't make any difference, he was our friend. Not everyone is as open-minded. What Nick was is a sin to some people and they won't buy tea from you if they see you as a party to immorality."

Fiona took his hand and squeezed it. "Don't desert me now, Teddy. I need you. You've always been there for me. Always. Be there now."

Teddy looked into her eyes, trying – she imagined – to fathom a reason for her obsession. "Don't do this, Fiona, it's madness," he said quietly. "You'll destroy everything you've worked for."

"You're wrong, Teddy," she replied. "This is everything I've worked for."

69

"Sure, but it's been awhile since I set foot in this particular shithole," Roddy said, looking up at the Taj Mahal's garishly painted sign. He shifted his gaze to the brick building's upper stories and saw a row of broken windows. "That the damage you were telling me about?"

P. C. McPherson nodded. "All them windows, plus the door, were pushed in, and the till was robbed."

"Just last night?"

"Aye."

"Did Quinn report it himself?"

"No, one of the neighbors 'eard the glass going in and started shouting for the police. I 'eard the racket and came running. Told Quinn I'd sort it out for 'im, but 'e didn't want my 'elp. Said it was 'is problem and 'e'd take care of it. Trouble with some local lads, 'e said."

"A pair of mischievous little tykes named Bowler Sheehan and Sid Malone," Roddy said grimly.

"Aye, but which one? I'd always 'eard Quinn was Sheehan's man. You think 'e switched sides?"

"I don't know, but I mean to find out. Somet'ing's up. What with Malone suddenly making appearances, and Quinn's windows going in, there's a battle brewing for East London. I feel it. Whoever this boyo is, he's got himself some big plans and they include our side of the river."

"You think Denny'll tell you what's what?"

"He will if he doesn't want his fine establishment closed down. Come on, let's go."

Roddy opened the door to the Taj and went inside,

followed closely by McPherson. He was prepared for the usual unpleasantries – the surly glances and muttered curses. The vulgar remarks. The remains of someone's supper thrown at his feet, beer sloshed on his jacket, a bottle aimed at his head. He was prepared for one of Denny's girls to offer her services. Even for Denny himself to collar him and ply him with offers of whiskey and beefsteak, all on the house. But he wasn't prepared for what he did see.

Nothing. Absolutely nothing.

There was no one around. Not a soul. On a flipping Friday night. The lights were out. The billiard tables were empty. There were no punters lined up at the bar. There was no barman. Nobody was tucking into a nice fry-up, nobody was traipsing upstairs after one of the girls. He turned around in a circle, astonished by the quiet.

"Quinn?" he called out uncertainly. "Denny?" He got no answer.

He looked at McPherson, but McPherson was no wiser than he was. Hands on their truncheons, the two men walked behind the bar and through a door that led into the kitchen. Nobody was there either, but the sink was full of peeled potatoes. A rope of sausages had been placed on a wooden board as if someone had meant to cut it up.

The hair on the back of Roddy's neck started to prickle. Something was very wrong. He led the way back out of the kitchen, through the taproom, and up the main staircase. Quinn's office was just off the landing. Quinn himself or Janey Symms, Den's lady friend and madam to his stable of whores, would likely be inside. They'd explain what was going on.

"Quinn!" he shouted, outside the office door. There was no answer. He turned the knob, but the door was locked. "Den? You in there?" he yelled, thumping on the door. Still no answer. He was about to knock again when he heard a low, faint groan. He backed up, then charged forward, heaving his shoulder into the door. It shuddered, but held. He did it again. The lock gave way. He rushed in.

Dennis Quinn lay on the floor, lifeless eyes staring up at the ceiling, blood pooling about his body like an obscene red flower.

"Jesus Christ," McPherson said.

Roddy knelt down and felt Quinn's neck for a pulse, causing fresh blood to trickle from the knife wound there. His eyes traveled down Denny's body; his shirtfront was red with blood. As he stood up, he heard the groan again. It took him a second to realize it wasn't coming from the dead man. It was coming from behind the desk at the far end of the room. He knew what he would see – whom he would see – before he even got there.

Janey Symms lay on her side, gasping for breath, her skin slick with sweat. One hand was pressed to the deep wound in her chest, the other was stretched out in front of her. She looked at Roddy with wild, glassy eyes.

"Janey, who did this? Tell me. Give me a name."

Janey swallowed, tried to speak, but could not.

"Hold on, luv," Roddy said. "I'm going to get you to hospital." He took off his jacket, placed it over her, and tried to lift her, but she screamed in pain and he had to put her down. "I know, Janey, I know it hurts, just hold on, you'll be all right . . ."

Janey shook her head. She raised her hand. Roddy took it. She pressed it against the floor.

"We've got to go, Janey. I'm going to pick you up again."

Janey closed her eyes. With the last of her strength, she raised Roddy's hand and slammed it down. He looked at his hand, pinned down against the pine boards by hers, saw her crimson index finger and saw, finally, what she wanted him to see. She'd written the letter S on the floor. In blood. Her own blood.

"Sheehan," he said.

"Or Sid," McPherson said.

"Which one was it, Janey? Was it Sheehan or Sid Malone?" Roddy asked urgently. He knew she couldn't last much longer. Janey swallowed again. Her chest rose and sank rapidly. "You hang on," he said fiercely, squeezing her hand. "I'm going to get you out of here." But even as he was talking, he felt the life drain out of her. She was gone. Roddy shook his head, cursing. He released her hand. Already, the blood from her wounds was seeping across the floorboards, blotting out her *S*. "What's your guess?" he said, looking at McPherson.

"Sheehan if Quinn turned against him. Malone if 'e didn't."

"That's a big help," Roddy said. "Almost as big a help as our dead witness here, and the evidence that just got blotted out and the fact that there were probably fifty-odd people downstairs when whoever did this came in, and not one of them is going to come forward. Two people were murdered and we've got not'ing to go on. Bloody not'ing."

"You're right about that, Sergeant. But you were wrong about what you said earlier."

"What's that?"

"The battle for East London's not brewing. It's already begun."

70

Neville Pearson, a chatty, portly, bespectacled man of sixty or so, ducked around a ladder, stepped over a bucket of paint, and reached for Fiona's hand. "Mrs. Soames, is it?" he asked, shaking it so vigorously that her teeth rattled. "A pleasure. Teddy's written. Told me all about you."

He wore a fusty brown suit that might have been stylish twenty years ago and a yellow tattersall waistcoat that sported tea stains and bread crumbs. He was bald except for tufts of pure white hair on the sides of his head and he had the florid complexion of a man who enjoyed his food and drink. He looked nothing like Teddy or any of the other New York lawyers Fiona knew with their smart suits and haircuts, their manicured hands and expensive shoes. With his worn briefcase under his arm and his glasses perched low on his nose, Pearson looked more like a befuddled academic than one of London's most esteemed civil-law barristers, a Queen's Counsel.

"The pleasure is mine, Mr. Pearson," Fiona replied.

"Hmmm. Yes, well . . ." he said, looking around himself, ". . . let's try and find a quiet corner, shall we? I'd take you to my rooms, but the builders are tearing them apart. Terribly sorry about all this. We're refurbishing. A junior barrister's idea. Says the place looks old, behind the times. Wants us to look modern. A misuse of money and a blasted inconvenience, I say. Edwards!"

"Yes, Mr. Pearson?" a young man behind the reception desk replied.

"I need an office."

"I believe Mr. Lazenby's is free, sir."

"Good. Follow me, Mrs. Soames, and mind your skirts."

He led her from the reception area down a long hallway, telling her all about the venerable Gray's Inn – one of the four Inns of Court – how parts of it had been built in the fourteenth century and enlarged under the Tudors, and how it had survived all these years very nicely, thank you, without the assistance of know-nothing renovators.

Fiona smiled as she followed him, enjoying the sound of his voice. She had missed the music of English voices. New Yorkers skated roughly over their words, rushing through their speech as they rushed through everything else. Londoners delighted in their language, every one of them. From the plummy-voiced concierge at her hotel, his lips crisply forming his consonants, giving his vowels their due, to the cabby who'd brought her here – a Lambeth man who chewed his letters with relish, as if he had a delicious bite of beefsteak in his mouth.

The trip to Pearson's offices was the first outing Fiona had taken since she'd arrived at the Savoy Hotel yesterday. In the last twenty-four hours, she'd seen a city of wealth and refinement – a London she'd never known. Her suite was sumptuous and she was waited on hand and foot. The streets her carriage had traveled to the Inns of Court were airy and graceful, the houses and shops upon them elegant.

She knew, however, that this was not all there was of London. Eastward was another city, one of poverty, struggle, hunger, and hardship. It was the very Janus face of this London and it was waiting for her. She would venture there soon, not to its heart – Whitechapel was a place she could not yet bear to go, but to Bow. To see Roddy. It was a reunion she both longed for and dreaded. She was happy at the thought of seeing him again, but she knew she would have to tell him what really happened to her father, and she knew it would break his heart.

"Here we are!" Pearson suddenly exclaimed, stopping a few feet ahead of her. He pushed a door open, then said,

"Oh, my! Terribly sorry, Lazenby! Good day to you. And to you, too, sir. My apologies." He quickly pulled the door closed, and as he did, Fiona heard a man she assumed to be Lazenby tell Pearson that he thought Phillips's office was empty. And then she heard another voice, Mr. Lazenby's client, no doubt, tell Pearson his apology was unnecessary.

Something about that voice made her stop dead. It was a man's voice. A warm voice. Lively and humorous, and very East London. She took a few steps forward and grasped the doorknob, entranced by the sound of it.

"This way, Mrs. . . . ah . . . Mrs. . . . oh, blast!"

"Soames," Fiona said, removing her hand from the knob. What on earth was she doing? She couldn't just barge in on a barrister and his client.

"Yes, of course. Soames," Pearson said, leading her toward a staircase. "Let's try the next floor. That office is occupied. Very important client. See him here all the time, but I can't remember his name. I'm terrible with names. Barton? Barston? Something like that. Owns a huge chain of high-end shops. What are they called? Montague's! That's it!" He turned to Fiona on the staircase and knocked on his pate. "Gears still work after all," he said, pleased.

Fiona wondered, not for the first time, exactly what Teddy had been thinking when he recommended this man.

"Very successful chap, that Barton," Pearson continued. "Pulled himself up from nothing. You're in the same line, aren't you? In addition to the tea business? I think I remember Teddy mentioning a chain of shops in his letter. You must make a point of visiting a Montague's. Very superior establishments." He stopped again at the top of the stairs. "I say – he's opening a flagship in Knightsbridge next week. Having a big do to celebrate. The whole firm is invited. Why don't you join myself and my wife? We could have supper somewhere first, then go on to the party."

Fiona politely declined the invitation – she had more important things to think about than parties – but Pearson persisted. It seemed as if the man would not budge until she agreed, and so, eager to discuss her claim, she did. Pleased by her acceptance, he ushered her into an unoccupied office, barked at a passing clerk to bring them tea, then settled down to business.

He reread the papers Teddy had sent, then asked her myriad questions. As he did, his absentminded air fell away and Fiona discovered that Teddy had indeed put her in the hands of an astute and experienced counselor.

"Your claim is most assuredly legitimate, Mrs. Soames," he finally said, still perusing the documents. "And it will certainly stand up in court."

"I'm glad to hear it," Fiona said, relieved.

"But, as Teddy surely told you, it will be a lengthy and expensive process."

Her heart sank. "Isn't there something you can do to hurry this, Mr. Pearson? Are there no corners you can cut? No way to push a claim through the courts quickly?"

Pearson looked at her over the top of his glasses. "One cannot hurry the law, Mrs. Soames."

She nodded, chastened. "How long do you think it will take?"

"I'll need a few days to study the documents in detail and make some inquiries. Then I'll be able to make an estimate. I feel I must caution you against being overly optimistic. I know Elgin's lawyers. I am confident we will win in the long run, but they won't make it an easy victory. Or a pleasant one. Do you take my meaning?"

"I do, Mr. Pearson, and I am prepared for the unpleasantries."

Pearson gave her a long look, gauging her sincerity, then said, "Very well."

He said he would contact her in a week's time, then stood to walk her to her carriage. On the way out they again passed Lazenby's office. And again Fiona heard the voice that had captivated her. It was slightly raised this time, yet muffled by the heavy door. It was foreign to her – she was certain she had never heard these measured,

648

authoritative tones – yet it was so compelling. Again her hand went to the knob.

"No, no, this way, Mrs. Soames," Pearson said, motioning her to him.

For the second time that day, Fiona wondered what had come over her. She followed Pearson to the foyer and took her leave.

71

Roddy O'Meara stole a sideways glance at the elegant woman on his arm. She was so polished and had such a commanding presence, it was hard to believe she was once a barefoot girl in a patched dress and pinafore, listening wide-eyed by the fire to his stories of fairies and leprechauns.

Until she turned those remarkable blue eyes on him. And then it wasn't hard at all. The girl was still there, in her eyes. The face was a woman's now, fine-boned and faintly etched at the brow by life's cares and concerns, but the eyes . . . they were still as excited, as lively as a child's. Warm, but full of steel, too. Defiance, even.

She has those eyes from her father, Roddy thought. The defiance as well. It was what had led Paddy to take up his union work, and what had led his girl to escape Whitechapel and make such an extraordinary success of herself.

He suddenly felt sad, thinking of his old friend, but did his best to hide it. He didn't want to depress Fiona by dwelling on painful memories and spoil their wonderful reunion. She had come to the house for dinner and Grace had cooked a proper English meal – roast beef and Yorkshire pudding with all the trimmings. There were tears and laughter all around when he'd opened the door to greet her. Neither he nor Grace could believe how much she'd changed. And Fiona, for her part, hadn't wanted to let go of either of them. She wouldn't allow him to take her hat or Grace to pour her a cup of tea until she'd hugged them and kissed them over and over again. Her driver had followed her in with parcel after parcel, each sporting the name of some elegant New York shop. There was a beautiful hat for Grace and a pair of ruby earrings, and for him a smart cashmere jacket and a set of gold cuff links. For the children – Patrick, the eldest at nine; Emily, who was seven; Roddy Junior, who was four; and Stephen, who'd just turned one – there were toys and games and sweets.

Over tea in the parlor, and then dinner in the dining room, they'd talked of the last ten years. He and Grace had told her of their lives, of his advancement in the force, and Fiona had told them of hers. When she'd finished, she paused for a few seconds, then said, "There's one thing I haven't told you about. The reason for my and Seamie's abrupt departure. I apologize for that. To both of you." Roddy could tell the words were difficult for her. He had started to shush her, but she persisted. "No, Uncle Roddy. I want to say this. It's bothered me for ten years. I'm deeply, deeply sorry to have run off without telling you where I was going, without thanking you face-to-face for all that you'd done for me. But there was a reason for it. A reason I can tell you about now . . . that I *need* to tell you about." Her eyes traveled from Roddy and Grace to the faces of their children. "But I don't think it's appropriate here."

"Why don't you and Roddy take a walk, Fiona?" Grace suggested. "That'll give me a chance to clear up the dishes and give you a chance to talk together. We'll 'ave dessert when you get back."

They had set off then, he and Fiona, to stroll in a nearby park. The July day was lengthening, but the sun was still warm and the sky cloudless.

"There's nothing quite as beautiful as summertime in England, is there?" Fiona said now, admiring a clutch of lupines. "I never noticed before. Whitechapel was dismal no matter what the season. But I rode through Hyde Park today and thought I'd never seen anything so lovely."

Roddy agreed. He listened to her chatter about the weather and flowers and London and wondered why she was talking about everything except what they'd come out here to discuss. Was it something to do with Joe? He purposely hadn't mentioned the lad, thinking she would bring him up herself if she wanted to. Or was it something to do with the money Sheehan once claimed she'd stolen from Burton? Whatever it was, her hesitancy to broach the subject told him it was still painful for her. He himself thought it was better to get such things over with. Like pulling a bandage off a wound. Best done quickly and all at once. "Is there something you wanted to tell me, lass?" he finally asked.

Fiona nodded. She was gazing straight ahead and he could see her jaw working. She turned to face him and he saw that a new expression had crept into her eyes. It was an unsettling mixture of sorrow and anger – no, not anger, *rage* – and it was new to him. He'd seen a harrowing grief in her eyes when she'd lived with him. He'd seen hopelessness there, too. But he'd never seen this.

"There is, Uncle Roddy. I've been wondering how to say it. Trying to find the courage."

"Fiona, lass, you don't have to bring up past ghosts –"

"I do. I wish I didn't." She gestured at a nearby bench. "Let's sit down." Once they were seated, she began to speak. Her story, confined deep within her for so long, burst forth. She told him everything and by the time she finished, Roddy was slumped against the bench in shock, feeling as if he'd just been kicked in the stomach. "I'm sorry, Uncle Roddy. I'm so sorry," she said, taking his hand.

It was some time before he could find his voice. "Why didn't you tell me this before?" he finally asked. "Why didn't you come to me instead of running away? We could've had them arrested."

Fiona shook her head. "No, Uncle Roddy. Think about it. There were no witnesses besides me. No one would've taken my word against Burton's. And I knew I was in danger."

"I would've protected you. I would've kept you safe."

"How?" she asked gently. "You would have had to stay with me every minute of every day. The minute you went to work, or out to the pub, or to see Grace, Sheehan would've made his move. I was already in danger and I didn't want to put you and Grace in danger, too. I had to get away. I did the best thing – the only thing – I could think of."

Roddy nodded. He could only imagine how frightened she must have been, and how devastated. Paddy. *Murdered.* Sorrow overcame him. He lowered his head and wept. All these years he thought he'd lost him to an accident – and that was hard enough. But *this*! Losing the best friend he'd ever had to a man's greed . . . it was incomprehensible. He cried for a long time, and even when there were no more tears left in him, he sat motionless. After a while, he heard Fiona ask if he was all right.

He lifted his head and wiped his eyes. "I was just . . . t'inking about it all," he said. "About the injustice of it. It happened ten years ago, and I know you said there were no witnesses besides yourself, but still . . . there's got to be *some* way to make Burton and Sheehan pay for what they did. I keep chasing it round and round in me mind, but I can't come up with one bloody way to get at them. Either one of them."

"I can. I think. I can get at one of them, at least."

"How?"

Fiona explained her plan to take over Burton Tea and her upcoming suit against Randolph Elgin. Roddy didn't entirely understand the workings of the stock market, but he knew enough to know that anyone who owned fifty-two percent of a company's shares owned the company.

"So," he said, "as soon as you get your shares, Burton Tea is yours, right? What does Pearson say? How long does he t'ink it'll take to get them?"

"He doesn't know. My attorney in New York thought it could take years."

"*Years?* Jaysus."

"And not only is this going to be a slow process, it may become an ugly one."

"What do you mean?"

Fiona had glossed over the truth about her marriage to Nick earlier; now she told him the whole story. She explained that Randolph Elgin would use Nick's homosexuality to argue that their marriage was a sham. The resulting scandal could damage – even destroy – her business.

"Could it really?" Roddy asked.

"Yes," Fiona said. She told him about the New York press and its insatiable appetite for gossip. "I got myself a husband by trying to avoid a scandal," she said, "but the truth is, Uncle Roddy, I don't give a damn about a scandal now. I'd willingly lose my business to obtain those shares, but even if I'm successful in ruining Burton, what about Sheehan?"

Roddy picked up a stick and fiddled with it, digesting all Fiona had told him. Then he said, "What we've got to do is pit one rat against the other. But I don't know how. At least, not yet. I do know one t'ing, though. I've never seen lawyers do anyt'ing quickly. There has to be a way to speed this up and nail Sheehan in the bargain. I'm just not seeing it yet."

Fiona sighed. "Nor I."

They were both silent, looking straight ahead in the gathering dusk, when the tolling of a nearby church bell told Roddy they should be getting back to Grace and the children. They stood up. Fiona looked so pale and broken to him now. He realized that she had carried this secret alone for ten years. And that he was the first person – the only person – she'd told. Standing there, watching her, his heart ached for her. For the grief and terror she'd suffered. For the fact that despite everything that had happened, she had not let bitterness and anger overwhelm her. Yes, there was a darkness in her eyes now, but there was light, too. The same strong, clear light that had shone when she was a girl.

Wordlessly, he pulled her to him. She had no father, no mother, this girl. Even the husband she'd loved was dead. But she had him. He loved her like one of his own and would do everything in his power to help her. They couldn't undo the past, but maybe they could change the future. "You're not in this alone anymore, lass," he whispered fiercely. "We're going to get them. The two of us together."

72

Fiona frowned, trying to remember the address of the advertising agency where she was supposed to be in ten minutes' time. "Number twenty-three Tavistock Street, right?" she said aloud, standing on the sidewalk at the intersection of Savoy Street and the Strand. "And Tavistock is off Southampton, which is off the Strand. Or was it number thirty-two Tavistock?" She sighed. "You do realize you're talking to yourself, don't you?" she whispered, digging in her purse for the address. She pulled out a scrap of paper. "Number thirty-two. Right then. Let's go. And no more muttering."

She continued west down the Strand, her lips clamped together. She would not talk to herself again. She hated the habit; it frightened her. It seemed like the first step on the road to insanity. Start doing it and before you knew where you were, you'd be one of those poor souls who shuffled down sidewalks ranting at invisible companions. Usually she controlled the impulse, but today she was so distracted, she'd slipped.

One whole week had elapsed since she'd met with Neville Pearson and he still hadn't gotten back to her. She took this as a bad sign. Things must be worse than he expected. What tactics were Elgin's lawyers cooking up? What on earth was going to happen to those shares? And when?

She hadn't heard from Roddy, either. Two days had passed since their reunion and she'd received no note, no visit, nothing to indicate that he'd thought of a way to go after Sheehan.

If she could only get her hands on those shares, if Roddy

could only figure out a way to nail Sheehan. If only, if only.

Fiona made a right off the Strand onto Southampton Street, heading toward Covent Garden. She looked at her watch – nearly four – and hastened her steps. She wanted to launch Quick Cup in England one day and knew it would serve her well to gain an understanding of how English advertising firms worked. She was meeting with Anthony Bekins himself, head of the firm and recommended to her by Nate Feldman, to see examples of his work and discuss costs and placement strategies. She knew that if she could get her mind focused on business, she would forget her other concerns. At least for a little while.

Lost in her thoughts at the corner of Southampton and Tavistock, Fiona never saw the market porter heading toward her, his dolly loaded high with crates of lettuce, until it was too late. Scrambling to get out of his way, she stumbled and fell against the wall of a brick building. The man whizzed by, missing her by a hair's breadth.

"Look where yer going, missus!" he shouted.

"Me?" Fiona sputtered, dazed by her fall. "*You* look where *you're* going, you bleeder!"

The man blew her a kiss and disappeared around the corner.

"Diabolical, they are," a voice said. Fiona turned and saw a woman carrying a basket of posies on her hip. "You all right, duck?" she asked, helping her up.

"I think so. Thank you."

"You want to mind yourself round 'ere. They'll run you down soon as look at you. Ta-ra, then."

"Ta-ra," Fiona said, turning to look for her purse. She spotted it on the sidewalk and bent to pick it up. As she did, a pain shot through her shoulder. Must've banged it when I fell, she thought. She straightened, pausing to rub it, and saw the cause of her discomfort. A hard brass plaque. It was polished to a sheen and read: BRISTOW'S OF COVENT GARDEN WHOLESALE PRODUCE, JOS. AND JAS. BRISTOW, PROPRIETORS. She stared at it for a full minute, reading the words over and over again, then whispered, "It can't be."

It's not him, she told herself. Why would he be out on his own? He works for Peterson's. Probably runs the place by now. But it must be. Who else could it be? He had a younger brother named Jimmy – she vaguely remembered him – that would be the Jas. Bristow. And sisters, too. She couldn't picture either of them. It had been too long. She tried to swallow, but her mouth had gone dry. And her hands were trembling. She told herself it was because of her fall.

Men and women, market workers all, passed her on the sidewalk, some ignoring her, others giving her curious glances. She looked at the door. It was painted a rich hunter green, just like the fronts of her and Michael's grocery shops. She remembered seeing that same color on the facade of Fortnum & Mason's. On the outing they'd once taken. They'd both liked it, both thought it was a wonderful color for a shop door.

She wanted to go upstairs. She wanted to see him. But she was afraid. She took a step toward the door, then stopped. Don't, she told herself. There's no point. You'll only hurt yourself. Turn away and start walking. Then at least you can say you've never seen him with her ring on, happy. But she didn't move. "Go," she hissed at herself. "Now, you bloody fool!"

She walked on. Woodenly at first, then more decisively. She got to number thirty-two Tavistock, twisted the doorknob, then turned and ran back to the building on the corner. One thing she had never given in to was fear. She could handle this. She was past it all now – the anger, the sorrow. She just wanted to see him again. As she would any old friend. Just to catch up and see how life had treated him. "Liar," she whispered. What she wanted to see was those laughing blue eyes.

She stopped outside the building, winded, and looked at it. Huge doors, partially opened, revealed a warehouse. She doubted he would be in there. The hunter-green door must lead to the offices, she reasoned. She would try that. Taking a deep breath, she pushed it open and walked up a flight of stairs to an open reception area awash in light from a row of tall windows. There was a long wooden counter, behind which two young women sat at desks, typing furiously; a third desk had two telephones on it, which rang continually and were attended by a harried young man who kept glancing at the large clock on the wall. Fruit and vegetable crates, full of fresh produce – to be inspected and sampled, she guessed – were stacked haphazardly.

A boy in kitchen whites, who'd just arrived with an envelope under his arm, stood in the center of the room, refusing to relinquish his missive to an angry clerk. "It's the menu for the party," he said defiantly. "Chef Reynaud said 'and it to the guv'nor 'imself and not no poxy clerk." The clerk threatened to wring the lad's neck for him. The boy manning the phones never looked up, neither did the typists. Fiona began to despair of getting anyone's attention when she noticed a pretty young blond woman talking to two porters near a second stairway that led directly down to the warehouse. The woman handed them a lengthy order sheet, then turned toward her. She stared for a few seconds, then, with a strange look of what Fiona thought was almost alarm, said, "Can I 'elp you?"

"I'd . . . I'd like to see Joseph Bristow," Fiona said.

The woman hesitated. "I'm sorry," she said, "but 'e isn't in right now."

"Tell me, is Mr. Bristow . . . is he from Montague Street? In Whitechapel?"

"Aye."

Fiona, her heart hammering, opened her purse and dug out a calling card. "May I leave this for him?" she asked.

"Of course."

She felt the woman's eyes on her as she scribbled a quick note on the back of the card. She handed it to her. "If you wouldn't mind."

"Not at all. Ta-ra."

"Yes. Well . . . ta-ra," Fiona said, feeling awkward and

disappointed. Then she headed for the staircase and Tavistock Street and her appointment at Bekins and Brown.

Cathy Bristow stared after the beautiful black-haired woman as she disappeared down the stairwell then looked at the card in her hand. MRS. NICHOLAS SOAMES, it read.

It's her. Fiona. I'm sure of it, she said to herself. She has a face that's hard to forget. Though she's obviously forgotten mine, she thought, irritated. Then again, I was probably what? Eight years old the last time we saw each other?

"Cathy!" a voice bellowed down the hallway.

"What is it, Joe?" She looked past the reception desk, down the hallway. Her brother was leaning out of the doorway to his office.

"I need the guest list. For Saturday. Can you bring it, luv?"

"Right away," she said.

He vanished back into his office. Cathy looked at the card again. This is none of your business, she told herself. She read the message anyway. "Dear Joe, I'm in London for a few weeks. Staying at the Savoy. Would love to see you. Best regards, Fiona Finnegan Soames."

She bit her lip. You should've had her wait, her conscience said. You should've fetched Joe. He'll be furious if he finds out what you've done. You can still catch her, it's not too late. Go after her!

She started for the stairs, then stopped. Why? she asked herself. What for? To rip open old wounds? Fiona Finnegan is married. Mrs. Nicholas Soames, that's what the card said, didn't it? There's no point in going after her. None at all. And why does she want to see him? Maybe she's still angry at him, she reasoned. Maybe she wants to have some kind of revenge. To show him that she's happily married and quite unavailable.

Cathy could imagine her brother's expression when he saw the card. The bloody fool would leap up and run all the way to the Savoy. And after he'd seen her, after she told him all about her husband and her wonderful life in

New York, he'd be devastated. Cathy loved her brother very much and it pained her greatly to see the ever-present sadness in his eyes. She knew it would go away if only he could fall in love again. And she knew he never would if he saw Fiona.

She'd promised Sally Gordon she would help her catch Joe and she meant to keep her word. They'd talked at Jimmy's wedding and it seemed to go well. Joe had been very charming and Sally looked so sweet and pretty. How could he not fall for her? They'd make such a good match. Joe just had to be brought round to seeing it. And Fiona's reappearance in his life would only derail things.

"Cathy!" Joe shouted again. "Where's that guest list?"

In a flash, she made her decision. She tore up the card and tossed the pieces away. As they fluttered to the bottom of the rubbish bin, she shouted, " 'Ang on a mo', will you! I'm coming!"

73

"It's 'im, Sergeant," P. C. McPherson said, waving a sheaf of paper in the air.

Roddy turned from the small rectangular mirror hanging on his closet door and regarded the man. "Except it's not," he said. "Because it can't be. Because he's dead."

"Aye, right you are," McPherson said dutifully.

"But, just between you and me . . ."

". . . all 'ypothetical like . . ."

". . . the coroner's report indicates . . ."

". . . that the fucker's alive and well and at it again."

"Good Christ," Roddy sighed. He turned back to the mirror and resumed fumbling with the metal emblems that were supposed to sit straight on his collar. A letter had just arrived, not ten minutes ago, summoning him to his superintendent's office. He was to leave immediately. He had been expecting the summons, but he was not looking forward to answering it.

Two days ago, McPherson and another police constable had been alerted to the presence of a decomposing corpse stuffed into a privy in the back of a derelict house in Thrawl Street. A group of boys had discovered it. McPherson had recognized the jacket, a gaudy purple thing, and had identified the body as that of Maggie Riggs, a streetwalker. Her throat had been cut and an attempt had been made to cut off her face. Her dress pocket was ripped open and she'd had no money on her, so Roddy put out the word that she'd been the victim of a robbery that had turned violent. He gave the press no description of her wounds, hoping to quell any comparisons between this crime and the Ripper murders. He'd managed to keep it pretty quiet, but the superintendent had gotten word. Now he would have to present the coroner's report to the man and assure him that his officers were patrolling the streets night and day and that everything was under control.

He gave himself an appraising look, shifting this way and that, trying to see as much of himself in the small glass as he could. Then he turned to McPherson and said, "Are me badges straight?"

McPherson looked at Roddy's collar, his shoulders, his front pocket, taking in the various insignia of his rank. "Right as rain."

"What about the Quinn murder? Anyt'ing on that?"

"Not a sausage."

"Not'ing at all? Nobody heard anyt'ing? Saw anyt'ing?"

"Sergeant, does anybody ever see anything round 'ere? You'd think every man, woman, and child in Whitechapel was deaf, dumb, and blind. A murder could happen in the middle of Commercial Street at noon on a Saturday and nobody would see nothing."

Roddy nodded. It never rains in Whitechapel but it pours, he thought. First the double murder at the Taj and now the butchered prostitute.

"Keep the pressure up, McPherson," Roddy said. "It's possible that we're barking up the wrong tree t'inking it's Sheehan or Malone. Could be anyone. Who had a grudge against Denny? Who'd he owe money to? Who owed him? Squeeze the bartender. Potter's his name. Runs a lucrative sideline in opium, I'm told. T'reaten to choke it off."

"You know where 'e lives?"

"Dean Street."

"Thanks, guv. I'll leave the Thrawl Street report on your desk."

McPherson left. Roddy stole one last glance at himself in the mirror, glad that he'd gotten his hair cut and his beard trimmed the day before. He looked tired, but there wasn't much he could do about that. Ever since he'd seen Fiona and learned what had really happened to Paddy, he'd had trouble sleeping. Try as he might, he could not come up with a way to nab Sheehan. He was desperate for a solution. He wanted to help Fiona, he couldn't let her down, but four whole days had passed and he still had nothing. He picked up his report. He would attack the problem again tonight when he was home and his mind was clear. Right now, he had an appointment to keep. But just as he was about to leave his office he heard shouting from the front of the station.

"Get in there, you fucking bastards! Go on – both of you!"

"Oi! 'Old on a minute . . ." he heard one of his officers yell.

There was the sound of scuffling, then a crash. A man yelped in pain, and then: "Try and run again and I'll break your leg."

"Ripton! What the hell is going on?" Roddy shouted, striding down the hall toward the station's receiving area.

"I'm not sure, sir."

Roddy looked toward the doorway. Two men were standing in it. Staggering in it, to be exact. Their faces were pulp – running messes of blood and bruises. Their clothing was torn. Roddy shook his head, dazed by the sight. He approached the men and suddenly realized he knew them – they were Reg Smith and Stan Christie. Bowler Sheehan's men.

"Good morning, Sergeant O'Meara," said a voice from behind them.

A young man, fearsomely muscular, wearing narrow-cut trousers and a red kingsman, stepped forward. He was followed by another man wearing similar attire.

Bully boys, Roddy thought. You can tell by the clothes. They just can't help themselves. Might as well wear a sign. "Do I know you two?" he said, taking in the scar across the first lad's chin and the doughy fighter's nose on the second one.

"Tom Smith," the first lad said, perfectly straight-faced.

"Dick Jones," said the second one.

"So all we're missing is Harry Bollocks," Roddy said.

"Beg your pardon, Sergeant?" Tom said.

"Don't play the smart-arse with me, son. What are you doing here?"

"They 'ave something to tell you," Tom said. He gave his captives a shove. "Speak up, you gobshites. Nice and loud so the whole place can 'ear you."

Neither Reg nor Stan spoke. Tom, looking murderous, gripped one of his hands with the other and cracked his knuckles loudly. Reg winced. Stan, through livid, swollen lips, said, "It was us who did for Den Quinn and 'is tart."

"And who else?" Tom prompted.

"Bowler Sheehan."

Roddy looked at Reg and Stan in disbelief. "Are you prepared to write that down and sign it?"

They nodded miserably and Roddy had the officers who'd gathered lead them away. Tom and Dick moved off toward the door.

"Hold on a minute," he ordered. "How did they get like this?"

Tom shrugged. "Don't know. We found them that way. Outside a pub."

"Outside a pub? Which pub?"

"Anyone you like."

"Who are you working for?" Roddy asked.

Tom smiled. "I don't follow your meaning, Sergeant," he said.

"Ah. You don't follow my meaning." Roddy walked over to the door, slammed it shut, and locked it. "Do you t'ink a few days in the nick might help make it clear?"

"On what charges?"

"On charges of I feel like it and there's no one to stop me. How's that?"

Tom looked at Dick. Dick nodded. "For a friend of Denny Quinn's. For a man who don't think it's right that Bowler Sheehan gets away with murder."

"Friend, my arse. You work for Malone. Your man wants Sheehan out of the way. He's given me Reg and Stan and now he figures I'm going to do the rest of his dirty work for him, doesn't he?"

Neither lad answered. They just stared at Roddy with a gaze that was polite and respectful, patronizing and infuriating.

"What I can't figure out, though," Roddy continued, "is why Malone didn't just kill Reg and Stan. And why he doesn't just kill Sheehan. Unless Sheehan's gone to ground and Malone can't find him. Maybe that's it. Maybe he's using those two yobs in there as bait. He knows Sheehan wouldn't want them in the nick. He'd be too worried about them talking. He'll come get them. He'll show himself and Malone will put paid to him. Am I right, lads?"

Tom swallowed. Dick blinked. Neither said a word.

Roddy unlocked the door. He had his answers. "Be good lads," he said, "and tell Mr. Malone to stay on his side of the river. Tell him if he doesn't, he's going to be very sorry."

Tom paused on his way out. "Can you convict them, Sergeant?" he asked.

"If they sign confessions, yes."

"And Sheehan, too? For Quinn's murder?"

"If we can get enough evidence against him, or get his confession, then yes," Roddy said.

Tom nodded. "Denny Quinn was a good man. And 'e didn't deserve to die like that. Bowler Sheehan deserves it, though. 'E's going to 'ang for this." He smiled tightly. "One way or another."

"You leave that to us," Roddy cautioned. "Sheehan turns up dead, it's you I'm looking for."

But Tom and Dick were already heading down the street. Roddy stood looking after them for a few seconds. He was so distracted, so completely astonished by the enormity of the gift that they had just unintentionally dropped into his lap, that he forgot he was holding the report on the murdered prostitute and that he was supposed to be on his way to the superintendent's office.

Tom was right. Bowler certainly would hang. Not just for Den and Janey, but for Paddy Finnegan, too.

He had it. At last he had a plan to help Fiona. A longshot plan, admittedly, but a plan nonetheless. He would have to act quickly. Before word of Stan's and Reg's arrest spread and Sheehan went so far underground he'd never find him.

"Ripton!" Roddy shouted.

"Yes, Sergeant?"

"Get half a dozen men and bring Bowler Sheehan in. Look under every cobblestone, every dog turd in Whitechapel if you have to, but find him."

"Right away, sir."

"And Ripton . . ."

"Sir?"

"Do it before those two do," Roddy said, hooking his thumb in the direction of the door. "I need him in one piece."

74

"I say!" Neville Pearson declared, squinting through his spectacles. "Terribly dramatic, aren't they?"

"They're the four seasons!" his wife Charlotte exclaimed. "See? That one's spring, that's summer, there's autumn, and that's winter. Each is offering her bounty. What a clever idea!"

"They're absolutely enormous," Neville said. "Must be what . . . twenty feet by thirty? At least!"

Fiona said nothing. She turned in a slow circle, spellbound by the beauty of the unframed murals on the four opposing walls of Montague's produce hall. She recognized the artist – John William Waterhouse – one of the English Pre-Raphaelites. Nick had owned two of his romantic canvases.

Her eyes lingered on each season in turn. Summer, a brunette, wore a vibrant green gown and stood in a meadow, berries in her hands, her face lifted to the sun. Autumn gathered pears in an orchard. Her copper hair was long and flowing like her crimson dress. Winter was a pale blond snow queen in a white gown. She stood among evergreens wearing a crown of holly. And Spring was a lithe black-haired girl, a water sprite in a pale blue dress, with eyes of deepest indigo. She held rosebuds in her hands and stood by a stream. Cherry trees flowered behind her. Green buds poked up out of the black earth under her feet. Hers was not the harvest or winter's respite, but the promise of things to come.

Who would have thought to hang paintings in a grocery

shop? Fiona wondered. The same person, no doubt, who'd put iridescent blue and green tiles on the floor instead of white ones. Who'd lit the place with chandeliers and sconces shaped like lilies. Who knew enough to put mirror glass in back of his food cases to make the displays look twice as big. Who gave his sales staff silver name tags with the word "Specialist" engraved under their names, not "Clerk." Who'd situated the stairs to the upper levels of the shop at the back of the main floor, making it necessary for shoppers en route to the florist or tobacconist to wend their way past myriad tempting goods.

Whoever he is, he's a bloody genius, Fiona thought. Everything he'd chosen, every decision he'd made – from the paintings to the glorious flower arrangements to the artful displays of exotic fruits and vegetables – raised the tone of the place, elevating it from a loud and clanging food hall to a refined, luxurious emporium. Neville had promised her an introduction as soon as they could find the man . . . this Mr. Barston or Barton – he still couldn't remember which.

"Looks like you, Fiona," Neville said, pointing at Spring.

Fiona looked at the painted girl. "She's much younger. And far too pretty," she replied.

"Nonsense, Neville's right. She looks exactly like you, my dear," Charlotte Pearson said.

Fiona flapped her hand and told them they were seeing things. A waiter passed by with champagne. Neville plucked a glass from his tray and took a sip. Fiona took one, too, to be polite, but declined the lovely petits fours that followed. She was too tense to eat. She had far too much on her mind.

First, there was Neville. During the dinner she'd shared with the Pearsons at the Savoy before the party, he'd told her that he believed it would take him six months to get the Burton stock. He suggested they meet on Tuesday afternoon at his office to discuss the details. Six months seemed impossibly long. She wanted the shares now, not half a year from now. How would she run her businesses from London? She'd have to travel back and forth constantly – a prospect she did not relish.

Then there was Roddy. She'd received a note from him yesterday. "Got him," it read. "Give me two days." One day had already elapsed. One more to go. How had he nabbed Sheehan? And what on earth was he doing with him? She couldn't sleep at night for worrying. What was he plotting? And would it work, whatever it was? The wait was unbearable, but she would have to be patient. With any luck, she would know by Monday.

And then there was Joe. She looked around the room again, at the displays, at a woman's dress, at anything at all to take her mind off the fact that it had been three whole days since she'd left her card at his office. Three whole days in which she'd heard nothing from him. She was foolish to have done it. He obviously wanted nothing to do with her. Of course he didn't. He'd made that perfectly clear ten years ago. He'd probably thrown the card away the second that woman had handed it to him. She cringed at the very thought. She had tried to shrug his silence off, tried to tell herself it didn't matter. But it did. It hurt. Still.

It seemed she was spending all her time waiting these days. For a reply from Joe. For a resolution of her suit against Randolph Elgin. For further word from Roddy. She wasn't accustomed to waiting for solutions to her problems; she was used to taking action. And being forced to sit still, to be useless and idle, was driving her mad.

"What do you suppose this is?" Neville asked, a ribbed green pod pinched between his thumb and forefinger. He'd wandered off to the fruit and vegetable displays and come back again.

"Okra," Fiona said. "From America. It's grown in the Southern states." She wondered how it had remained so green and fresh. She and Michael often had difficulties getting good produce from Georgia and the Carolinas. They rejected much of what their wholesalers supplied. It must've come over on ice on a very fast boat directly out of a Southern port, she decided.

"Okra. How unusual," Neville said. He took a tentative bite, made a face, and tossed the offending vegetable onto a waiter's tray. "You must come with me, all of you," he said, "and see what I've discovered. It's remarkable! I was standing by a vegetable case wondering how they've kept everything so fresh in the summer heat when all of a sudden fog started coming out of it."

"Fog?" Charlotte said. "That can't be right."

"Yes, fog, my dear. It's most ingenious! Come see."

"That's all we need in London, more fog," Charlotte said, trotting after her husband.

Fiona followed the Pearsons and saw what Neville was talking about. The produce was displayed in tall, raked cases made of enameled metal. Someone had devised a way to make the cases release a gentle mist over the produce to keep it crisp. She reached up under the top and felt around. "There's a hose here," she said. "There must be tiny holes in it. They're forcing water through it somehow. A pump, maybe. But where is it?" She ducked her head into the case to try and get a better look, but got a face full of mist instead. "You're right, Neville, it *is* ingenious!" she said excitedly, dabbing her wet cheeks with her sleeve. "I must find out how it's done. Where is this Mr. Barton?"

"I don't know," Neville said, frowning as he searched the crowd. "He must be here somewhere, but I haven't seen him. Let's walk around, shall we?" he said, offering her one arm, and his wife the other. "We're bound to bump into him."

As they strolled off in search of the proprietor, the threesome investigated the rest of Montague's main floor, marveling at the immense variety of breads – Charlotte stopped counting after forty – the mouth-watering display of cakes, puddings, and biscuits; the beautiful mosaic of fish and shellfish; the wealth of game birds, venison, elk, and boar; the luscious cuts of beef and pork; the prepared foods – rich pâtés, salads, aspics, meat pies decorated with pastry garlands and hunting scenes; and the towering display of cheeses.

As Fiona took everything in, captivated, she managed to forget about her Burton Tea shares, and Joe's snub, and Roddy and Bowler Sheehan for a little while. It was impossible to worry while tasting a sliver of fine aged Parmesan, or questioning a clerk – no, a *specialist* – about a type of coffee she'd never seen before. She was full of admiration for this remarkable merchant Barton and quite impatient to meet him.

Charlotte spotted a friend and broke away to chat with her. "Let's go upstairs," Neville said to Fiona. "I want to visit the tobacco shop. Our secret, my dear. Charlotte doesn't approve."

Fiona laughed. Her mood had lightened. Heads turned as they walked up the large marble staircase. People stared, not recognizing the lovely smiling woman on Pearson's arm. She wore a summery gown of cream silk mousseline trimmed with Chantilly lace and cinched at the waist with a narrow length of satin. The open collar showed off her long graceful neck, its delicacy emphasized by a necklace and earrings of pearls, opals, and amethysts. Eyes darted toward her, attracted by her beauty, then lingered, enchanted by the spirit and animation evident in her every gesture.

At the top, the railings branched off to the left and right, creating little areas where people could stand and watch the scene below. Fiona accompanied Neville into the tobacconist's, which boasted a built-in humidor. She observed, curious, as he passed several cigars under his nose, pressing them slightly to ascertain their freshness, before making his selection. The cigars were paid for, then promptly secreted in his breast pocket.

Back outside, Charlotte was nowhere to be seen. Fiona and Neville walked back to the railing to wait for her. Fresh glasses of champagne were brought. Fiona had abandoned her first, undrunk, downstairs. More relaxed now, she sipped from this one. A handsome young waiter handed her a perfect crimson rose. "A gift from our florist," he said.

"Quite a do," Neville said.

"Isn't it?" Fiona agreed, inhaling the scent of her rose. "What an extraordinary shop."

Neville leaned his forearms on the railing. "Just look at all the people. Must be costing the chap a fortune in champagne."

"Yes, but he'll earn it back in spades when they all become customers," Fiona said, her eyes roving over the glittering, glamorous crowd below. These were people with money. Socially prominent people. She could tell by the richness of their clothing, their upper-crust voices. They would be dazzled by tonight's party, then go home and tell their housekeepers to buy at Montague's. Whatever its owner was spending now was only a small investment against his future profits.

"Shall we visit the restaurant?" Neville asked. "It's on the next floor. It's supposed to be extraordinary."

"Yes, let's. I'll just finish my drink . . ." Her words suddenly trailed off. Her eyes – locked upon a face in the crowd, a man's face – widened.

The ponytail was gone. The blond hair was neatly cut now, but still thick and curling. The threadbare shirt, the cap, and the red kingsman were gone, too. He wore a suit. A perfectly cut gray frock coat and trousers. But the wide, generous smile was the same. And the eyes, as blue and limitless as a summer sky, were the same. The boy was gone. A man had taken his place. The most beautiful man she had ever seen.

She heard a voice in her mind, the one she'd heard during her visit to Neville's firm. She'd been inexplicably drawn to it. Because it was *his* voice. "Barton or Barston," Neville had said. "I'm so bad with names." No, Bristow. Joe Bristow. Her Joe.

She could barely breathe as she watched him. He was talking to a couple, smiling, his hand on the man's shoulder. Her heart was so full of emotion that tears suddenly came to her eyes. The other day, in his Covent Garden office, she had told herself she could handle seeing him again. Handle it? She could barely stand up straight. The mere sight of him left her overwhelmed by feelings of love and longing. Feelings she thought she'd conquered long ago. She wanted to go to him, to hear his voice, touch his hand, and look into his eyes once again. To put her arms around him and feel his arms around her and pretend, if only for a few seconds, that they had never parted.

As she continued to watch him, drinking in every detail of his appearance – the way he stood, the way he jammed his hands in his pockets as he talked, the way he cocked his head to listen – he was suddenly mobbed by three boisterous blond children. He bent down to pick up the youngest, kissed her cheek, then plucked a sweet from a passing tray for her. As he put her down again, Fiona realized the little girl must be his. All three children were his. His and Millie's. Because he was married to Millie and had been for the last ten years and didn't want anything to do with her.

She backed away from the railing feeling physically ill. She had to get out of here. Now. Before he saw her. Or she'd look like some lovesick idiot who just couldn't stay away. A desperate, pathetic woman.

Neville noticed her stricken expression. "Fiona? What is it? What's wrong?"

She forced herself to smile. "Nothing, Neville. A touch of vertigo, that's all. I can't abide heights," she lied. Then she told him that she'd enjoyed herself immensely, but that she was tired and had a busy day ahead of her, so she had to get back to her hotel. She asked him to please tell Charlotte good-bye for her and said she would see him at his offices on Tuesday.

Then she started down the long, sweeping staircase. She'd

seen a side door and planned to make a beeline for it. She wanted to run, but forced herself to descend at a proper pace. When she finally reached the ground floor, she quickly threaded her way through the crowd toward the door. It opened into an alleyway that ran alongside the Montague's building. Once outside, she did run. Out of the alley and into the street, where she found a hackney immediately.

Inside the carriage, she gave vent to her emotion. The cabbie heard her choked sobs. Concerned, he turned and asked if she was all right.

"No, I'm not. Not at all," she said, too upset to be mortified that she was crying in front of a total stranger.

"Don't tell me – it's a bloke, ain't it?" the man asked.

She nodded.

"You're daft, missus. Fine woman like yourself . . . why, you could do better than 'im any day of the week. I don't give a toss who 'e is."

Fiona sighed. "That's what I tell myself. Maybe some-day I'll believe it."

"It was 'er," Joe said to himself, standing on the street outside his shop, frantically looking for a woman in a cream-colored dress among the crush of people. Those blue eyes, that face . . . it was Fiona. She was *here*.

He'd glimpsed her on the stairs. The sudden shock of seeing her had been so great, he'd dropped the glass he was holding. It had shattered at his feet. Before he could even call her name, she was down the steps and out a side door. He'd run after her, but the crowd slowed him. By the time he made it down the alley to the street, she'd disappeared.

Fiona. Here in London. In his shop. He'd *seen* her. He took a few paces down the sidewalk, looking in carriage windows; crossed the street, looked up and down it, but he couldn't find her anywhere.

It *was* her, I'm certain of it, he told himself. The only thing is, she lives in New York, not London. With her husband.

"Joe!" someone shouted. "Joe . . . over 'ere!"

He spun in the direction of the voice. It was Cathy. She was waving at him.

"Where 'ave you been?" she asked after he'd crossed back. "I saw you run out. I thought something 'ad 'appened."

"No, nothing. Nothing at all. I just thought –"

"You're needed back inside. Lady Churchill's just arrived. She wants a guided tour." She gave him a close look. "Joe, luv, what's wrong? You look 'alf distracted."

He shook his head. "You won't believe this, but I could swear I just saw Fiona Finnegan."

Cathy cast an anxious glance down the street and then at him. He realized he must be worrying her. "You think I'm barmy, don't you?" he said.

"You're not barmy, luv. Just overworked. It's been eighteen-hour days, seven days a week for all of us for over a month. But the shop's open now, and it's going to be a smashing success if tonight's any indication. As soon as the dust settles, you should take a few days off. Stay in Greenwich and rest yourself."

Joe nodded. "Aye, I think I will."

"Come on, then," she said brightly. "Mustn't keep 'er ladyship waiting."

Cathy led the way back down the alley. It would be quicker than trying to get in through the main entrance. Joe paused at the door to allow his sister to go ahead of him. He was about to follow her in when he saw a red rose lying on the cobbles near his feet.

He picked it up. Fiona had loved red roses. He used to bring her one whenever he could.

"Joe? You coming?"

"Right away." He shoved the bloom into his pocket. He *was* going mad. No doubt about it. Cathy was right. A few days' rest would do him a world of good.

75

"You bastard! You pig-fucking, cock-sucking, shit-eating bastard! You can't keep me 'ere! I want my solicitor and I want 'im *now*! I know me rights! When I get out of 'ere, O'Meara, you're going to be out, too! Out on your spotty Irish arse! You 'ear me? I'll 'ave your badge, you fucker! Yours and the bollocks who 'auled me in 'ere . . ."

Roddy, arms folded across his chest, regarded the man on the other side of the iron bars with a smirk. He'd run out of steam in a minute or two. Two days without food or water left even the toughest men weak. And Bowler, for all his noise, wasn't that tough. He was nowhere near as big as Reg or Stan. He was wiry without much fat to absorb blows. Roddy guessed he'd bleed like hell.

He pulled his battered truncheon from his belt and took a couple of practice swings. Bowler saw him do it and unleashed another torrent of invective. It lacked the color and vigor of the previous one. The man was tiring.

It had been a long time since Roddy had conducted an interview of this nature. McPherson had offered to help, but he'd declined. He wanted Bowler all to himself.

He waited a few more minutes, until Bowler, finally exhausted, sat down on the bench inside his cell. Then he took a ring of keys from his belt, unlocked the door, and stepped inside. As he expected, Bowler rushed him the second the door, clicked shut. Roddy was prepared. He deflected the blow with his truncheon, grabbed Bowler's arm, spun him around, and threw him against the bars. Bowler bounced off and came at him again. Roddy brought his truncheon down on his skull, opening a gash above one eye.

Bowler shrieked. Roddy grabbed him by his shirt and pitched him back onto the bench. "Paddy Finnegan was like a brother to me," he said.

"What the *fuck* 'as that got to do with me?" Bowler shouted, wiping blood out of his eye.

"You murdered him. You and William Burton."

"I don't know what you're talking about."

"You also murdered Dennis Quinn and Janey Symms."

Bowler spat a gob of bloody phlegm. "You've got the wrong man. It was Sid Malone. 'E wants into the East End. 'E was trying to throw 'is weight around with Quinn, but Quinn wasn't 'aving it. So Malone did for 'im."

Roddy drew two pieces of paper out of his jacket pocket, unfolded them, and held them up before Bowler's eyes. "Can you read?" he asked.

"Fuck you."

"I'll take that as a yes," Roddy said. "Read these carefully. They're signed confessions made by Reg Smith and Stan Christie and witnessed by two of my constables. They say that you yourself stabbed Quinn and that Reg and Stan cut Janey Symms."

Roddy watched Bowler's eyes as he read the documents, pleased to see a flicker of fear in them.

"So what?" Bowler said when he was done. "That's what those two say. I say different. I was nowhere near the Taj when Den was murdered."

"Listen, Bowler, I'm going to make you an offer. We both know you did this. I've got Reg and Stan's statements to back it up. And if I need to, I'll get more witnesses. Potter the bartender will place you there. So will half a dozen of Den's girls."

Bowler smiled. "They wouldn't dare."

"Not if they t'ink you're going to get out," Roddy conceded. "But if I assure them you won't, you're done for. I hear Ronnie Black who owns that gin shop on Lamb

Street was playing snooker when you arrived. T'ink he liked paying you off all these years? I bet he hates your guts. Bet he'd sing like a budgerigar. Bet any bloke in the room would. They'd love to get shut of you."

Bowler took a deep breath, held it, then blew it out. "What do you want?"

"The truth. About Quinn. About Paddy Finnegan, too. I want you to say how the Finnegan murder happened. How William Burton put you up to it."

Bowler nodded. "That's exactly 'ow it *did* 'appen! 'E put me up to it!"

"I t'ought so," Roddy said encouragingly. "Burton's the one I really want."

Bowler leaned forward, eager now. "If I do this, what's in it for me?"

A place on the hangman's dance card, Roddy thought. "I'll take care of you, Bowler," he said. "I'm not one to hide my appreciation. I'll make sure the magistrate knows that you helped me out and I'll do my best to get him to go easy on you. You'll get prison instead of the gallows, with time off for good behavior. Ten, fifteen years, you'll be a free man." He paused, then said, "But if you refuse, I'll call in every favor I've ever done, every debt I'm owed, to make sure you hang for Quinn."

Bowler sucked his teeth, deliberating. "All right," he finally said. "I know when the game's up. But if I'm going down, Burton's coming with me. You 'ave some paper in this dog 'ole? A pen? Let's get this over with."

76

Fiona, wearing a somber gray suit, hurried down Commercial Street, past Christ Church, and into a tumbledown pub called the Bells. It was an overcast morning, not quite six o'clock. A few workmen, hard types, sat at the bar, washing down meat pies or Scotch eggs with tea.

"Fiona! Over here!"

It was Roddy. He was seated at a table in the snug. He'd sent her a note last night asking her to meet him here. He said he had information pertaining to her father's death. To their plan. He had a pot of tea and the remains of a cooked breakfast in front of him. She noticed he was unshaven and bleary-eyed. "You look like you haven't slept. What happened?" she asked as she sat down.

"More like what hasn't happened," he said wearily. "Got called out at two o'clock this morning." He glanced around the room, then lowered his voice. "A body was found in an alley off Fournier Street. A prostitute. Her t'roat had been cut. A man heard her scream, went to help her, and found her dead."

"You're joking."

"I wish I were."

"It sounds just like Jack."

Roddy scrubbed his face with his hands. "Aye, that it does," he said. "And the papers are going to have a holiday with it. Reporters were crawling all over the crime scene trying to get information. We're under orders not to give them anyt'ing, but that's not stopping them. What they can't find out, they just make up. Bloody Bob Devlin, the editor at the *Clarion*, will have the whole East End in a frenzy by evening. We've asked for reinforcements from Limehouse, Wapping, and Bow in case there's trouble. But none of this concerns you, lass." He paused as the barmaid brought a fresh pot of tea to the table and asked Fiona what she wanted to eat.

"Nothing, thank you," she said.

"This time of day, snug's only for customers who are dining," the woman said sulkily.

"Fine. Bring me a cooked breakfast."

"Do you want chipped potatoes or tomatoes –"

"Everything. I want everything," Fiona said, wanting the woman gone. She poured herself a cup of tea and sloshed in some milk while Roddy continued.

"I asked you to come down here because I knew I wouldn't be able to get to you today and I wanted to tell you what's happened," he said. "A few days ago, a man by the name of Dennis Quinn was murdered along with his girlfriend, Janey Symms."

Fiona nodded, uncertain what Quinn's murder had to do with her father's death.

"It was Bowler Sheehan who did it. Another criminal, man by the name of Sid Malone, gave him to me. In a roundabout sort of a way."

"Malone?" Fiona repeated. "The same Sid Malone who tried to drag me down an alley once?"

"I wouldn't be surprised, but I don't know for sure. Haven't seen the bloke in ten years." Roddy explained how Malone's men had brought Reg and Stan to the station and how his own men had found Sheehan holed up in his sister's house in Stepney. "I told him I had him for Quinn," Roddy said, "but that I'd get the beak to go easy on him if he confessed to your father's murder . . . and fingered William Burton."

Fiona clattered her teacup back into its saucer. Her eyes were enormous. "And did he?"

"Aye."

She sat back in her chair, floored by this sudden turn of

events. As she considered all the implications, she realized she didn't have to wait six months for Nick's shares. She didn't need them. Sheehan's confession would hang both himself and William Burton. "You can arrest Burton now, right? You can put him in prison and bring him to trial and hang him for what he did," she said.

Roddy hesitated. "I hope so, lass," he said, "but I can't guarantee it."

"But why?" she asked, distressed. "You have Sheehan's confession."

"All I've really got is the word of a known criminal against that of a respected merchant. There were no eyewitnesses to your father's murder. No way to prove what Sheehan says is true," Roddy said. "I've done the best I could do. And maybe with a little luck, it'll be enough. I've sent a pair of constables to Burton's offices to apprise him of Sheehan's confession and conduct a formal interview. Maybe we'll get a miracle. Maybe he'll confess. It's happened before. A person can only live with murder on his conscience for so long before the guilt does him in." He covered her hand with his own. "Try to have a little faith now."

Fiona nodded disconsolately. William Burton was not such a person and faith was not her strong point. She was close, so close to avenging her father's death. Roddy had done so much. He'd put most of the puzzle pieces in place. Now all she needed was a bit of additional leverage, some way to trap Burton, to compel him to confess. But what?

Her meal arrived. She picked at it. It's all right, she told herself. No matter what, Roddy has Sheehan. He's going to hang for what he did. And if Burton doesn't confess, then you just go back to your original plan – Neville gets the shares and you use them to get Burton. She took a sip of tea, trying to quell her disappointment. Her eyes fell on Roddy's newspaper. The *Clarion*. He'd placed it on the table. "Murder in Whitechapel!" the headline screamed. "Woman Slashed in Alley." Below that was one about a brawl. "Twenty-Five Injured in Public House Melee." And under that, "Scandal! Local Minister and Fallen Woman. Details on Page 5." With headlines like these, the *Clarion* makes the New York papers look downright restrained, she thought. She read them again. For some reason, one word in particular jumped out at her.

Scandal.

It was a word she was well acquainted with. She'd married Nick to avoid one. And over the next six months she might well lose her tea business if her father-in-law made good on his threat to create another.

Scandal.

Shouted or whispered, it was a powerful word. Intimidating. Terrifying, even. Marriages were ruined by scandals. Businesses, reputations, lives. A mere threat could be devastating. People went to great lengths to prevent them. Threaten someone with a scandal and you had power over him. Leverage. Control.

She pushed her plate aside. "We don't need a miracle, Uncle Roddy," she said quietly.

"No?"

"No. All we need is a friend at a newspaper. Any newspaper. How well do you know the man you mentioned? Devlin?"

"Very well. We've done a lot of favors for one another over the years."

She opened her purse, placed a few coins on the table, and stood up. "Let's go see him."

"Why?"

"To see if he'll help us engineer a scandal. We may not be able to convict Burton for my father's murder, but we're going to make people *believe* we can."

"I don't understand. What will that do?" Roddy asked, balling up his napkin.

"Everything, I hope. Come on, let's go. I'll explain on the way."

* * *

Roddy paused, his hand on the door to the *Clarion*'s offices. He turned to Fiona and said, "You know, lass, this just might work."

"It better, Uncle Roddy."

"Are you ready?"

"I am."

"All right, then. Let's go."

He pushed the door open and they entered a long, noisy room containing the printing presses. It smelled strongly of oil and ink.

"Come on," he said, leading her toward a flight of stairs. "The newsroom's this way."

He knew the building. He'd visited it many times. The *Clarion* was hardly the *Times,* but it was a feisty, two-fisted paper with a strong circulation. It broke all the local stories, many of which were picked up by the *Times* and other leading papers. It would serve their purpose well.

Fiona had explained her plan to him. It was brilliant, but whether it worked or not depended entirely on Devlin. He was generally an all-right bloke, but he did have a stubborn streak. Just in case he proved to be in a balky mood today, Roddy had stopped by the station on the way over to pick up some insurance. A little present. Grease for the gears.

Tobacco smoke hung thickly in the air of the newsroom, mingling with the smell of uneaten breakfasts. A dozen or so reporters sat hunched over desks typing, while in the middle of the room, a short man stood and yelled.

"Call yourself a reporter, Lewis? You're a peabrain! Where's the detail? Where's the color? You said her throat was cut? How long was the wound? How deep? Did he get the windpipe? Was there blood on the ground or did it soak into her clothes? These are the things our readers want to know. Now get out and don't come back until you've got a *real* story for me."

"But, Mr. Devlin, sir, the police aren't giving us a thing! I can't get a look at the weapon. I can't even get into the alley!"

"Are you a man, Lewis? Have you got anything in those

trousers? Stop whining and get the story! If the police won't help you, find someone who will. A lodger in a neighboring building. The coroner's assistant. The bloke who mopped the floor after the autopsy. A few coins in the right hand work wonders. Find a way!"

The reporter, a lad of no more than eighteen or nineteen, slinked off, his head down, his cheeks burning. Devlin watched him go, shaking his head, then spotted Roddy.

"Sergeant! To what do I owe the pleasure?" he asked, walking over.

"Got to talk to you, Bobby. In private."

Devlin nodded and ushered them into his office. Roddy introduced Fiona, then, before the man could start asking questions, said, "I've a story for you. A good one. And I need it to go on the front of tonight's paper."

Devlin angled his head, a puzzled expression on his face. "That makes a change," he said. "I'm used to you trying to keep the good stories out of the paper, not get them in. And with top billing, no less. What's it about?"

Roddy told him how a union leader named Patrick Finnegan had been murdered ten years ago, right before the dock strike, and that Bowler Sheehan had just confessed to the crime. The second suspect, he said, was William Burton – the tea merchant.

Devlin frowned. "It's an interesting story," he said. "But the accusations can't be proved. I'll put it in if it helps you, but not on the cover. Page four, maybe. Murdered whore's getting the cover. I'd hoped that's what you were here about."

Roddy had anticipated a negative answer. "Come on, Bobby. I've done plenty of favors for you. Given you plenty of leads. I gave you the Turner Street Murders in '96, remember?" he said. "Made your career, those did. And the Blind Beggar gang. You wrote a whole series of stories on those thieves. Got you promoted to editor."

Devlin, fiddling with a paperweight, huffed with irritation. "Why's this story so important to you?"

685

"Can't tell you that. Not yet. Just do it for me, Bobby. I'm calling in me debts."

"It's just not *bloody* enough! It happened ten years ago. It's too old. People want *fresh* murders. Like the whore with her throat cut. Now that's a good murder!"

Roddy played his trump card. "There were two," he said.

Devlin stopped fiddling with the paperweight. "Two?"

Roddy nodded. "The body found in Fournier Street last night was the second prostitute killed in a fortnight. Both had their t'roats cut."

"Jesus bloody Christ!"

"We didn't want a panic on our hands. We've tried to keep it quiet. Obviously, if *you* don't know, we've done a good job."

"But how did you –"

"We lied about the first victim's profession. Said she was a seamstress. It was half true. It's what she told everyone. We blamed her murder on a botched robbery."

"It's the Ripper all over again!" Devlin said excitedly. "Where was the first one found? Same area? How old was she? Same type of knife used on both of them? Any other wounds? Any bruising?"

Roddy answered by unbuttoning his jacket, reaching inside, and pulling out a sheaf of paper. "These are the coroner's reports on both women." Devlin reached for them, but he withheld them. "They're yours . . . *if* you put Sheehan and Burton on tonight's cover."

Devlin chewed his lip, deliberating. His curiosity finally got the better of him. As Roddy knew it would. "All right, all right," he said.

"And I need you to provide my colleague here, Mrs. Soames, with a hundred advance copies."

"Anything else you want? A picture of your kids on page two?"

"You'll do it?"

"Yes! Now give me the reports!"

Roddy handed them over. "I need these brought back to me in an hour, Bobby. One hour. Send one of the new lads. Tell him to bring me a bacon sandwich. Fish and chips. Anyt'ing. Make it look like he's delivering me dinner. He can't look like a reporter. You got that? I'm taking a risk giving you these."

Devlin nodded, his eyes trained on the documents. "Listen to this, O'Meara. Throat cut left to right . . . trachea severed . . . esophagus, too . . . knife marks on the vertebrae . . . facial mutilation . . . possible attempt at evisceration . . . it's him!" he said gleefully.

Roddy stood. Fiona did, too. He noticed she looked pale. He wanted to get her out of there. Given how her mother had died, he doubted she shared Devlin's enthusiasm for blood.

"You'll give your readers a straight story on the whores, right, Bobby?" Roddy said. "You won't do anything irresponsible, like blaming the murders on the Ripper when we all know he's dead?"

"Not a chance," Devlin said, still reading.

"Good," Roddy said, relieved.

Devlin looked up and grinned. "We'll say it's the Ripper's ghost!"

"I can't believe this, Roddy," Joe said softly. "Paddy Finnegan was *murdered*?"

"Aye, lad. To keep the dockers from organizing."

Joe was silent for a few seconds, then said, "She needed me, Roddy. She needed me so badly. And I abandoned 'er. I turned my back on 'er. I didn't 'elp 'er."

"Help her *now*. If you ever loved her, do what I'm asking."

"I will. And I'll see to it that 'Arrods and Sainbury's and a dozen others follow suit. 'E won't get away with this. Not if I 'ave anything to do with it."

"Thank you, lad. I knew I could count on you. I want to buy her a little insurance. From you and your fellow merchants. And from the union lads." He stood. He was in Joe's office, in Covent Garden, and he had a long ride ahead of him. "I've got to go. I've still got to find Pete Miller, the head of the Wapping local."

"Roddy, wait."

"Aye?"

"Where is she?"

Roddy shook his head. "I can't tell you that."

"Please, Roddy."

"I don't t'ink she wants to see you, lad."

"Let 'er tell me that. Let 'er tell me 'erself and I'll never bother 'er again."

"You can't just barge in on her, Joe!" Roddy said angrily. "Jaysus! Don't you t'ink she's got enough on her mind tonight without you turning up at her door?"

"I won't go tonight. I'll go tomorrow. When it's over. I want to go right now, I won't lie to you. But I won't. You 'ave my word."

Roddy stared at him. "The Savoy," he finally said. He was about to remind him of his promise, but Joe didn't give him the chance.

"Trudy!" he bellowed, running past him to his secretary's office. "Get me 'Arrods on the line. Right away!"

Lowering rain clouds, dark and ominous, swept in upon London. A sharp wind whipped them along, scudding them inland from the Thames, over the riverside slums, westward over City countinghouses, and farther inland still, over Westminster and St. James's – rarefied enclaves of privilege and power.

A storm's coming, Fiona thought, from the east. She could smell the river on the wind. Had that same wind which now swept about her gusted through the bleak streets of Whitechapel? she wondered. Had it blown through the thin walls of the crumbling houses there, through the ragged clothes of the people in them? Was it just her imagination, or did the wind carry the bitter stench of poverty?

Two men, well-dressed and well-fed, hurried by her and disappeared into White's, the exclusive gentleman's club outside of which she now stood. Her father-in-law, Lord Elgin, the Duke of Winchester, was inside, too. He dined there nightly. She knew this because Nick had told her the man spent more time at his club than he did in his home.

If all went well, in a matter of mere minutes she would come face-to-face with him. And then everything would depend upon her. Upon her ability to act, to posture, to feign a certainty about money and markets and the habits of English investors, to bluff a man who was the head of one of England's most powerful banks, a man more sophisticated in the ways of finance than she could ever hope to be. How on earth would she do it? She was terrified of failing when so much was at stake.

A sudden gust caught her skirts. She smoothed them. Her diamond, the one Nick had given her, flashed up at her as she did. Nick. How she wished he were here. She needed him now. From behind, a stronger gust blasted down upon her. It felt like a hand in the middle of her back, pushing her forward. She suddenly had a feeling – just as she'd had the day Teddy read her Nick's will – that he was with her. That he'd swooped in from Paris or wherever his soul resided now, to be with her, to bolster her. She could hear him saying, "Go on, old shoe, go knock the stuffing out of him!" It gave her the courage she needed to walk up the steps and into the club.

A steward met her in the foyer. "I'm terribly sorry, madam," he said sharply, "but this is a private club. For gentlemen only."

Fiona regarded him as if he were some particularly repulsive form of insect life. "I am the Viscountess Elgin," she said haughtily, the title tripping off her tongue as if she used it every day. "The Duke of Winchester is my father-in-law. I must see him immediately. It's an emergency. A private family matter."

The steward nodded, suddenly accommodating. "One

moment, please," he said, then disappeared up a flight of carpeted stairs, past wood-paneled walls hung with English landscapes.

Fiona took a deep breath. So far, so good. She had assumed her first role and played it well, but the next would be far more difficult. As she waited for the steward to return, Roddy's parting words echoed in her ears. "Be careful, lass, be damned careful. I've seen people murdered over a pound, never mind a few hundred thousand of them." She promised him she would be. Roddy had done so much for her. Without him, she wouldn't be here now, only inches away from seeing her fragile plan succeed. He wanted this, too. She must not fail.

The steward reappeared. "The duke will see you. Follow me, please." He escorted her up the stairs and down a hallway into a private room. The door clicked shut behind her and she was left alone. Or so she thought until a man's voice, clipped and cold, said, "You have a great deal of nerve, Miss Finnegan."

Fiona's eyes fastened upon him. He was standing behind a desk at the far end of the room, a squat, fleshy toad of a man in a black dinner jacket. His face was exceedingly unattractive except for one feature – his remarkable turquoise eyes. Nick's eyes.

"Elgin. Mrs. Nicholas Elgin," she said. "At least that's what it says on my marriage certificate. I go by Soames, however. My late husband preferred it."

"May I ask why you have interrupted an extraordinarily good supper?"

Fiona drew a copy of the *Clarion* from her briefcase and tossed it on the desk.

"I am not familiar with this publication," the duke said, eyeing it distastefully.

"You may not be," she replied, "but the editors of every major newspaper in the city are. I believe it would be in your best interest to read the lead story."

He bent toward the desk. She saw his eyes move across

690

the headline. "Tea Merchant Accused of Union Leader's Murder." And under that, "William Burton Questioned by Police." He turned the page and read the story. For a fraction of a second she saw a ripple of alarm disturb his carefully composed expression. As quickly as it had come, it was gone again, but a spark of hope flared inside her, giving her confidence.

"What, exactly, has this to do with me?" he asked at length.

"Nicholas called you many things, sir, but he never called you a fool. You know as well as I do that murderers are not permitted to remain at large. William Burton will be arrested, convicted, and hanged. His business will be ruined. I've had copies of the *Clarion* delivered to every single editor of every London paper, large and small. The story will be all over the city by tomorrow. Copies also went to Burton's other major shareholders. I should think they'd be appalled at the idea of investing in a company belonging to a killer. By morning, they'll be scrambling to unload their shares."

"Perhaps," the duke said. "What do you want from me?"

"Nick's Burton Tea shares."

"And if I refuse?"

"Then I will do everything I can to ruin Burton Tea. I own twenty-two percent of the company – that's without Nick's shares – and I promise you, I'll dump it faster than you can blink. By noon, the market will be awash in Burton Tea. The stock won't be worth the paper it's printed on. The company will be ruined. And Albion Bank will lose the three hundred thousand pounds it invested."

The duke took a cigarette from a silver box on the desk, tapped it, and lit it. He took a long drag, blew it out again, then said, "I don't think so. The police will question William. He will, of course, deny any involvement and within a few days the whole thing will blow over. No outraged investors, no panicked selling."

"I'll start the panic. The second the market opens."

"To what end? The fact that you own twenty-two percent, plus your rabid determination to get your hands on my late son's shares, tells me one thing – you want to take over Burton Tea. How will you accomplish that if you release all your holdings?"

"I won't. But I will have bankrupted the company. I will at least have that satisfaction."

Elgin mulled this. "Very possibly, but there are no guarantees. Someone could buy a large chunk of your shares, stabilize the stock, and save the company. I've seen it happen."

Fiona swallowed. She was losing her advantage. She dealt her trump card. "This is a banker's draft for three hundred thousand pounds," she said, pulling a piece of paper out of her briefcase and placing it on the desk. "The sum total of Albion's loans to Burton Tea. The minute you give me Nick's shares, it's yours."

Elgin raised an eyebrow. "You're willing to repay the entire loan?"

"All of it. I'll be at Albion at eight o'clock tomorrow morning. We can do the trade then – the Burton Tea shares for my money. He had other shares in the account. They're worth a a good deal. Keep them. All of them. I only want the Burton Tea stock." She paused to let her offer sink in. "What if you're wrong? And I'm right? What if Burton Tea does go under? There are people in this world who value morality and justice above profit."

"Are there? I'm sure I don't know any of them. A very pretty speech, my dear, but believe you me, investors care more for their purses than for some long-dead dock worker." He stubbed out his cigarette. "I have rather enjoyed our little interview – my evenings don't usually afford me such dramatic interludes – but I must return to my supper companions now."

The walls of the room seemed to close in upon Fiona. She suddenly found it hard to breathe.

The duke walked over to her. He stood close to her, so

close that she could smell the wine he'd drunk and the lamb he'd eaten. He gazed at her intently, then said, "Tell me something, Miss Finnegan. Are you a virgin?"

It took a few seconds for her shocked mind to register the question. "How dare you –" she began, but he cut her off.

"Did my son ever fuck you? Tell me the truth and we'll put an end to all this nonsense. Did he take you like a man, or did he jam his prick up your shapely ass? That was his preferred method, I'm told. At least that's what his roommate from Eton said. To my counsel. Just yesterday, in fact." He smiled as her face went white. "What? Cat got your tongue? Not to worry, I have other ways of finding out. That laundress you fired three years ago – Margaret Gallagher – she's a very talkative sort. And if all else fails, we can always get an independent medical authority to make an assessment. Some randy old codger who's only too eager to part those slender legs and get a look at what's between them."

"You bastard!" she cried, raising her hand to slap him. But he, surprisingly nimble for a heavy man, grabbed her wrist and jerked her to him. She struggled, but he held her fast.

"When you bluff someone, you silly bitch, you need to make him afraid. Make him feel he's got something to lose. I have nothing to lose. There may be a flap in the papers tomorrow, but it will pass. Burton Tea will survive. William will continue to repay his loan. I will retain the sum I spent on his stock, and you, Miss Finnegan" – he tightened his grip until she thought he would snap her arm – "will withdraw your foolish claim."

He released her and strode out of the room. Fiona's legs went weak. She slumped against the desk. It was over. She had failed. Utterly and completely.

77

Asleep in a chair in her bedroom, in front of a fire long since dead, Fiona twitched, then moaned piteously, "No . . . please . . . help me . . . somebody help me . . ."

The dark man had come for her and this time he had caught her. He'd followed her down winding streets, in and out of abandoned buildings, until she'd run into a warehouse with no way out. He held her fast now, despite her violent struggles. She screamed again, hoping that someone would hear her. But no one came. She felt his breath on her neck and saw the glint of the knife blade as he raised it above her. And then she heard it, a battering, loud and insistent. Someone was out there. Someone would help her. "Mrs. Soames!" the voice cried. "Are you there?"

"In here!" she cried. "Hurry!"

"Mrs. Soames, I must speak with you . . ."

"Help me, please!"

But it was too late. She felt a searing pain as the dark man drew the blade across her throat. She was in agony, unable to breathe, as her own blood cascaded down her chest, and then she heard the battering again. And the sound of glass smashing. And then she was awake, panting with fright, blinking into the feeble light of a rainy morning. She sat up and looked around, reassuring herself that she was alive, and alone. She saw a half-empty bottle of wine on the table before her, a crumpled handkerchief. She looked down at herself and saw that she was fully dressed. She remembered collapsing into the chair, spent and broken, when she'd gotten back from White's . . . hours ago . . . pouring herself a glass of wine, and then being overcome by a convulsive fit of weeping. I must've cried myself to sleep, she thought. And then she'd had that terrible nightmare. Just the memory of it made her shake. The dark man, the knife, all that blood. She vaguely remembered that someone had tried to help her. She recalled a voice, the sound of a fist battering on wood. She closed her eyes, trying to calm herself, then nearly jumped out of her skin as the battering started again.

"Mrs. Soames! Fiona, are you there? It's me, Neville Pearson. Please let me in!"

Neville? What on earth does he want? she wondered. She glanced at her watch. It wasn't even seven o'clock yet. She ran her hands over her hair. She could tell it was a mess. "Just a minute!" she shouted, trying to tuck the loose strands back into their twist. Glass crunched under her foot as she stood. Her wineglass. She looked at her skirt. There was a big wet stain on it. "Bloody hell!" she swore. "Coming, Neville!"

She hurried out of her bedroom, through the foyer, and to the door. Three men were standing in the hallway: her counsel; a well-dressed man in his fifties who was slight and anxious-looking; and a man with a thick dark head of hair, not yet out of his thirties, who had a brash and pugilistic look.

"Thank God you're here!" Neville exclaimed, relief washing over his face.

"Why are you here? What's going on?" Fiona asked.

"May we come in?"

"Of course. Forgive me." She ushered them in and led them to her sitting room.

Neville glanced at her. "Have you not slept?"

"Not really, I –"

He cut her off. "No, I can't imagine you would've. Not after last night. Terribly foolish of you, walking right into the lion's den. Terribly brave, too."

"How do you know –" she began, but Neville didn't let her finish.

"I've taken the liberty of having breakfast sent up," he said. "Should arrive any minute. In the meantime, I'd like you to meet Giles Bellamy, the chairman of Albion Bank . . ."

Fiona stiffened. She nodded at the man. This will not be good news, she thought.

". . . and David Lawton, Lord Elgin's counsel. David and Giles told me of your meeting with the duke last night. They are here to oversee the transfer of your late husband's shares."

"With the proviso we discussed, Neville," David Lawton quickly interjected. "Mrs. Soames must be willing to honor the offer she made to Randolph Elgin. The shares for the banker's draft. Those are the duke's conditions."

"Yes, but things have changed a bit since last evening, haven't they, David?" Neville said hotly. "I doubt the shares are worth a farthing now."

Fiona, tired, wary, and now terribly confused, could only say, "Wait a minute . . . what are you talking about? I saw Elgin last night, as you gentlemen somehow all seem to know, and he made it quite clear that he has no intention of giving me Nick's shares."

Neville blinked at her. "Have you not seen the morning papers?"

"No, I haven't. I was up late, and then I fell asleep, and I –"

"Here." He opened his briefcase, took out half a dozen newspapers, and slapped them on the tea table. "Read those, my dear." There was a polite tapping at the door. "Ah, that must be the breakfast. I'll see to it. Do sit down, Giles. David, you, too."

Fiona picked up the *Times*. She had no idea what she was supposed to be looking for. The dolorous headlines about the British economy? A report of unrest in India?

"Bottom right," David Lawton said, settling himself into a chair.

Her eyes traveled down the front page. And then she

saw it. "Burton Tea on Brink of Financial Ruin." She sat down, her eyes devouring every line of the story. Neville returned, leading the way for two waiters with a trolley. Tea was poured and breakfast served with great decorum, but Fiona was oblivious to it all.

Burton Tea was expected to declare bankruptcy by the end of the day, the lead said. Most of its major customers had canceled their orders. In addition, all of its inventory was destroyed by unidentified men who broke into its warehouse last night. Panicked shareholders were expected to flood the market with devalued stock as soon as it opened.

She gasped as she read the following paragraph.

When asked why Montague's, one of Burton Tea's most lucrative accounts, withdrew its order, Joseph Bristow, chairman of the popular chain, said, "I have spoken with the authorities investigating the case and I am convinced of William Burton's guilt. I would like to state, in the strongest possible terms, that Montague's will have no further dealings with Burton Tea. We make our profits honestly and in a moral fashion and we do not support any supplier who does not do the same. Our customers expect no less. I speak not only for myself but for the entire Montague's staff when I say that I am shocked and outraged that a member of the merchant class would employ such villainous means to derail the just cause of labor.

How had he known? she wondered, dazed. The story could not have made the evening edition of any other papers last night and she doubted he read the Clarion. How on earth had he found out? The article continued.

Many of London's leading retailers, as well as hotels and restaurants, eager to be seen in their *customers' eyes as inhabiting the same high moral ground as Montague's, followed suit.*

Fiona read the names: Harrods. Sainsbury's. Home and Colonial Stores. Simpson's-in-the-Strand. The Savoy. Claridge's. The Connaught. Even the Cunard and White Star Lines. She slumped back in her chair, her head reeling.

"Keep reading," David said. "You even got the union involved. Quite a feat, Mrs. Soames."

"Common vandals. Rabble-rousers." Giles Bellamy sniffed.

Fiona turned to page two and learned that overnight, dozens of men – their faces hidden behind scarves or sacking – had broken into Oliver's Wharf and tossed every single chest, box, and tin of tea into the Thames. They'd destroyed the packing machinery, too. Roving gangs had barged into neighborhood shops in East and South London and thrown any Burton Tea they'd found into the streets. Shopkeepers had been warned not to sell the tea; shoppers had been warned not to buy it. Workingmen and housewives were quoted as saying they didn't need telling, they wanted nothing to do with William Burton's bloodstained tea leaves.

The article mentioned that no one knew who the masked men were, but suspicion was being leveled at the Wapping chapter of the dockworkers' union. Peter Miller, its leader, angrily responded that the union did not condone lawlessness of any sort and that reporters might do better by hounding the real criminal, William Burton, instead of himself and his men. The article concluded with market experts predicting a staggering sell-off of Burton Tea shares fueled by an unwillingness on the part of merchants, and of the public, to patronize the company.

Fiona looked at Neville, then at Giles, then at David. She was no longer confused; she knew why they were here. Last night, she had suffered the deepest despair. She'd been convinced she'd failed. But now it was clear she'd succeeded.

She was going to get her shares. Because of three men – Joe Bristow, Peter Miller, and Roddy O'Meara. Roddy was behind this somehow, she just knew he was. Neither Joe nor Peter Miller could possibly know what they'd done for her, but they would learn. She would tell them. She would thank them. She would go to visit Peter Miller in person as soon as this was all behind her. He could say what he liked to the *Times,* those were his men who'd thrown Burton's tea into the river and he'd told them to do it. And as soon as she was back in New York, she would write to Joe. He did not want to see her, and she would not compromise her pride a second time by going to see him, but he had done an incredible deed for her and she owed him her gratitude.

"If we could get down to business?" Giles suggested, breaking the silence.

"Certainly," Neville said. "As I started to explain, Fiona, earlier this morning Lord Elgin authorized David to make a trade he says you requested – Nicholas Elgin's Burton Tea shares for a banker's draft for the sum of three hundred thousand pounds. David then came directly to me, accompanied by Giles, and we proceeded to you. I informed these gentlemen that I knew nothing of such an offer, and even if you had made it, I would advise against it. Those shares have little if any value now."

"Make the transfer, Neville," Fiona said.

"What! But why? The shares are worthless!"

David Lawton leaned forward in his chair. "But they're not, Neville. Not to Mrs. Soames," he said. "Did you know that your client already owns twenty-two percent of Burton Tea? Young Elgin's shares will give her fifty-two percent. You're looking at the new owner of Burton Tea. All she's doing by giving us the banker's draft is paying off the debt on her new company."

"Is this true?" Neville asked.

"Yes," Fiona said.

"Because of your father?"

"Yes."

He shook his head. It was his turn to look dazed. "Well then, gentlemen, let's get started, shall we? David, you have the shares?"

"I do."

David unbuckled his briefcase, pulled out a thick stack of stock certificates, and handed them to Neville, who examined them. "The duke has lost a fortune," he observed.

"The duke is a practical man," David replied. "He realizes his own money is already gone. He doesn't want to compound the mistake by losing Albion's money, too."

"Where is the draft, Fiona?" Neville asked. "In the hotel safe?"

Fiona shook her head. She reached into her skirt pocket and pulled out a crumpled piece of paper. "It's right here," she said.

"In your *pocket*?" he asked, incredulous. "You could've been murdered in your sleep for that. Are you mad?"

"After the last twenty-four hours, quite possibly," she said. "Before I hand it over, I have a request."

"What is it?" David asked.

"I would like you, David, and you, Giles, to accompany myself and Neville to Burton Tea. I'm going to confront him this morning. As soon as I've changed," she said. "Your presence will strengthen my claim. He and his board of directors may not accept the facts from me or from Neville, but they'll have to accept them from Elgin's solicitor and the chairman of Albion."

"Out of the question," Giles Bellamy sputtered. "This is nothing Albion should be associated with. It's a dreadfully ugly business, taking a man's company."

"Not nearly as ugly as taking a man's life," Fiona said quietly.

David Lawton gave her a long look. The hardness in his eyes softened, just for a second, to something like admiration. "Finish your breakfast, Giles, we're going," he said.

* * *

"What's happening, man? Why aren't we moving?" Neville Pearson shouted, leaning out of his carriage window. Rain, fierce and battering, forced him back inside.

"I'm sorry, sir," the driver yelled, his voice nearly drowned by the din of the storm. "The street's jammed! It's 'opeless! You're better off walking from 'ere!"

Umbrellas were located, briefcases gathered. Outside the hackney, Fiona surveyed the scene before her. The street was clogged with carriages. Scores of people, all pushing and jostling, were mobbing the Burton Tea building.

"Who are all these people?" she wondered aloud.

"Angry shareholders. That would be my guess," David said.

"And we're about to make them angrier still," Neville said grimly. "Come on. Let's relieve William Burton of his company." He turned to David and Giles. "You know the procedure. Mrs. Soames will do the talking. We are merely here to verify her claim."

Both men nodded. Their expressions were somber. Fiona's was, too, but her companions couldn't see it for her face was hidden under a black lace veil attached to a broad-brimmed hat. It matched the black silk suit she was wearing. A mourning ensemble.

As the party proceeded up the street, Fiona was shoved and elbowed roughly. The rain was still sheeting down and it was all she could do to keep Neville in her sights.

"Mrs. Soames? Where are you?" he shouted, turning to look for her.

"Over here!"

He was halfway up the steps already. She hurried to join him, wedging herself through the sea of shareholders – some shouting, some dumb with confusion – who clamored at the doors, imploring the beleaguered porter for answers. She suddenly felt desperately sorry for these people. Many of them were facing heavy losses, perhaps even the destruction of their life savings. Because of her. She vowed to herself that she would make it up to them by turning Burton

Tea into a profitable company. They would get their money back and more besides.

Interspersed among the investors were reporters, questioning anyone who would speak to them as to their views on whether William Burton was guilty or innocent. She saw Neville at the top of the steps now, gesticulating to the porter. Giles Bellamy was behind him. The plan had been for them to tell the porter that Giles wanted to see Burton. Burton was undoubtedly sequestered within his offices, but they felt certain he wouldn't dare refuse a meeting with the chairman of Albion Bank. Just as she was about to join the two men, however, a new turn of events overtook them all.

A harried clerk came out of the building, cleared his throat nervously, then bellowed at the crowd that Mr. Burton would give them all the information and assurances they required in half an hour's time in a shareholder's meeting. The meeting would take place in the company's boardroom, which was big enough, the clerk said, to accommodate everyone if they would all proceed to it in an orderly fashion. Reporters were not welcome, he added, only shareholders. At that statement, notebooks were surreptitiously dropped into coat pockets.

"Shall we still try to see Burton alone?" Neville asked as Fiona reached him.

"No," she said. "Let's attend the meeting." She felt a sudden deep relief that she would not be confronting the man in his office, the very room where she'd heard him laugh about her father's death. There would be people in the boardroom, plenty of them, and there was safety in numbers.

Slowly, the crowd filed into the boardroom. It was an impressive high-ceilinged affair with a dais at the front. Twenty large rectangular tables were arranged throughout it in rows of four across and five deep. There were chairs at the tables and more along the walls. Fiona and her companions seated themselves near the back. The room filled. Many stood. Anxious voices rose and fell trading hearsay. Ten minutes passed, twenty.

Fiona felt William Burton enter the room before she saw him. In the same way a gazelle at a watering hole suddenly knows the lion is near, she was acutely aware of his presence. He had entered through a side door at the front of the room and now stood on the dais, behind the podium, hands folded behind his back, watching. She stiffened instinctively at the sight of him. A raw, uncontrollable terror gripped her. The last time she'd been in the same room with the man, she'd nearly lost her life. With effort, she fought her fear down. It was different now, she reminded herself. She was not a teenaged girl anymore, set upon by two murderers. She was a grown woman now and in control.

He looked much as she remembered. Well-dressed, elegant, powerful. His face was older, but smooth, and completely expressionless. His eyes, even from a distance, looked as black and cold as a snake's.

"Good morning," he said crisply.

All talking ceased. Every eye was riveted upon him. He began to speak. His voice was calm and assured. Fiona was surprised at how well she remembered it, but then again, she'd heard it for ten years in her nightmares.

"I have been accused, as you know, of complicity in the murder of a former employee of mine, a union leader named Patrick Finnegan. I assure you that the charges, brought against me by a Thomas Sheehan of Limehouse, a notorious extortionist, are entirely spurious. I have never harmed any of my workers, I have sought only to improve their lives through fair wages and decent working conditions."

Upon hearing his words, the vestiges of Fiona's fear fell away and the old familiar rage, the one that had smoldered impotently for so many long years, caught fire.

"I first had the misfortune of meeting Mr. Sheehan two years ago," Burton continued, "after he informed my foreman at Oliver's Wharf that he would burn the place to the ground if I did not pay him one hundred pounds a month as protection money. After I was told of his demand, I sought the man out and made it clear I would never submit to such extortion. He threatened to damage my property and harm my person. I increased security at Oliver's, but, foolishly, never thought to do the same at a former tea factory of mine. Mr. Sheehan burned it down. How do I know this? The man himself told me so. And now, finding himself in trouble with the police, he has made these absurd accusations. Presumably in a bid for leniency in his role in the Quinn murder."

The smoking fires of Fiona's anger had become a conflagration. She sat rigidly in her chair, her eyes closed, her hands clasped tightly together on top of the table, willing herself to remain seated, to remain quiet, to remain in control.

Burton continued, acknowledging that his stock's value had indeed fallen that morning, but assured his investors that he would win back his former customers' goodwill as soon as his name was cleared, and asked them to hold their shares and keep faith in the company while he guided Burton Tea through what would be only a short-lived storm.

Fiona looked around and saw how readily his explanations and promises were accepted by people desperate for reassurances that their money was safe. They would believe his denials and discount the charges against him if it meant that their investments would survive. Well, she wouldn't let them. They would hear the truth.

When he had finished speaking, Burton accepted questions. One query after another was fired at him. He fielded them expertly, giving succinct answers and throwing in little jokes here and there to provoke smiles from his inquisitors. After he'd answered twenty or so, he announced he would take his last one.

"There's a rumor that Albion Bank is demanding full and immediate repayment of your loans, Mr. Burton. Is this true?" a man asked.

Burton laughed. "Where do you get your information,

sir? From proper newspapers or penny dreadfuls? Albion has made no such demand. I spoke with them early this morning and they voiced their strong support. And now, if there's no further business, I must leave you to attend to my firm and get your share values back up to where they should be."

In the heavy gloom of the gaslit boardroom, Fiona stood. A reporter for the *Times* would later write that she had looked like a modern-day Fury at that moment, a dark avenging angel.

"There is one more piece of business, Mr. Burton," she said. All heads turned toward her.

"Are you a shareholder, madam?" he asked dismissively, pausing at the podium. "This meeting is open only to shareholders."

"I am, in fact, your largest shareholder."

"Are you? I thought I was," Burton said, eliciting laughter from the crowd. "I don't believe we are acquainted. What's your name?"

"Mrs. Nicholas Soames," she said. "And I believe these good people should know that as of this morning, I possess fifty-two percent of Burton Tea. And as the new owner, I demand your resignation. Immediately."

Burton stared at her in disbelief. "A madwoman," he said.

"I am not mad, Mr. Burton. And I insist you step down."

"A lunatic's prank. Remove her!" he barked at two of his clerks.

Neville Pearson stood up and cleared his throat. Fiona heard his name pass through the crowd in whispers. An eminent man, he was recognized by many of the people present.

"Mr. Burton, this is no prank," he said loudly. "My client, Mrs. Soames, does indeed own Burton Tea. She holds fifty-two percent, as she said." He placed his hands on two thick leather files on the table in front of him. "The documentation is all here."

Burton's composure cracked. "That's impossible!" he shouted. "I've kept a close eye on my shares, Mr. Pearson. I know for a fact that no single investor owns more than five percent."

"Munro Enterprises . . . twenty-five thousand shares. Chelsea Holdings Incorporated . . . fifteen thousand shares," Fiona intoned. "Seamus Consolidated . . . forty thousand shares. The Thames Group . . . ten thousand shares."

Burton stared at her uncomprehendingly.

"All subsidiaries of a parent company named TasTea Incorporated. Those and many more. *My* company, Mr. Burton."

"That may well be, Mrs. Soames, but I myself hold the majority share of my own damn company!"

David Lawton stood. Fiona saw that Burton recognized him. "Not anymore, William," he said. "You *did* own the majority share. Until you sold four hundred and fifty thousand shares to my client, Randolph Elgin, several years ago. That stock was kept in a fund for Elgin's son, who passed away this spring. Nicholas Elgin, who used the name Soames, married unbeknownst to his family. He bequeathed all his property, including his investment fund, to his wife. It was transferred to her this morning."

"It's true, William," Giles Bellamy said quietly, as he rose from his chair. "Mrs. Soames now owns Burton Tea."

The room erupted. People leaped to their feet. Questions were shouted at Fiona and her colleagues. Burton leaped down from the dais and fought his way through the crowd, shoving aside the very people he'd sought to reassure only minutes ago.

"Giles, what is the meaning of this?" he demanded.

"The papers are all here, William. Read them," Giles said. He opened a file and removed the certificates. These, Fiona had brought from New York. Then he opened the second file. It contained Nick's shares. Now, her shares.

Burton picked them up, one after another. When he had

seen them all, he took a few steps backward, pressed his palms to his temples, and said, "This can't be. It *can*'t be." He squeezed his eyes shut, ignoring the shouts, the questions, the commotion all around him. Then he opened them again, looked at Fiona, and screamed, "Who are you?"

The room fell silent. Fiona lifted her veil and met his black, hateful gaze. At first, his face registered only confusion, but as he continued to stare at her, recognition broke across it. "You!" he hissed. The room was as silent as a crypt.

"You remember me, Mr. Burton?" she asked. "I'm flattered. I remember you. Very, very well. I remember standing in your office one night listening to you and Mr. Sheehan discuss my father's murder. I had come to beg you for money, for compensation for my father's so-called accident. So that my brother and I could buy food and rent a room. I got rather more than I came for. Do you remember that night? He was a union leader, my father. He wanted the dockers to have a penny more an hour. For a bit of extra food for their children, or a warm jacket to work in. One penny more. And you . . ." She paused, overcome. Her rage had filled her eyes with acid tears. She could taste its bitterness in her throat. ". . . you wouldn't pay it. Mr. Sheehan was telling you how he'd arranged my father's death. And you laughed. I still hear your laughter in my nightmares, Mr. Burton. I remember trying to get out of your office and stumbling. You heard me. You and Mr. Sheehan. And you came after me. Mr. Sheehan tried to kill me that night. But I was luckier than my father. I escaped. But I couldn't escape the memories. I vowed you would pay for what you'd done. And you have. Burton Tea is mine."

Again, the room fell into chaos. People babbled and shouted. Some pressed handkerchiefs to sweaty brows. Others scrambled to have a look at the certificates. Reporters shouted Fiona's name. She didn't even hear them. Burton's eyes were locked on hers. She gazed back at him, unflinching. A naked hatred – a black, roiling, tangible thing – moved between them.

"You conniving bitch. I wish I'd killed you when I had the chance," he said. "Then you'd be six feet under like your miserable father."

"William . . . dear God!" Giles Bellamy exclaimed. He stepped back from the table, ashen-faced.

"Mrs. Soames!" a reporter shouted. "Mrs. Soames, over here!"

There was a white flash, the smell of smoke. Someone had managed to sneak a camera in. Fiona blinked, blinded by the brightness. It was all Burton needed. In one quick, fluid movement, he pulled a knife from inside his jacket and lunged at her.

David Lawton saw it coming. He grabbed Fiona's jacket and pulled her backward. The blade missed her throat by a whisper. It sliced through her jacket, across her collarbone, and into the soft flesh below.

"Somebody stop him!" Neville shouted.

Brandishing his knife, Burton ran to the front of the boardroom and disappeared behind the dais through the side door. A group of men ran after him, but found that he'd locked it. The call went up to hunt for him throughout the building. Some joined the chase, others crushed around Fiona.

David had lowered her into a chair. He'd packed his handkerchief and Giles's against her wound but the white cloths had already turned red under his hand. "I need more handkerchiefs . . . a shirt . . . anything!" he shouted. A score of handkerchiefs were handed to him. He wadded some together and pressed them against the gash. Fiona cried out as he did. The pain was excruciating.

"We've got to get her to hospital now!" Neville ordered. "Giles, get the carriage –"

"There's no time," David said. "The street's jammed. It'll take ages for the driver to get here. We'll have to carry her. It's the fastest way. Come on!"

David hoisted her up and Neville led the way out of the boardroom, cutting a swath through the crowds of jabbering onlookers with his walking stick. Giles gathered up the certificates, now spattered with blood, and brought up the rear. He passed them on the sidewalk and ran ahead, shouting for the carriage. The driver spotted him and pulled into the top of Mincing Lane.

"London Hospital, right away!" Giles shouted. He climbed in, followed by Neville. They reached for Fiona and eased her into the seat. Neville held her in the crook of his arm. She closed her eyes, struggling against a sickening dizziness. Her chest felt as if it were on fire. She could feel her blood, hot and wet, seeping into her clothing. She felt David climb in, felt the carriage lurch forward, then pick up speed.

"Faster, man, faster!" Giles shouted out the window.

"Mrs. Soames . . . Fiona . . . can you hear me?" David asked, patting her face.

". . . hear you . . ." she mumbled deliriously.

"Hang on, please! We're almost there!"

"She's fainted!" Giles said. "Oh, God, Neville, she's white as a sheet!"

"Fiona!" Neville barked. "Can you hear me? Say something!"

"Does she have family in London?" David asked. "Is there someone who should know what happened?"

". . . tell my da, David," Fiona murmured. "Tell my da we won . . ."

78

"Oh, Jaysus! Look at you!" Roddy stood in the doorway of the hospital room, helmet in hand, devastated by the sight of the frail, ashen figure in the bed.

Fiona opened her eyes and gave him a weary smile. "I'm fine, Uncle Roddy."

"I came as soon as I got word. One of my men ran into the station with the news. I couldn't believe it. Christ, lass, I was terrified! T'ought you'd been killed. What the divil was I t'inking? I should never have let you go alone!"

"I wasn't alone, Uncle Roddy, I –"

"I should've gone with you."

"But I'm all right –"

"Aye, the very picture of health. Can I get you somet'ing? Some water? Are you t'irsty?"

"Parched."

He crossed the room and poured her a glass of water from the pitcher on her night table. "There you are. What did the doctors say?" he asked

"That I lost a bit of blood, but I'll be fine," she said, taking the glass from him.

"Why do they want you to stay?"

"Just to keep an eye on me for a day or two. Until I get my strength back."

"How do you feel?" He touched the back of his hand to her cheek. He didn't like her color at all. Or the deep shadows under her eyes. Or the spots of blood seeping through her bandages.

"Just a little dizzy now and again."

"Burton won't make it to the gallows, I swear to God he won't. When he's found, I'm going to personally rip his head off."

"He's still at large?"

"I'm afraid so. I went to Mincing Lane and talked to the men in charge before I came here. The entire Burton Tea building was searched; there was no sign of him. He's not been at his house, either. The City lads think he's going to try to head to the continent. If he hasn't already. They've got warnings out to all the ferry companies. And they've put out a reward."

Roddy was frustrated not to be on the case himself, but Mincing Lane, as part of the City of London, fell within the jurisdiction of the City's own police force. He was a member of the Metropolitan Police, which existed under the aegis of the Home Office, not the City, and policed the rest of London.

Fiona leaned toward her night table. She grimaced as she set her glass down.

"Does it hurt?" Roddy asked.

"A little. The doctor said the wound's eight inches long." She laughed wryly. "No more low-cut dresses for me."

"Fiona, do you have any idea how lucky you are? If you'd been standing any closer . . . if you hadn't been pulled away in time . . . if the knife blade had been half an inch longer . . ." Roddy shook his head. "Well, I'd be visiting you at the coroner's, not in hospital."

"But you're not," Fiona said. She smiled again. "We did it, Uncle Roddy."

"*You* did it, lass. God knows how, but you did."

"With your help, that's how. You made a few extra visits last night, didn't you?"

"One or two."

"Where can I find Peter Miller?"

"Down the Lion, your da's old watering hole."

"You talked to Joe Bristow, too, didn't you?"

"I did."

Fiona nodded silently and Roddy could see a deep pain in her eyes, one that had nothing to do with the wound on her chest. It still hurt. After all these years, it still hurt even to talk about Joe. He wished he'd never given the lad her Savoy address. He hoped he'd stay the hell away from her.

"I don't want to see him," she said at length. "He's done a great deal for me and I should give him my thanks in person, but I can't. I will write him, though. Once I'm home. I owe him that."

Roddy nodded. He was just about to ask her to go over the whole day's events for him, start to finish, when they heard a knock. A sister in a crisp white cap stuck her head around the door.

"How are you feeling, dear?" she asked Fiona.

"Fine, thank you. Much better than when I came in."

"I'm glad to hear it. Did those other gentlemen find you?"

"Gentlemen?" Fiona asked.

"The deliverymen."

"What deliverymen?" Roddy asked sharply.

"The two lads from the florist's. I found them wandering the hallway looking for Mrs. Soames's room. I gave them her room number."

"I said Mrs. Soames was to have no visitors. Not one." Roddy had told the sister on duty to restrict access to police officers. He was stepping on the City force's toes by doing so, but he didn't care.

"Don't you take a tone with me, sir!" the woman said, bristling. "They were very nice lads. Very polite. They had an enormous arrangement of roses. What should I have done? Taken it from them? I couldn't even lift it!"

Roddy was on his feet immediately.

"What did they look like?"

"I . . . I don't know," the sister said, flustered. "The roses were so lovely, I was looking at them, not the lads."

"Can you remember anything? Anything at all?"

"They had dark hair, I think . . . and were maybe twenty years of age. Maybe younger. They were big. Brawny."

You've just described half the toughs in Whitechapel, Roddy thought. "Does this door lock?" he asked.

"Yes," she said, rooting in her pocket. "Here's the key."

"Stay here with Mrs. Soames. Lock the door when I leave. My badge number is zero-four-two-three. Ask me for it before you open the door again."

"Uncle Roddy, what's wrong?" Fiona asked.

"Not'ing, I hope," he said, "but keep that door locked."

Every cell in Roddy's body sensed danger as he sped down the corridor toward the back stairwell. He pushed the door open and peered down the spiraling steps. He saw nothing, but he heard the sound of hurrying footsteps, and then a door slamming shut below him. He was down the stairs in no time and out through a side door, emerging in a foul alley where the hospital's waste was stored. Panting now, he ran to the alley's mouth, his trained eyes scanning the scores of pedestrians on the Whitechapel Road, looking for two men who fit the nurse's description. He saw several – one pair heading into a pub, another boarding a bus, a third talking to a costermonger. Not one of them looked suspicious. A few were laughing or smiling; all were easy and unhurried.

Maybe they *were* just deliverymen, he thought, feeling foolish. And maybe they had been lost. He turned and headed back up the alley, wondering if his sixth sense, the intuition he relied so heavily upon, was too tightly wound in the wake of the day's events and sending out false alarms. He felt bad that he'd snapped at the sister and alarmed Fiona.

As he passed a large metal rubbish bin, a brilliant patch of red caught his eye. He turned his head, steeling himself against what he was sure would be bloody rags or bedsheets. Instead he saw roses. At least two dozen of them. Not the wilted remains of some spent arrangement, but fresh, beautiful flowers. He reached in, looking for a card, a bit of wrapping with a return address on it, or even the florist's address, but there was nothing.

It didn't matter. He didn't need an address to know who'd sent them . . . and the two lads carrying them. The City boys were wrong. William Burton hadn't left London. He was still here. And he meant to finish what he'd started.

79

"Is there an address for the driver, Sergeant O'Meara?" the bellboy asked.

"No. I'll tell 'im meself. We're going to ride with 'im, Mrs. Soames and I."

"Very well, sir. I'll take some of the lighter things now. I'll be back for the trunks."

The lad tucked a hatbox under his arm and scooped up two suitcases. Roddy held the door for him, then locked it. He picked his way through the stacks of luggage in the foyer on his way to the sitting room, glancing at the door to Fiona's bedroom as he passed it. It was closed. She was still napping. He would let her rest until the trunks were downstairs. Packing had tired her. She'd only gotten out of hospital this morning and she was still weak.

Roddy worried about overtaxing her. He worried that the move he'd insisted she make would drain her fragile reserves, but he also felt he had no choice. Two days after he'd tried to murder Fiona, William Burton was still on the loose. The police were scouring the city for him. Constables were posted at his house, at Mincing Lane, and Albion Bank. His picture had appeared in several newspapers and appeals were made to the public to be on the lookout, but there had been no sign of him. Not one.

No one knew where he was, but he, if he wanted to, could easily find out where Fiona was. Plenty of newspapers had run stories about her. Readers wanted to know everything about the brave young widow who'd avenged her father's death. Some papers had even stated that she was

715

staying at the Savoy. All Burton had to do was pick one up and read it. And though the rooms were private, the lobby was open to the public. Anyone could troop through. Hundreds of people did every day. And a few coins in the hands of an unscrupulous bellboy or maid could easily buy information on one of the hotel's guests.

Roddy had decided that Fiona would be much safer in a private house. He'd engaged an agency in Knightsbridge and had told the proprietoress that he needed a place that was completely secure, and that he needed it immediately. She'd found one the same day – a beautifully furnished town house in Mayfair that was situated in the middle of a limestone square and could only be accessed from the front. It belonged to a diplomat who'd recently been posted to Spain. Roddy had also badgered Alvin Donaldson, the superintendent who was heading up the Burton investigation, to post two constables in front of it.

Fiona believed that Burton was long gone, that London was too dangerous a place for him. She told him he was being a worrywart, but Roddy had stood his ground. Burton had murdered her father merely because he perceived him as a threat to his company. What would he do to the person who'd actually taken that company? He'd kill her in the blink of an eye. All he needed was a chance.

As he searched the sitting room for any forgotten belongings, he heard a knock on the door. He felt for his truncheon. He was certain it was only the bellboy back for the trunks, but he was taking no chances. "Who is it?" he yelled, his hand on the doorknob. There was a slight pause, then a reply. "Joe Bristow."

"Bloody hell," Roddy said to himself. He opened the door.

" 'Ello, Roddy. Is . . . is she 'ere?"

Roddy shook his head. "She was," he lied, gesturing at the trunks piled up behind him, "but she left for America. Just this morning." He had no intention of letting Joe Bristow loose on Fiona. Not after she'd said she didn't want to see him again.

Joe looked crestfallen. "I can't believe I missed 'er," he said. "I tried to see 'er in 'ospital after I read what 'ad 'appened in the papers, but they weren't allowing any visitors. Wouldn't even send me name up."

"Aye, that was my doing," Roddy said. "I was worried about Burton, or someone working for him, trying to get to her. I'll let her know you stopped by, Joe. I'll give her your regards."

"I'd like to let 'er know myself," he said. "Can I 'ave 'er address in New York?"

Roddy deliberated for a second, trying to figure out what he could say to soften the blow, then decided to be honest with him. "Joe, she knows about our meeting, about everything you did for her and she's grateful to you. But she doesn't want to see you. She told me so herself. I'm sorry, lad."

Joe looked at the ground, then at Roddy again. "Would you at least tell 'er I called?"

"I will."

"And would you give 'er this?" He handed him his card.

"I'll send it to 'er."

"Thank you. Good-bye, Roddy."

"Good-bye, Joe." Roddy closed the door and jammed the card into his pocket.

The bedroom door opened. Fiona came out, her face puffy with sleep, her skirts creased. "I thought I heard voices," she said. "Was someone at the door?"

"At the door? Ah, no. No one. Just ... um ... just a barrow boy trying to peddle his rubbish."

Fiona blinked at him. "A *barrow boy*? In the hotel?"

"I told you the security here isn't all it should be," he said, then quickly changed the subject.

80

Fiona regarded the sad wooden crosses sticking out of the ground. The plots they marked were tangled and matted with long grass and weeds. Two stood crookedly. One had broken off at its base. A fourth was discolored by rust marks from the nails that held it together. She could just make out the remains of a name on it: "Patrick Finnegan."

She turned to her companion, a large East London man, whom Roddy had hired as her driver and guard. He was carrying a rake, a spade, a trowel, a pair of clippers, a watering can, and a bag of fertilizer.

"You can put them down right there, Andrew," she said.

"Shall I get your 'amper? And the rest of the flowers, Mrs. Soames?"

"If you wouldn't mind."

She set the parcels she'd been carrying down and unwrapped them. They were young rosebushes – tea roses. She'd spent her entire afternoon traveling from florist to florist hunting for just the right ones. The churchyard was small and Andrew's carriage was right outside the gate. It only took a minute before he was at her side again with a flat of colorful primroses and a wicker basket. He set them down, then stood close by, his hands on his hips.

"I'd like to be alone for a while, Andrew. Could you wait for me in the carriage?" she asked.

He frowned. "Sergeant O'Meara said I wasn't to leave you alone."

"I'll be perfectly fine. Unlike Sergeant O'Meara, I doubt very much that William Burton is still in London, and even if he is, he's not likely to be hanging about a graveyard, is he?"

"I guess not. All right, then. Just shout if you need me."

"I will."

She picked up her rake and started in. It was a clear, cloudless August day and the sunshine was hot upon her back. It felt wonderful to move, to use her body again. Her stitches had come out yesterday. She'd had very little exercise since Burton had put her in hospital nearly three weeks ago. She was chafing under Roddy's restrictions, and hungry for fresh air, freedom, and time to herself.

Roddy had not been happy about this trip. He was so certain that Burton was still in London, whereas she didn't see how he could be. Where could he possibly hide? Alvin Donaldson had visited her just that morning to apprise her of any new developments in the case – but there were none. Burton's home and office, and the bank where he kept his money, were under constant surveillance. Donaldson felt that his lack of access to his known destinations, coupled with the fact that no one had so much as glimpsed him over the past fortnight, indicated that he'd had a sum of money stashed somewhere and had used it to buy himself a private passage across the Channel. The French were looking for him now; it was only a matter of time until he was caught.

Roddy had been with her during Donaldson's visit. He'd heard everything the man said, and admitted his reasoning was sound, but he still hadn't wanted her to leave the house. He'd had obligations today and asked her to wait until tomorrow, when he could go with her, but she'd refused. William Burton, she'd decided, had overshadowed her life for far too long. She didn't want him to ruin even one more day.

After an hour Fiona had the weeds cleared away and the grass clipped back on the four plots. Next, she planted the roses, then the primroses, and then she filled her watering can from a nearby spigot and gave everything a good dousing. She had muddied her hands and her skirt, but she didn't care. After today she would arrange for a gardener to tend the plots, but these things she wanted to do herself. Needed to. She'd been away for far too long.

As she worked, she had the churchyard almost entirely to herself. Two old ladies passed by on their way to leave flowers at a grave, murmuring quiet greetings. Likewise a young mother dressed in black and her small son. And then two lads strolled by, hands in their pockets. They were stopping every now and again, examining headstones. She glanced at them once, watching them as they pointed at markers or toed aside weeds. The second time she looked up, they were closer. Much closer.

"Looks nice what you did there, with the roses," one said.

"Thank you," Fiona said, looking up at them. They were young lads, strongly built. They wore narrow trousers, collarless cotton shirts, vests, and red kingsmen. Their faces showed evidence of scrappy dispositions – one had a scar, the other's nose had obviously been broken.

"We're looking for 'is granddad," the same one said, pointing at the other, "but we can't find 'im."

"What was his name?" Fiona asked.

" 'Is what?"

"His name. What's the name on the headstone?"

"Smith, Tom Smith. Same as mine," the second lad said.

Fiona looked at the neighboring markers, but none had the name "Smith" on it. "I don't think he's here," she said.

"What's that name?" Tom Smith asked, pointing at her father's marker.

"Patrick Finnegan," Fiona said. "My father."

"Is that so?" Tom said. He stepped up next to her to peer at the marker, so close that Fiona could smell the smoke in his clothes and the beer on his breath, and for a split second she felt afraid. Roddy had told her about the two men – Burton's men, he'd said – who'd come looking for her while she was in hospital. What if these were the very same men? Then she spotted Andrew. He was standing only five or six yards away, watching the lads' every move. They saw him, too. Tom Smith touched the rim of his cap. Andrew nodded back, unsmiling, arms crossed over his chest.

"Well, we'll keep looking, I guess. 'E's bound to be 'ere somewhere. 'E surely didn't get up and walk out, now did 'e?" Tom said, grinning. "Ta-ra, missus."

"Ta-ra," Fiona replied, feeling silly. They were just a pair of friendly lads and had meant her no harm. Probably the one was sent by his mother to tidy his grandfather's grave or some such thing. Roddy's dire warnings were making her jumpy. She resolved to put them out of her mind. She returned to her work and after a few minutes, when the lads had left the churchyard, Andrew returned to his carriage.

When she finished tending the plots, she spread a cloth on the ground, fished out a flask of tea and some sandwiches from her hamper, and sat awhile with her family. As she ate, she told them everything that had happened to her. All about her visit to William Burton's office so many years ago and what had happened there. About New York and Michael and Mary and her entire extended family. She told them about her tea business. About Will and Nick. She told them about Seamie and how they wouldn't even recognize him, he was so American now. He was going to discover something someday, she was sure of it. A cure for a disease, or a dinosaur, or maybe a whole new country. He was handsome, she said, as handsome as Charlie had been. She told them they could be proud of her brother, every bit as proud as she was.

And then she told them how she'd taken William Burton's tea company. He was ruined, she said, and as soon as he was caught he would go to prison, and then the gallows. "It's not enough, Da," she said, laying her hand on her father's grave. "But I hope it's something. I hope it helps you rest a little easier." Tears stung behind her eyes as she continued. "I miss you, Da. I miss you every single day. And I love you. Kiss Mam and Charlie and the baby for me, will you? And tell them I love them, too."

She sat quietly for a few more minutes, watching the early-evening sun slant through the trees, dappling the grass, and then, after promising she wouldn't wait ten years to come back, she rose to go.

She called for Andrew and the two of them piled all her clobber back into the carriage. He helped her in, closed the door after her, then nosed his horses through the narrow streets of Whitechapel on his way back to Mayfair. As Fiona gazed out the window, she glimpsed familiar street signs and buildings. She saw men on their way home from work and heard their voices as they called to each other or greeted their children. She saw the brewery where Charlie once worked and realized she wasn't far from Montague Street. She was suddenly seized by an overpowering longing to see her old street, her house, the place where she had grown up.

"Andrew!" she yelled, rapping on the small sliding window at the front of her compartment. "Andrew, stop!"

The carriage came to a halt. "What is it, Mrs. Soames? What's wrong?"

"I want to get out. I'm going to walk for a bit. I'll make my own way home."

"You can't do that, ma'am. Sergeant O'Meara told me not to let you out of my sight. 'E said to bring you to the graveyard and straight back."

Fiona was barely listening to him. She had seen Whitechapel again. And heard it and smelled it. It was beckoning to her. "Sergeant O'Meara will never know if you don't tell him, Andrew," she said. "Please don't worry about me. I'll be home before dark." And then, over his protests, she was out of the carriage, her purse in hand.

As she disappeared down Brick Lane, she was glad she'd worn an older skirt and blouse. Glad of the dried mud on her hem and that her hair had come down while she was gardening and she'd only caught it up in a loose, messy twist. She fit in; no one looked at her twice. She hurried along, swept up in the current of workers.

As she finally rounded the corner of Montague Street, her breath caught. There it was, her house. It looked exactly the same. Sooty red bricks and black shutters, the steps scrubbed spotless. And just down from it, Joe's house. For just a moment, she was seventeen again, on her way home from the tea factory, hoping he would be out, sitting on his steps, waiting for her.

The street was full of people. She walked among the fathers hurrying home to their tea. Mams hollering for their kids. Little girls in pigtails; older ones with baby brothers or sisters on their hips. A group of young boys kicked a ball back and forth. One launched it through the open window of number sixteen. There was a crash. "Oh, me teapot!" a woman cried from within. Then the man of the house was on the step, yelling for blood. But the boys were already gone, dispersed like a flock of sparrows.

She marveled at the noise and the commotion. No one ever yelled on Fifth Avenue. At least not uptown, where she lived. No children kicked balls around or skipped rope. There was no bawdy laughter from housewives clustered together. No sympathetic clucking over a young wife with a big belly. No old men showing off a prize budgie.

There was so much life in these streets, so much heart. Had she always known that? As a girl, she'd only wanted to escape this place. Why? She had never been happier than when she lived right here. In a shabby two-up-two-down without even a room to call her own and a drafty privy in the backyard. She'd had nothing, nothing at all, and yet she'd had everything.

She reached the end of the street and looked back. She could almost hear her father singing as he walked home from the docks. And her mother, hands on her hips, shouting for Charlie. She could almost see a lad, tall and blond and heartbreakingly handsome walking toward her, his hands in his pockets, the whole world in his eyes.

She kept walking and eventually crossed the Commercial Road. She knew she should stop there and get a hackney back to Mayfair. The twilight was coming down now – she could just make out a few faint stars. Instead, her feet carried her south, toward Wapping and the river. She knew the way by heart, and though a pub or two had changed names, or a shop had been painted a different color, everything was completely familiar to her.

Wapping's High Street was nearly empty as she crossed it. Oliver's was still there. It was strange to think she owned it now. To the side of it, just as she remembered it, was the narrow passageway that led down to the Old Stairs. She stood at the top of them and the sight of her beloved London river, calm and smooth, darkening under the evening sky, took her breath away. Never had it looked so beautiful.

She trotted down the steps and sat at the bottom, resting her chin on her knees as she had when she was a girl. She watched the boats gently bobbing on the receding tide, saw the black cranes silhouetted against the dark blue sky. A hundred million memories filled her mind. She remembered sitting here with her father when she was little, nestled close to him, sharing a cone of chips or a pork pie, as he pointed out the proud sailing ships and told her where they'd come from and what they carried. She remembered sitting here with Joe when she was older, and she remembered the last time she'd been here, the night he'd shattered her heart. Where are the pieces? she wondered. Still here? Buried in the sand?

She tried to think of other times, better times. She remembered all the times they'd talked about their shop, the first time he kissed her, the first time he told her that he loved her. They had all happened here, by the river. She closed her eyes, felt the warm summer breeze on her face, heard the waves gently lapping. Just as it had when she was a girl, the river comforted her. Restored her. Inspired her.

She turned her thoughts to the future instead of the past. She had a new tea company to run now, new markets to conquer. The day after she was released from hospital, she had called a meeting of all her new employees and informed them that she was now their boss. She told them all about TasTea and assured them that she had both the business acumen and the financial muscle needed to make Burton Tea – now TasTea, London – stronger, better, and more profitable than ever before. Those who wished to stay were welcome to, she said. Those who were loyal to William Burton should leave. Not one person had.

There was much to learn. About the company. About its real estate, both in London and abroad. And about the English and European markets. She knew she would have to get Stuart Bryce over here immediately. She'd called him shortly after she'd taken over the company; she could still hear his voice: "Bloody hell, Fiona! You've done *what*?" He'd been beside himself when he learned they had a whole new tea company to run – complete with offices, a wharf, and a plantation in India. She had no doubts that with the acquisition of Burton Tea, she and Stuart could make TasTea not just the biggest tea company in America, but in the entire world.

Excited by the very idea, she slipped off her boots, peeled off her stockings, and jumped down on the pebbled mud flat. She walked for a little ways, then picked up a handful of stones and started skipping them just as hard and as fast as she could.

"What do you think, Alf?" Joe asked, holding a scoopful of green coffee beans under his foreman's nose.

Alf Stevens inhaled, then nodded. "A bloody sight better than the last batch we 'ad. Not a trace of mustiness. Good, bright color. Smooth skins. A nice, fresh 'arvest altogether. Oscar Sanchez's plantation, I'd say. Just north of Bogotá."

"Alf, you're a bloody amazement," Joe said, clapping the old man on the back. Alf Stevens had been the foreman at the Morocco, a wharf on the Wapping's High Street, for over thirty years and could name not just the country or region, but the actual plantation where the coffee had been grown with just a whiff and a glance. "We've found ourselves a new supplier. I'm through with Marquez. Last batch 'e sent was pure rubbish. I'll 'ave the lads from the roaster's come round with a wagon Monday morning."

"I'll be ready for them."

"Good man. 'Ow's everything else? Any trouble since the Oliver's incident?" Joe asked, referring to the damage done to Oliver's Wharf after William Burton had been accused of Paddy Finnegan's murder.

"No. Nothing, really."

Joe sensed a hesitancy in his reply.

"What is it?"

"Nothing, guv. It's . . . it's silly," Alf said, embarrassed.

"Tell me."

"You know 'ow when the lads broke into Oliver's, they tore off some of the loop'ole doors? Well, I was on me way 'ome a few nights ago – it was late – and I 'appened to look up at the building. I know this sounds barmy, but I saw a man standing there. In one of the loopholes. I was so bloody startled I tripped on a cobble and nearly fell on me face. When I looked up again, 'e was gone."

"What did 'e look like?"

" 'E 'ad an 'ard, pale face. And dark 'air. And 'is eyes, I remember those. They were like the river at midnight. If I believed in spirits and all that rubbish, I'd say it was 'im, that Finnegan bloke. Come back from beyond to 'aunt the place."

Joe gave Alf a skeptical look. "You're saying you saw a ghost?"

Alf shrugged defensively. "I'm not saying anything."

"It was probably the night watchman. Doing 'is rounds."

"They don't 'ave a watchman. Last one quit after the place was smashed up." Alf held his hands up. "I know what you're thinking, guv, but I was as sober as the Pope, I swear it."

"I'll 'ave a look for 'im myself on me way out. I'll give 'im your best if I see 'im."

Joe's teasing tone was lost on Alf. " 'E don't strike me as the sociable type," the old man said. "You do see 'im, I'd advise you to keep on walking."

Alf and Joe finished inspecting the new coffee shipment, cutting into random bags and assessing the contents. When they were satisfied, Joe took his leave, reminding Alf that the roasters would come for the beans on Monday. Alf grumbled that he didn't need reminding and that Joe wasn't to think he was soft in the head now just because he was seeing spirits.

As Joe walked west down the High Street, he made a point of looking at Oliver's upper stories. He saw nothing. Just loopholes. Some shuttered, some open. Spirits, he thought, shaking his head. The only spirits troubling Alf came from the whiskey flask in his back pocket. As he continued to stare at the building, he wondered why William Burton hadn't repaired the damage, and then it suddenly struck him that William Burton no longer owned this building. A woman by the name of Soames did. Fiona Finnegan Soames.

He tried to push the thought from his mind. It hurt so much to think that she'd been here, in London, and that even now, ten years on and widowed, she still didn't want anything to do with him. He'd read about her in the papers. He'd gone to her hotel room so full of hope. Ever since the night Roddy had come to him to ask for his help, he hadn't been able to stop himself from hoping again. If only they could talk. If she would just let him tell her how sorry he was, how he'd never stopped loving her. He would have done anything for a second chance with her. Anything to earn her forgiveness.

But it wasn't going to happen. He'd left her when she needed him most. Left her to struggle on alone in the slums of Whitechapel. Left her to the tender mercies of Bowler Sheehan and William Burton. Her heart was big, but not big enough to forgive what he'd done. And what he'd failed to do. No one's heart was that big.

As he stood by the warehouse, the door to the Town of Ramsgate opened. A man came out, doffed his hat and went on his way. The usual pub aromas wafted out after him – smoke, beer, and food. Joe realized he was hungry. He decided he'd just nip in and order something to eat. That would take his mind off things.

He ordered haddock and chips, and a pint of bitter to drink while he waited. He had to hold his glass; men were wedged in like sardines at the bar. He looked around for a table, but everything was taken. It was a busy Friday night. Workingmen and sailors had filled the place. He asked the barmaid if there were tables upstairs, but she said it was even worse up there. His best bet, she said, would be to eat his meal outside on the Old Stairs. She could wrap it for him if he liked.

The Old Stairs. Bloody great. They'd be just the thing to take his mind off Fiona. He drained his glass, took his meal – a hot, greasy little bundle – and headed outside. As he settled himself halfway down the stone steps, he was seized by a rush of memories. Her blue eyes widening with delight as he approached her. The smell of her after work – all tea leaves, and sweet, sweaty skin. The feeling of her hand in his. An old, familiar sadness stole over him.

Let it go, Joe, everyone said. His mum. Cathy. Jimmy, too. The past is long gone. Move on.

But to what? He had known the rarest of things – love, real love – he'd held it in his hand and he'd thrown it away. What was left for him? A lifetime of second-bests. Of dead dreams and painful memories. He remembered how the job at Peterson's, the money, Tommy's approval had once mattered so greatly to him. Now, nothing in his life – not the success he'd achieved, nor the money he'd made – meant as much to him as sitting on these very steps with the girl he'd loved. Just the two of them with nothing but a few pounds in a battered cocoa tin and their dreams.

Alf is right, he thought, unwrapping his supper. There

is a ghost here. A lonely, heartbroken spirit. The ghost of everything that could've been and never was.

He looked out at the boats, gently rocking in their moorings. Night had come down and silver rays of moonlight streaked the soft waves. The sky was full of stars. His favorite, the bright star, was twinkling magically. It was brighter, stronger than he'd ever seen it. His eyes traveled to the bottom of the Old Stairs. How many times had he come here, only to find her there, on that very step, watching the waves and dreaming?

As he continued to gaze at the stairs, he realized that there was something on the very last step. He shifted forward and squinted. It was a pair of black boots. Women's boots. One was standing up, the other had fallen on its side. Heaped next to them were what looked like stockings.

Oh, Christ, he thought, alarmed. I hope no poor lass has done herself in. He knew that river suicides often left their boots on the shore in the hopes that someone who could use them would find them. A sad little bequest. His eyes scanned the riverbank. About twenty yards to his left, he saw her. A slender barefoot woman standing near the pilings. She had her back to him, but he could see that she was skipping stones on the river, one after another, hard and fast. The moonlight glinted off her black hair as she bent down to scoop up more. He relaxed. A distraught person wouldn't be skipping stones.

Still, he wondered what she was doing alone by the river at this hour. It wasn't the safest place for a woman to be. He watched her, transfixed by her sure, graceful movements. He saw that her hair had slipped free of its knot, and that her hem was trailing in the mud. A water bird suddenly took wing. She lifted her head at the sound of its cry.

He stood. His meal fell out of his lap onto the steps. "It can't be," he whispered.

It was a trick. It was this place, all the memories. His longing heart and the darkness conspiring. But his eyes told him it was no trick. He jumped down off the steps and walked toward her. Hoping. Fearing. He'd done this before. So many times. Caught sight of a slender black-haired woman and impulsively called to her, only to have her turn and gaze at him with eyes that were questioning, coldly polite, and never, ever hers.

He drew closer to her, slowly, carefully, not wanting to scare her. Remembering a girl who stood here once, mud on her hem, vowing to become as big as all London one day.

Hearing his feet on the stones, she turned, startled. Her eyes widened. And then he heard what he'd longed to hear for ten long years . . . the sound of her voice calling his name.

"Joe? My God . . . is it you?"

Fiona stood mute. She heard nothing, not the drunken laughter from the Town of Ramsgate, nor the dipping oars of a passing wherry. She felt nothing, not the river lapping at her feet, nor the night breeze rustling her skirts. She saw nothing, nothing but Joe.

"Are you real?" she whispered, touching fingers smudged with river mud to his cheek.

That face, the one she knew by heart, was the same, but different. There were a few shallow lines, and the cheek-bones were sharper beneath the skin. But his eyes were the same – so blue, so beautiful, but sad now. So much sadder than she remembered.

He touched her face, then cradled her cheek in his palm and the heat of his hand told her he *was* real. And then he pulled her to him and kissed her and there was a roaring in her ears, and a long, juddering crack, like ice breaking in a lake, from someplace deep inside her. The smell of his skin, the taste of his mouth, the feeling of his body pressed so close, overwhelmed her. It felt as if ten endless years – ten years of longing for him, of loving him despite her sorrow and her anger; ten years of aching loneliness, of a barrenness in her heart and body fell away in the space of mere seconds.

Powerful, conflicting emotions, dammed up for a decade, burst their confines, flooding forth in a dangerous torrent, pulling her under, threatening to drown her, to tear her apart. She tried to pull away from him, but he grabbed her wrists.

"No! I'm not letting go of you. Never again. Do you 'ear me? Do you?"

He was shouting at her. She struggled against him, desperate to break loose, furious that she couldn't. And then she clutched at him, grabbing handfuls of his jacket, his shirt, the flesh underneath, not caring if she hurt him. She buried her face in his chest and sobbed his name over and over again.

He held her tightly, crushing her to him. "Don't go, Fiona. Please, please don't go," he whispered.

She sought his lips, craving his kiss. She knew she shouldn't do this. It was insane. It was wrong. He didn't belong to her. But she could no longer help herself. She wanted him so much. His shirt had come untucked. She moved her hand inside it. The feeling of his heart beating under her palm brought tears to her eyes. This is all I ever wanted, she thought, his heart in my keeping. And mine in his.

An ancient desire, one buried in the very core of her, flared. She wanted to feel his skin against hers. Feel him inside her. She needed to touch his soul again, and know he'd touched hers, just as they'd done once upon a time in a narrow bed in a Covent Garden flat. He wanted it, too. She could see it in his eyes.

Without words or questions, he lifted her up and carried her into the pilings. When they were underneath the jutting dock, far out of sight, he lowered her to the ground on top of an old tarpaulin. He lay on his side next to her, fitting perfectly to her. Just as he always had. She could smell the river, muddy and low, and hear the water softly lapping as he opened her blouse and then her camisole. He touched her scar lightly, a mixture of anger and sadness on his face. She tried to pull her blouse back over it, but he pushed her hand away and kissed the livid skin. He kissed her shoulder, her throat, and then her breasts. He was gentle with her and she didn't want him to be. She wanted the imprint of his hands, his lips, his teeth upon her skin. To remember this night by. Tomorrow and forever.

She pulled his face up to hers, twining her arms around his neck. She kissed him hard, wanting to devour him. She felt him fumbling with his trousers, felt him pushing her skirt up around her hips and tugging at her underthings, and then she felt him between her legs, and finally, finally inside her. Filling her. Making her whole.

"I love you, Fiona. Oh, God, how I love you . . ."

She shook her head. She didn't want to hear those words. He loved her and she loved him and it was all bloody hopeless, just as it had always been.

"Make love to me, Joe. Please, just make love to me," she whispered.

But he didn't. He stayed perfectly still, gazing at her. Even in the darkness, the passion in his eyes was fierce and frightening. "Tell me you love me, Fee," he said.

"Don't ask that. It's not fair."

"Tell me. Say it, Fiona. Say it."

She closed her eyes. "I love you, Joe," she said, her voice breaking. "I've always loved you . . ."

And then he moved, pushing himself into her deeper and deeper, cradling her head in his arms, telling her over and over again how much he loved her, until she melted into him, skin and bones and everything inside her. She cried his name out, and when they were both still, she began to weep. Deep, shuddering sobs that shook her whole body.

"Sshhh," he whispered to her. "It's all right, luv, it's all right. Don't cry . . ." He moved off her, propped himself up on one elbow, and pulled her to him.

The loss of him, the sudden feeling of emptiness made it all worse. It *wasn't* all right. She wanted him inside her again. She didn't want this to be over. She didn't want to see him stand up and walk away from her again. She wanted to stay like this, the two of them together. A breeze blew in off the river. She shivered. He pulled her closer.

"Stay with me tonight," he said. "Come 'ome with me."

Fiona wondered if she'd heard him right. "Come *home* with you?"

He kissed her forehead. "Yes, right now."

"Are you mad?"

He looked at her, puzzled. "No. What's wrong? Who's to stop you?"

"Who's to stop me?" she asked, hurt in her voice. "What about Millie, Joe? What about your wife?"

"Millie?" he echoed, still confused. Then his eyes widened. "Blimey, you don't know. You don't bloody know . . ."

"Know what?"

He sat up now, too. "Fiona, Millie and I divorced nearly ten years ago."

"You *what*?"

"We divorced before our first anniversary. And then I tried to find you. I went to New York. I looked everywhere for you."

"You went to New York," she said hollowly.

"In '89. Just before your wedding."

She suddenly felt lightheaded. "Bloody hell," she murmured.

"I think . . ." Joe said, pulling the edges of her blouse together, "I think maybe we should've talked first."

Joe leaned back against a brick wall, part of Oliver's Wharf that abutted the Old Stairs. He shook his head and laughed.

"What?" Fiona asked, biting into a salted, vinegar-soaked chip. She was sitting next to him, eating the fresh order of fish and chips he'd brought from the pub.

"You. This night. It's all a bloody wonder."

She smiled shyly. "A dream."

"One I never want to wake up from."

"Nor I."

He looked away, picked at a crumbling brick, then suddenly pulled her to him and kissed her. She snorted laughter, unable to kiss him back, as her mouth was full of potato. He laughed too, then looked away again. They were strange with each other. Reaching for the other's hand one minute, or staring, captivated, at the other's face. Blushing and awkward the next. So familiar and yet so strange.

They'd been sitting on the Old Stairs, talking, for the better part of an hour. To think he'd been in New York. To think they could've been together years ago. It had made her heart ache to know it, but those years were gone. Swept away like leaves on the water. And nothing would bring them back. But they were here now. Together. Sitting by the river once again.

She had told him everything that had happened to her, from the day he'd left her to a few hours ago, when she'd visited her family's graves and walked to the river. He had told her everything, too. All about the breakup of his marriage. Living in the stable at Covent Garden. Figuring out where she'd gone. Starting his business. Going to New York to find her, and all the dead, lonely years that came after. He told her how he'd never stopped thinking about her, never stopped loving her, and she told him the same thing. There had been some tears, some hard silences. It wasn't easy to talk about these things. There was still sadness, still anger.

But there was joy, too. She could still barely believe that this was Joe sitting next to her. The man she loved, the man she desired, but also her oldest friend. The lad she'd grown up with, the one person who knew her better than anyone else in the whole world.

She looked at him now as he stared out over the water. His eyes were so dark suddenly. They'd lost the light they'd had in them only seconds ago.

"What is it?" she asked, suddenly fearful that he was regretting what they'd done. That he didn't want her after all. That she'd only imagined the things he'd said to her under the pilings. "What's wrong?"

He took her hand. "Nothing," he said. "And everything."

"You're sorry about what happened, aren't you?"

"Sorry! For making love to you? No, Fiona, I'm not sorry about that. I'm scared. Scared you don't want me. Scared we'll leave this place and I'll never see you again. What I'm sorry for is what I did ten years ago, right 'ere –"

"Joe, you don't have to "

"I do 'ave to. I am so, so sorry. For everything. For all the pain I caused you."

"It's all right . . ."

"No, it's not. It's never been all right. Not since the day I walked up these stairs and walked away from you. I 'urt you that day, I know I did, but all you lost was me. I 'urt myself a million times worse because I lost you. I've wanted you, ached for you, every single day since. Living without you all these years . . ." He swallowed hard and Fiona saw a shimmer of tears in his eyes. "It's been like living in a dungeon, without warmth, or light, or 'ope." He took her hands in his again. "I'd give anything to be able to go back and undo it all if I could, but I can't. But if you let me, I'll try so bloody 'ard to make you 'appy. I meant what I said earlier. I love you, Fee. With all my 'eart. Do you think we could start over? Do you think you could forgive me?"

Fiona looked into the eyes she knew so well, the eyes she loved. They were full of sorrow, full of pain. She wanted so much to take that pain away. "I already have," she said.

Joe took her in his arms and held her. They stayed that way for a long time, then he said, "Come 'ome with me."

She was about to tell him she would when a pair of feet appeared at the very top of the Old Stairs and a voice bellowed, "There you are, you bloody stupid girl!"

It was Roddy and he was furious. "What the hell is

wrong with you, Fiona? Don't you have any sense at all? It's nearly ten o'clock! Andrew came to the station hours ago to tell me you'd gone off by yourself. I've been waiting for you at the Mayfair house. And worried sick! T'ought William Burton got you. Where have you been!"

"Just here . . . I was . . . um . . . walking along the shore. Looking for stones."

"She found a pair, too," Joe said under his breath.

Fiona gasped, choked, then started coughing. She'd forgotten about his wicked sense of humor. His bawdy, teasing ways. When she finally got her wind back, she started laughing hysterically.

"It's not bloody funny!" Roddy shouted. "I've told you five hundred times how dangerous it is for you to be out by yourself!"

"No, you're right. It isn't funny," Fiona said, struggling to control herself. "I'm sorry, Uncle Roddy. I didn't mean to scare you, but I'm fine. Nobody bothered me. I just walked here from Whitechapel, met up with Joe and lost track of the time."

"Aye, I can see that," he growled.

"Come and sit with us," she said, patting the step above her. "I've been perfectly safe all evening. Really."

"Depends on what you call safe," he said, giving Joe a pointed look. Still grumbling, he trotted down the steps and sat with them. Fiona handed him what was left of her supper. He ate a chip, then another, then finished her haddock. "I'm bloody famished, I am. Didn't have any supper. Spent the whole night looking for you. I was about to call out half the London police force."

"I'll get you a proper supper. Sit here. I'll be right back," she said, hopping up. She scrambled up the steps and headed for the pub, eager to escape Roddy's wrath. Hopefully, by the time she got back, he'd have cooled off a bit.

Joe and Roddy watched her go. When she was out of sight, they looked at each other, then stared at the black water.

"Gone back to New York, eh?" Joe said.

"If I see one tear on account of you, just one, I swear to God . . ."

"You won't."

There was a minute or so of silence, then Roddy said, "She needs her head examined. You both do. If for no other reason than sitting here eating greasy chips by this ugly river when you've both got brass enough to eat at a decent place."

81

Roddy toed the lifeless, blood-covered body of Bowler Sheehan as it lay prone in the exercise yard of Newgate Prison. A straightedge, still open, lay on the ground nearby. "I don't suppose anyone confessed to this?" he said to the guard.

The man snorted. "They're all saying 'e did it 'imself, sir."

Roddy raised an eyebrow. "He just took a razor that he surely didn't have on him when he came in here and cut his own t'roat. Right in the middle of the yard?"

The guard looked uncomfortable. "We know one of them did it, but no one's talking."

"What about the other guards?"

"None of them saw anything, either."

"That's bloody great," Roddy fumed. "As if I didn't have enough on me plate. Now this mess." He knelt down and gave the gash across Sheehan's throat a cursory examination. Why? he wondered. Why kill him? Sure, some of the other prisoners undoubtedly had grievances against him, but bad blood between criminals was nothing unusual and no thug with half a brain would stick his own neck out so far over a grudge. There was only one thing that could make a man take a risk like that – a very large sum of money. Someone had bribed one of the prisoners, or one of the guards, to do for Bowler.

On the way out of the prison, Roddy stopped by the warden's office to thank him for notifying him of Sheehan's demise. He'd been summoned to Newgate because the warden knew he had a special interest in the case and would wish to be apprised of any developments concerning the prisoner – such as said prisoner getting himself topped. In the warden's office, he met Alvin Donaldson. Donaldson had also been informed of Sheehan's death because of Sheehan's history with William Burton and its possible pertinence to his own case.

"You think it's Burton, don't you?" he asked Roddy as they walked out together.

"The t'ought had crossed my mind," Roddy replied.

"What does it take to convince you, O'Meara? The bloke's gone. We're certain of it. We're putting all our efforts toward working with the French. We've sent pictures. As soon as they see him, they'll nab him."

"Just because he didn't put in an appearance at his house or Mincing Lane you t'ink he's off holidaying on the continent?" Roddy asked. He didn't like Donaldson. The man was too confident in his own opinions. Too cocky.

"No, I think he's on the continent because he's got nowhere else to go. There's a reward out. You know that. Your own Mrs. Soames upped it to a thousand pounds," Donaldson said. "Let's just say for argument's sake that he was lying low here in some lodging house . . . you think his fellow lodgers wouldn't turn him in? For a thousand quid? They'd grab him so fast his head would spin."

Roddy made no reply.

"You know I'm right. And if you ask me . . ."

"I didn't."

". . . you should be looking at our friend across the river, Sid Malone. Word is he wanted to pay Sheehan back for topping Quinn."

"Tell me somet'ing I don't know."

"I should also tell you that we're removing the men we've had stationed at Mrs. Soames's house."

"What? Why the divil are you doing that?" Roddy asked angrily.

"Top brass says Burton's gone. And if he's gone there's

no further need to protect Mrs. Soames from him. We can't tie up men for no good reason."

"I don't t'ink that's a good idea. Not at all. What if you're wrong?"

Donaldson smiled. "We're not."

Then he left, and left Roddy fuming in the prison's vestibule. He looked over the visitors' log on his way out, but no names popped out at him. He hadn't really expected any to. Anyone smart enough to get Sheehan killed was smart enough to put a fake name in the log.

As he walked back to the station house, he turned Donaldson's words over and over in his mind. His intuition told him Burton had done for Sheehan, but intuition was only a feeling. Logic told him otherwise. Maybe Burton really was no longer in London. As he allowed this thought to sink in, Roddy realized how much he had wanted him to be. No matter how confident Donaldson sounded, if Burton was on the continent it would be very difficult, maybe impossible, to catch him.

He would visit Fiona later and tell her what had happened to Sheehan. She would want to know. He'd tell her Sid Malone was probably the one responsible.

It was a hard thing to face – the fact that Burton might never be apprehended, that he might never be brought to justice for what he'd done. But maybe it was time he accepted it. Maybe it was he himself, not Alvin Donaldson, who had too much confidence in his own opinions.

82

Joe took a mouthful of wine, swallowed it, and looked at the naked woman drowsing peacefully next to him. She lay on her side. Her black hair was loose and spilling across his white pillow. A sheet covered most of her body, except her lovely arms and one long, perfect leg. She was the most beautiful thing he had ever seen.

He had just made love to her. In his bed. With a fire casting its warm glow across her skin. She hadn't cried afterward, as she had at the river, and he was glad of it. He never wanted her to cry again. She'd just nestled into his sheets, flushed and smiling, sighed prettily, and closed her eyes.

Today was Saturday – a full week after they'd met again by the river. The happiest week of his life. He still couldn't believe what had happened, still couldn't believe that she was his again. Every morning when he woke, he was immediately gripped by panic, terrified that he'd only dreamed that night by the river and the glorious days that followed. But then he would roll over in his bed and pull her to him as she mumbled sleepy protests, reassuring himself that she was no dream, that she was real.

He kissed her head now. Her hair was damp. They'd been walking in his orchards, looking at the river, when the skies had suddenly opened. They'd run for the house, shrieking and laughing, and had arrived in his kitchen drenched.

He'd made a quick detour to the cellar for a dusty bottle of Haut-Brion before leading her upstairs to his bedroom.

There, he'd built her a fire and poured her a glass of the rich old Bordeaux to take the chill away. They'd sat talking by the fireplace, drying off, for all of sixty seconds before he had her up out of the chair, undressed, and in his bed. He was so hungry for her. So eager to see her lovely body, to hold her and touch her, to take his time as he hadn't been able to at the river. In her arms, looking into her eyes, it was as if they'd never been apart. Knowing that she forgave him, that she loved him and wanted to be with him, he had finally felt the sadness, his constant companion, leave him and an indescribable joy take its place.

Rain sheeted against the windows now. He looked out of one and saw the branches of an ancient oak tossing crazily in the wind. Let the bastard blow over, he thought happily, let the whole world blow away. This room, the two of them, was all that mattered. He pulled the sheet up over Fiona's shoulders, got out of bed, and slipped on a robe.

"Don't go," she murmured.

"I'm not, luv. Just putting another log on the fire." He put two more on, poking and prodding them until they caught and the flames were blazing nicely. He refilled their glasses, then padded across the bedroom to rummage in his highboy. He had something for her. Something he wanted so much to give her. Anyone in his right mind would say it was too soon. Far too soon. But he wasn't in his right mind. He was in love. And for him, it couldn't be soon enough.

He found what he was looking for, a small red leather box marked "Lalique, Paris." He placed it on his night table, shrugged his robe off, and climbed back into bed. Fiona stirred. He'd meant to put the little box in her hands and have her open it. But since he'd gotten up, she'd kicked the sheet off. He looked at her. Her round, luscious breasts were as beautiful as he remembered. His eyes traveled downward, following the contours of her body. He wanted her again. Very much. The box would have to wait.

He leaned over her and kissed her. She stretched lazily and smiled. He cupped her breast and squeezed it, bending his head down to tease her nipple with his lips. "Mmmmm," she sighed. His hand moved down, over her waist, to her thighs, and then between them. He stroked her there, gently at first, then harder. He slipped his fingers inside of her, into the sweet softness of her, making her wet and breathless, then stopped, pausing to kiss her belly, the smooth curve of her hip.

"You better finish what you started, lad," he heard her whisper.

He grinned at her, enjoying the fact that she was hot and bothered. He loved making her want him, loved knowing the heat on her skin, and inside her, and the low moans in her throat were all for him. He didn't want to be inside her now, though. Not yet. He wanted to feel her need for him, to hear his name on her lips. To know she was his again. Only his.

He bit her ear softly, making her giggle, then nuzzled her neck. He moved down, taking her pretty nipples into his mouth again, trailing his tongue over her rosy skin, lower and lower, until he was just where he wanted to be. Then he parted her legs and tasted her. She didn't protest this time as she had when she was a girl, instead she opened herself to him, shivering with pleasure as he explored her. After only a few seconds he heard a small cry, felt her body tremble, heard his name whispered.

Whispered? he thought, frowning. That won't do. Not at all.

She had rolled over on her side. Her face glowed, lightly sheened with sweat. He lay next to her, propped on his pillows, playing with strands of her hair. He waited until her breathing slowed, then pulled her on top of him.

"Oh, Joe, I can't . . ." she said, laughing, her voice husky, her eyes as heavy and dazed as an opium smoker's. She sat up, straddling him, trying to get her balance. "Don't move, I'll fall off," she giggled. He reached for his wineglass and handed it to her. She held it with both hands and took a big swallow. As she did, he guided himself into her. Her eyes closed. Her body arched against his. He took the glass from her just in time, before she dropped it on him, and put it down.

He grabbed her hips, pulled her tight against him, and rocked into her, slowly, rhythmically, coaxing the heat back into her body over her weary, sated protests until he heard her moans, louder than before, and felt her skin all slick. He pushed into her, deeper and harder, and she gasped, clutching at his hands. And then he felt her sweet, shuddering spasms, harder than before, and heard his name cried out instead of whispered. And then he let himself come, her name on his own lips.

When he could breathe again, and see again, he realized she was lying on top of him, utterly spent. She opened her eyes and looked at him. He pushed the hair out of her face and said, "That's enough now, Fee. You'll kill me."

She burst into laughter and was still giggling when he handed her the red leather box. "What's this?" she asked.

"Take a look."

She sat up, tucked the sheet around herself, and opened it. "My blue stone!" she cried.

He nodded. It looked much different than it had the day he'd pulled it out of the river mud. He'd sent it to Paris to have it polished and set into a ring. René Lalique, the celebrated French jeweler, had designed a special setting for it, one of twining rushes and river lilies.

"How did you find this?" she asked excitedly.

He told her how the private investigator he'd hired to look for her had found it in the pawnshop near Roddy's old flat.

"It's so beautiful!" she said, holding it up to catch the firelight. "It shines so, I can't believe it's just glass from the river."

"It's not glass, Fee. It's a scarab. Carved from a sapphire."

"You're joking!" she whispered.

"I'm not." He took the ring from her. "I 'ad it set as soon as I could afford to, then put it away 'oping that one day I'd be able to give it to you myself. A week after I'd sent the stone to Paris, the jeweler himself telephoned to tell me it was a sapphire. It's ancient. And very valuable, you know. You sold it far too cheaply." He shook his head, remembering all the years without her, suddenly sad again.

"Funny, 'ow you can 'old a jewel in your 'and, toss it away, and not even know what you 'ad until it's gone."

Fiona took his face in her hands and kissed him. "Don't," she said. "No more sad memories. Only the ones we make from now on."

He slipped the ring onto her finger. "Well then, this is the first one. An old jewel, but a new memory." He got up to pour them more wine.

Fiona admired her ring, then looked at him coyly. "Joe?"

"Mmm?"

"Does this mean we're courting?"

"That all depends."

"On what?"

"On whether or not you'd make a good wife. Can you cook?"

"No."

"Clean?"

"No."

"How about ironing? Can you do that?"

"No."

"What can you do?"

"Come here and I'll show you."

"Again? You're insatiable! As randy as a goat. I'd always 'eard older women were as keen as cats for it."

"*Older women!* You little sod! I'll show you who's old . . ."

She pulled him down on the bed and loved him and as the fire burned down and they fell asleep in each other's arms, he smiled, hopeful that what she'd said was right, that there would be no more bad memories, only the new ones they made. Nothing more to come between them. And no dark past to haunt them. Only the future they would make together. At long last, together.

83

"Bobby Devlin," Roddy said, looking up from the papers on his desk to the visitor in his doorway. "Always a pleasure."

"Save the malarkey, O'Meara," Devlin said. He tossed a copy of the *Clarion* onto Roddy's desk. "Tomorrow's edition."

Roddy stretched and looked at his watch. Three o'clock. "Christ, is it that late already?" he said. It was a Saturday. He'd come in at nine to catch up on a backlog of work. He'd been so preoccupied with William Burton's whereabouts during the last few weeks, he'd neglected his other duties. He motioned for Devlin to sit down. "You a newsboy now, too? Making deliveries?"

"Thought it might be of interest. Concerns your man Burton. Don't think you'll be seeing him again so soon."

Roddy peered at the front page. "William Burton, Impostor and Sham, Flees Country," the headline read. And below it, "Relative Makes Plea on His Behalf." The byline was Devlin's. Roddy quickly opened it and read the article. Devlin had ferreted out the existence of William Burton's elderly aunt, an eighty-year-old woman by the name of Sarah Burtt. Miss Burtt lived in a comfortable flat in Kensington. She had agreed to talk candidly to the *Clarion,* the story stated, because she was anxious to clear her nephew's good name.

In the ensuing interview, Miss Burtt completely controverted the known story of William Burton's rise from poverty to success – that he'd been orphaned as a young boy, raised by a kindly spinster aunt, and had risen above his humble origins to become a wealthy tea baron.

She said that she had indeed taken William in. Not because his mother had died, however, but because she had abandoned both William, who was five at the time, and his three-year-old brother Frederick. She had left the boys in a filthy room, in a rank lodging house, with no food or money. Told not to make a sound or they'd be beaten, William and Frederick had waited silently for her return. Several days elapsed before the lodgers in the neighboring room, alerted by a foul smell, figured out something was wrong. By then it was too late for Frederick. When they broke down the door, they found five-year-old William next to his brother's decomposing body. He was delirious with hunger and illness, mumbling about rats. It was then that they noticed Frederick's right foot had been chewed off.

Devlin had asked Miss Burtt why their mother had abandoned the boys. Could she not care for them? Had they been unable to live on her seamstress's wages? Miss Burtt told him that her sister, Allison Burtt, had begun as a seamstress, but ended up as a prostitute. She was a mean-tempered woman who was addicted to drink and beat her boys mercilessly. She had been disowned by her family before either of the boys was born.

Devlin then asked if Burton's father had really been a sea captain who'd gone down with his ship. "Could be," the frank Miss Burtt said. "Or a butcher, baker, or candlestick maker." She had no idea who had fathered her sister's boys, and doubted if her sister had known, either. She then asserted that none of that was important. What mattered was that William had always been a good boy, always good to his Aunt Sarah. He had excelled in school. And he'd worked hard. He'd taken a job at a corner shop, in Camden Town where they lived, when he left school at fourteen, and by the age of seventeen he'd saved up enough to buy the place from its elderly owner. That shop had been the beginning of Burton Tea.

Devlin then asked if a search had ever been made for Burton's mother. Perhaps she still lived in Camden Town, he suggested. Miss Burtt replied that her sister had never lived in Camden Town. She'd resided in Whitechapel, in Adams Court. "You might recognize the name," Miss Burtt had said. "It's where the last of those awful murders happened. A dreadful place."

"I can't believe this!" Roddy exclaimed. "Burton lived in Adams Court. That's where Fiona's family lived!"

"He lied about that and everything else," Devlin said.

Roddy kept reading. His eyes skimmed over the part where Miss Burtt told the paper that her nephew had changed his name from Burtt to Burton because he thought it sounded grander, to the end, where Devlin had asked the woman to tell him truthfully whether she'd seen her nephew at any time during the past month.

Miss Burtt said she had not, but two weeks ago she'd received a letter from him stating that he was going abroad. He didn't say where. She was very worried about him. He'd always been a good man, she said, always good to his Aunt Sarah. She didn't believe that he'd stabbed that Soames woman, or that he'd murdered a dockworker. The interview ended with Miss Burtt appealing to her nephew to return to London and clear his good name.

"He's the target of one of the biggest manhunts in London's history, and he slips right through the net. He could be anywhere. France, Italy. Might be halfway to China by now. Wonder how he did it. A disguise, maybe? A fake name? That bloke's nothing if not clever," Devlin said.

"Oh, he's clever, all right, but he's not on the continent," Roddy said. The prickling had started. On the back of his neck. Along his arms. Deep down in the very marrow of his bones. His sixth sense, pushed down ever since his conversation with Donaldson, had sprung back up with a vengeance.

"I don't follow you."

"Somet'ing's not right, Bobby. It's all too neat and tidy.

The doddery old aunt. His letter. It's all too convenient."

"You think the letter's a setup?"

"I do. I t'ink he realized that sooner or later someone would discover Sarah Burtt's existence. The police or the press. He made sure she had that letter to show them. It's a false lead. He wants us to t'ink he's gone abroad, but he hasn't. He's been here all along. Waiting. That smug bugger of a Donaldson! I knew he hadn't left. I bloody well knew it!"

Roddy stood up and shrugged on his jacket. His sixth sense wasn't just prickling anymore. It was tapping him on the shoulder. With a sledgehammer. He wanted to show Fiona the Sarah Burtt interview. Since her scar had healed, and since she'd met Joe again, she'd been going out and about with much greater frequency. He had to warn her, to tell her that she must continue to be extremely cautious. She was even talking about dismissing Andrew. He couldn't let her do that.

"Where are you going in such a hurry?" Devlin asked.

"To Fiona's house. To show her your paper. She doesn't believe Burton's still here, either. Says it's too dangerous for him. That he has no home here anymore, no tea company, no reason to stay. She's wrong, though. He does have a reason. And she's it."

Davey O'Neill sat in his local, where he'd been drowning the voice of his conscience nightly for the past ten years, and fingered a crisp fifty-pound note. It was enough to send his daughter, eleven now and still not strong, to a sanitarium in Bath for a year. Paid to him for yet another task he hadn't wanted to do. He smiled bitterly at that. What had he ever wanted to do for that man except bash his rotten head in?

Davey tucked his money safely away, ordered a pint, and downed it. He immediately ordered another, trying to silence the voice inside that nagged at him, asking him over and over again what the consequences might be of the delivery he'd just made.

I don't know and I don't care, he told the voice. It was

an errand, that's all. Nothing to do with me. And besides, it was the last one. He said he was going away. I'm finished now. I'm free.

Free? the voice mocked. You'll never be free, Davey. You sold your soul. You sold her, too. For a handful of silver. Like the Judas you are. Only Judas had the good grace to hang himself.

"It's only a letter," he muttered angrily. "For God's sake, leave me alone!"

"What's that, Davey?" the publican asked. "You ready for another?"

"What? No. Sorry, Pete. Talking to meself."

The publican moved off to dry some glasses. Davey caught sight of himself in the mirror behind the bar. He was gaunt, hollow-eyed. His face was lined. His hair had gone gray. He was only thirty-four.

He scrubbed his face with his hands. He was weary. It had taken him days to find Fiona Finnegan. He'd tailed her. Twice from Oliver's, and three times from Mincing Lane – losing her carriage in traffic each time. Then, on the fifth try, he'd gotten lucky. His cabbie had managed to stay close behind her all the way to Mayfair. He'd seen her carriage pull onto Grosvenor Square, seen her enter number sixteen. And after he had her address, he'd gotten Joe Bristow's at Covent Garden. Then it had just been a matter of finding out where Bristow landed his tea shipments.

He means her harm, the voice said. You know that, don't you?

It's just a letter, Davey said again, silently. What harm can there be in a letter?

It's a death warrant. That's blood money in your pocket.

I did it for Lizzie. Everything I've done, I've done for Lizzie.

Did you kill for Lizzie, too?

"I didn't kill anyone!" he said aloud.

You stood by when he killed her father. And now you're doing the same thing all over again.

"No!" he shouted, slamming his fist on the bar.

"Davey, lad, what's ailing you?" the publican asked.

"N-nothing, Pete. 'Ere's for me pint," he said, tossing a coin on the bar. "I 'ave to go."

Davey left the pub walking, but soon broke into a run. He had lived the last ten years of his life knowing that he'd played a part in Paddy Finnegan's death and the knowledge had eaten him alive. He wouldn't spend the rest of his life knowing he'd helped Burton to murder again. He figured he had one slim chance – only one – to stop what he had helped put in motion. And he was going to take it.

The hackney slowed as it neared the corner of Southampton and Tavistock. Davey threw money at the driver and was out the door before it could stop.

The return address on the letter had read "J. Bristow, 4 Tavistock Street, Covent Garden." But Bristow hadn't sent that note and Davey had to tell him who had. Maybe he would know what to do.

He ran the few yards to number four. BRISTOW'S OF COVENT GARDEN WHOLESALE PRODUCE, JOS. AND JAS. BRISTOW, PROPRIETORS, the nameplate read. He turned the doorknob, but the door was locked. He pounded on it. "Mr. Bristow!" he shouted. "Mr. Bristow! Anybody!" But there was no answer. It was late on a Saturday afternoon, most businesses were closed, but maybe there'd still be a porter about or a clerk, someone who could tell him where this J. Bristow was. "Mr. Bristow!" he shouted again.

"Mr. O'Neill," a voice said quietly from behind him.

Davey spun around expecting to see William Burton standing behind him, staring at him with his awful black eyes. But it wasn't Burton. It was a lad. He was wearing a flat cap and a kingsman. He had a mean scar on his chin and was built like a bull. Another lad was standing at his side.

"Would you come with us, please?" the first one said.

" 'Ow do you know my name?" Davey asked them, backing away.

"Let's go, Davey," the second lad said.

"I'm not going anywhere with you . . . I . . . I need to find Mr. Bristow," Davey stammered. And then he bolted.

The lad with the scar tackled him against the building. "Don't do that again," he warned.

"Let go of me!" Davey shouted, struggling.

"In good time. We've a few questions need answering first." He gave Davey a shove toward a waiting carriage. "Get moving," he told him.

"You tell Burton I'm all through," Davey said, his voice rising. "I want nothing more to do with 'im! We 'ad a deal –"

The lad grabbed Davey's arm, twisted it up his back, and marched him to the carriage. "We don't work for William Burton, you stupid cunt. By the time we finish with you, though, you might wish we did."

"Ow! Fuck! Me arm!" he screamed. "Where are you from? Who sent you?"

"The guv'nor sent us, Davey. Sid Malone."

Joe loped up the steps to number sixteen Grosvenor Square, a bouquet of crimson roses in his hand. He rang the bell, expecting Mrs. Merton, the housekeeper, to open the door. Instead a big mustached face greeted him.

"Joe? What the hell are you doing here?" Roddy asked.

"Nice to see you, too," Joe said. "Mind if I come in? Where's Fiona?"

"I might ask you the same t'ing. She's supposed to be with you, and you're supposed to be at Oliver's."

Joe laid his roses on the hallway table. "What are you talking about?" he asked. "I'm not supposed to be anywhere. I finished up early at work and came by spur-of-the-moment to see if she wanted to get an early supper and ride out to Greenwich with me."

Roddy looked confused. "I don't understand this. I got here a few minutes ago and Mrs. Merton told me Fiona had left to go meet you. She said you'd sent her a note. Something about a tea shipment."

"I didn't send a note," Joe said, confused now himself. And worried.

"Hold on . . . maybe I got it wrong," Roddy said. "Mrs. Merton!" he yelled. "Mrs. Merton, are you there?"

They heard brisk footsteps and then the housekeeper appeared. "Yes? What is it?"

"You said Mrs. Soames was going to Oliver's, didn't you? That she'd received a note from Mr. Bristow?"

"Yes, that's right. That's what she told me. She said she wouldn't be gone long and that she planned to return here with Mr. Bristow."

"But I didn't write any note," Joe said, feeling fear's first greasy waves ripple through him.

Mrs. Merton frowned. "I'm sure Mrs. Soames mentioned your name, sir. I didn't read the note myself, of course."

"Is it still here?" Joe asked. "Did she take it with her?"

"I don't know," the housekeeper said, sorting through the mail scattered on top of the hall table. When she didn't find any opened envelopes there, she pulled a lacquered waste-basket out from under the table and reached into it. "Here it is," she said, handing him a crumpled envelope and card.

He smoothed them out on the table so Roddy could see them, too. The envelope had his office's address on the back. It had been typed. The card, also typed, said that a large shipment of tea had arrived earlier than anticipated and that there was no room for it at the Orient Wharf, where he usually landed his tea. It asked if he could store it at Oliver's and asked her to meet him there at six. There was an apology for the typing, saying he was pressed for time, that he'd dictated the note. By the time Joe got to his own typed name, his fear had turned to full-blown terror.

"Christ, Roddy . . . it's Burton," he said.

"He's at Oliver's . . ."

". . . and she's on 'er way to meet him."

And then they were out the door and down the steps, shouting for Joe's driver.

*　　*　　*

Andrew Taylor sighed, then ploddingly said, "Sergeant O'Meara said I wasn't to let you go anywhere alone. I 'ave to stay with you at all times."

"Andrew, I'm just going inside the wharf," Fiona said. "Mr. Bristow's inside already. And the foreman, too."

"Mrs. Soames, can't you wait one minute till I tie the 'orses?"

"Don't be silly! Look, the door's three yards away! There it is, Andrew, wide open! Tie the horses and come in," Fiona said. Andrew was getting to be as impossible as Roddy. He knew she was meeting Joe. He'd been standing right next to her as she told Mrs. Merton she was taking the carriage to meet him at Oliver's. It was all getting to be too much. Burton was gone. Sheehan was dead. Donaldson had dismissed the constables who'd been guarding her house, but Roddy still insisted Andrew accompany her everywhere. If she wanted to have afternoon tea, he went to Fortnum & Mason's with her. If she wanted to buy a new dress, or some pretty underthings, they both went to Harrods. As if William Burton were going to hide himself under a tea table or pop out from a pile of bloomers!

She twisted her beautiful scarab ring around her finger in irritation as she headed into Oliver's, but the frown on her face quickly dissolved. She was happy, far too happy these days, to be angry about anything for long. Sometimes, when she thought about the last few weeks, about everything that had happened to her – it all seemed so incomprehensible – she felt so overwhelmed, that she tried to stop thinking about it. Instead, she gloried in it. In the warmth of Joe's love, and in her own newfound capacity for happiness.

She looked at her ring now. Though she had teased Joe about their courting the night he'd given it to her, it had indeed turned out be her engagement ring. They would be married in a fortnight's time, she and Joe. And whenever she thought about how it had all been arranged, she couldn't keep from laughing.

A week ago, they'd gone to visit his parents. Fiona was so eager to see them again, she'd barely been able to contain herself on the ride over. As soon as the door to number four Montague had opened, and Rose had come rushing out, both women had burst into tears at the sight of each other. Rose had smelled so wonderful, of all the memories of Fiona's childhood – lavender soap cut from a huge block at the corner shop, roast potatoes, stewed apples with cinnamon, strong tea. Her embrace, so fierce and so soft all at once, felt just like her own mother's. When they could finally bear to release each other, Rose led her inside to see Peter and the rest of the family, and Joe trailed behind them. She met Joe's grandfather again. Jimmy and his wife, Meg, who was expecting their first child; Ellen, her husband, Tom, and their three children; and finally, Cathy, who'd been studying the floor during the greetings and introductions.

"Sorry about the card," Cathy said awkwardly, finally glancing up at her. "Friends?"

"Friends," Fiona said, reaching for her hand. Cathy took it in her own. "Cor, what a pretty ring!" she said, admiring Fiona's scarab. "I've never seen anything like it."

"Isn't it lovely? Joe gave it to me," Fiona said, without thinking.

"Did 'e? Are you engaged, then?" Cathy asked.

Fiona didn't know what to say. They'd only joked about it. There was a dreadful silence, then Ellen hissed, "Crikey, Cathy, what a thing to ask!"

"Why? 'E gave 'er a ring, didn't 'e? And 'e's only been mooning after 'er for the better part of the century. Of course 'e wants to marry 'er."

"Good Lord," Peter sighed, looking at the ceiling.

"Cathy, you are the rudest, most ignorant little . . ." Rose began. Then she stopped and turned to Fiona. Her expression softened. "Are you, luv?"

Fiona waited for the floor to swallow her up. When it didn't, she said, "I don't . . . we haven't . . ."

"Well, I know 'e wants to marry you," Rose said anxiously. "It's all 'e's ever wanted. You will marry 'im, won't you, pet?"

Fiona blushed crimson, then smiled. "If it'll make you happy, Rose, I will."

Rose whooped and hugged her. "Did you 'ear that, lad?" she shouted. "She's going to marry you!"

"Aye, so I gathered. Thanks, Mum. Last thing I wanted to do was ask 'er meself," he'd grumbled.

By the time they'd sat down to dinner, it had been decided that she and Joe would be married in three weeks' time, for that's what Rose thought it would take to get family and friends assembled and a proper wedding breakfast arranged. Fiona caught Joe's eye in the midst of it all, silently beseeching him to rescue her or at least help to change the subject, but he'd simply smiled and shrugged, defenseless against his mother and sisters.

She'd had the most wonderful afternoon with the Bristows. She felt so at home with them and couldn't remember the last time she'd laughed so hard. They were such a loud, roistering bunch. Somebody was always saying or doing something completely inappropriate. It was from costering, she was sure of it. You couldn't put people in front of a cart day after day, tell them to sing their wares, then expect them to be quiet simply because they were at the table. Soon they would be her in-laws. And Joe would be her husband. How had this all happened? she wondered. How could one person suddenly be granted so much happiness?

She shook her head and laughed, unable to answer her own questions. She walked past the wooden stairs that led to Oliver's second floor and into the large ground-floor room. It was darker inside the wharf than it was outside and her eyes took a few seconds to adjust. Looking across the room, she could see tea chests, just arrived from her new estate in India. She saw, too, that the new loophole doors had been hung, replacing the ones Pete Miller's men had torn off.

"Joe?" she called out. "Mr. Curran?" There was no answer. The wharf was very quiet. The street had been, too. A half-day, she thought, remembering her father's Saturday work schedule.

"Anyone here?" she shouted. Still no answer. They must be on one of the upper floors, she reasoned. She was about to head up the stairs when she noticed a light was on in the foreman's office. It was all the way on the other side of the floor, near the river. Maybe they were in there and hadn't heard her.

She picked her way around tea chests. The office door was open a few inches. "Mr. Curran? Are you in there?" Thomas Curran was sitting in his chair. His back was toward her. "There you are," she said. "Has Mr. Bristow arrived yet?"

But Curran didn't answer her. His head was bowed. He looked as if he were sleeping.

"Mr. Curran?" She put a hand on his shoulder and gave him a gentle shake. His head lolled forward, then rolled back. Too far back. There was blood down the front of shirt. On his blotter, his typewriter. His throat had been slashed.

"Oh, no . . . no . . . oh, God," she whimpered, backing away from him. She banged into the door, unable to tear her eyes away from the ghastly sight, then turned and ran. "Joe!" she shrieked. She didn't see the tea chest in front of her and smashed into it, crying out with pain. "Joe!" she screamed again, panic-stricken. "Joe, please! Come quick!"

But there was no answer. She hobbled toward the street-side doors, her leg throbbing. "Joe! Andrew! Is anyone there?"

Ten yards away from the door, she heard them. Footsteps. Slow and measured.

"Oh, thank God," she sobbed. "Joe, it's Mr. Curran. He's dead!"

But the figure walking toward her in the gloom was not Joe.

Fiona squeezed her eyes shut. This isn't happening, she thought. This can't be happening. He's not real. He's only a nightmare. He doesn't exist.

Shaking and sick with fear, she opened them again and gazed into the mad, hateful eyes of the dark man.

"Joe!" Fiona screamed. "Help me!"

"He's not here," William Burton said, walking toward her, his hands at his side. "He never was. I sent you the note. No one's here."

Her mind tried to understand what he'd said. Joe wasn't here. No one was here. But he was wrong. "Andrew!" she shouted. "In here! Hurry!"

Burton shook his head. "He can't hear you, I'm afraid." He extended his right hand toward her and she saw he was holding a knife. Its silver blade was wet with blood.

"Andrew . . . oh, no!" she cried, her hand coming to her mouth. He was dead. Andrew was dead. All because he'd been trying to look out for her. "You bastard!" she screamed, suddenly furious. "You filthy, murdering bastard!"

He made no reply, just smiled. While she'd been screaming at him, he'd been advancing. He was now only yards away.

Move, you fool! a voice inside her ordered. She edged around the tea chest in front of her, trying to judge the distance between herself and the door. If she could only get outside. The Town of Ramsgate was right next door. If she could get to it, she'd be safe.

Burton saw where she was looking and stepped aside to afford her a clear view. "Locked," he said. "You could try the stairs, I suppose. If you think you can get to them before I get to you. But what's the point, really? They lead up, not out. You'd only be prolonging things."

She glanced around herself frantically. There was nowhere to go. The sides of the building were solid brick. In the back left corner was Curran's office. Hope flared

759

briefly. She could lock herself inside it. He wouldn't be able to get to her through the thick oak door. As if reading her mind, he cut to his right, blocking her way. She looked behind herself. The riverside wall had loopholes but they were locked. Iron padlocks on chains hung from their handles. There was nothing on the right wall, no office, no loopholes, no windows – nothing. Just a grappling hook someone had left hanging on a peg on the wall and a few tea rakes leaning up against it.

And still Burton advanced, pushing her farther and farther back toward the wall. And suddenly it was right behind her. She hit her heel against it and there was a sharp, sudden pain in her shoulder blade. She tried to flatten herself against the bricks like a cornered animal, but she couldn't. Something was sticking into her, hurting her.

The grappling hook.

She didn't dare risk a look. She bent her arm up behind her back, forcing her hand higher and higher until her muscles were screaming with pain.

He was only ten yards away now.

"I'm going to slit your throat and watch you die, Mrs. Soames," he said. "And then I'm going to burn this place to the ground."

"You won't get away with it. They'll find you," she said, struggling to keep her voice even. Her joints were on fire. Where was it? Where the hell was it? Just when she thought her arm would surely rip free of its socket, her scrabbling fingers touched metal. Easy, she told herself. Don't drop it, don't you dare drop it.

"They won't. I'll be on a boat to Calais in an hour."

Nine yards, eight.

"Did you know that after your father fell, he lay in his own blood, his legs broken, for a good hour before his screams attracted attention?"

For a second, Fiona's courage failed her and she almost crumpled. Don't listen to him, she told herself. Don't listen. She coaxed the hook off its pegs, then twisted it around in her hand until the smooth wooden handle was in her palm and the curved iron jutted out between her fingers.

Seven yards, six, five.

"It doesn't take as long to die from a cut throat as it does a fall," Burton said. "But it isn't instantaneous, as some people believe."

She squeezed her hand into a fist. Every fiber in her body was snapping and sparking with fear. Four yards, three yards, two . . . she knew what happened next, she'd seen it in her dreams . . . night after night for ten long years.

Except this time, she wasn't sleeping.

With a yell, she swung the hook. The curved metal bit into Burton's cheek and ripped it open. He roared in pain. His knife clattered to the floor.

She darted past him, weaving her way in and out of tea chests, and bolted up the wooden stairs to the second floor, then the third, where new chests were piled three and four high. She heard his feet pounding up the stairs, heard him shouting on the second floor. The tea chests weren't piled on top of each other down there; they'd been opened for inspection. It wouldn't take him long to see she wasn't there. Moving quickly, she made her way to the center of the room and crouched behind a tall stack.

And then he was on the landing. "Come out!" he shouted. "Come out now and I'll make it fast. But if I have to find you, I'll carve your thieving heart out!"

Fiona pressed her hands over her ears and hunched into a ball, numb with fear. There was no way out. She had seen the new loophole doors, they were locked. And even if they weren't, she couldn't jump. The dock was below. The fall would kill her as surely as Burton's knife. All she'd done was buy herself some time. In another minute or two, he would find her and when he did it would be all over. Silently, she started to weep.

There was an earth-shaking crash. A stack of chests had gone over. "Stinking little bitch . . ." he cursed. Another crash. Closer to her this time, much closer. "This is *my* warehouse . . . *my* tea . . ." he thundered. She squeezed her eyes shut. He was on the other side of the chests, only feet away. All he had to do was take two more steps and he'd find her.

And then he stopped. And she heard a noise. From downstairs. A steady pounding. No, not a pounding . . . a battering. Coming from the front of the building. From the doors. As she listened it picked up in tempo. She realized it was the sound of axes. Someone was chopping at the doors.

She heard a scream of rage, felt the chests next to her shake, then topple. Two crashed down beside her. A third clipped her shoulder, tearing through her jacket and into her skin, before smashing open only inches behind her. She bit down on her bottom lip to keep from crying out. Tea dust swirled all around her.

The chopping stopped. "William Burton!" a voice boomed from below. "This is Sergeant Rodney O'Meara. Open the door and give yourself up!"

Hurry, Uncle Roddy! Hurry! Fiona silently begged him.

She heard Burton run toward the street-side windows, heard him enter the stairwell, heard his shoes on the steps. After a few seconds she risked a glance. He was nowhere in sight. She fought the impulse to crawl out from behind the chests and bolt down the steps. She could only see the top of the stairs from where she was, and he might be hiding halfway down them. It would be safer to remain here, out of sight. All she had to do was wait for Roddy to break the door down. Once the police were inside, she would be all right. The chopping started again.

Sweat beaded on her forehead and rolled down her face as she waited. She felt breathless and hot. Tea dust, still floating in the air, stuck to her skin and got into her eyes. The chopping continued. The wooden doors were huge and thick, built to keep people out. "Oh, hurry," she whispered. "Please, please, hurry."

Her eyes started to water. Her throat burned. Where are they? she wondered anxiously. What's taking so long? She took a deep breath, trying to calm herself, and realized it wasn't tea dust she was breathing. She scrambled out from behind the tea chests and looked at the landing. It was filling with smoke. Burton had set the wharf on fire.

Fiona knew she had to get off the third floor. The wharf was a tinderbox filled with wooden chests and dry tea leaves. It would go up in no time. If the fire reached the stairwell, she'd never get out. Steeling herself, she stood up and dashed across the room. Smoke obscured the stairway. She took off her jacket and held it over her nose.

She was shaking with fear as she descended, expecting Burton to rush at her from below, his knife drawn. But he didn't. She made it down safely to the second floor and looked around. In the center of the room, chests had been pushed together and set on fire. The flames burned brightly, leaping toward the plank ceiling. As she started down to the ground floor, she heard a voice shout, "We're almost in, Sergeant!"

She sobbed with relief. All she had to do was get to the door – just a few more steps – and she'd be safe. The smoke was thick and black as midnight now. Her eyes were running; she could barely breathe. "Uncle Roddy!" she shouted. "In here!"

She stretched her hand toward the door, and just as it gave way under the ax, a face came roaring at her through the smoke, a hellish mask of rage and madness, streaked with ash and blood. Its black eyes were blazing, its torn cheek hung open, exposing teeth and bone.

Burton grabbed her by her hair and pulled her, screaming, up the stairs after him.

"Let 'er go!" a voice thundered.

It was Joe. He was fighting his way through the smoke toward them.

"Joe! Help me!" Fiona cried. She kicked and struggled, trying to slow Burton down, but he was massively strong and he dragged her up the stairs until they were on the empty fourth floor where the builders had not yet made repairs. Pieces of smashed tea crates littered the floor. Loopholes stood unshuttered. He hauled her over to one and stood in it, his left hand braced against the brick arch, his right arm around her neck in a chokehold.

"Stay back!" he shouted. "Stay back or I'll jump and take her with me!"

Fiona could barely move, but she managed to twist her head far enough to look down and see the river churning below. They were standing in the easternmost loophole, right at the edge of the building. The dock ended directly below it. If she fell, her only hope of survival would be to clear its edge and hit the water.

"You won't get the chance to jump, Burton, I'll kill you first." It was Roddy. He had a pistol drawn and aimed at Burton's head.

"Let 'er go. It's over," Joe said, walking toward them.

Fiona felt the arm around her neck tighten. She looked at Joe and her eyes filled with tears. All Burton had to do was take one step back and she would never see Joe again.

Roddy kept yelling. Joe kept talking, kept walking. Fiona saw that though he was addressing Burton, he was looking at her. She could feel him willing her to be strong, to keep her head. She nodded at him, then saw his eyes flick to her right. To the side of the loophole. Once. Twice. She followed his gaze and glimpsed a large iron ring, used for tying ropes, mounted into the brick.

Joe drew nearer. Roddy yelled louder. "You won't jump, you son of a bitch! You'd kill anyone who got in your way, anyone at all, but you wouldn't kill yourself!"

"Stop!" Burton shrieked, his eyes flicking from Roddy to Joe. "Don't come any closer!"

"Now, Fiona!" Joe yelled.

With every ounce of her strength, Fiona lunged forward and grabbed the ring. In the same instant, Joe rushed Burton and pulled his arm from her neck. The two men scuffled. Burton stepped backward, but his foot found only air. He lost his balance. His hands scrabbled for purchase.

And found Joe.

"Nooooo!" Fiona shrieked as both men plunged out of the loophole. She lunged after them, but a strong pair of arms grabbed her and held her back.

"No, Fiona, no!" Roddy shouted, pulling her away.

Wild-eyed, screaming, she pummeled him, trying to break free.

"Come on!" he yelled. "We have to get out now or we won't get out at all!"

He dragged her across the room. Smoke was billowing up between the floorboards. The third floor was in flames. Tongues of orange licked at the stairwell. When they reached the second floor, they saw that the stairs to the ground floor were engulfed.

"Run! Fast as you can!" Roddy shouted, putting her down. "It's the only way!"

Covering her head with her hands, Fiona barreled through the flames. She heard a loud roaring, felt an incredible heat. There was a blistering pain on her leg, and then they were outside and a dozen hands were slapping at their clothing.

She pushed past the constables and bystanders and ran for the Old Stairs. She flew down the stone steps and had just reached the riverbank when a sound like the end of the world hit her, flinging her forward like a rag doll, into the mud and water. For a few seconds, she could neither see, nor hear, nor move her limbs. Water filled her mouth and nose. Then suddenly her senses returned. Coughing and spitting, she raised herself to her knees and looked back. The Old Stairs were gone, ripped away. In their place was a mountain of bricks and flaming timbers. Where the west wall of Oliver's had been there was now a hole at least two stories high. Smoke and fire were pouring out of it. Fiona could no longer see the Town of Ramsgate, or the alley that had led from the Old Stairs to the street. Where was Roddy? Had he stayed with his officers? Or had he run after her?

"Roddy!" she screamed, starting back toward the stone steps. "Uncle Roddy!"

"Fiona! Are you all right?" The voice was strong, but distant. He had to be on the other side of the rubble. "It's the gas lines! Get out of there before the whole building goes!"

"I can't! I have to find Joe!"

The tide was coming in. Fiona ran under the pilings, into the murky water, calling for Joe. Farther and farther she went, the waves buffeting her against the tall timbers. She was trying to get to the easternmost end of the wharf, where there was a patch of riverbank to the right of the dock itself. If Joe had cleared the dock and hit the water, he might've had a chance. As she finally struggled out of the pilings, the river swirling and sucking around her knees, she saw a figure lying still on the mud bank, half in and half out of the water. His leg was at a funny angle to his body.

"Joe!" she screamed in despair. "Oh, no . . . please, no!"

Joe groaned and struggled to sit up. Fiona ran to him. She kissed his face, sobbing. "You're all right! Please say you're all right!"

"I'm fine, I think. Except for me leg. Snapped it on the edge of the dock on the way down. Just below the knee. I can't move it."

"What happened to Burton?" Fiona asked, looking around fearfully.

"I don't know. 'E wasn't 'ere when I pulled myself out of the water. I think 'e 'it the dock." Joe tried to pull himself farther up on the bank, but fell back into the mud, racked with pain. Fiona saw that his face had gone gray and though he was shivering, his skin was slick with sweat.

"Lie still," she said. "I'll get you out of here."

But how? she wondered frantically. The tide was rising by the second. She had five, maybe ten minutes before the rest of the mud bank was completely under water. She couldn't go back the way she'd come. The Old Stairs were

766

useless and beyond them were only the high sheer walls of the treacherous Wapping Entrance. Out on the river, she could see barges, but they were all moored midstream, too far away to be of any help. The only other way out was the Wapping New Stairs, but it was well east of where they were now. Between Oliver's and the New Stairs were half a dozen large wharves, all abutting one another with no alleyways between them. By the time she got to the New Stairs and brought help back, it would be too late, the tide would be in. And then there was Oliver's itself. One more explosion might level the entire wharf. Fiona realized that she had to get Joe into the water. The New Stairs was their only way out.

She told him of her plan. "Can you find me some boards or sticks?" he asked her. "To brace me leg?"

Fiona ran toward the Orient Wharf, desperately searching for bits of wood. She found part of a tea crate and a piece of driftwood. They would have to do. She ran back to Joe and knelt beside him. As she was ripping a length of fabric from her skirt to secure the splint, Joe's head snapped up. His eyes widened.

"Fiona, look out!" he yelled, pushing her away.

As she tumbled sideways, she felt something swish by her cheek.

"Run, Fiona, run! Get out of 'ere!" Joe shouted.

She staggered to her feet, felt a searing pain across her shoulder, turned and saw William Burton, bloodied, broken, his knife in his hand, lunging for her. She screamed and backed away from him. She felt what he'd done, felt the hot blood on her back. He kept coming, forcing her back toward the Old Stairs, away from the Orient Wharf, away from the river and any hope of escape.

"Leave 'er alone, Burton!" Joe shouted. He was trying to raise himself, trying to get to her.

Burton swiped at her again, grinning, pushing her farther and farther away from Joe.

"Help! Help me, somebody!" Fiona screamed.

"I looked for you in streets in alleys in houses and rooms. There were so many like you, whores all," he said.

Still backing away, she banged into the wall of the Wapping Entrance. There was nowhere else to go. It was over, all over. He was going to kill her. She turned and tried desperately to scrabble up the wall, then reached down, grabbed stones and handfuls of mud and blindly threw them. "Murderer!" she sobbed.

Burton kept advancing, mumbling his strange litany. "Polly, Dark Annie, Long Liz. Catherine with the little red flower. Marie who sang me a song while she still had her throat. Pretty Frances. And the one who meddled, a dead redhead . . ."

Fiona knew these names. They were all prostitutes. Except one. The one who meddled. A dead redhead. She sank to her knees in the mud, beyond fear now. Beyond terror. He was only five or six feet away now. A sickening certainty had taken hold of her. "Are you Jack?" she rasped.

Her eyes found his. Darker than heart's blood. Bright and black and insane.

". . . you ran, but I found you. My knife is sharp and ready for new work. You won't escape, I'll tear your heart out, tear it out . . ."

"Are you Jack?"

He raised his knife.

"Answer me, damn you!" she shrieked.

There was a sharp crack in the air. And then another, and another. Six in all. Burton's body twitched and jerked with every report. He stood motionless for a few seconds, then pitched forward and dropped to the ground. Behind him stood a man with a pistol in his hand. Fiona looked from the pistol to Burton, at the blood oozing over his lips, seeping from the holes in his body. She started screaming then and could not stop. She cowered against the stone wall, her eyes closed, but felt hands under her arms, pulling her up. "Come on, Mrs. Soames, we've got to go," a man said. Oliver's was an inferno now.

"No!" she cried, scrabbling away, delirious with fear and pain.

There was a wild, metallic screech as a winch pulled free of its anchors. It came crashing down into the dock, sending shards of wood flying. The man yanked Fiona to her feet and pushed her into the water.

"Joe!" she screamed, lurching toward the pilings. "Let me go! Let me go!"

The man held her fast. " 'E's all right, Mrs. Soames. We've got 'im. 'E's on the boat. Come on now, luv."

Fiona, shaking and in shock, looked up at the man. He was young and muscular and had a scar across his chin. "I know you," she said. "You're Tom. Tom Smith. From the churchyard."

Tom Smith smiled.

"How did you get here? Did Roddy send you? My Uncle Roddy?"

Tom laughed. " 'Ardly. Sid Malone sent us. 'E's been looking out for you. Bloody good thing, too."

Sid Malone. The man who'd tried to force himself on her. The man who'd killed Bowler Sheehan. What did he want with her? She did not want to be trapped in a boat with the likes of Sid Malone, but she had no choice.

Tom walked her to the boat's edge. It was a large wherry. Hands immediately reached down for them, plucking them out of waist-high water. When they were in, oars dipped down and the boat pulled away from Oliver's. There were five men in the boat – two near her in the stern, two rowing, and one more, his back toward her, in the bow.

"Where's Joe? Where is he?" she asked, looking from one unfamiliar face to the other. Tom pointed behind himself. Joe was stretched out on the bottom of the boat with a blanket over him. His eyes were closed. She knelt by him and saw that he was in a great deal of pain. She took his hand and held it to her cheek, frightened by his pallor, then sought Tom again. "Thank you," she said to him. "I still don't know how or why you did this, but thank you."

"Wasn't me, Mrs. Soames," Tom said, nodding at the figure in the bow.

He helped Fiona make her way over to him. "Mr. Malone?" she said to his back, trying to keep her voice even, to not show any fear. There was no answer. "Sir, where are you taking us? My friend needs a doctor."

" 'E'll be taken care of," the man said.

His voice was strongly Cockney. And familiar. So familiar.

"I don't think you understand. He needs to go to hospital." She touched his arm. "Mr. Malone?"

He took off his cap and turned around.

Fiona gasped. Her legs buckled. If Tom hadn't been at her side to catch her, she would've collapsed. "It can't be," she whispered. "Oh, God, it can't be . . ."

" 'Ello, Fiona," the voice said.

The voice of a dead man.

The voice of a ghost.

The voice of her brother Charlie.

84

"And the returns on Quick Cup, they're absolutely phenomenal! We're feeding ten tons of tea through the machine a week and we still can't keep up with the demand. The new machine's on order, and Dunne promised it'll be in New York by November. Just in time for the holidays! Maddie's designed the most beautiful gift tin for Christmas. You've got to see it. I brought the sketches –"

"Oh, never mind the tea, Stuart. How are *you*?" Fiona asked. "How are Michael and Mary and Nate and Maddie? How's Teddy? And Peter?"

"I'm fine. They're fine. Everyone's fine, Fiona. The bigger question is, how are *you*? No one really believes what's happened, you know. Michael kept telling us installments and we kept saying he was making it up. I mean, really! First a whole new tea company, then a husband . . . everyone thinks you've gone bonkers!"

Fiona laughed. She was so happy to have Stuart here. He'd just arrived from New York that morning. She'd arranged to have him met at the station, and have his things taken to the Savoy, and then she'd gone to see him herself, arriving there only half an hour ago. She'd planned for them to have a nice, civilized luncheon, but he said he was tired of sitting and insisted they go right to Oliver's and then Mincing Lane. A tea man through and through, he was much more interested in business than lobster salad.

They were walking down the Wapping's High Street arm in arm now, catching up.

"Really, though, Fiona," Stuart said, suddenly serious.

"All jokes aside, it sounds like you almost lost your life."

"Found it, rather."

"But the man nearly killed you! William Burton, of all people. I almost went to work for him once. As a lad. Years and years ago." He shook his head. "It defies comprehension. And you say they never found the body?"

"No, by the time they got the fire out, the tide had come and gone. It took him with it."

"And the man who killed him?"

"They never found him, either," Fiona said, looking away.

"He just shot William Burton, rescued you, and kept on going?"

"He was a wherry captain. He'd just taken passengers across the river," she said quietly. "He saw the fire, heard me screaming, and stopped to help."

"I didn't know wherry captains carried firearms."

"He said he was robbed once too many times."

"He never gave you his name?"

"He didn't. On purpose, I'm sure. He'd killed a man. To save myself and Joe, but nonetheless, he'd killed a man and he wanted no visits from the police. He saved our lives, Stuart."

"It's like something out of an adventure story," Stuart said, and for a moment Fiona felt as if a dark cloud had passed overhead, blotting out the sun.

"There's a happy ending, though, isn't there?" Stuart asked. "You were married soon after, right?"

"Yes," she said, smiling. "At Joe's house. In Greenwich. Where you're going tonight."

"And this is a lad you knew when you were a girl?"

"Yes."

"A good lad?"

"A very good lad."

"I can tell. You're simply blooming, Fiona. I've never seen you happier."

"Thank you, Stuart. I can't wait for you to meet him."

He patted her hand. "Nick would be happy for you. You know that, don't you?"

Fiona nodded. She looked down at her hand, resting on Stuart's arm. She had retired Nick's wedding band to her jewelry box, where she would look at their initials engraved inside of it sometimes and remember her first husband and dearest friend. She wore Joe's wedding ring now. And his beautiful blue scarab. But she still wore Nick's diamond – on her right ring finger instead of her left. Joe didn't mind. In fact, he often said he owed Nicholas Soames for taking such good care of her.

"Now, when are we getting you back to New York?"

"In a month's time. Now that you're here, I was hoping to get the London company back on track. I've only been able to hold it together these past few months, not make it as strong as I'd hoped. We've got so much to do, Stuart. But the resources are all there. We've even got our own estate! Can you imagine? But we're going to have to completely start over. Everything's in disarray. I was wondering . . . would you mind staying here for a while? Possibly a long while? There would, of course, be added compensation. A new title. President of TasTea, London. And a new salary."

"Mind? Fiona, from the moment I got your telegram asking me to come over, I hoped you'd ask me to run the new company. I miss old Blighty horribly. I think I'm getting soft in the head. Nearly cried when I got off the train. I'd love to come home."

"Oh, Stuart, that's wonderful! This couldn't have worked out better! I'm delighted!"

"What about you, though? Won't you mind leaving London?"

"I'll mind leaving Uncle Roddy and my in-laws, but I miss the rest of my family so much, Stuart. I can't wait to see Seamie and Mary and the children." She grinned mischievously. "Even Michael." And she did miss them all. Horribly. When she left, back in July, she'd only planned to be gone a month at the most. Now it was nearly October. She missed TasTea, too. Stuart had handled everything beautifully in her absence, but she was eager to see her warehouse again, her freight cars and wagons.

"What about your husband? Won't he mind losing you to New York?"

"Oh, I'm not leaving him!" she said, laughing. "He's coming with me. We're going to try spending three months in New York, then three in London, and so on and see how it goes." She stopped him and pointed at the red brick building in front of them. "Here we are," she said. "This is it. Oliver's Wharf."

"Bloody hell! It's enormous!" Stuart exclaimed, leaning back to get a better view.

Fiona looked up at it, too, pleased to see that the work was progressing rapidly. Oliver's was looking proud again. The black soot stains had been scrubbed off its exterior. The shattered wall had been reconstructed. Windows and loophole doors had been replaced. Inside, the support columns and joists had all been rebuilt and the builders were currently laying new plank floors. Already, tea was in the warehouse again. Assam leaves that she'd ordered for TasTea, London's new signature blend were sitting in chests on the second floor. As she stood watching the workers winch boards up to the fourth story, she felt a fresh breeze blow in from the river.

"Let's go in," Stuart said.

"Go ahead, look all around. I'll be right behind you," she said.

He disappeared and she headed for the Old Stairs – the new Old Stairs – to sit by the water for a bit. She needed to see her beloved river, to collect herself and calm the strong emotion stirred up by recounting what had happened the night Oliver's burned. She walked to the top of the steps and took a seat in her usual spot, halfway down.

She watched the gulls for a while, saw a mudlark digging for treasure. When she could bring herself to, she gazed across

774

the water to Cole's Wharf, a grain warehouse on the south side of the river, and the last place she had seen her brother.

Tears came to her eyes, as they always did when she recalled hearing his voice, then seeing his face, and feeling his strong arms around her. She had wept and wept, undone by her emotion and exhaustion, her wounds, the terror she'd suffered, and finally, the joy.

During their boat ride, Charlie told her how he'd read about her in all the papers after she'd taken Burton's company from him. He told her what he'd felt upon learning that Burton had murdered their father – the shock and rage and grief. And he told her how happy he'd felt to know she was alive and well. He'd instructed his men to keep an eye on her, and to find Burton. But they couldn't; he'd hidden himself too well. It was only when Tom and Dick had grabbed O'Neill, after tailing him to Fiona's house and then Covent Garden, that they learned Burton had been living in a hidden room on the top floor of Oliver's. By then, it was nearly too late. They'd had the foresight to telephone Charlie, and he'd gotten himself and some more of his men into a boat. By the time Tom and Dick had arrived at Oliver's, having figured out what Burton meant to do, the wharf was in flames. They'd run down the New Stairs and slogged across the riverbank just in time to stop Burton from killing her.

While Charlie talked, his men rowed south across the river. They'd disembarked at Cole's Wharf and entered through a side door. Fiona had been astonished to find herself in a comfortable, well-lit room with tables and chairs, food and wine. Joe was carefully laid upon a settee and given laudanum for his pain. A doctor was speedily brought. His leg was straightened and set. He could have received no better care if he'd seen the Queen's own surgeon. The doctor, Wallace was his name, cleaned Fiona's wound, too, and stitched it closed. Burton's blade hadn't cut as deeply as it had the first time, and she hadn't lost nearly as much blood.

Then, while Joe was resting and Tom Smith and the

others were eating, Charlie took Fiona into a smaller, more private, room. It contained a large desk, some club chairs, and a couple of settees. They'd embraced again, and she had wept again, clinging to her brother as he stroked her hair and shushed her sobs. He'd led her to a settee, bade her sit, and poured her a glass of port.

"Fee, you've got to stop crying. Please. Your eyes are swelled shut. I'm 'ere, it's all right," he'd said.

She'd nodded, but kept crying anyway. Between great, gulping sobs, she babbled a million questions at him. "Charlie, where were you? We thought you were dead. Where did you go? They pulled a body from the river. It had Da's watch on it. Where have you been all this time? Why didn't you try to find us?"

He'd gulped down the contents of his own glass, then, with obvious difficulty, told her about the last ten years, beginning with the night of Jack's final murder.

He'd been on his way home from the Taj, where he was celebrating a win. It was late and dark and he'd been surprised to see a crowd gathered in Adams Court. He'd pushed his way through and saw his mother lying lifeless on the cobblestones, her blood running into the cracks between them. He'd heard Fiona shrieking, heard the baby wailing. He remembered trying to hold his mother, to keep the constables from taking her away. And then he remembered running. Away from the horrible scene. Away from himself. He kept running until his legs were aching and his lungs were on fire and his heart was screaming for him to stop. Deep into the dark heart of East London. All the way to the Isle of Dogs. There, he crawled under a fence and found himself in a shipyard, where he holed up in the remains of an old trawler. How long he stayed there he didn't know. Hours, maybe. Or days. When he crawled out of the hulk, cold and hungry, he didn't know where he was or who he was. Something had happened to his mind – to this day, he didn't know exactly what. Denny Quinn told him it was called amnesia.

He wandered the shipyards and wharves. He slept rough, eating whatever he could dig out of rubbish bins. Then he moved west again, hugging the river. Bit by bit, his memory returned. He'd have an image now and again of his old street, his family, his friends. But as soon as it came, it was gone. And then, finally, it all came back, and he remembered that he had a brother and two sisters, that his mother had been murdered. His grief had overwhelmed him.

He told Fiona how he'd gone back to Adams Court one night to look for them, but they had left. He realized then that he had no one, and nowhere to go, so he returned to the streets.

"But why didn't you try to find Roddy?" Fiona asked. "He would have been able to help you, to tell you where Seamie and I had gone."

"I did try," he'd answered evasively. "I looked for 'im at his old flat, but 'e wasn't there."

Fiona persisted. "But after you disappeared a body was found in the river. Roddy identified it. It had red hair and Da's watch was in the jacket pocket. The watch he gave you. We thought it was you. Charlie, who on earth did we bury if it wasn't you?"

He had looked away.

"Who, Charlie?"

"Sid Malone."

Fiona had slumped against the settee, aghast. "How?"

He told her in a rush. One night, when he'd first regained his memory, he'd found himself on the Wapping's High Street. He was rooting through some pub rubbish when a lad grabbed him by the neck. It was his old antagonist, Sid Malone. "Well, well, if it ain't you! Everyone's wondering what 'appened to you. I 'eard you ran. Always knew you was a coward," Sid had said. And then he'd punched him in the nose, breaking it. The pain blinded him for a few seconds, long enough for his attacker to gain the advantage. Sid went through his pockets. There was no money to be had, but there was his father's watch. Sid pocketed it, then rained down punches on him. He said he was going to kill him and throw his body in the river. He would've too. His punches were vicious; they forced him to the ground. Charlie tried to stand up. As his fingers scrabbled for purchase against the cobbles, they found a loose one. He clawed it free and aimed blindly. There was a soft, wet crunch.

He had hit Sid in the head. Stoved it in. He tried to bring him round, but it was useless. He was afraid that if anyone found out, they'd never believe he'd done it in self-defense. They'd hang him. Panicking, he did what Sid said he was going to do: he dragged the body to the river and heaved it off a dock – forgetting in his haste to take his watch back.

"That's the real reason I didn't go to Roddy," he admitted. "I was worried that someone 'ad seen me do for Sid. I didn't want to involve 'im."

"Roddy would've believed you, Charlie," Fiona said, bursting into fresh sobs. "He would've helped you."

"I went to Denny instead. It was 'is idea for me to take Sid's name. Said the bloke 'ad no family. Said for me to lay low, to go south of the river where no one knew me. Den took care of me. 'E looked after me all these years. We was about to go into business together. The two of us. About to take on all of East London, north and south of the river. 'E taught me 'ow to survive, Fiona. 'E treated me like 'is son."

"And turned you into a criminal," Fiona said softly.

He turned away at that, then swiftly rounded on her again, pointing a finger at her. "I 'ad nothing! No one! I 'ad to *survive*, Fiona. And I did. Not your way, maybe, but my way. The East London way."

"By thieving, Charlie? By breaking heads? By doing the same things Bowler Sheehan did? Sheehan, remember? The man who killed our da?"

Charlie's jaw tightened. "I think it's time I got you 'ome," he said. "Tommy! Dick!" he barked.

Fiona realized she had cut too deeply. "No, Charlie, not yet. Talk to me, please."

"Charlie who?" he'd said, a mixture of grief and defiance in his eyes. "My name is Sid. Sid Malone."

He'd kissed her good-bye and told her not to try and find him. Then his men ushered her out of his office over her tears and protests.

The days that followed had been tremendously hard. She had called Roddy's station as soon as Charlie's men delivered her and Joe to Joe's house. Roddy wasn't there, but an officer found him and told him where they were. He was in Greenwich before daybreak, barely able to believe that they were alive. Fiona told him everything that had happened. And he, one of the hardest, toughest men she had ever known, cried like a child when she told him who Sid Malone really was. They had gone back to Cole's Wharf one night – she, Joe, and Roddy. The watchman hadn't wanted to let them in, but Roddy had persuaded him by flashing his badge. They searched the entire wharf – every floor – but found only cargo. All the furniture, all the food and drink, every sign that anyone had ever been there, was gone.

There had been an inquest and many difficult questions. Fiona had refused to identify any of the men involved in their rescue and Joe followed suit. They didn't remember much, they said. It was dark; they had both been suffering from shock.

In her heart, Fiona knew the truth and did not flinch from it. Her beloved brother was a criminal. A thief. A smuggler. An extortionist. A handsome, deadly, emerald-eyed thug.

And yet, she knew another truth, too – Charlie had saved her life. And Joe's. She had no doubt whatsoever that without him, they would both be dead. And he had done what she, in ten years of trying, had failed to do – he had destroyed William Burton.

She still shuddered when she thought about Burton's

final moments and how close he'd come to killing her. Or when she thought about the things he'd said before Tom had shot him. She'd told Joe and Roddy about his mad ravings. Roddy had had his house searched, but his men had turned up nothing incriminating. The knife Burton had planned to use on her had disappeared with him. Roddy'd had her describe it and concluded that the type and length could certainly have produced the injuries sustained by the women in '88, and by the two streetwalkers whose bodies had recently been found.

"It could be him," Roddy had said. "I, for one, wouldn't put it past the man, given the things we know he's done. But without him here to answer questions, we'll never know for sure, will we?"

No, Uncle Roddy, she thought now as she gazed at the river, we never will.

Sometimes she still imagined she saw him . . . Burton . . . Jack . . . the dark man. Walking along the riverbank in his black frock coat and top hat, hands clasped behind his back. He would turn to her, as if suddenly aware of her gaze, doff his hat, then disappear into the dark waters of Wapping Entrance or the shadows of the Orient Wharf. Roddy said he was dead; that no one could survive six gunshots at close range. She knew he was dead, too. And yet, he lived on. In the scars he'd left on her body. In the scars he'd left on her heart.

In the weeks that followed the investigation, Roddy had put in for a transfer. He'd told his superiors that he'd had enough of the East End and wanted to take his family out of London. He was hoping for an assignment in Oxfordshire or Kent. He'd told Fiona that if he stayed, he and Charlie would certainly cross paths and that the prospect of arresting Paddy's son was too much for him. He'd told her that the real Charlie Finnegan was dead. He'd died back in '88.

"We all did, didn't we?" she'd said ruefully. And in a way they had. Not one of them – not she herself, nor Roddy,

Joe, or Charlie – were the same people they'd been ten years ago.

Tears came again. What would she tell Michael? And Seamie, who had so adored his older brother? "Tell them nothing," Joe had said. "Let Seamie keep his memories. At least give him that." Fiona had accepted his counsel. But only for now. Only for today. She wouldn't stop trying to find Charlie, no matter what he said, no matter what he did. She loved him. And she'd get him back one day. The real Charlie, not Sid Malone. She wouldn't give up hope. She'd never do that.

As the river's breeze dried her tears, she heard footsteps on the stairs behind her. She turned, expecting Stuart, but saw a little red-haired girl, perhaps nine or ten years of age, instead. The girl smiled shyly at her. "I sit 'ere sometimes and watch the boats," she said. "The air smells good today, don't it? Like tea."

Fiona smiled back. "Yes, it does. It should. Oliver's Wharf had fifty tons of the best Assam landed yesterday."

"I like tea," the girl said, a little bolder now. "Tea comes from the East. From India, China, and Ceylon. I know where they are on a map."

"Do you?"

"Aye," she said excitedly. "I'm going to India someday. On a boat. And I'm going to 'ave my own tea plantation and be a grand lady like that woman in the papers, Mrs. Soames."

"I think it's Mrs. Bristow now," Fiona said, her eyes shining with delight at the spunky little thing in her worn cotton dress and threadbare jacket. "Are you really going to India?"

"I want to," the girl said, but doubt had crept into her large brown eyes. "But I don't know . . ." She looked down at her boots, scuffing the toe of one against a step. "Miss says I'm silly. Says me 'ead's full of dreams and cobwebs."

"Oh?" Fiona said, her eyes narrowing. "Who's Miss?"

"Me teacher."

"Well, she's wrong. You're not silly. People with dreams are smart."

"Really?"

"Really. The day you let someone take your dreams from you, you may as well head straight to the undertaker's. You're just as good as dead."

"Is that true?" the girl asked, wide-eyed.

"Absolutely. A very wise man told me that. A wonderful man who used to come here and watch the boats. Just like you. What's your name, lass?"

"Daisy."

"Well, Daisy. If you want your own tea garden someday, you're going to have to know a lot about tea."

"Do you know a lot about tea?"

"A thing or two."

"Tell me!" Daisy said.

"The first thing you have to know is how to tell a good tea from a bad one. And there are a few ways of doing this. Come on, I'll show you."

Fiona offered her hand and Daisy took it. They walked up the Old Stairs. Behind them, scores of derricks rose and dipped, barges jostled with ferries, a chantey carried on the breeze, and the silvery Thames flowed on. Immutable, implacable. Straining at its boundaries, reaching past its shores. Always and never the same.